THEY WERE MEN  ...Y,
TRUSTED THEIR C... ...D
TO PAY THE U...
CONVICTIO...

Major Paul "Lucky" Anderson—His face horribly disfigured in a near-fatal flying accident, Anderson must channel all of his energies into becoming the consummate professional warrior . . . and keeping his men alive.

Major Glenn Phillips—Once an arrogant, hotshot fighter pilot, he will learn the true meaning of heroism in the dismal cell of a brutal prison, clinging to his code of honor as he watches his fellow POWs suffer and die.

First Lieutenant Billy Bowes—He lost his father in Korea and a brother in Vietnam. Driven by frustration and outrage, this descendant of Cherokee warriors vows vengeance in the skies over North Vietnam at the controls of the world's deadliest aircraft.

Quon—The famous North Vietnamese fighter-pilot ace had shot down Germans in World War II and Frenchmen in Indochina. Now the Americans have taken the life of his only son . . . and Quon is obsessed with his desire for revenge against the American Thunder planes and an American pilot named Lokee.

"Peacemaker"—Through an API reporter who has contacts with the Viet Cong, this outwardly upstanding airman is doing the unthinkable: providing target information to the enemy in the North.

ALSO BY TOM WILSON

Termite Hill

LUCKY'S BRIDGE

TOM WILSON

Tom Wilson (signature)

BANTAM BOOKS
New York·Toronto·London·Sydney·Auckland

LUCKY'S BRIDGE
A Bantam Book/October 1993

ISBN 0-553-29311-7

Published simultaneously in the United States and Canada

Bantam Books are published by Bantam Books, a division of Bantam
Doubleday Dell Publishing Group, Inc. Its trademark, consisting of the
words "Bantam Books" and the portrayal of a rooster, is Registered in
U.S. Patent and Trademark Office and in other countries. Marca Reg-
istrada. Bantam Books, 1540 Broadway, New York, New York 10036.

This work is dedicated to Tom (USAF), Mike (USN), Gavin (USAF), Chris (USMC) and Diane (USAF)—five strong, patriotic and yet very different individuals—and to all the sons and daughters who would dare to fight to keep the American dream alive.

ACKNOWLEDGMENTS

As *Lucky's Bridge* was conceived, and then as the writing progressed, I received constant support, and valuable criticisms and ideas from Andrea. After the work, originally entitled *Bridges*, was submitted, Mr. Joseph Pittman suggested the new title as well as several beneficial changes. Mr. Greg Tobin, and then Mr. Tom Dupree, worked to smooth the way at Bantam.

Several close friends reviewed the manuscript for authenticity. Lieutenant Colonel Billy Sparks, USAF (Ret.), put his uncannily prodigious memory to work on historical background. Colonel Jerry Hoblit, USAF (Ret.), was also, once again, a lifesaver. Although the first time, when we flew a combat tour over North Vietnam, was more dramatic, this one was also appreciated. Both of those former combat fighter pilots, to whom their country owes so much, provided technical details about tactics, military aircraft, weaponry and support equipment which I had either not known or had long forgotten. Lieutenant Colonel Ed Gamble, USAF (Ret.), contributed information about Special Operations aircraft and procedures, and covert insertion and withdrawal of Special Forces long range reconnaissance patrols. Colonel Chuck Sloan, USAF (Ret.), supplied details about RF-4C combat recce efforts. My buddy, Colonel Mike Gilroy, USAF (Ret.), once again reviewed and corrected descriptions of sophisticated enemy weapons. Any errors should not be blamed on them, but on my indiscretion, hard-headedness, and desire to weave a somewhat simplified tale.

I would also like to acknowledge the present and former maintenance, weapons, logistics and support men, pilots, Wild Weasel bears, aircrew members, POWs, intelligence officers, Special Forces members, grunts, wives, and many others, whose war stories and vignettes were borrowed, reshaped, disguised and included herein.

Thank you all.

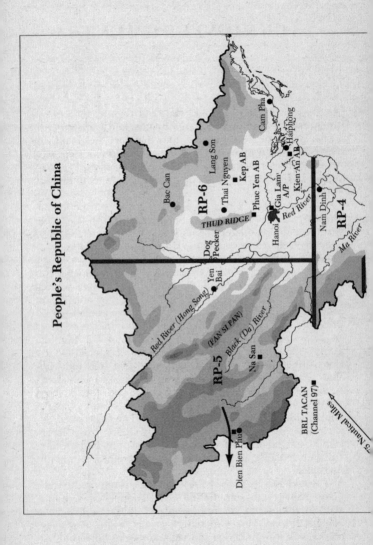

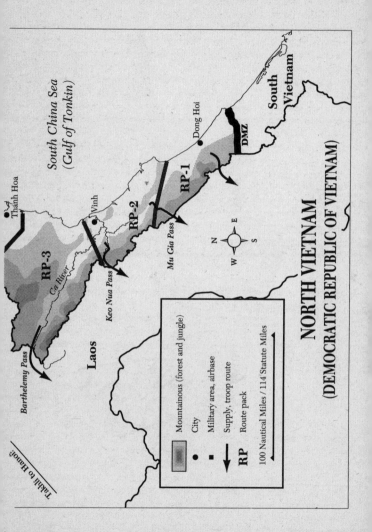

BOOK I

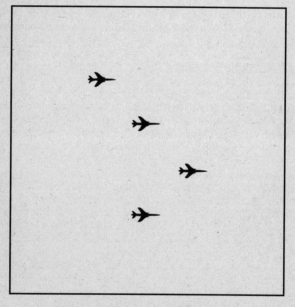

Fluid Four Formation

Headquarters Seventh Air Force, Tan Son Nhut Air Base, Saigon, Republic of Vietnam

Peacemaker toiled diligently through the day, maintaining the war plans with the finickiness of an old-maid librarian, ensuring that each change and deletion was properly logged and inserted into its document.

When he finished with his labors at an hour well into the evening, for the volume of his work was endless, he again examined the latest entries on the primary-targets list, paying special attention to the ones just approved for transmittal to the units. His final official act of the long workday was to survey his desktop carefully and then those of his co-workers, to ensure that no one had left out a classified document. He went around the large office and twirled the knobs of the seven safes and penned his initials on their cards to show he'd checked that they were locked. Only then did he sign off the room as secured.

He trotted down the stairs and hurried down the hall to the security desk, where he showed his badge to the security policemen. They joked about him working late to brownnose his boss, and he told them not to get too much sleep on the job.

Peacemaker emerged from the building thinking he was

surrounded by Stone Age military mentalities. As he walked toward a nearby base bus stop, he ran the target coordinates over and over in his mind.

Ten minutes later the blue Air Force bus dropped him off at his barracks. His buddy Gino was there, champing to go downtown and griping because he was half an hour late. He changed into civvies. Gino didn't quit bitching until they were outside and quick-walking toward the gate.

They took a taxi to the Blue Pheasant and sat in their customary dark corner near the loud and awful live band. He quietly drank Pepsi while Gino guzzled beer and whooped at the strippers, whom they knew by their Americanized first names. Suzee, Doreece, and then Katee smiled plastic expressions and moved woodenly as they took it all off.

By the end of a second tune Katee was nude, and she'd begun to caress herself with handfuls of mineral oil. She glistened and dripped as she moved her hands over herself, and Gino sucked on appreciative breath. She cupped her small breasts and aimed pelvic grinds toward the audience, and that caused Gino to glaze over. He stood and tottered toward the side entrance. He'd go around to the back, where they'd open up for him so he could claim her. Gino boasted he was so well liked by the girls that he could take his choice, and that furthermore he got it free. The simple shit didn't realize he was being subsidized by the American press.

Someday when it was all over, maybe he'd tell Gino how he'd unwittingly helped to bring truth to Americans back home.

Peacemaker drained his glass of Pepsi and casually turned to look at the man sitting at the bar. The skinny reporter from API glanced at him, then back to Katee as she squirmed and dripped her oil onto the filthy stage floor. Finally the tune ended, and Katee abruptly stood and scampered backstage to Gino. Another stripper took her place, wearing an abbreviated cowgirl outfit and grinding to the tune of "Rawhide."

Now began the dangerous part of the game.

If Americans were truly free, Peacemaker would simply go over and chat with the reporter. But Americans were not free. They'd been maneuvered into an evil war by the lies of the political/industrial/military establishment, and the fascists were jealous of their secrets. The cretins at his workplace, starting with the stupid colonel who ran his department, *were paranoid about information leaks, and if they knew what he was doing . . .*

But it was his right—no, his duty—to help bring truth to the people. The reporter was an American, for Christ's sake, and the American public should know what their own military was doing. It wasn't as if he were passing information to the North Vietnamese, although he'd wondered if even that would really be so wrong. Perhaps if they knew, the civilians could be moved from the target areas and innocent lives saved.

He gave Gino a couple more minutes to connect with Katee, then carefully flattened a bar napkin onto the tabletop and pulled out his U.S. government–issue pen. He carefully wrote:

20/210753–1055108, 205054–1064323—NEW TGTS BE-ING PLANNED: KEY BRIDGES IN RP SIX

On the twentieth, three days hence, American pilots would bomb the thermal-power plants at the coordinates in Hanoi and Haiphong. He felt bad that he couldn't provide Time Over Target information as the reporter also wanted. He didn't know if the tidbit about the plan the colonel was working on, to destroy critical bridges in North Vietnam, would be useful, but the reporter said he could use such nuggets. Good background, he'd called them.

He double-checked his figures, looking closely in the dim light to make sure they were legible. He liked his handwriting to be as orderly and precise as his mind.

He wadded up the napkin and placed it into the empty ashtray, then motioned carelessly toward the bar. A grinning waitress hurried over. She cleaned the table thoroughly before taking his order for another Pepsi. When she left, the apprehension left him, replaced by a serene knowledge that he'd done the right thing.

A few minutes later Peacemaker watched the reporter stroll out without a backward glance. He would take the crumpled bar napkin to this fancy apartment across town and begin to write his press release. After the airplanes had flown their bombing missions, the reporter would file an in-depth report that the Americans had bombed the power plants and killed innocent humans there. He might even say that he'd gained his information through an anonymous high government official.

Peacemaker felt a tingle of conscience about what he'd

done, but he quickly tempered it. They were printing all sorts of military secrets in the newspapers back home, and those had to be coming from others such as he. A surge of righteousness coursed through him, smothering the doubts.

The Pepsi arrived, and he sipped and watched with a bored expression as a new dancer took the stage. He hoped Gino would hurry with Katee so they could find a restaurant, eat, and get on back to the base. He had a busy day facing him tomorrow, and Peacemaker was never late.

CHAPTER ONE

Thursday, April 20th, 1220 Local—1967, Takhli Royal Thai Air Force Base, Thailand

The noonday sun permeated every substance and shadow, creating raw heat, which rose in shimmering waves from the tarmac spiderweb of parking areas, taxiways, and the long runway. It was the dry season, and with each puny stirring of wind, red dust boiled up to cover everything with ancient Siamese grime.

Like other peoples native to tropical areas, the Thais knew to live and move slowly and to conserve their energies when the sun was high overhead. The loud, profane men who had come from halfway around the world toiled doggedly in spite of the heat, as if challenging the sun's authority over the world below.

From birth the men had been taught that anything was possible if they wanted it bad enough and worked hard enough to get it.

Staff Sergeant Larry Hughes

"She's loaded and ready, Sarge," said the brawny and sunbronzed load-team leader.

Staff Sergeant Lawrence (NMI) Hughes looked over the Aircraft/Ordnance Load form. "Any problems?"

"Nope. Had a little trouble crankin' in the ammo, but the problem's with the autoloader, not your bird."

Larry Hughes nodded. The M-61 Gatling cannon had better be okay. A week earlier a pilot had reported that his rounds had gone wild when he'd taken a high-angle snapshot at a MiG. The gun shop said they couldn't find a problem. At his insistence and under his watchful eye they'd boresited the gun again. Then he'd personally tweaked and fine-tuned until he was convinced the six spinning barrels were precisely aligned. Hughes was satisfied only when everything on his airplane worked, and worked right.

He watched as the motorized MJ-1 loader roared off for another cradleful of general-purpose bombs and the load crew trudged to the next bird in the line, joking and laughing with the crew chief there. One more and they'd be finished reloading all the squadron aircraft. Seventeen of the 354th's twenty-five assigned airplanes had flown this morning. Sixteen would fly combat sorties to various North Vietnamese targets in the afternoon. Eight of the sixteen would, like Larry Hughes's bird, join aircraft provided by the other two squadrons to make up the alpha strike, which meant they'd be sent to bomb the most dangerous targets. He'd been told this one was a particularly difficult mission. It was unlikely all the aircraft would return.

Like the load crew, Larry Hughes was stripped to the waist. His coal-black skin glistened. Sweat tickled as it ran down his chest and his back, soaking his fatigue pants, gathering in rivulets to flow down the insides of his legs. Ropes of muscles bunched and played across his back and shoulders as he moved. He was rock-hard and lean, surely in the finest physical condition of his life. Eighteen and twenty-hour workdays had done that for him. Once-pleasant features now looked habitually weary, and the mouth, once graced with an easy smile, was entirely too serious. He was twenty-three years old, but worry lines had formed and were beginning to mar his handsome face.

Hughes had been at Takhli for three months, and this was his third assigned aircraft. Two months earlier he'd waited for his first one to land after the early-morning combat mission, watched as other aircraft taxied in and were parked, and heard the voice inside him say it would be okay,

that the pilot had likely just been delayed or maybe taken a
hit and been forced to land at one of the forward bases.
Then reality had arrived as the line chief drove up in his
battered pickup to give him the bad news. His bird wasn't
coming back. When Hughes asked one of the pilots, he
learned the airplane had been hit by a surface-to-air missile.
When he asked if the lieutenant had been rescued, he'd
been given a terse shake of the head.

Hughes had turned in the aircraft forms. Then, feeling as
if he'd been punched in the stomach, he'd wandered aimlessly to the NCO Club bar. After his fifth Budweiser he'd
realized the beer was just screwing with his mentals, making
him sadder and the pictures of the lieutenant sharper. He'd
left the club and begun to walk and think.

*Had it been something he'd forgotten or done or not
done?* He'd walked all the way to the main gate, then several miles around the inside perimeter road, walked until his
legs felt like lead, until a security police patrol stopped to
tell him to get the hell off the perimeter road before he surprised one of the sleepy Thai guards and caught a load of
double-aught buckshot. They'd given him a ride back, and
he'd returned to a lonely corner of the all-night NCO Club
bar to drink a few more beers.

The next morning the gruff line chief had assigned him a
new bird, just flown in from the overhaul depot in the
states, and Larry Hughes had begun the acceptance inspec-
tions with a king-sized hangover. He'd not stopped checking
and tightening and tuning and fussing over the aircraft until
0200 the following morning. Only then did he declare the
immaculate airplane ready for its maiden combat flight.

That afternoon a swarthy captain had crawled out of the
crew van wearing his parachute, survival vest, and g-suit
and hauling his map bag. He'd acted especially nervous, so
Larry had guessed they were going to another tough target.

He thought often of that afternoon, how he'd apologetically mentioned the aircraft's few remaining minor problems, how the pilot had listened with less than full attention.
Remembered the captain crawling up the ladder and into
the cockpit wearing a distant, wistful look. Recalled the
whine of the start cart, the engine start-up, and running
smoothly through the ground-check procedures while he
spoke on intercom to the pilot. Finally the big fighter was
taxied out of its parking place, and he'd saluted, the sharpest

he could muster. The swarthy captain had acknowledged with a grim-faced nod.

Major Lucky Anderson, who'd been leading the flight just behind the captain's, had searched Hughes out after that mission to make sure his questions were answered. The big bird had come apart in the air in a violent explosion just as it settled into its dive-bomb attack on the target. *That's when we're most vulnerable,* the major had told him, *because we're predictable and make an easy target. Probably a direct hit from an antiaircraft artillery round in some vital area.* It was nothing Hughes could have prevented, he'd told him.

But Larry Hughes would never know for sure. The Thunderchiefs were rugged and built for combat, and seldom just blew up like that.

After that second one, the gruff line chief, a canny senior master sergeant fighting his third war, had sent Larry off to Bangkok on a three-day R and R he'd neither wanted nor enjoyed. When he'd returned, he'd found himself assigned to aircraft 59-1820, an aging hangar queen with too many flying hours and a reputation for developing unexplainable gremlins at precisely the wrong moments. After forty-two hours of constant labor, the squadron maintenance officer, a major, had ordered him to return to his quarters and get some sleep. Eight hours later he'd been back at work because, just maybe, if he toiled hard enough, his airplane would bring back the pilots who flew it.

The former hangar queen had now been flown on forty-three consecutive combat sorties and had neither been hit nor received a serious write-up from a pilot. Every time one of them mentioned anything, any slightest complaint, Larry Hughes tackled the problem as if it were real and serious. The pilot who'd flown aircraft 820 that morning had congratulated him on having the best bird in the squadron, maybe in the entire wing.

Now she was reloaded with bombs and ammo and again prepared for combat. *Was she really ready? Had he done everything possible?*

He examined the first lieutenant who crawled out of the crowded squadron crew van. Tall and rugged looking, with a hawk's beak, eyes that were dark and flat, and a copper hue to his skin, he walked with the graceful, sure strides of an athlete. Expressionless at first, he finally swung the bulky parachute from his back and cast a smile toward Hughes.

First Lieutenant Billy Bowes

First Lieutenant William Walter Bowes propped his parachute at the base of the ladder leading up to the cockpit and nodded to the black staff sergeant waiting nearby with the Form One, the loose-leaf document that gave the history of the aircraft and its various past illnesses.

He looked up at the fighter. He'd been flying F-105's for four months, had started his checkout in Thuds shortly after Christmas, but he was still impressed. It stood so tall you could walk upright under its nose and wings, and you had to climb up twelve feet before you could crawl over the canopy sill into the cockpit. It weighed fifteen tons when it was clean and dry, and you could add several tons of fuel and weapons before it began to strain under the load. Sixty-seven feet from Pitot boom to tail. Only thirty-five feet between the tips of the sharply swept wings, but they were sturdy and carried no fuel cells, and if you took a flak hit in a wing, you didn't care nearly as much as you would in a wet-wing fighter like an F-4 Phantom. It was big, yet a radar reflector came down when you extended the nosegear, because the Thud was so sleek the radar-approach controllers had trouble picking it up on their precision radars. So fast and stable, you could fly it at Mach one right down on the deck and feel easy doing it, making tiny corrections that would be impossible with other fighters.

The F-105's cockpit was armored to protect the pilot from small-arms fire, and the instrumentation was superb. The avionics, indicators, and controls were made for flying fast and sure with only an occasional look inside the cockpit. Controls knobs were sturdy and easily memorized. The primary instruments used vertical tape readouts rather than round dials and could be interpreted at a glance. The radio electronically tuned to frequencies preset before takeoff, so you didn't have to dial in numbers laboriously while you were flying. Air-to-air and air-to-ground radar modes were controlled by finger switches beneath the throttle. Other avionics included a radar altimeter, Doppler navigator, a sophisticated weapons-release system, and a good stability-augmentation system. All were easily monitored and simple to operate. The Thud was forgiving, which meant you could ham-fist it around the sky and make a screwup or two and it wouldn't go bananas on you. The pilots said it was the most honest airplane in the sky, because it wouldn't spook you with adverse yaw and control reversal as some fighters did, and it always warned you before you got into deep trouble.

"She ready to fly?" Bowes asked in his Oklahoma accent. His speech included that curious midwestern mixture of southern y'awl and western yep.

"Yes, sir," answered the crew chief.

Billy took in the flight line's pungent kerosene and hydraulic fluid odors, and the raucous human and mechanical noises. They were the same as he'd smelled and heard at other airfields throughout the four years of his Air Force flying career. He pulled on calfskin driving gloves, which gave him a better feel of the airplane's controls than did the cloth and leather ones they were issued. Billy liked to sense every nuance the bird could pass to him. He was a good pilot and had known it two weeks after reporting for pilot training at Laredo, Texas, as a second lieutenant fresh out of ROTC.

Don't give yourself time to get nervous, he reminded himself. Which was why he was keeping his mind busy with trivial bullshit.

He started his walk-around inspection, the black crew chief following closely behind. They started at the shiny Pitot boom extending from the pointed radome and moved back past the Gatling cannon gunport, walking slower as they looked over the six M-117 750-pound bombs on the multiple-ejector rack hanging beneath the belly. Then all the way back past the aft-air inlets that purged the electronics bays of dangerous gases, and the fuel vent pipe to the shiny petals of the speed-brakes. When closed, the petals covered the eyelet exhaust of the huge J-75 turbojet engine. When you opened them in the air, they blossomed and the aircraft instantly began to slow. Out to the right wing's outboard station, where he examined the ECM jamming pod, then to the inboard station with its 450-gallon fuel tank. Around to the port-side wing, then to the other 450-gallon tank and the lone AIM-9 Sidewinder.

At Takhli they called the load, the centerline 750-pound bombs and inboard fuel tanks, the standard combat configuration. Clean, the F-105 Thunderchief could be flown at more than a thousand knots of airspeed, but the M-series bombs, built for internal carriage by World War II bombers, slowed you down with their high drag and presented bright returns on enemy radar scopes. More aerodynamic bombs, the Mk-series, had been developed for jet fighters. Sleek 500-, 1,000- and 2,000-pounders. But someone up there said they had to carry the old M-series bombs to save taxpayer money since so many had been stockpiled after World War II and Korea, and that they would continue using them until they ran out of the damned things.

He kept his mind preoccupied with thoughts like that, and with double-checking bomb fuze settings and fuze wires, and inspecting for hydraulic and fuel leaks. The Thud looked good. The crew chief had his shit together.

Satisfied with his preflight inspection, Billy returned to the yellow boarding ladder and prepared to mount up. He removed his blue service cap. It was well-worn, as a fighter jock's should be, the cloth stained, the officer's piping frayed, and the silver first lieutenant's bar scratched and dull. He folded it in half, then tucked it into the pocket on the leg of his g-suit and zippered it inside. *It's time*, he told himself. He hefted the parachute and began to strap it on, more nervous than he'd anticipated.

"How you doin', Bowes?" an unexpected voice sounded from behind him.

Major Lucky Anderson was standing a few feet away peering at Billy, likely checking to see how rattled he was, since this was his first combat mission.

Billy was careful to keep his voice even. "My airplane looks good, Major. Yours?"

Anderson grimaced, but it was difficult to tell if he meant the expression. His features were ill defined, a sheath of thin, transplanted skin stretched over bone and muscle. The nostrils were small, unprotected holes, the lips scarred and misshapen. Beneath his strong chin, the skin of his neck was crinkled, as an old man's might be. Until you were used to it, the sight of Lucky Anderson's face was startling.

That's what a fire could do to you in a fighter . . . if you were fortunate enough to survive being burned by the syrupy, clinging jet petroleum. Billy had met other pilots around the Air Force who'd suffered bad burns like Lucky Anderson's, but very few who'd been able to stay in fighters.

Most had been permanently grounded, or at least restricted to flying less demanding birds.

The damage to Lucky Anderson's face had been limited to the area unprotected by his helmet and visor, for his short brown hair, brows, and eyelashes were healthy and normal. His mood was best determined by examining the pale-blue eyes, with their innate intelligence and piercing stare.

Except for the face, Lucky Anderson appeared normal. He was tall, with a strong neck, broad shoulders and a narrow waist, and ample muscles of upper arms and thighs bulged under his flying suit. It was obvious he worked to stay in shape.

"Too bad, you having to go to pack six on your first mission," said Anderson in his pleasant voice. "It'd be better if we could get you a few missions down in the lower packs before throwing you into the frying pan."

North Vietnam had been separated into six route packages by the headquarters planners. Route pack one was just north of the demilitarized zone with South Vietnam and was considered a low-threat area because most of the big guns were massed up north. The defenses were said to get tougher as you progressed northward through packs two and then three. Next there was pack four, just south of the badland, and pack five, just west of it. The old-timers said flying in packs four and five could get as hairy and dangerous as you wanted. But it was pack six, the Hanoi-Haiphong area, that had become legendary among Air Force and Navy pilots. It was the most lethal flying area in the world. There, in the broad Red River Valley, were found more hostile surface-to-air missiles, antiaircraft artillery, and interceptors per square mile than anywhere else in the world.

"I'm a quick study," Billy said cockily.

"You just hang on my wing," said Anderson. "We start maneuvering too hard, drop back in trail. Try not to fly directly behind me, or they'll shoot at me and hit you."

Billy kept his face impassive.

Continuing to measure Billy carefully, Anderson stripped the cellophane sheath from a cigar, a fat one shaped like a torpedo, and then mouthed it, not lighting it but savoring the taste. By regulation you couldn't smoke within fifty feet of an aircraft. Lucky Anderson was C-Flight commander, Billy's superior officer and reporting official. He likely followed the rules down to the dotted *i*'s, thought Billy Bowes.

Anderson was about to lead Ford flight, four F-105 fighter-bombers, into aerial combat, and Billy would fly as his wingman. Bowes didn't know Anderson, but he knew his own capability. "I'll be there on your wing, Major," he said confidently, careful to keep his voice free of the irritation he felt, "and you don't have to worry about your six o'clock."

A wingman's primary responsibility was to continuously check the airspace around his leader and make sure no one crept up on them unannounced. His job going to and from the target area would be to stay in position, keep a good lookout, and gain experience.

Anderson pursed his scar-twisted lips thoughtfully, his gaze still squarely on Billy Bowes, then nodded abruptly and growled, "Engine start in ten minutes." He strode off toward his own aircraft, slowed, and called back over his shoulder, "And get rid of those fucking unauthorized gloves."

Billy burned, first with anger, then with embarrassment as he realized the crew chief had overheard.

"You could do worse than to listen to Major Lucky," said the black sergeant with a measure of respect. "He's got a reputation for knowing what he's talking about."

"Well, you heard the man," Billy barked in a piqued tone. "Let's get the show started." He would make his own judgments about Anderson.

He paused for another judicious moment, then resolutely crawled up the tall ladder, still wearing the driving gloves. He wanted every possible advantage when he flew to pack six, and the gloves just might provide a tiny edge.

1310 Local—Green Anchor Air Refueling Route

Major Lucky Anderson

After takeoff from Takhli, the four-ship strike flight called Ford flew north-northeast on a heading of ten degrees and contacted Brigham. The ground radar gave them vectors toward their assigned KC-135 air refueling tanker, where it orbited in a long racetrack pattern along a route called "green anchor." When they'd approached within a couple miles of the tanker, Lucky throttled back, depressurized his cockpit, ensured that everyone had their weapons' master-arm switches in the SAFE positions, and called "*Noses Cold*" to

the tanker. Then he sucked in 100 percent oxygen as he
jockeyed his fighter behind the tanker. The enlisted operator, lying on his belly and clearly visible in his glass cage at
the aft of the big tanker, deftly jabbed the nozzle of the tele-
scoping fuel boom into the opened receptacle beside Anderson's cockpit. When the boom's nozzle was latched into
place, the operator activated a pump and began to transfer
fuel.

Unlike many pilots, Lucky enjoyed aerial refueling. Maneuvering smoothly at the slower limits of flight was a challenge, and there was little about flying he did not savor.
After several minutes he finished topping off with the kerosene mixture called JP-4, and the operator disconnected and
swung the boom up and away. Lucky moved to his left and
watched with a critical eye as Bowes, his newly arrived
wingman, maneuvered into position behind the big tanker.

Satisfied the kid was doing okay, he looked upon the
larger scene, at the sleek fighters and the silver tanker
against the background of white clouds and blue sky. If you
flew fighters, you *knew* there was a God, because your view
of the world was so delicately detailed, so spectacularly
beautiful, that it could not possibly exist due to the random
mistakes attributed by science.

As some men treasured other aspects of life, Paul Anderson loved flying fighters. Each time he retracted the gear
and pointed the radome skyward, he experienced a rush and
thrill that lingered until long after he'd landed. He enjoyed
flying in clear or stormy weather, day or night, over deserts
or snowcapped mountains. To him there was nothing to
equal the spectacular views of blue skies and cloud-swathed
earth, the alternating moments of serenity and exhilaration,
of taxing his mental and physical resources to the utmost. To
be able to do so in the F-105 was especially pleasing, for he
believed the Thud was the ultimate fighter-bomber. To be
able to fly the big war steed into combat to do battle with
a canny and capable enemy who he felt were bestial assholes especially pleased him.

Other than flying, few pleasures were left to him. There
was his physical training, but it was done to condition his
body and reflexes, and therefore to enhance his flying skills.
There had once been other personal pleasures, but that
seemed long ago and in another life. He neither dwelled on
the past nor disliked his present life. Flying jets and fighting

communists—these were enough for a man who thought of himself as a professional warrior.

In the pursuit of his calling, especially given the ferocity of the present combat, the odds were not good that he would die of old age. Even that factor, of death residing in such proximity, somehow pleased him. He regarded death as not especially chilling, only infinitely final. He was appropriately prudent in his flying—only a fool would do otherwise in a high performance jet—yet there were worse ways to go than in a sudden, fiery crash.

Lucky considered himself to be a good military officer, but the other duties of a major in the Air Force paled when compared to the flying. The fact that he was a field-grade officer did not impress him, for he despised the accompanying bureaucratic paperwork and silly protocol. He believed heartily in what Manfred von Richthofen had once said, that the fighter pilot's job was to fly and to fight, and all else was rubbish. Except to improve their flying skills, he did not enjoy leading the men assigned under him. If someone ruled that only sergeants were to fly fighters, he would give up his major's leaves in an instant. But since he'd been appointed as a leader of men, he would lead them to the best of his ability.

Lucky enjoyed the camaraderie of his fellow pilots at the O' Club bar, but voluntary socializing ended there. In peacetime he'd tried to avoid all social functions . . . dinings in, hail-and-farewell dinners, change-of-command ceremonies, squadron parties, and such. Those demanded by military protocol he'd attended, but he'd left as early as possible without unduly offending his hosts or the attending brass. Some military men and most civilians felt uneasy around Lucky Anderson because of his disfigured face, which was just as well, for it made it that much easier to maintain his privacy. At Takhli their pitifully few social functions featured discussions of flying and fighting, subjects that pervaded the minds of combat pilots, and these he attended. There were no American females assigned at Takhli, for there was a shortage of adequate quarters and sanitary facilities, and Lucky was pleased with that. For the past eight years women had been repelled by his burned face.

Ford two was doing well with his refueling. Lieutenant Bowes maintained a steady position in the center of the boom's reach, easily matching the wallowing motion of the tanker. The boom operator signaled that the refueling was completed, disconnected with a spray of fuel from the boom, and Billy Bowes smoothly slid back and crossed over to Anderson's wing. He'd made a good first impression. Lucky hoped he would prove as steady when they got to pack six and the test of combat.

It was Ford three's turn, and Lucky had no worries there. Turk Tatro was a capable and likable captain in Lucky's C-Flight, a southerner with a quick wit and slow speech. He easily moved his fighter into position and began to take on fuel.

High on the tail of each bird of the four-ship flight were the large white block letters *RM*, topped by a wide band of bright blue paint, showing they came from the 354th Tactical Fighter Squadron. They called themselves the Fighting Bulldogs, and their squadron emblem showed a tough English bull defending the Statue of Liberty. The pilots were dedicated to flying, and the crew chiefs of the 354th were a hardworking group who maintained their birds with pride. It was a good squadron, thought Lucky. They'd taken too many losses during the past few months, lost too many good pilots, but that was because they'd given the North Vietnamese hell.

The previous month they had methodically leveled the big steel mill at Thai Nguyen, thirty-five miles north of Hanoi, while the North Vietnamese had furiously protected it with every resource they could muster. The 354th, along with the other two fighter squadrons in the wing and the pilots at their sister wing at Korat Air Base, had kept bombing relentlessly, day after day, until the steel mill, as well as the enemy defenses there, had been beaten to pieces. It was still tough, flying to pack six, but they'd instilled a measure of respect and caution in the gomers and were confident that they could destroy any target, regardless of the sophistication of the enemy's defenses. With the showdown at Thai Nguyen behind them, they now knuckled down to the tasks of slowing the flow of supplies and generally making life miserable for the North Vietnamese. Most of the pilots felt they'd entered a tedious home stretch of the air war.

Today's mission was against the Hanoi thermal-power plant, just north of the capital city. Not a great, war-stopping target, but its destruction would make the Hanoi leaders' lives less tolerable, and that was part of their objective. It was certainly better than some of the targets, like bombing a canopy of treetops under which intell thought might be located a truck park.

The big efforts like this were called alpha strikes and featured a composite force. First to arrive at the target would be a flight of fighters led by SAM-hunters, two-man crews flying dual-seat Thuds called Wild Weasels, who threatened and thus preoccupied the gomer SAM sites during the strike. Overhead, flying much higher than the Thuds, was a flight of F-4 Phantoms from Ubon Air Base, to engage any MiGs they found there. Next would come the flak-suppression flight, carrying cluster bombs to drop on antiaircraft guns, which the enemy massed about every potential target in pack six. Then the main players, six four-ship flights of Thuds, would dive-bomb the target. Lucky Anderson's Ford flight would be the first strike flight on the target.

The strike force would fight their way through the MiGs, SAMs, and flak to bomb the power plant. Considering the proximity of today's target to the thick defenses surrounding Hanoi, there was a probability they would lose an aircraft or two. Lucky hoped the losses would not be from his flight.

Ford four, a new lieutenant named Francis, was finishing with his refueling. Twice during the fuel transfer he'd gone into an up-and-down roller coaster, and the boom operator had been forced to disconnect quickly and stop refueling until he settled down. Anderson penciled a note on his flight plan card to work with Francis on his refueling technique.

When Ford four was clear, Lucky again moved behind the tanker. He and Lieutenant Bowes would top off their fuel tanks, then Ford flight would break away from the tanker to fly the final 200 miles to the western border of North Vietnam. He began to tingle with anticipation.

1352 Local—Channel 97 TACAN, Laos

First Lieutenant Billy Bowes

"Ford is at the checkpoint," Billy heard Major Anderson call on the radio.

They'd been flying at 480 knots calibrated airspeed in a loose fingertip formation. Billy was on Anderson's right wing, keeping his mind occupied with flying the aircraft and going over the weapons-release procedures during the half-hour lull between drop-off from the tanker and arrival at the navigation checkpoint.

Bowes had been told that the TACAN ground station, sited on a flat, barren hilltop deep in the hostile territory two miles below Ford flight, was manned and protected by friendly tribesmen under contract to the CIA. They said its presence was known to the enemy, that periodically it had come under attack by Pathet Lao troops, and that once it had almost been overrun and was saved only after a massive display of air-power support.

The world below was colored by tawny elephant grass when they'd dropped off the tanker in northern Thailand and proceeded northeast into Laos. Next they'd overflown the purplish-brown hues of the vast Plains des Jars. Now, as they approached the tall, western mountains of North Vietnam, the earth was changing to dark green, the color of the tall teak trees and jungle thickets.

Just as Billy felt they were crossing into North Vietnam, Anderson made another radio call. *"Ford flight, push 'em up. Let's go to button three."*

Anderson sharply increased his airspeed, and Billy kept abreast by adjusting his own throttle forward. With the same hand, Billy switched until the indicator before him showed the number 3, and heard a buzzing as the radio tuned. It was a little touch, having the radio so easy to operate, but one the pilots appreciated.

"Fords, radio check," called Anderson on the combat frequency.

Billy was quick with his response, *"Two!"* then the other two flight members chimed in. *"Ford three!" "Four!"*

A glance at the instrument tape showed they had settled at 550 knots airspeed, yet the huge J-75 engine was not yet straining.

"Let's green 'em up," called Anderson.

Billy's heart thumped. He set up for EXTERNAL BOMBS and switched on the master-armament switch. A green light told him he was ready to fight.

After another long moment Anderson called, *"Fords, turn on your music."*

Billy was confused, then he remembered. He located the ECM control panel and rotated the wafer knob from

STANDBY to TRANSMIT. A green light illuminated, indicating the ECM pod was operating properly. The pod, loaded out on the right wing and powered by a small ram air turbine propeller, generated electronic noise to help confuse enemy radar.

Billy heard a crackling sound from the radar homing and warning equipment, called RHAW. Its purpose was to alert you when an enemy radar scanned your airplane with its beam. A telelite panel would indicate the type of radar, whether from AAA, SAM, or a MiG, and a strobe on a small CRT would point in the clock-direction of the radar. This was Billy Bowes's first experience with the thing, but he felt that something must be amiss to make it act up like this.

The crackling sound continued. Bright green strobes sputtered at the center of the CRT scope, and periodically the AAA and SAM lights flickered on.

Billy had been briefed that all threats should be called over the radio. *Why wasn't Anderson calling them out?* He paused, unsure of what to do, not wanting to do anything dumb but determined to give warning if there was impending danger. They were over enemy territory, and the RHAW was picking *something* up.

More crackling sounds and flashing lights. To hell with it, he told himself.

"*Ford two has a RHAW indication,*" he broadcast over the radio, since he was unsure whether it was an artillery or SAM radar.

He was answered by silence.

The CRT continued to flicker. "*Ford lead, two has a RHAW indication,*" he repeated.

"*Ford two, maintain radio silence unless you see something,*" replied Anderson.

"*Ford two's got intermittent SAM and AAA lights,*" Billy called stubbornly, unable to keep his voice from rising. Anderson was ignoring him.

"*Ford four has the same,*" came an even shriller radio call from the other lieutenant in the flight. Like Bowes, it was also Fred Francis's first time in pack six. They'd known one another at McConnell, where they'd checked out in Thuds. Billy felt vindicated now that Francis had seconded his observation.

The good feeling didn't last.

"*Ford two and four, unless you've got at least a two-ring*

strobe and a solid light, ignore it," Anderson called impatiently. *"Your receivers are picking up the jamming from your own pods."*

Billy's face flushed hot with embarrassment.

"THIS IS BIG EYE. BISON IN QUEBEC GOLF THREE. I REPEAT. THIS IS BIG EYE. BISON IN QUEBEC GOLF THREE," came a blasting radio transmission over the emergency frequency. Big Eye was an airborne radar aircraft, and—Billy looked at the card on his kneeboard—"Bison" was the code name for MiGs. He fumbled and opened his map to find out where the hell the Q-G-3 coordinates were.

"Fords, keep a good lookout for MiGs," radioed Anderson.

According to Billy Bowes's map the Q-G-3 sector was not far ahead.

"Cadillac lead has two MiG-21's at our three o'clock. Prepare to engage, Cadillacs."

He looked again at his kneeboard. "Cadillac" was the Wild Weasel flight, flying a dozen miles out in front of them. Excitement welled within his chest and he felt his heart quicken.

He moved his gaze about the sky, staring hard, shifting, staring hard again. Concentrating on his area of responsibility, the airspace from dead ahead, around to the left, to their rear. He nudged left rudder and craned about. Nothing behind them. He swept his gaze slowly back toward the forward quadrant.

"Move it around, Ford two," Anderson barked at him. *"Keep jinking."*

Damn. He'd forgotten to keep his aircraft in motion. He banked, first one way and then another, as Lucky Anderson was doing. An old-hand combat pilot had told him to avoid abrupt movements, to make smooth, yet unpredictable adjustments to create tracking problems for enemy gunners.

Ford flight continued toward the target area. Billy's mind computed. *Four minutes since they'd crossed into North Vietnam. Flying at nine nautical miles a minute.* He estimated they were ten minutes from the ridge of mountains north of Hanoi.

He peered at the terrain. Ahead was a wide flatland checkered with multihued rice paddies. A wide, muddy river writhed snakelike through the valley. The Red.

It was pack six, and just as he'd been briefed, it looked

very different from the green mountainous jungles covering
pack five. It was the pulsing, vibrant heart of North Vietnam. Fifteen million people, three fourths of the country's
population, lived on the tiny farms and in the crowded population centers of that single great valley. All of the country's
industry was located there, as were their two primary cities,
Hanoi and Haiphong. Except for the single ridge of mountains that ran north of Hanoi, it was mostly flat. So flat that
the elevation, from the coast to the western mountains more
than one hundred miles inland, was less than fifty feet above
sea level.

*"THIS IS BIG EYE. BISON IN ALPHA GOLF FOUR. I
REPEAT. THIS IS BIG EYE.- BISON IN ALPHA GOLF
FOUR."* The radar aircraft, again announcing MiGs, broadcasting with their directional antennae, which made the
words so loud they hurt your eardrums.

He lifted his head, saw motion in the distance, and focused on three delta-wing forms. MiG-21's!

Billy hit the mike button and stuttered, *"B'Bogeys at ten
o'clock."*

Anderson asked quietly, *"Who's got bogeys at ten
o'clock?"*

"Ford two has three MiGs in sight at ten o'clock," he announced in an unnaturally high voice. It was hard to restrain
himself from pulling up and into the MiGs.

"High or low, Ford two?" asked Anderson in the madden-
ingly calm tone.

"High," he shouted.

"Take a closer look, two."

"Lead, I see four of them now. Request permission to . . ."
Billy stared harder, saw the bogeys continue serenely, weaving and jinking on a high flight path that paralleled their
own. There was something about them. . . .

"See the smoke trails, Ford two?"

Billy saw the wisp of black smoke and wanted to hide in
a hole. *"Roger, sir."* His voice was much quieter.

*"MiGs don't smoke like that, Ford two. I've been watching
the F-4's for a couple of minutes now. You just see 'em?"*

He paused to swallow. *"Yes, sir."*

"Keep up your lookout for MiGs, Fords," said Anderson
with a hint of sarcasm.

*"Ford three's got two bogeys at two o'clock, ten degrees
high, 'bout six miles, lead,"* came Captain Tatro's lazy voice.

Billy snapped his vision around, searching the sky, saw two specks in the distance. He swung his head back toward lead and . . . Anderson had turned directly toward him! He immediately banked hard left, reefing on the stick to avoid being hit. Then, adjusting his composure and ungritting his clenched teeth, he closed to fly a hundred yards off lead's wing.

"Keep your airspeed up, Fords," Anderson calmly called, *"and prepare to engage. Select left outboard station for a missile shot."*

Billy excitedly reset his weapons-panel switch, wondering if they shouldn't drop their bombs and fuel tanks to prepare for hard maneuvering.

"Ford lead, this is three," sounded Captain Tatro's southern draw. *"The MiGs are turnin' south."* Tatro's "south" came out sounding like "sowf." His Mississippi accent was sometimes difficult to interpret.

"I've got 'em in sight, Ford three," said Anderson, and led Ford flight into a slow turn back to course.

Billy glanced back at the MiGs and studied them for future reference. He had exceptional eyesight and would not mistake them again.

He overheard the flak-suppression flight talking about SAMs up ahead, saying something about preparing to "take it down," which he knew was a maneuver to evade surface-to-air missiles. He felt ill prepared and now wished he'd been given the practice missions Lucky Anderson had spoken of.

Ford lead altered course and Billy easily corrected, vowing not to be thrown out of position again.

As they crossed the wide, muddy river, groups of white puffs sputtered over a riverbank village a few miles to their right. They did not appear menacing, for the explosions were not close, yet his heart betrayed him and thumped harder. Billy Bowes had seen his first flak.

"Fords two and four, that's Yen Bai at our four o'clock," explained Lucky Anderson to the two new men. *"They shoot like that when we go by. Don't hit much, but they shoot a lot."*

"Ho Chi Minh's got a cathouse set up there," drawled Captain Tatro, the word pronounced "kayut-hayous."

How the hell could they be cracking jokes? Billy's stomach felt as if something was clawing to get out.

A squealing, chattering sound broke the solitude. The CRT on his RHAW showed a dancing electronic strobe which extended to the third concentric ring. There was no problem discerning between the real thing and the random noise he'd seen before.

"*SAM activity at one o'clock, Fords,*" radioed Anderson, still using the calm, conversational tone.

"*Ford three's got a SAM launch indication,*" called Tatro in a distinctively higher pitch.

"*Prepare to maneuver, Fords,*" called Major Anderson, and Billy Bowes's heart flooded with adrenaline.

1411 Local—Route Pack Six, North Vietnam

Major Lucky Anderson

Lucky watched distant flurries of dust and smoke as the SAMs blasted off their launch pads, then carefully kept his eyes glued on them as he lowered the nose of his Thud a few degrees and nudged the throttle forward to the stop. They'd fired a group of three missiles, with six seconds between each launch. He estimated the SAMs to be ten to twelve miles distant. He couldn't see the missiles themselves yet, only the fiery plumes of their boosters.

His Thud was building speed. He didn't know how much, because he didn't dare take his eyes off the SAM plumes to look inside the cockpit. Speed meant maneuvering energy, and more was better than less, so he kept the throttle pressed to the limit.

The secret now would be to keep their cool, to continue building up their energy until the last split second, when the missiles were too close to react, and then to maneuver hard.

The missiles were shooting toward them at incredible speeds, the combined closure rates now more than four times the speed of sound. He slowly sucked in a breath of air and waited—waited until he could see the missile clearly—waited until—*NOW!* He pulled the control stick sharply back, and the Thud skidded and slewed upward. A fuzzy cloud of white formed at the canopy bow, condensation from the muggy air. He maintained the sharp climb, then banked first left, then hard right before rolling the Thud over on its back.

"*Ford lead, I saw all three missiles go by,*" called Turk Tatro, his voice calm again.

"*Roger, Ford three,*" Lucky replied, rolling out wings level. He glanced out to his right and was amazed to see Lieutenant Bowes moving back into position. If Bowes could stay in place through that sort of wild-assed maneuvering, Lucky thought, he was one hell of a pilot.

He adjusted course toward Thud Ridge, the line of mountains north of Hanoi, and the prominent knoll that was to be their turn point, pushing the throttle forward to the stop, then easing off a single notch. They were flying at 630 knots, almost Mach one, and were only a couple miles south of their preplanned course.

Cadillac, the Wild Weasel flight, called from the opposite side of Thud Ridge that the target weather was CAVU, *clear and visibility unlimited*. That was partly good, for they'd have no trouble seeing the target, partly bad because the gunners would be able to see them as well.

A flight behind them announced they'd spotted MiGs. Lucky looked about and again caught his wingman flying straight and level, as if he were flying an airway in the States. "*Ford two, keep it moving around,*" he chastised.

Bowes immediately resumed his random maneuvering. He'll be a good combat jock, thought Lucky. He had reservations about Lieutenant Francis, who was only now joining up with Captain Tatro after the defensive maneuvering.

They approached Thud Ridge at equal altitude with the knoll, skimming over the trees on its left side. Lucky turned hard right and descended. He flew southward toward the target, dropping and rising, using the contours of the ridge as a shield from defenses, the remainder of the flight trailing out behind him. The tactic was called terrain masking, for while they were flying this close to the mountains, they would remain hidden in the ground clutter on the gomer radar scopes.

The flak-suppression flight, thirty seconds in front of them, announced they were popping up for weapons delivery.

Lucky looked ahead and saw the sprawling city of Hanoi. Dark 57, 85, and 100mm flak bursts formed in dense groups of fours and sixes over the Red River, wide and pocked with islets here, where it meandered through the northernmost part of the city. As Ford flight passed the last green hillock of the ridge, Lucky Anderson pushed the throttle outboard into the afterburner detent and pulled back on the control stick, then felt the kick in the ass as the burner lit.

"Ford lead is in the pop-up," he announced, then added for the benefit of the two new lieutenants: *"I'll offset to the west of the target, over the river. Two, follow me in, but not down the same chute. We'll recover on the east side of the ridge."*

He was climbing fast, jinking sharply to his left, then to his right, as he passed through 10,000 feet and approached the perch. He saw the dancing sparkles of cluster-bomblet units going off at his eleven o'clock, where the flak-suppression flight had dropped on the guns.

He rolled the Thud over on its back and hung in the straps, carefully searching the earth below, letting his eyes drift up the north side of the riverbank, then settle on white smoke issuing from two stacks. The thermal-power plant? He studied the shape and convinced himself it was the same structure he'd studied in photos before takeoff.

Smoke from the power plant's stacks was blowing gently to the east, toward him. Ten knots of wind?

"Ford lead's in the dive," he announced, again for the benefit of the green lieutenants. When they were more experienced, it would all be done silently.

He heard the rattling sounds of a SAM tracking radar over his RHAW system.

"Ford two has a SAM light," called Lieutenant Bowes. A good call, for this time the kid was right.

"Ignore it, Ford two. The missiles won't be able to keep up with our maneuver."

Lucky tucked the stick back into his lap and nudged it against his leg. He rolled out wings level, in a steep forty-five-degree dive in the direction of the target area, pulling his throttle halfway back, settling the pipper short of the target, adjusting slightly for the wind. As he continued diving, the pipper crept upward toward the target. He was flying straight and predictably, now in the most hazardous period of a dive-bomb combat mission. If he jinked now, the bombs would be thrown off target. Time to grit his teeth and press on.

Black and ominous flak bursts walked about the sky,

searching for him. The RHAW squealed and chattered. He
ignored it all, maintaining the steady sight-picture, waiting
as the pipper slowly crawled toward the power plant. *Pipper
on target.* He waited for a split second longer, a final com-
pensation for the wind, then pickled. The bombs departed,
his bird jolting with the relief, and he immediately banked
hard one way and then the other as the flak bursts tracked
closer. He'd begun his pullout lower and faster than normal.

Breathing hard now. The controls mushing as the Thud
was buffeted by flak bursts. BOOM—BOOM. So close, he
could hear the muffled noises over the screaming turbojet.
Climbing out slowly, still going fast, he rolled up on his left
wing and flew an arc, staring back at the target. The power
plant was lost in towering columns of gray smoke and rusty-
brown dirt. His bombs and his wingman's had done that.
More explosions, then more, as the rest of Ford flight's
bombs found the target. A furious white vent of steam spat
out of the carnage as a boiler was split.

He glanced up and saw the next flight starting its dive toward the target. Then, much closer, a bright light flared.

"Ford four's hit," came the shrill voice of Lieutenant
Francis.

"It's your main fuel tank, four. Eject!" called Captain
Tatro.

The Thud was streaming brilliant fire from the top portion of its fuselage.

"Get out!" radioed Tatro.

Lucky Anderson saw the flash of the ejection rocket as
Ford four punched out of his aircraft.

"Weeep, weeep, weeep, weeep . . . ," the sounds of
Francis's emergency locator beeper sounded. The beeper
came on automatically when the parachute opened, and
broadcast its plaintive cry on 243.0, the emergency frequency.

Anderson continued his slow bank, shutting off emergency-
guard frequency to eliminate the irritating noise of the
beeper.

"They're shooting at him in the chute," sounded Captain
Tatro's outraged southern voice.

Anderson saw that Lieutenant Bowes was pulling into
position on his right wing.

"Ford three," Lucky radioed. *"Let's go home. Nothing we
can do to help here."*

"The bastards are shooting at him. I can see the tracers."

"Join up, three," ordered Major Lucky Anderson in a firmer voice.

Except for a smattering of flak when they crossed back over the Red River into pack five, and a single sighting of a distant MiG-17, the flight home was quiet and uneventful.

As they crossed the border into Laos, Lucky radioed the success code to Red Crown, indicating they'd destroyed the target. They found the tanker at the end of the refueling track, where the ground-radar controller said it was waiting, checked their switches and told the tanker pilot that their noses were cold, and took on enough jet petroleum to make the trip home.

During the final hour of the flight, from tanker drop-off until they made their visual approach at Takhli, the three men in the cockpits of Ford flight became lost in their thoughts, remembering the young man named Francis and wondering about his fate.

1930 Local—Hoa Lo Prison, Hanoi

Major Glenn Phillips

A guard harshly pushed the door open. Fishface, the chief interrogator at the Hanoi Hilton, whose chinless face and puckered lips made him resemble a carp, stepped inside, staring at the prisoner with a look of expectancy. Glenn stood, staggered once because his leg, though healing, was unstable at the best of times and had been immobilized for the past several days. He steadied himself, then tried to bow sharply at the waist as was demanded and expected of him, and staggered again. Fishface nodded to the doorway, and guards dragged a prisoner into the cell. Blood drained from the man's legs, leaving bright snail's trails.

With a mocking expression, Fishface said, "Here is *Pra-ans*, another Mee cow-ard," which meant he'd been able to question the poor bastard. "Mee" was the Vietnamese word for Americans, and they spat out the word with a hateful tone. Fishface's English was improving. Likely, thought

Glenn, because he was interrogating prisoners more often than before.

When Glenn had first arrived at the stark, gray-walled Hanoi prison, the guards would just beat the hell out of the pilots who arrived in the New Guy building until they bent them and got them to talk, and then, except for periodic re-education sessions, would generally ignore them. Now there seemed to be less meaning to the beatings. The gomers weren't any more sophisticated about their questioning, they just seemed more methodical. They'd beat a guy good when he first came into the New Guy building, to break him down and get all the target information and personal data they could. Then they'd just keep at him for a couple more weeks to destroy any vestiges of pride. Before they'd move him to another building or one of the other camps, they'd slack off some, just beat him every once in a while. Without purpose or reason they'd take him and bend him for a few days, then get him to write a letter or propaganda statement to make sure his mind wasn't healing before they moved him along.

The pilots hadn't expected to be treated well when they were shot down. Some had even expected to be tortured for information and then killed. But none had expected the degree of savagery, the constant mistreatment and humiliation they had to undergo, or the relish with which the officer interrogators and enlisted turnkey guards enjoyed tormenting them.

The gomers dropped the new man onto the second bunk, an elevated concrete slab with its wooden slat mattress on top.

He was Air Force. Glenn could tell by the blood-soaked gray flight suit. The fact that he had a flight suit on at all was a bad sign. If a prisoner was lucid and in good condition when they captured him, the gomers would often strip off his flying suit as a humiliation measure. If the guy was bad off, they'd just take his watch, dog tags, and the stuff from his pockets, zip off his vest and g-suit, and leave on the flight suit while they decided what to do about him. This one was worse than bad off. His flight suit was dark and wet with blood, and he was unconscious, his face chalky pale as if no blood was left in there.

After Glenn had been shot down, the gomers had mistreated his broken leg so badly that death had seemed a sure thing. Then, inexplicably, they'd taken him to the Bach Mai

Hospital, where a Russian doctor had repaired his leg and inserted a metal rod to give it strength. After a questioning period at the hospital they'd left him alone and he'd slowly mended. Since his return to jail, they'd put badly wounded prisoners in with him, as if he were a doctor. Kept him at Hoa Lo, instead of taking him to the Zoo or the other outlying prison camps where the other guys were sometimes moved. Glenn didn't know why the gomers were acting so strangely, acting as if he were a healer or a priest or something, and the one time he'd asked Fishface, the interrogator had done his rope tricks and hurt him so badly that he'd decided it would be unwise to ask again.

Glenn had been alone for the past week, since they took away a badly burned Navy lieutenant who had somehow survived. He'd spent the entire week in wood and iron leg-stocks, holdouts from the previous century, that were so rusty they had to use heavy hammers to open and close them. His legs had grown progressively more painful and stiff until the feeling was gone, his miserable solitude interrupted only when the turnkey arrived with a plate of roach-infested, tasteless gruel, or let a prisoner in to haul out his *bo*-bucket of piss and shit. They'd given no reason for the punishment. Neither had they explained why they'd arrived a couple of hours ago and removed the leg-stocks and walked him around the room, ignoring him as he cried like a baby from the pain. Now he knew why.

Phillips began to examine his new roommate with the guards still there. One started to chastise him, but Fishface growled something obviously funny to them and they left, laughing.

No chance, was Glenn's immediate thought about the new prisoner's condition.

A loud, shrill voice boomed from the speaker box in the hall, announcing the daily propaganda and listing the American soldiers killed in South Vietnam.

"What's your name?" he whispered in the flier's ear.

No response.

He inspected closer and found multiple wounds in the chest and stomach. Before they'd captured him, the guy had somehow taken the two rolls of gauze and the elastic bandage from the survival kit and wrapped them tightly around the outside of the flight suit to form pressure bandages. The wounds were so bad that all the poor bastard had done was delay death long enough for Fishface and his crew to torture him.

Glenn was surprised they brought the prisoner to him. Most of the ones this bad they just threw out next to the trash pile at the west side of the prison to be hauled off. He started to inspect the man closer and jumped when the body began to thrash about, feebly and without reason. Glenn tried to hold him down, then realized that it was for no good purpose, so he just stepped back and spoke a simple prayer as the limbs convulsed in their dance of death.

The thrashing was feeble and quickly ceased. A gentle, sighing sound issued from the dying man's throat. Glenn watched for a while longer, then leaned over the still body.

"Pra-ans," he muttered to himself, repeating what Fishface had called the man and wondering what the name really was and how it was spelled.

The primary task the prisoners had assigned themselves was to return home with their honor intact. Another was to memorize the names of all men taken prisoner. Once a prisoner's location and status was known, he was said to be "in the system," and his name was added to the list. The list had grown so long that ranking officers had assigned different portions of the list for various of the men to memorize.

For Glenn Phillips to get and disseminate the name of the dead man was crucial.

He found a laundry mark on the bloody T-shirt that tracked with Fishface's fractured mispronunciation. He wished he had more, like an initial, but it was all he could find.

He went to the wall later that night and, using a tap-code developed in American prisons and adopted by the POWs, entered Francis's name into "the system."

"N-U P I-S D-E-D. N-A-M-E W-A-S F-R-A-N-C-I-S."

The captain in the adjacent cell tapped his acknowledgment.

"See, buddy," Glenn told the body, which stank of blood, urine, and feces, "there was a reason you came to visit."

CHAPTER TWO

Major Lucky Anderson

The morning following the mission to the Hanoi power plant, Lucky called a meeting of his C-Flight. There were many new faces in the group, and it was time to introduce them to one another, explain the rules, and start the process of getting them to pull together as a unit.

The men chattered as they settled into the theater-style seats set up in the squadron pilot's lounge.

Lucky went to the refrigerator and pulled out a frost-coated bottle of Coke. As he returned to the front of the group, organizing his words in his mind, Lieutenant Bowes hurried in, carrying a bulky sheaf of papers in a folder. He was finishing with the shitty details of clearing onto base.

"C-Flight's all here now, Major," Turk Tatro announced.

Lucky eyed the six pilots. Three captains and three first lieutenants. Only he, Captain Tatro, and Lieutenant Horn had any combat experience to speak of. Lieutenant Bowes and Captain Liebermann had only one or two missions under their belts. Captain DeVera and Lieutenant Walker had yet to fly their first mission. A somber thought preoccupied him. After he'd helped the new guys with the basics and got them working together, they'd still be beating the odds if half of them made it through their hundred-mission tours.

"Once a week," he began, "we'll have these meetings. Not because I like them . . . I don't, and I've got plenty of other things to do. But the nature of the air war changes fast and often, and we've got to stay on top of things. So every week we'll sit down together, talk about flying combat, and go over any new restrictions they've thought up."

"Restrictions?" asked Manny DeVera with a raised eyebrow. He'd been quick to pick up on the thing that stuck most in their craws at Takhli.

"By damn, Manny, you'll wonder who's on our side when you hear the bullshit you've gotta remember when you're flying up there," said Turk Tatro in a southern accent so thick he could transform three-letter words into three-syllable ones.

"What kind of restrictions?" growled Manny.

"You can't fly within thirty nautical miles of Red China or within twenty miles of Hanoi unless specifically directed on a JCS target. You can't fly within twenty miles of a noncombatant ship, even if they're bringing ammo and missiles to shoot you with. You can't shoot MiGs on the ground, because all their bases are restricted. You can't bomb dams or dikes that might cause flooding. You can't . . ."

Lucky lifted his hand and interrupted. "We'll go over them all later, Turk."

Manny obviously didn't like what he'd heard. "And we've gotta obey all those restrictions? How the hell do we get air superiority if we can't take out the MiG bases?"

"Yeah," said Anderson, with a trace of impatience, "we've gotta obey all the rules. No, it doesn't make a hell of a lot of sense."

Manny glared. "Who makes that shit up?"

Lucky ticked his answers off on his fingers. "Starts with the President. Passed to the Secretary of Defense, through the JCS offices at the Pentagon, out to CINCPAC, who's a four-star admiral based at Pearl Harbor. From him across the harbor to Headquarters PACAF at Hickam Field, General Roman's group. From PACAF to Seventh Air Force in Saigon, where Lieutenant General Moss runs things. From Seventh Air Force to the flying units, like the 355th Tactical

Fighter Wing here at Takhli, and the 388th at Korat. Every
general and staff puke in that chain gets a crack at interpreting the restrictions and coming up with ways to make sure
you don't cheat. So don't."

"Jesus," snorted DeVera. "You'd think they'd take away
the Mickey Mouse bullshit when we go to combat, so we
could do our jobs."

"Yeah, Manny," Lucky said, "you'd think they'd do that."

He leaned against a table placed in front of the theater
seats, examining the men of C-Flight and sipping his Coke.
They were the seeds of a good combat unit, each man pos-
sessing his unique skills. It was up to Lucky to mold and
tune them into a single aerial machine that was much more
than the sum of their potentials. He would have to build on
their strengths and compensate for their weaknesses. The
day before, he'd worried about the flying skills of First Lieutenant Fredrick G. Francis, but Francis had been weeded
out before Lucky had gotten a chance to teach him the
ropes. Thinking of that . . .

"Any of you guys know Francis?" he asked.

Walker and Bowes raised their hands.

"You two help Captain Tatro get Francis's things sorted
and boxed up. Turk, I'm appointing you as summary-courts
officer. Tell the admin sergeant to type up the orders."

Turk Tatro grimaced. No one liked summary-courts duties. Going through the personal effects of the guys who
were shot down and making sure they were forwarded to
the family, ensuring the family had been properly notified,
was truly miserable work. But Turk was reliable and thorough, and Anderson knew it would be done right.

Lucky returned to the immediately task. "I've met you
all," he started, "but I want everyone in C-Flight to get to
know one another like brothers. I want you to learn each
other's birthdays, and what everyone drinks at the bar. One
guy's girlfriend walks out on him, I want you all feeling
shitty. The six of you will be moved into three adjoining
rooms at the Ponderosa, that's the new air-conditioned pilot's quarters between here and the main gate. I know some
of you asked to room with guys you knew from before, but
I had that changed."

Lucky Anderson shucked the cellophane wrapper off a
cigar and mouthed it as they bitched about the sleeping ar-

rangements. He savored the tobacco taste until the noise subsided.

"I've also posted two notes," he continued, "one at the command post and the other at the squadron duty desk, telling them I want C-Flight to stay together on the flying schedule."

No one complained this time, and it began to sink in what Lucky was about. To make sure they understood, he explained. "All of this togetherness isn't because I'm trying to promote brotherly love. I don't give a diddley shit if you hate the sight of each other. But I insist you learn what to expect from the guys you'll be flying combat with. We don't need surprises up there. The worst thing imaginable when you're flying in pack six, is to depend on someone and have them let you down."

"Amen, by damn," muttered Turk.

"I want you to learn to fly *standard* missions, with *no* surprises. That's the only kind I'll stand for. Remember . . . *no surprises.*"

Lucky paused. "You won't always get to fly together. There are five flights in the 354th squadron: A, B, C and D flights, *and* a Wild Weasel flight. All three squadrons in the wing have that extra flight, because each squadron has its own Wild Weasel airplanes and crews assigned. We're down to two Weasel crews in the 354th now, not even enough for their own four-ship flight, so periodically you'll be scheduled to fly with them. But other than augmenting the Weasels and occasionally getting tapped to fly with the brass, I intend to keep C-Flight flying together."

"What do the Wild Weasels do?" asked Lieutenant Walker, who had not yet flown combat. He and Manny were both scheduled for tomorrow's morning mission.

"They fly two-seat F-105Fs," Lucky said, "with electronic equipment installed so they can home in on SAM site radars. They precede us going to the target area and trail us coming out, and try to keep the SAM operators busy while we're bombing. The Weasel front-seaters are high-time Thud pilots, and the backseaters are electronic-warfare officers, called bears."

"Do they really help?" asked Manny DeVera with a dubious tone. Wild Weasel was a new concept. Fighter pilots were a conservative group and were often suspect of changes from traditional ways of doing things.

"When they're in the area, we see fewer SAMs targeted for us, because the Weasels get the gomers to fire their missiles at them. And you'll celebrate every time they find and bomb a site, because there'll be that many fewer missiles launched at you. They're effective enough, but they take a lot of combat losses, and there's seldom enough of them to go around."

"Everything about flying here can be measured in degrees of bad," interjected Turk. "It's damn hairy flyin' in pack six, even with the Weasels with us. Without 'em, it's worse."

Lieutenant Bowes stirred, then spoke in a quiet voice. "I had a cousin who was a Weasel stationed here. Got shot down last month."

"They've got a tough mission," said Turk Tatro, squinting hard at Bowes as if he recognized something but couldn't place it.

They waited for Bowes to elaborate, but he'd returned to his silence. *A loner?* Lucky wondered. He nudged them back on track.

"Time for introductions. I'm Paul Anderson, and I'm called Lucky by those who can't pronounce my one-syllable first name. I've got fourteen hundred flying hours in the Thud, mainly at McConnell Air Force Base, Kansas, and Nellis Air Force Base, Nevada. Before that I was in Huns at Luke, where I got six hundred hours in the F-100D, and before that I racked up three hundred hairy hours in bent-wing F-84Fs at Sembach Air Base, Germany."

He paused, eyeing them. "I'm a believer in flying safety, which I learned the hard way, and you'll hear me bitch if I see you flying in unauthorized gear like Captain DeVera's silk scarf or Lieutenant Bowes's driving gloves. You ever get in a bad cockpit fire, you'll wish you'd listened. But I will forgive you if you ignore that counsel. I will *not* forgive other things, however—like failing to support your flight in the air."

Captain DeVera was frowning, which didn't surprise Lucky. Manny was a good pilot, but like many fighter jocks his ego was such that he required special handling.

"What's wrong with my scarf?" Manny growled. The silk cloth around his neck had the black-and-yellow checkerboard pattern worn only by fighter weapons school graduates.

"It's flammable, Manny. Get in a fire and it'll either torch or smolder. Wear it when you're on the ground, but not in the air. You can give it to your crew chief before you take off. He'll keep it for you until you land."

DeVera looked disgusted. He was something of a non-conformist, which Lucky felt was acceptable as long as he performed well in the air. Manny had a reputation as a ballsy and capable pilot.

"It's a good-luck thing," Manny said finally.

A number of fighter jocks carried good-luck pieces of one type or another. People who lived on the fine edge weren't especially more superstitious than others, it was just that they didn't see wisdom in pissing off the fates.

Lucky decided enough time had been spent on the flying-safety issue, so he left it with a parting shot. "Manny," he concluded dryly, "you want to ignore what I'm telling you about fires, think about this lovely face of mine, then do what you think's best."

DeVera looked embarrassed, an emotion alien to his brash manner.

"Let's get on with the introductions," said Lucky. "Captain Tatro is assistant C-Flight commander. Once you get so you can understand his Confederatese, you'll find he knows what he's talking about. Turk?"

Tatro, lounging easily in his seat, turned toward the others. He was short and slight, burr-headed and pug-nosed, with the fiesty air of a gamecock. His wide grin was seldom far from the surface.

"The name's Turk Tatro," he said. "I came over from Kadena on the original Thud deployment in 1964. We flew mainly in Laos then, but I got in more'n a dozen missions to North Vietnam before they rotated us home. That was before the gomers got SAMs or even any MiGs to speak of, and we had ourselves a turkey shoot. When I returned here four months ago, I found everything had changed. In those two years they got everything imaginable to shoot us with, and by damn, we've got to be prepared for every bit of it. The best way is to do everything you'd do if you were going to fly a combat mission to Moscow and back."

"Turk's flown a total of seventy-two missions over North Vietnam," interjected Lucky. "More than any of the rest of us."

To complete a combat tour they were expected to fly one hundred sorties *up north*. That meant over North Vietnam. Lesser hazardous sorties, those flown over South Vietnam or Laos, did not qualify as *counters*. Twenty-eight more counters, and Tatro would be celebrating and going home.

Turk continued. "One thing you guys should know," he said, "is that most pilots get shot down on their first twenty missions, while they're still learning the ropes. Which means you've gotta learn as much as you can, as quickly as you can."

Next Lucky came to a skinny, freckled redhead with a studious mien. "Captain Liebermann?" Lucky had flown once with him, as had Turk, and they'd concluded that he was both nervous and entirely too serious. They'd also agreed that he listened hard and was learning at a phenomenal rate.

"My name's Bob Liebermann," he said to the group, "and I upgraded into Thuds out of SAC. I flew B-52's at Loring Air Force Base, Maine."

Manny DeVera stared at him uneasily, as if Liebermann had committed the sacrilege of even *speaking* of bombers.

"Bob escaped, by damn," said Turk. Most fighter jocks distrusted bombers and all things about them, but Tatro had told Lucky that Liebermann was okay since he was so happy to be out of the eight-engined behemoths.

"Yeah," agreed Bob Liebermann, " 'escaped' is a good word for it. I just hope they don't send me back to BUFs when I finish my tour here." "BUFs" was an acronym assigned to B-52s, short for "big ugly fuckers."

"You feel easy flying Thuds?" asked a skeptical Manny DeVera.

"I've been trying to get into fighters since I got out of pilot school," said Liebermann. "I like the Thud. It's a complex airplane, though, and I've got a lot of catching up to do. I read the Dash-One day and night, even take it to the shitter with me. I think I've damn near got it memorized. I don't want to give *anyone* reason to send me back to BUFs."

The Dash-One was the three-inch-thick technical publication that described all aircraft systems and included detailed checklists, and safety and flight data for the aircraft.

"You're up," said Lucky, nodding to DeVera.

"Call me Manny," said the big and beefy captain, showing a glittering smile of even white teeth. He looked like a youthful, very sure and very handsome Anthony Quinn.

"I immigrated to the States by way of a shallow river crossing when I was about two years old, and"—he waved his arms expansively—"in our wonderful land of opportunity, I've gone on to become the world's greatest fighter pilot."

"The Supersonic Wetback," said Turk, calling Manny by the nickname he had himself fostered, "does not suffer from lack of ego."

Manny, who had glowing reputations both as an adept pilot and an uncannily successful womanizer, grinned wider. "When you got it, why hide it? I've got fifteen hundred hours of fighter time. Huns and Thuds ... upgraded from F-100's to F-105's four years ago. I've had tours at Hahn, Germany; Nellis Air Force Base, Nevada; and Wheelus Air Base in Libya."

"Tell 'em about Wheelus, Manny," said Lucky. "Some of the lieutenants probably didn't even know we had a base in Libya."

"We maintain a big gunnery range there for the fighter jocks stationed in Germany to practice on. The country's run by King Idris, an old codger who likes Americans. We have a support base just outside Tripoli called Wheelus, with half a dozen fighter jocks to monitor the weapons programs and run the range. The squadrons from Germany rotate in and out of Wheelus so the jocks can stay proficient in bombing and gunnery."

Lucky noted how the others hung on to his words. Manny had a bucket of charisma, one of those guys people liked being around and listening to. When Manny went to the bar or the squadron-duty desk, others gathered to hear about his latest exploits. It was difficult to explain his charm. Someone could tell an off-color joke, and females within earshot would frown. Manny could follow with a downright raunchy line, and the same women would giggle and give him wicked little smiles.

"Lieutenant Walker?" urged Lucky Anderson to keep

things moving, motioning to a handsome, light-skinned black man with even features.

"My name's Joe Walker," he said in a quiet, mellow voice. "I'm from Pasadena, California, and I attended the Air Force Academy before I went to pilot training. This is my first operational assignment."

Turk snapped his fingers. "You played football at the Academy! *That's* where I heard of you."

Walker looked about shyly, until his classmate, Lieutenant Henry Horn, spoke up boldly. "Joe played end and set school records that'll be around for a long time. He caught everything they threw his way and then some."

"By damn," admired Tatro, an avid football fan.

Horn wasn't done. "The Baltimore Colts tried to sign him. Offered him a big cash fee so he wouldn't be hurting for money while he finished his service commitment. But Joe turned them down and applied for pilot training."

"How come you didn't take 'em up?" Manny asked.

Joe Walker grinned and shrugged. "I wanted to fly fighters," he said simply, and gained instant kinship within the group.

"Henry?" Anderson urged.

"I'm Henry Horn," answered the sturdy lieutenant with the shock of blond hair, "from Boulder, Colorado. Married a Denver girl when I graduated from the Academy, and she's got a tiny fighter pilot in the hangar."

"And that's all he talks about," interjected Turk.

"This is my first operational assignment," continued Horn. "I've been here three months, since January, and so far it's been a hell of an experience." He looked around at the three new members of C-Flight. "One thing I've learned. We're fortunate to be working for Major Lucky. Listen to him, because he's got a lot to teach us."

Anderson wondered about that. Counting Francis, C-Flight had now lost four pilots in the two months since his arrival. He spent a lot of miserable hours thinking about the lost men.

"Lieutenant Bowes?" he said to the tallest of the lieutenants.

Bowes's look was intent, as if he were quietly taking in everything and carefully evaluating it. Bowes, Lucky remembered, had exhibited superb flying ability. He was going to be very good, possibly the best pilot in the group. Maybe, someday, as good as he was.

"I'm Billy Bowes," he announced softly. "I attended the University of Oklahoma. I was an instructor pilot at Moody Air Force Base, Georgia, then at Vance in Oklahoma. I volunteered for F-4's because I'd rather be killing MiGs than dropping bombs, but they sent me to Thuds. Then I asked for Korat, because I heard it was a nice base next to a big city, so they sent me to Takhli."

He was joking. Anderson had seen his dream sheet, where they listed their choices for assignment. Lieutenant Bowes had wanted action in a hot charger unit and had specifically requested Takhli.

Lucky said, "You'll get your chance at MiGs. We go where they are, or rather they go where *we* are. They're after our big, overweight asses when we're loaded down with bombs and fuel tanks on the way to the target."

Turk Tatro again looked closely at Bowes, as if he couldn't quite place him. "You had a relative here in Wild Weasels?"

"Malcom Stewart was his name. My cousin."

"Bear Stewart over in the 357th squadron?"

Billy Bowes nodded. His look was unwavering, eyes flat and inexpressive.

Turk Tatro's face brightened with recognition. "Yeah. When he and his pilot were shot down, the Bear decided to shoot it out with a squad of gomers. He had a pistol and they had AK-47's." He shook his head sympathetically. "Big balls, but he didn't have a chance."

"The North Vietnamese are a tough, determined enemy," said Lucky as he studied Bowes. "They work hard to kill you in the air, and once they get their hands on you on the ground, they're brutal. You can't afford to give them an inch."

"I hadn't planned to," said Billy Bowes, and Lucky Anderson liked the answer.

He regarded his group of war eagles. They were a cross section of young pilots you might find anywhere in the Air Force, but they were assigned to his C-Flight, and for that reason they were special in his eyes. "Let's go over the rules and restrictions," he said to them, "and what we *can't do*. Then we'll talk about combat flying and what we *have to do* to survive and get our bombs on the target."

1120 Local—Vietnamese People's Army Headquarters Hanoi, Democratic Republic of Vietnam

Colonel Nguyen Wu -

Nguyen Wu was tall and wraith thin, with a sunken face and eyes that darted nervously. He despised all Tay, the Vietnamese word of scorn for Westerners, and especially the Mee, the word for "Americans" taken from the French word *ami*. Yet he was the sort who would instantly embrace them as brethren if such was to his advantage.

Like the others in the room, he'd been called to a meeting chaired by General Van Tien Dung, the most powerful of the generals working in the shadow of General Giap. Wu sat immediately behind General Luc, his superior officer and commander of the People's Army of National Defense. General Tho, seated beside General Luc, was commander of the People's Army Air Force. Those two were entrusted with the protection of the Democratic Republic. General Tho controlled the bases, aircraft, pilots, and their support, General Luc the antiaircraft rocket, radar, and artillery defenses, as well as the home militia. Behind the two generals sat the colonels who made the generals' wishes happen.

They all waited patiently for General Dung.

Colonel Nguyen Wu had risen quickly to his present rank and position. At thirty-three years of age he commanded all radars and guided rocket defenses. An important position, but one not to his liking. He was too visible, his failures too difficult to hide from the eyes of superiors. He intended to remain in the position only long enough to find a more suitable, less vulnerable one.

Wu's attention was focused upon a fighter pilot sitting to his immediately right, a man known simply as Quon, who was one of the best-known heroes of the Democratic Republic. Quon's exploits were frequently cited in *Nham Dan*, the official party newspaper, and his background was familiar even to schoolchildren. The tale had appeared numerous times, for Quon was a model for the propagandists. His life's story was only slightly less familiar to the public than that of Ho Chi Minh.

In 1943 the eighteen-year-old son of a respected Saigon family had stolen into the jungle to join one of the several guerrilla units resisting the occupying Army of Japan and their Vichy French collaborators. He'd picked upon the Viet Minh, the military arm of the secret Lao Dong party. The leader of the Lao Dong was an elusive communist named Nguyen Thanh, who had changed his name to Nguyen Ai Quoc, "the Patriot." He'd just talked his way out of one of Chiang Kai-shek's prisons in Nationalist China and announced that henceforth his name would be Ho Chi Minh, "the Enlightened One." Ho's military leader was a former history professor, Vo Nguyen Giap, and shortly after his arrival Giap had appointed Quon to join nine other bright young men on "a very special assignment." The leader of the group had been a nephew of one of Ho Chi Minh's inner circle, and he'd answered their questions vaguely and revealed little. Lieutenant Tho told them only that they'd be departing immediately, and there was a likelihood they would not come back . . . ever. He'd added that any who desired to do so could drop out without censure. None did.

Propaganda writers liked to pause at this juncture to explain how a truly dedicated communist must, like Quon and the others, ask only to serve.

They'd ventured north to China, then westward to the border with the Soviet Union, where Lieutenant Tho had shown letters granting them safe passage. On toward the setting sun, across the huge expanse of barren steppes. They'd walked, taken ox carts, and once ridden in a large, open trailer pulled by a wood-consuming, steam-driven tractor with huge iron wheels. Two of them had been struck down by sickness on the long trek and left behind. Just before the snows came, they'd arrived at the furiously busy airfield of Kamensk-Uralskii on the eastern slope of the great Ural mountain range, and Lieutenant Tho had finally told them the nature of their special assignment.

They were to become pilots. At the end of the war a socialist republic would emerge in Vietnam, and as Ho Chi Minh had convinced the right people within the Soviet Union, they would need a military air service.

Another facet of the Enlightened One's wisdom, the writers interjected here, was his ability to determine the needs of future generations.

The Soviets had agreed to train them to fly, then assign them to combat units to gain operational experience. The seven standing before Lieutenant Tho had turned gleeful, caught up in their sense of self-importance and sacrifice.

At Kamensk-Uralskii they were provided with rudimentary flight instructions. Quon's were given by an elderly Russian pilot with one eye, the other lost in some earlier war for red socialism, in a battered, dual-seated I-15 biplane with canvas-enclosed cockpits and no heat except that inadvertently supplied by engine exhaust.

The writers included Quon's joke that it had been so cold in the old airplane that their words came out frozen and had to be passed between cockpits and thawed out to hear.

After they'd been trained in the basics of flight, they endured the remainder of the terrible Ural Mountain winter, waiting to be checked out in operational aircraft and assigned to a combat unit. Finally, and it was early 1944 by then, Quon and the others had hastily been taught to fly the sleek and powerful YAK-3 fighters, similar in appearance to British Spitfires. Then they were told they would not be joining a Soviet unit but a group of Free French pilots already fighting alongside the Russians against the Germans.

By this point it was clear that the *Nham Dan* writers were intimating . . . never openly saying it, of course . . . that the Russians had been prejudiced against the Vietnamese pilots. This drew somber nods from readers who had experienced the Soviets' disdain for East Asians.

Lieutenant Tho had briefed them. Do not, he had said, let the French know we represent a new Vietnamese order. Tell them nothing. Remember that we shall kill Germans to save communism, for the Nazis are trying to destroy the cradle of Marxist-Leninist socialism. We would never help the French. We spit on the French. But do not let them know . . . yet.

The group of eight, immortalized by *Nham Dan*, flew new Yakovlev fighters to an airfield west of Moscow to join the Normandie-Nieman Group, the Free French contingent that flew agile YAK-3's and better-armed YAK-9's against the Germans. There they'd been welcomed by the pilots who'd escaped France to carry on the fight.

Three of their number had been quickly lost before they could acclimate to the furious tempo of combat flying, and two more killed as the war ground on. Together they accounted for 19 of the 273 Luftwaffe aircraft claimed by "the Group." Quon had been the youngest man in the unit, but during his fourteen months of combat he'd shot down four Ju-87 Stukas and three Bf-109 Messerschmitts. He'd gained the respect of the pilots of the Group, and his name had been read into their honor role.

Seldom did they receive word about home. It was as if a veil covered Indochina. In mid-1945 the victorious Normandie-Nieman Group flew their Yakovlev fighters to Le Bourget airfield in Paris. Only after they'd been mustered out did they learn how things were at home. Then they celebrated as enthusiastically as the French, for Ho Chi Minh had taken charge of all of Vietnam!

Largely due to assistance from the Americans, the Viet Minh had grown into the best equipped and best organized of the irregular military units, and at the end of the war the Japanese had turned the keys of government over to the only organized enemy group in sight: the Viet Minh. Ho Chi Minh had immediately created the new Democratic Republic of Vietnam and established his capitol in Hanoi. The Americans had supported him in all of this.

Let us toast the Mee! the three surviving Vietnamese pilots had said.

Getting to Vietnam hadn't been easy. Discrimination against them was open, and there seemed no way to gain passage home in the face of French outrage over the loss of their colony. Finally Tho had made arrangements on a freighter bound from Marseilles to Saigon. Each day of that voyage they'd anticipated their return, to pluck the heady fruits of victory.

Instead they returned to find only turmoil.

When the British had arrived to accept the Japanese surrender officially, they'd declared martial law and used that pretext to release the Vichy French and even some Japanese troops from their prisons to restore order.

In Saigon, Quon found the situation desperate. As British Gurkha troops fought vainly to keep peace in the streets, various bands of nationalist groups, criminal gangs, and just-freed French legionnaires wandered about, looting, fighting each other, and hunting down sympathizers of Ho's government. Old mandarin families, Viet Minh appointees, and French administrators vied for control, creating more confusion. In the north Chiang Kai-shek's troops crossed the border to convince Hanoi to change from their communist ways. The new French government, anxious to regain their

Indochinese Empire, informed Washington that they were supporting a communist regime. Recoiling, the Mee had withdrawn support and began turning over surplus war materials to the French. Ho Chi Minh's pleas to Moscow and Washington went unanswered, and his coalition government was left without support.

For Quon the personal tragedy was complete. His father had disappeared without a trace. His mother's family had sided with the Viet Minh in 1944 when Giap's men had attacked the outposts of the Vichy French. One by one they'd been hunted down and assassinated.

He'd stood watching the flames of a fire started by a drunken legionnaire and realized that only through subjugation to the Lao Dong party would his people be able to cast out the French oppressors. Then he'd walked northward, abandoning Saigon with no backward look. During the trek he assumed his mother's ancestral name of Quon and dedicated his life to their revenge. When he reached Hanoi, he offered his services to Ho Chi Minh and the party.

Now General Tho commanded the People's Army Air Force, and Quon the air regiment at Phuc Yen. Quon carried the authority of a colonel, or perhaps even a general, but disdained badges of rank. It was a part of his mystique, so admired by the readers of *Nham Dan*. Now he hunted Yankees rather than Germans or Frenchmen, and his weapon of choice was a sleek MiG-21, silver but with a special splash of red on the fuselage. According to *Nham Dan* he had destroyed countless numbers of Yankee pirates.

Quon's only son had just graduated from pilot training in Russia, as Quon had done twenty-three years before. A recent issue of *Nham Dan* had featured the story of the avenging father-son team. Quon the elder, and Thanh the son, valiant protectors of the Republic.

Each time the inspirational saga was printed in *Nham Dan*, young men clamored to be accepted for pilot training. Quon was a national asset, thought Nguyen Wu. He wondered how much of the heroic accounts were truth, and how much invented for the purposes of the party.

Since taking his seat, Wu had tried to speak with Quon, for he was a good man to know, but thus far his friendly words had been thoroughly ignored. Was that the way of the famous pilot, or was it disdain for the political way Wu had been promoted?

Nguyen Wu's aunt was one of the powerful who directed international activities at the Ministry of External Affairs, soon to become the newest member of the Central Committee of the Lao Dong party. It had been at Li Binh's insistence that the Lao Dong party had urged the Army to promote him.

He remembered General Luc calling him in and telling him of the promotion with a bewildered air, obviously uneasy that he would fill such a critical position. But Nguyen Wu felt relatively secure. Day-to-day control of the People's Army was exercised by General Van Tien Dung, the man for whom they now waited. The wily general had seemed pragmatic about Wu's promotion, and no one was likely to change things without his approval. Nguyen Wu's aunt had told him that, and she knew of such matters.

Li Binh was highly regarded for her ability and widely feared for her ruthlessness, both with just cause. That fear kept even the boldest wolves from challenging him. A few grumbled about incompetence, but they did so quietly. Still, Nguyen Wu knew he must tread cautiously and not anger the generals. Their mentor was General Vo Nguyen Giap, and Giap was tremendously powerful. He was Minister of Defense, Chief of Staff of the People's Army, trusted advisor to the Enlightened One, a founder of the Lao Dong party, and a ranking member of the Central Committee. With a single word from Giap, regardless of his family connections, Colonel Nguyen Wu would find himself a humble foot soldier . . . or worse.

I must not tarry long in this position, he told himself. There were too many jealous colonels, too many watchful generals.

On Nguyen Wu's left sat Colonel Trung, who controlled the country's antiaircraft and antiship artillery units. Trung was twenty years older than he, a traditionalist who openly disdained him. But everyone knew old Trung distrusted sophisticated weaponry as much as he disliked the young colonels promoted to control them, and his grumbling was often ignored.

General Luc turned in his seat, spoke pleasantly to Trung, then regarded Nguyen Wu. He was still uneasy around his newest colonel. Finally, "How is your aunt faring, Colonel?"

As always, Wu tried to search for hidden meanings in the general's words before he responded. "She is doing well, considering her grief, comrade General. As you know, she just left for Paris to attend important talks."

Luc nodded. "And Colonel Xuan Nha?"

Wu's uncle was a Hero of the Republic. Educated in physics and electronics, he was one of few senior Vietnamese officers who understood the complex new systems supplied by the Soviet Union. It had taken such a man, with his technical knowledge and acceptance by the generals, to establish the networks of radars and surface-to-air rockets. But a month before, Xuan Nha had taken control of one of his rocket batteries and engaged a group of Mee warplanes. Severely wounded by Mee bombs, he was now a bundle of splints and bandages languishing in the sprawling Bach Mai hospital.

Xuan Nha was an official dichotomy, admired by the generals because he got results, distrusted by the party because he'd allowed foreigners, Russians and North Koreans, to control Vietnamese defenses. The generals wanted him to recover and return to duty. The party hadn't yet decided how to handle him *should* he recover.

Wu spoke in a woeful tone. "Xuan Nha is alive, comrade General Luc, but that is all. We hope for his recovery, but . . ." He shrugged helplessly.

Following his uncle's misfortune, Wu had moved into his beloved aunt's villa. He said he was there to help console her. That was certainly true, and both he and his aunt were delighted with the arrangement. Li Binh had gone to see Xuan Nha only once and reported he was a vegetable hidden within a swath of gauze. She had not returned.

"We miss Xuan Nha's technical wisdom," General Luc observed. "He had a special understanding of radars and guided-rocket systems, and how to get the most out of them."

Was it a thrust at Wu's competence? The results Nguyen Wu had thus far provided were discouraging, for the rocket batteries had not yet recovered from the battering they'd taken when the generals had thrown in everything to stop the Mee at the Thai Nguyen steel mill. Wu knew he must improve the rocket force, but the key to that goal had been elusive. In the meantime, while he sought solutions, he must stall for time.

"We work relentlessly to rebuild," he told General Luc, "and often I ask my staff, 'What would my uncle have done in this circumstance?'"

"Yes," said General Luc, "you should do that." He raised an eyebrow as he paused meaningfully. "The Mee are increasingly successful. During yesterday's raids on the power plants here and in Haiphong, we lost much of our electrical generating capacity."

"We shot down three air pirates," said Wu. Actually Trung's artillery had shot down two Thunder planes, and his cautious rocket commanders had made an unfortunate error.

"That was what I was briefed," said Luc drily.

Did the general know he'd altered the report? Nguyen Wu hastily started to explain, "My rocket batteries at . . ."

Quon interrupted, his voice as emphatic as the crack of a pistol. "One of my interceptors was lost to your fornicating rockets! He was closing with a Phantom north of Hanoi, and your rockets hit the wrong target. Could *that* be one of the aircraft you are claiming?"

Nguyen Wu was startled at the outburst, and it took a moment for his thoughts to settle. He didn't wish to antagonize Quon, but neither could he allow himself to be criticized before the generals. "Let us speak about it later, comrade Quon," he hissed in a low voice.

Quon persisted. "I *demand* to know why your radar operators cannot identify our aircraft! We fly with transponders turned on, yet your people *still* confuse us with the enemy."

Wu wanted to ignore the question, but he realized that the generals were looking on and waiting for his answer.

"In the heat of battle," he reasoned, "the radar operators at the rocket batteries sometimes make mistakes. They are increasingly under attack themselves, and . . ."

"Perhaps you should do something about it and not simply make excuses," Quon snapped, staring directly at Wu.

Nguyen Wu's anger flashed. "Perhaps you should train your pilots better. Your MiGs were flying in an area assigned to my rockets."

A smile flickered at Quon's lips, happy that he'd elicited the outburst. He continued his baiting. "Send your radar operators to visit my pilots at Phuc Yen," he said, "so we will be able to recognize our *other* enemy."

Wu looked sheepishly toward the generals. "I apologize for our outburst, comrades."

Quon snorted. "I do not apologize, Colonel Wu. I *demand* that something be done. When Colonel Xuan Nha controlled the long-range radars, he operated them under a centralized control center for both our pilots *and* his rocket operators. We *all* got results. We *all* shot down many enemy fighters, and there were no mistakes like this one. Since you have taken over, there has been only confusion. Your radar controllers provide my pilots with poor instructions and often simply ignore us. It *cannot* continue."

Nguyen Wu looked to the generals for support, then realized there would be none. He sputtered, "The control center was damaged and had to be dismantled, and we are still reorganizing. But"—he tried to puff himself out importantly—"I have taken control from the foreigners and returned it to our people."

General Tho spoke to General Luc, ignoring Nguyen Wu. "Quon believes we should bring both of the long-range radars back under the People's Army Air Force. Since they are located at our MiG bases, it would be a simple matter. Our interceptors must be able to operate in harmony with the rocket and artillery batteries without being threatened."

General Tho explained further, "The Russians refuse to supply us with more fighters until they reequip their own units. We may get a few more MiG-19's from the Chinese, but that is all. We cannot afford to lose more aircraft needlessly."

"I must retain control of the long-range radars," Wu tried to interject. "Only my people have the technical training required to pass information to the rocket batteries."

"The radars *must* be returned to the People's Air Force," Quon said doggedly, "so we can be assured the controllers will work with our interceptors."

General Luc knew to listen. Tho and Quon were favorites of the general staff and not to be ignored. He mused silently for a moment longer, then he and Tho turned forward again.

Shaken, Wu felt a wave of helplessness. He opened his mouth to argue further, but judiciously closed it. A sideward glance showed that Quon was smiling.

Was the pilot trying to disgrace him?

For a moment he was consumed with worry; then he began wondering how he might deal with the fighter pilot. *Perhaps his aunt?* Not possible. She'd be away in Paris for weeks, and he might not have that much time.

General Dung's aide hurried through the door. "The general arrives," he announced.

Chairs scraped as the officers stood and bowed sharply as Van Tien Dung entered and stood by his chair at the head of the room. He wore an immaculate white-dress uniform, and each epaulet was adorned with three gold stars.

Ho Chi Minh, Vo Nguyen Giap, Le Duan, Le Duc Tho, Pham Van Dong, and the remainder of the Lao Dong party's vanguard sprang from affluent parentage, conspiring as students while attending French schools. The exclusion of the poor from their group was not by design, only because none were within their circles of trusted friends. The Workers' Party, the Lao Dong, was begun and thereafter controlled by the children of the privileged.

Van Tien Dung, with his peasant's roots and crude manners, had become the exception, and was living proof of the Lao Dong's commitment to The People. Despite his obscene jokes and loud guffaws at the most improper times, Dung had prospered in their ranks. After the Viet Minh had attacked the French garrisons and then fled into the Viet Bac mountains north of Hanoi in 1947, Dung had become their chief logistician. In early 1954 he'd been a critical factor behind their decisive victory at Dien Bien Phu. At the end of the great War of Liberation, he'd been Giap's right hand, and there he remained. Now, in the War of Unification, Giap worried about grand strategies and interfaces with the party, while Dung provided day-to-day control of the People's Army.

Van Tien Dung was methodical, wary of bold moves and given to conservatism. Always a survivor, he was a master at manipulating people and situations. He stood for a moment, quietly surveying the men in the room. For a split second Nguyen Wu felt the gaze resting on him. He could not quell an inner shudder, for the eyes had been hard.

Then Dung sat and did not wait until the others took their own seats before he said, "I have received reliable information that the Mee will soon begin bombing our bridges."

1210 Local—HQ Seventh Air Force, Tan Son Nhut Air Base, Saigon, South Vietnam

Lieutenant Colonel P. S. Gates, Assistant Chief of Plans and Programs at the headquarters, was far more important to the war effort than his humble title described.

Since its inception in 1947, superbly capable men had been assigned at all levels of the United States Air Force. Unfortunately, the skills of many were never realized. This was particularly true within the middle-management ranks, where competition for promotion was fiercest. Of the officers who entered the Air Force, fewer than half would be selected for lieutenant colonel. Only a third of those would make colonel. Less than five percent of those would wear stars. It was called the "up-or-out" system, and you were either promoted or left in the dust with your friend's toe in your eye as he scrambled over you.

Due to the competition for promotion, superb fighter jocks who could hardly write their own names without feeling uncomfortable, asked to be transferred to high-visibility positions at headquarters. Too often their flying duties were then assumed by pilots who were uneasy with flying, but who, given the chance, would have been very good staff officers. Thus the anomaly of superbly coordinated officers manning fifty-dollar desks at headquarters, while awkward bookworms flew multimillion-dollar aircraft about the sky.

Yet there were happier truths. Within each flying squadron there was one junior pilot who was a natural entrepreneur, who *should* have been placed in charge of the squadron snack bar. His efforts were seldom applauded, but were appreciated by thirsty squadron pilots who found plentiful supplies of chilled Coors and Heineken in snack-bar refrigerators on bases that had not received a beer shipment in weeks. Similarly, in every headquarters there were thorny and difficult problem areas, and for each of these there was an officer who could quickly and accurately interpret the vast regulations and written guidelines, relate these to the real world, and advise the generals what they should or should not do. Successful general officers searched for and found these men, nurtured and listened closely to them, and were seen to make superb judgments. Stupid ones did not.

Richard J. Moss, the three-star commander of Seventh Air Force headquartered in Saigon, was not stupid. Among

the experts to whom he listened was Lieutenant Colonel
P. S. Gates.

P. S. Gates had been stuck with the nickname of "Pearly"
since he'd been an ROTC corporal. He'd resisted it, for he
was from a proud and old Philadelphia family, and his name-
sake grandfather had been a rather famous state governor.
Regardless, Pearly remained "Pearly." Few of his Air Force
friends knew that the *P* really stood for Phillip, and fewer
yet gave a shit about politicians.

At the Seventh Air Force headquarters in Saigon, Pearly
Gates was the Out-Country (meaning out of South Vietnam)
expert, who knew more about OPlan ROLLING THUN-
DER, the bombing campaign against North Vietnam, than
anyone.

When Pearly had been assigned as Assistant Chief of
Plans and Programs, he'd been as bored as any human
would be with the dryly written conventional war plans, operations plans, contingency plans, supplements, and ad-
denda. But *someone* had to become familiar with them, and
he felt it should be someone who understood the consequence of a poor interpretation, who realized that a single
screwup transmitted from the Tactical Air Control Center to
the flying units could cost the lives of good men and destroy
the careers of men who deserved better. So Pearly had taken
a deep breath and thrashed through the reams of type-
adorned paper until he could navigate deftly through the
tomes filling the safes and cabinets of the back rooms and
the Top Secret tank.

Assistant Chief of Plans and Programs was not a coveted
position at any headquarters, but since Pearly Gates's assignment the desk at Seventh Air Force had become a powerful one. On paper he worked for a full bull, who worked
for a one-star, who worked for Lieutenant General Moss,
who was boss at the headquarters that supervised the air
war in Southeast Asia. The brigadier general, the Deputy
Commander for Plans, spent his time attending mandatory
staff meetings and answering the mail. The colonel, the
Chief of Plans and Programs, was immersed in the rules
concerning the air war in South Vietnam. They both de-
ferred to Lieutenant Colonel Pearly Gates to answer the
general's tough questions about North Vietnam.

It was Pearly who interpreted the regulations and operations plans, who revealed the implications of new bombing

restrictions passed from the President through the Air Staff, and who estimated the impact of various target assignments upon the North Vietnamese. He did his homework and seldom opened his mouth unless he was positive his answer was correct according to all available information. He kept himself and his staff of two officers, five noncoms, and nine airmen working long hours to make sure of that.

Pearly held a Top Secret clearance, had access to SI/TK/SK sensitive, compartmented information, and joked that he was cleared for the ridiculous. A sergeant in the comm center covertly tagged every classified scrap concerning North Vietnam that came in addressed to *anyone* in the headquarters. Pearly Gates scanned through each of those at his 800-words-per-minute reading rate, then pored more deliberately over the important ones.

He also spoke often to the flying wing commanders to gain their impressions and input, and argued on their behalf at the headquarters staff meetings. Those favors generated trust, and he was told things other headquarters pukes were not. He read the after-action summaries transmitted from every wing, every day, and compared those to reports and estimates generated by the half-dozen Saigon intelligence sources he considered credible. He did all of those things in order to remain aware, to be able to put two and two together, and to provide informed answers to General Moss's tough questions.

The field grades, from major through full colonel, were watershed ranks for officers in the military services, the shining time in a career when it was decided whether one was to progress to more important positions. Most Air Force light colonels believed success would come only by commanding a flying squadron or managing a highly visible department in a major headquarters. Neither of those were offered to Pearly, so he dedicated himself to a boring job no one else wanted and became indispensable.

Lieutenant General Moss used Pearly Gates's knowledge as he might an encyclopedia, for he'd assigned him to the handful of trusted advisors that he called his mafia. If he had a question, Moss would call out his name, and a few minutes later Pearly would appear in his office to answer his question. To show he *truly* knew his subject, Pearly would sometimes add the volume, chapter, page, and paragraph number

of the reference. General Moss knew he had his man, and
Gates knew he was going to enjoy a more prosperous career.

Pearly was an unlikely candidate for his role, for except
for their dedication to duty, he and Richard J. Moss were
opposites.

Moss was tall and lean, exuding a sensitive, patrician air,
and possessed the aura of a man born to command others.
The extent of his intellectual bent was to quote, inaccurately
if it met his purpose, historical military figures. He was vain
and had a terrible, quick temper. He looked particularly at
ease on a tennis court, but his staff members hated playing
him, for he refused either to win or to lose graciously.

Conversely, Pearly Gates was of average height and battled constantly to remain within official weight limits. He
had a bulbous nose, a receding hairline, impossibly curly
hair, and wore plastic-framed issue glasses to correct 20/100
nearsightedness. Pearly prided himself on being a steady, reliable, and reasonable man.

It was a pilot's Air Force, a fact nurtured by the generals
who had run the service since the first U.S. Army Signal
Corps officers filched flights aboard the Wright Flyer. The
great bulk of the aircraft assigned to Seventh Air Force units
were fighters, and General Moss left no doubt that he was
a fighter pilot. He believed strategic bombers and missiles
should be transferred to the Army as part of their long-range
artillery, and berated the dumber shits and clumsier oafs on
his staff by saying they acted like "goddamn navigators."

Pearly Gates was an unrepentant navigator. He knew that
airplanes flew because of a nebulous thing called lift, but
did not care to further explore the physics of flight. As a
navigator he'd worked in the bellies of B-29's and nose compartments of B-47's, and then had been upgraded to become an electronic-warfare officer stuffed into darkened
compartments in B-52's. All this had been done while he
was assigned to Strategic Air Command. He'd never flown
in a fighter aircraft and possessed no slightest wish to do so.
Yet for some unfathomable reason, Pearly liked the obnoxious, superegotistical fighter pilots he met around the bases.

Pearly carefully studied the traits of the fighters assigned
to Seventh Air Force units. He learned their weapons configurations, their best and worst maneuvering regimes, and
their peculiarities, strengths, and vulnerabilities. He knew
to question when someone tried to assign F-4's to low alti-

tudes or F-105's to the higher ones. He knew that fighter pilots preferred to fly at seven or eight nautical miles per minute in low-threat environs, and at nine or ten miles per minute in the presence of heavy defenses, to simplify navigation and fuel-flow computations. From the pilots in the various units he learned which weapons were appropriate for the various aircraft and targets, and he argued with the headquarters weapons people, often fruitlessly, to obtain them.

Once he'd discovered an oddball weapons configuration directed in an air tasking order being prepared at the Tactical Air Control Center and had corrected the error before the ATO had been sent out to the fighter wings. General Moss had learned of it and had bestowed his highest compliment. "I don't care if you can't see jack-shit, Pearly," he'd said with a sincere smile, "they should've made you a fighter pilot."

As soon as it had become clear that Pearly was Moss's chief mafioso of the North Vietnam bombing campaign, the general had grown protective. A new full colonel named Tom Lyons had learned this the previous week at the weekly ROLLING THUNDER recap meeting.

For the dozenth time in as many weeks, Pearly had voiced his opinion that using F-105's and F-4's to bomb camouflaged jungle truck parks was too often a waste of munitions.

Colonel Tom Lyons had interrupted Pearly to ask where he'd gained his information.

Pearly had replied that he'd canvassed wing and squadron commanders and a number of unit pilots, had gone through a number of intell reports and that he'd concluded the results just weren't worth the resources they cost.

Lyons, although new to the headquarters, had responded by admonishing him, speaking slowly as he might to a child. "We've got to stop the trucks *some* way, Gates, and fighters can bomb more accurately than the other birds over here."

General Moss often argued the same point, but he'd regarded the colonel with the look he'd once given to dog mustard he found on his shoe after he'd walked across a Persian rug.

If Lyons had not been so new and had known him better, he would have immediately stopped. Instead he'd shaken his head slowly, staring at Pearly's chest and his star-and-

wreath-adorned Master Navigator wings. "You've got to be a
pilot to understand that sometimes squadron jocks don't
want to do the tough things it takes to win a war."

Moss had grown pale about the ears as he continued to
stare at Tom Lyons, who did not realize that his status had
just dropped *even lower* than that of dogshit. Lyons had
glanced about, smiled brightly at General Moss, then at his
own two-star boss, the Deputy for Operations. He'd finished
with a grandiose and self-important flick of his wrist to show
that *he* would handle this minor irritant.

"I'll speak to the commanders and reemphasize just how
essential it is to continue the antitrucking campaign, and put
a stop to these complaints," he'd said.

The two-star DO started to give a terse warning to his
man just as Moss's jaw began to quiver. Too outraged at first
to speak, Moss had stabbed an angry forefinger at the colonel before gaining his voice. "Get the hell out of my
meeting!" he'd roared.

Lyons's jaw had drooped. He'd started to respond, but
the DO quickly interrupted. "You heard him, Tom. I'll talk
to you when we're done here."

Moss had glared, and the colonel had slunk out of the
room without understanding that by criticizing the general's
handpicked mafioso, he had criticized Moss.

"Who the hell was that fool?" Moss had snorted at the
Deputy for Operations, still angry and not to be fooled with.

"Colonel Lyons, sir. Fresh from the Pentagon. He's taking
over the Out-Country plans desk at the Tactical Air Control
Center."

Moss had snorted again. "Bullshit. Get him out of my
headquarters and off my base!" Then the general's eyes had
glittered. "Send him to Takhli. They don't get many colonel
volunteers. Maybe B. J. Parker can use him."

Colonel B. J. Parker was wing commander at Takhli Air
Base, considered the shittiest assignment in Thailand for
staff officers. Located in the boondocks in the middle of the
blistering Thai savanna, Takhli had few amenities and no
frills. There was no city there, only a small farming community, and the area's claim to fame was that it nurtured the
world's largest king cobras. It was unbearably hot in the dry
season and miserably wet during the monsoons.

"Good choice, sir," said the Deputy for Operations. "Colonel Lyons checked out in the F-105 before coming over. He'd planned to get out periodically to fly with the units."

Moss had nodded and returned his attention to the briefing. "Go on, Pearly." Then he'd growled at the audience, "And no more interruptions until he's done."

While it had been confirmed that Lieutenant Colonel Pearly Gates was firmly entrenched on the general's list of good guys, Moss didn't agree to stop the fighters from bombing suspected truck parks. He made the same argument Colonel Tom Lyons had. Stopping the shipments of supplies to South Vietnam was too critical to allied efforts, he said.

Lieutenant Colonel Pearly Gates

A little after noon on Friday, Pearly sat waiting in the general's outer office, knowing he should move cautiously for what he was about to request. The importance of his business made him pause, for if properly pursued, the campaign he was about to suggest might make a great difference to the war effort.

After ten long minutes the general's secretary spoke quietly on her intercom, then nodded at Pearly. "The general will see you."

He stood, smiling appreciatively. He'd learned that an important key to getting things done in any headquarters was a good rapport with the secretaries. The fiftyish secretary had been with Moss since he'd been a colonel and zealously controlled access to his office.

"He's *not* in a good mood," she whispered. Pearly was one of her favorites.

Pearly pushed his glasses firmly into place, hitched and smoothed his uniform trousers, drew a breath, and then walked resolutely through the open doorway of the lion's den.

Moss refocused his attention from the several-page message spread before him on the massive teak desk and nodded at Gates.

"We're working for fools, Pearly."

Gates stared without comment.

"The President refuses to listen to anyone, and the Edsel mechanic's so convinced we're going to lose that he won't turn us loose to win."

Gates swallowed, feeling uneasy. The general despised politicians and berated them mercilessly when he was with his mafia members. He especially disliked the Edsel mechanic, which was what he called the SecDef.

"They want us to stop the supplies coming south, but they won't let us do it where it's easiest. Dammit, the supplies are on the docks at Haiphong and in the streets of Hanoi."

Gates nodded glumly.

Moss calmed himself a bit. "You here about this dumbshit LOC message?"

"Yes, sir."

"They think it's a big deal, authorizing us to mount a campaign against the lines of communications. Hell, we've been bombing LOCs, especially roads and rail sidings, since before I got here last year."

Pearly spoke cautiously. "They also want our ideas on how the campaign should be run. And it reads 'throughout North Vietnam,' so it's not as restrictive as we've seen."

Moss snorted. "We've given 'em campaign plans before, but they've been ignored."

"I think they may be prepared to listen, General."

"Soon as they take the restrictions off and untie our hands, we'll give them all the results they want, but you and I know damned well they're not going to do that as long as Russia and Red China make sounds like they might step in. That's all bullshit, but they don't have the balls to ignore them." Moss tapped the message. "So what does that leave us?"

"Perhaps there's something, sir. Back-channel I'm hearing that the President needs results because the voters are restless and it's getting close to election time."

Back-channel messages were nonattributable, sent between individuals at the different headquarters without record and with no copies made. Back-channel info was what a headquarters puke like Pearly could learn from his contacts, unofficially and off the record. While sometimes speculative, back-channel information was often accurate.

Moss brooded. "We're already hitting LOCs. How about the railroad sidings? Hell, we're hitting them every week."

"Yes, sir, and those generally give us good results. We destroy considerable tonnages of war matériel that way."

"When they let us hit the right ones, we do."

Pearly sucked a breath and plunged in. "I want to concentrate on their bridges, sir."

Moss narrowed his eyes. Gates had mentioned such a campaign before. Moss had discouraged it because he hadn't believed that, one, the brass would allow a concerted effort, and, two, that they could do it without taking undue losses because of all the restrictions.

"Bridges are critical chokepoints on the lines of communications," said Pearly.

"And what makes you think *your* plan won't be just another exercise in futility?"

Pearly was ready. "I spent the night talking on the scrambler net. PACAF and CINCPAC thought a bridges campaign was a good idea, but they didn't believe the Pentagon would buy it. XOOF at the Pentagon thought it was an okay idea, but they thought it might piss off the JCS."

Moss gave his *I told you so* look.

"So I said screw it and used a shekel." Pearly Gates measured the give-and-take between staff officers at the various headquarters in imaginary shekels. "I called a friend at the joint-plans office at the Pentagon. He said they'd purposefully left the options open, that the President wants results so badly he'll even consider targets inside the restricted areas."

"So it's up to CINCPAC?"

"I called back to CINCPAC and told them what I'd learned. They said they'd consider the idea if *you* request it. Then they asked if it was you or me I was talking for."

Moss waited.

"I had to tell him that so far it was just me talking."

Moss stared at him. "And that's the end of it?"

Pearly nodded. "Anything more has to come from you, sir."

"Give me the gist of *your* plan."

"We keep bombing until we knock out the critical bridges between Hanoi, Haiphong, and China to slow down the surface shipments."

Moss sighed, not excited with the idea. He stared at the window and the glare of the sun against the mesh curtains. "We'd need Navy support," he said begrudgingly.

"Yes, sir. Especially for the bridges near Haiphong."

Pack six, the Red River Valley of North Vietnam, was divided into two parts, six alpha and six bravo, separated by the railroad running northeast from Hanoi to China. The Air Force was generally responsible for the targets in six alpha, the western half of the valley. The Navy bombed mostly in the east, in six bravo. Since they both had their own jealously guarded bombing plans, the boundaries were sometimes crossed.

Moss finally sighed. "Come on, Pearly. I know you've already brought it up to them. What's the Navy's reaction?"

"Their targeting officers think it'd be a good idea, if . . . ah . . . we'd take care of our part."

Moss glared. "We fly seventy-five percent of the combat missions, but the Navy gets seventy-five percent of the credit. We should keep them out of a few big ones, just to show the press who's doing the *real* work up north."

"They're critical on this one."

"We took the Thai Nguyen steel mill down . . . flew *ninety* percent of those missions, did most of the damage, and took most of the losses. But who got the credit in the press?" He snorted. "Our damned PR officers have to get off their asses."

Pearly was prepared to use even inane arguments. "This time there'd be plenty of PR for everyone, sir. There'd be a lot of bridges to destroy."

Moss stared at the window. "I don't know," he muttered, still unconvinced.

"The wing commanders believe we can knock them all down, sir. They think some of them would be difficult, but they feel we can do it."

Moss grunted. "It'd be harder than they think, especially if the North Vietnamese brought in large numbers of defenses. It takes big bombs to knock the things down, and it's no fun lugging them around when they're shooting like hell."

Pearly released another tidbit. "My contact at PACAF thinks we'd be directed to use AGM-12 Bullpup missiles."

Moss snorted again. "That's dumber than dirt! You've gotta get in close and guide them all the way to the target, for Christ's sake. Our pilots would be sitting ducks."

"Maybe there's another option. A captain from Nellis Air Force Base came through the other day to brief us on a new family of weapons he's working on. He calls them 'smart bombs,' and from what he told me, they'd be perfect for targets like these."

Moss narrowed his eyes. He'd come to Saigon from Nellis. "What was his name?"

"Diller, sir. Captain Diller. He wanted to brief you, but you were unavailable."

Moss chuckled. "Moods Diller. Used to work on projects with my fighter mafia guys there at Nellis. He's smart, but he's got his head up in the clouds, always coming up with ideas no one can understand or afford. I wouldn't get too excited about what he's got."

"The people in our weapons shop here and at PACAF liked the sounds of them."

"Has he got hardware, or is he just pipe-dreaming?"

"From the sound of his talk, they're close to having hardware, sir. He'd like to get our support so he can get a higher priority to finish development."

"Don't hold your breath. Moods Diller gets intoxicated with his ideas."

"The PACAF Deputy for Operations liked the sound of his briefing."

"The PACAF XO is a pipe dreamer just like Moods."

Pearly shrugged. "May be, General. The PACAF XO's also the one who wants us to start using Bullpup missiles. His staff says he thinks they're high technology, and that things like that can give us the edge over the enemy."

"He's never flown fighters. Spends most of his time at Anderson and U Tapao giving World War II pep talks to B-52 crews. How would he know anything about Bullpups?"

"His staff says he gets excited whenever they brief them, and he's looking for something to try 'em on. They say if this campaign's approved, he'll want to use them."

The idea did not please Moss, and Pearly wondered if he hadn't just lost his whole argument because of it.

"What's the Navy say they'd use?"

"They'd try their A-6's with the new precision radars, and go in at night with one- and two-thousand-pounders."

"They're smart about that one. In France we used the biggest damn bombs we could hang on our airplanes. So big that even if we missed, sometimes the concussion would knock them down."

"Perhaps you could call the general at PACAF and get him to change his mind about the Bullpups, General?"

Moss sighed, as if Pearly were trying to sucker him into

something he wasn't sold on. Finally he asked, "How about the other thing?"

The "other thing" was taking the losses required to get the job done. The general was always concerned about the "other thing" when they considered difficult targets. When they'd made up their minds and the targets were hit, it was different. Once committed, Moss didn't seem to worry as much about actual losses as he had the forecasts.

Pearly was good at determining loss rates for the various targets. Using historical statistics, pessimism, and a bit of bullshit, he was usually accurate within a single percent.

"I feel it will cost us between five and six percent attrition for each mission, sir, with the present numbers of guns defending the bridges. I can give you better numbers when I look at the individual target photos."

Now they *both* stared at the window, and Pearly found his own enthusiasm flagging. He hated talking about losses.

"How many bridges are we talking about?" asked Moss in a quieter tone.

"So far I've identified eleven big ones for us and nine for the Navy. There's more like two hundred if we include elevated railroads and bridges across the smaller streams."

"It wouldn't be easy, even if we just concentrated on the major ones, Pearly. They'd be hard to knock down, harder than you think, and once we start, we'd have to keep knocking them down because they have the manpower to repair them."

"Yes, sir."

"Even if we knocked down *every* bridge, would it really stop the supplies from getting through?"

Pearly shook his head. "If it was anyone else, I might say so, sir, but the North Vietnamese are damned resourceful. All I'm predicting is we'd slow them down."

Moss sighed. "You know, Pearly, in 1944 we were sent out to stop the supplies from coming up to the front at Normandy. We flew our asses off and took our hits, but by God we stopped them." He paused in memory. "Sometimes we'd knock out a single bridge and stop an entire tank or truck column."

Pearly Gates remained quiet.

Moss shook his head sadly. "But I suppose if we'd given the Germans sanctuaries and reassurance that we weren't *really* going to hurt them, and plenty of time to regroup between bombings, they'd have figured out ways to resupply too."

"General, one way or another the North Vietnamese would likely end up getting their supplies through. But they'd have to work for it, and I just can't think of any other way to slow down the flow without breaking the President's rules."

"How many troops are we tying up in North Vietnam with our bombing now?"

"Intelligence estimates are between four and five hundred thousand."

"What do you think?"

"I'd say half a million *minimum*, not counting the men, women, and kids on the repair gangs. I'm talking about the troops manning the defenses and the home-defense militia."

"And this would tie up even more?"

"Big-time numbers, general. They'd have to keep a tremendous work force in place fixing bridges, rafting supplies across the rivers, and carting the stuff between chokepoints. Even then the supplies would be slowed down."

A colonel wearing a white mess dress uniform with elaborate fruit salad came to the doorway and peered inside.

Moss waved him away. "I'll be a few more minutes," he called tersely, and that made the colonel look nervously at his watch.

Pearly's glasses slipped forward on his nose. He pulled them off and carefully polished them with his handkerchief. Moss stared incredulously at the thickness of the Coke-bottle lenses, then glanced away as if embarrassed. "How quickly could you put an OPlan together?"

"I've got the essentials already. Another couple of days?"

"I've got to be on time for a protocol function, but let me tell you something damn important." Moss looked evenly at him, and the muscles in his jaw bunched angrily. "Somehow our targeting information's getting to Hanoi. We've got a leak somewhere in the system."

Pearly stared at him, slowly pushed his glasses into position and blinked.

"I don't know how, but it's getting out," said Moss. "I've been shown photos of NVA defenses being pulled out of critical areas and built up around specified targets more than twenty-four hours prior to our strikes. Yesterday the numbers of guns around the power plants at Hanoi and Haiphong were trebled before our aircraft arrived."

Moss lowered his voice when he next spoke. "Who've you shared *this* one with, Pearly? If we went after their bridges, we sure as hell wouldn't want them knowing it."

Pearly knew it wasn't one of his own people leaking the information, so he tried to remember who else he'd told. "Intell. Some of the people at the Tactical Air Control Center. Staff officers in Hawaii and Washington on secure lines."

"Well, start keeping it closer to your vest. I'm tired of losing pilots. I've contacted the Smith brothers to see if they can find the leak."

CIA agents often introduced themselves as Mr. Smith. Collectively they were called the Smith brothers.

The colonel reappeared at the door.

Moss slowly gained his feet, still thinking hard. "I've got a reception with General Westmoreland and Ambassador Lodge. You keep working on our campaign, Pearly."

Our campaign? Relief swept over Pearly Gates as he realized he'd won. "Yes, sir," he said as he also stood.

"Call CINCPAC and tell 'em I'll request a trial bombing mission against one of the key bridges as soon as the OPlan's completed. You pick a good target and brief me. As soon as we've ironed out the wrinkles, I'll request a large-scale bombing campaign against every major bridge in pack six."

"I'll advise them, General."

"You brief your bosses about this yet?"

"No, sir. I felt it was your call and should come from you."

Moss looked pleased. "Tell them I called you in and told you to build the OPlan."

"Yes, sir."

Although it was Pearly Gates's idea, Moss would receive the credit, *especially* if things went right. But, of course, that was what generals and staff officers were all about.

CHAPTER THREE

Saturday, April 22nd, 0715 Local—Route Pack One, North Vietnam

Major Lucky Anderson

"This is Hillsboro, go ahead with your transmission."

Lucky had spent five long minutes trying to raise the airborne command post that controlled the airspace and monitored flights in the southern route packs. This portion of North Vietnam was too close to the demilitarized zone with South Vietnam to escape the interest of the brass, some of whom suspected that all fighter pilots were not great at navigation and sometimes lost track of precisely where they were over the ground. Thus all flights operating in pack one were closely monitored by Hillsboro, to make damn sure the fighters weren't near friendlies when they dropped their bombs.

A selection of command posts and radars, some airborne like Moonbeam, Cricket, Hillsboro, Ethan, Big Eye, and Crown, some on the ground like Motel, Invert, Viking, Waterboy, Lion, and Brigham, some on ships, like Red Crown and the two aircraft carriers presently on station, all controlled various portions of North Vietnamese airspace. Sometimes the pilots listened and at other times disregarded the advisories, but they knew if you ignored Hillsboro or its nighttime replacement, Moonbeam, and mistakenly dropped bombs on friendlies, you might as well take up hula dancing, because when you landed, your ass was going to be grass.

"Hillsboro, this is Reno lead. I've got four nickels loaded with hotel echo bombs and alpha-papa twenty mike-mike," radioed Lucky Anderson, introducing Reno flight as four F-105's carrying high explosive bombs and full loads of armor-piercing 20mm ammo for their guns. *"Do you have targets for us?"*

At times Hillsboro would have a good target, like NVA troops moving south toward the DMZ, gomer boats sneaking down the coast, or trucks spotted on the Ho Chi Minh Trail.

"Negative, Reno lead. Suggest you remain north, repeat north, of Dong Hoi. Hillsboro out." Which meant that some sort of operation was in progress near the DMZ and they were to stay clear of it, and also that Hillsboro was busy and didn't have time for them.

Anderson led the flight into a slow turn back toward Dong Hoi, a seaside fishing community thirty nautical miles north of the DMZ. He tried calling Cricket, the other daytime C-130 flying command post in the area, but got no response.

They flew at 6,000 feet in a loose fingertip formation, with 500 feet spacing between aircraft. On Lucky's wing was Lieutenant Walker, and the descriptive word for his flying was "smooth." He was jinking nicely, moving his aircraft about the sky unpredictably but not jerking around like a fish out of water. Manny DeVera was number three, leader of the second element, and Billy Bowes was on his wing. He had no complaints about either man's flying skills. Lucky was smugly happy about the abilities of his C-Flight. After a few more indoctrination missions such as this, they'd be right up there with the best in the wing.

They flew north, only five miles from the coastline, passing over the heavily pocked fields of pack one. The craters were created by U.S. Navy ships as they blasted away at vehicles or troops with their big guns. A great number of the holes were nowhere near a roadway, just out in the wide expanses of sand and scrub brush. Lucky suspected the Navy used the area for training and to zero in their guns. The roads themselves were kept smooth by construction gangs, swarms of worker ants the pilots only periodically glimpsed.

"*Dong Hoi,*" announced Lucky as they passed by. Dong Hoi was built at the mouth of a river that emptied into a small harbor, protected by land on three sides. A ferry hidden somewhere in the area was used to transport people and vehicles across the mouth of the river at night, but no big convoys passed through the open and vulnerable area. Instead they moved in great numbers forty miles to the west, where the Ho Chi Minh Trail snaked through a dozen heavily forested mountain passes into Laos. From there they flowed southward and then poured through a hundred sieve openings into South Vietnam.

After ten minutes of looking about, examining the coastal flatlands and low hills, Lucky began to look for a particular phenomenon to show them.

Thirteen miles north of Dong Hoi, on a section of the coastal highway, sat an A-1 Skyraider, a World War II vintage prop aircraft the pilots called a Spad. From the air it appeared in good condition, as if it had just landed and was waiting for its pilot to climb back in, crank up, and take off. Two years before, after taking a critical hit, its pilot had landed on the roadway and abandoned it. Now the gomers used it as bait for inquisitive pilots who were tempted to take a closer look. A few antiaircraft guns were hidden about the area and fired upon any fighter that drew near.

Lucky explained the flak trap. He ended by telling them, "*They're either entry-level gunners, or simply very poor shots, because they've never hit anyone.*"

"*Reno four,*" he said then, "*I want you to swing out solo and fly a couple miles north, then drop down to a thousand feet and come back up the road . . . fast.*"

"*Four,*" Billy Bowes replied cheerfully, reefing his aircraft into a hard left turn.

"*Renos, keep an eye on the trees at the sides of the road down there,*" radioed Lucky to the remainder of the flight.

Thirty-five seconds later the Thud flown by Reno four came streaking down the roadway. Bees zipped upward out of light foliage on either side of the road.

"*That's twelve point seven and fourteen point five millimeter, Reno flight,*" called Lucky. "*Every seventh or tenth round is a tracer, so there's a lot more of it than you can see.*"

A few white puffs formed above and aft of Reno four, now well past the flak trap.

"*That's thirty-seven millimeter, Renos, aimed with iron sights, with manually preset burst altitudes. Up in pack six, they have so many of them, they don't aim. They use barrage fire. Just point the barrels up toward a common sector, and maybe fifty or a hundred guns pound away at that section of sky. Then another group of guns fire at the next sector and others in the next ones. That way they can pretty well cover the sky over a target and boost their odds of hitting someone. Barrage fire can be damned effective, so try to avoid flying through it.*"

Bowes was circling and climbing to join them.

"*How about fifty-seven and eighty-five millimeter?*" came a radio call.

He knew the call had come from DeVera, but Lucky was trying to teach them the way it should be done. "*Reno flight, every time you push a mike button up here, identify yourself.*"

Silence.

"*Right, Reno three?*" Lucky prodded.

"*Roger, Reno lead,*" said Manny DeVera.

Bowes was pulling back into place off Manny's left wing.

"*As for your question, Reno three, fifty-seven and eighty-five use aimed fire, either optically or radar guided. The color of the flak bursts are determined by the warhead material. Fifty-seven is usually light gray, and eighty-five is darker, like one hundred and one hundred thirty millimeter. They use a combination timer and proximity fuze. The timers are preset by the gunners as the rounds are chambered.*"

They were flying eastward toward the high mountains when DeVera's aggressiveness bubbled forth. "*Lead, Reno three. Aren't we going to bomb the guns back there?*"

"*Negative, Reno three. I like having those particular gomers on the guns. Hurt them and they might bring in someone who can hit something.*"

They approached the mountains at 10,000 feet. Lucky described the limestone karsts off to their left as craggy, low hills that were honeycombed with caves.

"*You ever get shot down, there's a hell of a lot of hiding places in a karst formation,*" he explained. Then, after another minute, "*Over at your two o'clock, at five miles, is a canyon containing one of the branches of the Ho Chi Minh*

Trail. There's water buffalo, elephants, horses, trucks, jeeps, humans, handcarts, and bicycles thick as ants down there, carrying supplies to their gomer buddies in the South. They move at night or in bad weather. Only time you'll see them in the open is if you get down under a cloud deck or if you use flares at night."

They'd seen no good targets of opportunity during the flight, so Lucky reverted to a set of coordinates given them by intelligence before takeoff. He located the crook in the heavily treed canyon, double-checked to make sure they were at the right location, as if it made a difference, and then led the flight into a dive-bomb run on the suspected truck park. There was no ground fire, so Lucky figured there was nothing under the dense jungle canopy. Nine tons of bombs were released into the empty expanse of jungle.

Reno flight returned to base without incident.

0930 Local — Hanoi, DRV

Colonel Nguyen Wu

For the hundredth time, Nguyen wished his aunt was not away. She was so much better at things like this. But she would not return from Paris for weeks, and he dared not wait.

Through the long night, yesterday's argument with Quon about the long-range radars had festered and bothered him. He'd arrived at his office late, to find a message from the famous fighter pilot, demanding that they meet in General Tho's office to discuss the matter further. When Wu had gone there, he'd found that General Luc had also been invited, and the argument of the previous day had been resumed.

The Soviet tactics adopted by the People's Army Air Force demanded that the MiGs be closely tracked and directed by highly trained radar controllers. Since Nguyen Wu had taken over and removed the pilot controllers, radar control had been poor, almost nonexistent.

Nguyen argued that "Wisdom" had used North Korean and Russian controllers, and he had been told by "important people" never to again allow foreigners to control their defenses.

Quon, staring coldly at Nguyen Wu, said he did not care about politics, only about victories. Just who were these important people and he would speak with them. When Wu had refused to tell him, he had smirked and intimated that Wu was lying.

As Wu had left, his face had burned with helpless rage. He sensed that Quon was poised for the kill, that he was gathering his final ammunition to wrest control of the two long-range radars. He also knew he must act quickly and resolutely if he was to keep them.

But the previous night he'd worked out a solution, and as he strode to his waiting staff car, he decided that it was sound. Perhaps rash . . . but nonetheless sound. The kind of plan his aunt would surely approve of. Anything less might be too little to stop the fighter pilot, anything more, and the legend might be tarnished and the party angered. Best of all, Nguyen Wu would be uninvolved. Sergeant Ng drove him directly to the Russian embassy compound, then around the perimeter road to the building from which Colonel Feodor Dimetriev commandèd his contingent of Russian technical advisors.

There was no waiting to see Dimetriev. *The man knows the power wielded by Nguyen Wu,* he thought haughtily as he barged directly into the inner office and voiced his demand.

Feodor Dimetriev disliked him, a fact made apparent by his look of distaste. He refused him, saying that Wu must take up such matters with his own people.

At first Nguyen Wu almost panicked; then he calmed himself and lied and told the Russian that the demand did not come from him, but from his aunt.

Dimetriev changed his tone. He hedged that Madame Li Binh should speak for herself, since it was such a sensitive and unorthodox request.

Wu sensed the change in the Russian and resumed his confidence. He said she had relayed the request from Paris, and that the entire matter must be held in the utmost confidence. After a short argument the chief of Russian advisors agreed to take action.

When Nguyen Wu rose to go, he looked at the Russian colonel evenly and told him, "This conversation did not occur."

Dimetriev looked away, muttering in Russian. Nguyen

Wu translated. The Russian wished by all that was decent that it had not.

As Colonel Nguyen Wu was driven across the central and northern quartiers of Hanoi, back toward the two large buildings housing the Vietnamese People's Army headquarters, he felt increasingly pleased with himself.

The plan would work. The death of Quon's only son would surely distract him from a minor problem such as control of the two radars.

1445 Local—Air Battalion Briefing Room, Phuc Yen People's Army Air Force Base

Kapitan Aleksandr Viktor Ivanovic

Most officers of the Soviet Air Force went through thirty years of faithful service and were never faced with a choice between duty to the party and preservation of personal honor. Aleks Ivanovic, a capable fighter pilot sworn to remain a "brave and diligent warrior in support of the constitution and Soviet law," was not so lucky. On Saturday afternoon he came nose to nose with the ugliest face of political reality and was never again the same.

Ivanovic was completing his briefing to the Vietnamese pilots. Subject: Positioning for attack upon a force of aircraft. He'd finished with the "use of clouds for cover" and was about to review the afternoon's lessons when a clerk slipped into the room.

He was passed a note telling him to proceed immediately to Hanoi, that a driver from the Soviet embassy was waiting in front.

Two hours earlier, during a break, the ranking pilot advisor assigned to the Phuc Yen air regiment had come by to ask Aleks about the new batch of Vietnamese *leytenants*, fresh from flight training in Russia. Since the same *mayor* had also signed the note, Aleks assumed the invitation was related to that conversation.

The driver was a junior enlisted man, a Lithuanian with only a single gold stripe adorning his blue shoulder boards. He was young, with fuzz on his chin and a few wayward hairs on his upper lip showing he was trying to grow a mustache. He was rather dull and kept his conversation to a

minimum, answering Aleks's questions only after prodding.
A harbinger of trouble when they arrived in Hanoi? Aleks
could think of nothing he'd done to warrant disciplinary action. He liked his vodka and the company of females, and he
occasionally sang a bit loudly at parties, but those were expected of an interceptor pilot of the Soviet Air Force. Reassignment to another unit? He did not like that idea, for he
was only now, after six weeks, feeling at ease with the pilots
of the air battalion to which he'd been assigned.

The twenty-kilometer drive between Phuc Yen and Hanoi went very slowly due to the teeming road-repair gangs.
Main highways were damaged more by heavy usage than by
bomb craters. Traffic moved in great surges at night and
during bad weather, creating oversized ruts and great pot-
holes in road surfaces. During the daytime the traffic was
light, but that time was reserved for the road-repair gangs,
hordes of old people, women, and children driven by bullies
wearing militia uniforms. The occasional vehicle, such as the
one occupied by Aleks, was stopped again and again. If you
wanted to get somewhere quickly, you obtained proper authority and waited for darkness.

By the time they'd crossed the small bridge over the Canales des Rapides into the Gia Lam area, he'd learned only
that the driver had been born and reared in a farm town in
northeastern Lithuania, that he disliked the fact that the
windows of his vehicles had to remain open due to the terrible heat, and that the dust that billowed inside was dirtier
than that found in Lithuania. When Aleks asked how he
liked Hanoi and his assignment, the driver clenched his jaw
and did not answer. Aleks thought that odd. Most Lithuani-
ans enjoyed complaining about anything at all.

They passed Gia Lam, Hanoi's busy municipal airport,
and approached the Long Bien bridge, which spanned the
wide river the Vietnamese called the Hong Song. On a concrete pillar at the northern end of the bridge he read the
French words *"Riviere Rouge . . . un homme grand . . .
Governeur Paul. . . ."* His French was spotty, but he finally
interpreted that this bridge crossed the Red River and had
been erected in honor of a governor named Paul something.
The rest of the name had been obliterated, so he assumed it
was not a popular one.

He shifted his attention back, again asked, and was again
told that the young driver had no idea why he'd come for

Aleks. This time he grumbled, more like a true Lithuanian, that he'd been told to wait for Aleks and take him back to Phuc Yen when his business was done. Two trips instead of one, he complained.

Aleks felt better. If he was being called in to be disciplined, it was nothing serious or he wouldn't be returning so quickly. He still wondered what it was about, but with less foreboding. He looked out at the scenery with more interest.

Aleks Ivanovic was a happy man, not only contented but excited about his lot. And why shouldn't he be? He was young, in superb health, was a better than adequate jet interceptor pilot who loved his job, and was sufficiently appealing to females that his sexual appetites seldom went unfulfilled for long.

The wide river they were crossing was the color of old rust on a sheet of iron. His attention was drawn to construction along the riverbank. Rough shanties lining the sides of the shore, both up- and downriver, were being cleared from the area within a kilometer of the bridge. Strange, he thought, as he watched the beehive of activity at locations throughout the cleared area. He searched with inquisitive eyes until he realized they were preparing hundreds of gun positions. Artillery pieces were already installed in some, and more were being drawn into place by a motley collection of vehicles, water buffalo, and swarms of humans.

An American air attack was obviously expected upon the bridge. Then he remembered similar activity around the bridge over the Canales des Rapides, so he supposed they expected an attack there too.

Intelligence obtained by the North Vietnamese was uncannily accurate. In the South they usually knew when and where the American soldiers were about to attack. Here in the North, they often knew bombing targets even before the American pilots were briefed.

The driver left the big bridge and drove into the city, then abruptly slowed to a crawl behind an endless convoy of heavily laden, Chinese-manufactured six-by-six vehicles and trailer trucks, all belching black smoke and moving sluggishly through the central *quartier*. Each night hundreds of them were loaded at the railroad sidings at Yen Vien and Gia Lam to move almost endlessly through the city, protected from bombing attacks by the sworn word of the American President himself. They would gather and wait in the southern suburbs. Then, during darkness or bad weather, they would move southward in a great, relentless tide.

Aleks was amazed by the spectacle of the vast lines of supplies rumbling through Hanoi, but the Lithuanian driver only smoldered with anger at the slow convoys and was not at all impressed. When they finally turned off the main artery onto a cross street, he released a loud curse and mighty sigh that he was rid of the traffic.

At the tall green-painted gate to the Soviet embassy, a guard peered and nodded in recognition at the driver, then glanced at Aleks's identification and waved them through. They drove around the tree-lined perimeter road to a large building, where the driver stopped near the double-doored entrance.

"Where do I go?" asked Aleks.

The driver shrugged. He'd delivered him.

Aleks opened his door and got out, looking about warily and wondering whether he should go inside. A meticulous and stiff *serzhant*, three gold stripes on blue shoulder boards and wearing a rope of braid, came out of the door and looked about.

Two officers passed, resplendent in crisp green uniforms and wearing the black shoulder boards, collar tabs, and hatbands of missiles-and-artillery men. Another passed, wearing the red of combined arms, and two more the light blue of aviation. You could tell the headquarters men from the advisors, Aleks decided, because of the advisors' hungry look and the important expressions of the staff officers.

The meticulous *serzhant*, definitely a headquarters type, allowed his eyes to settle upon Aleks. He likely had fifteen years' service, but Aleks would bet he'd never served in the field. Too soft and too neat.

Aleks felt uneasy. He'd worn his flying suit, and now it was rumpled and sweat soaked from the drive. He ran his hand through his hair, then placed his service cap atop his head to hide as much of it as possible.

Eight weeks earlier they'd cut his hair stubble-short in preparation for the Asian tour, telling him it would help him cope with the infestations of lice he'd find in the tropics. When he'd arrived at Phuc Yen, the Russian advisors already there had joked about his hair. The only great infestations of lice they knew of came from the crotch of a Vietnamese girl working in the laundry who'd tumble in the mounds of dirty bedding for a couple of cigarettes. A short haircut *might* protect you from her lice, one wag had said, if you used your tongue on her, and he'd extended and quivered his tongue suggestively. Another said if he did that, he'd better check his mustache and nose hairs for the little beasts.

Since experience was measured in degrees of baldness, the advisors allowed their hair to grow too long. Aleks's hair looked strange, still too short on top, but much too long at the sides, and he was ashamed he'd come to the Russian embassy compound looking like this.

"Kapitan Ivanovic?" the immaculate *serzhant* asked.

"Yes."

"This way, please." He led the way inside, then down a wide hall with a high-gloss floor. The *serzhant's* shoes ticked as he walked. *He's had metal inserts added to the soles,* Aleks noted. How strange headquarters people were. More clerk than warrior, yet they wore the gaudiest uniforms of all.

POL. FEODOR DIMETRIEV, the sign in the hall announced. They turned into the open doorway, passed through one room into another, and finally into a large office.

Aleks glanced back to see the *serzhant* slip out and close the door behind himself. The full colonel sat quietly, reading from notes and ignoring Aleks, who stood awkwardly.

He'd recognized the name, and he now recognized the man he'd met at the embassy reception shortly after arriving in North Vietnam. *Polkovnik* Feodor Dimetriev was in charge of the 300-man Soviet advisory contingent. He coordinated all surface, naval, and aviation matters with their Vietnamese hosts and passed on requests for support from Moscow. An influential man. Not a pilot, but an administrative officer wearing the red tabs of combined arms, he'd made it obvious that he believed that Aleks and the other fighter pilots were rather mindless. In an endless introductory speech he'd told Aleks's group to do their duty for the motherland by helping this brave Republic, a new anchor of socialism in Asia. Aleks and the other pilots had waited until Dimetriev had left before laughing at his theatrics.

Dimetriev looked up from his desk and *almost* stared at him. Not quite, for his eyes did not meet Aleks's.

Aleks waited for another long moment, then barked out

his name, "*Kamerade Kapitan* Aleksandr Viktor Ivanovic. Sir!"

Dimetriev lifted his hand and dropped it, as if to say he already knew that. "Do you know a pilot named Thanh?" he asked quietly.

Aleks replied that he knew Thanh, a *leytenant* second grade who'd recently returned from Russia, where he'd been trained to fly the MiG-21 interceptor. He started to add that the *leytenant*'s father was their air regiment commandant, but Dimetriev cut him off.

"It is reported that you know him well," Dimetriev said, frowning and staring as he spoke, still looking not at Aleks's face but just above it.

Aleks paused to think of an appropriate response. It was not exactly correct that he knew the young *leytenant* well, although he spent a great deal of time with him.

Upon his return from pilot training in Russia, the *leytenant* had dramatically broadcast that he was forsaking his formal name as his father had done years before and was dedicating his own life to vengeance. He'd first taken his father's name of Quon, then had changed it to Thanh, which was Ho Chi Minh's family name. He'd confided to Aleks that although as far as he knew, the Enlightened One's family had never suffered at the hands of *any* oppressor, his father had suggested the idea. That made the idea a sound one. The propaganda writers who swarmed to Phuc Yen loved Thanh just as they did his father, but seemed not to notice that the son was not at all sure of himself, or that he eagerly listened to advice from just about anyone.

Young Thanh needed people and their inputs. Guidance from Aleks about flying skills, from his commander regarding his duties, from his father about the directions of his life. Aleks felt that good interceptor pilots required few reassurances, for they *knew* they were good. The only people they needed were adversaries, so they could prove it. Thanh's dream was to make his father proud of him. But Thanh was a poor pilot, and left to his own devices, he would fail them both.

Aleks started at the beginning. "The *leytenant* was checked out in big-tail PF-model MiG-21's, and has had certain problems getting accustomed to the small-tails here," he told Dimetriev. "He has not . . ."

Dimetriev interrupted. "But do you know the *leytenant* well?"

"He asks many questions and trusts my advice. Nothing more."

Feodor Dimetriev continued to refuse to meet his eyes as he considered the answer. Aleks became increasingly disconcerted. *Was he looking at his hair?*

Then, as if he'd made a momentous decision, Dimetriev warily dropped his voice. "Very important people among our hosts," he said, "wish for the *leytenant* to become a Hero of the Republic. You"—he still avoided Aleks's eyes—"have been selected to help with the task."

"They want him protected?" Aleks asked. Photographers from the government news agency and reporters from *Nham Dan,* the party newspaper, lurked about Phuc Yen and made a great fuss about Thanh. It wasn't so surprising the party wanted him protected. He started thinking of ways he might shield the *leytenant* from danger.

But *Polkovnik* Dimetriev was frowning with some emotion Aleks could not define. "You must learn to listen, *Kapitan* Ivanovic," he hissed. "They mean they want a Hero of the Republic. I would guess that if he was to become a hero, it would require more than hiding from danger. I might think it would require a degree of boldness."

His sarcasm stung Aleks, who hesitated for only a moment before impudently retorting, "And if the *leytenant* does not wish to be bold, or to become a hero?"

"Then you must *help* to make him bold," Dimetriev said in a louder, almost angry voice. He was testy.

Dimetriev brandished a French cigarette, readily available in Hanoi and fast becoming a favorite of the Russians stationed there. He carefully lit it, sucking avidly on the thing. Smoke trickled from his nostrils as he spoke. "The matter is of importance to their party, but it is just as important to maintain secrecy. His father, his fellow officers . . . *no one* . . . must know what you are doing."

Aleks was bewildered about just what it was that Dimetriev was ordering him to do. "Do they wish for me to help him destroy an enemy aircraft?"

"That might be acceptable . . . if he was seen to actually destroy an American aircraft. But of course, that would lead to the requirement to shoot down another and then yet another, and you cannot do it all for him, can you?"

"Perhaps I could help him shoot down one airplane," mused Aleks. "Two would be ambitious."

"Then find another way," Dimetriev snapped.

Aleks was staring, wondering just what it was that the ground-loving, sister-fucking *polkovnik* in the too-neat uniform had called him in for. Why wasn't he coming out with it? And what was there about it all that kept the man from looking him in the eyes?

"He is not a good pilot," Aleks confided. "It may be difficult to get him to do anything requiring skill."

"It was pointed out to me," said Dimetriev in his lowest and least audible tone, "that many glories may be accorded to a *dead* man."

Aleks stared.

"I believe you understand me now, *Kapitan*." Then, just as suddenly, still unable to look him in the eye, Dimetriev curtly dismissed him from his office with a flick of his wrist and a shower of French tobacco sparks. He cursed as he picked a glowing coal from his shirt front. "You'll know when you have your chance," he said in the low voice as Aleks prepared to leave.

Aleks would not forget the shower of sparks and the shaking hand as Dimetriev plucked the ember from his shirt. He finally understood what it was that Dimetriev wanted.

He had just been told to kill the *leytenant* in such circumstance that Thanh would appear to have died heroically.

"The chance may come very shortly," said the chief advisor.

Damn the sister-fucking . . . "I cannot do this thing, *kamerade Polkovnik*," he spouted, not caring that his voice was shaking and his tone disrespectful.

"It must be done, *Kapitan*," said Dimetriev, ignoring his words. "Tomorrow you and the *leytenant* will deploy to Kep. Perhaps you will find your chance there."

"I am not on the list to go to Kep."

"The list has been changed. Wherever the *leytenant* goes, you shall follow until your task is done."

"I cannot do what you ask," Aleks repeated, drawing himself up to his tallest, numbed with outrage.

Dimetriev sighed.

"I must confer with the *mayor* at Phuc Yen about this request, *kamerade Polkovnik* Dimetriev."

"You shall speak to *no one* about it. That is an order."

Aleks's anger seethed and his voice trembled. "I must return to my unit, *kamerade.*"

"Salute me first, *Kapitan,*" Dimetriev said, his voice low, as if searching for something familiar and honorable in the situation.

Aleks saluted crisply, unable to keep repugnance from his expression, then turned and strode, head high, from the office.

Barbaric, he thought as he stepped out of the outer office and down the hall. *If the sister-fucking dandy of a staff officer wants Thanh killed, he'll have to do it himself!*

Aleks saw the exit doors ahead and stopped cold, wondering what he should do next. He turned several courses of action over in his mind. Perhaps he should find the vehicle and driver and go to the home of the Eurasian girl a departing advisor had passed on to him along with the hovel she maintained near Gia Lam.

Yes!

He'd fuck her until the unclean feeling left him, regardless of how the Lithuanian driver complained of the delay. Then he would return to Phuc Yen and speak with the major in charge of the group of pilot advisors there. He would know what to do.

"*Kapitan!*" The meticulous *serzhant* caught up with him as he approached the outer doors, holding a sealed folder out to him.

Aleks turned.

"*Polkovnik* Dimetriev asks that you open this during your return trip. He said that the original of *one* of the two copies inside is to be added to your official records. He asks that you decide which."

"What does this contain, *serzhant?*" Aleks's voice crackled with residual emotion.

The *serzhant* shrugged politely, but Aleks sensed that he knew. He nodded to where the Lithuanian driver sat waiting in the shade of a tree. "Have a pleasant trip."

Aleks did not visit the Eurasian girl.

Of the two papers, one was a glowing report of his superb performance and unswerving dedication to duty, with a recommendation that he be considered for early promotion to the rank of *mayor*. The other spoke of his unreliability and mentioned the names of three women he had fucked before leaving his base in Russia, including the insatiable wife of a superior officer. It detailed the times and dates he had forced his will upon each woman, and the things he had demanded that each do for him. The paper concluded that Aleks must be summarily relieved of duty and court-martialed, and suggested his family be investigated for a background of depravity. Both papers were signed by *Polkovnik* Dimetriev, countersigned by the embassy political officer.

Even before they'd left Hanoi, Aleksandr Viktor Ivanovic began wondering how he should go about complying with Dimetriev's order.

2050 Local—Officers' Club Stag Bar, Takhli RTAFB, Thailand

First Lieutenant Billy Bowes

When he had finally signed onto the base and settled into the bachelor officers' quarters, a concrete building that looked like a bunker, and which the guys called the Ponderosa, Billy decided to look up one of the friends his cousin had written about in his letters. He wanted to know more about what had happened when Mal had been shot down. Thus far the information had been sketchy, except for three letters from Mal's squadron mates telling them he was surely dead.

His cousin had been in the 357th squadron, which the pilots called the clit-lickers. The 357th patch showed a dragon with a long red tongue. The association was inescapable.

At first Billy decided to go to the 357th squadron building, not far from his own 354th, but then it became too late, so after dinner he went into the Officers' Club stag bar and looked there. Since the bar was crowded, Billy looked for the biggest guy in the bar. He found him sitting alone at one end of the long bar, a drink cupped in a huge paw.

Billy approached, pushing past a couple of jocks gesturing with their hands, waving them around like airplanes, which was the way fighter people supplemented their verbs.

"You Tiny Bechler?" he asked.

The big lieutenant turned and peered. "Hi, Bear," he said. He started to turn back, then stopped and paled. "Jesus Christ," he muttered.

"Billy Bowes. I just signed into the 354th squadron," he said.

The lieutenant looked closer. He shook his head to clear it. "You look a lot like someone I knew," he mumbled.

Billy edged in beside him and motioned to the bartender, who wore a plastic name tag with JIMMY etched into it. "Scotch and rocks."

"No hab rocks," said Jimmy the bartender.

"Th' fuckin' ice machine's broke again," grumbled the big lieutenant.

"Just Scotch then," said Billy Bowes to Jimmy.

"*Damn* if you don't look like someone I used to know," said the big lieutenant.

"And the guy I look like is Malcom Stewart?"

Tiny drew back and looked hard at him. "How'd you know?"

"He's my cousin." He did not add that Mal's mother was his father's sister, and that they'd both looked a lot like their grandma, right down to big ears that stuck out like handles on a water pitcher.

"You sure as hell look like him."

"He wrote about the guys in his squadron. Said you were a friend."

"Bear Stewart had his shit together." Tiny pushed his face closer, peering hard and remembering. "You the IP who was stationed at Vance?"

"Yeah," said Billy.

Tiny's face brightened. "Bear told me about you. Said you were on your way over." He reflected on something else. "Your father was military, right?"

"Marines. He was killed at the Chosin Reservoir in Korea."

"Then your family went home to Oklahoma and ended up living with the Bear and his mother. He told me about that."

They'd all lived together. Mal and Ma Stewart, and Billy with his mother and three little brothers, in the old farmhouse on the south side of McAlester. The rest of the Bowes

clan, including cousins and various aunts and uncles, all re-
sided within a few miles.

Mal had worked like hell to help take care of them all,
even though he'd been just a kid himself. Until he'd enlisted
in the Air Force, he'd done everything from picking cotton
to working in a slaughterhouse to help fill the table. During
that time Mal and David Bowes, another cousin, had pushed
Billy to study hard in school, and even worked with Billy's
teachers to clear the way for the scholarship to Oke U. Billy
owed them both . . . a lot.

"Mal and I were close," was all Billy said.

"The Bear said that."

They'd all gone into the military. Mal and he into the Air
Force, David and two brothers into the Army, another
brother into the Marines. Grandma Bowes said the family
had always been like that. Always patriotic and first to defend the clan. She said they came from warrior blood. She
was pure Cherokee, whom she called "the People," and was
fiercely proud of it.

Grandma Bowes had thought Mal was one of the best,
sort of a throwback to a time when the world had been a no-
bler place, and she'd been surprised that the North Vietnamese had killed him. It was her old-ways belief that if a
man was pure of spirit and strong enough, he would be invincible. She'd said, as if she'd known, that Mal had not
died easily.

Billy downed the Scotch whiskey and shuddered at the
raw, burning sensation.

"Mal's number three," he said.

Tiny Bechler looked puzzled.

"I got an uncle who was a regiment sergeant major in the
Army. He got screwed up by a mine explosion when he was
out visiting the battalions in the field. A fucking booby trap,
probably set by some kid. David, he's another cousin stationed over here with the army, wrote me about it. Said they
saved one leg, that his dad's in the VA hospital in Oke City
learning to get used to living with a plastic leg and no balls."

"Another drink?" asked Tiny, looking uneasy.

"Sure," said Billy Bowes. "Anyway, my uncle was number
one. Then seven months ago, my little brother was killed by
North Vietnamese Army regulars in South Vietnam. He was
a door gunner in a chopper." Billy didn't like to think about

the way the NVA had killed him. "Then Mal got killed last month. That's three."

"Maybe you shouldn't be here, Billy. There's programs that don't allow whole families to go into a combat zone."

"Bullshit. Like my cousin David, he's in Special Forces at Danang . . . like David says, sometimes revenge is sweet."

"Maybe so," said Tiny Bechler.

Billy felt drawn to Bechler, probably because of Tiny's friendship with Mal, but there were things best left unsaid, things that were the concern of the family alone. He'd spoken enough and even wished he could withdraw some of his words.

Tiny Bechler looked at him with an unhappy expression. "I guess you know what happened to Bear Stewart."

"Some," said Billy. "That's why I looked you up. I was on the way over here when it happened . . . heard about it when I called home from the Phillippines. The official notification said he was MIA, but the letters said there was no way he could've survived."

"He's dead," said Tiny. "He had a pistol, and there were about thirty gomers with AK-47's, so he didn't have much of a chance. The rescue people were right there and saw it. An A-1 Sandy pilot flew down low and said the gomers had him and were chopping him up with machetes. We went in and bombed and strafed the shit out of them."

Emotion glittered in Billy's eyes.

As Tiny ordered more drinks from Jimmy, Billy's mind churned. Hatred welled and made a bitter taste in his throat that he tried to wash away with another sip of whiskey.

"You flown here yet?" asked Tiny Bechler.

"Two missions so far."

"Learn as much as you can before you have to go up to pack six."

"My first mission was to the Hanoi power plant. Our squadron's short of experienced people, so we couldn't get an indoctrination ride first."

"Who's your flight commander in the 354th?"

"A major called Lucky Anderson."

Tiny nodded. "He's as good as they come. Listen to him and stay aggressive." He poked a big finger at Billy's chest. "That's good advice."

"Thanks." Billy appreciated it.

The drinks arrived and Tiny paid for them, then nodded

toward two colonels who had entered the stag bar and were standing near the door. "The shorter of the full bulls there is B. J. Parker, the wing commander. A fucking glory hound, but he's okay. He flies his share of tough ones and treats his men well."

Billy sipped more raw Scotch.

"I don't know the other guy. He's new."

As the colonels approached the bar, the wing commander motioned to a very attentive bartender. The wingco was in charge of all American military forces on the base.

"Give us a drink, Jimmy," he said. "A martini and . . . a manhattan, right, Tom?"

The second colonel nodded. He was tall and tanned, blond hair meticulously lacquered into place.

"How you doing, Tiny?" asked Colonel B. J. Parker.

"Just fine, Colonel," Tiny said pleasantly.

"Meet Tom Lyons, freshest cannon fodder among our crop of colonels," joked Parker. "He's taking over the command post, and I'll keep him busy with special projects until we come up with something more suitable for his talents. Tom, this is Lieutenant Tiny Bechler, one of our fine young Air Force Academy graduates."

As Lyons hesitantly proffered his hand, frowning as if the lieutenant's might be contaminated, the fighter jock behind Tiny Bechler jostled Tiny hard enough that his drink sloshed onto the sleeve of Lyons's flight suit.

"Sorry," mumbled Tiny, but Lyons's look was furious.

B. J. Parker was talking animatedly to a nearby major, and Lyons turned stiffly away from the lieutenants to join him. Then Jimmy came around the bar to personally bring the colonels their drinks, and they wandered away through the crowd, smiling benignly, like benevolent gods come to visit the mortals.

"That new colonel's bad news," said Billy Bowes, staring after them.

"Prima-donna asshole," snorted Tiny Bechler in agreement.

Captain Manny DeVera came in and beelined for the bar. Billy introduced him to Tiny.

Manny said he'd been to the on-base Thai market. He showed off his new go-to-hell hat, an Aussie-style bush hat with a cord that held both sides of the brim up and in place. He'd already pinned captain's bars onto its front.

"Some of the guys mark their missions on the band," said Tiny. He showed his own, with dozens of black marks. About half were twice as long as the rest. "Those are pack six missions, and I remember every damn one."

Manny showed a single line on his own hatband. He grinned at his handiwork, then saw the two colonels. His smile faded. "Shit, is that Lyons?"

Tiny nodded. "That's what Colonel Parker called him."

"And he's a full bull now? Double damn."

Lyons had turned back toward them, his gaze upon Manny. His eyes smoldered briefly; then he pursed his lips thoughtfully before looking back at Parker.

"Trouble with a capital *T*," moaned Manny. "He has regard for only one man, and that's the guy he loves—himself."

"You know him?" asked Billy.

"Wish I didn't."

"That bad?"

"He was in a flight of F-100's, getting his checkout at the Wheelus gunnery ranges. A buddy of mine was leading the flight. This asshole, he was a major then, fucked up when they were joining back in formation to depart the range. He overshot and ran right into lead."

"Jesus," muttered Tiny.

"Both of them went down, but my buddy was too low before he ejected, and he was still in the seat when he hit the ground. I was range officer and saw the whole thing. Jumped in my pickup and drove out to where they landed. My buddy was dead, of course, and when I picked up Lyons, he started babbling how sorry he was. Then all of a sudden his tune began to change and he started making excuses. By the time the chopper landed to take him back to Whelus, he was saying he'd had a problem with his airplane."

"Damn."

"That night I was in the Wheelus Officers' Club when he comes in and corners me. He said my buddy ran into him, instead of the other way around, and he wanted me to back him up. I got pissed off, but he was a major and I was a lieutenant, so I just told him to fuck off and went to my BOQ room."

"Didn't the accident board nail him?" asked Tiny.

Manny DeVera gave a sad shake of his head. "I was

about to go before the board and tell 'em what I saw, when he called me up and tried to convince me I hadn't seen what I had. Said I must've looked away or something, and that I'd better, by God, change my story. I kept my cool, just told him that I wouldn't lie."

"So it was your word against his?" asked Billy.

"Let me tell you something about Colonel Thomas F. Lyons over there. His daddy dabbles in politics. He was Ike's Secretary of the Interior for a year, but he quit when he decided he wanted to be ambassador to Italy, because they have a humungus place over on the Italian Riviera. His ma's family owns things, like a small county in Colorado and a couple of big ones in West Texas. They've got two town houses in New York, which they use only every couple of years when one of the family's in town."

Billy Bowes shook his head incredulously and wondered why the hell Lyons would choose a military career.

Manny answered his unspoken question. "I know of several guys who come from big money who are sent to the military. Most Air Force officers are from middle-class families. Then there's a few poor kids like me who get in because we're such superb pilots. . . ."

Tiny and Billy both grinned.

"But then there's a few ungodly rich bastards like Lyons who are here because it's a good place for their families to shuck 'em off to so they won't fuck up the family fortune."

Tiny stared at the colonels. "So they sent Lyons here to fuck up the Air Force?"

"Most of 'em don't give a shit about anything but themselves. They expect special treatment from the time they get to flight school, and unfortunately, sometimes they get it." Manny nodded at Lyons. "That guy can't fly worth a damn, but *somebody* let him through, and now he's a fucking full colonel."

"Why do the generals let it happen?" asked Tiny. Billy could tell that Tiny was caught up by Manny DeVera's spell. Manny was so outgoing and such an all-American fighter jock, it would be difficult not to like him immediately.

"Some senior officers like being around people with money. Makes them feel important to rub elbows with them, I guess. I know of a few more like Lyons. Most of 'em made colonel, and a couple are generals. A few have talent and deserve it. But there're others like Lyons there who haven't got the morals of a snake."

"So what happened when the accident board found out he'd fucked up?" asked Tiny, eyeing Tom Lyons as he accompanied Colonel Parker to the door.

"The board listened to me, took my written statement, asked a few more questions, then blamed it all on poor flight management. Said my buddy fucked up."

"I'll be a bastard," said Tiny.

"I only saw Lyons one time after that. He'd made lieutenant colonel and was about to leave for the States. He looked at me like I was scum, like you just saw. Told the major I worked for that we didn't need people like me in the Air Force."

They watched the colonels leave the bar.

"I hear there's a round-eye in the area," said Manny, changing the subject. He looked around inquisitively, as if he were trying to get the feel and layout of the Takhli stag bar, and acting like he was only casually interested in the female. His reputation preceded him; Billy had already heard he was a horny bastard.

"We've got *two* ladies on base," grinned Tiny Bechler, "both staying in the guest trailers. One's from Bangkok. Some kind of high-ranking USAID official. Colonel Mack, he's our squadron commander, thinks she's really some kind of spook. The other one's from the Peace Corps camp over near Nakhon Sawan." Nakhon Sawan was a city fifty miles northwest of Ta Khli Village.

"She's here trying to talk B.J. out of supplies for their camp," said Tiny.

"You guys ready for a drink?" asked Manny, happy with the news about the round-eyes. Billy said he'd had enough, but Tiny said sure, he'd take one. Manny ordered the drinks, then swung his attention back to Tiny. "How about the other one? The one from Bangkok?"

"The guys call her the Ice Maiden, because she's cool and collected. No one knows what she's here for, but it's nice having her on base. Except for a couple of USO shows and a wife who visited once," said Tiny, "this is the first time we've had round-eyes on base."

"What do they look like?" asked Manny, keeping his innocent look. "Heifers?"

"Nope. The Peace Corps dolly's a real fox. Sort of a

honey blond . . . maybe twenty-one or -two. Short and well stacked, and all her lumps are in the right places. The other one's older, maybe thirty, and she's got dark hair and the calm, cool look about her. Sorta tall and slender and on the quiet side, but she's sure no dog."

Manny smoothed his just-sprouting mustache, deep in thought. Billy thought the mustache made DeVera look like a Mexican bandit.

He drank down half of his drink.

Tiny Bechler turned and gave him a friendly look. "The Bear told me you guys were Indian. I thought Indians had trouble holding their liquor."

"Some I know can't drink worth a damn," Billy admitted. "People say they go berserk and do funny things like stick knives in people for no reason at all." He finished the Scotch.

Tiny regarded Billy closer. "You seem to be able to hold it okay."

Billy sighed contentedly as he savored the drink. "I'm only half-Indian, and we're different. It's never happened to me yet, understand, but I hear one minute we'll be normal, and the next we'll be asking the bartender for a paring knife."

Tiny grinned his disbelief, but he started when Billy pushed back from the bar.

"See you guys later. My hold baggage shipment arrived today, so I've gotta go back to the Ponderosa and unpack."

"Be seeing you around," said Tiny Bechler. "Sorry about what happened to your family. Gets you good and pissed off at the gomers, doesn't it?"

The big lieutenant didn't know the half of it, thought Billy. He walked out the door into the heat of the tropical night, deciding to write the others in his family to tell them what had happened to Mal. Then he'd get on with what was expected of him.

0920 Local—Regional Hospital, Travis AFB, California

Captain Benny Lewis

Benny lay flat on his back, as the doctors demanded, for just a month earlier he'd ejected from his burning fighter and experienced a compression fracture of the back. Painful, but they said it wouldn't be overly serious if it was allowed to heal properly. He'd judiciously spent the month strapped to the rock-hard hospital bed, just as they'd wanted.

He'd thought a lot during that time about much more than his physical problem. In fact, when it wasn't hurting, the injury had been far down on his list of priorities. At first he'd reminisced a lot about the Bear, the Wild Weasel backseater who'd been shot down with him, and who had died there in the western mountains of North Vietnam. Sometimes, in his mind, he'd even talked with the Bear, held sort of a conversation with a voice that had been inside him since they'd put him on the hard bed.

They'd been close, he and the Bear. So close that when they flew together, they'd hardly had to use the intercom to know what the other was thinking. On the ground they'd complemented one another, his stodginess offset by the Bear's devil-may-care cockiness. He'd tried to keep the Bear out of trouble when he flew off the handle, and the Bear had tried to teach him to loosen up and enjoy life.

Now it was the voice inside him that laughed at him when his thoughts grew *too* inflexible. The voice that told him to joke more with the nurses and nicknamed the floor nurse Lady Dracula. He knew it was just remembering the Bear and wondering what he would have thought of this situation or that, but it certainly *seemed* like a voice was coming from within.

After they'd been shot down, the Bear had saved him, had fought it out with the gomers, holding them off while he was rescued . . . and his last words had been to take care of his wife and the kid inside her.

He would.

The voice in him knew he would.

And as he was thinking about her, Julie Stewart, the Bear's vivacious wife, came into the room, nodding and agreeing with the nurse the voice called Lady Dracula.

"Use bigger ropes on him," Julie told the nurse.

"I'm about to use a mallet," said Lady Dracula with a grimace. She was tall and angular, with severe features, and was infuriatingly efficient. "Every time I think he's listening and staying put," she complained, "I find him moving around or trying to convince a flight surgeon he feels better than he does." The rawboned nurse was adamant when it came to compliance with rules, and she'd argue with any doctor who thought that Benny was mending, saying he was still very fragile.

Julie looked hard at him. "Do as you're told," she scolded.

"Yes, ma'am." He tried to look repentant.

The nurse checked him over, gave him a scathing look to tell him to remain completely still during the visit, and left.

"You really should do as they ask," Julie chided.

Benny sighed mightily. "I'm tired of reading, the local radio news is antiestablishment, antiwar and prohippie, and the nurses won't let me go to the lounge to watch television. I'm also getting tired of counting the two hundred seventy-two tiles on the ceiling."

"You'll only have to put up with it for another few weeks, and then . . ."

"Maybe just a few days. The doc told me they might put me into a brace next week."

Julie shook her finger. "Benny Lewis, you've been all over these poor people, and it's only because you're bored."

He felt sheepish. She could make him feel that way when no one else could.

"The doctor said no matter what, it's going to take ninety days for your back to *start* mending, then three more months before you can go back to work even part-time."

"I had another flight surgeon look at my last X rays, and *he* says I'm starting to heal. He's going to see if they can't transport me to my next assignment after they put me in the brace. Says I can heal anywhere. He's also saying I may be released for limited duty after sixty days, not ninety."

She raised an eyebrow. "They're going to move you to Nevada?"

"Maybe. I'm going to be reassigned to Nellis Air Force Base in Las Vegas, same place I was stationed before I went to Takhli."

"The nurse says you're not *ready* to be moved," she said.

Benny felt perversely pleased at her concern. "I'll be careful," he promised. "Anyway, nothing's definite yet."

He didn't tell her how he wheedled the flight surgeons at every opportunity, how he promised to take it easy and religiously wear the brace, but how much he'd like to be moved to the hospital at Nellis. He was anxious to get *closer*, at least, to a fighter base. The docs said it would be a year before he could return to flying status, probably longer. But surely, he thought, there were other things he could be doing.

He changed the subject. "How's the kid in the hangar?" She was four months pregnant.

"He's a hell-raiser," she said proudly. "I know it's early, but I'll swear he woke me up with a couple of good kicks last night." She laughed. "He's anxious to get on with things."

"Kid doesn't know when he's got it good," Benny joked. "Takes after his dad. The Bear was always in a hurry."

"Maybe, but Mal Bear knew a good thing when he saw it. He married me, didn't he?"

They laughed easily. They shared close feelings for the dead father. They'd gone through a long period of sadness together and only now were beginning to joke about things.

The Bear would have been disgusted with such behavior, thought Benny. The voice inside him told him so.

Benny had felt warm and at ease with Julie since the first time they'd met, and now his feelings for her grew in some indescribable manner each time she visited. He guessed it was protectiveness, but he knew he was happiest when she was around, somehow empty when she was not.

He thought of his possible departure in a week. He remembered the line he'd rehearsed. Then he muffed it.

"If they let me go, why don't you come to Vegas?" he blurted, surprised at the terse way the words emerged.

The voice inside groaned. *Dumb fuck.*

Julie was sitting in the chair beside his bed, staring at his face. She was likely startled by the boorish way he'd presented the offer, he thought, and he couldn't blame her for pausing for a long moment before answering.

"I'm a working girl, remember," she finally said. Julie was a stewardess with Pan Am.

"Quit," he croaked through his suddenly dry throat, again surprised at his boldness.

She just stared.

He tried again, using a different tack. "I'd worry about you if I was in Vegas and you were alone back here."

That's a little better, said the voice.

"The doctor says I'm a perfectly healthy specimen and should have no problems with the delivery. Anyway, you should stay here in the bay area until you're recuperated."

She glanced away, and he realized the conversation was becoming difficult for her. Still he couldn't help pressing on.

"I want to get to Nellis, so I'll feel useful again, Julie. But I treasure your visits, and . . . I want you around."

Not bad at all, said the voice.

She was quiet. Had he gone too far?

Words suddenly tumbled from her, and there was a catch in her voice. "I don't know *what* I'm supposed to feel, Benny, but lately I just feel numb when I think about Mal. He's listed as MIA, and even though I know in my heart that what you guys say is true, that he's really dead and gone, a tiny part of me believes he might be fighting to get back."

"He won't come back, Julie. He can't."

"But what if he *did*?" She sighed and shook her head sadly. "My mother doesn't help. Every time I talk to her, she tells me to be a good military wife and keep hoping for the best."

"He's dead, Julie."

"Not officially. Officially he's neither dead nor alive, just missing."

"And if his status was changed?"

"God, I loved him," she breathed. A long minute passed before she finally, sadly, shook her head. "But it would make things easier if I knew one way or the other, if they just called it like it is rather than generate this false hope."

He nodded.

She touched his arm reassuringly and spoke in a low, soft voice. "Benny, you're the best friend I could possibly have. I've relied on your moral support from the first, and I don't want that to change. I wish I could come with you, but . . . I just can't."

They started to speak about other things, and the air between them eased. At first they talked about his parents, who lived only an hour away in Santa Rosa and treated her like their own. Then she shared gossip about the various stews she worked with, and he told her the raunchy jokes passed on by a nurse on the night shift. A month before he'd never have shared the jokes with any female, but the voice was changing that. She enjoyed them and laughed with delight at the punch lines, which he was beginning to tell better each time she visited.

You're learning, said the voice.

After an hour she prepared to leave. As she rose, he said, "Julie, you make me feel good when you visit. I feel . . . easy around you."

She gave him her impish look. "Me too. If I didn't, I sure wouldn't be here. Why else would I visit a grumpy guy strapped to a board every single day I'm not flying?"

"Grumpy?"

"And who else could get away with asking me to run off to Vegas to shack up?"

He felt his face flush. "That wasn't what I meant."

"It's not?" She feigned surprise.

It's not? joked the voice.

"We'd get you an apartment," he sputtered, "and I'd stay on base."

She raised an eyebrow. She was back to her fun-loving self—which, since he was trying to make a difficult point, was downright irritating.

"No chance I could get you down there?" he asked a last time, wanting her to say yes.

She sighed and looked at him, then slowly shook her head. "I just can't, Benny."

"Then I'd better prepare for one hell of a telephone bill," he said.

"You'd better," she agreed, and then she got a catch in her throat and had trouble continuing. "You'd better."

That afternoon, after Julie had returned home across the bay in San Francisco and they'd given him his doses of muscle relaxant and painkiller, he napped and dreamed.

He heard the popping sounds of distant gunfire, and the sounds of the chopper coming for him.

When he awoke, Benny was determined to write the people at Takhli.

That evening, a Red Cross volunteer wrote a letter for him. It was addressed to Lieutenant Colonel MacLendon, his squadron commander at Takhli. He told him he'd met with Bear Stewart's wife, and how she was having a difficult time coping due to the confusion about the Bear's status. He wondered if Mack couldn't have the matter reopened, and suggested that the Bear's official status be changed to KIA.

The voice inside him was pleased.

CHAPTER FOUR

Sunday, April 23rd, 0700 Local—HQ Seventh Air Force, Tan Son Nhut Air Base, Saigon, Republic of Vietnam

Lieutenant Colonel Pearly Gates

This time General Moss had summoned Pearly, saying he wanted to talk about the new OPlan he was writing, so there was no waiting around trying to get in. Pearly Gates hustled through the outer office, noting the secretary's perfunctory nod and the whisper, *"He's smiling."* He hesitated at the door long enough to run his free hand over his uniform. After smoothing his shirt and aligning his belt buckle, he stepped inside.

The general was alone, poring over a document with a white-and-red cover sheet marked TOP SECRET—SENSITIVE INFORMATION. Moss glanced up and said, "Have a seat," then went back to his reading. Periodically the corners of his mouth would twitch. He was in a pleasant, almost jocular mood.

Two silent minutes passed. Pearly bided his time by mentally measuring steel mesh panels half-hidden under the Air Force–blue curtains at the sides of the room's single window. During emergencies they were swung closed. The window itself was multilayer safety glass, thick and shatterproof. The precautions were warranted, for the Viet Cong had made infrequent rocket and mortar bombardments, as well as two sapper attacks, on Tan Son Nhut Air Base. In January they'd launched a serious one that had lasted three days.

Moss grunted, drawing Pearly's attention. "Intell was right about the security leak. The Smith Brothers confirm the NVA are getting target information, sometimes even before it's released to the units."

Appropriately paranoid, Pearly wondered if it had been wise to let the CIA in on it, Saigon contained a quagmire of spies, sympathizers, and double agents of various allegiances and motivations. Pearly trusted absolutely *none* of them.

Moss put the paper away, thoughtful as he carefully replaced the classified cover sheet. "I told 'em I want the source found. Someone's putting a gun to our pilots' heads, Pearly."

"Yes, sir."

"The Smiths say they're trying to find the leak, but I told them to by God work harder. I also called in the OSI to see if they can help."

Pearly regarded the OSI's effectiveness as just lower than that of the Keystone Kops. The Air Force's Office of Special Investigations was a sort of in-service FBI, normally kept busy tracking which black-market items the South Vietnamese merchants were coveting and other problems unrelated to operations.

"Have you picked out the first bridge target yet?" Moss asked him.

"Yes, sir." Pearly walked around the desk beside the general, leaned over, and spread out a detailed map of Hanoi and the immediate surrounding area. He pointed a forefinger at the northeastern section of the city, and the bridge, almost two miles long, which spanned the Red River, crossing from one shore, over a large river island, to the other.

"It's a big one," Moss said.

"Their most important bridge, General. It carries both rail and highway traffic. Traffic from both rail lines to China and from the port at Haiphong get into Hanoi over that single bridge. So does most of their road traffic." Pearly added three photos of the structure, slowly so Moss could digest each one.

"It's built mostly out of brick and concrete. Multiple arches, like the Romans taught the Gauls two thousand

years ago. You see the same kind of construction in Rome
and Paris."

"It certainly looks sturdy enough."

"The arches give it strength. *Most* of the North Vietnamese bridges are well built. The credit goes to a fellow named
Paul Doumer, same guy they named this bridge for."

"French?"

"Right down to his spats. Doumer was an insufferable,
turn-of-the-century frog-eater who thought of himself as a
modern Napoleon."

Moss smiled, so Pearly continued.

"Back in 1897 the French were having trouble with the
locals when Doumer arrived as the new governor-general
for the Indochina Union. He'd just suffered a political set-
back in France, but he didn't let that dampen his ambition.
In fact, it just made him more determined to make a name
for himself here in Indochina."

"Trying to win the people over?"

"He didn't care what they thought. He was a dollars-and-
cents man, and only the bottom line counted. When anyone
interfered, he used legionnaires to kick ass and take names,
and they humiliated every prominent Southeast Asian that
got in his way. Within a couple of years he had South, Central, and North Vietnam, Laos and Cambodia, all of them,
saying 'yes, sir, three bags full.' He put French administrators in charge at every level of government and used the old
mandarin bureaucrats to tell the people what was expected
of them."

"A fucking accountant politician." Moss snorted. He'd
been known to call the SecDef by the same title when he
didn't call him the Edsel mechanic.

"Doumer set up complex infrastructures to sell off the
wealth and rake off the profits. In the northern part of
Vietnam, called Tong King, he shipped everything through
Hanoi, where his people sorted and inspected it, then forwarded it to Haiphong for shipment. That meant he needed
a good transportation network. Farm-to-market roads,
highways, rail systems, and bridges, everything going
through Hanoi. He had similar plans for the rest of French
Indochina, but Tong King was his showplace. He wasn't
doing the Vietnamese any favors by building bridges, just setting it up so France could take its share of everything."

"Imperialism."

"In its worst form. By the time he was done, Doumer had turned Indochina into a French money machine. He'd bred great animosity and created the environment for the various antiimperialist movements, including the "Workers' Party" set up by Ho Chi Minh."

"Why didn't the French get rid of him and bring in someone more popular?"

"Because he turned a hell of a profit. He made so much money for France, they recalled him and made him a senator. And his successors kept things going here just like he left it, because they were getting so much loot."

"Poison in the well."

"It's hard to fault the Vietnamese for hating the French. That's why the North Vietnamese call us imperialists when they want to rile up the people, and sometimes it works."

"Damned politicians'll screw it up every time, Pearly."

"When World War I came along, the only thing that kept France out of bankruptcy was their income from the Ministry of Colonies, and Doumer kept reminding them of that until they elected him president. The people here paid the price, but he got what he was after. The French kept his rules around and kept raking in the money right up to the end."

"What happened to Doumer?"

"A Russian anarchist killed him."

Moss peered at the aerial photos. "The Paul Doumer bridge," he muttered.

"The Vietnamese call it the Long Bien bridge. They think of Doumer about like we do Benedict Arnold, maybe worse."

"Poor bastards have had it tough. First the Chinese, then the French, next the Japanese, and now Ho Chi Minh and his cronies. Slavery, imperialism, or communism. Shitty choices, Pearly." Finished with philosophizing, Moss studied the map.

Pearly tapped the bridge symbol. "I picked this one for our debut. Hitting it should give us an example of what we'll be facing. And when we knock it down, it'll get their attention and slow down a lot of traffic."

Moss regarded the bridge's close proximity to downtown Hanoi with a wary expression. "You know I've got reservations."

"Still, sir?" Pearly returned to his chair.

"It'll be expensive," said the general.

Pearly wondered if he had to sell the campaign again, or whether Moss just wanted reassurance they were going in the right direction.

"We're already losing men and aircraft, sir. The difference is there's no coherent campaign now." When there was no explosion from Moss, he continued. "One time we bomb a barracks, next time a truck park, next time an overpass. There's no continuity, sir. Up in pack six, most of the meaningful targets are still restricted. Every now and then we get to bomb a JCS target the President or the SecDef believes will *verrrry* slowly add pressure, but even then we usually don't get to follow up."

Moss's expression darkened. He and most of the staff despised the SecDef. They felt he voiced his opinions that the war couldn't be won, then threw obstacles in their path to make his prediction come true. It was different when it came to the President. As a loyal soldier, Moss seldom came out and said that his commander in chief was a buffoon meddling in military matters he didn't understand. Instead he just said Johnson was a "consummate politician," but everyone knew his feelings toward that profession.

Pearly spoke slowly. "This campaign would let us pursue a real interdiction program. If we can keep going after the bridges until the important ones are knocked down, the enemy will be spending a lot more time and manpower trying to get supplies through."

Pearly paused.

Moss was looking at the photos of the Doumer bridge. He stared for a second longer, then abruptly nodded his head. "How soon before we can get approval?" he asked.

"I briefed CINCPAC like you said, and told them that today you'd decide *which* bridge to start with. The admiral's got it greased for a one-time trial strike. Once they've reviewed our OPlan, we should get approval within twenty-four hours."

Moss spoke reluctantly. "Go ahead and put the gears in motion." He pushed the photos across the desk toward Pearly. "How close are you to being finished with the plan?"

"Done, sir," said Pearly. He placed a spiral-bound document before Moss.

Combat Operation Plan
CROSSFIRE ZULU
HQ 7 AF OPlan 67-121

22 April 1967

Moss absently leafed through it, nodding. "Leave this copy with me and I'll read it later."

"Yes, sir."

"You mention Bullpup missiles in there?"

Pearly remembered that the general thought them a poor choice for this target. "Only as an alternative weapon, far down the list of options, sir."

"I called the Deputy for Operations at Hickam and told him I thought they'd be a pilot-killer in a high-threat area. I *think* he listened, but you never know about bomber pukes."

Pearly, being an ex–bomber puke, held his counsel.

"Go ahead and distribute the OPlan to all the players. Looks like you're ready for 'em, Pearly." Which meant that Moss thought he'd covered the right bases.

Pearly braced himself for what must be said. "The enemy are also ready, General. They've been stacking guns and SAMs knee-deep around every bridge between Hanoi and Haiphong. I haven't seen defenses this concentrated since we went after Thai Nguyen."

Moss grew an unpleasant expression. "They've found out," he hissed.

"Possibly, sir."

"Hell, the bridges aren't even approved targets yet."

Pearly remained silent.

"Are *your* people secure, Pearly? The leak could be right here in this building."

"It's not in my branch," Pearly said quickly. He had faith in his hardworking crew.

"No one wants to think it's their people." Moss gave him a sharp look. "Treacheries like this brew distrust, and we can't have that."

Pearly blew a sigh. "We'll need a diversion target, sir. Something important enough to get the enemy to draw their guns away from the bridge before we give the go-ahead."

Moss's angry look dissolved like a balloon with a slow leak, and a grin again began to tickle the corners of his mouth. "A diversion?" he asked slyly.

He obviously knew something Pearly did not. As a staff officer, that concerned him.

"Yes, sir."

"What kind of ... ah ... diversion would you suggest?" asked Moss, cocking his head and grinning and making Pearly wish he would go ahead and tell him what he knew.

He joined the game. "Maybe one of the targets off the new authorized list?"

"Have we received it yet?" Moss asked, too innocently.

"No, sir. I checked with the comm center this morning."

Moss tapped the Top Secret document before him. "Here's the list, couriered from CINCPAC in Hawaii. Same with the copies for General Westmoreland and Seventh Fleet."

Pearly was surprised.

"When the Smith Brothers confirmed the leak, General Westmoreland and Ambassador Lodge were appalled. They agreed that we have to take emergency measures. Until the problem's corrected, all critical information will be sent by courier."

Pearly thought about that for a moment. He wondered if that was really any better than the normal way of matching classified code words with a classified target list. Certainly it was not as timely, and he doubted the gomers had broken the cryptographic codes.

Moss was leaning forward now, an excited glitter to his eyes. "Let's talk about MiGs."

It was a subject Pearly knew well.

"How many do they have?" asked Moss.

It was a good question, for the estimates varied. They were restricted from bombing the enemy's military airfields, so the numbers had grown as the Soviets and Chinese granted North Vietnamese requests for more and more aircraft. But in the past few months the North Vietnamese had grown bolder with their tactics, and the Phantoms and Thuds had been steadily bagging MiGs. And for some reason the Soviets had recently stopped replacing the ones their clients lost. Those factors, combined with the fact that the North Vietnamese often hid or camouflaged their aircraft, made the problem difficult.

"Total aircraft, or just interceptors, sir?" The North Vietnamese had small numbers of light bombers and transports.

"Just MiGs."

Pearly calculated for a few seconds before he spoke. "CIA says sixty-seven, and our intell says eighty-nine. That's MiG-17's, -19's, and -21's."

"What's *your* estimate, and how'd you get it?"

"Ninety-two, with six more based in China for pilot-refresher training. They shuffle them around a lot, so I got my count by using multiple recce bird and satellite photos at a single, specified time. Then I added the ones Motel radar said were in the air and others intell said were probably hidden in hangars and under camouflage nets. I did that three different times and got very close to the same answer."

Moss wrote the number 92 on his pad, then frowned and underlined it.

"Did I authorize those reconnaissance requests?" he asked, and Pearly realized he was treading on treacherous ground. Moss had mood swings caused by God knew what, and too often the staff officer who happened to be before him suffered.

"Yes, sir." Pearly had buried the special request for recce sorties in a bundle of others for prestrike photos.

Damn, he thought. Moss hated to be given bad news and had been known to shoot the occasional messenger. What would he do to someone who manipulated him?

Moss shook his head ominously and his voice rose. "Next time tell me what the hell I'm authorizing. I'd have let it through." He paused and muttered, "Probably."

"Yes, sir." It was time for such a response.

"Be straight with me, and don't pull any of that junior-officer connivery. Don't start acting like a fucking navigator, Pearly."

"No, sir." Moss had surprised him with the light admonishment.

Moss's look brightened, so the dangerous time was over.

Change the subject, Pearly told himself. "When will we be cleared to bomb the diversion target, sir?"

"Tomorrow soon enough?" Moss was cheerful, as if the ass-chewing had been tonic.

Pearly Gates nodded. "Yes, sir. That should catch them with their defenses still bunched around the bridges."

"That's precisely what I want, to catch the bastards with their pants down for once. Hop on a T-39 and go out and brief the wing commanders so they can prepare, Pearly."

Pearly did not look forward to shuttling back and forth

between the bases as he'd done when they'd bombed previous hot targets. "Yes, sir," was what he said.

"Tell the commanders about the whole scheme, about this being a diversion target and about the bridges, but tell them to damn well keep it close to their vests. Tell them we won't officially release the supplementary air tasking order until in the morning, a couple of hours before takeoff, but that there won't be any surprises. And you can tell them to expect more of your visits while we get the CROSSFIRE ZULU bridge campaign going."

"Yes, sir, I will."

"Now I suppose you want me to pick a worthwhile diversion target from this list they've sent us." Moss was showing off again.

"Is there a suitable one, sir?"

Moss told him the target they'd been given. "You think that might get their attention?"

Pearly's grin widened until it matched the one Moss was wearing. "Yes, sir, it just might."

0815 Local—Kep PAAF Auxiliary Base, DRV

The dartlike silver jets made long, straight-in approaches toward the distant runway, flying with a kilometer's separation between aircraft. The Tumanskii turbojets were characteristically loud and high-pitched, and their sounds shattered the morning quiet. Flocks of birds flushed from freshly planted rice fields as each jet passed overhead. The six aircraft were so spaced that as the birds began to settle, another would scream overhead and rally them into yet another fervor.

At ten kilometers from the end of the runway, a position marked by the crossing of a wide irrigation canal, each pilot activated a paddle-shaped switch on his console, and the wing-flaps began to squeal and chatter as they slowly moved down grooved tracks.

The tracked flaps were one of several weaknesses in the early-production models. The MiG-21's aerodynamic design was clean, basic, and sound, a blowpipe with a small tail and a delta wingform. The engineers at the Mikoyan-Guryevich bureau had built an aircraft prototype; the bureau and military test pilots had flown it in 1956; and the engineers had made minor changes and so forth until the first MiG-21's were approved for production due to their superb speed and maneuverability at altitude. But when the mainline unit pilots received them, the first production runs of the sleek jets proved unstable and difficult to fly, and the flap mechanisms archaic and dangerous.

Because of the small surfaces of the tracked flaps, the early MiG-21's landed hot and fast and used an inordinate amount of runway for both takeoff and landing. The flaps also gave cause for another concern; if you did not watch carefully when they were activated and chattering along in their channels, you might end up with a "split-flap condition," meaning one had hung up while the other continued moving down. With split flaps you cannot fly straight and level or land. Instead, the aircraft will enter a constant and increasingly violent roll, and if you don't immediately correct the condition, you will crash.

The early MiG-21's, with their undersized tail assemblies and tracked flaps, were alternately called "small-tails" and "spin machines" by the pilots. The problems had been solved on big-tail MiG-21's like the PF and PFMA models. Their redesigned tails made them more stable, and their more powerful engines had been modified so air could be diverted to blow down their much larger flaps. Big-tail MiG-21's flew faster, landed slower, were easier to handle, and were equipped with radar and improved instruments.

The dangerous early-production models were shuffled off to the satellite nations, and the new big-tails given to the Soviet Air Force. The MiG-21's provided to the Vietnamese People's Army Air Force fell somewhere in between. They *had* been equipped with newer, more powerful afterburning engines, but they still had the small tails and the tracked flaps.

It took a special touch to fly small-tails well, and a number of the North Vietnamese pilots had great difficulty converting from the much simpler MiG-17's. Although they were daily engaged in mortal combat, no one had yet been able to convince the Soviet generals to provide big-tail MiG-21's. Moscow had felt the problem could be solved through better training and provided a cadre of experienced pilots to train the VPAAF until they came up to speed. They'd also requested volunteer pilots from their satellite nations in Eastern Europe.

German, Czech, and Polish volunteer pilots who had experience flying them made up one of the two MiG-21 air battalions at Phuc Yen, to be replaced by Vietnamese pilots as they gained experience and confidence. A cadre of Soviet pilot-advisors were assigned to assist the North Vietnamese pilots of the other battalion.

Aleks Ivanovic of the Soviet Air Force flew the small-tail very well and was one of the most skilled of the advisory group. In fact, he was very sure he was the best of them all.

Kapitan Aleksandr Viktor Ivanovic

Aleks flew last in the formation by choice, so he could see and monitor the five other silver aircraft strung out before him. Two were flying a couple of hundred meters higher than the rest, likely because they'd forgotten to readjust their altimeters for landing.

"Reset altimeters to seventy-five point four centimeters," he reminded the two three-ship flights. After a second thought he added, *"And check that flaps and landing gear are down."* He spoke Vietnamese, however poorly, for they were ordered to do so to keep the Americans from learning what they undoubtedly already knew, that foreign pilots were flying in North Vietnam. The Europeans in the other battalion spoke even poorer Vietnamese than Aleks, for they hadn't attended the four-week language course, but they tried to comply with the directive. When things got busy, the airwaves were filled with a polyglot of languages.

The fact that he'd found it necessary to make his last transmission was troublesome, for he'd done the job normally assigned to ground-radar controllers. The controllers at Phuc Yen should have advised them to descend and prepare to land at Kep and then should have followed them down carefully, barking out instructions as they passed through 8,000, 6,000, and 4,000 meters. Then he should have advised them about the altimeter setting, next to descend to 2,000 and then 1,000 meters altitude, and then to extend flaps and gear and prepare to land. But they'd not been instructed to descend, nor given any advisories or instructions. Which showed just how poor the radar control had grown. During the past month they'd retreated from highly centralized control, manned by Russian and North Korean pilot-controllers at the helm of the system they'd called "Wisdom," to the complete noncontrol they were now experiencing.

A flight of American F-105's had attacked and strafed the Wisdom control center. Since then aircraft accidents and mishaps had risen, and their combat effectiveness had been sharply reduced. It was a sad thing that the flight leaders now had to remind their pilots to check their altimeters so they could tell their proper height above the ground.

The rumor among the pilot advisors was that the Wisdom system had been dismantled because the Vietnamese hierarchy distrusted the foreigners who had been controlling North Vietnamese pilots. After Wisdom was damaged, the rumors said, the radars were placed under the command of a "politically reliable" officer who knew nothing about fighter aircraft. Soviet tactical doctrine demanded that controllers be fighter pilots. To have someone in charge who knew nothing about fighter operations ran counter to everything the pilots had been taught.

Aleks came from a family with strong party loyalties. Both parents were relentless workers for the regional political apparatus. Aleks was himself political, and his personal ambitions would increasingly require party support as he rose in rank and stature. Yet he despaired at the ways the party interfered with day-to-day operations in the Russian military, and in the Democratic Republic of Vietnam it was even worse. The Lao Dong party influenced every aspect of military life, regardless of the impact upon operational success.

Ahead, the first aircraft dropped from his vision, descending to land at the Kep auxiliary airfield.

The six MiG-21's, two three-ship cells from Phuc Yen, were replacing a contingent of MiG-17's. The VPAAF's two regiments of interceptors, one headquartered at Kien An and the other at Phuc Yen, kept a number of aircraft deployed at auxiliary airfields—most often at places like Kep, Hoa Lac, and Gia Lam, Hanoi's international airport, but occasionally even at smaller airfields like Yen Bai, Thanh Hoa, and others near the Chinese border. Aircraft could be launched more quickly from several runways and locations, but the dispersion was primarily a matter of force survival. If the Americans received permission to attack the MiG bases, they wouldn't find all the chickens in a single coop.

Aleks was last to land. He slid the throttle back, rotated

and held his MiG's nose up in a high angle of attack, and began a slow descent. Twenty seconds later the main landing gear made a mouse's squeak, kissing the runway less than five meters from his intended touchdown point. He dragged the throttle to idle and pushed the stick forward. The aircraft settled on its tricycle gear and rushed down the runway. He did not deploy the drag parachute, so there was only the friction of rubber against concrete to slow him. When the momentum was sufficiently drained, he used the brakes. A loud, squealing sound issued, another irritating quality of the small-tail MiG-21.

He turned off at the fourth exit, far down the runway, then rapidly taxied back toward the takeoff end. Finally he slowed, and a three-man ground crew waved him into a small taxi-through hangar, reinforced with sandbags and draped with camouflage netting. Nets were vaulted and strung about the area to hide the hangarettes and the small operations and sleeping dugouts.

Aleks motioned for chocks to be placed, then gratefully shut down the screaming turbojet. He waited in the cockpit a moment longer, until the engine had clattered to a complete stop and the ground crew safetied the rockets. His MiG-21F was equipped with two K-13a heat-seeking rockets, but the 30mm cannons in the wing-roots had been removed to conserve weight. Plans called for the aircraft to be modified to carry twin-barreled 23mm cannon packs beneath the vari-ramp air intake, but at the present the fighters carried only the guided rockets for armament. The aircraft were a mixed bag of D- and F-models, and you were never really certain of the configuration you might draw.

Ridiculous, he thought. Then Aleks stopped himself. Since his trip to Hanoi he'd been grumbling to himself about matters over which he had no control. Things like the ages of the aircraft . . . the awful radar control . . . the varying armament. Yesterday morning he had been pleased with his lot. Then he'd learned just how insignificant and vulnerable he really was, and how despicable he was about to become.

He tried substituting happier thoughts . . . feeling thankful he'd been selected to fly the only kind of combat available to Soviet pilots . . . reminding himself of the superb condition of the aircraft, congratulating the North Vietnamese mechanics and their watchful Russian tutors for that . . .

thinking that in a few more days he would return to Phuc Yen, catch a ride to Hanoi, and make the French-Vietnamese girl squeal with pleasure. But then he remembered that it had been sexual dallying that had been responsible for his current great dilemma, and he slipped back into gloom.

Aleks safetied the ejection seat by inserting a long pin into the initiator mechanism, then unstrapped from the parachute, removed and placed his helmet on the right canopy rail, and briskly rubbed his scalp to regain circulation. He carefully kept his hands off the canopy as he crawled out of the cockpit. Small-tail MiG-21's had a single-piece canopy that hinged from the rear and was actually attached to and a part of the ejection-seat assembly. *A silly idea,* he thought as he crawled over the side and down, using toeholds carved into the fuselage.

No more grumbling and complaining!

Back on firm ground he stretched, feeling good physically but still angry at the world . . . at *Polkovnik* Feodor Dimetriev and his ridiculous order . . . at himself.

A smiling young man wearing the double star-pips of a *leytenant* second class hailed him from the mouth of the hangarette. Thanh, the son of air regiment commandant Quon.

Thanh had been second to land and was one of those who'd failed to reset his altimeter until Aleks had reminded him. Enthusiastic, but neither intelligent nor a good pilot, thought Aleks. His flying was stiff and mechanical, his decisions slowly made, and if he did not soon improve, he would find himself in dire trouble. He was certainly not equipped to engage the enemy without proper radar control.

Fuck his sister, and why should Aleks care? Thanh would shortly be a dead hero.

Aleks nodded for the *leytenant* to wait, then told the ground crew to top off all tanks with jet fuel. He walked to the mouth of the hangarette to examine the draped camouflage net.

"The major has gone to advise Hanoi and Phuc Yen that we have landed and are in place, comrade Captain," *Leytenant* Thanh called to him. From his first days at Phuc Yen he'd attached himself to Aleks like a stray puppy, and he spoke to him in dutiful tones. "The major orders us to join him in the operations room."

"Very good," Aleks said. He pointed and called to the

ground crew to pull the net lower over the entrance to the hangarette, to better hide his aircraft.

He wasn't worried about being caught on the ground at Kep by enemy bombers. The precautionary launch procedures were explicit. As enemy aircraft approached any border or coast of the northern part of the country, the first alarm was sounded and an announcement made to stand ready. The ground crews would hurry to prepare the aircraft for takeoff as the pilots studied the weather and drank tea. When the enemy force approached within a hundred kilometers, the second alarm was sounded and the loudspeaker would order them to prepare to launch. The pilots would hurry to the hangarettes, excitement mounting, and start engines. A steady siren was next, advising the pilots to taxi and take off. After the aircraft were airborne, the controllers would radio instructions to either position for attack or withdraw toward China. Only a small number of the aircraft at the main bases might be ordered to take off, but at auxiliary bases like Kep all aircraft were launched. A primary purpose of being there was force survival.

That was the way it was planned, the way it had always happened. As worried as Aleks might be about the competence of the controllers, he at least knew they'd be advised when the Americans were on their way.

But the camouflage netting on the hangarettes and buildings kept enemy reconnaissance aircraft from discovering their true numbers and locations, and since Aleks could think of no reason to broadcast the information, he fussed at the ground crew until the net was in place. Finally satisfied, he joined the *leytenant*, and they began to walk toward the operations dugout.

"We had terrible radar control this morning," said Thanh disgustedly. It had become a favorite complaint of the pilots, especially the younger ones who'd been trained using strict radar control and knew nothing else.

Aleks grunted in response, not wanting to be drawn into the darker mood. He was known for his sunny nature, and the outrage he'd felt for the past twenty-four hours was alien to him.

"My father demanded that the radars be turned over to us." The *leytenant* spoke often of the legendary Quon, who was their air regiment commandant. "He said the rooster colonel in charge of the radars was shocked that *anyone*

would challenge his authority." Russian pilots called nonfly-
ing officers "roosters," and the Vietnamese had picked up
the expression.

Aleks said, "The rooster colonel's life does not depend
upon a radar controller. Perhaps we should take him flying
with us, eh, Thanh? He may strut and crow on the ground,
but he'd shit white droppings if they made him fly."

Thanh laughed loudly.

As they approached the molehole burrowed in the
mound of sandbags that served as an operations room, Aleks
wondered how he could best comply with Dimetriev's order. He also wondered, more casually, if the rooster colonel
they spoke of might be the one calling for the *leytenant's*
life. The rumor was that the inept colonel had powerful
party connections, and if he was angry at Thanh's father . . .

0945 Local—People's Army HQ, Hanoi

Colonel Nguyen Wu

He'd expanded the modest office he'd acquired from his uncle Xuan Nha to three times its previous size, as he felt was
befitting of a man with his responsibilities, and the briefing
was held around a large table there.

He listened with half an ear as his intelligence officer advised him of the strength and equipage of his rocket forces.
Twenty-one battalions, each with three firing batteries. Each
firing battery equipped with a radar, command trailer, and
six rocket launchers. There were six defensive areas, at
Vinh, Thanh Hoa, Hanoi North, Hanoi South, Haiphong,
and Thai Nguyen, but most of the rocket batteries protected
Hanoi.

The force had been larger before the air battle at Thai
Nguyen. Seven rocket batteries had been destroyed there, a
dozen more damaged. Since then three more batteries had
been destroyed by enemy bombs, and several others damaged by terror missiles, for the enemy had learned how to
find them. Wu and his staff had discussed the problem but
could find no solutions except to have the radars stay off the
air, and they could not fire their rockets with the tracking
and guidance radars off. They'd decided for the radars to remain on for the minimum time possible . . . make a habit of

coming on the air abruptly, and quickly firing rockets at the most vulnerable targets, so the radar-hunters could not find them. And to do that, they needed constant input from the long-range radars.

Despite promises to keep them at a full strength of twenty-five rocket battalions, the Soviets were dragging their heels, and replacement rocket batteries were slow coming. That was of little consequence, for the highly trained crews required to operate them had been killed at Thai Nguyen, and replacement crews would not arrive for another month.

Time was the essential thing Nguyen Wu needed, for only that could heal his rocket forces. In the meanwhile he had to monopolize the long-range radars, regardless of how much the interceptor pilots said they needed them. As the intelligence officer droned, Nguyen Wu could not keep his mind from wandering to the radars at Phuc Yen and Kien An, wondering if he would be able to keep them in the face of the fight being waged by Quon.

Quon's voice was being heard. Just this morning General Dung's office had queried General Luc about the operational impact of moving the radars to VPAAF control.

Nguyen Wu's anger flashed. He could not allow that to happen.

The pilot would not speak so forcefully when Wu's plan bore fruit. Everyone knew how he treasured his only son. Wu felt his smile grow as he anticipated results from the Russians. *But when?* he wondered. He hoped he would not have to wait long.

He wished Li Binh were there to advise and guide him.

Ugly thoughts began to nag.

Was his plan rash? Was it wise to use the Russians? The gnawing doubts grew. What if the Lao Dong party learned that he'd used a foreigner to kill a Vietnamese hero? And what of his aunt Li Binh? He'd used her position to force the Russian to agree. Should he have first consulted her? He doubted she could be harmed by his actions, but . . .

What would she say if she knew what he'd done?

Who was more powerful, Quon or his aunt?

"Are you warm, comrade Colonel?" the briefing officer asked solicitously, and Nguyen Wu realized he was sweating profusely.

"Continue with your briefing," he snapped.

He must maintain control of the long-range radars, but he now realized his plan was faulty, for there were too many difficult questions. He wished Li Binh were here to help him with it. She was a master at such things.

Wu decided that he must halt the present plan and take an entirely new approach.

The briefer asked something.

"Repeat that question!" he demanded.

"The area commandant at Thai Nguyen asks that we release a number of the mobile rocket batteries for the defense of his critical assets. He says the defenses at Thai Nguyen and Kep are inadequate."

Lieutenant Colonel Tran Van Ngo had been groomed to take Nguyen Wu's present position. Wu considered him as dangerous competition who would have to be dealt with.

"Tell Tran that I make such decisions, not he."

"He says he is left with only a few guns, comrade Colonel."

"He is fortunate to have those."

The briefer looked surprised.

Nguyen Wu sighed impatiently, as if having to deal with a child's questions. "The next targets for the Yankee pirates will be the bridges on the Hong Song, nothing in his area. General Dung has said that."

"Shall I tell that to Lieutenant Colonel Tran?"

"Tell him nothing."

The briefer stared at him for a quiet moment, then continued his briefing.

Wu's mind returned to worrying about how he should deal with Quon.

1445 Local—Route Pack Three, North Vietnam

Captain Bob Liebermann

He was not only getting the hang of it, Bob Liebermann was having one of the finest times of his life. He loved flying fighters more than anything he'd done since he'd entered the Air Force. His misfortune was that he had excelled academically when he'd attended pilot training seven years earlier, when the Strategic Air Command generals had a hammerlock on the Air Force. The top pilot school graduates had been skimmed off for SAC, and Bob had been sent directly to Castle Air Force Base, near Merced, California, to upgrade into B-52's.

Now Liebermann wheeled and soared with eagles, and felt invincible. He wondered why God had punished him for so long by not allowing him to fly fighters.

This was the first time he felt at ease with the Thud. On his first combat mission, he'd been stiff and ragged with his air refueling. During his second mission, the air refueling had been acceptable, but he'd had trouble with his jinking and staying in position during hard maneuvering. He'd improved little with his third and fourth missions.

Then last night Turk Tatro had come by his room and pulled him away from poring over the dog-eared Dash-One manual, and insisted he go downtown with him. Turk had introduced him to several sleazy bars and clubs in the village of Ta Khli, and they'd drunk at least one whiskey in each of them. By the time they reached the fifth such dive, Liebermann had forgotten about his intensity. They'd gotten thoroughly, knee-walking, dry-puking drunk, and all the while they'd talked about flying and fighting and Turk kept saying the secret was to ease up on the studying and let it happen.

"By damn, it isn't like you're going to build a Thud, you just want to fly the thing," he'd said.

Bob had stumbled back into the room late, waking up and pissing off Manny DeVera. Then he'd had trouble trying to get his socks off and had hopped around, banging into things and giggling. He'd fallen asleep at two A.M. At five A.M. Manny had delighted in waking him up and telling him, *oh yeah, you're supposed to get down to the squadron ops desk and help Major Lucky with the weekly schedule.* Bob had watched forlornly, cross-eyed tired and with a pounding headache, as Manny had gone back to sleep.

At the squadron he'd drunk a quart of coffee and worked with Major Lucky on the schedule, and listened to the same advice.

Loosen up, Lucky had told him.

So this afternoon he was trying what they said and was discovering they were right. He'd let things come more naturally, beginning with takeoff, and he figured it was that, maybe along with the hangover and not giving much of a shit, that made all the difference.

It felt glorious. After takeoff he'd slid into position on Major Lucky's wing just as a member of the Thunderbird aerial demonstration team might do and had stuck there like glue. His air refueling had gone so smoothly that he wondered how he possibly could have had trouble those other times. It was as if he could tell when he'd moved a couple of inches out of position.

Today's mission was to pack two. Officially they were fragged to locate and bomb "targets of opportunity" on specified "lines of communications," meaning trucks or vessels on the coastal highway, the Ho Chi Minh Trail, or the Ca River. Unofficially, Lucky was taking them for a look at the terrain and landmarks, at the city of Vinh at the northern edge of the pack, and at the defenses of pack two, which were concentrated around Vinh.

The gomer commander at Vinh was supposed to be one of the best. He had only one or two SAM sites and a dozen AAA batteries, but he'd shot down a large number of fighters.

All of that had been given during the flight briefing, and the members of Tinker flight had listened carefully.

Major Lucky was Tinker lead, with Liebermann on his wing. Tinker three was Captain Manny DeVera, and his wingman was Lieutenant Billy Bowes. They flew in a spread fingertip formation, watching out and looking where Major Lucky told them to, memorizing what everything looked like.

Get to know the terrain like a baby knows its mama's left tit, Tatro had advised.

Lucky had told them he'd had to finagle to get another training sortie for C-Flight, and not to waste it.

"I've got a feeling," he'd told Liebermann as they'd worked on the squadron schedule that morning, "we're about to get some hairy ones, so let's take all the easy ones we can get."

"Think it looks harmless down there, Tinker flight?" radioed Lucky Anderson.

They all looked at the barren fields below, pocked with bomb craters, and out at the mouth of the Ca River. The city of Vinh was clearly visible across the water.

"Reason we're keeping our Mach up and jinking like this, and looking out for threats even though it seems peaceful, is that eleven Thuds from our wing and a hell of a lot of other

friendlies of all description have been shot down here,"
called Lucky in a dry voice.

A chattering sound erupted and a strobe appeared on the
RHAW system.

After a few seconds Manny DeVera called, *"Tinker three
has a two-ring triple-A radar at nine o'clock."*

"Good call, Tinker three," radioed Lucky. *"That's a
Firecan radar on the other side of Vinh. He directs fire for
fifty-seven- and eight-five-millimeter artillery. Watch your
asses when you're anywhere close to a Firecan."*

They were flying near Vinh alone, with no Wild Weasel
flight to keep the defenses busy, so Lucky had told them
they would not dawdle in the area. He'd also briefed them
that he felt the area commander would pull some kind of
trick to get his quota, for it had been a week since he'd
bagged his last aircraft. They wouldn't chance bombing near
Vinh unless they found a good target, and thus far they had
not.

Major Lucky led them out over the water for a couple of
minutes, the AAA radar steadily tracking them; then he
made a lazy turn back toward the shore . . . directly toward
the city of Vinh. He throttled back, a fat and lazy target, and
they followed.

Another rattle, this one sounding like a rattlesnake, with
an accompanying flickering strobe and a SAM light.

They waited longer yet, felt increasingly vulnerable, and
then the ACTIVITY light illuminated, meaning the battery was
about to launch surface-to-air missiles.

"Push it up," was all Lucky said, but his voice was cool
and sure, and they all followed him as he slowly descended
and accelerated, faster and faster yet, until they were flying
just above Mach one, and descended lower and lower, until
they were less than 200 feet above the water.

"You are now bulletproof," came Major Lucky's laconic
call.

They streaked past the coast, still traveling at the speed
of heat and so low they barely skimmed over the swells in
the Ca River, ignoring the squealing sounds from their
RHAWs and watching only the man they were flying formation with.

"They cannot hit you if they cannot see you," called the
even voice of Lucky Anderson, and they knew they were a
fuzzy, noisy blur to anyone watching from the ground.

They followed the gentle S-curves of the river, still flying so low and so fast they were invisible. Too low for radar detection. Too low and fast for human detection. By the time human ears heard them, they would be past and going out of sight.

Then Lucky was climbing, and they were following. Up quickly, then leveling out at 4,500 feet, throttling back to five-fifty knots, now out of range of the Vinh defenses.

"That, gentlemen, is rule one. The laws of physics and logic do not change in combat. If they can't locate you, they can't harm you. The bad thing about flying down there is you have trouble finding targets and delivering bombs with any real accuracy. So we fly up higher like this most of the time to be able to see. Any questions, Tinker flight?"

"Tinker lead, Tinker three," called Manny DeVera. *"Are those barges I see down at our two o'clock?"*

There were five river barges being hauled by a tugboat, stacked high with barrels of fuel and headed up the Ca River toward the trucks traveling the Ho Chi Minh Trail. When Tinker flight finally pulled off ten minutes later, after their final bomb release and strafe pass, the tug was sunk and all five barges were burning furiously, floating aimlessly back toward Vinh and the sea.

1855 Local—355th TFW Command Post, Takhli RTAFB, Thailand

Lieutenant Colonel Pearly Gates

The thing that bothered Pearly most about the briefing was the presence of Colonel Tom Lyons, because Lyons regarded him with a sour frown throughout.

The thing he liked best about it was seeing a lot of faces among the key combat-operations staff that he remembered from earlier forays to Tahkli. Fiery Colonel B. J. Parker and his quiet Deputy for Operations. The heroic majors: like the weapons officer, Max Foley, who had shot down two MiGs, and badly scarred Lucky Anderson, who had pressed in close and taken down an entire blast furnace of the Thai Nguyen steel mill, then limped home with severe battle damage from his own bombs. He couldn't forget Lieutenant Colonel Mack MacLendon, regarded by some as the canniest combat squadron commander in the free world. But several other faces were unknown to him, and that was sad because they'd replaced others who'd been shot down.

The 354th TFS, for instance, presently had no squadron CO, for the last two commanders had been shot down in rapid succession. A new commander was in the pipeline, which meant he was being shipped over from the States, but in the interim one of the flight commanders was acting in his place. B. J. Parker had told Pearly he'd offered the interim job to Lucky Anderson, but that Anderson had asked *not* to be considered. He was happy leading his C-Flight. Lucky Anderson was a strange duck, he thought. Most men would have jumped at the chance to command a squadron.

Mack MacLendon handed him a cup of coffee, although he hadn't asked for it, and said, "You look like you need this." Pearly was indeed tired, having already visited Danang, Udorn, Ubon, and Korat.

"We've missed you, Pearly," said the quiet Deputy for Operations. "What's it been now? A month?"

"Six weeks since I was here last, sir," said Pearly. He took a sip of coffee and almost choked. Then he took a more appreciative gulp, for it was laced with good brandy.

"Great coffee," he said to Mack.

"What kind of bullshit target you got for us this time, Pearly?" growled B. J. Parker. "Another Thai Nguyen?"

He grimaced. "I sure as hell hope not, Colonel." He'd shuttled like this, between the headquarters and the bases, during the strikes at the Thai Nguyen steel mill. The enemy had dragged up every defense imaginable there, and the two sides had gone at it tooth and nail. In the end air power had won out, for the steel mill had been leveled and the SAM defenses punished and battered, but the losses had been heavy.

Pearly sipped his coffee. "Which targets would you like to take out most, sir?"

Parker narrowed his eyes and stared, afraid to say it unless it was true.

"How about a couple of MiG bases?" prompted Pearly.

Silence pervaded the room as B. J. Parker's mouth began to crinkle into the same smile General Moss had worn a few hours earlier. Some said it was because the politicians were afraid of harming Russian advisors, while others said it was because they feared the appearance of escalating the war.

But for *some* reason, until now they'd been restricted from striking the enemy's air bases.

"How about Kep and Hoa Lac?" Pearly asked.

"Hot damn!" whooped Major Max Foley, seated beside Parker.

"Are Phuc Yen and Kien An on your list?" asked Lucky Anderson. Those were the two primary MiG bases, the first just north of Hanoi, the other immediately south of Haiphong.

"They're not on *this* list. So far they've just authorized Kep, Hoa Lac, and a few smaller fields like Vinh, Yen Bai, Dien Bien Phu, and Dong Hoi, which are pretty well unusable anyway. Kep and Hoa Lac are the biggest ones on the list."

"Lucky, don't question," grinned Mack MacLendon. "We'll take 'em, Pearly."

"Damned right." Parker had found his voice. "But as soon as we've wiped these out, get us permission to bomb their main bases."

"You don't have to encourage us, sir. General Moss would love to turn you loose on Phuc Yen. He asks for authorization almost weekly."

"Okay, tell us about Kep and Hoa Lac," Parker said, sitting back with his arms folded across his chest and peering up at the large map of North Vietnam behind the podium.

Pearly paused to double-check his data. He'd just briefed at the other bases, but he liked to be meticulously correct when men's lives might depend upon him.

"Both bases are near Hanoi. Hoa Lac's fifteen nautical miles west, and last Thursday there were eight MiG-17's there. Kep is thirty-three miles northeast of Hanoi. We don't have a current estimate, but a week ago Motel radar reported six MiG-17's had landed there."

"Everything you're saying is a week old," grumbled Colonel Tom Lyons, speaking up for the first time. "Don't you have any current information?"

"Not really," said Pearly.

"Haven't you learned what tactical recce's about? Get us some current photos, dammit. How else are we going to know what we'll find there?" asked Lyons. His tone was increasing in both volume and nastiness.

Pearly looked directly at Lyons. "Colonel, we're trying to keep this one from the enemy. If we sent in recce birds, it would be like sending them a telegraph we're coming. Right now their defenses are bunched around other areas, and that's where we want them."

"What areas?" asked Lyons, spitting out the words as if he didn't believe him.

Pearly hedged. "That's really not a part of this briefing, Colonel."

"You mean," said Lyons with disbelief, "that you've got information about defenses that you're going to withhold from the combat units? Unbelievable."

Pearly opened his mouth to answer, then realized Lyons had him trapped, that anything he said would appear trite.

"I'll provide a follow-on briefing for Colonel Parker's ears only," he finally said.

Lyons shook his head in disgust.

"That's okay, Tom," said B. J. Parker, his brow furrowing at the undercurrents. "We'll take these targets, no questions asked. You don't realize how long we've been waiting to knock out the MiG bases." Parker paused, then sighed. "But I agree it'd be nice if we knew whether we were going to find MiGs there."

"Amen," Lyons snorted, glaring at Pearly.

"I sincerely doubt you'll catch any aircraft on the ground at either place," said Pearly. "They flush everything at their dispersal bases well before our strike missions arrive. The only places we'd find MiGs on the ground would be at the big bases, Phuc Yen and Kien An."

"How about their bombers?" asked Colonel Parker hopefully.

"Four operations IL-28's are based at Phuc Yen. When they fly, which is seldom, it's usually on short training missions up toward China. They're big enough we can track them using Motel, and we've never seen 'em go into either Kep or Hoa Lac." "Motel" was the call sign for the sensitive over-the-horizon radar set up at Udorn Air Base, Thailand.

"Well, hell," said Parker. "When do we get turned loose?"

"Tomorrow morning, sir. We'll be hitting both bases off and on all day long. Your wing is assigned to strike Kep in the morning and Hoa Lac in the afternoon."

Parker stared. "Will we be first to strike Kep?"

"Yes, sir, you will."

That made B. J. Parker look happier.

"You won't receive official tasking until after midnight tonight, sir, but General Moss said to assure you that there'll be no surprises."

"What are the weapons loads, so I can alert the munitions people and the load crews?" asked the Deputy for Maintenance.

Pearly reached into his briefcase for the information sheets he'd made up before leaving Saigon.

Later, when there was only B. J. Parker and himself left in the room, and as he sipped from the third cup of coffee provided by Colonel Mack, Pearly allowed himself the luxury of relaxing. He explained that, though bombing the MiG bases was something they'd waited a long time for, they were intended mainly as a diversion, to draw the guns away from the bridges before that campaign was begun. Then he went over the upcoming strike at the Paul Doumer bridge and mentioned that PACAF wanted them to use Bullpup missiles.

Parker stared up at the map. "So you're saying the word got out somehow, and the gomers are piling their defenses around the bridges? Where's the leak, Pearly?"

"God only knows, Colonel. The General's got half the spooks in Saigon tripping over one another trying to find out."

"If their intell's so good, what makes you think the gomers'll sucker for this one and pull their guns away from the bridges?"

"I don't know they'll fall for it at all, sir."

Parker was frowning. "A bridge might look big from the ground, Pearly, but from the air it's damned small. You want to hit it with a Bullpup, you've got to fly straight and level enough to keep your eye on the missile until it hits. If we use bombs, some of the guys'll end up pressing too low . . . all of which means they'll be vulnerable. That'll be doubly so on smaller bridges that are heavily defended. Is the general aware of all that?"

"Yes, sir." Pearly cocked his head inquisitively. "Are you against this campaign?"

B. J. Parker mused for a moment, then shook his head. "I'm just telling you there'll be losses. If I could read the future, I might be against it. Like if I knew this was just another stop-and-start campaign. If we're going to go out and bomb a bridge, then give 'em time to repair it, then maybe bomb another one, or stop bombing them altogether, then I'd say it's another bunch of bullshit. You've got to admit that so far no one's been very persevering at waging this war."

"I concur, sir."

Parker shook his head. "If they don't turn us loose and let us fight, the people back home are going to get sick and tired of it all and say that's enough. Then someday someone'll look back and believe we failed and not know it was political lack of purpose."

Before he left to return to the flight line and the T-39 waiting there to take him back to Saigon, B. J. Parker asked what was going on between him and Colonel Lyons. Pearly told him what had transpired at the meeting at Seventh Air Force headquarters, without casting blame. Parker took it in without comment.

CHAPTER FIVE

Monday, April 24th, 0350 Local—Command Post Briefing Theater, Takhli RTAFB, Thailand

Major Lucky Anderson

The men were restless. They knew the target was a special one because the eight flight leaders had spent part of the night planning the thing. Lucky hadn't gone to bed until one and had left a message for the squadron orderly to wake him at three-fifteen.

B. J. Parker came into the briefing theater and peered about. "Looks like a happy group," he said.

A weary-looking tech sergeant entered behind him and went to the backlit Plexiglas board. He started writing target coordinates, and the muttering got louder.

Parker had told the flight leaders he personally wanted to break the news about the target. He'd wanted to bomb the MiG bases since he'd gotten to Takhli, had requested that permission from the generals from the various headquarters every time he got his chance. Now B.J. felt a personal triumph that they were getting to go after them, even if they were limited to the small ones. But the wing commander hadn't mentioned telling the men about another directive received from PACAF, which Lucky had just heard about. He wondered if Parker would cover the bullshit news as well as the good.

B.J. waited for a couple of last-minute stragglers to take their seats, nodded to the lieutenant from intell to shut the door, then pointed his finger out at the fighter pilots in the room. The muttering subsided.

"Wars are won by the troops on the ground, but since 1917 we've realized that we can make a hell of a difference by supporting them from the air. Air support is vital to modern conflict, but to properly provide that support, we must first gain air superiority. The first step of gaining air superiority is to take out the enemy's airfields and not give his aircraft a place to land or hide. Every war plan we've ever devised has targeted enemy airfields. Yet whenever I've asked for that authority in this conflict, I've been told no."

B.J. nodded at the backlit Plexiglas board.

"We've wanted this every time we watched the MiGs taxi out while we flew by, every time they jumped us when we were on our way to a target loaded with bombs, and every time one of the bastards popped out of a cloud, fired an Atoll missile at one of our buddies, then ran like hell for his base, where we couldn't shoot back. Now you're going to remove one of the enemy's sanctuaries. Gentlemen, today, all day, we'll be going after two of their MiG bases."

The pilots' whispering grew loud.

Parker said he'd wanted to lead this one himself, but had been restricted because of the sensitivity of certain information he'd recently received. Parker gave the men a few more rah-rah words, then turned the briefing over to Mack MacLendon, commander of the 357th.

As Lucky had anticipated, the wing commander had presented the good news and left the bad stuff for Mack.

Colonel Mack was an experienced fighter jock, liked and admired by Lucky and most of the other combat pilots. He'd flown P-47's in North Africa and Europe in World War II, and was regarded as both a fine leader and a competent pilot. No one complained when Mack was placed in charge of a tough mission.

But then Colonel Mack gave them a surprise. The commander at Headquarters PACAF, the general with the bomber background who thought fighter jocks were dumbshit cowboys and called them that, had changed the way they were going to fly. At their sister base at Korat, the Thud drivers had been trying a formation designed to baffle the sophisticated SAM radars, where everyone flew in a single giant gaggle with their ECM pods turned on. The message from PACAF had directed that Takhli fly the same formation.

"Horseshit," said Captain Turk Tatro, who sat beside Lucky. Like Turk, Lucky preferred the flexibility of the fluid-four formation, but he remained quiet.

"Dammit to *hell*," exploded Major Max Foley from nearby. Max had been at the club eating breakfast when the other flight leaders had been told about the PACAF message, so this was the first he'd heard of it. They'd had their chance to cool off while he had not. "What kind of lunacy is this?" he raged.

"Fucking bomber generals at PACAF headquarters, I'll bet," growled Turk Tatro. "Betcha Bomber Joe Roman got nostalgic thinking about the great B-17 formations of World War II, so he decided we oughta fly the same way."

B. J. Parker charged to the forefront of the group, glaring at Turk and Max and then at the other pilots. "The *fucking generals* you're talking about are your superior officers, and by God I won't hear any more words like that."

Very slowly Major Max Foley, the lanky wing-weapons officer who had always been a good and loyal officer to Parker, rose to his feet. He sighed and looked the wing commander squarely in the eye. "Colonel, there's just no sense in flying up high, straight and level, and putting our faith in a jamming pod that may or may not be working. Even if it works against SAMs, it's a dogshit formation for fighting MiGs."

"Our job isn't to fight MiGs, it's to drop bombs," snapped Parker. "Anyway, you don't *have* to like the formation, Max. I got your recommendation that we continue to fly the fluid four, and I agreed and forwarded it to PACAF. Now they're telling us no, that we've got to do it their way. It's time to bite the bullet and play soldier, not to be insubordinate."

"It's not their asses getting shot off." Max Foley's voice was even. He was still staring Parker in the eye, and the level of tension mounted until it almost crackled, like static electricity.

Colonel Parker had recently recommended that Max be awarded a Silver Star Medal for gallantry in action for shooting down his second MiG-17. Unofficially, the two men were friends. Officially, Max was the wing commander's advisor when it came to selections of weapons and delivery tactics. In both capacities Max had advised B. J. Parker that he thought it would be a mistake to change to the big formation. This directive ran counter to everything his training and experience told him was right, everything he'd briefed Parker, everything he personally believed, and was a slap at Max's pride.

"You want off the flight, Max?" B. J. Parker asked in the quietest of voices.

Max stared for a moment longer.

Don't do it, Lucky's inner voice yelled at Max.

Someone coughed.

Lucky cautioned softly, "Max!"

Max Foley blew a disgusted breath of defeat, broke the visual lock, and slowly sat down.

"How about the rest of you? Anyone want off the mission?" Parker asked, looking first at Turk Tatro, then around at the others.

It was quiet in the room. In that minute of silence the 355th Tactical Fighter Wing changed its primary tactic for flying in high-threat areas. Until then they'd flown over the Red River Valley in a series of four-ship flights, each flight leader eager to challenge anything the enemy threw at them. These were the men headquarters relied upon to press in and destroy the toughest targets. Their Wild Weasels found and bombed yet another enemy missile site every few days. Their pilots had the highest MiG shoot-down ratio of any unit in Southeast Asia, including any of the F-4 wings whose *specialty* was fighting MiGs. They'd suffered considerable losses, yet they'd taken great pride in fighting not to just participate, but to win, and in being known as the "hot-charging 355th." But the bomber generals had pulled back on their leash, and from that day on they would fly their four-ship fingertip formations only to the edge of North Vietnam, then join into a huge gaggle of fighter-bombers. They would simultaneously turn on their ECM pods and fly at 20,000 feet to the target area, scarcely banking or turning, for whenever an aircraft rolled even slightly, it reduced the collective effectiveness of the jamming pods. It would be hard to be a hot-charger if you were tied to flying straight and level in the midst of a sixteen-ship gaggle and depended on Phantoms to shoot the MiGs for you.

Parker was obviously torn. He alternately glowered at a

diagram of the Korat gaggle the intelligence lieutenant had placed in front of the room, and mellowed when he regarded the backlit Plexiglas listing Kep airfield as the alpha-strike target. After a full minute of silence, he nodded toward Colonel Mack and abruptly hurried from the room.

It was not a time of confidence. The pilots had great faith in themselves, but not nearly as much in the ECM pods, the devices hanging out there on the outboard pylons, built by a division of the giant Hughes Corp, that all too often did not work.

Colonel Mack briefed as if they'd been flying the formation all along, as if today would be just another mission rather than a watershed event. He said the eight four-ship flights would remain in their individual formations to the Channel 97 TACAN navigation station on the border between Laos and North Vietnam. There the flights would form into two loosely amalgamated sixteen-ship formations. They could have joined a single thirty-two-ship mob, but he felt they'd better try something more manageable their first time out, and sixteen airplane groups would prove unwieldy enough.

Then Mack motioned to the intelligence lieutenant. His last name was DeWalt, and he was skinny and had a teen-ager's baby face, complete with runaway acne. The lieutenant took the podium and energetically began to brief what the ECM pod formation would look like, and the merits of flying it.

As they approached the Red River, they would close to the precise spacing called for by the formation, wingmen 1,500 feet and forty-five degrees back, and proceed across the valley that way. He said the formation was designed so that, when viewed from any direction or elevation, an aircraft would be flying in each resolution cell of the enemy radars and would thus present a large white blob on their scopes.

The noise level of muttering and low cursing continued to swell.

One of the Wild Weasel backseaters muttered to his pilot, "I'm sure as hell glad we don't have to fly in that stupid formation. The pods don't put out enough power to create white blobs on anything."

The Wild Weasels would be flying well out in front of the gaggle.

One pilot just shook his head and kept whispering, "This is pure horseshit."

Lucky Anderson had decided early on that, horseshit or not, if they were to fly the formation, and the fate of his C-Flight depended upon doing it right, he wanted to learn all he could. He gained the attention of two captains in Max Foley's flight who were bitching loudest and growled, "Dammit, be quiet."

One started to argue, but Max whispered for them to listen up. Then Max looked at Lucky and nodded solemnly, obviously having come to the same conclusion.

But other voices drowned out Lieutenant DeWalt, who was still trying to brief details of the formation. Finally Colonel Mack got back up in front of the group and raised his hands.

The noise level diminished.

Mack wore his poker face, neither smiling nor frowning. "You guys remind me of a story this guy told me back in 1944, about a briefing that went something like this one. This bunch of B-25 crews were going to fly into Ploeste on the first large-scale, low-level bombing mission. First time it had *ever* been done, and the guys didn't like it one bit, so by God they didn't listen to the briefing officers."

The muttering grew even quieter.

"This guy I talked to drew a bad airplane, so he didn't have to fly on that mission. Anyway, that's all I had to say. Let's get back to the lieutenant's briefing, so you can continue to ignore what he's trying to tell you." He started to return to his seat.

A captain from the 333rd squadron asked, "How'd the low-level attack work out, Colonel Mack?"

"The guy didn't know if it worked or not," said Mack.

The pilot looked puzzled.

"None of them made it back. Not one."

That got their attention, and it became quiet.

Mack stared out at the men until he knew that his point was sinking in, then added, "Since you don't want to listen to the lieutenant about this formation, I guess you're all hoping you'll get a broken airplane, like that guy I talked to back in 1944."

"Not a bad idea," muttered someone. This generated a few laughs.

"I don't think maintenance can break that many airplanes," said Mack.

"I've got faith that our maintenance can break anything we give 'em," said Turk Tatro in his southern drawl, eliciting a roar of laughter.

Mack shook his head. "Nope. Some of you are going to have to fly. Tell you what, only the guys who are going to get good airplanes have to listen . . . the rest of you go on into the next room and talk."

"That room ain't big enough," growled Turk Tatro.

More laughter.

"On the other hand," said Mack, casting his eagle's stare out at the men, "I'm awfully intrigued to see what Kep runway looks like from a new perspective . . . say from a forty-five-degree dive-bomb delivery?"

"Amen," said Max Foley. "Lieutenant, tell us more about the silly-assed formation."

Colonel Mack nodded for Lieutenant DeWalt to continue his briefing and sat down.

The pilots remained attentive throughout the remainder of the briefing. Mack had given another of his not-too-subtle lessons in leadership, and like the others in the room, Lucky thought it had been rather neat.

First Lieutenant Billy Bowes

At the mission briefing Major Lucky Anderson had handed out flight plan and lineup cards to the members of Shark flight. Bob Liebermann would fly Lucky's wing. Turk Tatro was number three, and Bowes number four. They would be a four-ship flight only during the first and last parts of the mission. The rest of the time, going to and from the target, Shark would be at the tail end of the second sixteen-ship formation and would be last to bomb the target.

The gaggle provided one advantage the pilots liked. They would ingress at higher altitudes, so there would be no need to pop up to delivery altitude when they approached the target. The aircraft could simply wing over into their dive-bomb deliveries. On the flip side, it would be more difficult to pick out the target from the higher altitude. As Colonel Mack had pointed out, it was a good thing they were starting out with an easy target. It would be hard to miss the long runway at Kep, even from 20,000 feet.

The various flights would break away, dive-bomb the target, then rejoin the gaggle on its way back to the west, toward Laos. First on the target would be Mack's Tuna flight, and they would attack the gun emplacements around the periphery of the air base. Next would come five flights of Thuds carrying 500-pound Mark 82's with delay fuzes. The weapons were sleek, had good accuracy, and with the delay fuzes, were good at penetrating hard surfaces. Those Thuds would attack and crater the runway.

The final two flights, including Shark, would carry CBU-29's, which were clamshells containing hundreds of cluster bomblets, baseball-sized frag grenades. After release the clamshells would start to spin, and after a few revolutions they'd open and spew out the bomblets. Then the bomblets would themselves spin and become armed. Some of the bomblets would detonate upon contact with the ground, spraying the area with deadly fragments. Others would lie there for up to half an hour, like grenades with their pins pulled, and randomly explode. The CBU-29's would destroy aircraft or personnel that happened to be in the open.

After the mission briefing, when the men believed they knew what the lieutenant had been trying to tell them about flying the Korat gaggle, they broke up for individual flight briefings, and Major Lucky led them to a smaller room and shut the door.

As soon as the door was closed, Turk Tatro erupted, "By damn, I don't like that formation one bit."

"Why?" asked Bob Liebermann. "Everything the lieutenant briefed was correct. I've studied the effects of jamming for large aircraft, and its got to be even easier to mask a fighter. I think it makes sense."

"Doesn't really matter what we think," said Major Lucky. "We're going to fly it."

"Doesn't mean I have to *like* it," grumbled Turk stubbornly.

Lucky Anderson reviewed the mission data, then used the blackboard as he talked about weapons delivery.

"We'll be last. Fifteen seconds after the previous flight enters its maneuver, we'll drop our CBUs on this area adjacent to the north end of the runway."

"I don't see anything there," complained Billy Bowes, peering at a recce photo.

"Remember what intell said? The reason the photos look so fuzzy's because the gomers have camouflaged the areas around both ends of the runway."

"It just looks indistinct to me," frowned Bowes, "like a bad photo."

Lucky smiled at him. "Let's drop our CBUs there anyway, okay Billy?"

"Okay." He thought of something else then and asked, "You think we're going to catch any MiGs on the ground?"

"The guy from Seventh Air Force who briefed us last night said they flush the MiGs at Kep when we're on the way in. So no, probably no MiGs."

"And if there are?"

"What do you mean?"

"Say we spot MiGs when we're recovering from the dive bomb . . . ?"

"Yeah?"

"Seeing how we're last in on the target, can we go back and strafe the bastards?"

Lucky stared at him. As always, Billy had difficulty reading the expression on the ruined face. Finally Lucky nodded. "You see any MiGs, call 'em on the radio. If the ground fire's not too bad, we'll swing around and shoot 'em. Just one pass, though, then we'll haul ass out of there and rejoin the gaggle."

Yeah, grinned Billy. *I'm in the right flight.*

0420 Local—Flight Line

At Billy's request the squadron-maintenance officer had permanently assigned him number 820, which had been the first aircraft he had flown at Takhli. Not only was he a bit superstitious about such things—he'd escaped without a scratch on that hairy flight—he also knew Staff Sergeant Larry Hughes was fastidious about his work and felt that was a commendable trait for the man in charge of the airplane upon which he bet his life.

When he went out to the aircraft that dark morning, he found that his name had been painted in bold letters on the left canopy rail. **1/LT W. BOWES.** The letters were white against a bright-blue background, the same shade as the banner of blue paint across the top of the tail. The color differentiated their aircraft from those assigned the other squadrons.

Billy inspected the aircraft closely, with Sergeant Hughes at his side holding a flashlight. As they checked and double-checked, he noticed the crew chief seemed happier than usual.

Billy finished with the walk-around inspection, then headed toward the boarding ladder, pulling at the cinches of his parachute. You knew the leg straps were tight enough only when you were so uncomfortable you had to hobble around half bent over. Which was sure as hell better than the alternative—ejecting at high speed and having the blast of air break your arms and legs, maybe even pull you out of the parachute harness.

The pilots flew with a lot of gear strapped to their bodies. First there were the flight suits and web-sided jungle boots. Next came the g-suits, which zipped tightly over their legs and around their waists, designed to inflate and keep the blood from migrating to their legs when they were maneuvering hard. They wore nylon-mesh vests, with pockets for two survival radios, a couple of plastic baby bottles filled with water, other miscellany that would be valuable if they were shot down, as well as shoulder holsters for their Combat Masterpiece .38 Special revolvers. By the time the parachute was added, it was quite heavy, and the pilot was miserably hot inside it all.

Billy glanced again at the crew chief. "Okay, what's the smile for, Sarge?"

"Didn't realize I was," said Hughes.

"You look awfully pleased about something."

"We heard about your target. You guys going after a MiG base?"

"Yeah."

"Feels damned good that we're finally doing it, sir."

0500 Local—People's Army HQ, Hanoi, DRV

Colonel Nguyen Wu

Nguyen Wu had spent an awful night living a nightmare and thinking of the flaws in the plan he'd set in motion. An attack upon Quon's son was the wrong approach. It would create sympathy, making Quon even more popular and his requests more irresistible.

But Quon was attacking his competence and trying to pull his command apart, and Wu knew he must do *something*. As Sergeant Ng drove him to the headquarters, he decided upon an entirely new solution to his dilemma.

The next series of large-scale attacks would be upon the bridges, and Dung had impressed upon them the importance of defending them. So Wu had massed *all* the mobile rocket batteries to protect them and told the battalion commanders to defend the bridges with everything they possessed. He'd ordered them to attack relentlessly, to fire rockets as rapidly as enemy targets could be acquired on radar and the launchers could be reloaded, and to ignore all firing doctrines they'd previously learned or been taught by the Soviet advisors.

Several commanders had intimated that Wu was wrong both about the firing doctrine and the way their batteries were deployed on top of one another. He'd made an example, had one of the majors removed from command and demoted, before the others had grown silent.

He told them he would not condone questions, or failure, or losses of more rocket batteries. They must be accurate, destroy more enemy aircraft than ever before. They must provide the enemy with no respite, for the Mee must not be allowed to destroy a single bridge. He had seen his uncle spur the same commanders using threats and cajolery, and *he* had obtained superb results. The fact that his uncle had once commanded a rocket battery himself and spoke from experience did not impress him.

But good results alone might not be enough to stop Quon. While Wu's rocket forces must shoot down great numbers of enemy aircraft, Quon's MiGs must shoot down none at all.

That was the crux of his new plan.

The answer had been so obvious, he wondered how he'd missed it. His long-range radar controllers would delay alerting the MiG bases of the Mee air strike. They would delay notification until it was too late for the interceptors to position for attack. As a result, the rocket forces would get their kills, and the MiGs would not.

There was little time to set it up.

He thought about it again and realized a new problem, for it must be done so he could deny all blame if something went wrong. A breakdown of equipment?

He went up the stairs to his offices feeling pressured to hurry.

Nguyen Wu immediately called in his communications officer and carefully passed instructions, then accompanied him to the radio room. There the lieutenant spoke to carefully selected communications officers at the Phuc Yen and Kien An radars, and they to their most trusted maintenance technicians.

Certain radios and land lines would be conveniently made inoperative due to problems with untraceable causes. At the critical moment the communications officers at the long-range radars would be unable to relay directions to the interceptor units, and communications between Hanoi and the bases would be broken as well. The problems would be such that no one would suspect. When the lieutenant finished with each call, he ascertained that no record of their communication had been written down. *Indeed, no such conversations had occurred.*

Colonel Wu was comfortable with the new plan. The first one had been born too much of emotion. This one was potentially more fruitful and less damaging if something went amiss.

Word from the command center began to pour into his office for his attention, relayed by the communications lieutenant.

Report: Agents disclosed increased activity at all four Thailand fighter bases. Large numbers of aircraft were being loaded with fuel and munitions. *Report:* Seven refueling aircraft had taken off at varied time intervals from Takhli. *Report:* Thunder planes, first at Takhli, then at Korat, were taxiing in preparation for takeoff. *Report:* Kien An radar detected increased air activity over the three Mee aircraft carriers.

It was surely to be the first large-scale raid upon the bridges. Wu inwardly exulted.

Report: At Ubon, some Phantoms loaded with bombs and others with rockets were starting engines. *Report:* Reconnaissance Phantoms were preparing for takeoff at Udorn. He smiled, called for tea, realizing that he'd moved none too soon. Another hour and it would have been too late.

Sergeant Ng, the scarred and aging warrior who acted as his personal servant, driver, and even tended his more personal needs, hurried in with a cup of bitter tea, which he sipped with satisfaction as he took a moment to relax.

Then he remembered something else, something critical. He'd implemented the new plan, but had not yet dismantled the old, much more dangerous one. He quickly telephoned Feodor Dimetriev at the Soviet embassy, but was told the colonel was not yet in his office.

Wu covered the telephone's mouthpiece as his intelligence officer interrupted to say that the command center had requested authorization to make phase-one alert notifications.

Nguyen Wu returned to the telephone and told the embassy operator that it was most important that he speak to Dimetriev as soon as he arrived. He said he'd be in the command center for the next few hours, and to have Dimetriev phone him there. He hung up.

The intelligence officer awaited his answer.

"Tell the command center that I shall hurry there to verify things for myself," he said. He glanced at the communications lieutenant, who gave an almost imperceptible nod. He needed a few more minutes to sever the communications links with the bases. It would take them that long to go to the basement.

At just after six-o'clock Wu and his communications lieutenant entered the command center. As the senior officer present, Wu would now make all decisions until one of the generals arrived. A captain there saw them and came over to advise Wu that four minutes earlier listening posts at the border had reported large formations of aircraft passing overhead.

Wu continued toward his seat at the rear of the large room.

"Shall we call the first phase of alert, comrade Colonel?"

Wu stopped, acted as if he were considering, then shook his head. "Wait for confirmation by the Phuc Yen P-1 radar," he said. "They may not be coming this way."

Such a procedure was not uncommon. When Phuc Yen radar confirmed the attack was coming toward the Hanoi area, they would be ordered to assume responsibility for notification of first the MiG regiments, then the rocket and artillery battalions. But of course that first communication would be impossible.

Phuc Yen radar would be able to talk *only* with his rocket sites.

The stage is set, thought Wu, and nervousness began to tingle at his spine.

Quon and General Tho came in the side door, engaged in deep conversation, and Wu's heart began to crawl toward his throat.

What are they doing here?

Quon's eyes searched, then found Nguyen Wu's. A slow smile formed at the fighter pilot's lips, and a crawling feeling of fear begin to permeate Wu's being.

Did he suspect something?

"Communications to the Phuc Yen P-1 radar have been interrupted. Their last transmission said that a large strike force is approaching the Hong Valley from the west," said the captain from beside him.

"Have them alert all defensive units," sputtered Colonel Nguyen Wu in a high-pitched tone. He was unable to wrest his eyes from Quon's stare.

"Yes, comrade Colonel," said the captain. He nodded and motioned to several men, who spoke excitedly into their field telephones.

They began to speak about communications problems, with only static on their lines.

Quon continued to pin Wu with the look.

Quon knew something. He was sure of it!

The communications lieutenant motioned to him, holding out a telephone. "It is the Russian colonel," the lieutenant told Colonel Wu.

Panic seized Wu as he took the receiver, remembering that he had not yet shut down the first plan. Then he calmed himself. Surely there hadn't been sufficient time for anyone to set up Quon's son for the kill.

The babble in the room grew, for now there was no contact with the interceptor bases.

"Good morning, comrade Colonel," said Feodor Dimetriev on the telephone. His voice contained the same loathing as Quon's stare.

0617 Local—Kep PAAF Auxiliary Air Base

Kapitan Aleks Ivanovic

Aleks took the cup from the cook, swirled the tea residue about in the bottom, and noted with satisfaction how dark the liquid was. He drank and sighed.

The major, leader of the two cells of interceptors, was at the door staring out. They waited patiently for the first siren. A few of the maintenance people had even wandered out to the aircraft in anticipation.

"Perhaps they will not come today, *kamerade mayor*," said Aleks.

The major glanced back at him and nodded. "Perhaps you are right." He stared for a split second longer, then turned back to look out toward the camouflaged hangarettes. "Perhaps," he iterated in a mutter.

The major did not like Russians, but that did not concern him. Aleks's easygoing nature made it easy for him to build rapport, and the major was warming, already friendlier than he'd been in the beginning.

Aleks joined the major. Like him, Aleks was surprised they hadn't yet been alerted.

The sirens for the three alert stages would be activated from the operations room, the dugout a hundred meters south of them. Thus far there had not been a murmur.

In the distance Aleks heard a faint Klaxon, likely from one of the artillery batteries ringing the base. Not as many as normal. He'd seen only two batteries of S-60 57mm guns and a single SON-9 artillery-guidance radar. Aleks had noticed it when he'd gone for his run around the base perimeter the previous evening. But . . . the SON-9 was the only radar he had seen. The rocket battery, with its advanced radar and six firing units, had been removed from the usual position on the east side of the base. Aleks supposed it had been moved to another nearby location. Air bases, he knew, ranked high on the list of assets to be protected.

He'd asked Thanh to accompany him on that evening run, and the first time they'd slowed their pace to rest, Aleks had begun to work on him.

"I am honored you have come with me," he'd said.

"Honored?" Thanh had asked incredulously. He'd always fawned on Aleks, amazed that Aleks could wring so much performance from the small-tail MiG-21 when he could only flounder about the sky, continuously wary that he might induce a spin. He'd repeatedly asked for advice, as if Aleks might hold some secret to make him a better pilot.

"Of course I'm honored," Aleks had replied. "Everyone knows how you've offered your life to the party. We read in the newspapers about you and your father."

Thanh had avoided his look.

"I am sorry I did not respond earlier to your requests for advice," Aleks had said, "but truthfully, I did not believe you needed anything I could offer."

The young lieutenant had looked surprised.

"You are doing well, much better than any of the other new pilots."

"I've only flown in combat twice," the lieutenant had mumbled, "and we did not engage the enemy."

"But I can tell such things. The others are still fearful of combat."

"Are they?" Thanh had murmured.

"I suppose you have also already guessed that *your* natural flying skills are much greater than theirs."

Thanh had been bewildered, yet increasingly pleased as Aleks continued to praise him. He was a dull and unimaginative young man. If it had not been for his father, there would have been little chance he would have been selected for pilot training. But it was precisely that slow wit that would make Aleks's task easier.

While they were flying, it should not be too difficult to scrape the trusting *leytenant* off on a mountainside, Aleks had thought. He had not yet concluded how he could make him into a hero, but he believed that idea would come.

"Great pilots realize that there are no limits on their capabilities," Aleks had told him as they'd continued walking. "They do not recognize impossibilities, only challenges." He had continued in that vein for half an hour, alternately bolstering Thanh's ego and telling him he must be very bold. Thanh had listened intently, nodding more vigorously at each pause. He was giddy to be singled out for such praise from the man he admired so, and he swelled with pride about capabilities he'd never dreamed he possessed. And he nodded just as vigorously each time Aleks told him that he must be bold.

It had been so easy to change the young pilot's perception of himself that Aleks began to feel he might not have to do much more than continue to build his overconfidence. Thanh might not have to be killed after all . . . with only a little more prodding and manipulation, the fool would be pushed into a frame of mind to do it to himself.

The next time they'd stopped running, when they were approaching the sleeping quarters, Aleks had placed his hand on the young man's shoulder in a moment of intimacy and stopped, as if overcome with emotion. "I feel there is a moment of greatness coming very soon for you, my friend." He nodded, eyes piercing into Thanh's.

The young pilot had stared back, breathless and in awe of the moment.

"You must be equal to the occasion when it is presented, as your father was when *he* was young."

Thanh swallowed and stared.

Aleks whispered, "You will be even *greater* than your father."

Thanh had been stunned into silence for a long moment, and it was obvious that Aleks had told him something he had not dared even dream.

Aleks had known he'd discovered the key. Thanh wanted to emulate his father and would do *anything* to achieve it.

The rest would be easy. "I will help you," he'd told him.

When they'd returned to the sleeping dugout, Thanh had advised the major that he wished to fly with the Russian advisor. The major was to lead the first section, and Aleks the second. Thanh would fly on one side of Aleks, another *leytenant* on the other.

As he sipped his morning tea, Aleks thought of all that and concluded that the killing of Thanh must not be delayed. Only after he'd finished the distasteful task would he be able to begin cleansing himself. Since the meeting with *Polkovnik* Dimetriev, time had passed miserably slowly, and he'd felt very unclean.

Thanh came into the kitchen, yawning and stretching in the dim morning light. He stood beside Aleks and frowned.

"I am surprised that there is no phase-one alert," said Thanh. "I heard sirens from the artillery batteries."

The major came back inside and impatiently motioned for the cook to refill his cup with tea. He looked displeased at a *leytenant* who came into the kitchen to join them wearing rubber clogs.

"Where are your boots?" the major snapped.

"On my cot. Since the first siren has not yet sounded . . ."

"Get them, you fool. Do you think we should all wait for you to go to your cot before we take off?"

The *leytenant* hurried out.

Another siren in the distance. They waited, but there was still nothing from the operations building.

The major could stand it no longer. "I am going to see if there is a problem. Perhaps the line to Phuc Yen is out. If it is the sirens that are malfunctioning, listen for my voice."

Today's takeoff might be more hurried than normal, Aleks was thinking. Perhaps in the confusion following a hurried takeoff . . . He glanced at Thanh.

The major left.

"An old maid," whispered Thanh, smiling secretively to Aleks.

Aleks leaned toward Thanh and placed a hand on his shoulder, as he had the evening before. "I feel it again. When we are in the air, follow me very closely. Keep your eyes on me, *Leytenant*, for this will be the start of your greatness."

He felt unclean.

"We will shoot down a Mee fighter."

The *leytenant*'s eyes glittered.

"Perhaps not just one."

Thanh's eyes grew wider.

"Try to stay with me. We shall be flying at the edge of performance."

Thanh spoke quietly. "I shall be there on your wing."

Aleks stared at him. "Do you feel it too? The sense of destiny."

"Yes, I . . . I do."

"There is *nothing* you cannot do when you have that feeling," said Aleks gravely. "Your father will be proud of you, Thanh."

The young pilot beamed his pleasure.

0619 Local—Route Pack Six, North Vietnam

First Lieutenant Billy Bowes

Flying the big formation was difficult, especially doing it for the first time in combat. Trying to get sixteen fighter pilots to fly in a predictable manner, to maintain 1,500 feet and forty-five-degree separations in all planes, to preserve radio silence when they saw the others around them screwing up, not to jink when they saw flak down below, just to keep flying straight ahead like a bunch of bomber pilots, was almost too much to ask.

Before they'd left the flight briefing, Turk Tatro had said it would be like trying to get a group of nymphomaniac hookers to give up fucking and sew doilies for a church benefit.

But they'd turned on their ECM pod switches, gritted their teeth, and tried it.

By the time they approached the Red River and watched the smattering of flak, low and to their right at Yen Bai, the aircraft in their formation had finally formed into a semblance of what they thought the intell lieutenant had tried to explain. The separation looked fairly even between all the aircraft Billy could see, and a number of the ECM pods must be working, because the scope of his RHAW receiver was sputtering with static from the noise jamming.

Then the Wild Weasel flight, which ranged several miles ahead of the first gaggle, called back that the target area was CAVU, and that no SAM sites had been detected. Which was very good, because Billy would have hated to see them flying the new formation that no one trusted and trying to cope with shitty weather and SAMs, all at the same time.

But regardless of all of that, he hoped there'd be a MiG left for him at Kep.

0629 Local—Kep PAAF Auxiliary Air Base, DRV

Kapitan Aleks Ivanovic

The distant sirens continued to wail, yet there was still nothing from the operations building.

"Come," said Aleks to Thanh, "let us walk over toward the hangarettes."

The early-morning sky was spectacular. Dark in the west. Vivid blue, with alternating streaks of orange and smoky haze in the east, where the sun's form was not yet visible.

"It will be a good flying day," said Aleks.

"You are right, comrade Captain. Today will be a day of mourning for Mee families."

Aleks studied the wind banner, flapping high over the camouflage net covering the operations building. "Notice the wind direction? We shall take off to the south."

"That is where the Mee will be bombing. My father said the bridges of Hanoi and Haiphong will be next. He warns to expect a great campaign from the Mee, like we saw at Thai Nguyen. I am anxious for it to start."

The fool, thought Aleks.

The siren at the operations building wailed, picking up decibels until the sound was very loud. "Finally they come," yelled Thanh.

They watched the remaining maintenance personnel, the ones who hadn't already gone out to their aircraft, hurrying from their sleeping quarters.

"Hai yaaa," Thanh yelled playfully as the crew for his aircraft hurried by.

The lieutenant seemed more at ease than he'd been before Aleks had flown with him on other occasions. His words had instilled even more confidence than he'd imagined.

Aleks settled his eyes toward the northwestern horizon and tried to focus upon something there. A puff of smoke? A contrail?

"I wonder how long they will be," said Thanh as they walked.

The contrail arced quickly across the sky toward them, then began its descent.

"A terror missile!" yelled someone, meaning the guided rockets the Americans fired at radars, and Aleks thought of the SON-9 he'd seen the night before.

A muffled explosion in the direction of the artillery-directing radar.

The American radar-hunters. They were soaring now, sweeping around the base in a great circle. Not far behind would be the attack aircraft.

It was then, as he watched the birds up there circling

their prey, that Aleks realized *they* were the target. There would be insufficient time to take off.

His mind raced.

"Quickly," he cried to Thanh, motioning toward the hangarettes where the MiGs were parked. "Start engines and taxi at your first opportunity. Do not wait for another siren," he yelled. "Today is your day of destiny, Thanh. I will meet you at the end of the runway, and together we will take off and hunt the enemy."

Thanh looked at him and a smile crept onto his face. "Good hunting!" he shouted, then began to lope purposefully toward his interceptor.

Yes, thought Aleks, his heart thumping wildly as he hurried toward his own hangarette, *the* leytenant *may have the stuff of heroes after all.*

Aleks looked up as he hurried. High in the western sky were a group of small specks. Two were already detaching themselves and plummeting earthward.

He began to worry then about his own survival.

0637 Local—Route Pack Six, North Vietnam

Major Lucky Anderson

The Wild Weasels up ahead called back that they'd silenced a Firecan, which was the only threat radar they'd found in the target area.

The strike proceeded as briefed, and the bombing of the base went even more smoothly than they'd thought it might. As Lucky had suspected, it was easier bombing a big, apparent target when you didn't have to pop up to delivery altitude.

It started with an eruption of gunfire from around the perimeter of the airfield, obviously meant to discourage them when they were still several miles away. The bursts were fuzed wrong, and mostly went off far beneath them. The gunners were having a difficult time judging their altitude without the assistance of the Firecan radar.

Colonel Mack's Tuna flight peeled off from the gaggle and did creditable work silencing the guns ringing the base. Next came the flights with their hard bombs, all in rapid succession. They blasted a series of craters along the length of the runway, then gouged such a redundancy of holes at either end that Turk Tatro marveled over the radio that *"not even a blimp could take off on that thang."*

When the final two flights dropped their CBUs and Lucky pulled out and started to climb toward the west, he felt the CBUs had been dropped in vain, that there'd been nothing there to destroy. Then he heard the call from Lieutenant Billy Bowes, who'd been last to drop. As the last man in the last flight, Bowes could afford to take a more leisurely look and not worry that someone might drop bombs or CBUs on him.

"Shark lead. Shark four's got an aircraft in sight down there, taxiing."

Incredible, thought Lucky, but as he turned back and circled, staring at the area of netting they'd blown down with the CBU-29's, he saw a single delta-winged MiG-21 hurrying down a taxiway, dodging craters and trying to make it to the end of the runway. He strained to look out to his nine o'clock and could see Lieutenant Bowes's Thud in a tight turn, precisely as if he were flying a visual overhead pattern and preparing to land.

"Shark four's turning back for a low-angle strafe pass," called Bowes, his voice muffled by the G-forces. He was setting up for a standard ten-degree strafe run, which would take him dangerously close to the ground.

"You're cleared, Shark four," said Lucky, because it was now mostly a fait accompli. It would be equally dangerous for Bowes either to continue or to break it off and climb out to join the rest of them.

For the benefit of the others, he radioed, *"Shark two and three, set up for guns-ground and prepare for a thirty-degree, high-angle strafing run."*

"Shark two," called Bob Liebermann.

"Shark three," drawled Turk Tatro in his most eager voice.

A flew flak bursts began to walk across the sky toward them as they perched at 5,500 feet, banking around toward the taxiing MiG-21. They would wait until Bowes had finished his low-angle run, then make their higher, steeper strafe passes on the MiG.

Poor, dumb bastard, thought Lucky Anderson as the taxiing MiG began to zigzag down below. The pilot had obviously seen Billy Bowes's Thud as it rolled out, stabilized, and began to close for the kill.

0642 Local—Kep PAAF Auxiliary Air Base, DRV

Kapitan Aleks Ivanovic

Aleks had huddled, rolled into a ball in the hangarette near his MiG-21 as the bombs rained on the airfield, sending concussive waves, one after the other, to pummel his senses. He'd looked out only periodically, and each time another explosion had rocked the ground he'd pulled back, turtlelike, and huddled again.

He wore his flying helmet, for he'd made it into the cockpit acting as if he were considering starting the engine when the first bombs exploded on the runway. Then he'd scrambled down to find an unoccupied corner.

A lull, and he cautiously looked out the mouth of the hangarette. An explosion shook the hangarette, and a spray of sand spewed down through the wooden ceiling. Then *plop, plop, plop* as sandbags fell through to land beside a terrified, screaming maintenance man.

Aleks was facing the taxiway and could see a great gouge 200 meters distant where the closest bomb had impacted. Probably that last, great explosion, he thought, which had also loosened the sandbags.

A rain of smaller explosions blanketed the operations building.

Cluster bombs!

He backed another meter into the sanctity of the hangarette, but still cautiously peered out.

Some of the bomblets exploded as they rained down, while others bounced about the tarmac before they came to rest. *Are they duds or delayed fuzes?* he wondered.

More raining bomblets, some exploding, some just bouncing and lying there. Then, down the flight line, he could hear one of the MiG-21 engines whining to life. Even above the awful din of the exploding bomblets and the artillery bursts far overhead, he could hear the distinctive, shrill call of a lone Tumanskii turbojet.

Thanh?

"Don't go out there!" he yelled at the maintenance crew,

who'd heard the jet engine and were edging toward the
door. "The bomblets have time-delay fuzes!"

At the corner of his vision he saw a silver MiG taxiing
out. It had emerged from Thanh's hangarette.

The young Vietnamese pilot left the hangarette's mouth,
then swung into a hard right turn up the taxiway. Aleks
watched without smiling, his heart crawling toward his
throat.

Dimetriev's hero.

Mechanics cheered from the hangarettes.

The lieutenant gunned his engine and sprinted his
MiG-21 forward for twenty meters, then slowed to avoid
taxiing over a piece of net that had been tossed there by an
explosion.

Aleks watched as the MiG drew abeam the mouth of his
hangarette, and he saw Thanh peer quizzically, then frown
as he saw Aleks's aircraft still inside. He waved frantically
and pointed energetically toward the runway end. His
breathing mask hung to one side, his expression was one of
bafflement.

A mechanic ran from Aleks's hangarette toward the taxiing MiG, waving and cheering.

A hero. The sick feeling continued to crawl in Aleks's
stomach.

He watched then as a Thunder plane descended, extended for distance, then turned sharply toward the taxiway
as if the American pilot were going to land there. There was
no doubt that he was positioning for a low-angle strafing run
on the taxiing MiG-21.

The moment became frozen. Both hunter and prey were
aware, for Thanh had seen the Thunder plane and was zig-
zagging wildly, still a hundred meters from the end of the
runway.

*The sister-fucking idiot doesn't realize the Thunder planes
have destroyed the runway. There's nothing to take off on!*

"*I'll meet you at the end of the runway,*" he'd told Thanh,
"*and we will take off together.*" So Thanh had taxied.

The fool! That moment marked the end of Aleksandr
Ivanovic's naïveté.

Mesmerized, he watched as the Thunder plane drew
closer, saw a stream of smoke from its gunport, and a second
later heard a loud *braaa-aaat*. It was the same gun that ter-

rified all sane pilots when they studied it. This was the first time Aleks had actually heard one.

The Thunder plane was already by, but its image was fresh in his mind's eye. Big and angry looking, with green and black and tan camouflage paint and a splash of bright blue at the top of the vertical stabilizer.

He dared to look and saw that Thanh's aircraft was still taxiing. Had the Thunder plane missed?

"Thanh! Get out!" he cried.

The MiG-21 continued in a straight line, off the pavement and toward the sleeping quarters . . . slowing in the grass, stopping finally beside the entrance to the dugout. The hardy Tumanskii engine continued to squeal as smoke began to curl from the right wing-root.

Did Aleks see a shrug of movement from inside the cockpit?

"Get out of the aircraft!" he heard himself hoarsely yell again.

A roar of dismay erupted from the throats of a dozen maintenance men, who began to run from the hangarettes to help Thanh get out.

Aleks stood, wanting to run out and join them . . . hesitating.

A bomblet's timer expired and it exploded with a loud bang, and two of the men dropped in their tracks. Two others turned to scramble back to the safety of the hangarettes, but the remainder screamed defiantly and kept running toward the young hero.

More smoke trickled from the wing-root. There was indeed movement from within the cockpit. The canopy cracked open and started slowly to lift.

He was alive. Aleks began to smile. Thanh was alive!

Nine maintenance men had made it to within twenty meters of the aircraft with its still-squealing engine when the sky again began to rain bullets.

"Nooooo," moaned Aleks as he watched.

The downpour was intense, making the turf pop and sputter, and the maintenance men fell in their tracks as if swatted by a giant hand. The small-tail MiG-21 jumped and shuddered, then knelt onto its right wing before spouting flame from the fuselage aft of the now-opened canopy. The Tumanskii engine stopped dead.

Braaa-aaa-aaat. The sound followed the spectacle.

Aleks glanced up, saw a Thunder plane pulling away, another diving in its place. Tears were awash in his eyes. He could not remove the mental image of the young lieutenant as he'd looked at him with trust in his eyes. He stifled a sob.

"Forgive me!" Aleks moaned.

More deadly hail. Thanh's aircraft danced and shuddered from side to side with the impacts. Its remaining gear collapsed and it settled onto the grass.

Braaa-aaaa-aaat.

A final fury, this one walking and stirring angrily about the entire area, making the tarmac pop and jump just as the sod had done.

Braaa-aaa-aaa-aaa-aaat.

The small-tail MiG-21 was burning fiercely. Once Aleks thought he saw an arm slowly rise from the inferno of the cockpit, but he doubted that could be so.

He began to cry.

The siren at the operations building again sounded, and through his grief Aleks wondered if it was the alert for the attack that had just occurred, or if another was beginning.

It was the latter, for a few minutes later Phantoms began to dive-bomb the runway. Again Aleks Ivanovic curled into a ball, still sobbing, but his sadness was quickly replaced by terror as bombs again began to rain upon the airfield.

CHAPTER SIX

Air Regiment Commandant Quon

Quon stared out the open door of the big Russian helicopter, dazed in his grief, mind racing with self-incrimination and memories of his son.

The boy had been conceived the year of Quon's heroic return from Europe, the seed energetically pumped into a lively fifteen-year-old offspring of Lieutenant Tho's stodgy uncle, as it was into a dozen other daughters eager to please the dashing young pilot. But then the revolt had come, and he'd hurried into the mountains to hide and fight for the Viet Minh. He'd not learned of the girl's condition until several months after their frolic, and by then he'd not been able to remember what she'd looked like.

The girl's father had been a high-ranking Lao Dong party official, sufficiently important that when hostilities began, he and his family had been imprisoned in Hanoi by the French. When Quon learned of her pregnancy, he'd been told the girl was already swollen like a melon and daily announced to Frenchmen within earshot that the child's father was a brave pilot named Quon who would soon come to rescue her. He also heard that her important father was pleased with neither his daughter's condition nor her suitor. That was all. News from Hanoi had been shut off because of the war, and he'd forgotten the affair as he learned to fight on the ground like an elusive mud-hog, rather than in the sky like a great predatory bird.

By the time he'd heard about the Hanoi girl, Quon had already plucked another from a nearby village to keep his campsite neat, prepare his food, and help carry his belongings when they moved by night. Many Vietnamese men were either very shy in the presence of females, or looked upon them as shallow and useless objects. A considerable number of Viet Minh were more sexually attracted to their fellow warriors with whom they shared hardships than to the women in the villages. But Quon liked females and preferred them young, and by the end of that long conflict, he'd gone through several girls, none older than sixteen. One had been killed as she hurled herself, screaming defiantly, upon an advancing platoon of legionnaires. That one had likely saved his life as he escaped. But the fourteen-year-old girl had sacrificed herself willingly, and he'd understood it as a reasonable and necessary act. He'd mourned only because she'd been especially obeisant and might be hard to replace. That worry was proved unfounded when he took an equally humble and dedicated girl, gangling and wonderfully elastic-limbed, from the next village they passed through.

He thought hard before he remembered what had become of that one.

She'd allowed herself to become pregnant, this only a few months before he and Captain Tho had started on the long trek from the mountains northwest of Saigon to China. By the time they'd walked 200 kilometers, she was slowing them down. She'd grown plump and waddled along, complaining about her discomfort as well as the weight of the camp goods, until they'd finally grown exasperated and traded her to a small, nomadic Lao tribe.

The tribesmen had been short and misshapen from inbreeding, with pronounced noses, muscular bodies, and small arms and legs. Fierce and peacock proud, they wore metal jewelry that dangled from their ears and outsized, tatooed noses. Three naked and slack-jawed women busily attended the needs of the sixty men, each as pregnant as the girl with Quon.

Like other nomadic tribes, they traveled exceedingly light, carrying few luxuries. Sickly males and most female infants were cast out to die. Only one female was spared for each ten males, to become a communal seminal vessel and mother to the future tribe.

The previous year catastrophe had struck when four of their adult women were killed by a relentless fever. Since their replacements were very young, only the three adult females were left to them, and they were severely overworked. Every minute they were not moving, during the several days they were with them, at least one was on her hands and knees at a corner of the camp, lurching and grunting as she was serviced by one of the males whose jewelry jangled gaily as he howled and rutted.

Taller than the tribesmen by a head, Quon's gift was a curiosity appreciated by the village men. As he'd prepared to leave, he'd heard her wailing for him to take her, but her voice had come in starts and jerks accompanied by a lively, jingling sound. They'd received one of the tribe's shaggy pack horses for her, which he and Tho quickly decided was a good trade. The horse neither nagged nor complained and easily carried their load.

They'd continued through north-central Laos, then into southern China, where in mid-1953 Captain Tho had wheedled the Chinese People's Army into donating two vintage fighter aircraft to the Viet Minh cause.

Quon stared out the window and saw Kep in the distance. The trip would soon be over.

Quon remembered the child he'd acknowledged. The one who had grown up to die in a hail of American cannon rounds! He groaned at the thought, and his adjutant looked at him with an embarrassed, sympathetic look.

In 1954 they'd quickly lost their two aircraft to French gunfire, and both Tho and Quon had only narrowly escaped death. When the Viet Minh had marched victoriously into Hanoi, he and Major Tho had hurried to the Gia Lam airport to observe the facilities and inspect the military aircraft abandoned by the French, some battle damaged and others victims of cannibalization. He'd still been there when the message from the child's mother had arrived, passed to him by her party-official father, who was Major Tho's uncle. Le Duc Tho was a prominent member of Ho Chi Minh's entourage, a resolute, often-jailed martyr of the Lao Dong party, and a man to be reckoned with.

Quon had judiciously wed the woman he did not remember and acknowledged the son he'd never seen. Later the party newspaper *Nham Dan* had published the first of dozens of articles about the great hero Quon. Mostly lies, but always flattering. According to *Nham Dan* the marriage was solemnized by the girl's father, and the couple bade to keep the covenants of marriage so long as the Republic breathed freedom into the breasts of Vietnamese people.

Le Duc Tho had certainly been solemn, but the only words he'd spoken to Quon had been a terse threat to bring no more shame to his family. While he doted on his grandson, after the hasty marriage he paid little attention to either his daughter or Quon.

Le Duc Tho had gone on to become the most trusted confidant of the Enlightened One, and it was now rumored that he might even replace him as president. He was in the South as Ho Chi Minh's on-scene agent, orchestrating the war effort and keeping the military activities in tune with the political ones. His nephew was General Tho, commandant of the People's Army Air Force, and his son-in-law was Quon, Hero of the Republic. But the only one of the group he cared for greatly, his only grandson . . . was now dead.

The helicopter engine surged and clattered, and they settled toward the end of the battered runway below. The Russian helicopter pilots were wary, looking about nervously for enemy fighter-bombers, although the Phuc Yen radar continued to announce that all was clear.

The Russians build fine helicopters, Quon thought, trying to keep his mind busy with inconsequentials.

He studied the damage to the airfield. The Americans had continued bombing throughout the previous day, and the previous night the damnable Navy Intruders had bombed even more, killing many of the repair crew trying to patch the holes in the tarmac runway.

The runway was still unusable, but no air raids had been made today, and if their luck held, they'd be able to repair it sufficiently for the three undamaged Mig-21's to take off and return to the safety of Phuc Yen. Two other MiGs would be transported by giant Russian workhorse helicopters to the Gia Lam aircraft-repair facility.

Below them he saw the MiG that had been attacked and destroyed. Burned to skeleton and ashes. As was his son.

He wished he could recall the boy and tell him to ignore the lies created by *Nham Dan*.

In his shaken voice he directed the helicopter pilot to fly the length of the runway before landing, so he could further survey the extent of the damage.

The work gangs are making progress, he finally decided.

He held his face stony then as they circled back and descended to land near the demolished MiG-21, where it rested in the grass near the end of the runway. He no longer appeared distraught. An observer would have believed him to be in complete control.

What sort of feelings should he hold for a fool who insisted on following in his father's footsteps?

Sadness. Utter sadness. He caught a breath.

The boy had attended pilot training and taken up the ridiculous false name his father had suggested. The father had encouraged him even though he'd suspected his limitations. Self-recrimination nagged unmercifully until he again convinced himself the American assassins had somehow singled out his son for death.

Quon remembered meeting the frightened eight-year-old, so full of stories planted by his mother. The awkward child with bright eyes. He remembered the boy's childhood, remembered ignoring him again and yet again, always in a hurry to attend to important matters.

During puberty Buddhist sons would go into the mountains for a month of seclusion and prayer with their fathers to learn humility, how to lead a righteous life, and whatever other nuggets of wisdom the father wished to impart. What had *he* taught his son? How to strut like a peacock infatuated with its own legend? How to smile enigmatically when awed fools asked about the lies printed in *Nham Dan*? He'd done such a good job of it that the boy had wanted to be like him.

When his son was fifteen, Quon had decided it was time to participate in his tutelage and had excited him with the news. Time had not allowed it. He'd promised to take the boy with him on this or that trip. He'd never done it. He'd spent his available leisure hours with his latest concubine rather than his wife, leaving her to maintain his home and raise their son.

Guilt flooded him, made his chest hurt with emotion as he realized how much he missed the foolish, fawning boy.

He crawled from the helicopter while the rotors were still turning and hurried to the wreckage to stand dumbly before it and stare. Smoke still issued from here and there. Only a few ribs and part of the tail section remained intact.

Several men stood about, staring awkwardly.

"Where is the major?" he asked quietly.

"Here, comrade Quon," replied a nearby, fearful voice.

"My son?"

"We placed the body in a box and put it in the hangarette there." He paused. "There is not much."

He pondered for a moment. Then, "Place him aboard the helicopter." His chest ached more deeply. "I shall take him home," he said.

"Yes, comrade Quon."

He questioned the officers and senior mechanics and asked what they'd seen. They explained the horrors of the bombing, the heroism of his son, and then the strafing attack.

Why did he taxi from the shelter? he asked himself. He'd never known his son to be that brave. But then, he'd not really known him.

He spoke with the operations sergeant manning the telephones and radios, who confirmed they'd received no notification from either Phuc Yen or Kien An radars. When the major had tried to contact them on the radio, they'd not been able to get through until it was too late. Repair technicians had explained that the problems had been caused by a series of electrical-power surges.

Quon did not understand such things, but he resolved to tell the communications people to make sure it could not happen again.

He spoke with the Russian, Ivanovic, and the man kept repeating something about blue tails.

Then Quon spoke to a maintenance sergeant, who told him the Russian had cowered in his hangarette and shouted for them not to go out to assist his son. But Quon remembered how highly his son had spoken of the Russian captain with the ready grin, and it was a time to honor his son's memory.

He asked more and found that only the last four attacking American Thunder planes had done the strafing, and that those aircraft had bright-blue paint at the tops of their vertical stabilizers.

When the big Russian helicopter lifted off for Hanoi, Quon huddled inside beside the small box containing his son's remains: slivers of charred bone and teeth, and scorched cloth with unrecognizable fragments of meat. He'd seen other such victims.

He averted his eyes from the others aboard the helicopter, for he could not quench a sudden flood of tears. *Oh my son!* he wailed inwardly, agony gripping his chest. He felt a last flash of guilt and again replaced it with accusation. The American flight leader had somehow known it was his son. He wondered how, but knew he would never know unless . . .

Two challenges were presented him, at first incoherent and ajumble due to his misery, then increasingly clear. He would do both in memory of his son.

First he must gain control of the radars and correct the command-and-control problem. Second, he must find the man who had led the flight of Thunder planes—the man who had killed his son.

He vowed to deal with Nguyen Wu, the inept colonel who had allowed the operation of the radars to sink into such disarray.

And he vowed to shoot down and capture the American flight leader.

He would bring him here where he'd assassinated his son, and he would kill him . . . here where his son had died.

Both were very personal challenges.

Immediately after transporting his son's remains to Ba Dinh Hall, where a party official spoke of arrangements for a proper eulogy and acclaim, perhaps even a hero's state funeral, Quon set up meetings, first with General Tho and then with General Dung.

That should get things moving on the first matter. The other would take more thought.

1100 Local—354th TFS, Takhli RTAFB, Thailand

Major Lucky Anderson

Lucky felt that part of the price an Air Force pilot should pay to fly fighters was to stay in good physical condition, and since a pilot's day often involved a lot of paperwork and little free time, he carefully scheduled a daily exercise regime and religiously maintained it. Whenever alone, whether at a desk or in a fighter cockpit, once each hour he would tense the muscles of his back, then his arms, his stomach, and his thighs, each for fifteen seconds, then he would grasp his buttocks and tense and pull. Each morning or evening, as the flying schedule permitted, he spent an hour running and working out. Because of these rituals, he remained in superb physical condition.

That morning he'd started at his trailer with the isometrics, then ran a three-mile course that ended at the base gym, where he immediately did twenty-five sit-ups followed by twenty-five repetitions with 100-pound weights. He'd jogged back to his trailer, showered, and walked to the squadron for the first meeting of the flight commanders with Lieutenant Colonel John Encinos, who'd just arrived at Takhli to take over as their new squadron commander.

Encinos had served on wing-staff organizations from Yokota Air Base, Japan, to Bitburg Air Base, Germany. He was a too-quiet, too-withdrawn man, who'd made his way to light colonel not by virtue of his accomplishments, but by not making mistakes. He wasn't a bad guy, but neither was he one whose subordinates could warm to or call a "good shit." John Encinos openly favored those whom generals and colonels liked, and disregarded the others.

Three of the five flight commanders knew John Encinos from other places in the Air Force, for the fighter pilot community was not large. Before his arrival the commanders of A, B, C, D, and the Wild Weasel flight of the 354th had gotten together and talked about how it would have to be when Encinos, with his peculiar ways of doing things, came aboard. They'd decided it would work out best if they just continued making the tough decisions as they'd done since they had lost their last squadron commander over Thai Nguyen. So when John Encinos called the meeting, they were ready.

Encinos was slight, nervous, swarthy, and of average height, and could easily be lost in a crowd, because that was precisely what he wanted. He had made lieutenant colonel, which had been his career goal, and now he wanted to coast until he had his two years in grade and was eligible for retirement, which was less than a year away. That was what his fellow officers believed, for he didn't hesitate to tell them. They also knew him as a mediocre pilot who cared little about flying.

At his in-briefing he did nothing to dispel their notions. After shaking the hands of the men he knew and being introduced to the ones he did not, Encinos stumbled through a short, standard speech about how he expected them to give him their best.

"I expect you guys to run your flights," added John Encinos, "and I'll stay out of your hair so long as things are going well."

That much was true, thought Lucky. It was unlikely they would even see him in the squadron very often. He would probably find some full bull colonel on the wing staff and spend his time trying to impress him. B. J. Parker, the wing commander, heartily disliked Encinos, so it would have to be one of the others.

Encinos rambled on some more, then the two flight commanders who didn't know him began asking questions, and each time Encinos would pause thoughtfully and then say he'd get back to them with the answers. Glances between the flight commanders intimated that no one believed he would get back to anyone with anything.

"What's your policy on upgrading the guys to flight-lead status?" the exasperated D-Flight commander finally asked. "I'm facing that right now, and I need an answer."

Encinos furrowed his brow, as if he'd been asked for an alternative to the theory of relativity. He looked about and finally turned to Lucky. "What procedure have you been using, Major Anderson?"

Lucky was glad to give the answer. The D-Flight commander was new at his job and needed guidance.

"I don't upgrade my pilots until they've got twenty missions here, regardless of experience," he said. "I keep a book on 'em and try to write down something about every man's performance each time we fly. He has any problems with anything, I try to get it ironed out before we go up the next time. Then, before I upgrade 'em, I try to give them a couple checkout rides down in the easy packs."

Encinos nodded sagely, as if Lucky had given the correct answer, and turned to the other flight commanders. "You guys keep a book on your guys, too. When you feel they're ready, tell the admin sergeant, and he'll type up the orders."

Having John Encinos for a commander was much like having a parrot around.

After half an hour they broke up the meeting, and Lucky walked with two of the other flight commanders toward their trailers, which were nestled beside the Officers' Club.

"Jesus," chuckled one. "The Bad Injin is more wishy-washy than ever."

"Bad Injin" was Encinos's nickname.

Lucky Anderson knew he'd have no problems with Encinos, because it was known that General Moss and a couple of other fighter generals held him in high regard. Encinos would give him wide berth, for he did not want anything to hurt his chance for on-time retirement.

Which was just fine with Lucky. He held no particular animosity toward the man.

As they approached the club, the other flight commanders went to their trailers. Lucky continued on to find a few of his C-Flight members and have lunch.

Turk, Manny, Liebermann, and Billy Bowes were arriving as he rounded the corner of the club. They traded salutes and greetings, then walked in together.

1205 Local—Officers' Club Dining Room

Turk joked, "I saw you running, Lucky. Keep it up with the exercises, and by damn, you're going to end up muscle-bound."

Lucky's rigorous exercising made him look like a model for a body-building magazine. At least from the neck down.

"You oughta try it, Turk," laughed Manny DeVera. "Then the big guys would quit kicking sand in your face."

"I get my exercise chasing little women," said Turk. "They're a lot quicker than the big, slow ones you guys go after."

Turk Tatro stood only five six and was kidded a lot about his size. He was happily married, and every day he wrote a letter, alternately addressed to his wife and two daughters waiting back in Mississippi. Turk didn't *really* chase little women or any other kind, for he had his hands and time filled by the three he doted on. His infrequent visits to the whores in Ta Khli were purely for physical relief, but even those had now stopped. Turk had put in for an R and R to Hawaii next month, to take a break from combat and bask in the sun with his wife and daughters, and was abstaining from *all* contact with the girls downtown—just in case they left him with an undesired memento, like the hardy strain of gonorrhea the guys called "killer clap," which was becoming prevalent in Thailand. His wife would not understand at all.

When Lucky had told him his R and R had been approved, he'd thought Turk was going to grin his ears off. Tatro was seriously in love with his family of little women.

They took a table at the side of the dining room, and all waited as Manny DeVera joked with No Hab, the waitress. He looked primly down his nose at the well-worn bond-paper menu. "I'd like sautéed escargot, a lobster tail with freshly drawn butter, and a bottle of your finest 1959 Auslese," Manny told her.

"No hab," she said with a special smile for the handsome pilot.

"How 'bout a hamburger with fries?"

"No hab flies."

"How about beetles?"

"Hab beetles," she joked, and scribbled as if she were taking the order.

"Hamburger and fried rice?" he asked.

"Hab flied lice."

"And a glass of milk?"

"Hab grass of milk!" she announced proudly.

The others then went through the drill of what was and was not available with No Hab. Ordering lunch was a lengthy and often arduous drill at the Takhli O' Club.

As she left, No Hab waggled her butt and glanced back at Manny.

"She likes you," said Lucky with a grin.

"No Hab's got good taste."

"My God, the women here are pretty," said Bob Liebermann with a shake of his head.

"You're just getting horny," observed Manny.

"I agree with Bob," said Billy Bowes, and Turk echoed him.

"I think it's something in the water," Billy said.

Turk turned from staring after No Hab and motioned across the table at Major Lucky. "So how's the Bad Injin these days?"

"Bad as ever," said Lucky.

"Bad Injin?" asked Bob Liebermann. "Who's Bad Injin?"

"Lee-ootenant Colonel John Encinos," said Turk. "Real name was Juan Carlos Encinos-Testaverde, I think. That right, Lucky?"

"Something like that. I remember he was once called Carlos."

Turk grinned. "Then someone told him the gringos got the promotions, so he decided to join 'em. Started carrying a little sissy briefcase everywhere, even when he went down to the squadron to fly. Got his name officially changed to John Anthony and asked everyone to call him John. He'd get howling mad when anyone called him Carlos."

"That's when everyone started calling him Bad Injin," said Lucky.

Turk nodded. "Which really pissed him off, seeing all the work he'd gone to to get his name changed. Then he was sent to Bitburg and went to work for Colonel Alonzo Bautista, who's very proud of his Latino blood, and he almost shit bricks trying to get everyone to call him Carlos again, so he could impress Al Bautista."

Lucky was smiling at the memory. "But by then *everyone* called him Bad Injin."

Turk continued. "So *then* he got his name officially changed to John Encinos, which he figured was halfway in between and ought to please everyone."

They were all chuckling. Manny was laughing loudest, because he already knew about the Bad Injin.

Turk looked at the others, drawling out the story in his Confederatese. "Bad Injin Encinos has been a wing staff puke since he was a lieutenant. Always got just the minimum flying time possible to collect his flight pay and squeak through his instrument checks. Spent the rest of his time hiding from responsibility and trying to impress the colonels."

Lucky smiled at the astute description.

"But now," said Turk Tatro with a smirk, "the Bad Injin's

our squadron commander, and he's got a *real* dilemma on
his hands. He's spent so much time with his nose up different colonels' asses, telling 'em how the squadron commanders *ought* to be doing their jobs, they started to believe he
could do it better. Poor fellow's got himself promoted too
high, and now there's no way to avoid the spotlight."

"Jesus," said Liebermann, "is he really that bad?" Bob
tended to think the best of everyone. Now that he'd made it
into fighters, he wanted to believe all fighter pilots and their
leaders were great fellows.

"Is he that bad?" reflected Turk Tatro. "Naw, not really.
He's *worse*."

Manny DeVera broke in. "Don't worry, Bob. The Bad
Injin's so wishy-washy he won't be any trouble unless you
want him to answer a question."

Liebermann looked at them as if they were surely joking.

Turk Tatro peered over at Lieutenant Bowes. "I hear your
cousin's been put in for an Air Force Cross."

"I heard the same thing," said Billy.

"They don't just hand those things out," said Lucky.
"From everything we heard, Bear Stewart earned it. He was
flying with a good friend of mine, fellow named Benny
Lewis. Benny wrote me and said the Bear deserved the
Cross. Maybe even a Medal of Honor."

"They keep those for guys who can make nice speeches
to the VFW," said Turk.

"No one who lives through it should get a Medal of
Honor," said Manny DeVera, reflecting the thinking of a lot
of military men. "He didn't, so *maybe* he deserves it."

A side discussion sprang up. The Medal of Honor ranked
just higher than the Air Force Cross, but with the Medal,
politics became involved. It wasn't often awarded to a hell-
raising, hard-drinking fighter jock. If you got a Medal of
Honor, it meant you deserved a medal, but it also meant you
could be trusted to make a speech to a ladies' tea group
without saying "fuck" or letting on how much you enjoyed
killing communists. Politics and protocol, not heroism, was
the difference between the two medals.

Turk Tatro explained how medals were decided upon at
Takhli.

"Let's say you do something great and someone thinks
you deserve a Distinguished Flying Cross," said Turk.
"Flight lead will write up what happened and give it to Ma-

jor Lucky, who puts some flowery words on it and turns it in to the squadron awards-and-decorations officer, who is some poor bastard unlucky enough to be assigned the additional duty. If the awards-and-decs officer's busy or has a hangover, you won't get anything. If he can't interpret Major Lucky's writing or understand his lousy spelling . . ."

Anderson winced dramatically and they laughed.

". . . then either wing headquarters or Seventh Air Force will disapprove it or downgrade the DFC to a Bronze Star. If he adds the *right* words and the write-up's got lots of adverbs, the staff pukes'll get all misty-eyed and approve it or even upgrade it to a Silver Star. Some well-deserved medals disappear in the bureaucracy. Other times guys get medals because they happened to be along on a mission the brass likes. But by damn, when you see someone get an Air Force Cross, you know he did something special."

"No one alive deserves a Medal of Honor," iterated Manny.

"I wouldn't mind pinning a medal on *that*," said Turk Tatro, staring at a group coming into the dining room, and Manny DeVera almost suffered whiplash turning his head.

B. J. Parker and Tom Lyons entered, ushering two pretty, yet entirely different females. One was blond and petite, with a tiny waist, rounded breasts that stretched her cotton blouse, and a sexy derriere tightly encased in khaki pants. The men in the room were staring appreciatively, and though it was obvious she knew it, she didn't appear unhappy or embarrassed. Lucky's attention shifted to the other woman, and he inhaled sharply. She was taller, thinner, very striking, and wore a sophisticated, no-nonsense air.

What the hell was she doing here?

She saw him, paused, then waved, and Lucky felt a bubble of excitement build in his chest before he pulled his eyes away.

"The Ice Maiden waved," announced Manny in a hushed voice. Then he realized it was Lucky she'd waved at. He frowned. "You know her, boss?" he asked.

"Yeah," mumbled Lucky, troubled. "At least I used to."

GS-15 Linda Lopes

Linda looked at Paul Anderson, examined the ravaged face, and felt her stomach lurch. *Funny how your heart seems to affect your stomach*, she thought. Lucky glanced back at her, and their eyes locked for an instant before he looked away again.

Colonel B. J. Parker led them to his private table at the rear corner of the room, and Tom Lyons waved imperiously to a flustered waitress, who hurried over to hand them all a menu typed on a sheet of folded bond paper.

"The selection is abominable," announced Lyons, letting a smile play across his pretty-boy features, "but it tastes worse."

She'd grown an instant dislike for Tom Lyons the moment they were introduced. Too oily smooth and sure of himself. Although he wore no wedding band, Linda had pegged him as married, regardless of the constant come-on. After she'd spoken a few caustic words of discouragement, he'd switched his attentions to Jackie, the shapely young Peace Corps administrator. He now hovered over her and pointed out various menu items, as if the girl couldn't choose between a hamburger, fried chicken, and a Salisbury steak, which was all the Thai waitress said was available.

Linda observed Paul Anderson again.

Still as shy as ever, she thought. She wondered if he was over the bitterness or whatever it was that had taken him from her.

In 1959 she'd been a GS-8 working for the Defense Intelligence Agency at Wiesbaden Air Base, Germany, trying to make sense of the electronic intelligence gathered by aircrews flying very special aircraft on the airway into Berlin and the embassy run to Moscow. She'd been twenty-three years old, attractive, unattached, living in exciting Europe, doing exciting work, and out to prove to her parents that she could manage just fine for herself in the big world outside Big Spring, Texas.

Then one evening she'd agreed to a night out at the Von Steuben with a male acquaintance, a co-worker civilian employee at Wiesbaden Air Base. The Von Steuben was a military hotel for officers and civilian equivalents located in downtown Wiesbaden, and the master chef there prepared some of the finest entrées in Germany. After dinner they'd gone to the bar, where they'd danced and had a drink or two, and then the boyfriend had put the moves on her, and she had told him not only to forget about what he was after, but to go far away, like maybe to hell or Amarillo.

To impress her and try to return to her good graces, her co-worker had then made a tactical error, for he'd introduced her to "this fighter-pilot guy" he'd met who was there on temporary duty from Sembach Air Base.

The young captain was tall and movie-star handsome, with a breath-catching physique. He'd been charming yet wonderfully shy, and as they were still being introduced, she'd gotten the warm, moist feeling her mother had warned her about, precisely where she'd said it would be centered.

He was from Dayton and had gone to school at the University of Ohio at Athens, where he'd gained a mechanical-engineering degree, then had wasted it by going directly into the Air Force's flight cadet program. He flew F-84's at Sembach Air Base, a few miles south of Wiesbaden, but shortly he would return to the States to be checked out in the F-100 Super Sabre. *He was available.* His wife, having endured enough military life, had returned to the States and was filing for divorce, which he agreed was the best course for them both.

Linda had breathlessly learned all of that within their first five minutes of discussion, and then he'd listened just as raptly to everything about her boring childhood in Big Spring, Texas, and her education at Texas Woo, which is what they'd called the women's university at Denton, north of Fort Worth.

The guy she'd come with had finally wandered away muttering, but she'd scarcely noticed. At the end of the evening she'd accompanied the fighter pilot to his third-floor room in the Von Steuben as if it were the natural thing to do, because it was, and found that losing one's virginity to the right man was more sharing than giving.

Every weekend for the five wonderful weeks following that night, she'd hopped into her VW bug and flown south, for she was sure the tires hardly touched the autobahn's surface, to Sembach Air Base.

On the Monday following her final visit, he'd taken off in his F-84 "bent-wing thunderhog," as he called it, on a routine training mission to a gunnery range in the Netherlands. They told her that on his final approach back at Sembach the engine had belched fire and quit, and that he'd ridden it in, landing in an open field so the aircraft wouldn't crash into nearby homes. She was told the fuel tanks had ruptured during the crash landing, and that he'd been extremely fortunate to be able to stagger out and get away from the aircraft, even if he was drenched with jet fuel and burning like a human torch. They said his oxygen mask had been torn away when he'd egressed the airplane, and that his face was horribly burned.

He'd been allowed no visitors after they'd taken him to the big Wiesbaden Hospital. Except for a single peek at a mound of loose bandages with tubes extending from it, she'd been unable to see him before he was flown in a med-evac aircraft to the burn center at the Brooks Air Force Station hospital in San Antonio.

The doctors at Wiesbaden told her that since he'd survived the initial shock and the critical first week with no infections or complications, it was possible he might recover. Regardless, they said, he'd be kept for a very long while at the burn center for reconstructive surgery, and that he'd never fly again. They said that when he was in his worst pain, he'd called her name.

She'd immediately requested a leave of absence to be with him during the difficult period. The international tensions were hot, and the Soviets were acting up, so Linda had been unable to get leave right away, but she'd written him every day for the next month. Then she'd received a single-liner from him saying:

> *Dear Linda,*
>   *I'm getting back together with my wife.*
> *Best regards,*
>
> *Paul Anderson*

When the leave of absence finally came through, she took it, staying in her apartment for a solid, lonely week to cry and try to get over him. It had been nine more months before she heard more, and that was by accident, through a pilot a girlfriend was dating.

He said that Lucky Anderson had been released from the burn center and was spending his days going between the Air Force Military Personnel Center and Wilford Hall, the Air Force's largest hospital, both located right there in San Antonio, fighting to get back on flying status. When she asked *very casually* how he was getting along with his wife, the pilot said Lucky and his wife had split when he was still in Germany, and as far as he knew, she'd never even visited him at the burn center. He said Lucky's face looked like hell, but that except for some initial skin grafts he'd turned down more reconstructive surgery because he was afraid a further healing period might keep him from getting back on flying status.

Linda had seen him only once after that. Two years ago when she'd flown to Las Vegas.

She'd been working in Washington, D.C., in the State Department information office. It was a boring, dead-end job, screening inputs for Voice of America broadcasts, ensuring their accuracy and then analyzing embassy reports to measure the reactions in Eastern Bloc nations. Trapped in a field that would not allow her to rise above GS-11, she'd decided to return to the intelligence collection-and-verification business because she knew she'd been damned good at it. But she was having trouble with a guy in State Department intelligence who thought women weren't mentally equipped to serve as anything more than secretaries.

That had all accumulated to put her in a funky, down mood when she heard from a friend working across the river at the Pentagon that a Major Anderson—*"I'm just sure it's the same guy you had the hots for over in Germany who was burned so horribly"*—was assigned to Nellis Air Force Base in Las Vegas. He was now flying F-105 fighters and teaching aerial gunnery to other pilots and had recently been presented with some kind of flying award. Her friend had seen his picture in the *Air Force Times. "Awful!"* she'd said.

Linda had convinced herself that a trip to Vegas was just what she needed, and maybe if she just relaxed some there, she could figure out how to handle the male chauvinists at State. She'd signed up for a Las Vegas tour package offered by a local travel agency. Upon arrival at the desert city, she'd immediately rented a car, and then, when she realized she wasn't fooling herself, drove directly to Nellis and used her State Department ID to get on base.

From the arched doorway of the Officers' Club dining room she'd seen him having dinner alone in a corner.

His face! She'd known it would be bad, but it was much worse than she'd expected—so disfigured that *no* one could have been prepared for it. She'd caught her breath a couple of times and started to cry, then turned and fled, to stand outside and sob and feel sorry for him, *he'd been so hand-*

some! and for herself, *she'd loved him so!* . . . and for both of them together for what should have been.

Several officers in flying suits had stopped and tried to help, but she'd ignored them and kept on sobbing until she was devoid of sorrow, dry of tears, and quite ashamed. She started to go in to him, knew she looked awful from crying so much, and retreated to the safe haven of the ladies' room for repairs.

He'd already left the dining room when she finally emerged, which was not surprising because she'd taken so long.

The billeting office had given her his room number in the bachelor officers' quarters, but when she'd gotten there, his roommate told her Lucky had come back, grabbed a pack and some gear, and had immediately taken off for "Mount Charlie or up north somewhere" in his Jeep. Lucky went camping alone like that every now and then, the friend said, but this time he'd acted as if he were in a particular hurry.

She'd felt awful and wondered if Lucky had seen her crying.

I'm Glenn Phillips, the guy had said. *Why don't you come in and wait, and we can share a drink and see if he comes back for something.* She had judiciously left and the next day had cut the trip short and returned to Washington.

Now he was here in the same room, and Linda felt as giddy as she had the first time they'd met. She was staring at him, she realized, so she looked away.

"Unsightly, isn't he?" said Tom Lyons, who had reached over and was patting her hand reassuringly, as if he were protecting her from something.

She pulled her hand away. "Pardon me?"

"The major with the burns. We've got a few like that around the Air Force."

She nodded, and then the impact of what he'd said struck her, and she bristled.

"That's Lucky Anderson," said Colonel B. J. Parker, whom Linda had not yet made up her mind about. She had him pegged as a climber. He'd been *too* impressed when she had first arrived and introduced herself as country coordinator for the USAID program. He was obviously aware that the country coordinator position was much different and more important than it sounded and had little to do with handing out foreign aid packages to Asians; that it was a front title for a senior State Department intelligence official.

"He looks awful," said the Peace Corps administrator. Jackie Bell was cute and sexy, and Linda had liked her from the moment she'd met her, but she had a lot to learn. Like to stop listening to the showcase colonel, who was now trying to imitate an intrepid Steve Canyon look and at the same time peek into her blouse.

"Major Anderson's one of the finest pilots we have here," said B. J. Parker, and with those words of defense Linda decided she liked him after all.

"But definitely not very pretty," quipped Colonel Lyons.

You low creep! thought Linda.

"Who's the dark-haired captain with him?" asked Jackie Bell, and Linda saw Lyons stiffen. Jackie was demurely eyeing a virile-looking captain who steadily returned her gaze.

B. J. Parker chuckled. "That's the Supersonic Wetback." Then he glanced at Linda and looked embarrassed, remembering her name was Latino.

Linda smiled to show she wasn't offended.

"He calls *himself* that," said B. J. Parker awkwardly.

"He's a hunk," Jackie said. Linda noted that Tom Lyons was looking sullen.

"His name's Manny DeVera," said Colonel Parker, "and he's a self-centered, show-off, hot-rod pilot." He nodded his approval. "I wish more of my pilots had his spirit."

Lyons was frowning at Parker's description, obviously in disagreement.

"You'll have to introduce me," said Jackie.

"If I know Manny, he'll do it himself. You'd better watch out for him, young lady. He'll charm your socks off."

"Mmmmm," mused Jackie wickedly. "Is that all?"

Colonel Parker chuckled. Jackie was young and open and could get away with such a remark. Linda's female's antennae picked up that Jackie might not be quite as naive as she let on.

"Maybe I'll have to visit your base more often than I thought, Colonel," said Jackie, as she cast another glance at Manny DeVera.

"The guest trailer is yours anytime you wish," said Colonel Parker. Linda felt he was being fatherly toward Jackie Bell. Some one probably should be, she thought.

"Sometimes," said Tom Lyons, trying to recapture center stage, "I wish I hadn't made full colonel so quickly. Captains seem to have all the fun."

Could Lyons be such an egotist that he'd brag so openly? She decided he was.

The men at the other table stood as if preparing to leave, and Linda nodded to Parker. "Excuse me for a moment. I'd like to say a word to an old friend."

Jackie Bell surveyed her sharply, wondering, and the men stood politely as she rose. He was on his way to the door with the others, so she had to hurry.

"Paul?" she called in a voice louder than she'd intended. He turned and stared, and it was difficult to tell his expression because of the mask of scars.

"No time to say hi to an old friend?" she asked.

"I thought you were busy over there." He watched as his friends left.

She sucked a breath and lowered her voice. "Have I ever been too busy for you?"

He glanced about awkwardly.

"How long have you been at Takhli?" she asked, forced to carry the conversation.

"Not long."

"I've been here since Saturday. If I'd known you were here, I would have gotten in touch." She glanced at the patch on his shoulder, held there by Velcro tape. *354th TFS* it read, and she made a mental note.

"Good to see you, Linda," he said, but there was little conviction to his tone.

"I'm working in Bangkok, running the USAID mission at the embassy." She said it hoping to get him to display at least a trace of interest.

"Uh ... I've gotta go and plan a combat mission. See you."

"It's good to see you again, Paul," she said, but he'd already turned and was hurrying toward the door. She stood planted for a moment longer, then returned to the table where the waitress was delivering their Salisbury steaks.

"You know the major?" asked Tom Lyons, looking at the door with distaste.

"The major," said Linda Lopes firmly, "is probably the finest man I've *ever* known."

Jackie Bell was looking at Linda softly, as if she were observing something very nice. "I'm sorry I reacted like I did, Linda. It was thoughtless of me."

"He was in an aircraft accident in Germany."

"Not exactly the sort of thing you'd like to meet up with in a dark alley," Lyons joked to Jackie, with a short laugh at his own wit.

Linda looked down at the table, eyes brimming. She wanted to cry, just as she had two years before at the Nellis Officers' Club. The sexy kid, Jackie Bell, reached over and gently patted Linda's hand. "If you say he's a nice person, hon, he's okay by me, and his burned face doesn't make a damn."

B. J. Parker looked on with an embarrassed, yet sympathetic, look. *Why am I being this transparent?* she wondered, for both Parker and Jackie Bell seemed to know exactly what she felt. She was normally much more collected.

"Like I said," Parker said kindly, "Lucky's one hell of a fighter pilot."

Tom Lyons shook his head, exasperated that they would waste valuable time discussing anyone with a disfigurement. While Jackie Bell was turned away, he stared sidelong at her full blouse. He grew a calculating look and sucked in a breath to flatten his soft belly. He saw Linda looking and smiled.

A true creep, she thought.

"How much longer are you going to be with us, Miss Lopes?" asked Colonel Parker.

"I'll stay in the area for another week on this initial visit," Linda said.

She would be working with local Thai government officials, ostensibly to observe their foodstuff-distribution networks, but also to set up a dialogue with certain key civilians. She'd work quietly with contacts across the field from the U.S. Air Force flying unit: with the Thai base commander to determine who might be asking questions about U.S. military matters, at the Air America compound to establish a radio listening post. Shortly she would have a local information net established here, as she already had in the areas surrounding the other American military bases. Within three months she wanted to have a good idea of every possible source of trouble that might emerge for the 355th Tactical Fighter Wing. If she was fortunate, she might even get a lead on enemy agents they believed were reporting on base activities.

"I'll leave next Monday," she told Colonel Parker.

"Will you be visiting often?"

"Monthly, once I get everything set up. At first it will be more often. If you don't have room for me here, I can find something in Nakhon Sawan."

Nakhon Sawan was the provincial capital, located fifty miles to the northwest.

"No need. Since you'll be in and out, I'll tell the base commander to permanently assign you the guest trailer you're occupying now. We're getting more and more facilities built, and there's plenty of room for our field-grade officers."

"That's most gracious of you," said Linda. She and Jackie occupied either end of one of the trailers reserved for majors and lieutenant colonels. Her GS-15 grade authorized Linda the same courtesies provided to an Air Force full colonel, but she wouldn't complain.

An idle thought struck her. She wondered how far from Lucky Anderson she'd been sleeping. It would be more difficult to drop off at nights, now that she knew he was so close.

Lyons interrupted her thoughts with his smooth voice. "We're honored to have you ladies here. We don't get many female visitors at Takhli, and it's tonic just to get a glimpse of a pretty American woman every now and then."

Creep, Linda thought again. He'd been here less than a week, yet he was acting like a deprived war hero.

He eyed Jackie. "How long will *you* be with us, Miss Bell?"

"Just a couple more nights, Colonel. But our camp's not far away, and we do have a telephone." Linda could have sworn that Jackie batted her eyes.

Tom Lyons was grinning appreciatively at the young Peace Corps administrator, and Jackie Bell seemed to be thoroughly enjoying herself. Linda decided to have a private talk with her about fighter pilots in general and the creep colonel in particular.

CHAPTER SEVEN

1345 Local—HQ Seventh Air Force, Tan Son Nhut Air Base, Saigon, South Vietnam

Lieutenant Colonel Pearly Gates

A hot message from CINCPAC, the four-star admiral in Hawaii, was waiting on Pearly's desk when he returned from lunch at the Tan Son Nhut Officers' Club.

```
SECRET
IMMEDIATE—TIME SENSITIVE
DTG: 250600Z APR 67
FM:  USCINCPAC CO CAMP H.M. SMITH, H.I.
TO:  CINCPACAF CC/XO/XP HICKAM AB, H.I.
     CINCPACFLT CO/XO PEARL HARBOR NS,
     H.I.
     7 AF CC/DO/XP/TACC SAIGON, RVN
     7 FLT CO/XO/FO
INFO: JCS/JTO PENTAGON
      USAF CC/XO PENTAGON
      USN CNO PENTAGON
      HQ TAC CC/XO LANGLEY AFB, VA
      TFWC CC/TA NELLIS AFB, NEV
      NOTS CO/VX-5 CHINA LAKE NAS, CAL
```

REF 1: (S) OPLAN CROSSFIRE ZULU
REF 2: 7AF CC (S) MSG DTD 230450Z APR
67
REF 3: 230535Z APR 57 MOSS/RYDER/ROMAN
(S) TELECON
REF 4: 240930Z APR 67 ROMAN/RYDER
(S) TELECON
SUBJECT: (SECRET) 7AF OPLAN CROSSFIRE
ZULU COMBAT TEST
1. (S) 7AF/CC IS AUTHORIZED TO STRIKE
TEST TGT (REF 1, PARA 12A(1)) AS
REQUESTED (REFS 2 & 3), TO INITIATE TEST
PHASE (PH 1) OF CROSSFIRE ZULU.
2. (S) WPNS LOADS FOR COMBAT TEST
W/BE AS PER (REF 1) PARA 4C(5), AT
DIRECTION OF (REF 4) CINCPACAF/CC.
3. (C) WPNS SETTING PARAMETERS &
DELIVERY PROFILES ARE AT DISCRETION
OF 7 AF/CC.
4. (U) SECDEF HAS DIRECTED THAT
MAXIMUM PRECAUTIONS BE TAKEN TO AVOID
HARM TO CIVILIANS AND FOREIGN
NATIONALS AND DAMAGE TO
UNAUTHORIZED TARGETS. MSN SUCCESS IS
TO BE CONSIDERED OF SECONDARY, REPEAT
"SECONDARY," IMPORTANCE TO THESE
CONSIDERATIONS.
5. (S) THIS AUTH IS FOR ONE-TIME, RPT "ONE-
TIME," TEST ONLY. TEST MAY BE CONDUCTED
N.E.T. 26 APR & N.L.T. 28 APR AT
DISCRETION OF 7AF/CC. STRIKE ACFT
ARE AUTH TO ENTER HANOI RESTRICTED
ZONE FOR PURPOSES OF TEST ONLY.
6. (C) RESULTS OF TEST W/BE REPORTED
SOONEST TO SENDER AND ALL
ADDRESSEES VIA CLASSIFIED COURIER.
7. (S) UPON EVALUATION OF COMBAT TEST
RESULTS, DECISION W/BE RENDERED
WHETHER TO PROCEED WITH PHASE TWO
(SUSTAINED AERIAL STRIKES) OR PERFORM
FURTHER TESTING.
8. (C) FOR NELLIS & CHINA LAKE: FOR
THIS PROJECT, USAF AND USN HAVE

```
AGREED THAT TFWC IS ASSIGNED AS LEAD
WPNS TEST AGENCY, WITH SUPPORT BY VX-5
AS REQUIRED. DIRECT CONTACT WITH 7AF
IS ENCOURAGED FOR DURATION OF
CROSSFIRE ZULU. SUPPORTING TEST
PROJECTS ARE ASSIGNED PRIORITY 1B BY
DIRECTION OF JCS.
9. (U) FOR 7AF/CC: GOOD HUNTING.
SECRET
```

Using a copy of the OPlan to check the referenced paragraphs, Pearly interpreted the message. They'd been authorized to start the test phase of the bridges campaign, to strike the Paul Doumer bridge on a one-time basis, as per General Moss's request.

General Roman, commander of PACAF, had personally called the admiral and suggested the weapons load. He looked it up and grimaced. For the initial test the Thuds would be carrying AGM-12 Bullpups, the air-to-ground missiles both General Moss and Colonel Parker had not wanted. General Moss's staff could dictate the tactics to be used to deliver the Bullpups. Moss would likely delegate the formulation of specific tactics to the flying units involved.

As a CYA measure, they'd included the standard executive directive to avoid injuries to civilians and foreign nationals.

The timing window for the air strike would start tomorrow, Wednesday, and would continue through Friday. General Moss would likely opt to strike as soon as possible to minimize any possible effects from the security leak.

The test facilities at Nellis, as well as the weapons specialists at China Lake, would be made available to them. That was good news, because Pearly wanted every possible edge, *and* he wanted to know more about the smart bomb project the captain from Nellis had told him about. He felt a tingling sensation run along his spine. The campaign was his idea. With the approval from the brass the OPlan had taken a grandiose flavor, but . . . it was still his baby, and he must be mentally prepared for the losses that would surely come.

He carefully replaced the red cover atop the secret message and tried to capture the attention of the WAF admin sergeant who was talking on her telephone.

"Call the general's office and see if you can . . ."

She shook her head. "It's General Moss's secretary on the line, Colonel. He's yelling for you to get up there *pronto*."

Pearly nodded and absently pushed his glasses back onto the bridge of his nose, gathered the message and rose. "I'm on my way."

The WAF staff sergeant hung up her phone. "His secretary says he's *definitely* not in a pleasant mood."

Pearly nodded absently, thinking about the Bullpup missiles that had been directed in the message. General Moss had said they were the last thing he'd want to use on a big bridge smack in the middle of the Hanoi defenses. He'd personally called the Deputy for Operations at Hickam to try to get them to think differently, but PACAF XO was General Roman's protégé, and like Roman, he was another bomber general, and he had obviously not listened.

Fucking bomber people, Pearly thought as he went out the door and down the hall. He wondered how he'd ever gotten along with them before, when he'd been one of them.

As he hurried up the stairs, he girded himself with mental armor for the discussion with General Moss.

1420 Local—Bach Mai Hospital, Hanoi, DRV

Colonel Xuan Nha

Boredom was Xuan's principal enemy, and to fill his hours, he exercised his mind.

Xuan Nha was a short, barrel-chested man, handsome if one disregarded the sharp sparrow's nose. He was purposeful, educated, and intelligent, and without doubt the most knowledgeable man in the Democratic Republic regarding the employment of sophisticated defenses. He'd been the key figure in the establishment of the highly successful rocket forces.

Yet for the past several weeks, Colonel Xuan Nha had been slowly returning from the brink of death.

His right eye had been exploded from its socket and both eardrums punctured by awful overpressures, and his left arm had been severed at the elbow by a cannon round, all within bewildering seconds during a bombing-and-strafing attack on the rocket control van he'd taken command of.

Those, and the fire-charred flesh of his legs and torso, had given him intense pain for the past weeks. The doctors at Bach Mai hospital had not believed he could endure it. His hardy body had proved them wrong. But though he was now healing and a number of bandages had been removed to allow the skin to be exposed to the healing air, the pain, while diminished, remained constant. Those portions of his scorched body exposed to the air felt as if they were crawling with insects. The doctors said that was a part of the healing process. He'd told them he was ready to endure the removal of his cocoon of bandages from his burned torso, but the doctors would not allow it, and each time he moved, he felt as if something in there were tearing. Sometimes blood would seep through a portion of bandage, for there was no skin to keep it from happening.

He waited and played mind games as he slowly healed.

He was a far different man than he'd been only a few months before. Then he'd been confident and sure, knowing how to use just the right mixture of terror and cajolery to get the most from his technical warriors in the People's Army, ready to make any sacrifice for the glory of the party . . . and himself. But he'd changed. Not because of the wounds. Injuries and even death were to be expected in his profession, and he was not a cowardly man. He'd been taught that politics were more deadly to an officer of the Vietnamese People's Army than any enemy.

If he was given the chance to return to his military duties, and he would work relentlessly to do so, he would never place his trust in anything, not his superiors or subordinates or even his own abilities, without first measuring the political impact.

His wife Li Binh had visited once, but he remembered it only vaguely because of the pain. When he'd become lucid, there had been two visits by Tran Van Ngo, the lieutenant colonel he'd once groomed to take his place. Tran was commandant of Thai Nguyen Area Defenses and a busy man, but he had taken time to visit and whisper the sad state of things since Colonel Wu had been appointed in Xuan Nha's place.

The rocket forces were in utter disarray due to lack of direction, like a group of ships with wildly fluctuating rudders, and radar control of the interceptors was even more dismal.

"What can I do?" Tran Van Ngo had asked.

Xuan Nha had only shaken his head sadly, for he knew no appropriate response.

So the mind games had begun. And during the long periods of idleness, Xuan Nha had thought of the quickest and most efficient ways to repair the networks of defenses. There was little chance he would be able to implement the changes, but he thought of them anyway.

Colonel Nguyen Wu, the ambitious nephew of his wife, was now filling his former position at the head of the radars-and-rocket forces, and until Wu was gone, there would be no chance of his returning, and no chance for the improvements he had in mind.

His communications officer, Lieutenant Quang Hanh, had been wounded at his side in the control van and now recuperated from burns and a mangled leg in a crowded ward not far from Xuan Nha's room. He was scheduled to be released shortly. Each day he dutifully hobbled down the hospital hall to visit and tell him what he'd heard during his family's visits, and from faithful reading of *Nham Dan*, the party newspaper. Thus Xuan Nha knew a bit of what was happening on the outside, but not nearly enough. He wished Li Binh would visit, for she was a fount of information, but his messages to her went unanswered.

But that hot Tuesday afternoon things were changed, and were never again the same.

He'd once known Quon well, yet he was surprised when the fighter pilot came into his room and stared down at him, a grim expression on his face.

"So the great legend visits," croaked Xuan Nha. His larynx had been damaged, and his voice came out in a rasp. The doctors said it would always be like that.

Quon leaned against the bed. "When can you return to work?"

Xuan Nha grimaced. "It is my stomach and chest. The skin was burned away, so there is nothing holding it all together except scar tissue, and that forms slowly. I will be a long time healing." His doctors said *if* he healed, but Xuan Nha was an optimist.

Quon eyed the bandages encasing Xuan's torso.

"I can walk," said Xuan Nha. "Not fast, but if I am very careful, I can endure it for a short time. The Americans won that skirmish, Quon."

"The article in *Nham Dan* said you destroyed a dozen Mee air pirates before they were lucky enough to find you."

"And they say you have destroyed two dozen Mee fighters, but that you are too modest to claim them all."

"Do you doubt the party newspaper?"

"Never," Xuan rasped.

Quon cocked his head inquisitively. "I hoped I might find you ready to return to duty, Xuan Nha. The defenses have suffered greatly since you left us."

Hope fluttered momentarily, then abruptly subsided. "My wife's nephew is in control of all that now," he said finally. "You must speak to him if you wish for improvement."

Quon eyed Xuan Nha. "I would much rather deal with you. Nguyen Wu will be removed from his position, and I would like you to return to duty."

Xuan Nha's heart pumped faster. Quon was well connected with both the general staff and the party. Even the Enlightened One had congratulated him on his patriotism and selfless contributions to the Republic. Could he do it?

"Will you help me, Xuan Nha?"

He pondered, not wishing to speak rashly. This was a political move, and Xuan had been betrayed by party politics. Finally he said, "The doctors say I must stay here for a long time. They worry about infections if I leave."

"Does it concern you that I plan to have Colonel Wu removed from his position?"

Xuan Nha sucked a breath. Although Wu had connections in the party, Quon could easily challenge Wu's authority. But Li Binh was squarely behind her nephew, and he doubted that even Quon could match her power. He was certain he could not match her manipulations.

"I have just come from General Dung's office," Quon said. "He agrees that steps must be taken to improve the defenses. Nguyen Wu must go." Quon related what had happened when the Americans had attacked Hoa Lac and Kep air bases, and then, more haltingly, what had happened to his son.

Xuan Nha expressed his sympathy.

Quon's eyes narrowed bitterly in response, so Xuan Nha steered the conversation to other things. "What about Li Binh?" he asked. "My wife is powerful, Quon, and she supports her nephew totally."

"And you?"

Xuan Nha paused. He wanted to agree with Quon, yet he was fearful of Li Binh's vengeance. He tried to explain. "My wife will not allow harm to come to her nephew. Beware of her, Quon, for she is powerful and her anger can be awesome."

Quon smiled. "Li Binh is in Paris, coordinating a series of meetings with American diplomats."

"Ahhh. I did not know," Xuan Nha said. "We . . . have not been talking recently."

"I believe she *talks* with your nephew," said Quon, and there was a glint in his eye. "I regret to tell you this, but it is best coming from a fellow warrior. It is widely rumored that your wife and her nephew are sharing more than is respectable."

Xuan Nha felt dismay. He'd had suspicions even before he'd been wounded, but each time they surfaced, he'd rejected them because of what he knew about Nguyen Wu.

Soon after Wu had come to work for Xuan, his driver had told him that Wu enjoyed sex with men. Such behavior was casually accepted among Southeast Asian cultures and not discouraged by field commanders whose men might be without women for extended periods. But Sergeant Ng had told him that Nguyen Wu liked *only* men, and Xuan had believed him, for periodically the gnarled old sergeant would himself single out a young soldier for his use.

Yet however unlikely, somehow Xuan knew that what Quon said was true.

He paused for a moment to allow the churning in his stomach to subside. "Still," he said, "I cannot return to my office until the burns heal."

"But you will help me?"

He spoke carefully. "I will not stop you." Then Xuan told the fighter pilot about the things he'd been thinking of while he'd lain there, how the network could be reinstituted by establishing regional control centers at Phuc Yen and Kien An, both receiving inputs from the other and the midrange acquisition radars as well, and to coordinate interceptors, AAA and rocket batteries alike. Somewhat like his old Wisdom system, but not as sophisticated. Then he began to list the equipment and personnel they would need.

Quon interrupted. "We cannot allow foreigners to control our forces. Wu said the party would not allow it, and *there* I believe him."

"Then we will use the Vietnamese pilot controllers we trained at the Wisdom complex. They were preparing to take over when Wisdom was bombed and destroyed."

He realized that Quon only half understood what he was saying. "When you have . . . ah . . . worked things out with my nephew, bring Lieutenant Colonel Tran Van Ngo to me. He is commandant of Thai Nguyen Area Defenses. I will explain it all to him, and he will understand. Tran should be placed in charge."

"Only temporarily, and only if you agree to work closely and provide him with advice. I trust you, Xuan Nha, but I do not trust any other of your rocket people."

"You must move quickly with Wu, before my wife returns from Paris."

"Tomorrow it shall be done. I have the assurance of General Dung. Things are critical, Xuan Nha." Then Quon told him about the intelligence report that warned of a campaign against the bridges, and the Americans' bombing of Kep instead.

"Was the intelligence report about the bridges from a reliable source?"

"The best, a source so sensitive that very few know about it."

Xuan Nha remembered being told by Li Binh of it. A Mee journalist relayed secrets provided by an American serviceman assigned to a Saigon headquarters.

Quon continued, "Last week Wu and Colonel Trung prepared to defend the bridges by placing tremendous numbers of rocket-and-artillery batteries around them. Now they are convinced the Americans have changed their minds and that the same defenses should be moved to the air bases. We do not know whom to believe."

Xuan Nha thought hard before answering, remembering first what Li Binh had told him about the reliability of the intelligence source code-named Peacemaker, and then about his knowledge of the Western mind. He motioned vaguely toward his bandaged torso. "I feel it in my chest, Quon. It was a diversion. If they had attacked the big air bases at Phuc Yen or Kien An, it might be different."

Quon looked at him thoughtfully.

"If they cut our supply routes to Hanoi by destroying the key bridges, it will become a critical matter. Now they are trying to get us to move our defenses so they can do it."

"Perhaps," said Quon. He did not appear convinced. "I would hate to be the one to suggest that we keep our defenses at the bridges if they came to bomb Phuc Yen."

"The Mee politicians authorized them to attack the auxiliary air bases only. They are still frightened of bombing airfields with civil aircraft present. Trust me, Quon, for I've grown to know how they think. Advise Colonel Trung and General Luc that the guns must remain around the bridges. Have them bring even more. If the Mee attack on the first bridge is very costly and unsuccessful, they will think twice before continuing such a campaign. It would be foolhardy for them to continue to attack the bridges in the face of a thousand guns."

"We heard through our source that they may use air-to-ground guided rockets."

"Even better!" exclaimed Xuan. "The Mee must fly predictable paths to succeed with their guided rockets, which will be perfect for our gunners." He nodded, gaining enthusiasm. "Have them keep the artillery at the bridges. Protect other targets with rocket batteries and interceptors until the Mee attack the first bridge. If you can keep them from being successful on the first one, you will stop the campaign. The Mee politicians will force them to stop."

"I hope you are right."

"I am." Xuan felt confident.

Quon stared evenly, then nodded. "I will speak with the generals."

A flush of exuberance washed over Xuan Nha. It was like old times, when they'd listened and heeded his advice.

Then Quon told him about the Mee pilots who'd murdered his son. "I want them, Xuan Nha, especially the flight leader. He knew it was my son's aircraft and ordered the attack."

Xuan Nha doubted the Mee could single out any particular person for death, but Quon insisted they'd done precisely that and would not debate the point. After a thoughtful pause Xuan decided to help Quon in this matter, which required no political danger. Revenge was a powerful emotion that he understood well.

He mused over Quon's description of the blue-tailed American aircraft. "Some of the Thunder planes have squadron markings like that. I have seen various colors on aircraft we shot down from the base called Takhli in Thailand."

"Which ones have the blue?"

Xuan's memory was flawless, but it took a moment to bring up that particular tidbit. "There is the Dragon Squadron. They have the large letters *RU* in the middle of the vertical stabilizer and yellow paint at the top. The Lancer Squadron is red, I believe, and the letters are . . . *RK*. And the Pig Squadron? Yes, their color is blue, and the letters are *RM*. You can verify all this by asking the guards at Hoa Lo Prison. They get such information from prisoners when they interrogate them."

"The Pig Squadron?"

"Their squadron emblem shows an animal that looks like a pig with fangs, so that is what our intelligence people call it. Actually, the Tay raise ferocious-looking dogs that look like that, but our intelligence people have never seen them. Ask the prison interrogators about the Pig Squadron. You can find out many things by speaking with them."

Quon listened intently.

"Perhaps you can even learn the name of the man who led that particular flight of Thunder planes. Was anyone shot down in the attack on Kep?"

"None," Quon said bitterly.

"Then have the interrogators interview the next pilot they get from Takhli. The prison officials are only lieutenants and sergeants and are fearful of anyone with rank. Pass them your request, and they will get the information."

"I will tell them to question the next Mee prisoner who flew a Thunder plane with a blue tail." A bitter expression grew on Quon's face. "And I shall speak with him myself."

When Quon had left him, Xuan continued with his mind games. He willed the outrage over Nguyen Wu and Li Binh to diminish until it simmered in a recess of his mind. There were important duties to accomplish. His time was returning. In the meanwhile he must carefully wend his way through a maze of intrigue. With General Dung involved, perhaps Quon *could* deal with Nguyen Wu. Xuan Nha would distance himself from such activity, yet remain in a position to prosper from it. Once he'd regained his place within the People's Army, he would continue to be cautious. He had learned that lesson.

0915 Local—Regional Hospital, Travis AFB, California

Captain Benny Lewis

The colonel from the Tactical Fighter Weapons Center at Nellis telephoned him in his hospital room.

"How're you coming along?" asked the man he would be working for.

"I talked with the flight surgeon again, and he says they may fly me to Nellis as early as next Monday."

Benny didn't add that the flight surgeon said he'd be assigned not to work, but to be an in-patient at the Nellis Hospital. He'd be fighting that dragon when he got there, to be changed to out-patient status as quickly as possible so he could come and go freely from the hospital and perhaps be assigned to limited duty.

"That's awfully quick. How's the back?" asked the colonel.

"It's a lot better now," answered Benny. He fibbed a little. It was not really much better. Of course it was hard to tell, when your time was spent flat on your back.

"So you think you'll be ready for limited work in a week or so."

Benny gambled, "It shouldn't be *much* longer than that, sir."

The colonel paused, as if trying to interpret what he meant. He'd known Benny Lewis before and knew he was both a die-hard optimist and a dedicated workaholic. Finally he said, "We're reorganizing. I'm putting you in charge of one of the new SEA liaison teams."

"Sounds *great*, Colonel."

"You'll have two guys working for you. One knows you. You remember a young pilot named Moods Diller."

"Sure," said Benny. "He was a lieutenant in our air-to-ground flight at the Fighter Weapons School." The FWS was the graduate school for top Air Force fighter jocks.

Benny remembered Moods Diller as being extremely bright and totally captivated with advanced technologies, convinced that the magic of electronics and computers would change the face of air power. Moods was an unorthodox officer who cared not at all about military niceties, who became so involved with his various schemes that he'd forget the world around him existed. Some of his fellow pilots mistook this for moodiness, for he'd grow silent and not answer their greetings or questions, so they'd tagged him with the nickname. The fact that Moods had an IQ of 175 impressed few of them.

"Moods is a captain now," said the colonel. "He's flying an F-4 to Travis this morning so he can talk with some engineers there in the bay area. I asked him to stop by and tell you about your new team and what you'll be doing. I think you'll find the work interesting."

Benny felt elated. Not only did the job sound promising, he'd shortly be meeting with a friend who could talk knowledgeably about flying airplanes. The hospital staff was an okay group, but he missed his own kind.

"I'm looking forward to seeing him, sir."

"Another thing. Have you had a chance to look at the promotion list?"

"No, sir." Benny didn't yet have the required minimum time for promotion to major, so he hadn't been overly interested. In two years, when his turn came, he *thought* he'd have a fair crack at making it.

The colonel tried to tell him he was on the list.

"I . . . uh . . . think that's a mistake sir. I don't have the time-in-grade yet."

"You're on the below-the-zone list, and you'll pin on the oak leaves sometime in June or July. Congratulations."

Benny was stunned. He was well regarded in the fighter community, but he hadn't expected this. Two years below the zone? The majority of the one-year below-the-zoners were bomber pilots. Less than 2 percent of eligible captains made major two years below the zone, and most of those were headquarters pukes. Were things changing?

But the colonel was not finished. "You also have some medals waiting for you. They'll be properly presented when you get here."

"They already gave me my Purple Heart, Colonel." A local congressman had walked through with the hospital commander, doling Purple Hearts out of a box and giving a silly spiel about it being a pity they'd had to go to Vietnam to fight somebody else's war.

"How about two Silver Star medals?" asked the colonel.

"Two Silver Stars?" *Jesus!* He didn't even *know* anyone with two Silver Stars.

"And three Distinguished Flying Crosses . . . so far. Every

couple of days personnel calls up to tell us you got another medal approved, so there'll probably be more. Right now the total is two Silver Stars, three DFCs, eight Air medals, and a Bronze Star for your work as a flight commander. When you get here, the general will be laying on a parade to honor you and a couple other guys who just got back from SEA."

Although he was more excited about the medals than was modest, Benny would rather have had eyeteeth pulled than endure a military parade.

He had an immediate excuse. "I don't think the flight surgeons are going to allow me to stand at attention for that long," he tried.

"Then we'll strap you to the flagpole and raise your hand when it's time to salute. The two-star here wants a parade," said the colonel.

"Yes, sir." His head spun from all the revelations.

They talked a while longer before Benny hung up and lay there, mind whirring as the rawboned nurse he called Lady Dracula angrily disconnected the telephone extension.

"If you think you're going to be returning to work in the next couple of weeks, you're *wrong*," she chided.

"You were listening?"

"Just to your end," she said. "I keep trying to tell you your back injury is serious, but still I don't think you understand."

"I'm improving fast."

She shook her head and gave him a knowing look. "Not as fast as you're telling the flight surgeons. By the way, you've got a visitor."

He smiled. "Mrs. Stewart?"

Julie Stewart visited every day she had off.

"Nope. She said she was flying today, remember? This time it's a Captain Diller." Then, totally out of her bitchy role, she lowered her voice and casually asked, "Is he single?"

"He was when I saw him last." He could not visualize Moods Diller as a married man.

She left and a few minutes later returned with Moods, with his long, serious face and nervous air. The nurse had obviously prebriefed him, for he very carefully kept his distance.

"Good t'see you," he said. Moods Diller spoke in unique,

choppy machine-gun bursts, as if his mind were racing ahead of his ability to express himself. He also shortened words and eliminated those he considered unnecessary to convey his meaning.

The nurse lingered, smiling serenely as she busied around the room with minor chores usually left to hospital techs. Moods didn't notice. Benny did, for there was something very different about her, something that transformed her plainness.

Benny grinned up at his old cohort. "I hear we're going to be working together."

Moods made a lopsided grin. "Together as captain and major can get.... Dammit, Benny ... just when I thought I was catchin' up, you get promoted."

"I just heard about it myself."

"Congratulations."

"Thanks."

Moods paid the slender nurse no attention as she flitted about the room. Finally she reached in front of him and *accidentally* brushed against him.

"Excuse me." Nice smile.

"Sure." Moods finally took notice.

Lady Dracula regarded Benny, but the inhaled breath and expanded chest were for his visitor. "If you need anything at all, just push the buzzer," she said in a melodic tone he hadn't heard before. Then she turned her smile on Moods, said, "Nice t' meetcha," and glided from the room on her skinny legs.

Moods watched her go. "Nice lookin'." Moods's tastes were often peculiar to himself.

Benny felt he should say something complimentary. "She's dedicated," he said.

"You're first of th' fighter mafia t' return t' the States," Moods said abruptly. "The others're still in Southeast Asia."

Moods Diller, he remembered, switched subjects easily. You had to stay on your toes to keep up.

"Yeah," said Benny, "we were together at Takhli for a while. Then Glenn got shot down, and I *almost* finished my combat tour."

Four of them had worked closely together at Nellis for two years prior to leaving to fly combat: Lucky Anderson, Glenn Phillips, Max Foley, and Benny. Although he wasn't part of their group, when they needed heavy brainpower for a project, they'd called on Moods. He'd always acted honored, because the four pilots in the fighter mafia had been well regarded by both the brass and their fellow fighter jocks.

Moods lifted an eyebrow. "North Vietnamese . . . released Glenn Phillips's name on their latest POW list."

"Hey, shit hot! That's *great* news."

They spoke about Glenn and several other mutual friends who'd been killed or captured in SEA during the past months, then became lost in private remembrances.

"Anyway," said Moods finally, "y' made it. . . . Too tough t' kill."

Benny remembered the ballsy way Bear Stewart had exited life.

"Tough helps," he said, "but it's not enough. My backseater was plenty tough, but he's dead."

"Yeah, I heard," said Moods. "Major Sam Hall came through on his way t' Luke . . . down there checking out in F-4's . . . tol' us about it at th' bar. Said your bear left a pregnant wife b'hind. Said he hated it . . . said she's a good lady."

Benny nodded, started to add that he saw her almost daily, but decided against it. It might not look good, with her being a recent widow and people perhaps not realizing there was nothing going on between them.

"That's bad," said Moods, "leaving a wife 'n' kid on their own like that."

"She'll be okay," Benny said firmly.

"I hear you split, you 'n' your wife."

"It was a long time coming," said Benny.

"Women're jealous of airplanes," said Moods. He nodded at his wisdom.

After a pause and still being unable to decipher what Moods had meant, Benny changed the subject. "What's this new office supposed to be like?"

Moods told him they were setting up liaison teams at Nellis to interface with the guys flying over North Vietnam. One team concentrated on air-to-air to help the F-4 pilots, and another assisted the Wild Weasels with the SAMs. The third one was theirs. "You'll be boss . . . air-to-ground team," said Moods.

"Sounds good." Although he'd killed a MiG, and although he'd been a damned good Wild Weasel pilot, Benny's forte was dropping bombs. His friends said he had velvet hands, that he could thread a needle with a bomb from 5,000 feet.

"Message came in las' night," said Moods. "Our first task. Supposed t' help on some kinda combat test . . . set up an OPlan. . . . Prove they c'n knock out a big bridge in Hanoi."

"The Doumer bridge?"

"That's th' one. . . . Dumb shits're gonna try AGM-12's in a high-threat environment."

"General Moss knows better than that." Moss had been their two-star boss at Nellis, which was the reason their foursome had originally been called Moss's Fighter Mafia before he'd pinned on his third star and left for Saigon.

"Anyway, OPlan's name's CROSSFIRE ZULU."

"You'll have to carry the ball until I get there."

Moods nodded. "Colonel already sent th' message namin' me contact officer."

"There's three of us in the office?"

"You . . . civilian analyst to crunch numbers . . . me. We're supposed t' end up with four, five more pilots but that may take a while. . . . Ever' swingin' dick experienced fighter jock that's not in a critical position's on his way to combat." Moods grinned. "That's how you got t' be boss. . . . Down t' the sick an' lame." Moods grinned.

"Thanks a lot. What's *your* job?"

"Worker bee. Attached t' th' test-and-eval squadron for flyin' . . . keep up with anything's being developed might give our guys the edge in combat . . . fly on the tests . . . work on projects like this CROSSFIRE ZULU thing."

"Sounds good."

"Maybe. Guys at TAC headquarters hold an awfully close rein on us at Nellis. The President and the SecDef micromanage the air war . . . tell our pilots what they *can't* do . . . targets they *can't* hit. . . . New buzz word's 'command 'n control.' Ever' headquarters, large 'n' small, wants in the act. . . . We fart, they ask why our gas is odious. . . . We try to work out tactics 'n' develop weapons for combat, but TAC keeps their nose in everything. . . . Roll up your flight-suit sleeves on a hot day, someone says t' roll 'em down 'cause someone at TAC likes 'em like that."

Tactical Air Command, with its headquarters at Langley Air Force Base, Virginia, was commanded by a four-star. Nellis only had a two-star, so they were often overridden by headquarters pukes who flew desks at Langley.

But Moods bitched entirely too much.

"It's always been like that," said Benny. "We'll work around 'em like we did before."

"Worse 'n before, Benny.... There's only th' one war, and ever'one wants to make the most of it like they're the only ones with answers. Ever' time we give a high priority to a project th' guys flying combat need ... sure as hell someone at TAC will downgrade it 'n' push their own idea. Then the bomber people running things at the Pentagon get pissed off 'n' say something else's more important. It's fucked up royal, like nobody gives a shit about th' jocks over gettin' their asses shot off."

"Sounds shitty, but not abnormal. We'll make it work." Benny tried to remain upbeat.

Moods shook his head. "Wanta hear shitty? Last week they presented two DFCs to a captain just back from flyin' a tour in F-100's. Nex' day th' promotion list came out ... wasn't selected for major, so he's being booted out of th' Air Force."

"Get off it, Moods. Save the sad stories for the chaplain."

Without changing his tone, Moods fired three measured machine-gun bursts, "Th' skinny nurse fuck? ... I like 'em thin so I c'n feel what they got.... She married?"

Moods Diller was not the most romantic person in the world.

"The answers are *I dunno ... that's interesting ... no.* Anything else?"

Moods shook his head, looking analytical. His mind worked in strange and disjointed ways.

Before Moods could take off in yet another direction, Benny asked, "Are we going to get to go over and fly with the guys in the combat zone?"

"That's th' good news. Every couple months we c'n send someone over to fly a few missions ... keep our hand in so we'll know what they're doin' and how we can help."

Benny nodded and hoped he wouldn't have to wait long before getting back into the cockpit.

"But there's paperwork ever' damn time we wanna send someone over."

Moods complained about filling out request forms until Benny stopped him by asking, "What are you working on that brings you here?"

Moods lowered his voice. "You won't believe it."

"Try me."

"Terminally guided bombs, Benny, so accurate we c'd use a single sortie . . . knock th' wick off a candle."

There'd been such dreams since the first pilots in biplanes had tried dive-bombing through flak.

"What kind of CEP are you talking about?" "Circular error probability" was the average miss distance.

"Zero. I'm talking about bombs hitting *precisely* where we want 'em to. Things'll damn near think for themselves, Benny, so I call 'em *smart bombs*. . . . You just fly along straight and level, pickle 'em off 'n' go home, 'cause you'll know the target'll be destroyed."

"Standoff weapons?" That was what they called munitions that could be released beyond the range of hostile fire.

"Standoff *smart* weapons. So accurate, we'll never hafta go after th' same target twice."

"Have you got hardware?"

Moods deflated a little. "Not yet . . . won't be long. Right now a few guys 'n' me're trying to iron out the bugs on paper . . . but we're buildin' a workin' model."

"What kind of guidance are you talking about?"

"Two kinds. I gotta Texas team 'n' a California team . . . both workin' on their own thing." Moods started to add more, then looked around and shook his head. "Wait'll you get to Nellis. We keep it classified right up there with nukes. . . . When I tell you 'bout it, you'll understand. They'll be that accurate, Benny."

Benny was interested. Their friends were having to dive-bomb through flak and SAMs and then go back again. Numerous sorties were often required to knock out a single target.

"When will you be ready to put one of your smart bombs together?"

Moods calculated, then whooshed a breath. "Dunno. . . . Not long if we c'n get the proper priority, but like I tol' ya . . . that's not easy. Hardest part's gettin' th' brass to listen, if you c'n imagine. Be easier when we get a couple prototype kits put together."

"Kits?"

"It's a modular concept . . . sort of like building blocks

that let you mix and match 'n' build your own bombs. Each kit'll contain two modules we'll attach to th' bombs."

Benny had difficulty trying to envision it. "What size bombs?" he asked.

"Doesn't matter. Any bomb you choose. You pick th' right size bomb for a particular job ... bolt on th' module with movable fins, then screw on another module that provides terminal guidance and fuzing."

"A homing bomb," Benny said. "Why not use missiles?"

"There's more bang in bombs ... and they're a lot cheaper. I'm using ever' bit of math I ever learned, and I got a master's degree in math, Benny ... still a lotta problems with it ... biases and keeping the dam' things locked on to th' aim point ... things we're tryin' to anticipate before we build 'em for testing."

Benny was utterly baffled. "Have you live-dropped anything?"

Moods sighed again. "Not yet. It's hard t' get funds, and ... ah ... not *everyone's* convinced they'll work. We'll need your support 'n' more, we're gonna continue with it." He raised an eyebrow. "When you think they'll let you outa here?"

"I'm trying for next Monday."

Moods looked at him lying there flat on his back and not moving and cocked his head to emphasize a puzzled look. "The nurse tol' me more like a couple months."

"She's a pessimist. I'm working some angles."

Moods glanced at the door. "I'd like t' work on *her* angles." That, for Moods, was romantic talk. "Know when she gets off?"

"Any time now. She's on the early shift."

Moods opened his mouth. . . .

"She lives in an apartment in Fairfield. Alone."

"You after her?"

Benny almost shuddered. *After Lady Dracula?* "No."

Moods glanced at his watch. "I'm meetin' some guys at Stanford in a couple of hours ... maybe she'll come along." Moods raised a hand. "I'll drop by in th' morning before I crawl back in my trusty jet."

"You flying with anyone?" The F-4 was a two-place bird.

"Guy from procurement. Th' general sprung a few bucks from his discretionary fund ... enough so we might interest some Stanford engineering support."

"Then you've got *some* support for your project."

"Not enough. I'm serious about this modular smart bomb bein' the answer for th' future. . . . Preach to ever' general I c'n get into a classified briefing room." He nodded at Benny. "Maybe if you'd been carrying one of *my* bombs . . . you wouldn't be layin' here like a fuckin' radish."

"Maybe."

"I think this CROSSFIRE ZULU campaign's a perfect vehicle to try out my smart bombs. . . . I'm pushing it with th' Seventh Air Force project officer."

Benny should have picked up on that, and later he would regret not doing so. But his mind was on other things.

"When you drop by tomorrow," he said, "I should know more about when I'll be getting out of here."

"Don't press it, Benny. Soon's I heard you were in th' pipeline, lobbied to have you put in charge of the team . . . we need you. But don't try to get outa th' hospital too early . . . not if it might screw you up later on."

"Don't worry. I don't intend to do anything that might keep me off flying status a day longer than necessary. I like the extra hundred and eight-five a month, and I like to fly. I'll take care."

Moods nodded and waved a hand. "See you tomorrow."

"I'm looking forward to it. Good luck with your engineers."

Moods gave him a secretive look. "Electro-optics experts . . . work with lumens 'n' contrast 'n' background shadows . . . anything that'll show up on a videcon tube."

"What's a videcon tube?"

"Sensor for a television camera."

Benny narrowed his gaze. "Television?"

"Think it over. We'll talk when you get to th' office . . . see if you've figured it out."

"You've flipped your wig, Moods. Television?"

Moods Diller laughed. "Texas team's working with lasers."

Benny had never heard the word. "What's a laser?" he asked.

" 'Bye."

As if on cue the nurse popped in, the special smile glued to her face.

Moods cleared his throat and looked very seriously at

her. "Could I ... ah ... speak to you 'bout my friend here before I leave?"

"Sure," she said.

"In private?"

She smiled wider. "Of course."

CHAPTER EIGHT

Wednesday, April 26th, 0345 Local—Briefing Theater, Command Post, Takhli RTAFB, Thailand

Captain Manny DeVera

When the air tasking order had been received at 2100 the previous evening and fragmented to show their part of it, they'd called Max Foley, the wing-weapons officer. After he'd read it, he contacted Manny DeVera, for Manny was as close to an expert on the AGM-12 missile as they had at Takhli, and they'd been directed to use Bullpups to attack the Doumer bridge the next morning.

When Manny got to the command post, they'd talked about the hand-guided missiles at length, and the more they'd talked, the more they'd disliked the idea of using them for *any* target in a high-threat area. When they reread the tasking order, they found that the headquarters weaponeers had discouraged arguments by including the remark that the missile had been *designed* for point targets such as bridges, and its use had been *directed* by PACAF.

"Bullshit," Manny told Max. "They were designed for use against tanks and buildings, not for big bridges located in the middle of a bunch of guns and SAMs."

At 2300 Manny had stood by while Max Foley spoke on

the scrambler phone to the fighter duty officer at Seventh Air Force's Tactical Air Control Center. Max complained that the short-range, data-link-guided AGM-12 was good only for unprotected targets, for the pilots couldn't deliver them and take proper evasive action. He added that even if they were successful and hit the target, he wasn't convinced the small warhead would take down a sturdy structure like the Doumer bridge. The FDO told him to hang up and stand by for a response.

At 0015 they'd received a message from the Seventh Air Force Directorate of Intelligence pinpointing the critical stress points of spans near the northern and southern ends of the bridge. The message directed them to forward a detailed postmission report.

It was time to salute and execute, so Manny and Max had hurried to their quarters to get a couple hours of sleep, for both had volunteered to fly on the mission.

As the pilots filed into the briefing theater, they stared hard at the mission board.

It was again show-and-tell time for the 355th Tactical Fighter Wing, for again they'd been picked to fly a most dangerous mission. The pilots had seen the Doumer bridge as they'd set up to bomb other targets, had even used it for a visual reference. The big bridge spanning the Red River between Hanoi and Gia Lam would not be difficult to find. It was located smack in the midst of heavy defenses, however, and they didn't relish going there.

The briefings started early, because there was a lot for the pilots to discuss and digest.

Colonel B. J. Parker was mission commander, and he opened by stating the importance of the mission to higher headquarters, and quite possibly to the war effort. He looked out upon them proudly and said he'd assigned his best men to lead and fly this one.

They were briefed that the test was important, and that General Moss was "extremely interested" in the outcome.

Several of the more knowledgeable pilots muttered that the "important test" was a bunch of bullshit, for they didn't agree with the weapons selection.

The alpha strike force would include KC-135 tankers, F-105F Wild Weasels, F-4D Phantoms, a flak-suppression flight, and eight strike aircraft, called "shooters" in this instance.

Captains Holden and Watson, an experienced Wild Weasel crew from the 357th squadron, would lead their four-ship flight of two-seat Thuds, call sign Red Dog. They would enter the target area first and would rove about the periphery of Hanoi during the period of the strike, firing radar-homing Shrike missiles in broadsides to keep the SAM operators busy.

Two F-4D MiG-CAP flights from Ubon Air Base would provide escort, with one flight preceding and the other following the strike force. All MiG fighting would be left to the F-4's.

The F-105Ds would ingress to the target area at 18,000 feet in a twelve-ship formation and would feint toward another target before turning toward the Doumer bridge. Eight miles from the bridge the shooters would break off and descend to set up for their AGM-12 deliveries. The flak-suppression flight would continue for five more miles, then push over and dive-bomb their cluster bombs onto the guns to soften up the target before the shooters arrived.

Colonel B. J. Parker would lead the flak-suppression flight, call sign Trout. They'd drop CBU-24's on concentrations of guns along the banks of the Red River, one Thud concentrating on the northwest side of the bridge, another on the southwest, and so forth around the quadrants. They would be careful to release at the right altitude for optimum dispersion of the bomblets, for the recce photos showed large concentrations of guns.

As the eight shooters descended to 15,000, then to 10,000 feet, they would first swing south toward Hanoi, then around to the north, and one by one would break off to attack the target. Lucky Anderson would lead Tuna flight and would concentrate on knocking down one of the northern spans. Major Max Foley's Guppy flight would attack a southern span.

Lieutenant DeWalt took the podium and stretched a one-liner into a fifteen-minute harangue on bridge construction techniques. There were precisely twenty spans, he said, eight of which had been reinforced by dumping what appeared to be old vehicles into the water beside the pilings.

Few were interested, and the muttering in the room grew louder.

Annoyed that his words were being ignored and drowned out, DeWalt looked for support and found that B. J. Parker was holding his *own* side discussion. DeWalt concluded abruptly, repeating the direction from Seventh Air Force to aim for the critical stress points, the pilings over the deepest water.

Colonel Parker thanked him and said they'd now discuss the short, pudgy 570-pound star of today's show, the AGM-12.

Captain Manny DeVera, like Lucky Anderson and Max Foley, was a Fighter Weapons School graduate, but he'd also helped run the Bullpup missile program at the El Uotia gunnery range in Libya. He gave the pilots a thorough run-down on the AGM-12, describing its strengths and weaknesses, and everyone listened closely. They'd all sat through hours of simulator time, going through the Bullpup firing and tracking procedures, but Manny DeVera had actually launched and guided three of the things.

First he gave a brief description of the weapon. He explained how the data-link signal was transmitted from the aircraft and entered the missile's antenna, and caused the missile's fins to move and guide it. Then he talked about weapons delivery, saying that for best effectiveness they should set up at least three miles out and fly a straight-in, twenty-degree-dive attack. For *this* mission, since there were a hell of a lot of guns along the delivery track, which was southeast down the Red River, they would begin their runs at 10,000 feet, fly a thirty-degree dive, and release when they had a good sight picture, about 9,000 feet slant range from the target.

Max Foley interjected that it would be dangerous not to jink at all as they were diving, since the thirty-degree profile would make them very visible and vulnerable to the gomer defenses. But the shooters should jink *very little* between missile release and missile impact if they were to hit anything, because the Bullpup should remain between the aircraft and the target to receive proper steering corrections. The Bullpup's rocket motor burned brightly and would be easy to see. After motor burnout they'd see flares mounted on the fins and guide the bright dot into the bridge using a controller handle, giving *up-down-left-right* steering information.

"Just like you practiced in the simulator," said Manny.

Max and Manny tried to convey confidence, but few of the pilots were fooled. It was going to be damned dangerous to use the Bullpup missile in the high-threat area over Hanoi. More pleasing were their light and relatively aerodynamic configurations. Other than the Bullpup and its adapter, they would carry only a 650-gallon fuel tank on centerline and an ECM pod on the right outboard station.

Colonel B. J. Parker got up next and briefed that after delivering weapons, the flak suppressors and shooters would rejoin over Thud Ridge. Then he paused before telling his pilots to "kick 'em in the ass," as he sometimes did on tough ones, and sent them off to their individual flight briefings.

"Good briefing, Manny," Lucky said as the mission briefing broke up.

"I dunno, boss," said Manny. "I don't have a good feeling about this one."

Turk Tatro and Henry Horn, who were the second element of Tuna flight, waited for them near the doorway, and Lucky nodded in their direction. "Like B.J. said, we've got one edge. We've got good pilots flying this morning."

As he followed Lucky toward the door, Manny hoped to hell they and all the other "good pilots" would return. A sudden wash of apprehension swept over him, and he shuddered.

0718 Local—Route Pack Six, North Vietnam

Major Lucky Anderson

The Wild Weasels were beating up on the Hanoi SAM sites with salvo after salvo of Shrike missiles, and twice the MiG-CAP Phantoms had chased off MiGs, so thus far the Thuds had not been directly threatened. They flew at 18,000 feet as planned, easterly and directly toward the big MiG base at Phuc Yen.

"Probably scaring the shit out of the gomers," announced someone, for it was likely the North Vietnamese thought the target was their biggest air base. Lucky knew the someone was Turk Tatro, for he could never mask his heavy southern drawl.

Then B. J. Parker, flying at the forefront of the group, announced, *"This is Trout lead. Turning, now!"* and the Strike force abruptly banked right and rolled out on a heading of 140 degrees, toward a point just north of Hanoi, a colorful amoeba sprawling in the distance.

Abeam Phuc Yen, eight nautical miles from the bridge, it was Lucky's turn.

"*This is Tuna lead. Descend,* now!" he radioed, and both Tuna and Guppy flights nosed over into a rapid descent. A few seconds later Guppy disappeared behind as Max Foley led them into an S-turn for separation from Tuna.

It became the four of them. Lucky, Manny, Turk, and Henry Horn. Lucky looked his brood over carefully, feeling intense pride heightened by the surge of adrenaline that accompanied imminent danger. They were all jinking now that they were away from the collective protection of the gaggle, twisting and turning as they descended. Smoothly yet unpredictably, as the book said.

Through seventeen thousand feet.

Manny flew on his right wing, in perfect position. Turk and Henry Horn were to his left. It would come quickly now, but he felt his men were ready.

Sixteen thousand feet.

He turned hard right, toward the heart of Hanoi on another diversion feint, and they flew toward the largest buildings there. Two of them were headquarters for the NVA, intell said, and he hoped the bastards were sweating bullets or maybe shitting their pants.

Fifteen thousand feet, and he leveled.

His RHAW receiver rattled with a SAM indication, showing a LAUNCH light and making a squealing sound. He looked out, waited, then saw three missiles rising toward them, their fiery boosters still attached.

The brightly burning boosters dropped away into an eastern suburb of Hanoi.

"*Dumb shits're doin' our work for us,*" someone drawled, and Lucky wished Turk would stay off the radio with his comments. He'd speak with him about it when they landed.

As the flight paths of the SAMs were bending toward them, they crossed over the edge of Ho Tay Lake.

"*Tuna flight. Turn and descend,* now!" he called, then shoved the throttle forward, pulled the control stick hard left, and entered a steep dive.

A long moment later Turk Tatro called that the missiles were clear, and Lucky was damned happy he had this team with him. As they passed 11,000 feet, he began to level out, and as they reached 10,000, he looked right and saw the big bridge clearly.

"*Tuna lead's in,*" he called, and turned, leaving the others. He dived for the northern end of the bridge and was pleased when the gyro settled and read precisely thirty degrees.

He could see a couple of Thuds from Trout flight pulling up from their weapons deliveries. Their CBUs would be exploding among the guns. *Good timing,* he thought.

He was jinking smoothly, concentrating his vision on the northern end of the bridge and ignoring the random flak bursts. Not much longer now. He fingered the pickle button in anticipation.

The sky erupted, filling with fire and fury. Flak bursts so thick, it seemed there was no place left to fly. He heard Parker's flak suppressors calling on the radio, but whatever they'd dropped had little effect, because there were more explosions going off around and before him than he'd ever seen. Not even at Thai Nguyen had he seen such flak. He jinked harder.

"*Tuna two's in,*" called Manny DeVera, meaning he was turning toward the target.

"*Tuna lead has very heavy gunfire,*" Lucky radioed, and his voice was shrill. He could no longer see the target through the white blankets of popcorn, the red flashes, and the big gray and black bursts, which seemed to be everywhere.

"*Jesus . . .*" Manny's voice.

Lucky looked frantically for the obscured target.

"*Weeep, weeep, weeep . . .*"

Someone was down! He thought it might be DeVera, then heard Parker calling about his number three, so it was one of the flak suppressors. They were less vulnerable than the shooters, but one of them had been hit. *Damn!* he thought. How the hell were *they* supposed to make it?

"*Tuna three's in,*" called Turk Tatro's voice, not nearly as lazy as normal. The flak was an attention getter.

"*Weeep, weeep, weeep . . . ,*" the emergency beeper continued to wail.

"*Guppy lead is in hot,*" called Major Max Foley, although Tuna four hadn't yet turned in. The Guppys were going after the southern end of the big bridge, so that was okay.

Lucky strained and tried to see the target through the stuff, and he finally did. Too close. He pulled his wings level and pickled off the Bullpup. He felt it release, then saw the plume merge into his vision, wondered how *it* could not be hit by the flak. He steered and corrected with the controller handle.

"Tuna four's in," called Henry Horn, hardly audible over the noise of the beeper and radio chatter.

A fireball. Lucky's missile had hit the bridge. And just after he saw the Bullpup's warhead explode, his Thud lurched and slewed sideways. He was hit.

"Guppy two's in," called Foley's wingman.

Lucky was able to overcome the yawing motion by using rudder. He glanced to his right as a new hole was punched through the wing joining several others already there. "Damn!" he shouted to himself.

"Weeep-weeep-weeep . . ."

His airplane was still flying, so he pulled hard to his left to get away from the terrible flak.

"Guppy three's in."

Another burst hit his Thud, and as he heard the muffled boom, a shard of shrapnel sliced a hole in his canopy and struck his headrest, jarring him violently.

"Damn!" he yelled again, and his adrenaline pumped even more wildly, but his voice was lost among the shrill call of the beeper, the jabbering on the radio, and the roaring sound from the canopy hole.

He flew free of the worst of it, and it was as if he'd emerged from a thunderstorm.

"Guppy four's in hot," could hardly be heard. Then he realized that a second beeper had joined the first one.

"Weeep-weeep, weeep-weeep, weeep-weeep . . ."

Whose? he wondered. He swiveled his neck back toward the inferno. The flak was so intense that he could make little sense of what was going on there. He saw that a Thud had broken off its attack early, and he could not fault the pilot. Manny DeVera?

Then he stared and saw that the span was still standing. He'd hit the damned thing squarely, but it was still standing!

Someone shouted excitedly on the radio, but through the wailing of the beepers and the wind noise he couldn't make it out. He turned up radio volume and listened.

The Weasels were dive-bombing a SAM site.

One of the beepers shut off. *Whose, dammit?*

He looked back again. A Thud was zooming upward trying to get out of the flak, torching brightly from the main fuel cells. The stores dropped away, and just afterward the Thud nosed over, going down.

Again the sounds of two beepers rent the airways.

"*Weeep-weeeeep, weeep-weeeep, weeep-weeeep . . .*"

"*Guppy three . . . down,*" came a call through the noise. Who was the one not yet identified?

He shut off the emergency-guard radio channel to eliminate beeper noise and slowed a bit. He flew in a long arc so his men could cut him off and join up. Then they would fly together to Thud Ridge, where Colonel Parker's flight orbited and waited.

Only two Thuds pulled in beside him. The other had been lost.

0945 Local—People's Army HQ, Hanoi, DRV

Colonel Nguyen Wu

He was in his office, demanding more information from his intelligence officer about the morning's air attacks on the Long Bien bridge, pleased about the three Thunder planes shot down by Colonel Trung's artillery. He would take credit for at least one of those. They'd lost a rocket battery to bombs, and another had been damaged by a terror missile, but that didn't bother him, for the generals were growing to expect such losses. His anger was directed toward those rocket-battery commanders who had shut off their radars and not fired at the attackers.

As he lowered his voice and asked the intelligence officer which of the downed aircraft they could most credibly claim, the door opened. General Dung's aide, a captain, peered into the room.

Wu stood. "Can I help you?" he asked. He provided the general's aide with much more respect than he'd give another junior officer. He noticed that two brawny men in plain uniforms and bearing sidearms stood behind the captain. Very odd.

"Please come with us," the captain aide said, motioning to the two men, and realization flooded numbly through

Wu, for those were the nondescript uniforms of secret policemen!

"Ohhhh," he moaned. They'd found him out, and his beloved aunt was not there to help! He felt his bladder loosen and was unable to stop himself from urinating.

"Please," he cried in a piteous mew.

The two secret policemen showed no surprise, but the aide stared in disbelief at the growing puddle. Then the captain regained his voice. "Comrade Colonel, we are only going downstairs so the general can ask certain questions."

Liar! "I did not do it," whispered Wu, cringing.

"Please follow me, comrade Colonel," said the aide, and led the way out the door. The policemen surrounded him, and one wordlessly motioned that Wu should follow the captain.

He hesitated until one man supported either arm and they assisted him.

Out into the hallway, then down the flights of stairs. Were they taking him to the interrogation rooms at the Ministry of Internal Affairs, or to the common ones at Hoa Lo Prison?

"No," Nguyen Wu periodically wailed, but he was gently urged to continue downward.

"This way," the captain said when they arrived at the main entrance and they continued on down the stairs to the basement, which housed the intelligence offices and the command center.

They will shoot me in the basement! Wu's chest was heaving with panic, his eyes furtive. He stumbled once, and a wordless policeman roughly caught him.

This treatment is for others, not me!

"My beloved aunt!" he shrieked, startling two young officers who judiciously averted their eyes and continued up the stairs.

At the basement level the captain led the way into a small office, where Generals Dung, Tho, and Luc waited. Beyond them Wu saw Quon and Colonel Trung.

"I am sorry," he babbled at Quon, then began to sob, wondering how he could atone for killing the pilot's son.

"Colonel Wu!" exclaimed General Dung, and Wu cringed. Dung nodded toward the door, and his aide and the policemen hurried out and closed it behind themselves. Wu was left with the generals, Trung and Quon.

"Comrade Colonel," General Luc said in greeting as Wu continued to cringe.

Wu looked fearfully around at the group.

"We came here," said Dung quietly and without expression, "to tell you we have an emergency at hand that requires your expertise."

Nguyen Wu shook his head to clear it, then stared with drooping mouth at the general.

General Luc picked up the conversation. "The helicopters in the South give our ground forces more and more problems. They provide great mobility for the Mee troops. Also, their fighters are very responsive and increasingly dangerous. We must do something."

"Another challenge is presented by the new Mee dragon ships," said General Tho, "cargo aircraft that carry rapid-firing guns and cannons. We thought it would be prudent to seek your advice on these problems, since you are our expert on antiaircraft matters."

Wu stared at them incredulously. *Is it a trick?* He swallowed and tried to think. *What were they talking about?* Hope tried to glimmer through his confusion.

"How do you think we should approach this problem?" asked Dung.

Wu realized they were serious about the discussion. He thought of the wetness of his trousers, but his mind was still preoccupied and not yet prepared for embarrassment.

"General Dung is reluctant to move rocket batteries or heavy guns south," said General Luc, "even though the commanders there ask for them."

"Yes," began Wu, trying to think. "I . . . ah . . . agree with the comrade general. The . . . ah . . . rocket sites would be . . . difficult to move there."

"And would be endangered if we did?" prompted General Dung.

"Yes . . . ah . . . they would be in danger."

"I told you," said Dung, looking at the others.

Wu wondered. It was unlikely they didn't see the wet stains on the front of his trousers, but they acted as if this were just another casual conversation. And why the secret policemen? He began to recover a degree of aplomb, but he was still terrified whenever he glanced to the rear of the room into Quon's stony gaze. *Why is he here?*

"General Giap says we *must* do something about this problem in the South," said Dung.

Wu tried again to concentrate on what they were saying.

General Luc said, "I told General Dung that you would know what we should do."

It is true! They are only talking business. Giddy with relief, Wu gave a last shudder.

"I told him you would study the problem and recommend positive action," continued Luc, "and that we should put our faith in your superb judgment." He smiled at Nguyen Wu as proudly as a father might.

"I would . . . ah . . . be honored to study the problem and give you my . . . best opinion," stammered Wu.

"See," said General Luc, beaming at the others. "He wishes to *study* the problem."

"You must leave immediately, Colonel Wu," said General Dung. "I will have my driver take you to the convoy."

"Convoy?"

"While you are on your way south, it will be safer if you accompany one of our groups going there. Of course, you will be convoy commander."

"South?"

"I assume that this very thorough study of yours will take several months," said Luc, "therefore I will find it necessary to temporarily assign someone to replace you as commandant of radar-and-rocket forces."

Wu opened his mouth to protest, but his mind was reeling, and he could not think of appropriate words. Surely this was a farce . . . but would such high-ranking generals take part in such at thing?

"My aunt . . . ," he began.

Dung cheerfully broke in, "You bring great honor to your family, Colonel Wu. Your assistance may save the People's Army in the South."

Wu sputtered, "Thank you, comrade General, but . . ."

General Tho nodded, still smiling. "By volunteering for this hazardous duty, you have set an example for others to aspire to. Don't you believe so, Quon?"

"As I suggested earlier," Quon said quietly. "I do not doubt that Colonel Wu will serve us well when he goes south."

Air Regiment Commandant Quon

When Wu had departed from the room, shepherded by General Luc and dour old Colonel Trung toward the waiting staff car, General Dung turned to Quon and General Tho. He pursed his pudgy lips thoughtfully. "I believe your problem is solved."

Quon looked at the door in disgust. "He watered his pants."

It had been Dung's idea that the burly staff officers remove all trace of rank, as if they were secret policemen. Quon no longer doubted that Dung was a master of manipulation.

"There was no lie spoken," mused General Van Tien Dung. "We do have a problem with the American air forces in the South, and I truly hope he will be able to assist us there."

"And," said General Tho to Quon, "now you can get on with repairing the damage he has done to the defenses."

"I shall begin immediately."

"General Luc tells me you were the one who advised him to keep the guns around the bridges," said Dung as he delved into his pocket for a cigarette pack.

"The credit must go to Colonel Xuan Nha. He is astute about such things."

"How many Mee aircraft were confirmed shot down this morning?"

"Three at the Long Bién bridge," said Quon, "all by Colonel Trung's guns. Since the Mee paid so dearly and had such little success, Colonel Nha believes they will think hard before trying again." Dung lit an American Salem and sucked in a satisfying lungful of smoke. He smoked the brand incessantly. He looked at Quon. "I am sorry about what happened to your son," he said.

Quon nodded wordlessly.

Dung pointed the forefinger of the hand with the cigarette, dropping ashes. "But do not allow revenge to consume you, Quon. There is still much we must do."

"The matter shall not interfere with my duties, General Dung."

"You must see that it does not."

Quon scarcely heard, for he'd just learned that the top of

the vertical stabilizer of one of the Thunder planes shot down by artillery was painted bright blue.

1100 Local—Hoa Lo Prison, Hanoi

The prisoner was understandably confused and frightened when they dragged him in. He'd been followed closely as he floated down in his parachute, captured as his feet touched the ground. Then, when the blue markings had been verified, the prisoner had been beaten into submission, stripped and shackled, beaten again, and driven to Hoa Lo. Quon had been waiting outside the gray-walled prison and had watched as the truck arrived with him.

They'd dragged him inside, into the admittance building's interrogation cell, a room so unkempt that Quon wrinkled his nose in distaste.

When a prisoner was first brought to Hoa Lo, Quon learned, he was taken to a cell in this building and shackled to a concrete bunk. Then he was relentlessly interrogated for several weeks until the jailkeepers had learned the military secrets, such as his unit and information about it, the next targets the Americans would attack, and so forth, to be used by People's Army Intelligence. Personal information about his family and home life was also elicited and provided to the Ministry of External Affairs for propaganda purposes. Yet as he looked about at the disorder of the room, Quon doubted they were efficient about their jobs.

He heard loudspeakers spouting a cacophony of scratchy music and American words.

The nervous prison commandant, a senior lieutenant wearing a wrinkled and grubby uniform, eyed Quon continuously, obviously impressed.

"What is that?" asked Quon, frowning and waving a hand toward the source of noise.

"We reeducate the prisoners to become sympathetic to our cause."

Quon snorted. "Does it work?"

"Sometimes a little, General Quon."

"Did I say I was a general?" snapped Quon.

The senior lieutenant looked confused.

"Have them stop that noise," said Quon, looking again at the prisoner.

"At once, comrade Quon," said the lieutenant, and he shouted shrilly at the open doorway. After a few moments the sound abruptly stopped.

The prisoner was very short for a Westerner, red-faced and ugly as Americans are, with blue eyes and close-cropped hair. He'd been stripped to undershorts and socks and looked ill at ease, yet there was something still defiant about him.

"What is his name?" asked Quon.

An interrogator, a man with a pronounced and rounded upper lip, barked Mee words and gained a series of clipped responses from the prisoner.

The interrogator turned to Quon. "He is a captain, and his name is *Tai Tro.*"

"Shut the door," commanded Quon, not taking his eyes from the prisoner's.

The interrogator hurried to do so.

"There is certain information I must have regarding the air attack at Kep airfield on Monday." He spoke slowly, eyes still locked on the American's, telling the men precisely what he wanted and taking enough time for the prison commandant to write it all down.

When he'd finished, the senior lieutenant bobbed his head energetically. "We shall get it for you, Colonel Quon!"

Quon gave him an exasperated look.

"Ahh . . . comrade Quon?" the man corrected.

"How long until you have the information?"

The senior lieutenant, looking as worried as the American prisoner, calculated. Finally he answered. "Three days?" The lieutenant looked at Quon proudly, as if that would be a feat.

"I will give you one hour."

The prison commandant's eyes bulged comically.

"In one hour I will return to this room, and you will give me the answers to my questions." He turned without ceremony and left.

Quon did not care for either the dismal place or the men assigned there. The guards and officers of Hoa Lo were obviously People's Army, yet were a motley-dressed and sniveling group. They had likely volunteered for the duty so they wouldn't be sent to fight alongside *real* soldiers in the South or to man Colonel Trung's artillery.

He went outside, spoke with his driver, then sat in the rear seat of the utility vehicle and went over paperwork he'd brought with him. *It never ends,* he decided. If the bureaucrats had their way, commanders would sign authorizations before their men were allowed to shit.

He heard screams in a foreign tongue, then loud sobbing, and then more screams, and knew it was the Mee pilot named *Tai Tro.* It was no way for a fighter pilot to be treated, but as he listened he felt no pity.

His vehicle was parked in the shade of trees on the side of the prison near a long gray concrete wall. Watchtowers were at either end, and guards in them were peering toward Quon's vehicle and chattering. None appeared interested in watching the grounds inside. His feeling of disgust at the sloppy operation intensified.

He returned his attention to the paperwork, marking notes here and there with a black pen stenciled U.S. GOVERNMENT. American supplies captured from ARVN puppet soldiers or pilfered from the Mee themselves, even air conditioners destined for the offices of high government officials, were brought north in returning trucks.

The screams became constant and Quon absently wondered how the man could do that without taking a breath.

Precisely an hour after he'd emerged, he went back inside, ignoring the fawning guards, past the prison commandant's office and directly into the interrogation room. The Mee pilot's arms were tied at the elbows behind him, and he was strung up, arms pulled out of swollen sockets. Two guards were pummeling his torso, although the man was oblivious and only grunted weakly now and then.

"Stop," said Quon, and they did. The Mee pilot swung there, his chest and stomach a mass of livid blue and red bruises, his face bloody and puffed.

Quon glanced at the senior lieutenant, who stood rigidly at attention. "What have you learned?"

The senior lieutenant nodded to the interrogator, who was still puffing from exertion. As he waited, Quon decided that his slackened jaw, oversized lips, and bland expression made him look like a grinning carp.

"He *is* from the pig squadron," the interrogator finally panted.

"The rest of it!" demanded Quon.

"He flew on the attack on Kep you spoke of, but he has not yet told us the names of the other members of the flight."

Quon glared at the interrogator's incompetence. "Was he the leader of the last four aircraft?"

"No, comrade Quon, he was third in the blue-tail flight. But he admitted firing his gun at a taxiing aircraft."

Quon's chest tightened convulsively and he looked again at the Mee pilot, this time with revulsion. This . . . *thing* . . . had helped kill his son.

"How soon before you learn the other names?" he whispered in a hate-filled voice.

The carp-faced interrogator looked troubled. "Soon, comrade Quon," he said. "He is . . . ah . . . a difficult one."

The prisoner groaned in his semiconsciousness, smelling of dung and piss.

"I will give you one more hour," said Quon to the interrogator. "You must give me the information then."

The senior lieutenant intervened. "Comrade Quon, it will mean we must use such force that the prisoner may not survive. We have been ordered to keep the Mee alive. We can kill none of them except those brought in dying or with missing limbs."

Quon brought the full fury of his gaze to bear on the man.

The senior lieutenant began to plead. "If you give us more time, only a few days, we can get the information for you and the prisoner will live."

"One hour, and when I return, I also want the prisoner to be able to understand what I will say to him," said Quon. He stalked from the room.

An hour later he returned to find the Mee pilot still hanging there, mouth open and drooling blood, chest and belly whipped to raw meat. His fingernails were gone and blood ran from his scrotum down his legs.

The senior lieutenant was sweating even more than before. He silently handed Quon a piece of paper upon which was written a list numbered one through four, with several lines of details written at the side.

Quon read and asked, "What does this one mean? No face?"

"His leader was burned in an aircraft fire."

"Major . . . *Lokee*," said Quon aloud. He repeated it again and felt pleased. The man he hated most had a name.

The Mee pilot said something. The words came out in a series of gasps scarcely louder than the whisper of leaves falling.

"What did he say?" Quon asked.

The carp-faced interrogator smiled humbly at Quon and moved closer as the broken prisoner whispered again. He turned back toward Quon. "He mentions something about his God," he said. "They often do that, comrade Quon."

"Will he live?" asked Quon, peering at the Mee pilot.

"I think perhaps so," said the senior lieutenant. "I've seen others this bad, and some of them survived. The Mee are stubborn about living."

Quon drew his sidearm, a well-tended Makarov 9mm automatic pistol.

The senior lieutenant looked alarmed.

"Raise his head!" demanded Quon.

The carp-faced interrogator tried to grasp the prisoner's hair, but it was too short. He lifted his chin.

The Mee pilot's eyes dilated blindly, flickered, then settled upon Quon's.

"Tell him to think of the time he fired his cannon at Kep," Quon said in a quiet voice.

The interrogator babbled something in the Mee language.

The prisoner continued to stare into Quon's eyes as the pistol was raised, continued even as it was placed against his forehead.

"Ask him if he fears death," said Quon in a tight voice.

The interrogator spoke, and shortly thereafter came a ragged, four-syllable response.

"Fuck you, by damn," were the words, and while Quon did not understand them, he heard the contempt in the voice.

The 9mm bullet blew away the rear portion of the Mee pilot's head, spraying blood and matter on the wall behind him.

1640 Local—Trailer 5A, Takhli RTAFB, Thailand

GS-15 *Linda Lopes*

She knew he was staying in Trailer 5A, for she'd asked Colonel Parker. The wing commander had pointed it out, and like a gentleman he'd not mentioned it since.

She'd wanted to go there the previous evening after her discussions with the Air America administrators, but pride told her to wait for him to make the first move. He had not. She'd spent her evening grumbling at herself. Hadn't he made it clear enough during the past seven years that he wanted none of her?

Not clear enough, she'd decided over today's lunch at the Air America Pilots' Club. She'd finished her day's business early and returned to her trailer. There she'd showered and changed into a fresh blouse and slacks, and then marched over to see him.

She rapped at his door, then knocked again with "shave and a haircut, six bits."

He should be in. A call to his squadron had revealed he'd gone there. Then she heard him moving around inside and felt a jolt of panic.

He opened the door and grew a surprised look. He was wearing khaki shorts, T-shirt, and clogs.

"He, neighbor," she said with a smile, waving two cans of Budweiser. "See, I was sitting in my trailer right over there . . . 9A if you've wondered . . . and I said to myself I'll bet there's a poor ol' thirsty Air Force major somewhere around here who . . ."

"Hello, Linda."

She grinned. "You gonna ask a girl in out of the hot sun?"

He paused.

"Well?"

He opened the door and she handed him the two beers and went inside. She removed a set of dumbbells from a chair beside the table and sat. As he closed the door, she appreciatively eyed his build. Eight years older now, he looked to be in even better condition than when she'd known him in Germany. He'd always been serious about staying in shape. *It's all a part of flying fighters,* he'd told her.

"What can I do for you?" he asked awkwardly.

"How about sharing a beer, for starters."

He found a church key, used it, and brew sprayed wildly. He tried to cover it with his mouth, and she laughed as the stuff bubbled down the front of his T-shirt.

"What'd you do, shake 'em up?" he asked.

"Hey, it's free, fella."

As he was getting two more beers from his refrigerator and opening them, she looked around his trailer, observing the homey appearance. The basic half trailer was a mirror of the one she inhabited, but a few neatly arranged knick-knacks and a couple pictures of old biplanes on the wall had transformed it to look much better.

"You've got it set up nicely."

He sat down opposite her, took a drink, then looked around as if seeing it for the first time. "It's where I live," he said simply.

"Nice," she repeated, wishing he'd help carry the conversation.

"You'll start people talking, coming to a guy's trailer like this," he said.

"That's not what you used to say when I came to your BOQ room at Sembach."

He shook his head. "That was a long time ago."

"Sure was." She wished she could think of something just a bit more intelligent. She had a graduate degree and fifty-odd credits in communicative skills, and all she could think of was *sure was?* She lifted her own can and sipped heartily, laughing at herself.

"Just a second," he said. He retrieved a clean glass and set it in front of her. "Sorry about that. My manners have gone to hell."

She poured her beer into the glass and wondered how long they were going to keep up the silly small talk.

"I see you're a GS-15 now. That's great for someone as young as you."

"I'm thirty years old, Paul."

"Still awfully young to be a GS-15. Congratulations."

"Thank you." Since he knew her general scale grade, she thought, he must have at least asked about her. She smiled and kidded, "Or is that sour grapes because I'm a mere woman?"

"You've always been capable, so I'm not really surprised. Still working for the spooks?"

"Of course not. I'm in charge of distributing food and essentials to the poor, deserving wretches of Asia."

He smiled, or at least she thought he did. It was difficult to tell.

He caught her looking at his face and held her eyes with his.

At least he's no longer ashamed of it, she thought, but then he spoke and she was no longer sure.

"You didn't have to come here, Linda. That's beyond the call of duty."

"What do you mean?"

"I mean that I'm doing fine. I get to fly a lot, and I'm doing what I was trained to do." He searched for words. "I don't need moral support for anything."

"You think I'm here because I feel sorry for you?" she asked.

He laughed, but she heard no joy in it. "Sure you are."

"That's ridiculous."

"I thank you for caring, but I just don't need it. Honest, I'm doing fine."

"That's *not* the reason I came," she argued.

Lucky stared at one of his prints, a World War I combat scene. "This morning I lost a good man in my flight. He'd become a close friend."

She felt awful. "I didn't know."

Silence.

"What was his name?"

"Turk Tatro. We believe he's alive. The guy in the airplane behind his said he had a good chute. He was likely captured, but he got out of the airplane okay."

"Thank God," she said.

"Turk's a feisty little guy from Mississippi who likes to make people laugh. Has a wife and two little girls." He motioned at a pad of paper. "I was trying to write them."

"It must be difficult."

"Yeah." He looked at his beer can and brooded. "Damned difficult."

She felt mushy about it, but she also thought he was beginning to accept her presence. "Something like this has to be hard on the family," she said.

"His wife's a nice lady. A cute little southern belle who hasn't stopped flirting with him. I met her a few years back."

"You knew him before you got here?"

"I've known Turk since sixty, when we were checking out in F-100's at Luke. I'd just come from the burn center, and . . ." He looked at her strangely, as if he'd just realized he was opening up.

She sipped her beer. "So you met him at Luke. Go on."

Lucky shrugged, withdrawing into his shell. "That's all. He's a good guy and I like him."

"That's hard, isn't it? To lose a friend and not know what's happening to him."

"Yeah, it is." He decided something then and resolutely drained the beer. "How long are you going to be at Takhli, Linda?"

"Until Monday."

"I've got to struggle through this letter to his wife now. I'll see you before you take off for Bangkok, okay?"

She smiled. "How about dinner tomorrow?"

He paused, then nodded.

"Promise?"

"Yeah. I don't think you ought to be seen coming to my trailer again, though."

"Well, I've been thrown out of better places." She stood and walked over to where he was sitting. "I'm sorry about your friend," she said softly. Before he could react, she brushed his forehead with her lips, lingered there for a moment, then straightened and made her way toward the door. He looked confused, and she felt a bit of triumph that she was able to interpret his expression.

He stood awkwardly. "It's a bad time to talk, while I've got all this on my mind."

She fluttered her fingers in a wave and went out, still smiling.

1815 Local—Officers' Club Dining Room

Captain Bob Liebermann

Manny was brooding. So when he'd asked him if he'd like to go to the club for dinner, Bob had said sure, even though he'd already eaten a candy bar and wasn't particularly hungry. He just didn't like seeing Manny alone with his crummy mood.

The members of C-Flight are growing closer, he thought

as they walked into the O' Club dining room, *just like Major Lucky planned it.*

When they were seated in the busy room, Bob brought up the gossip concerning Lucky and the Ice Maiden from Bangkok, but Manny kept talking about Turk Tatro and how shitty it was he'd been shot down. They'd all liked the little southerner, but it was something more with Manny. He'd pulled up and out of the flak and missed the target while Turk had pressed on and been shot down.

Every one of the shooters except Guppy lead had been hit at least once. When the maintenance men had seen Lucky Anderson's flak-shredded Thud, they said he'd been fortunate to make it home, which was an understatement. His bird had taken multiple hits in both wings, and a piece of shrapnel had missed his head by inches.

Manny said something about Turk Tatro.

"Bad luck," said Bob.

"No luck to it. We shouldn't have been using fucking Bullpup missiles, flying straight and level like that, with all the fucking guns in the world shooting at us. Jesus," said Manny, "I wonder what genius came up with that one."

"I thought you said it was the people at Seventh Air Force."

"They're blaming it on the staff pukes at PACAF, but I don't know who to believe and I don't care. Headquarters pukes use their dorks to do their thinking."

It didn't matter much to the fighter pilots *which* headquarters pukes came up with the stupid ideas. They lumped them together as "they" and regarded them as cretins.

"I got some friends at Seventh Air Force," said Manny. "Most of them have a *pu-ying* set up downtown in an apartment. I wonder if the assholes even realize there's a war going on."

"What's a *pu-ying?*"

"Hell, Bob, that's the first Thai word you should've learned. It means girl, for Christ's sake."

"I've learned *kop koom krup.* That means 'thank you,'" he said proudly.

"Yeah Bob, I know what it means." Manny looked at him and sighed, making him feel even more naive. "Anyway, I figure all those guys think about is Saigon pussy. They oughta get their heads outa their asses." Manny shook his head sadly. "Bullpups."

No Hab came and took their orders, and this time Manny didn't joke with her as he usually did. He just kept brooding and talking about losing Turk and the two other guys in the heavily defended target area, and nothing Bob said seemed to help.

Colonel Lyons came in then, ushering the blond Peace Corps administrator. Manny stared at them, eyes blazing. "And that cowardly asshole doesn't help anything," he said.

"What do you mean?" asked Bob.

"Did you know he hasn't flown anywhere outside of route pack one yet?"

"You're shitting me."

"Hell no, I'm not. He's flown seven missions so far, and every one of them have been just north of the DMZ, where there's no guns."

Bob frowned. "Colonel Parker says his colonels are leaders both on the ground and in the air, so he'll *have* to fly up there sooner or later."

"Then it'll be a hell of a lot later. I overheard the chief master sergeant who works for him in the command post complaining to Major Lucky. He said Lyons gave him an *order* to make *sure* he's only scheduled to fly in pack one. He said flying anywhere else takes up too much of his *valuable* time."

Bob's frown grew deeper.

"The chief said he'd had one too many bosses like Lyons, and he didn't feel like taking any more of their shit. Major Lucky told him if he felt that way, he should go to B. J. Parker, but the chief said he didn't need the hassle. He's going to cut his tour short and retire."

Bob had trouble believing him. In his years in the Air Force he'd never met anyone like Manny described. Maybe, thought Liebermann, he was just jealous about the girl.

Manny was still staring at the nearby table where Lyons huddled close to the blond, expounding about something. Then Bob saw the girl glance over at Manny DeVera and give him a distinct flutter of eyes.

A change crept over Manny's angry face, like a chameleon switching colors. His expression grew softer and so charming, Bob would have bet he could have calmed a rhino.

Lyons was so busy talking and striking poses, he didn't see the girl nod a greeting and cast a warm smile at Manny.

"I talked to her yesterday afternoon," said DeVera. "Name's Jackie Bell. Great body."

"Very nice."

Manny grinned. "I dunno if I'd get *that* carried away."

"Wonder what she's doing with the colonel?" asked Bob.

Manny didn't answer, but continued to stare at her until Bob became embarrassed. Then Manny stood, wearing a purposeful expression, and Bob grew horrified as he realized what his roommate was about to do.

"Manny," he hissed, but DeVera was already walking the several paces to the "Reserved for Colonels" table, staring the entire time into the bright blue eyes.

"Hi," he said, ignoring Lyons, who was in the middle of a statement.

"Hello there yourself," the girl said in a husky voice.

"You had dinner yet?" Manny asked.

"No," she said, beaming at him.

"What do *you* want, *Captain?*" asked Lyons, who had recovered from his initial shock.

"Just talking with the lady, sir," Manny answered happily, "and asking if she'd care to accompany this poor *bachelor* to the fine metropolis of Ta Khli for a steak."

Lyons's eyes smoldered. "I do not remember inviting you to join us, *Captain.*"

"I just thought the lady might like to accompany a *bachelor* downtown to see the lights," said Manny, placing as much emphasis on the word "bachelor" as Lyons was on "Captain."

"I would love to join you," replied the blond.

Lyons's mouth sagged.

Manny very formally put out his arm. She stood without hesitation and took it.

"Captain!" sputtered Lyons.

"I shall return the lady in fine repair, Colonel," Manny said, and steered her toward the door.

Jackie Bell laughed from deep in her throat, then looked back toward Lyons. "Sorry to run so quickly, Colonel, but I've wanted to see what the village is really like since I got here, and I just *can't* turn down the captain's offer."

Most of the men in the room had noticed, and were grinning and whispering, telling the others.

A few minutes later No Hab arrived with the two hamburgers and glanced around for Manny. Then she looked over at the "Reserved for Colonels" table and smiled know-ingly. By then the room was abuzz with low voices, and a couple of times Bob heard a loud laugh.

Liebermann could eat only half of one hamburger, and he decided to give Manny hell about having to pay for both of them.

Colonel Tom Lyons ate his own meal quietly, periodically glaring at the captains and lieutenants in the room, who looked away with great innocence. Bob couldn't tell if Lyons was angry, embarrassed, or both.

CHAPTER NINE

Colonel Xuan Nha

Xuan Nha came instantly awake. Someone had cracked the door open and was peering inside. He felt at his side and grasped the familiar handle of the Tokarev pistol.

"Colonel Nha?"

"Enter," Xuan croaked warily.

Quon switched on the dim light and led Tran Van Ngo inside. The pilot seemed happier than on the previous trip, but, of course, then he'd just come from delivering his son's body.

"It is good to see you, comrade Colonel," said Tran, staring. More bandages had been removed from Xuan's body to allow it to heal better, and his protégé's eyes were drawn by the scarlet hues of his chest.

"The matter with Colonel Wu is done," said Quon, "so as you asked, I brought Lieutenant Colonel Van Ngo from Thai Nguyen."

"Nguyen Wu was relieved of duty?" asked Xuan. He was surprised it had happened so quickly.

Quon gave a lift of an eyebrow. "Off to the South to plan

the air defenses there. I hope he is not taken seriously, or all may be lost."

Xuan thought, and worried. The action was not nearly final enough. He wondered if Quon realized the threat Wu would pose so long as he lived and was supported by Li Binh? He'd been doubly cautious since Quon's previous visit when he'd learned of the power struggle, for his assassination might somehow serve his nephew. With Nguyen Wu still alive, he would rest no easier.

"Tran Van Ngo will be placed in charge of the radars and rocket defenses until you return to full duty," announced Quon. He looked at Tran. "I expect you will coordinate all matters with Colonel Nha."

"I have always listened to the Tiger of Dien Bien Phu," Tran replied.

Xuan Nha had once been called that, and the sound of it was tonic to his ears.

"And, of course, you will keep me informed." Quon stared at the younger man.

"Of course."

Xuan watched the interchange, then motioned Tran closer. "You must locate the pilot controllers trained at the Wisdom complex," he told him, "and immediately place them in the P-1 radars at Phuc Yen and Kien An."

Quon interrupted. "I have already contacted them at their units. They are waiting at Phuc Yen for instructions."

"Very good," said Xuan Nha, still eyeing Tran Van Ngo. "Now we will discuss what must be done. Time is our enemy. You will have to act quickly to repair the damage to both the interceptors and the guided rocket forces."

Tran nodded briskly, eyes pinned upon his leader, ears tuned to the rasping voice.

Xuan continued to voice instructions and ideas.

Quon listened for a while, then nodded toward the door. "There are too many confusing things being discussed. I must leave for Phuc Yen and things I understand, like pilots and aircraft."

Xuan Nha regarded him evenly with his remaining eye. He felt gratitude of such depth that he could not fully express it. He'd been provided with a second chance, something he had thought was impossible only three days earlier.

Tran Van Ngo voiced his words. "We shall provide your pilots with the best possible control, comrade Quon."

"That," said Quon evenly, "is what I expect." He paused for yet another moment, to stare at the men before leaving.

Tran turned to Xuan Nha and shuddered. "I would not want him angry with me."

Xuan Nha agreed. Yet he also wondered about Colonel Nguyen Wu. When Li Binh returned from Paris and heard what had been done with her nephew, things would surely change.

1415 Local—Route Pack Six, North Vietnam

Major Lucky Anderson

Friday's target was the Gia Lam rail-repair depot, close to the Doumer bridge they'd attacked with such awful results on Wednesday, but far enough away that they would be out of the coverage of at least some of the tremendous buildup of guns.

Lucky had been shaken by the visit from Linda. He had to admit that she'd left a warm, inexplicable glow in him, and somehow even the difficult letter to Turk Tatro's wife had been made easier, but he knew it would not last. During their dinner the next evening he'd reined in his emotions and kept things on an impersonal basis as she tried to drag them into nostalgic discussions of times past . . . but it had been hard not to join her.

Even in the air his mind sometimes betrayed him and reverted to warm thoughts of her, but then he would exercise an inner discipline and concentrate on the challenges of flying. Yet though his mind was preoccupied with details of flying and fighting as they approached the target, the pleasantness was somehow with him.

He looked out and around, making his visual check of things, and saw that the flight was properly spaced within the gaggle.

The loss of Turk Tatro had intensified his fierce protectiveness, for it reemphasized how vulnerable even the best of them were. Today Henry Horn flew in the number-two position. Manny DeVera, now the most-discussed stud bachelor at Takhli, flew as number three. Billy Bowes was last.

Henry had become even more steady and reliable, as if he'd picked up the mantle left by Turk Tatro. And Billy

Bowes? Lucky did not believe he'd ever observed a better display of flying ability than he saw there. Something troubled Billy, but it was neither fear nor lack of skill. If Lucky was to worry about anyone in the group, it would be Manny, because the personable and outgoing captain was more nervous than Lucky had ever seen him.

If he didn't watch himself, Manny could lose his confidence and enter an even worse depression. Lucky had seen it before and recognized the initial symptoms. The solution was sometimes easy, like sending a pilot off to Bangkok or the Philippines on R and R. Sometimes the pilot should be scheduled on some easy counters down in the safer route packs for a while. Other times it was like being thrown from a horse, you just had to get them back in the thick of things so they could prove they could defy the defenses and hit the target.

He felt the latter was the best course. Manny was a good man, well worth whatever it took.

First Lieutenant Billy Bowes

Their Tiger flight was at the tail end of the gaggle, and by the time it was their turn, the guns were shooting furiously, and gray flak bursts blossomed in the sky below them.

As their leader Lucky was first to enter his dive toward the big railroad-repair depot. Billy watched him, admiring the sure way he handled his bird, snapping over on his back as he did, pulling the nose through until he was at a forty-five-degree angle and sharply rolling out wings level. He was good, and his bombs would likely be squarely on target, which was where Lucky usually put them.

Which meant it would be okay to do what he had planned.

Billy had spent a long time studying the map and photos, concentrating on areas adjacent to the rail yard. Then he'd found a group of warehouses beyond the repair depot, almost at the river's edge.

He was to be dead last to bomb the target. The last aircraft of the last flight.

If he destroyed his private, extracurricular target, he just might feel a little better the next time he thought about the gomers killing Mal and his little brother. He would have picked the big Gia Lam international airport and maybe a

Soviet cargo plane parked there, but the repercussions would have been too great. The warehouses would have to do. He eyed them down there and saw the flash of a big gun coming from their midst.

Henry Horn was nose down in his dive-bomb maneuver, and it was Manny's turn to roll in, but for some reason DeVera was holding up.

They circled the target, and Billy watched Lucky's bombs hit squarely on a repair building, just as he'd thought they would.

Henry Horn had already released his bombs when Manny finally rolled over and entered his dive. A few seconds later Billy followed him down the chute, offsetting toward the warehouses but keeping an eye on DeVera's bird.

As he passed through 9,000 feet, a group of flour flak bursts went off not far from DeVera, and he jinked away hard, then corrected back toward the target. Four bursts surrounded Manny's airplane, and Billy saw it stagger and almost immediately afterward saw the bombs release. Manny must have flinched or been hit as they released, for they went flying in the direction of the airport.

Billy watched DeVera begin his pullout through the middle of a layer of barrage flak. Then he concentrated on his own sight picture and the warehouses that were creeping up toward the pipper. Several bundles of 57mm flak went off close by, but he ignored them and pressed. Perfect. He pickled, felt the 750-pound bombs release, then pulled off, jinking hard and looking back.

The bombs flew true and detonated into one of the warehouses, sending up a shower of wood and debris. Then a much larger explosion reached out in a giant fireball as something volatile exploded in the next warehouse. The concussion swatted his Thud, and yet another explosion buffeted him.

Shit hot! he told himself as he fought the controls.

"Damn," someone radioed. *"Look at that baby blow."*

Billy felt smug about what he'd done, but realized it hadn't been very damned covert. He decided to tell them he'd jinked to avoid a flak burst just as he'd pickled, and that his bombs had been thrown wide. As he eyeballed around for the rest of the flight, he wondered about Manny DeVera.

Billy watched as Henry Horn throttled back and slid in

beside Major Lucky, then spotted Manny to the north of them. A trace of black trailed behind his Thud.

The smoke grew more pronounced as Billy keyed his mike. *"Tiger three, this is four. You're trailing smoke,"* he called. He knew better than to mention the word "fire" unless an aircraft was obviously burning.

"This is Tiger lead, Manny. I'm confirming the smoke," called Major Lucky.

The dark trail grew more pronounced, and Billy saw a bright spot near the center of the Thud's fuelage.

"Tiger three, you're burning," he called.

"I'm going to try to blow it out," came Manny DeVera's high and frightened voice.

A couple of seconds later Billy watched as the Thud's afterburner lit and spouted blue flame, then as Manny accelerated sharply and began to climb northward. He would be going high, to thinner air, trying to blow out the fire.

"Tiger three, this is Tiger lead," radioed Major Lucky in his calmest tone. *"Turn thirty degrees port and fly northwest."*

There was no response, but Manny's bird altered course.

"Tigers, let's keep up with him," said Lucky, and they all lit their burners.

Captain Manny DeVera

I'm about to die! thought Manny as he looked wildly about, sucking hard on 100 percent oxygen. *Oh, God, please don't let me die here.*

His calibrated airspeed was . . . 520 knots? *Yeah.* Altitude was . . . passing through . . .

The awful fear washed over and consumed him. It was the worst thing he'd ever felt, invading his mind with unreason. A couple of minutes ago they'd been trying to kill him. Now he was on fire and would have to eject. His head hurt and he was shaking all over. He tried to calm himself, succeeded for a second, then shook again.

Get control of yourself.

He was soaring higher, still in burner, with the nose of his jet held up at . . . fifteen degrees climb angle? The altimeter showed 26,000, then 27,000 feet.

Can't let them kill me, he thought, and wondered if he

should be jinking. *Stupid thought. Just get the fucking fire out!*

Lead was calling someone, and he wondered who. His chest rose and fell mightily, and the hissing and sucking sound was loud to his ears.

He remembered that the air-turbine motor pumped a lot of hydraulic fluid around the airplane, and he started to shut it down because hydraulic fluid burned just as well as jet fuel if it got hot enough. He stopped, remembering that he'd lose a lot of critical systems if he lost the ATM, including gauges and hydraulics.

I can't think straight, he wailed to himself. God, but he was scared.

Altitude? Thirty-something. Thirty-four thousand? It was hard to see.

He felt numb, and his vision left him except for gray spots dancing before his eyes.

I'm dying. Oh, God, I'm dying!

He breathed even more harshly.

Lucky Anderson was calling again, this time more stridently. Calling for three to respond.

I'm three, he remembered. *What's happening to me?*

In a lucid moment he realized that he was hyperventilating and in the process of passing out. He slowed his breathing and pawed at the oxygen panel. He switched off the pure oxygen, then remembered he was flying damned high and was unpressurized and had better keep it there. He switched back, wondering why he was having trouble with simple thoughts.

Slow down the breathing, he told himself.

He regained his eyesight and the numbness went away.

Tiger three, Tiger lead. What's your altitude, Manny?"

He found his voice, but heard himself spitting words in shrill bursts. "*Thirty-eight thousand feet, going to thirty-nine,*" he blurted.

That's real good, Tiger three. Better come out of burner pretty quick now. You're using too much gas. The fire's out. No visible smoke now."

Manny's hand shook hard as he pulled the throttle out of burner and leveled off. Then he blew a couple more breaths and looked about the sky. God, but he was scared. He was so fucking scared! His stomach began to flip-flop wildly, and something was squealing loudly in his headset. *A man doesn't do this,* he thought, but then his gorge rose and he could not help himself. He fumbled off a glove, then leaned forward and puked into it. He gushed vomit, groaned, and heaved again.

Lucky Anderson called, and Månny realized it was for the second or third time, and that Lucky was excited, but it was hard to hear over the squealing sound. He answered.

"Repeat for three, Tiger lead," he radioed.

You've got a SAM, three! Break left and down!"

It took a second to digest it, and as he did, his eyes rested on the solid red telelite before him that read LAUNCH.

He slammed the stick hard left, and pulled, and his Thud entered a steep dive. A missile flashed by his cockpit, so close he could see the canard fins moving.

"Oh shit!" Manny screamed to himself, and continued his descent.

"Tiger three, Tiger lead here," Anderson radioed in his casual tone. *"You're clear of the missiles."*

But Manny continued through the split-S maneuver, and when he leveled at 11,000 feet he sped at full throttle toward the western hills. As he did so, shivering and feeling awful, flying at more than 700 knots, he puked into his glove and stifled sobs.

When they landed, Manny told Lucky about hyperventilating, joking about his still being green at this stuff and concentrating on the target so much, he'd forgot and let his breathing get away from him. Lucky told him that was an easy thing to do, but to control his breathing better and watch for the symptoms. You black out at the wrong time and it's fatal, he said. He also told him he'd been damned fortunate to be able to blow out the fire.

His bombs had been thrown into an open field beside Gia Lam airport, and he told the debriefers he'd jinked to evade a flak burst and just flat missed. Billy Bowes said he'd done the same thing. Then everyone began talking about the spectacular secondary explosions from Bowes's errant bombs and about Manny's fire, and forget about the rest of it.

Manny never mentioned that he'd puked. Nor did he reveal how terrified he'd been or how very afraid he was to fly up there again.

• • •

That evening the awful remembrance of fear was hard to shake. Manny tried to drink it away, had put away half a dozen MiG-15's when Bob Liebermann came into the stag bar looking for him. He said Jackie Bell was in the outer "gentlemen's" bar, asking for him and complaining that he'd missed their six o'clock dinner date.

Manny blurted, "Oh shit, I forgot," and hurried to the other bar, where he found her being sweet-talked by another pilot, who was very willing to fill in for him. Manny cut her away from him and patiently listened to her bitch about his tardiness as he bought them both another drink. She stared and asked if something was the matter.

Jackie Bell was perceptive.

"Yeah," he said, but he couldn't and wouldn't tell her what it was. It was shitty enough trying to accept what he'd learned about himself.

She looked at him with her little-kid eyes, asked in a small voice if he'd walk her to her trailer, and then watched closely as he blinked and slowly nodded.

2030 Local—Guest Trailer 9B, Takhli RTAFB, Thailand

When they arrived at her trailer, Manny stumbled and had to put out his hand to the side of the trailer to steady himself.

"You drank too much, hon," said Jackie, inserting the key and jiggling it until it turned. She opened the door. "Watch your step."

"Sorry," he muttered. He wondered if she had the same thing in mind that he did and let his excitement grow. *Forget the fucking mission, Manny,* he tried to tell himself, *and let's see the old pro in action.* He stepped up and tripped again, and when he fell against the metal of the trailer, it made a loud, clanging sound.

"Shhh," she said. "Someone's going to hear you."

"Then let me in," he reasoned.

She led him inside and pushed the door closed so they were in the dark. She kissed him soundly, then more coquettishly as she took more time and parted her lips, held them slightly away from his and caressed his tongue with hers. She was very good at it.

When they broke, he blew a happy but noisy breath, wishing there was less fog in his brain.

"Shhh. Linda's next door."

"Say," he whispered, "has the Ice Maiden got something going with Major Lucky?"

Jackie ignored him and he heard rustling sounds. He peered until he could make out her shape in the darkness, and the shape was fumbling with buttons. *She's taking off her clothes, for Christ's sake.* He grinned as widely as possible without tearing the sides of his mouth and began undoing the side zippers and pulling off the fancy flying boots he'd had custom made by Herr Probst in Germany. He hopped about to remove the second boot.

"Hon, be quiet."

He shucked his flight suit from his shoulders and fell against a chair as he tried to step out of it. "Turn on a light," he suggested, wishing he hadn't drunk quite so many MiG-15's.

"Be quiet," she hissed. She'd removed her blouse and was reaching for a chair to place it on.

"I'm sure glad you stayed over a day," he said, and in the dim light he could see she was removing her bra. He watched her breasts bob free, and exulted because they were as magnificent as he'd imagined. He felt a wash of drunkenness as he reached out to her, then moved closer and moved his hands over her body, anticipating, wanting to use her to cleanse the memory of the fear and restore his manhood.

"Your shorts," she whispered.

He reached down and began rolling down her panties. "I'm busy," he said, so she began to fumble at his waist.

"Oh God, Manny," she whispered. "I want you so *badly*."

They fell on the narrow bed and kissed hard as their hands explored. He pushed his tongue into her mouth, and she caressed it lovingly with her own. He succeeded with her panties, but she was still struggling with his shorts.

He helped her.

"God, it's *huge*." She inhaled a sharp breath.

Manny worried about hurting her and felt to see if she was lubricated. Moistness squished noisily when he probed. She trembled and sucked a breath. He slid wet fingers about her bottom, feeling and caressing and listening to her low moans each time his fingers penetrated an orifice or brushed her clitoris.

She was panting and arching her body. "Hurry," she whispered.

"Be patient," he whispered back, anticipating.

It must be so wonderful that it erases memories.

He moved his hands over her and felt her firm flesh, dropping them now and then to make her moan and shiver. "I can't stand any more, Manny," she whispered finally. She was trembling, caressing the length of him.

"Now?" he whispered.

"Yes!" she cried hoarsely.

As he positioned himself, she pushed her knees up and out and held them there. She sucked a sharp breath at first contact. He had never felt more engorged. *I've got a prick of steel,* he crowed to himself, and very slowly pushed into the moistness. It slid in easily at first, but then she tightened and gripped him like a powerful fist. He stopped, groaning and praying he wouldn't lose it, afraid that if he pushed harder, he might hurt her.

She clutched him about the back of his neck, moaning from the pressure, gripping relentlessly with her vaginal muscles. He pressed lightly to no avail. She only tightened more.

Are you a man? Manny asked himself. He pushed with all his might. She gasped and released, and he pushed on, powerfully, until he was fully lodged and they were belly to slippery belly. But then she somehow constricted again and captured him, and he felt as if his organ had been squeezed into an impossibly small glove.

"Oh, God," she moaned, shuddering uncontrollably, and the muscles held him tight.

He reached to each side and held her knees, one in the crook of each arm, and slowly pulled them upward. When they were breast high, he slipped his arms around her and held her. He felt the pressure relaxing, then lifted her knees higher yet. When she was fully vulnerable and unable to tighten herself, he felt a sigh shudder through her.

My turn, he thought, and pushed deep, feeling the heat that radiated from within her.

She moved her head slowly from side to side, moaning her pleasure and speaking love lies in small rushes of words. He held her tightly and hardly moved except to breath. He could feel the blood pulsing as it grew larger and began moving as of its own will, seeking the source of her fever.

Something inside her surrendered, and she cried out.

"Jesus," he gasped in a croaking sound, for he was into the center of the heat.

She sobbed, and he knew he'd hurt her and hated himself. Then she began to move her hips and make incoherent sounds and progressed into a grand, shuddering orgasm. As her joy continued, he pulled his arms up farther, lifting her knees and positioning her heels over his shoulders. He slowly withdrew, then pushed harshly into the fiery heat, again withdrew and again went in, establishing a rhythm. With each thrust she shuddered and tossed her head in yet another orgasm. He'd never experienced a woman who did that, and it mystified him. He moved faster, and her orgasms became smaller but still joyful.

Then he reared back, almost full-length, and rammed hard, not stopping until their lean, slick bellies slapped together, and she squealed, "Oh God." He did it again and then again, driving her into the mattress, and each time she squealed her pleasure.

He counted five orgasms for her, and by then his testicles were aching, and he knew he must have his own relief. He drove harder.

It wasn't working.

What kind of man . . . ?

Manny stifled a sob. He was still hard, and his balls throbbed unmercifully.

Don't quit.

He deftly rolled her onto her stomach and heard her whisper encouragement. His breath was coming fast, almost in gasps, and some inner wildness would not let him pause. He lifted her onto her knees and spread her legs, then stroked and caressed with trembling hands as her spoken desires increased in urgency. She told him she loved him as he pushed in. When he was sheathed, she screamed, holding her face against the pillow to muffle the sound.

He had to make it.

He worked, driving harder and harder into the heat, jarring her, hearing her animal sounds each time he was deep.

It was no good.

He withdrew almost frantically and turned her again. She was not as wet as before, but there was little obstacle as he rammed fully in and then frantically began to fuck.

She began to cry. He stopped, thinking he'd hurt her.

"It's . . . wonderful," she whispered between sobs, and he realized she was experiencing a big kahuna orgasm. He pressed and stayed there long enough for her to finish.

She subsided finally and spoke between huffs of breath. "I've . . . never . . . never . . . had anything . . . like this."

He lay there, calmly cursing himself, fully extended into a lovely and desirable woman and unable to finish. He wondered if it would always be like that now that he was not a man. He tried to start again but knew it was no good, so he slowed and then stopped.

It was over.

He decided to have a cigarette and try to forget this failure, just as he wanted to forget the other.

She blew out a long breath. "You were wonderful."

He was still atop of her, still in her, but was relaxing and losing his tumescence, thinking about the cigarette, when she suddenly, violently, whispered, "Oh, Manny!"

"Huh?" he asked. She'd bent her knees at his sides and was reaching down to grasp her ankles.

"Huh?" he exclaimed again, because he'd never seen a girl do that. She began to rock, ever so slowly to and fro, as gently as a mother might tend a cradle, and at the same time she was kissing and suckling on his chest and nipples.

"Jesus," he said, for it all felt very good.

"Hush."

She continued to rock slowly and established a steady, serene, and increasingly wonderful tempo. He felt himself growing in her again.

He relaxed and enjoyed, periodically groaning as the heat inside her would engulf him. Freed, she worked the inner muscles, tightening and then loosening and moving up or down on him, then tightening again, and then she began to ripple and quiver inside. She worked silently as her mouth suckled on his chest.

Once, as her muscles relaxed, he started to move, and she stopped cold. "Don't."

She pulled and twisted until he was rolled over onto his back, then she lowered herself on him, catching her breath and moving her hips from side to side as she did so. When she had fully succeeded, she reached back and again grasped her ankles and went back to work, carefully attentive and responding to his every quiver and gasp, for the inner muscles worked even better when she was on top.

The pleasure turned almost unbearable. It intensified until he was hoarsely yelling, "ah . . . ah . . . ah," as she tightened and pulled and rippled. Then she could stand it no longer and released, convulsing again and again, moaning through gritted teeth, helpless as she carefully and methodically milked his juices.

Finally he lay still, head back and utterly contented.

"Okay, hon?" she asked primly as she ran her hands over his chest, still straddling and pinning him with her knees.

"Jesus," he said. He *really* wished he had a cigarette now and wondered if she would mind.

"Feel better?" she whispered.

"Yeah. I feel a hell of a lot better. You?"

"You were wonderful."

"Yeah? You too."

She shuddered. He started to lift her off, but she resisted, wanting to stay connected. He slowly rolled over and lifted onto his elbows, wondering where he'd left his flight suit, for his cigarettes were in the shoulder pocket. She relaxed and sighed.

"So good," she whispered. Then she began to bring her knees up at his sides and reached down for her ankles.

"Jesus," he said groggily into the first dim light of morning. "That was five times."

She stretched lazily and snuggled. "That was six times, hon."

"Jesus," he said again, wondering where he'd lost track. She kissed his chest. "I feel *wonderful.*"

"Dinner tonight?" Manny asked to get her mind off sex, because she was licking his nipples and squirming against his leg as if she were becoming aroused again. *Didn't she sleep?*

He was exhausted.

"I've got to go back to the camp today, hon," she said.

"That's too bad." It was okay by him. It would take weeks to get back into shape.

"We've got a phone at the camp. I'll write out the number and put it in your pocket so you won't forget it. Will you give me a call tomorrow?" she asked in the little girl's voice.

"It's not easy to get an outside line from the squadron."

"Colonel Lyons said *he* would call."

"Hell, Jackie, the bastard is married with three kids. You oughta stay away from him."

"Why? Do you intend to marry me?"

"Maybe I'd better go."

"Just joking, hon. I don't like Colonel Lyons. He's too egotistical. But I've got to get some things for my camp, and Colonel Parker says to work it through him."

"Lyons is an asshole."

"Will you call?"

"Yeah," said Manny. "There's a Thai pay phone at the Service Club."

She mewed some more and began to slip down under the sheet.

"I don't think I can do it, Jackie."

She proved him wrong.

When they emerged from the air-conditioned trailer, the heat of the morning sun was startling.

They walked toward the nearby O' Club for breakfast.

"It's hot today," she complained.

"Hell," he said. "It's hot every day."

"Not long until the monsoon rains arrive," she said. "They should be here within the month. Maybe that'll cool things off some."

A voice sounded from in back of them. "Could I speak with you, Miss Bell?"

It was Colonel Tom Lyons, and he looked irritated.

Manny saluted.

Lyons did not return it. "Where's your hat, Captain?"

Manny pulled it from the leg pocket of his flight suit and put it on.

Lyons shook his head at Manny as if exasperated, then motioned to Jackie. "I'd like to speak with you at my office. It's concerning your requests."

Manny bristled until Jackie patted his arm. "Since I'm going back to the camp today, this is my last chance to get the things I came for." Then in a lower tone she whispered, "Call me," and went with Lyons toward his blue staff sedan.

Colonal Lyons gave him one last hard look before he opened her door and began his smooth line. Jackie waved to

Manny, then joined in the conversation, making her pitch for as much support for her camp as she could get.

Manny wandered on toward the Officers' Club. He thought about how he still owed Bob Liebermann a burger, and wondered if he hurried if he might find him still at breakfast. He also remembered that there were some things he needed to pick up at the base exchange. He didn't reflect on the fact that Jackie Bell's solution had worked, for it had been so effective that he'd utterly forgotten about the previous day's problem. At least for the present his fear had been washed away.

Later that morning Lucky Anderson told him it was time to send someone from C-Flight on rest-and-recuperation leave, and offered it to him. Manny thought about it for a moment, then shook his head. Too many things that needed to get done, he told him. He didn't tell him that one of those would be to explore how any female could grab her ankles and make Manny DeVera alternate between snorting like a bull and squealing like a happy baby.

CHAPTER TEN

Monday, May 1st, 1005 Local—HQ Seventh Air Force, Tan Son Nhut Air Base, Saigon, South Vietnam

Lieutenant Colonel Pearly Gates

The general saw him at the doorway and waved him into his office. "I've got ten minutes before my next meeting."

Pearly hurried inside, eyes feeling grainy and his body near its limits of exhaustion.

"You got the recce photos?" Moss asked.

"Yes, sir," Pearly mumbled.

Pearly pulled them from the folder and placed them side by side before the general. There were six in all, and they created a montage of the bridge and its surrounding area.

Moss leaned over them. "You said there were three hits?"

"Two on the bridge surface and one on a piling." He pointed them out. "Here on the northern span, here on the southern span, and this concrete piling on the island's damaged."

"Not only is the damned thing still standing, you can hardly tell it was hit."

"You were right about the Bullpups being inadequate, sir."

"Damn right I was."

"The railroad side's damaged on the southern span, sir. And on the northernmost span there's a hole penetrating through the highway surface. The damage is worse than it appears."

Moss shook his head. "Don't try to make ice cream out of horseshit, Pearly. We may have inconvenienced them, but we didn't stop much traffic. How long until it's repaired?"

"Intell figures the road traffic was shut down for six to eight hours. The rails were repaired in less than twelve hours."

"So it's *already* back in operation?"

"Yes, sir. And we lost three pilots." Pearly's voice cracked on the last sentence.

Moss pursed his lips thoughtfully. "You ready to forward the results to CINCPAC?"

"Yes, sir." Pearly didn't try to hide his disappointment.

Moss leaned back in his chair, and Pearly swallowed under the scrutiny.

"You look tired, Pearly. You getting proper sleep?"

"Not much, sir."

"What is it? Losing the pilots?"

"That and wondering if I didn't screw up by picking that target."

"You didn't make the decision, I did, and I sleep just fine, Pearly. We lost some good men and I hate it, but I'm able to sleep at night and function and get on with things. And"—he looked Pearly in the eye—"I expect my key staff officers to do the same."

"Yes, sir."

"Don't blame yourself for having qualms and second thoughts. We all do. But once a decision's made, you've got to learn to put your faith in the guys with the stick in their hand. The whole difference between good men and good military men is that from time to time we have to be able to overcome the Judeo-Christian heritage we've been taught since childhood. We've got to be able to kill our enemies. And . . . we've got to be able to send men out knowing some aren't coming back."

A colonel, Moss's chief of staff, came to the door and looked in. It was time for Moss's meeting. Moss waved him away and continued to eye Pearly Gates.

"You keeping up with what's happening here in South Vietnam?"

"Not really. I'm busy enough with what's going on up north."

"There's a big fight going on at Khe Sanh. Our Marines are engaging a regiment of NVA regulars in the mountains there, and they're taking losses. They'll probably lose a hundred fifty or more, with maybe four times that many wounded. Good, brave men, Pearly. Tough guys, and they'll win like they usually do. There's three strategic hills there, and they'll take them all."

Pearly nodded.

"You know what we'll do then, within a month or two, maybe less?"

Pearly cocked his head.

"We'll abandon the hills. See, our soldiers here have no front lines, and there's no real objectives except to kill enemy soldiers and try to keep them out of key areas. We're kicking the shit out of them here, then going over there to whip 'em again, but we're not taking anything and holding it. Our guys are fighting a war of attrition against an Asian enemy, which is precisely what General Joe Stilwell said never to do some thirty years ago. And Joe Stilwell likely knew Asia better than any American military man ever, including MacArthur."

"Doesn't make much sense, does it, sir?"

"Right now there's four hundred thousand enemy troops here in the south. Maybe three hundred thousand are operational fighting men. Every day they receive reinforcements and supplies from North Vietnam. And every few months General Westy asks for more American ground forces to fight them with. Hanoi sends more NVA troops, we send more American military men. It could keep going like that until the American public gets tired of it."

Pearly nodded.

"So what's our ace in the hole? How the hell can we turn a fucking no-win, two-bit war in Asia into something manageable? Which really means, how the hell can we get the North Vietnamese to back out of the fight and let this country decide its own fate?"

Pearly stared.

"We've got an Air Force that could do it. You know that. All we have to do is convince the politicians to let us act like we're at war and turn us loose to cut off the snake's head up north. I'll bet it wouldn't take you a week to build a plan that would force Hanoi's hand. Hell, I'll bet you've already *got* one."

"Yes, sir," said Pearly. "I do. Although it's very rough and would need a lot of work."

"What's the first step of your plan?"

"Counter-air. We'd take out their air defense network."

"What aircraft would we use?"

"The Wild Weasels would lead the way, but we'd use everything we've got. B-52's to fighters. We'd also use short-range missiles, decoys, and the entire conventional arsenal."

"And second?"

"Take out the hundred strategic targets the JCS said were critical to their war effort."

"And then?"

"Destroy the reservoirs and dikes and flood the country. The whole place sits right at sea level, and that would paralyze them. We'd also mine their ports and waterways, destroy their military headquarters and centers of government, take out their . . ."

Moss interrupted. "How long would it take us to force North Vietnam from the fight?"

"Within three weeks their infrastructure would be destroyed."

"Our losses?"

"Eight percent of our strike force the first week. Down to less than one percent after we've destroyed the defenses."

Moss stared. "Do you believe that scenario?"

"Yes, sir, I do."

"Between you and me, I briefed something similar to your plan to the Air Force Chief of Staff," said Moss. "Only I told him it might take as much as four to six weeks before the North Vietnamese would say uncle."

Pearly caught his breath. He wondered. . . .

"He said the timing's wrong, that the political environment is sour. The President's scared of the Russians and Chinese, the SecDef's determined we can't win and he's suspicious of military advice, and Congress is increasingly fed up with the whole thing."

Pearly deflated.

Moss was slowly shaking his head. "A recent poll showed that more than sixty percent of the American public support a vigorous air campaign to win the war, but the people who can make it happen are either too frightened or too political to let us do it."

The colonel reappeared at the door, looking nervous.

"Just a couple more minutes," called Moss.

"We'll be late, General."

"Won't be the first time I've kept a politician waiting."

The colonel backed from the doorway.

"Another delegation of truth-seekers from Washington," explained Moss.

"I'd better be going, then."

"When I'm finished."

"Yes, sir."

"I was once a pretty damned good squadron commander, Pearly, so every now and then you've got to put up with me trying to act like a leader. I envy the commanders in the operational units. I manage assets while they lead men into air battles."

Pearly waited as Moss reflected.

"But then every once in a while I get to hand out advice to you guys on my staff. One of my strong points when I *was* a leader was that I knew to keep my men informed and then back off and give them a chance to get the job done."

Pearly nodded.

"Try it yourself. Give the wings the best advice and the best plans you can, and then get out of their way and let them fly and fight."

"Yes, sir."

"We can win this war, Pearly, and we will once the politicians give us the nod. They'll come around. Until then we've got to keep as much pressure as possible off the backs of our ground troops. One good way is to carry out our new OPlan."

"Then you're not canceling the campaign?"

"Of course not. Go ahead and send the results to CINCPAC, bad-news photos and all, and I'll make a call to the admiral this afternoon before it gets there. I'll tell him we proved we could hit the damn bridge, but the weapons we were *directed* to use were too light and made us too vulnerable. He's still a Navy fighter jock at heart, and he understands glitches like this. For the next couple of weeks we're going to pound on the small airfields, enemy electrical plants, and chokepoints in the new authorized-targets list.

Then we'll go after that damnable bridge again, but we'll do it with *bombs*, like we should've the first time."

Pearly was beginning to feel better. The general, he decided, was indeed a leader.

"When I was commander of the Fighter Weapons Center at Nellis," said Moss, "I had a group of fighter jocks who were damned good with tactics. I want you to work with a few of them, and for you guys to iron out the glitches before we go back to the Doumer bridge. Once we've knocked that one down, we'll go to work on the others."

"Yes, sir," said Pearly.

"A few of my old Nellis mafia are stationed over here. You know Lucky Anderson?"

"He's a flight commander at Takhli."

"Then there's Benny Lewis. . . ." Moss frowned. "But he's in a stateside hospital."

Lewis had been a Wild Weasel pilot. Pearly Gates had met him and had known his backseater well. The combat theater was a small world.

Moss went over a few more names, then settled on Anderson again. "Lucky's as good as they come. You want me to call B. J. Parker and get him sprung loose to work with you?"

"No need to, sir. I've a good working relationship with Colonel Parker."

The colonel was back. "The congressman from New York's asking for you, General."

Lieutenant General Moss sighed. He rose to his feet, glared at his chief of staff, then turned back to Pearly and pointed at the recce photos still arrayed on his desktop.

"Next time we go after that damned thing," he said, "I'll expect better news."

"I sure hope I can give it to you, General."

"Now get your ass out of here and go get some sleep."

1040 Local

Five minutes later Pearly entered the administrative section of his branch, fully intending to spend only a few minutes before taking the general's advice. But when Pearly asked the WAF sergeant if there was anything going, she motioned her head at a visitor seated in his office, wearing a civilian safari outfit.

"Says he wants to speak with you, Colonel," she said.

"Who is he?"

"Special agent's all he said. Didn't give a name."

"Anything else?"

"Staff Sergeant Slye went to his barracks a few minutes ago saying he was sick."

"That's twice this week for him."

She nodded.

Slye was a sometime eight ball and borderline malingerer. The master sergeant he worked for said his frequent sicknesses were the result of too much partying, too late. He said he'd seen him in some pretty shabby joints downtown. When Pearly, tongue in cheek, had asked what he'd been doing there himself, the sergeant hadn't smiled. He'd said he liked to keep tabs on his people.

Pearly stepped into his office, wondering how quickly he might be able to get rid of the spook. No telling which agency he worked for. They all liked the title of "special agent," and to Pearly's mind they were all quite alike.

"Can I help you?" he asked.

The man looked up lazily from the *Time* magazine he'd taken from Pearly's in-basket.

"You Lieutenant Colonel Gates?"

Pearly sighed and chose to ignore the question. He was obviously a light colonel, and the name tag on his right breast pocket was not misspelled.

He took his seat behind his desk. "I've not had the pleasure," he said.

The man's brows furrowed.

"Who are you?" Pearly asked.

The man brightened. "Special Agent Brown."

"Identification?"

The man fumbled, then held up a leather case with a badge and card. He was OSI, and his last name was York.

Not too tricky. Pearly figured he was here to look into the security leak that was compromising the target list. The agents were becoming a pestilence within the headquarters.

"We'd like to question the men in your branch, Colonel."

"Is it really necessary?"

The spook grimaced. "We believe so."

"Concerning what?"

"Routine security inspection. We'll start with a general rundown of your organization's function. Manpower. List of personnel. Duties. That sort of thing."

Joe Friday was alive and well.

Pearly told him there was a total of seventeen people in his branch. Including himself, there were three officers, five noncoms, counting his admin sergeant, and nine airmen.

The agent took out a notepad and pen. "Names?"

"The staff sergeant out front will give you a roster."

The spook leaned forward, trying to pin him with a confidential stare. "Anyone acting suspicious lately? Anyone I should be concentrating on?"

"What do you mean?"

"You know."

"No, I don't. Tell me."

When the agent was more specific, Pearly told him he didn't know if any of his people were homosexuals, alcoholics, or narcotics users. He didn't believe so, but who could really know? Nor was there any unpatriotic talk that he'd heard of.

"Anyone reporting in sick a lot? Taking an excessive amount of time off?"

Pearly thought of Sergeant Slye, then decided that even if he was somewhat of an eight ball, there was no way the angular young man from Arkansas could be a spy. Anyway, he wasn't gone *that* often. "Not really," he answered.

"How many have access to classified material?"

"All of them," replied Pearly.

"Any Top Secret material stored here?"

"Yes."

The Agent brightened. "How many Top Secret documents?"

"You have no need to know that."

"I can show you my security clearance."

Pearly sighed. "You still have absolutely no need to know, and that's prerequisite. Much of our material is compartmentalized and source sensitive, requiring special clearance."

"Can I see the document logs, showing who handles what?"

Pearly nodded. "I'll have them brought to you."

"I'll need to see where you keep the documents."

"They're in a classified vault and you can't go in there."

The agent's voice was rising. "I can go anywhere in this building. I have an order signed by Lieutenant General Moss."

"We control documents that even General Moss can't see."

The agent looked exasperated.

"Look, let's start this entire thing over. You tell me what you're after, and I'll make sure you get to see what's necessary for your investigation. We'll even sanitize the vault and escort you in there, if it's really necessary."

"It's not an investigation," argued Special Agent Brown/ York. "Just a routine security-procedures check."

Again Pearly sighed, feeling the weariness creeping over him. "Then you tell me what your routine check's about, and I'll give you all the help I can."

The agent would not tell him what the check was about, even though Pearly knew. Ten frustrating minutes later they walked down the hall to the other facilities of Pearly's domain.

"We work in four different rooms, all in this wing of the building," Pearly told him. "My office, two working offices, there and there, and the classified vault on the end."

"Your men work in three different groups?"

"Two. Combat Programs, and Documentation." He pointed at one door. "There's a major, a captain, and seven enlisted men working in the Combat Programs section. They build the operations and logistics plans." He pointed at another. "Documentation section's run by Master Sergeant Turner. His five men keep track of all the material. They post amendments and changes, run the vault, and make sure the compartmentalized documents stay that way."

"Where do you keep your classified material?"

Pearly pointed again at the massive steel door. "Top Secret and Sensitive documents are kept in the vault, controlled by the Documentation section. Secret and Confidential material's in safes in the various rooms. Which are you interested in?"

The answer, Pearly knew, was Top Secret, -Sensitive, for that was how the targets were classified until they were attacked. After they were bombed, they were downgraded to Confidential.

The agent surprised him. "All of it," he said.

"You want to include every classified document we've got?"

The agent nodded. "Past, present, and future."

Pearly stopped, then slowly took off his glasses and began to polish them. He was dog-weary from the lack of sleep, and increasingly impatient with the OSI agent.

"Something wrong with that?"

Pearly held the glasses up to inspect them. "I won't tell you the number of Top Secret documents we've got on hand, but in all we have more than nine thousand classified manuals, plans, and pieces of correspondence. Probably more like twenty thousand, if you count amendments and changes."

The agent's mouth dropped.

"So where do you want to start?" Pearly asked wearily.

"First with your people, then with the classified." The agent was frowning. "Maybe I'd better call in a couple of other agents."

"Maybe so. Or enlist some of my men to help. You've bitten off a big chunk."

Airman First Class O'Neil came out of the Documentation office and started down the hall.

Pearly called his name.

O'Neil turned and saw them, and hurried back. "Yes, sir."

"You going somewhere important?"

"Just down to the cafeteria for lunch."

"Special Agent . . . what did you say your name was?"

"Jones."

"Special Agent Jones here is helping to conduct a routine security procedures check in the headquarters. Wants to make sure we're handling our classified material properly."

O'Neil did not bat an eye. He was one of Pearly's sharpest young airmen. He had two years of college, and his NCOIC, Master Sergeant Turner, was trying to get him into the airman's education-and-commissioning program.

"Is Sergeant Turner in?" Pearly asked.

As his name was spoken, Turner came down the hallway toward them.

Pearly introduced them. The NCOIC appeared more nervous than O'Neil, Pearly observed, likely because he knew the turmoil that was about to beset his section. Turner was an orderly man with an orderly mind and did not like interruptions in the routines he'd established to handle the tremendous work load.

"Why don't you begin with the Documentation section," Pearly told the agent, "so we can get that part over with and things back to normal. Sergeant Turner will help you."

He told Turner to sanitize, if necessary, and show him the vault.

"Will do, Colonel," said the master sergeant. His look remained grim.

"Now," said Pearly Gates, "I am going to follow a direct order and go to the BOQ to get some rest."

1400 Local—Route Pack Five, North Vietnam

Major Lucky Anderson

The big formation was over the western mountains, still twenty miles from the flatlands of pack six. There were a number of cumulus clouds at their altitude and more up ahead, and that fact was cheerful to no one.

But Lucky's ECM pod was working, his flight was precisely spaced and positioned in the middle of the twenty-ship gaggle, and there was no flak at the height they flew at, so all was not amiss. They were on their way to the power-transmission station in a northern suburb of Hanoi to complete the destruction of the area's power-distribution network, and were flying in a beeline for the thing.

Red Dog flight, the Wild Weasels, was ranging out a few miles ahead and called that there was only a single SAM radar signal on the air.

So far so good. The Weasels should be able to deal with the single site. There were likely to be others, but according to the bomber generals all they had to do was sit back in their big formation and whistle, and the missiles would miss. But SAMs were all they were likely to have to worry about until they dived into the flak. The MiGs had been inactive for several days now.

"*THIS IS BIG EYE. GOPHER AT ALPHA FOX ONE. I REPEAT. THIS IS BIG EYE. GOPHER AT ALPHA FOX ONE.*" The volume over the emergency channel was loud.

I was wrong, he thought as the airborne radar, call sign

Big Eye, made its MiG warning call. He glanced at the small map on his kneeboard to find the A-F-1 sector.

"THIS IS MOTEL. GOPHER AT ALPHA GOLF THREE. I REPEAT. THIS IS MOTEL. GOPHER AT ALPHA GOLF THREE." Motel radar's transmission was less booming, but the words were spoken just as emphatically.

Were the MiGs in A-F-1 or A-G-3? he wondered. Then he realized they were probably in both sectors, and he wondered if it wasn't going to be a MiG day.

The radio channel became busy as flight leaders encouraged their pilots to maintain a lookout for MiGs.

Lucky glanced out to the left side and saw the Red River in the distance. In a minute or so they would enter pack six.

1403 Local—Hoa Binh Province, DRV

Air Regiment Commandant Quon

He piloted his distinctive MiG-21F, with its brightly polished aluminum and the red sash painted across the fuselage. Today they would use stealth, and he wished he could somehow become less visible. The previous week he'd ordered that all the MiGs be painted dull green, but it would take several weeks for the job to be completed.

The small-tail MiG-21 was goosey, and the nose tended to wander in a tight turn, but Quon liked the aircraft's speed and had taken it to its limits on several occasions. Handled properly, it could turn like a nimble acrobat.

He flew at the edge of a large cloud and listened to the voice of the radar controller. The Mee radar-hunters were in a four-ship formation a few kilometers to his right, the bigger formation a dozen kilometers to his left. He was between them. Quon's three-ship section of MiG-21's were to attack the radar-hunters. A larger group of MiG-17's was just now turning toward the rear of the larger formation.

"This is Red Quon. Directions to target?" he radioed, asking the Phuc Yen radar controller to steer him toward the stern of the radar-hunters. The P-1 radar tracked his datalink return, and the controller knew his position as well as the location of the Thunder planes. The enemy jammers were set to confuse rocket and artillery battery radars, but didn't affect command-and-control radars such as the P-1.

"*Red Quon, turn and fly nine-four degrees,*" came a quick response from the controller. "*Target at five kilometers, one hundred meters low.*"

Good. It was time to turn, and the entire approach had been fortuitously hidden by clouds. He'd seen no Thunder planes; therefore, he was confident they hadn't seen him.

He deftly motioned to his two wingmen to drop back, then flattened his hand and moved it downward. He wanted them behind and slightly lower, prepared to pull up and fire rockets when his own were expended.

He abruptly turned the MiG on its right delta wing, and in the harsh turn grunted as the gravity forces pressed him. The Russian advisors tried to convince him to wear one of their full-body antigravity suits, but he shunned it as too hot and unnatural. He liked to feel the gravity forces, wanted to remain aware of every slight nuance of flight.

He was in a slight dive, picking up speed, for he wished to be lower than his quarry. He interpreted the indicated speed to be 1,220 kilometers ground speed, likely a bit faster than the Americans would be flying, and checked the weapons wafer switch to ensure he'd set it properly. The number-one K-13 heat-seeking rocket was indeed selected. Unlike later models that used audio, the early MiG-21's used a light to show when the missile was locked on. It would remain off until it detected heat from a target, then would flicker until it locked on, at which time the light would become bright and steady.

He flew at the edge of the cloud, moving in and out of its wispy reaches, steadied on a heading of 100 degrees, then called again for directions to target.

The controller was excited. Quon was within 3,000 meters and slowly closing, the Thunder planes ten degrees left.

He corrected, broke out of the clouds, and saw the big planes before him. He slapped the paddle switch to activate the rocket head, and throttled back ever so slightly, tracking precisely on the rearmost aircraft, which was slightly high and dead ahead.

The amber-colored tracking light flickered, then came on steady. He pulled the trigger, felt a slight tremor, then watched the K-13 rocket flash into view, tracking true.

A hit! The Thunder plane slewed and began to disintegrate.

No time for celebration. He'd already shifted his atten-

tion to the next aircraft in the flight, selected right outer station, and slapped at the spring-loaded tracking-head switch.

The radar-hunters before him hadn't realized they'd lost
their fourth ship, for they continued as if nothing were
amiss.

The Phuc Yen radar controller was shouting instructions,
but Quon ignored his calls.

He closed on the third aircraft, this one a two-seater.
Well within 1,000 meters now. The light blinked, steadied.
He fired and watched the white trail of the rocket as it
sprinted forward.

Another kill! The Thunder plane staggered and fire-
torched behind the rear cockpit. A split second later he saw
first one and then another flash as the pilots ejected.

He was about to call for his wingmen to pull forward to
join him when the lead Thunder plane turned hard right,
followed closely by his number two.

Quon broke left and down, not bothering to select
reburner boost.

Not a bad afternoon, he crowed as he saw that both of his
wingmen were with him. They sped northward toward the
safety of the areas restricted to the Mee by their own rules.

1407 Local—Route Pack Six, North Vietnam

Major Lucky Anderson

In a matter of twenty seconds they'd lost three aircraft, two
in the Wild Weasel flight and one in the strike force. Counting the two men in the dual-seat Weasel bird, there were a
total of four people swinging in four parachutes, all floating
earthward at the same time, and the strident squeals of four
emergency beepers were raucous and confusing.

No one knew exactly what to do for a moment, except to
circle the chutes, wonder what had happened, and look out
for more of whatever the hell it had been.

Lucky felt it had likely been MiGs coming up from their
six o'clock, so he called for everyone to stay on the lookout
for them. Tiny Bechler, flying in one of the rearmost flights
in the gaggle, said he saw a flight of MiGs north of them
running like hell. Knowing he'd been right didn't make
Lucky feel better.

Colonel Mack was mission commander, and after a minute or so, when he'd gotten things fairly well in hand, said he felt they just might luck out and pick up the pilots, all of whom had survived their shoot-downs and were in radio contact. He canceled the strike mission so they could concentrate on the rescue effort.

The Wild Weasels, both the Weasel crew and their wingman, were down in the flats thirty-five miles west of Hanoi. The strike pilot was not far away, nearer the base of the mountains but also in the flatlands. Those were bad positions, for there was little cover to hide in, but Mack said that with a fighter force as big as theirs they could surely keep the gomers away while the rescue force came in and picked them up.

But shortly it became apparent that the rescue aircraft, especially the choppers, didn't wish to venture over the valley regardless of *how* many fighters were protecting them. They came in partway, then hemmed and hawed and made various excuses, and Lucky couldn't fault them. Out over the flats the rescue would have been a hairy one on a good day, and if the rescue pilots had an unlucky feeling, they might end up with even more people on the ground than were down there now.

Finally a chopper pilot said he had a fuel-flow problem, and the aircraft commander of the other chopper said he couldn't go in alone, so the rescue effort was scrubbed.

Colonel Mack told the guys on the ground—there were so many of them it was hard to keep them straight—that they'd try to put together another rescue attempt in the morning.

On their way back to the air-refueling tanker, Lucky thought a lot about what had transpired, for he felt that after such a debacle you should certainly learn *something*.

Lesson one was that the gomers had gotten their shit all together in one bag regarding MiGs and how to use them. No one had seen any of them during the fight—if you were generous enough to call it a fight—and the MiGs had cleanly gotten away. That confirmed the big ECM pod gaggle was no good for seeing and fighting MiGs. Lucky thought about it and decided to tell his C-Flight to become more wary, to keep checking their six o'clock positions, and to keep a plan in mind at all times.

Lesson two? Well, the guys had floated down in their

parachutes and were likely seen by every gomer within a dozen miles. If he was unlucky enough to go down in an inhabited area like that, he decided to put as much real estate as possible very quickly between himself and where the gomers *thought* he'd come to earth. It would be dangerous moving fast through the vast populations down there, but it was a hell of a lot better than just hunkering down and hoping rescue would get there before the bad guys did.

His third and final lesson was that the MiG alerts had to be changed. They had to find a way to advise the pilots of precisely where the MiGs were without their having to look up some obscure quadrant on a map. He decided to call Pearly Gates in Saigon about that one.

On their return trip, as they neared the Laotian border, the individual flights slowed and circled the Termite Hill, where a guy from the 357th squadron had been mutilated by a group of enemy soldiers. In a dark and angry mood they armed their weapons switches and one by one dived at the mountain with their unused ordnance. There was no reason for accuracy, so they just generally aimed for any remaining patches of jungle growth on the mountainside. As each of them felt their bombs release, it somehow made them feel better. The 750-pound bombs were tail-fuzed for good penetration, so when they exploded, they created great spouts of red dirt and green trees. By the time they left, much of the eastern slope of the mountain had been denuded of trees, and a pall of red dust drifted eerily through the small valley.

1430 Local—Phuc Yen People's Army Air Force Base, DRV

Air Regiment Commandant Quon

Quon held his forces back as the attack force of Thunder planes milled about in the area where they'd lost their three aircraft. Finally, when the controllers confirmed there were no enemy aircraft left around, Quon directed all fighters to land.

The Mee rules said they could not shoot them down during final approach, for Phuc Yen was restricted to Mee fighters.

As he listened to the controllers give crisp instructions to descend and land, Quon felt a puff of pride. After only two days Xuan Nha and his protégé were *already* turning things around, and he had made it possible. He'd already sensed a surge in his pilots' confidence. After today it would be even better.

Quon made his approach, but pulled up the last moment before touchdown and smoothly performed a crisp four-point victory roll and then another, for the benefit of the men who would be observing below. He sharply turned the MiG-21 back on a downwind leg and prepared to land, feeling good about what he'd done.

With the reestablishment of radar control for his MiGs now accomplished, he could turn more attention to settling things with the man called *Lokee*.

1850 Local—Officers' Club Stag Bar, Takhli RTAFB, Thailand

The atmosphere at the O' Club bar reflected the successes or failures of the fighter pilots and their missions. Following a good day, such as the raid on Kep airfield, the atmosphere would be jolly, and you would hear a lot of laughter and horsing around, and the jocks would relate how they'd discovered this new tactic, or that new fact about the enemy. On the first day of May in 1967, there was little of that, for that particular Monday the MiG drivers had kicked the shit out of the strike force.

The mood of the men was downbeat, angry, and a little perplexed. They were educated and canny, the cream of America, and to a man they did not like or accept failure.

As often happened, the men shot down had been especially capable and well liked. The Wild Weasel crew was the most experienced in the wing, flying in the number-three slot only because they'd been filling in for another crew. The Weasel pilot had just been put in for the Medal of Honor for destroying a SAM site and killing two MiGs on a single, very hairy mission. The two single-seat fighter jocks had been among the best in the wing.

They'd all been lost in pack six, and the men in the bar knew that none of them would be picked up, and they spoke glumly about their downed comrades.

In corners of the bar two different groups held small celebrations. One was for a pilot of the 333rd TFS, a popular major who'd been named squadron-operations officer. The other, smaller gathering was for Billy Bowes of the 354th squadron, who had been promoted that day.

Captain Billy Bowes

The C-Flight pilots were gathered in a group, celebrating his promotion. Manny DeVera led them, and others in the bar joined in to sing the promotion song:

"Oh, he climbed up on the steeple,
and pissed on all the people,
but they couldn't piss on himmmm.
Fuck himmmmm."

Major Lucky held a pair of sterling-silver insignia before Billy Bowes. "I suppose you think you deserve these?"

"Well, sir, I was beginning to think I was a permanent lieutenant." During the past ten days they'd all developed an intense respect for Major Lucky Anderson, and the captain tracks meant more coming from a man Billy looked up to.

"You guys are pampered," growled Major Lucky. "It took my group six years to make captain."

"Only takes us four and a half years now," said Billy Bowes. "Shows you how much more valuable we are."

"Wiseass," Lucky grinned, then shook his hand. "You're a hell of a pilot, Billy. Congratulations." He dropped the shiny insignia into Billy's hand. "This particular pair of tracks came from a long line of fighter jocks, starting with Tommy McGuire."

The group was awed. McGuire had shot down thirty-eight Japanese aircraft in World War II and was the second leading American ace of all time, topped only by Dick Bong. If he'd lived longer, many pilots from that time felt he would have surpassed Bong.

Billy peered down at the captain's bars with a reverent expression.

Lucky nodded at him. "There's a lot of proud history that goes along with them. When it's your turn to pass 'em on, pick some young pilot *you* think will honor them."

Billy felt such emotion that it was difficult to answer, so he just nodded. The group remained quiet as everyone stared at the captain's bars.

Henry Horn finally spoke solemnly. "Billy, you've given me confidence. I used to worry about making captain. Now I know *anyone* can make it."

The others laughed and the awkward moment was past.

"A toast!" cried Bob Liebermann, and it was so out of character for the quiet captain that he gained everyone's attention.

They waited as he looked about at them, gaining courage to continue.

"C'mon, Bob," encouraged Manny DeVera, who was Liebermann's roommate, "he doesn't deserve much."

The others howled in happy agreement.

Liebermann lifted his beer bottle and looked at Bowes. "May you have a fast jet and blue skies...."

"Hear, hear!" chanted the others.

"May your enemies falter and fall before you...."

"Hear, hear!"

"And may your nerves and your prick turn to *steel*."

They laughed.

"By damn," concluded Bob Liebermann.

They looked at him inquisitively.

"Turk Tatro taught me that one, and I thought it was appropriate," mumbled Liebermann, looking about for reassurance.

"Hear, hear," they said in quieter voices.

Joe Walker looked sad. "Sure be nice if Turk was here with us."

"I'll bet he's giving the gomers fits," said Manny, "trying to understand him. Probably can't figure out why it takes him half an hour to give his name, rank, and service number."

"Yeah," agreed Henry Horn, "and he's probably got 'em shook up with his jokes about chasing little women. Hell, that's the only kind of females they've got."

They laughed.

Joe Walker grew wistful. "Turk's tough. They question him, I'll bet he doesn't give them the time of day."

Billy started to say something about everyone having a breaking point, then shut up. They all knew that was true.

Lucky Anderson clapped a heavy hand on Billy's shoulder. "I've got an appointment."

Manny DeVera raised an eyebrow. "Wouldn't be with a certain person from Bangkok, would it, boss?"

Major Lucky ignored the question. "Congratulations, Billy. Next week I'm putting DeVera on flight-lead orders. You'll be next."

Bob Liebermann listened with a frown. It was common knowledge within the flight that he wanted, very badly, to lead a flight of fighters. It was also known that Lucky wanted him to become more at ease with the Thud and to gain more experience first. So Liebermann studied relentlessly and learned the flying rules and regs as well as anyone in the squadron, and hoped he wouldn't have to wait long before Lucky relented.

Lucky Anderson left the stag bar through the side door leading to the trailers.

"Bet he's going to say good-bye to the Ice Maiden," said Manny. "She's leaving on tonight's base flight to Don Muang." Don Muang was the Bangkok airport.

"How the hell do you know that?" asked Billy.

Manny cast him a funny look, and Billy realized that he'd taken it as his mission to know everything possible about round-eyes who ventured onto the base.

"Lucky doesn't talk much about personal relationships with women," mused Henry Horn. "Because of his face, I guess."

That gave them all pause.

"Yeah," Manny finally muttered. "Maybe you're right."

Billy furrowed his brow at the thought. He'd met few officers in the Air Force like Lucky Anderson. He looked up to him, as he might have looked up to his father if he'd known him better. They all felt like that. They seldom spoke, or even *thought* about Lucky's deformity, for there was so much to admire in him.

It was known that even while recuperating from his accident, he'd battled to be returned to flying status. It was also accepted by most that he was probably the most tenacious combat pilot in the wing. But Lucky was also regarded by his men as a good guy and a superb leader who gave an honest shit about their welfare. The burned face didn't figure into any of the factors of being a fighter pilot, a leader, or a man. Even Bob Liebermann, in his zeal to be placed on flight-lead orders, never doubted that Lucky Anderson would make the correct decision.

"I suppose," said Henry Horn, "women get turned off by his burns. I noticed that No Hab doesn't like to look at him. He is pretty ugly."

Bob Liebermann had been drinking beyond his tolerance level. "He's not really *ugly*," he said. "He just doesn't have a face."

Manny DeVera looked troubled. "It isn't right. A guy like him who's got more ability than anyone I know, living like a fucking monk. I know for a fact he hasn't gone to the Ice Maiden's trailer with her."

Bob Liebermann spoke up. "Turk Tatro said Lucky went downtown with him once, but he wouldn't go into the bars. Said he joked about there being no reason to scare the whores."

"Guess there's nothing we can do to help," Captain Billy Bowes finally said.

"Your blond girlfriend gone now?" Joe Walker asked Manny.

"She's at a Peace Corps camp not far from here. I called her a bit ago."

"Maybe she could tell the Ice Maiden what kind of super guy Lucky is," said Walker.

"I think she already knows. When I asked Jackie about what was going on between them, she just got all swimmy-eyed and said it was *nice* and wouldn't say anything else."

"Maybe," said Joe Walker, "they're already getting it on."

Manny shook his head. "He's got some kinda hang-up. He's not getting any."

"You guys act like we're a bunch of matchmakers," said Bob Liebermann uneasily. "Major Lucky wouldn't like us doing this."

"Hell," said Manny with a wry grin," he works his ass off trying to keep us alive. Least we can do is a little pimping for him."

Billy bought another round in celebration of making captain, and the conversation continued about how they might help get Major Lucky laid, then shifted to stories about how each of them had scored or missed out with females of the world's various nationalities.

A couple of times during the increasingly loud conversation, Billy fished the captain's bars from his pocket and looked at them. He was still awed by them and impressed about what Lucky had done.

Then Tiny Bechler, the huge lieutenant from the clit-licker squadron, moved out to the middle of the room with a couple of friends and started to sing about the mouse.

Oh, the likker was spilled on the barroom floor,
  And the place was closed for the night,
When out of his hole crept a little brown mouse,
  And he sat in the pale moonlight. . . .

A circle of men were gathering, adding their voices to the song. Manny and Henry Horn joined them.

Then he lapped up the likker on the barroom floor,
  And back on his haunches he sat,
And all night long you could hear him roarrrr . . .
  BRING ON YOUR GODDAM CAT!
Hic . . . cat,
  Hic . . . cat.

Then they sang the ballad of the young pilot who lay dying by a Laotian waterfall. The song had first been sung in World War I clubs, but then it had been a Belgian waterfall. In World War II it had become a New Guinea waterfall, and a few years later a Korean one.

Billy had another Scotch and rocks and was mellowing nicely when Tiny Bechler came over and joined him in his corner of the long bar.

"Congratulations on making your tracks," said Tiny, shaking Billy's hand in his ham-sized one.

"Thanks."

Tiny peered closer, and Billy realized he had more on his mind than congratulations.

"You know I'm an Academy grad?" said Tiny.

"I heard that."

"Well there's four of us here now, and once in a while we get together to talk. Just sit down and shoot the shit about what's going on here."

Billy wondered what Tiny was about.

"Henry Horn thinks you're okay, and so does Joe Walker, but Henry told us something that concerns me."

Billy finished his drink and tried to get Jimmy the bartender's attention. "Two more," he called.

"Henry says he saved your ass the other day."

"I don't doubt it," said Billy. "We fly together a lot."

"This was different. Lieutenant DeWalt in intell was going through your strike-camera film, and when he looked close, it was apparent you'd set up on the wrong target."

Billy remained silent.

"Seems you were lining up on a warehouse that wasn't the target, and the film showed it wasn't a mistake at all that you'd bombed it."

Billy remembered that the Thud he'd flown that day had a KA-71 strike camera mounted under its chin. Only a few of the aircraft were so equipped. Periodically the strike cameras were loaded and used to get target photos. He hadn't realized it was operating.

"DeWalt wanted to turn the film over to Colonel Lyons."

Billy felt a lump grow in his stomach. "Yeah?"

"He showed the pictures to Henry first, to get his opinion, and Henry had to talk fast to convince him it was a mistake."

Billy took the two new drinks from Jimmy and paid for them.

"Henry wasn't sure how to tell you."

Billy looked at Tiny squarely. "Henry's a good man," he said.

"But he doesn't like to cheat."

"I wouldn't ask him to."

"I'm leaving pretty soon," said Tiny. "I've got eighty-two missions now. I've been here long enough to know one thing, Billy. No matter how fucked up the political restraints, there isn't room for a private war. You'll end up dragging other guys into it and fucking them over. We all have to depend on each other here."

Billy dwelled on that thought.

"Just passing on advice. Henry felt it was best left alone, but I thought different."

A moment of silence passed before Billy finally said, "I called my cousin David today. He's a sergeant first class in Special Forces based in Nam."

Tiny Bechler furrowed his brow, probably wondering whether Billy was leading up to something or just crawfishing and changing the subject.

Billy continued. "Back when I was a kid, my two cousins, David and Mal, they helped me a lot. Now Mal's dead."

"Bear Stewart, you mean?"

"Yeah. I talked to David about that, then we talked about

how my kid brother died. You remember, the one I told you about that was killed when his chopper went down?"

"I remember you saying he'd been killed."

"He was an assistant crew chief and door gunner. A rescue patrol found his body. When they brought him back, the only way they could identify him was by his dental work."

Tiny looked uneasy. "The chopper burn when it went down?" he asked.

"No. The NVA captured him and skinned him."

Tiny Bechler grimaced.

"Strung him up like an animal, skinned him alive, and left him hanging in the sun. My cousin found out from the guys who brought him in."

"Jesus."

Billy regarded his drink, feeling very sober. "My family's been fucked over by the gomers, Tiny, and the way things are going with all the restrictions, I'm worried about the way this bastard war's going."

"They'll wake up and turn us loose."

"I sure hope so. I'd sure as hell like to even the score a little."

Tiny shook his head. "You keep it up and someone's going to get hurt, Billy, and it won't just be the gomers."

Bowes tried to joke. "Captain Billy now, Lieutenant."

As he left him, Tiny didn't smile.

The mood of the bar remained downbeat. At midnight the pilots on the morning schedule began to trickle out and return to their hootches to get their four hours of sleep. The others continued to sip their drinks, commiserate the losses of their buddies, and talk about how from now on they were going to check their six o'clock positions more often.

0925 Local—Tactical Fighter Weapons Center (TFWC), Nellis AFB, Nevada

Captain Benny Lewis

He'd signed into the Nellis Hospital after the med-evac flight dropped him off the previous day, just as the doctors at Travis had ordered him to. Then he'd immediately called an old buddy, a flight surgeon he knew there, and pleaded

to be changed to out-patient status. Now that he was wearing the back brace, he told him, he felt just great.

The ploy had worked only after Benny had promised to
spend all of his nights and most of the daylight hours in the
rigid hospital bed, and most of his up time in a wheelchair.
He'd also agreed to toe the line on certain other restrictions.

Promise them anything, the inner voice advised him.

The metal brace they'd strapped him into held his back
perfectly rigid and made it difficult to get around, and he'd
promised neither to remove it nor to try to adjust it. They
would continue to run periodic tests on his back, and he
agreed to show up promptly for each. Miss just *one* appointment and the deal was off. He was to take muscle-relaxant
pills religiously every four hours, day and night, take pain
pills as required, and advise them whenever the pain increased, however slightly.

He'd told his flight-surgeon friend that his back seemed
to trouble him less every day. *No kidding,* he'd said when
his friend shook his head and said he was full of shit.

You fuck it up bad enough, said his friend, *and you'll*
never *get back on flying status.* That got Benny's attention.
He vowed, no matter what, never to tell them if he felt pain.

But the flight-surgeon friend had agreed that Benny
could check into his new office and spend a couple of hours
a day working at a desk, so long as he stayed off his feet
most of the time and hotfooted it back to the hospital whenever his back acted up.

The Fighter Weapons Center building was only a block
from the hospital, and that helped him get his compromise.
He'd take a wheelchair both ways, he said.

As soon as he was released on Tuesday morning, he broke
the agreement and walked, ever so slowly, to the Fighter
Weapons Center building to report for duty to the colonel.
Then Moods Diller came up from the basement and took
him down to his office.

The basement was a huge classified vault, with heavy-
gauge steel doors that locked at each end to seal off the men
and their classified projects. The small offices were not
posh. The three men of his air-to-ground team shared a single room, and their gray metal desks were crowded together.
Their secretary was in a separate room, her services shared
by the two other liaison teams.

Benny sat at his desk, and his back relaxed a little. It had been hurting more than normal, even though he was taking double doses of relaxant pills. He huffed a breath.

Moods shook his head. "Sure you're okay?"

Moods spoke so rapidly that his sentence-burst phrases often sounded like single words.

Benny nodded. "Fill me in on what's happening."

"Nothin' good."

"How'd the combat test go on the Doumer bridge?" Benny asked.

"Three Bullpups hit th' thing 'n' did some damage . . . not much. . . . Lost three Thuds. . . . Lions three, Christians zip."

Moods went over it in more detail, describing the run-ins and the releases, and the concentrations of flak. Then he listed the names of the downed pilots.

Benny knew them all. "That's got to be a top priority, helping them with the bridge campaign."

"I agree. . . . Last night I talked on the scrambler phone . . . lieutenant colonel at Seventh Air Force named Gates."

"We've met."

"He said we'll get another chance in a few weeks. . . . Gave him a rundown on my smart bombs . . . told him you'd be here this week, and he passes his regards."

Benny nodded. "Who's he working with in the flying units over there?"

"Lucky Anderson . . . said that's what General Moss wanted."

"Good choice," said Benny. "What can we do to help?"

"Lucky may want some tests run on th' ranges." Moods paused a heartbeat. "You gonna take the project, now you're here?"

Benny thought about it. He wanted to, but . . . "You ready to give it up?"

"Hell no," said Moods. "Fits in with other things I'm doing."

"Then you stay with it. I'll only be working a few hours a day."

Moods nodded happily.

"How's your smart-bomb project doing?"

"Workin' away on it, Benny."

Moods showed him pen-and-ink diagrams. The concepts for the guidance modules were interesting. One type used a sensitive television camera.

"Idea's to get it to lock on and track th' contrast." Moods

explained in more scientific detail, but the explanation was beyond Benny's comprehension. The essence was that the camera in the bomb's nose could be made to track man-made objects.

"So you need sunlight?"

"But not too much. . . . Cameras we've been using become distracted if th' background glare's too great."

"How do you keep the thing concentrating on that particular shadow?"

"Alter the field of view. . . . Backseater searches for the target using wide angle. . . . Once he finds what he wants, he slews the camera till it's centered, and narrows the field of view till th' target presents th' most contrast in the picture." He grinned. "Pilot pickles off the bomb and it steers to the contrast. Boom."

"Sounds impressive." Benny tried to keep skepticism from his voice.

"I'm setting up a model in a room at th' squadron. . . . Circuitry for th' guidance module fills th' room . . . California team's gotta reduce it to fit the module."

"Interesting, but will it work?" asked Benny.

Moods drew back and gave him a look of astonishment. "Of course it will."

"Might be different, once you load it onto a fighter that's vibrating and pulling g's."

Moods looked wounded that his project was being questioned. "It'll work."

"Tell me about the other concept."

"It's a light sensor. . . . Steers toward a bright dot of light on th' ground. . . . Guy in one airplane flashes a bright dot on th' target . . . the bomb on th' other airplane sees the light and steers to it."

"What's your release altitude?"

"Eight or ten thousand feet . . . that's slant range."

"How're you going to get the dot that small and bright? That'd take *some* spotlight."

Moods *aha'*ed. "You discovered it, Benny. Needed something to give us a bright, focused dot of light. . . . So happens we've got just th' thing . . . called a laser."

"How big is this . . . laser?"

Moods sighed. "Laser itself's not big, but the power supply and electronics take too much room. . . . I've got the Texas team working on making 'em smaller."

Benny very slowly shook his head. "You can go ahead and play with these things, Moods, but you're going to have to concentrate on tactics for the CROSSFIRE ZULU project."

Moods's feelings were hurt. "Benny, my smart bombs are precisely what they need. . . . Told Colonel Gates about 'em . . . he thinks they'd be just the thing."

"You're mixing oranges and apples. They can't wait for you to develop something."

Before Moods could respond, the civilian analyst came in. After the initial introductions they began reviewing the various projects they expected to be assigned.

As he listened, a spasm clenched Benny's back, making him stiffen and grunt with pain. The others stared at his face, for it was contorted and spotted with beads of sweat. After a moment it eased, and he stopped Moods from dialing for an ambulance.

"Don't *ever* do that unless I tell you to," Benny snapped, still catching his breath.

Moods appeared hurt.

"I'll wait a few more minutes, then go on back to the hospital," said Benny Lewis, "and crawl back on my torture bed. You guys go ahead and get back to what you were doing."

The two launched into a discussion about the blast criteria required to knock down a large concrete structure such as the Doumer bridge.

The inner voice reminded him about something.

He'd called Julie the night before, to tell her he'd made it okay and give her his new phone numbers. She'd still received no new word about the Bear.

As Benny waited for the spasm to relax further, he penned another letter to Colonel Mack, asking about his request to have Malcom Stewart's status changed to KIA. On his way out, he dropped the letter by the secretary to be typed and was gratified to find that she was friendly and seemed efficient. As he started to leave, she called after him.

"I received a phone call this morning from the lady you mention in this letter," she said with a smile.

He peered at her. "Mrs. Stewart?"

"She said you shouldn't be here, but if you *did* show up, she didn't want you to overdo it. She asked if I'd make sure you do everything the doctors say."

He grimaced.

"I told her I'd do just that, Captain Lewis, so I called over to the hospital and they gave me the lowdown. One or two hours a day at work and that's all, and you're supposed to be in a wheelchair both coming and going. I'd appreciate it if you'd cooperate."

He nodded, but before he turned to go, he noticed that she'd grown a vague resemblance to Lady Dracula, the nurse at the Travis Hospital who'd given him a hard time. He wondered if Julie Stewart hadn't given the nurse and the secretary the same request.

Damn, grumbled the inner voice.

He left the Fighter Weapons Center building and walked back toward the hospital.

BOOK II

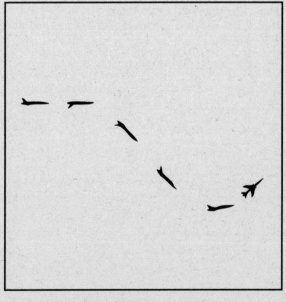

45° Dive Bomb Maneuver

HQ Seventh Air Force, Tan Son Nhut Air Base, Saigon, South Vietnam

Peacemaker was concerned. Agents from the OSI, the Air Force Office of Special Investigations, had been going through the headquarters questioning everyone who had access to the target locations. They said it was just a routine security exercise. When they'd talked to him, he'd remained calm, but something inside him told him it wasn't routine at all.

When he'd passed word at the Blue Pheasant bar that he would have to cool it for a while, the API newsman sent back a note telling him to meet him at his apartment. Peacemaker had ignored the note, and the next day he'd told his buddy Gino he didn't feel like going to the Blue Pheasant, as they'd been doing every Monday and Friday night like clockwork. Gino had grumbled about having to go alone, and when he'd gotten in that night, he'd bitched that he'd had to buy the girls drinks and then pay full price to take one to bed.

The next time Gino had gone off to the Blue Pheasant, he hadn't returned at all.

The security cops had come to their barracks and questioned Gino's friends, and Peacemaker had been truthful with them except he hadn't dared to mention the Blue Pheasant . . . and he certainly hadn't told them the reason for going there.

A full week passed, and still no Gino. Finally Peacemaker decided that one trip downtown, to visit the Blue Pheasant and ask about his friend, would be okay.

He walked through the doors into the darkness and loud music, and when his eyes had adjusted properly, took his old seat in the corner near the band. Cindee was performing, removing the last scraps of clothing and trying to make her plastic smile look sensuous. As he was ordering a Pepsi from a waitress, the API newsman came in and sat at the bar. This time he was not discreet, for he just sat there staring at him. Peacemaker tried to ignore him.

When the waitress arrived with his cola, Peacemaker asked if she'd seen Gino lately. She gave him a blank stare, as if she didn't understand English, and hurried away.

A pair of well-dressed Asian businessmen came in and took an adjacent table, looking odd in the sleazy bar among the American servicemen and Vietnamese whores. Peacemaker glanced at them and found one was staring in his direction.

The newsman came over to his table and sat, which annoyed Peacemaker, and asked when he would resume with his reports.

Peacemaker asked if he knew what had happened to his friend Gino, and the newsman said he had no idea what he was talking about. He just wanted more of the target information for his news releases. Peacemaker said the OSI agents were thick in the headquarters building, asking a lot of questions, and he didn't want to press his luck.

The newsman laughed at the mention of the OSI and told him not to worry. He motioned at the next table and said both of the gentlemen were regular informants to the OSI and were thought to be highly reliable sources. He said the gentlemen were also founts of information for his own uses.

It was a trade, he said. He gave them certain things, and they give him insights for blockbluster stories for his news agency.

It's harmless, the newsman said.

Peacemaker said he didn't care about any of that. He'd just come downtown to learn anything he could about his friend who'd disappeared.

The newsman persisted that he needed the targeting information, as Peacemaker had provided before. He leaned toward Peacemaker and told him he was in too far to back out.

All the newsman had to do was name him as his source of classified information, maybe turn over certain bar napkins he'd received with Peacemaker's printing on them, and . . .

For God's sake, keep your voice down! Peacemaker blurted, running his hand nervously through his hair.

Look at the gentlemen at the table there, the newsman told him, indicating the Asians. They're your so-called enemy. They're officials of the National Liberation Front.

Peacemaker whipped his head about. The men staring back with the friendly expressions were Viet Cong?

The newsman said they gave him information as reliable as his own. Next week they might even take him on a tour of an underground headquarters located a few miles from Saigon. They weren't afraid of truth being printed. Why was he?

The OSI agents are closing in, Peacemaker reminded him, as he stared as the businessmen.

The newsman said his friends at the next table could stop the investigation . . . if Peacemaker cooperated again.

How would they do that? he asked incredulously.

The newsman said he never asked, but they always did as they said in such matters. The Vietnamese businessmen at the next table continued to smile openly at them.

Two nights after Peacemaker's meeting with the newsman, an ARVN major who liaised with the Seventh Air Force headquarters was found with incriminating information in his possession detailing one of the following day's bombing targets in North Vietnam. He'd been fingered by a Saigon taxi driver who had long been a reliable source for the OSI. Unfortunately the major had obviously discovered they were onto him, for while American and South Vietnamese agents were on their way to his quarters, he'd held his .45 automatic in his mouth and pulled the trigger.

With the matter wrapped up, the OSI agents curtailed their investigation of Peacemaker's office and quietly took credit for their achievement.

The following evening Peacemaker visited the API newsman's sumptuous Saigon apartment with detailed information about the next week's North Vietnamese targets. In trade for those coordinates, the newsman was given his tour of the un-

derground Viet Cong headquarters. The story under the newsman's byline was featured in more than a hundred major newspapers in the United States and Europe.

Gino, Peacemaker's friend, was never seen or heard from again.

CHAPTER ELEVEN

Major Lucky Anderson

Lucky was mission commander for the morning alpha strike. They were to attack targets of opportunity on the northeast railroad, the rail line that crossed from Hanoi over the Paul Doumer and Canales des Rapides bridges and then snaked a hundred miles across a broad flatland into China.

The pilots disliked going out over the flats, for large numbers of gun and SAM batteries were lined up along the railroad and the sidings. It was so flat and without terrain features, the gomer SAM and AAA radars easily painted and tracked them, and when the guns and missiles were fired at them, which was frequent, there was no place to hide. They simply had to do their damnedest to outmaneuver them. A respectable number of Air Force and Navy pilots had been shot down there, and none had been rescued. In order to give the rescue forces a chance, they would have had to walk back as far as the mountains to the west or the South China Sea to the east, and both routes were considered impossible.

The sixteen strike pilots flew in four-ship fingertip formations, one behind the other, and Lucky had briefed that the various flights should rove over different portions of the rail line between the Hanoi restricted area and the Chinese buffer zone. They carried standard combat loads, six 750-pound bombs, and were to bomb or strafe any rolling stock they found.

As they approached the Red River, Lucky had to force himself to remain alert and ignore the false serenity of flying in the early morning. *It's visual trickery,* he thought as he looked down upon the world in its semidarkness. The sun had not risen sufficiently to light the earth below, but their Thuds were bathed in a gentle yellow glow. High above them golden-hued tendrils of cirrus clouds streamered against a gentle blue background. It was difficult to think of killing and friends dying with all the beauty surrounding them.

Except for the Wild Weasels flying up ahead, trying to sucker the SAMs into firing at them, Lucky's Talon flight was leading the way.

"Talon lead, Talon two. I've got the MiG-CAP in view at eight o'clock high," called Captain Bowes in his Oklahoma drawl.

Billy flew on Lucky's right wing and was doing his usual good job. His chore was to view the sky about them and keep lead informed, and Bowes had exceptionally good eyes to do it with. He routinely spotted aircraft long before the rest of them.

DeVera was to his left, flying as number three, and Joe Walker was Manny's wingman. Both were in proper position.

During the past three weeks the Supersonic Wetback had mastered his problem, whatever it had been. He'd been cocky and sure of himself, and on two occasions had led flights into the lower packs and done a good job of it. His recovery had undoubtedly been accelerated by the sexy blond, for Manny spent most of his free time on five baht buses to Nakhon Sawan, where her Peace Corps camp was located. If that was what it took, Lucky was all for the tonic she offered him.

Manny returned from his overnighters looking as if he'd been chased by a pack of sex-crazed, three-peckered gorillas—and they'd caught him. Or at least that's what Henry Horn liked to say. But Manny took his job as assistant

C-Flight commander seriously and lifted much of the dreary administrative load from Lucky's shoulders.

"Talon lead, Talon three. I've got three bogeys in the distance at our ten o'clock, going away." Manny's voice was businesslike.

"Roger, three. You hear that transmission, Pistols?" Lucky asked the MiG-CAP flight.

"Pistol has them in sight," the F-4 leader replied. *"They're headed toward the buffer zone. No threat to you guys, but we'll keep 'em in mind."*

The last flight in the series, Wolf, reported that a lone MiG-17 had made a single pass across their stern, had quickly flashed by, and then dived for the deck.

"Wolf, Talon lead. Keep a good eye out for his buddies," called Lucky, and felt the uneasy tingle that something was going on that he didn't understand. That sort of fast flyby had been occurring relatively often during the past weeks, as if the MiG pilots were looking for something. Some of the pilots thought the MiG drivers were checking out their weapons loads.

The four flights of Thuds crossed over the Red River twenty miles north of Yen Bai, keeping their vigil. Except for a few high cirrus clouds, the weather was clear.

0629 Local—Route Pack Six

Captain Manny DeVera

When Manny had spotted the MiGs in the distance, the old knot had threatened to return to his stomach. But the MiGs had flown on without turning and he'd calmed his stomach and the strike force had continued across the Red River Valley without incident. By the time Talon flight crossed over Thud Ridge, headed for the southernmost sector of the northeast railroad, and was still unchallenged, Manny was feeling better about it all, and even began to think it might be an easy day.

He needed a few more of those.

Of course he was over and done with whatever it had been that had caused the suffocating, puking fear, but he would not at all mind easier missions. He'd almost asked Major Lucky for a couple of more missions in the lower packs, but he'd realized he might be cheating some new guy out of his first indoctrination missions. And, of course, there was no reason to broadcast the fact that his nerve had gone on him that time.

The Wild Weasels, flying a dozen miles out in front of them, began to call out threats. They announced several Firecan artillery radars and at least two active SAM radars in the area they were flying toward, and Manny felt his hair tingle and the knot growing again.

Steel up, dammit. The Supersonic Wetback doesn't come unglued.

And suddenly he knew he hadn't shaken his fear at all. He'd been flying down in the easy packs, and you don't learn fuck-all about flying in pack six when you're down there. All he'd done was keep the others from learning how chickenshit he really was. He felt increasingly shaky as he realized the truth, and began to dart his eyes about, imagining the worst. How the hell could he steel himself when he knew the gomers had a silver fucking bullet with his name on it?

They'd know . . . the fucking gomers would know . . . and they'd pick him from the group and kill him. Or maybe they wouldn't know he was shaking like a fucking idiot, but he'd screw something up . . . and they'd kill him.

He found he was sucking and wheezing, just like the other time. *Dumb shit. Keep it up and it won't take gomer bullets. You'll kill yourself.*

Still forty miles from the railroad.

He monitored his breathing and forced himself to do the things that had to be done.

Christ almighty, but I'm scared.

The Wild Weasels began dueling with a SAM radar, and in the distance he saw missiles arcing upward. He sucked a breath and a cold shiver racked his body. He wanted to turn and run, thought hard about it, but knew he'd have an even poorer chance if he left the safety of the group. *Maybe it'll go away,* he thought, but he knew it wouldn't, and that Manny DeVera was about to die.

They flew on toward the battle, and he tried to think of ways to chicken out gracefully, but all he came up with was a bunch of jumbled, dumb-shit ideas.

The Weasel flight leader radioed that he'd seen rolling stock moving south between Bac Giang and Bac Ninh. Major Lucky asked how many, and the Weasel leader said he'd counted about a dozen boxcars.

Fuck! Now they had a target, and Manny still hadn't decided on a way out of the mess.

Bac Ninh was at the edge of the Hanoi restricted zone, so the train was fair game. No piece of cake there, for a lot of guns were deployed around Bac Ninh.

Manny's breath came faster, and the hissing sound became louder in the helmet's earphones. He looked over and found he was too far forward, was almost line abreast with Lucky. When he eased the throttle back, he noticed his hand was unsteady.

Maybe something was wrong with his airplane?

Coward! he raged at himself.

Lucky told the other flights to continue searching, then led Talon flight into a right turn, descending toward Bac Ninh. After a few miles they'd likely turn northeast, and the train would be coming toward them, Manny thought, trying to keep his mind busy. Now he just wanted it to be over with, so they could fly back toward the west and away from the dangerous flatlands, and so his heart might quit pounding. Maybe if it all went very quickly, he'd be able to see it through without getting too clanked up.

Shee-it, man, you're already clanked. You're going to die!

They were at 7,000 feet when he saw, first, the railroad, a dark thread against the yellow-brown fields, then the city of Bac Ninh through which it passed.

Was it a smudge of smoke beyond the city?

"Talon two has the train in sight," called Billy Bowes in an even voice, as if he were Chet Huntley giving the evening news. The guy had eyes like binoculars. All Manny could see was the tiny smudge.

They flew around Bac Ninh to avoid its guns, then northeast, parallel with the tracks, and the smudge grew until it was clearly billowing from the front of a line of rail cars. Some trouble or other had obviously held the train up during the night, for they normally moved them only during darkness and heavy weather. Likely the engineer was trying to dash the remaining distance to Bac Ninh and safety. The gomers knew about their restrictions.

Lucky began to climb and Manny followed, stroking in and out of burner to keep up.

"Talons, this is lead. First element will drop on the front

*part of the train, near the engine. Manny, you and Joe drop
on the aft section. Then we'll circle around and strafe.*"

"*Three,*" Manny answered, hoping his voice hadn't betrayed him.

As they climbed, his RHAW system came alive with the
unnerving sounds and strobes of distant SAM and AAA radars, and he was sucking and hissing hard in his mask.
Again he had to slow his breathing consciously. He could
see the train clearly now as it hurried toward Bac Ninh.
*Were those muzzle flashes coming from Bac Ninh or glints
from water?*

The first element, Lucky Anderson and Billy Bowes,
went into their dive. Manny held high, delaying the moment
as long as possible as he stared down at the train.

Flak bursts puffed in the sky around Lucky and Billy.
The guns from Bac Ninh were reaching out for them.

He sucked a final breath and held it, wishing he could
wait longer, then rolled onto his back and tucked the Thud
into a steep dive. He picked an aim point a hundred feet
west of the cars, because the smoke was blowing hard to the
east and that should correct for the wind. He eased back his
throttle and the Thud settled comfortably into its dive. *Concentrate on the bombing problem,* he told himself, *like you're
on a gunnery range in the States.*

Fifty degrees dive angle, he noted. Good, that meant
they'd have less time to shoot at him. He would be steep
and fast, and there was no reason to press lower than was
healthy.

*Passing through 9,000 feet, altimeter unwinding like a
fucking banshee, pipper climbing steadily toward the aim
point.*

He pickled at 7,500 feet, pipper squarely on the aim
point, and immediately threw the throttle forward and
reefed the control stick back and left, gritting his teeth and
groaning as he endured seven gravities. And he flew right
into it.

Flak bursts exploded directly before him. The windscreen immediately turned opaque, and a jagged piece of
alien metal lodged and sizzled there, smoking; then something else penetrated through the side of the cockpit, and a
wasp stung his right hand.

Oh sweet Jesus.

He panicked. *Not here. Don't let me die here!*

He pulled harder yet on the control stick.

"Good bomb, Talon three," he heard Lucky call in his too-calm voice.

Lucky didn't know.

The alien shard of hot metal stuck in the top of his windscreen fluttered, then dislodged and flew back to strike his helmet visor and drop down against the side of his seat.

"Oh shit. I'm hit!" he cried out over the radio.

He cautiously peered down and saw the small, twisted piece of metal lodged between his ejection seat and the bulkhead. He looked forward and watched as beads of Plexiglas separated from the edges of the two-inch hole and zipped over his right shoulder . . . like white beebees. He ducked lower into the seat.

Someone called but the words were dim, and he couldn't understand them over the sound of air rushing into his cockpit.

All of that had happened within a few seconds after he was hit. It was as if he were moving in snapshots of time, like a movie pausing on each frame.

He maintained the hard turn.

". . . right two o'clock," he heard.

He strained to hear better.

"Talon . . . heading of . . . repeat, heading . . . zero . . . zero." Lucky Anderson's voice was calm and reassuring.

"I'm hit!" he called again, wanting *someone* to know. Then he remembered his call sign. *"Talon three is hit!"* he cried out.

He dialed in more radio volume with his trembling throttle hand.

Lucky's calm voice again. *"You're not smoking, Talon three. No fire. Turn to a heading of zero, niner, zero. Fly due east, Talon three. Zero, niner, zero."*

They knew.

He'd begun to turn to the easterly heading when his body betrayed him and convulsed in a shuddering spasm. He rolled out, trying to control himself, then corrected to ninety degrees.

The other Talons closed in around him, shepherding him toward the coast.

A bracket of four 85mm rounds exploded in the distance, and although he was already crouching behind his combining glass to avoid the windblast, Manny hunkered even lower into the ejection seat. Heart pounding, he pushed the throttle outboard to select afterburner, and when it lit, he heard Major Lucky tell Talon to do the same so they could keep up. As he accelerated, the force of the wind blowing through the hole in the windscreen created more and more pressure on his body, but he tensed himself and endured it.

Six awful, long minutes later they passed over the coast and Lucky called "feet wet."

Manny DeVera began to sob.

Lucky called for him to come out of afterburner, and after a fearful look back at the enemy coastline he did so. But he continued sobbing.

He was safe. They couldn't shoot at him over the water because the U.S. Navy controlled both the surface and the air here. And if he *did* go down, they'd pick him up. He tried to stop crying, but could not. He tried again and felt a final grand shudder. It was as if his mind and body had been taken from him, but were given back.

He began to pull himself together.

Red Crown gave Talon vectors toward an emergency tanker on brown anchor, the air refueling track that would take them down the coast toward South Vietnam. Manny looked, and for the first time noticed that the map as well as all the papers that had been clipped to his kneeboard were gone. Siphoned out the small hole at the top of the windscreen? Impossible. Then he saw them scattered about at his feet, covered with red. Hydraulic fluid?

Lucky was calling, but Manny was too busy recovering his composure to answer.

The pressure was still tremendous, for the hole at the top of the windscreen continued to funnel air into the cockpit. He throttled back again, down to less than 400 knots.

"What's your status, Talon three?" Lucky called for the fourth time.

But Manny had noticed something bizarre. It was not hydraulic fluid on the maps and papers. He carefully switched to fly with his left hand, then lifted his right hand up before his eyes and turned it over and stared in amazement.

The glove was shredded on top, and bright liquid oozed down and dripped from his wrist. The web between thumb and forefinger had been sliced, and the meaty part of his thumb gaped in an open wound. Blood had obviously flowed more profusely at first, for the glove was thoroughly soaked. Now, with the hand held high, it was slowed to a trickle.

He'd been so frightened that he hadn't noticed. He remembered only the wasp's sting. He looked closer, wondering if they might send him home. The thought was pleasant.

Then Manny remembered Lucky's radio calls and carefully looked beyond the raised hand to survey the telelite panel and gauges. He spoke a few sounds into his mask to get the burrs out of his voice before broadcasting to the world outside.

"Talon three's bird is responding to the controls," he called, his voice increasingly sure. *"Oil and hydraulic pressures are good, and I've got enough fuel to make it to the tanker."*

He flexed his fingers and they seemed to work. He'd be able to handle the refueling. Everything was going to be just fine.

1054 Local—Danang AB, South Vietnam

Major Lucky Anderson

Lucky had checked out the rattletrap pickup kept at base ops for transient aircrew use and followed the field ambulance to the Danang hospital. Then he'd waited for fifteen minutes while they examined Manny's wound.

A crusty major came out and waved Lucky into the examination room, where a hospital tech was cleaning Manny's wound. The flight surgeon said there was no real damage to speak of. Although the hand looked gory, he said it should heal quickly. He'd just need a lot of antiseptic, a couple dozen stitches, and a penicillin shot, followed by a handful of aspirin and a good night's sleep. Nothing critical had been severed, so there was no reason to med-evac him to the regional hospital at Clark Air Base. Couple of weeks to let it heal, and he'd be back on flying status. He added, with a Santa Claus smile, that Manny would get a Purple Heart.

Manny had remained quiet through it all, too quiet, Lucky thought, and tried not to look crestfallen when he found he wasn't going to Clark. Lucky reasoned that there

were a lot of pretty Filipinas and a few round-eyes at Clark,
and as hot-blooded as Manny was, it wasn't so surprising he
was let down.

Then he reflected about how Manny had failed to answer the repeated radio calls and how he'd stayed in afterburner when it was uncalled for and he was only using up
precious fuel, and Lucky grew concerned again. But *then*
he wondered how any of them might act if they thought
they were bleeding to death in a lonely cockpit over enemy
territory?

Fuck it, Lucky concluded. When he returned to Takhli,
he'd send Manny off on a good R and R, maybe to Bangkok
or the Philippines. Get Doc Roddenbush to call it some kind
of recuperative leave. He'd probably come back rearing and
ready to fight.

He left Manny at the clinic, said he'd be back, and drove
the battered pickup to the command post to find out how
the rest of the mission had gone.

Bad news.

Wolf, the last flight in the strike force, had lost two birds
when they'd been setting up to bomb a rail siding. Just
when they were most vulnerable, two different sites had
fired SAMs, and to evade them, they'd dived into a mael-
strom of flak. Both Thuds had taken multiple 57mm hits and
had climbed out trailing smoke and fire. The first pilot had
made it only a few miles before he'd had to jump out. No radio contact, so he was thought to have been immediately
captured. The other pilot had ejected into the foothills of
Thud Ridge and was on the run.

Lucky felt shitty about losing the two pilots. He knew
them both, from A-Flight of his own 354th squadron. He
found he'd thoroughly chewed up the cigar he'd been
mouthing, and angrily shucked cellophane from a new one.

He called the Takhli command post, and the deputy
for maintenance said he'd send a team to Danang to patch
up Manny DeVera's Thud so it could be flown home. Then
B. J. Parker broke in on the line and curtly told Lucky to
return to Takhli ASAP with the good birds, because with the
two losses they were running short of airplanes.

So Lucky hurried toward base operations, where they'd
parked the aircraft. Halfway there an Army MP stopped him
and gave him a ticket for speeding.

"Where's your driver's license, sir?"

All Lucky had on him was his Geneva Convention ID card, which gave only name, rank, and service number. He tried to explain the rule about having to leave their wallets behind when they flew combat missions. The MP was unsympathetic and told him he shouldn't be driving without a military license, and added that violation to the ticket.

"Where are you stationed, Major?"

Lucky lied and told him he was stationed at Phu Cat Air Base and flew F-100's there. The MP should forward the ticket to his commander at Phu Cat, Lucky said. Before he let him go, the MP told him he'd likely have to attend a safe driver's course.

Lucky impatiently hurried into base ops to find that one of his pilots was missing. Joe Walker said Billy Bowes had gone to look for his cousin, an Army Special Forces NCO stationed at Danang. Lucky angrily mouthed his cigar and told Joe to go find Bowes and tell him to get his ass back to the flight line, then to file a VFR-Direct flight plan for Takhli, with takeoff at 1315. When Lucky went out to the transient area where their Thuds were parked, Joe was anxiously asking a base-ops sergeant where the Special Forces unit was located.

After a twenty-minute search Lucky found the transient crew chief taking a smoke break and told him to refuel the Thuds, repack their drag chutes, forget about topping off the liquid oxygen and all the other shit, and be ready to assist with engine start at 1300. The crew chief told him his F-105's would have to get into line, as his men would be launching a flight of transient F-4's at that time. Lucky went over the crew chief's head to the line chief and threatened and cajoled and finally convinced him that his three Thuds had priority. The transient crew chief was pissed off and stomping around angrily when Lucky left them.

Lucky drove the rattletrap pickup back to the clinic, opening yet another cigar and tossing away a soggy one, wondering what the hell he'd done to deserve all this shit.

Manny DeVera just nodded with a vague expression when Lucky told him to take his time getting back to Takhli. He loaned him twelve dollars, which was all he had with him, so Manny could buy cigarettes and a hamburger or two on his way home.

Driving back to base ops, Lucky was stopped and given another speeding ticket by the same Army MP, who gave

him even unfriendlier looks and an even windier speech
about driving safely at Danang. Yeah, he told Lucky, he
knew to forward the ticket to Phu Cat. He said Lucky could
now look forward to having his license suspended, and
maybe even receiving a letter of reprimand because *two
speeding tickets in one day is serious shit . . . sir*.

At base ops he found Billy Bowes waiting with his
cousin, a hawk-eyed and savvy-looking sergeant first class
who looked more Indian than Billy. The SFC saluted crisply,
then pumped his hand and told him he'd heard a lot about
him.

Lucky felt his indigestion worsen. "Where's Joe?" he
asked Billy.

"Got me, Major."

"Dammit!" exploded Lucky, then sighed and just shook
his head. He gave Bowes the keys to the pickup and told
him to find Walker, who was searching over in the Special
Forces unit, wherever the hell that was, for him.

"And *I'll* file the fucking flight plan," he yelled angrily as
Billy and his cousin "yessired" and fled in a belch of blue
smoke.

At 1310 Lucky was sitting in the cockpit of his Thud, ignoring the malevolent glares of the transient crew chief
when Bowes and Walker showed up wearing dogshit-eating
grins.

On the flight back to Takhli, Bowes radioed his excuse for
being late. He'd found Joe Walker right away, but an Army
MP had stopped them for speeding and had seemed to delight in issuing them a ticket and lecturing them. When
they'd said they were from Takhli, the MP had threatened to
haul them in to the provost marshal's office, because he by
God knew they were from Phu Cat.

Billy asked if Lucky would help handle the matter, because Colonel Encinos, their new squadron commander,
was concerned that the pilots were getting too many tickets.

Lucky blew up over the radio. He shouted and chewed
Bowes's ass down to the bone. Then he remained in his foul
mood and both Bowes and Walker kept their mouths shut
during the remainder of the flight.

1200 Local—HQ Seventh Air Force, Tan Son Nhut Air Base, Saigon, South Vietnam

Lieutenant Colonel Pearly Gates

A month had passed since the disastrous attempt on the Doumer bridge with Bullpup missiles, and that morning General Moss had again pulled him aside and asked if he wasn't ready for another combat test. If they delayed much longer, Moss told him, the entire idea would likely be shelved.

But again Pearly had put him off.

Just as General Moss had told him to do, Pearly had formed his team of staff officers and experts to help with CROSSFIRE ZULU. There was a major at the Pentagon, working in USAF/XOO, the ops shop there, a Navy lieutenant commander at Camp H. M. Smith, the USCINCPAC headquarters base adjacent to Pearl Harbor, and a major at PACAF headquarters at Hickam. Those three would deal with his requests and help to smooth the way through their respective bureaucratic mazes. At Takhli, Lucky Anderson and Max Foley, the wing-weapons officer, were excellent contacts, for they were experienced with the ways the various weapons and fuzes worked and with the tactics required to deliver them.

But the focal point had shifted to Nellis Air Force Base, where Moods Diller was working with a new family of smart bombs. From his first contact with Captain Diller, when Pearly had learned about the capabilities of new launch-and-leave weapons that would allow the destruction of point targets with a single bomb and a single sortie, he'd been intrigued. He called Nellis Air Force Base and talked to Captain Diller almost nightly, and each time he was again encouraged to wait "just a little longer" for the new bombs.

His latest contact had been even more encouraging, for Moods told him they were live-dropping test bombs, and that the results were surpassing even his own lofty expectations.

Pearly had tried briefing General Moss on the smart-bomb development, but the general had snorted and said there were just too many variables that could go wrong, and that they didn't have time for the weapons wizards to come up with the secret of the universe. *Let's get on with the test,* he'd impatiently repeated, *so we can get the campaign under way*.

But Pearly was both obstinate and optimistic. The use of smart bombs, with their one bomb, one target capability, sounded too promising. He envisioned sending just two aircraft out on a bridge mission, endangering only those men, and dropping a bridge every time they flew.

If they could wait just a *little* longer, they would save lives. He wished he'd been able to pin down just how *much* longer they might have to wait, but Moods Diller refused to be specific. Pearly supposed that was how development people were, never wanting to make guesses and stray from scientific fact. He'd delayed the second combat test for weeks now, to wait on the smart bombs and avoid pilot losses. He knew he did not have much longer or the entire campaign would be in jeopardy.

But *damn* if the smart bombs didn't sound intriguing.

He decided to call Captain Diller again that night and tell him he *had* to have a firm estimate, for they simply couldn't afford to wait longer.

1315 Local—Hoa Lo Prison, Hanoi, DRV

Air Regiment Commanding Quon

As soon as Quon was told that two blue-tail Thunder planes had been shot down on the morning raid, he'd canceled all staff meetings and told his driver to take him to Hanoi. When the sergeant cautioned him about the ban of surface travel for senior officers during daylight hours, Quon had shouted at him. It was not his normal behavior, for Quon treated his men well, but during the past month he had been driven as never before.

As he strode disdainfully past the guards at the door to the prison's entrance, he wondered at his continuing good fortune. That very morning could have been used as a lesson on how defenses should be run.

Quon visited often with the Phuc Yen radar controllers. They knew of his quest for a particular Mee pilot of a blue-tail Thunder plane, and even knew the man's name was *Lokee*, and eagerly joined the game. The controllers had given crisp directions to his pilots, telling them precisely how to make their flybys of the Thunder planes to pick out the blue-tails. Then, since Phantoms were protecting the Thunder planes, they held the MiGs well north in the restricted area and concentrated the efforts of the gun-and-rocket crews on the aircraft known to be blue-tails.

One of the Mee blue-tail pilots was already in custody, the other being sought in the foothills of the Viet Bac, the mountains immediately north ·of Hanoi and very near Phuc Yen. Quon felt happy with his good fortune and knew that even if neither man was *Lokee,* he was somehow closer to him.

The prison commander met him in the hallway outside his office, preening and smiling solicitously.

"The prisoner is in the interrogation room, comrade Quon," he announced proudly.

"Is this one *Lokee?*" Quon asked.

The senior lieutenant looked sorrowful. "No, comrade, but he is a pilot of the Pig Squadron." As he led the way into the dismal and dirty interrogation room, Quon hoped the lieutenant was wrong, and that his search had ended.

It was not *Lokee*. The Mee stretched to the ceiling hoist was a black man with very dark skin and no scars on his face. His arms were disjointed, chest and stomach ablaze with livid bruises. He panted as he looked about with a frightened, dazed expression.

Quon sighed. So much for hope.

"We began the questioning almost an hour ago," said the prison commandant.

"Did he fly on the mission to Kep?"

"Not that day, comrade Quon. He flew there on a later date, though."

Quon went closer to the prisoner, and the man tried to concentrate his vision on his features.

"Ask him about the man named *Lokee*."

The interrogator struck the pilot in the chest with a length of pipe and barked meaningless words in the guttural Mee language.

The prisoner cried out, then sobbed as he began to suck for breath in short gasps.

The interrogator spoke again. The prisoner answered. They conversed more, the interrogator barking questions, the prisoner gasping answers.

Finally the interrogator turned to Quon with a look of triumph. "He says that *Lokee* is the commander of a flight in the Pig Squadron."

"I know that," Quon snapped.

"*Lokee* was not in the other blue-tail we shot down."

Quon huffed an unhappy sigh, mused for a moment, then turned to the prison commandant. "Interview this man further, and then all of your pilots from the Pig Squadron again and again until you find out everything there is to know about *Lokee.*"

"I have sent you all we have found, comrade Quon," said the senior lieutenant.

"I want to know everything. What he eats, how often he shits, the women he fornicates with. Everything, do you understand?"

"Yes, comrade Quon," smiled the senior lieutenant.

Quon started to leave, but then turned back toward the prisoner, who was alternately sobbing and gasping in the short breaths. His ribs had obviously been damaged, for several poked out unnaturally.

For a quick moment their eyes locked, a private moment between victor and vanquished. Then the prisoner's dilated and could not see.

Quon nodded, pleased with what he'd seen, his hatred momentarily satisfied. He thought again about the man called *Lokee* and frowned, then abruptly turned and hurried out. His senses were offended by the stench in the room.

CHAPTER TWELVE

Captain Benny Lewis

Benny had been back to part-time work for three weeks when Moods Diller laid on his grand exhibition. He hadn't been able to spend more than an hour a day in the office, and often spent no time at all, because his flight-surgeon buddy had caught him overdoing it and pulled in the reins. Which had left Moods Diller to run the office and maintain the contacts with the outside world while Benny continued to mend.

But that morning Benny had taken a call from Lieutenant Colonel Pearly Gates in Saigon, and he was damned mad. He hadn't yet told Moods of his anger because he didn't want to screw up his show. But he was angry, and after the exhibition they would talk.

Moods had invited delegates from Air Force Systems Command headquarters, the Air Weapons Lab, and from Tactical Air Command and Pentagon requirements offices. There were also U.S. Navy representatives from the Naval Ordnance Test Station at China Lake. In all there were twenty test, development, and evaluation people in attendance, and several held Ph.D.'s in physics, math, or engineering. All appeared kindred in spirit, and Benny wondered about the shared IQ in the room. Likely, he thought, it was phenomenal. It would also be nice, he thought in a less charitable vein, if the common-sense quotient was half as high.

Moods intended to show that his smart bombs worked and prove his project merited a much higher priority, to provide the dollars and emphasis he needed to build and test them.

Diller wasted no time with protocol, even to acknowledge the presence of two colonels and assorted lesser ranks, although all were senior to him. Fortunately, they seemed much like Moods in their disdain for the unscientific world and did not complain.

He opened with a soliloquy about the numbers of bombs required to knock out a single point target. Benny immediately noticed that he'd slowed his speech and pronounced each word very correctly. The briefing was important to Moods.

Consider the destruction of a ruggedly constructed bridge in the face of heavy flak.

The fact that Moods had picked a bridge for his example was not lost on Benny.

In World War I such a task was impossible, for the aircraft could not carry that kind of tonnage. During World War II it took as many as a thousand sorties of B-24's and B-17's to eliminate a single bridge, and most times it was not even attempted. In Korea the number decreased some, because dive-bombing F-84's were more accurate. Say three hundred sorties. In Vietnam it is estimated that ninety to a hundred sorties will be required to destroy a single bridge. With a standard attrition rate for a point target in a high-threat environment, that means seven aircraft will be lost.

With those figures in mind, watch this.

An enlisted projectionist switched on a 35mm slide projector.

A photo of a laser generator, then another showing it was mounted in a small shed on a hilltop at a bombing range at Indian Springs, north of Las Vegas.

There were several appreciative nods from the eggheads in the room.

"We call this our 'zot machine,'" quipped Moods in his

slow voice. "It will generate a light beam that will illuminate . . ."

A photo of the outline of a bridge, etched onto the desert
floor by bulldozers.

". . . the target."

A photo of a 1,000-pound concrete bomb shape, with
makeshift, stubby, movable wings fixed to its top and a bulbous apparatus on its nose.

"This is a full-scale practice bomb, equipped with a light
sensor, steering circuitry, and movable fins."

Another shot of the shape fitted under the wing of an F-4
test aircraft, with a grinning Moods Diller standing beside
it.

"I flew this test last Saturday. Takeoff was routine, although I couldn't rotate the nose quite as much as normal
because of the size of the bomb's seeker-head. When I was
in the air, approaching the range . . ."

A photo of the F-4 when it was airborne, taken by a pho-
tographer in a chase aircraft.

". . . I enabled the weapon's circuitry, and called for the
zot machine to be turned on."

A shot of a bright bead of red light on a reflective surface
at the center of the "bridge."

"Then I positioned my aircraft at four thousand feet in a
slight dive at the target, and . . . released."

Two shots in succession. One of the bomb in the air, the
next of it impacting not more than ten feet from the bead of
light.

"One sortie, one bridge."

The audience was delighted.

Three hours later the impressed action officers promised
Moods Diller a *much* higher priority. Immediately after they
left, Benny Lewis confronted Moods back in the office.

"You like it?" asked Moods happily, reverting to his
machine-gun bursts of speech.

"It was great. I liked it."

"We've got the go-ahead . . . all the way up th' ladder,
Benny."

"Not me, you. It's been your baby all the way."

"I'll need your support."

"You've got it."

Moods beamed.

"I talked to Lieutenant Colonel Pearly Gates this morning," said Benny.

"I'll call him right away. . . . He'll wanna know we're on track with the smart bombs."

"I'm taking you out of the loop on CROSSFIRE ZULU, Moods."

Diller's jaw dropped in astonishment.

"Colonel Gates thought you had something he could use on his campaign tomorrow, not next year. You don't have anything like that. You've got a concept, not a weapon."

"You can't do this, Benny. You can't! . . . I've got the perfect weapon to use on the bridges. . . . It'll reduce losses and . . . you can't do this!"

"I did. I briefed our bosses already, and I'm sending a message to Colonel Gates. A no-shit message, Moods, telling him to forget about your smart bombs until they're ready. It's no game over there. Guys are betting their asses trying to fight the war, and Gates thinks you've got something that can do the job."

"I do!"

"Bullshit. You've got a concept."

"You saw the results. . . . The bomb hit squarely on th' bridge. . . . I plan to send pictures to Colonel Gates to *show* him we've got the right weapon."

Benny ticked off on his fingers. "One, you aren't even close to operational testing of a real kit. Two, the target illuminator is too big to be carried in a fighter."

"They're working on it! . . . They promise a zot machine that can be carried in the backseat of an F-4 within weeks."

"Three, you dropped from unrealistic parameters. Hell, I can hit a bridge in the sand at Indian Springs from four thousand feet without a laser or anything else."

Captain Moods Diller clenched his teeth in anger. "I'll take it to the general."

"If you think that's wise, go ahead. But first let me caution you. If you do, you'll risk having your project terminated, and I'd hate to see that happen."

Moods was too angry to listen. He stormed off to the general's office upstairs.

"Shit," muttered Benny Lewis. He'd been up for too long, and his back was beginning to throb. He took another muscle-relaxant pill.

A few minutes later the secretary stopped by to admonish

him for exerting himself before she left for the night. He nodded absently.

The telephone rang. It was the two-star who ran the Fighter Weapons Center.

Twenty minutes later Moods was back downstairs in their vault office, looking forlorn.

"Sorry I blew up like that," he muttered.

Benny shrugged. "I should've been on top of things better. I've been spending too much time at the hospital and forgetting to mind the store."

"You got a broken back, for Christ's sake." Moods looked at him. "I fucked up, huh?"

"Yeah. You're the best there is at what you do, Moods, but sometimes you lose track of what's happening in the world."

"The general told me to get my head out of my ass."

"I wouldn't put it like that." Benny grinned at Moods. "Not exactly."

"Thanks for coming to my rescue so he didn't kill th' project."

"I want you to work full-time on your smart bombs, Moods. It's a hell of a concept, but that's what it is right now. A concept."

Diller bristled for a moment, then shook it off.

"And in the meantime, I'll show up in the office more often and run CROSSFIRE ZULU. They need inputs, so I'll put a message together suggesting regular hard bombs on the next test."

Diller sighed.

"Cheer up. You put on a good show today and convinced a lot of people you're onto something more than a wild-assed scheme."

1430 Local—HQ Seventh Air Force, Tan Son Nhut Air Base, Saigon, South Vietnam

Lieutenant Colonel Pearly Gates

There were several classified messages in Pearly's in-basket when he returned from his afternoon meeting. One was of particular interest, because it regarded CROSSFIRE ZULU. When he'd called the Fighter Weapons Center tactics office night before last, which was daytime in the states, Moods had been out and he'd been connected with Captain Benny Lewis. He'd explained as much of his dilemma with timing and what Moods Diller had been telling him as he could on a nonsecure line, and Benny had quietly taken it all in. Then Lewis had told him that as of now he was taking over the project as Pearly's contact, and that he'd send a back-channel message outlining the status of various projects and giving him better answers.

Good, Pearly had thought. Captain Diller was undoubtedly bright, but he was also temperamental and disliked reports and dealing with headquarters. Perhaps Benny Lewis would keep him better informed. Anyway, Pearly had a hard time interpreting Moods's strange bursts of speech.

"Will the new family of smart bombs be ready within a couple of weeks?" Pearly asked Lewis in a hopeful tone.

Benny had again told him he'd explain it all in the back-channel message. He'd added that Captain Diller was conducting a briefing on his project that day, and he'd include any new data that came out of the meeting.

So Pearly had waited impatiently for the message to arrive.

When he read it, he felt betrayed, for it was not at all what he'd expected.

SECRET—SENSITIVE DATA—INCLUDES
WEAPONS TESTS RESULTS
PRIORITY MSG—ADDRESSEE'S EYES
ONLY—NO FURTHER DISSEMINATION
DTG: 242203Z MAY 67
FM: TFWC TAF/CAPT B. LEWIS NELLIS AFB,
NEV
TO: HQ 7AF DPP/LT COL P. GATES SAIGON,
RVN
SUBJECT: (U) CROSSFIRE ZULU (C-Z)
1. (C) AS PER OUR TELECON, SENDER IS
NEW C-Z CONTACT OFFICER, REPLACING
CAPT DILLER.
2. (S) "SMART WPNS": TO DATE ONLY LAB
ANALYSIS & PRELIMINARY TESTING HAS
BEEN PERFORMED. THERE HAS BEEN NO
OPERATIONAL TESTING & NO KITS EXIST
IN FINAL FORM. WE ARE PRESSING THE

STATE-OF-THE-ART IN SEVERAL
TECHNOLOGIES & CANNOT EXPEDITE THE
DEVELOPMENT PROCESS OR GUARANTEE
SUCCESS.

    A. (S) "LASER-GUIDED BOMBS": LGB'S
CANNOT POSSIBLY BE AVAILABLE IN
TIME FOR THIS OPLAN (UNLESS DELAYED
FOR "MINIMUM" OF 120 DAYS).

    B. (S) "E-O GUIDED WPNS": EXPECT AVAIL
N.E.T. 12 TO 18 MO.

3. (S) IF C-Z TEST IS HELD IN NEAR
FUTURE, SUGGEST USE OF "DUMB WEAPONS,"
AS FOLLOWS:

    A. MK-83 1000 LB BOMBS—GOOD
AERODYNAMICS, GOOD PENETRATION,
FAIR BLAST EFFECT FOR LARGE TARGET,
PRESENTLY AVAILABLE IN ADEQUATE
NUMBERS.

    B. M-118 3000 LB BOMBS—GOOD
BLAST EFFECT, FAIR AERODYNAMICS—BUT,
REQUIRES 30" LUG ADAPTER, MUST BE
CARRIED ON WING STATION, POOR
PENETRATION, IN PIPELINE BUT WILL
NOT BE AVAILABLE IN S.E.A. IN ADEQUATE
NUMBERS UNTIL AUGUST.

    C. MK-84 2000 LB BOMBS—GOOD
AERODYNAMICS, ADEQUATE BLAST
EFFECT, ADEQUATE PENETRATION—BUT,
"POOR AVAILABILITY IN SUFFICIENT
NUMBERS" DUE TO OTHER HIGH-
PRIORITY REQUIREMENTS.

4. (C) WILL REVIEW DELIVERY TACTICS FOR
USE OF "DUMB BOMBS" LISTED ABOVE
AGAINST C-Z TGTS & FORWARD DATA
DIRECTLY TO MAJ ANDERSON AT TKL,
AS PER OUR TELECON.

5. (S) WILL CONTINUE TO MONITOR SMART
BOMB TESTS & ADVISE OF PROGRESS.
ANTICIPATE THEY WILL BE CARRIED
ONLY ON F-4 AIRCRAFT SINCE TWO PILOTS
W/BE REQUIRED TO OPERATE SYSTEMS.
SUGGEST DANANG OR UBON (AN F-4
BASE) BE DESIGNATED FOR

OPERATIONAL COMBAT TESTING "IF & WHEN"
KITS ARE AVAILABLE.
6. (U) WILL REMAIN IN CONTACT. REGARDS.
SECRET—SENSITIVE DATA

Pearly was shattered. He cursed Captain Moods Diller soundly for misleading him. General Moss had *told* him this could happen, but he'd been convinced otherwise.

There'd be no magical weapons for their next try at the Doumer bridge. The message suggested 1,000-pounders, so it meant the same routine, pilots running the gauntlets of guns. Which also meant there'd be more losses while they carried out *his* plan. He tried to temper his dejection by remembering General Moss's pep talk, but he knew that with every pilot lost, it would be that much harder to sleep at night.

When he called his contact at CINCPAC that evening, to try to get CROSSFIRE ZULU turned on for another combat test, he received further bad news. He'd waited too long.

The Navy commander said the admiral had questioned him about it, and about the delay, and when the commander had waffled as Pearly had asked him to do, he'd been told to shelve it. The target list was established and approved, and it would be mid-July at the earliest before CROSSFIRE ZULU *might* be turned on again.

Pearly was despondent when he hung up. The project was delayed, and it was his fault for not looking closer into what was really happening.

It was late when he went up the stairs from the command post where he'd used the scrambler phone, to retrieve his hat and briefcase. As he started down the hall, he saw Master Sergeant Turner, NCOIC of the Documentation section, locking up his office.

"You're working awfully late, Sarge," he said.

Turner looked surprised. "Yes, sir," he muttered.

"Any special reason?"

Turner abruptly shook his head. "Just double-checking things. I've been a lot more cautious since you told us about the . . . ah . . . problem."

After the OSI investigation Pearly had called in his officers and ranking NCOs and told them there had been a leak somewhere in the system. The OSI had plugged it this time, he'd said, and told them what he'd found out. That it had been an ARVN major who'd somehow gained access to targeting documents.

He'd told them to stay on their toes, that American pilots' lives depended upon their maintaining strict security. A loose tongue, even an innocent who talked too much about innocuous, unclassified material, could break their trust with the men flying the missions.

Pearly had thought his briefing had gone over poorly, that his audience was bored with yet another harangue about security, but now he wondered. Ever since the investigation and Pearly's briefing, Master Sergeant Turner had acted nervous. Like now. Turner was fidgeting and appeared anxious to leave.

"Your guys have been under a heavy work load recently," Pearly said.

The master sergeant shrugged. "We can handle it."

Pearly motioned at the room. "Find anything out of place in there?"

"Not really. Sergeant Slye's desk's a pigpen, like always, but I didn't find anything except a few candy-bar wrappers. I'll chew his ass in the morning."

"Tell him to get rid of the symbol," said Pearly. Staff Sergeant Slye had a metal peace symbol propped on a corner of his desk that was upsetting some of the men.

"Says his brother sent it to him, that he keeps is there as a joke."

"I know. Just tell him to get it out of sight or take it to his barracks so the guys here don't bitch." Airman First Class O'Neil had complained to Pearly about the symbol, saying he thought it was inappropriate. When Pearly had gone to see what was causing O'Neil's heartburn, Sergeant Slye had told him the story about his brother. He'd called his brother a dingbat who didn't know what was going on, but he hadn't offered to remove it.

"Slye's the kind who'll argue," said Master Sergeant Turner. "He's a bit of a barracks lawyer. Always talking about his rights and how the Air Force is trying to screw him."

"Is he doing his job?"

"Yes, sir. He hangs around with the wrong crowd downtown, but Slye gets his work done. Sometimes it takes him longer than the others and he has to work late, but he gets it done. Like tonight. He worked a couple of hours later, then took off for downtown."

Pearly decided it wasn't worth the hassle. He had bigger problems. "Forget it, then."

Turner made his farewell and departed.

Half an hour later, as Pearly Gates continued to mourn the delay in the CROSSFIRE ZULU plan, coordinates of the following week's bombing targets were passed from an American serviceman to a Saigon taxi driver.

2355 Local—Hoa Lo Prison, Hanoi, North Vietnam

Major Glenn Phillips

They'd had trouble getting news recently, for the turnkeys had been trying to shut off communications between the prisoners. When they heard talking, or even the tapping sounds, they'd storm in and give a beating to whomever they suspected. Whenever the prisoners tried to leave a note in the *bo*-dump, the guards would find it and take it and beat someone. Until the guards got off this kick and onto another, it was a time for innovation.

Glenn peered out his peek hole across and into the gloomy light of another cell. At night the gomers, whom they collectively called V during their abbreviated communications sessions, kept a dim light bulb burning in the occupied cells. For the past half hour Glenn and the other prisoner had been "talking" by alternately covering and uncovering their peek holes.

The final communiqué from the Navy lieutenant across from him had been worrisome.

354 P IN IMMED DANGER. V TLCNG TO ALL 354 P. ASCNG ABT 354 SQ AND LUCCY ANDERSON.

There was no *K* in their code. They substituted *C*'s. They also abbreviated a lot: "354 P" stood for prisoners from the 354th fighter squadron. The guys from his sister squadron at Takhli were getting special "attention" from the interrogators.

They heard a guard approaching on his round, so both prisoners scurried to their bunks. Phillips crawled under his mosquito net and feigned sleep, thinking hard about this latest news. Lucky Anderson was a close friend and his former boss. They'd been stationed at Nellis, both of them instructors in the air-to-ground flight, and had worked together on tactics-development projects. For a while they'd even been roommates in the BOQ.

Since as far as he knew Lucky hadn't been shot down, he wondered what the gomers wanted with him. It could be nothing good.

CHAPTER THIRTEEN

Air Regiment Commandant Quon

As he entered Xuan Nha's hospital room, Quon noted that it had been transformed into a functional field headquarters. An entire wall was covered with maps of the Democratic Republic of Vietnam. Maps of the various provinces were sprinkled with colored markers, showing radars as well as permanent and deployment sites for rocket and artillery batteries. A composite map showed the communications net, and as the net expanded, so did the spiderwebs of red lines. Another showed where Mee aircraft had been hit by defenses and where they'd gone down. Green safe zone had been liberally watercolored onto all the maps, areas restricted from Mee bombing by Mee politicians.

Xuan Nha's young and badly crippled communications officer had set up business in a corner, on a table sporting two field telephones and a radio receiver, and a profusion of cables were bundled and run out of the room's single window to antennae and power supplies.

Visitors' chairs were set up before Colonel Nha's bed. He was meeting with Colonel Trung when Quon entered.

Xuan Nha's torso had been exposed to healing air, and Quon examined the sheath of gnarled and discolored scar tissue still forming there. The last time he'd seen him, Xuan had rasped that he didn't care what it was that held them, so long as his organs didn't spill out.

Quon had dropped by on other occasions during the past weeks, but this time it was for an entirely different and less official reason. Xuan Nha's wife, Li Binh, had visited the day before, following her return from Paris, and he was curious to know what had been said. He'd heard that she'd acted as concerned as any wife might, but that report only made him more suspicious. Li Binh was no dutiful spouse.

How was she reacting to the news that her nephew had been sent south into danger? General Dung had engineered it, but Quon was a rational man and knew that generals were political and that politicians rarely accepted blame. He also remembered that Dung had insisted that Quon be there when Nguyen Wu was brought before him.

Xuan Nha turned from Colonel Trung, the aging warrior who commanded the artillery forces, and greeted Quon warmly.

Quon glanced warily about the room, and Colonel Nha's communications officer hastily shut off the noisy radio and announced he would get tea for them.

"I was just congratulating Colonel Trung," said Xuan Nha. "His artillery are doing well. We've agreed they will bring him even greater glories when they are tied more firmly into the communications network."

Quon nodded impatiently. He was pressed for time and could not dally long.

Colonel Trung eyed him and interpreted his desire to be left alone with Xuan Nha. He rose slowly, not to be hurried by *any* younger officer, made his excuse, and left.

Quon closed the door behind the grumpy old warrior. "I thought you disliked him."

Xuan Nha's voice emerged in the raspy whisper, sounding like a huge rice-paddy toad. "A better relationship was needed. Our forces, yours and mine, cannot work independently of his guns. So I have been acting the part of the dutiful junior officer."

"I was told he distrusts your rocket systems."

"Colonel Trung is suspicious of all weapons he does not understand, and that includes anything more complex than

a gun. He once told me he believes it is unnatural for men
to fly in aircraft. He refuses even to get into a helicopter."

"I agree about helicopters. Their propellers are on the
wrong ends."

Xuan Nha smiled at the quip.

Quon could think of no reason to be indirect. "I have
heard that your wife visited."

Xuan stared back, the single eye unwavering, but Quon
could not read what was there.

"Were your discussions pleasant?" Quon asked.

"Yes," Xuan carefully croaked. "She was pleased with the
results of her trip to Paris. She worked not only with Tay
diplomats, but also with representatives from various peace
groups. A delegation of Swedes will arrive here next week,
and then a group of Canadian and American activists. Her
office will organize their tours."

Quon waited for him to continue.

"Premier Pham Van Dong applauded her accomplishments. I believe she is briefing the Central Committee now.
Tomorrow she will join them as the newest member."

The words weren't lost on Quon. There were eleven people on the committee whom Lao Dong party leaders trusted
to run the Republic. Li Binh would become the twelfth and
youngest member, firmly ensconced within the government
hierarchy. She'd make it to the top.

"Did you discuss Colonel Wu with her?" asked Quon.

"She asked about her nephew, and I told her what I'd
heard. That he had volunteered for a mission in the South."

"And did you discuss my visits?"

Xuan Nha pursed his lips thoughtfully. "I do not believe
so. If we did, I do not remember it."

Xuan Nha had an astounding memory and forgot very lit-
tle. By his hesitancy was he trying to tell him something?
Quon felt uneasy about what might have transpired with Li
Binh.

The lieutenant arrived with hot tea, and they sipped it
and spoke of how well the radar controllers were communi-
cating with all the elements of defenses, and how they were
better coordinated now than they had been in months.

When Quon left to return to Phuc Yen by helicopter,
since daytime surface travel was discouraged for senior officers, he wondered what had gone on between Xuan Nha
and his wife. By that afternoon he was immersed in the de-

tails of his job and had pushed the discussion with Colonel Nha from his mind. He'd decided there were more important matters to think about than the worries of a woman over the treatment of her worthless nephew lover.

Later Quon came to think differently about that decision.

0930 Local—Ta Khli Village, Thailand

Major Lucky Anderson

When they climbed off the bus, Linda immediately pointed out the row of tents set up across from the Ta Khli market-place.

"That's where the work's done," she said. "The priests are in there praying for rain."

Lucky felt dubious about the entire thing. An hour earlier Linda had barged into his trailer and *insisted* they go into Ta Khli Village to see the rain festival, and he had not been able to dissuade her.

"Everyone says its something we mustn't miss," she'd said.

"Who's everyone?" he'd tried.

"Paul Anderson, you've got to realize there's more to life than flying airplanes. There are so *many* interesting things here. Don't you want to learn about the local culture?"

"Sure," he'd said wryly. Then he'd told her he shouldn't go because one of his lieutenants had some questions about his next assignment, but he knew it was a weak excuse. So he'd resigned himself, thinking he'd come back as soon as she was satisfied they'd assimilated enough local color, and changed into *very* casual clothing as she suggested.

He'd been surprised by her visit, for during the past month he'd not answered her telephone calls or the two letters she'd written. But she'd mentioned none of those, only told him to hurry so they wouldn't miss anything. Then she'd called through the door of the bathroom as he'd dressed, saying she'd come early for her monthly visit so they could attend the festival. As soon as he emerged, she'd hurried them out of the trailer, saying they *couldn't* be late or they would miss *everything*.

And here we are, he thought. He had about the same interest in a Thai rain festival as he'd have had for a botanical field trip, yet somehow it was impossible to remain glum around Linda when she was enjoying herself.

"Let go look," she said happily, pulling him toward the tents.

He resisted, eyeing the swarms of people ahead. "What's this rain festival about?" he asked sourly. "I went to a *water* festival once, but that was a girls' swim-team demonstration."

"The Thais need rain. It's been dry since December. All the rivers and *klongs* are very low, and they use them for transportation and irrigation . . ."

"As well as for their drinking water and sewage system," he added.

She frowned at him for interrupting. ". . . so the people hold this ritual and it rains."

Lucky looked at the flawless, balmy blue sky. "It's almost summer-monsoon season, so it'll rain sooner or later, but it sure as hell isn't going to be today."

She sighed dramatically. "You're just one big wet blanket, Paul Anderson."

"But why did they pick today? The weather forecasters say it's going to be clear."

"Their priests tell them when to hold the festival, not your weather people."

They watched as a Buddhist monk in a saffron-colored robe came out of a tent and gawked at the bright heavens.

"Maybe he's going to call it off," said Lucky. He peered again at the cloudless sky.

"Come on, let's look." She tugged on his hand and led the way into the crowd.

Children slithered through the masses, squirting everyone with water pistols. A five-year-old boy ran up and started to squirt Lucky, then stopped to stare at his face.

Lucky growled.

The kid fled.

"Meanie," said Linda, pulling him along.

She'd advised him to wear clothing he did not treasure, so he'd put on a cotton shirt, chino trousers, and sandals. When an old woman gleefully tossed a dipperful of water on them, he was glad he'd done so. The woman happily delved into her pail for more water, and Lucky picked up his pace to get away. Then another woman splashed them, and a more fearless kid squirted them unmercifully.

Lucky sputtered water. "What the hell's this all about?"

Several young boys gathered around them and squirted away until their guns were empty. Obviously poor kids, filthy, ragged, and without pistols, blew water out of their mouths, then squirmed away through the crowd, laughing shrilly.

"The people are showing they have plenty of water and don't need rain," said Linda, her white blouse drenched and sticking to her skin. "If it looks like they need it, it won't rain, so they throw it all away. They're using a sort of reverse psychology on it."

"What's *it?* Who're they trying to impress?"

"The fates. Buddha's spirit. They're vague on *it. It* is what makes things happen."

The crowd grew thicker as they approached the tents, so they tried to push their way through. When that failed, they just stayed close and went along with the ebbs and flows.

"I thought you said they need every drop?" he yelled when someone tossed an entire bucketful on them.

Linda shouted back at him. "That's why they throw it away. So it'll rain."

"That's dumb."

They heard sounds of a propeller aircraft. A Royal Thai Air Force T-34 flew low overhead, dumping water from a belly tank onto the boisterous crowds.

"These guys are just wasting water," yelled Lucky. "I tell you the weatherman says its gonna be just another dry, hot day."

"You probably think Santa Claus is a fantasy for kids!" shouted Linda. "You probably think the Easter bunny's a fake!"

He watched as she turned her smile toward a group of shouting children they were passing. Although she had a graceful bearing and a look of class, Linda could transform herself into an excited little girl. He found himself smiling at the thought, infected by her cheerful enthusiasm. She'd affected him that way the evening they'd met.

He'd not allowed himself to think of that night for a long while. Had they really been apart all those years? He remembered the bad time, when he'd wanted to think about her but knew he could never again allow it. He'd become master of himself. With time it had been easier. *Now I'll have to do it all over again,* he thought as he watched her and felt the warm glow.

They were still being swept along as the crowd entered through the opened flap of the end tent, several of which had been joined together to form a single, long enclosure.

"Are the tents here to protect them from the deluge?" he joked with Linda, who gave him a glare.

A raised platform had been built on one side, extending the length of the interior. On it sat a row of Buddhist monks, hands held piously before themselves, chanting and diligently bobbing their shaven heads. Once inside, the crowd grew quiet, watching and moving in a long, silent wave past the praying monks.

"Our American Indians do it better," Lucky whispered. "I should get Billy Bowes to teach them a *real* rain dance." Then he noticed that Linda was glaring again, and hushed.

After they'd passed by the dozen praying monks, a young one climbed down and preceded them outside, and when he emerged, his robe fluttered, for a slight breeze was stirring.

Then they were also outside.

"I'll be damned," said Lucky in mock amazement. "It's not raining."

Linda peered upward, as the monk was doing. "Look." She pointed to the south, at a few small clouds gathering in a vertical formation there.

"They're too scrawny to hold rain," joked Lucky, but it was enough to make him wonder.

As they walked toward the marketplace, they saw a group of children in rags, spitting water at better-dressed kids with water pistols.

"Wait here a minute," he told her, and edged his way through a crowd to an open-air stand. He bought a dozen brightly colored water pistols and two lukewarm Singha beers.

Linda smiled when he returned juggling the bag of water guns and the beer bottles. "You going to play with the kids?"

"Nope." He gave her the bag. "Give 'em to the ones without guns, okay?"

She passed them out to the group of squealing ragamuffins, then returned for her beer.

"That was a nice thing to do," she said. "Keep it up and you'll ruin your Uncle Scrooge image."

"Just thinking of your Easter bunny."

They walked, sipping beer and joining the flow of various mobs of people, then stopped before a platform where three teenage girls danced amateurishly to music from a scratchy record player.

"Sounds like a bunch of tin cans being rattled in a garbage can," observed Lucky.

"It's called exotic music of the East, Uncle Scrooge."

A high-pitched voice accompanied the music.

"Now it sounds like they threw in a cat."

"You're impossible."

A drop splatted on her nose. They both looked up.

"What the hell?" he asked in an unbelieving voice. The southern clouds had become gray and were closer.

"There is too a Santa Claus," she whispered, as awed as he.

The clouds moved closer yet, and gusts of wind blew more of the large droplets upon the villagers of Ta Khli.

The crowds shouted joyously and began to throw away water in even larger amounts.

"Unbelievable."

"Come on, Uncle Scrooge. Let's get out of the rain."

A few minutes later the clouds arrived and it began to pour in earnest.

1330 Local—Ponderosa, Takhli RTAFB

Captain Manny DeVera

The base operator put Jackie's call through to the phone in the day room.

"Hello," said Manny reluctantly.

"Oh, hon. I heard about you being wounded and I've been worried sick."

He felt queasy. "Oh?"

"God, but it's good to hear your voice."

"Yeah, yours too." His voice came out as flat as he'd intended it to.

"When did you get back to Takhli, hon?"

"Yesterday."

"And you didn't call?" she pouted.

He started, by reflex, to apologize, then thought about it and kept quiet.

"Is it bad, hon?"

"Not really." Manny looked at his bandaged hand.

Her voice became kittenish. "I'll come over to the base just as soon as I finish with a little more paperwork. I cleared it with my boss, because I figured you'd be in need of TLC."

He took a breath. "I'm gonna be busy, Jackie. I'm behind on paperwork too."

"Then I'll help you write. I heard it was your right hand."

"I can write with my left hand. I can use either one about equally, and . . ." His voice trailed off.

A pause.

"You don't want to see me?"

Silence.

Her voice was sadder, searching for an answer. "Are you in pain, hon?"

"No. They gave me some codeine pills, but I haven't had to take any for a while."

"I can get off. No trouble about that. I told the project leader here about you being hurt, and . . ."

They both grew quiet.

She tried again. "Sure good to hear your voice."

Silence.

"Well, I'll see you, Manny. Give me a call when you're feeling better, okay?"

"Yeah, sure," said Manny.

She hung up.

He stared at the wall. He'd handled it precisely as he'd decided he would during the trip back from Danang. He and Jackie had grown close during his several visits to Nakhon Sawan. It wouldn't be right to saddle her, or anyone else he cared about, with the problems he'd faced when it became known that Manny DeVera was a coward and wanted out.

At least he was man enough to let her go. The thought didn't make him feel better.

He decided to go to the squadron and see if there really *was* any paperwork pending. Lucky hated the stuff and sometimes let it pile up.

"Who's got the keys to the van?" he yelled out.

Bob Liebermann, lounging in a nearby chair, held up the keys without raising his head from his book.

"Anyone need a ride?" Manny asked.

There were no takers.

When he went outside, he found that the sky was as dark and foreboding as his mood. He walked toward the blue van, still thinking as drops of rain splatted down on him.

It would be hard to admit to being a chickenshit coward.

Might as well go all the way. Tell them he wasn't a coward at all, but a conscientious objector, or maybe a high priest of the Fuh King Temple. Get out and join a peace movement and learn to smoke dope and drop acid. Let his hair grow and refuse to wash it or anything else about himself, so he could stand the smell of his new buddies. Wear a peace symbol around his neck and carry a gomer flag. Learn to say *Ommmm* and enjoy blow jobs from hippie broads with blackheads and hairy armpits who'd be grateful he wasn't exploiting them. Wear an American flag on the ass of his jeans and . . .

Wasn't that what all chickenshits did who had the crap scared out of them when they thought about real bullets?

God, it was going to be hard.

He crawled into the van and adjusted the seat.

No more Supersonic Wetback jokes, or singing songs with his buddies in a fighter bar. No more landing after a fur-ball practice dogfight with a friend, thinking he just might be the best fighter jock in the world. No more feeling proud he was returning just a little of what the best fucking country in the world had given him.

So hard.

He started the engine, still thinking, and as he drove toward the flight line, he decided not to hurry with his announcement to quit. He had the bandaged hand for an excuse. Later, when the docs put him back on flying status and they wanted to place him back on the schedule, he'd tell Major Lucky and take his lumps.

No way he'd fly with them and endanger someone with his cowardice.

He thought about how much he was going to miss the guys from C-Flight, and how he didn't deserve to breathe the same air they did.

354th TFS Duty Desk

Captain Billy Bowes

He was surprised to find the special orders in his cubbyhole at the squadron. On them was a list of unit pilots qualified to lead combat flights. Among them was *Name: Bowes, William W.; Rank: Captain; SN: FR52221; AFSC: 1115E.*

He was frowning and examining the orders when Captain DeVera came in.

He glanced at Manny's bandaged hand. "How's the paw?"

Manny shrugged and started past him toward the C-Flight commander's room.

"Something wrong?"

Manny paused and turned. "Sorry, Billy. I've been thinking."

"Bad habit." Billy grinned. "I try to avoid it as much as possible."

Manny nodded at the orders. "Congratulations on making flight lead. Major Lucky told me."

"Yeah?"

They went into the C-Flight commander's office, and Manny sat behind the desk while Billy slouched in a chair. Manny shuffled through the papers in the in-basket.

"He had to hurry your orders a little," said Manny, "what with my being off status. He can't fly every mission, so he needed someone to lead the guys when he's on the ground."

"Hell, you're not going to be off flying status that long, Manny. Doc Roddenbush says you'll probably be back on in a week or so."

DeVera shrugged, as if to say "who knows."

Billy tried crawfishing. "You *really* think I'm ready for it?"

"Flight lead? Damn right I do."

Billy Bowes did not wish to be ready. He'd thought Lucky would give him some sort of check ride before he issued the orders, and that he'd be able to make a few stupid decisions and get it put off. That having failed, he now opted for a verbal tactic with DeVera, who, after all, *was* assistant flight commander.

"I dunno, Manny. I think I could use a few more rides

flying on the wing. I haven't been flying the Thud very long, you know."

"You've got nothing more to learn on the wing. Anyway, won't be long and all the high-time Thud guys will have finished their combat tours. Then there's going to be a hell of a lot of guys from other airplanes coming over to fly one-oh-fives"

Billy grumbled, "I should at least get a few more missions as element leader."

"Whenever Lucky's along, you'll fly as number three, Billy. And before you take the guys up to pack six, you'll lead a mission or two in the lower packs."

Maybe, thought Billy, he should fuck up bad enough in the lower packs that Lucky would take him *off* orders and let him return to flying on the wing. That was the only way he'd be able to sting the gomers some more without having to worry about someone else's ass. Flight leads came under too much scrutiny, being out in front as they had to be. Hell, if he dropped a bomb on an illegal target, the rest of them might follow him in and do the same.

Then it would be as Tiny Bechler had said. He'd be hurting his friends. All in all, the flight-lead orders presented a shitty problem.

Henry Horn peeked his smiling face around the door. "What're you guys up to?"

"Telling secrets," said Billy. "Got any?"

"Yeah. Weather officer's all fucked up. Said it was going to be clear, and it's raining so hard the frogs are carrying umbrellas."

"Weather people are always fucked up," said Billy. "I think they shake up a bunch of Ping-Pong balls and read forecasts off 'em, like bingo callers. Makes me suspicious when I ask for a weather forecast and they say 'bee-five.'"

"Where's Major Lucky?" Henry asked.

"Got me," said Billy. "You know, Manny?"

DeVera had been uncharacteristically quiet throughout their exchange. "He's not flying. You try his trailer?"

"Yeah. He's not there."

"Maybe he went downtown."

"Major Lucky doesn't *go* downtown," said Henry Horn, taking a seat beside Billy. "You're assistant C-Flight commander, Captain DeVera. I'm supposed to put down where I want to be reassigned when I leave here, and I need some advice. I want to stay operational, but I want to consider my family too."

"Try a stateside base. Europe's got good wine and horny women for the single guys, but the flying is shitty because of the congested airspace and the awful weather. You'd be gone from your family a lot, because you have to go to Italy or Libya to find good weather and gunnery ranges. But then there's . . ." He stopped midsentence.

Henry was listening hard. "Go ahead. You've been there, and I value your judgment."

That seemed to shake Manny even more. Finally he resumed, in a quieter voice. "I think . . ." His voice trailed off oddly then, and he just stared at Henry Horn.

"Yes, sir?"

"Wait for Major Lucky," Manny mumbled. Then he bolted from his chair and hurried from the room.

Henry gave Billy a surprised look. It was obvious that something was bothering Manny DeVera.

2350 Local—Trailer 5A

Major Lucky Anderson

They'd drunk too many Singha beers and laughed too often, had eaten too much hot Thai food and become too intoxicated with memories. They'd also forgotten too many years and too many things in between, and acted as if they were still very young and in love.

That was how he explained it to himself. Otherwise there was no reason for what they'd done, or at least no reason that made sense.

They had returned to his trailer and without hesitation had stripped and made love. Gentle love, with no rushing, but also with no doubts or hesitation. Easy and natural love. Giving generously and taking selfishly. It had been as if she'd just driven down to Sembach, as she had back then, and they'd felt the first thing they must do when they got to the room was prove it all still worked.

Dammit! Lucky cried from within.

Rain began to fall again, in the big drops of the tropics that made soft, pinging sounds on the trailer's metal roof. It was dark, but not so dark he couldn't see her shape beside him, breathing softly and sleeping as if she were utterly without worry. As she'd drifted off, she had made the happy sounds of a fulfilled woman, sounds he'd remembered and which made his own satisfaction more complete.

She smelled of pleasant, feminine odors that he hadn't known for a long time. Aromas he'd forgotten, that he had never again expected to sense.

Stop it.

A particularly strong gust made the trailer tremble, and he wondered if the morning mission would be canceled. He hoped not. He needed to fill his mind with the things you must concentrate on to fly a jet.

What was it she'd said, when she'd snuggled close to sleep, and the impact of what they had done had begun to sink into his brain?

He remembered. "I'm home," she'd said in her sleepy voice.

They'd made love twice, just as they'd always done before. The first time stridently to tend the urgent needs, and the second time more softly. *My time,* she'd always said of the second lovemaking, and she'd repeated it tonight. Then, as he had begun to gather his wits about himself, she'd whispered that she was home.

Maybe it could work.

No! he raved at himself, struggling toward reality.

He'd realized it when he'd begun to recover from the accident, when he'd lain there thinking too much. He'd known exactly what he would do if they released him from the burn center and he could not get back on flying status. A flight nurse he'd known had told him how to do it.

He would get a Texas fifth of good Scotch and find a secluded spot on a nice beach. Then he'd drink the whole son of a bitch down in a single, grand chugalug and lie back and pass out and not wake up, because that much whiskey would kill a horse.

It was just after making that decision that he'd written the letter to Linda Lopes back in Germany, to stop things between them.

He'd known that he would never be accepted by a society that revered beauty and was repulsed by ugliness. He refused to face life as a second-class citizen, which he would become once he was cast out into the civilian life, and he

also refused to put Linda Lopes through the hell of being
tied to life with a monster.

She moved and came half-awake. Snuggled closer and
murmured his name. He held his breath . . . then her breath
evened, and he knew she was asleep again.

Several times during and after their acts she'd said she
loved him.

Do I love her?

He quickly pushed the question from his mind, refusing
to consider it. It was an unreasonable, treasonous thought, a
ruse to make him disavow his promises.

Nothing's changed.

He had a treacherous thought. *What if I was wrong?*

But he knew he was not.

Sleep was slow coming, fitful when it arrived.

Knocking on the door. He slipped out of bed and padded
over to open it. The rain had stopped.

The squadron orderly grinned at him. "It's four o'clock,
sir. Briefing's at four-thirty."

"Thanks." He yawned and closed the door.

She was stirring.

He went to the bathroom and was shaved and showered
in less than five minutes. He returned to the darkness of the
bedroom then and pulled on his flight suit and socks. He
was lacing his flight boots when she came awake.

"It's early." Her voice was sleepy.

"That's when we fly here, Linda, so we won't screw up
the enemy. They can set their clocks by the sound of our
bombs, every morning at seven, every afternoon at two."

"You're flying this morning?"

"Yeah. And you'd better slip out of here before everyone's up."

She was sitting and the sheet had fallen away, but he
carefully kept his eyes averted.

She stretched and shuddered. "I'll be talking to the
mayor in Takhli this morning and then with the provincial
people at Nakhon Sawan."

"Busy day?"

"But it'll be an easy one." She stretched again, slowly and
languorously. "*God* I loved last night." Her voice carried a
trill.

It was time for him to speak up, to stop it before it went further.

"It was all wrong, Linda. I shouldn't have let it happen."

"Bullshit."

The word startled him, for he'd never heard her curse.

"I'm not going to let you start your silly interfering again. Dinner?"

"No," he said.

"It's not going to work this time, Paul Anderson. I refuse to let you get away with it again."

"Get away with what? I'm not trying to get away with *anything*."

"Bullshit."

"Stop that."

"Bullshit, bullshit, *bullshit!*"

He finished lacing his boots and stood up.

"Dinner?" she asked again.

"Dammit, I do not want to have dinner with you."

"Why? Getting together with your ex-wife?" she asked in a mocking tone.

"What?"

"That's what you told me last time you wanted to get rid of me. That won't work again. *Nothing* you say is going to work."

"No dinner, Linda. And I don't think we should be seeing each other."

"Paul, I just spent eight years believing that and being miserable." Her voice rose angrily. "Guess how many men I've been to bed with in that time?"

Lucky winced. He was angry at himself because sometimes, in moments of weakness, he'd wondered. "That's none of my business," he finally said.

"Bullshit."

"Quit that."

"Zero, that's how many men I've been to bed with."

He was quiet, not about to allow himself to feel good about it.

"I almost slipped, Paul. I wanted to slip *so bad* sometimes that I cried. I wanted to feel like a woman again, to go to sleep all content and feeling like I belonged to someone. I wanted to feel wanted and needed. I didn't do anything to deserve being cheated out of that, did I?"

He refused responsibility. "You'll find someone," he said.

"Don't try to lay the blame on anyone else, Paul Anderson. It was you who took it away from me."

She did not cry, for she was not that kind of woman. Her voice was strong and her words so sure that it was obvious she meant what she was saying.

"You lied to me. I believed your wife was there helping you. I wanted it to be me at the burn center with you, but you even took *that* away from me."

He felt harried, as if he were being chased. "Dammit, Linda, what do you want?"

"To get back together. For things to be like they were before."

"It can *never* be like before."

Linda peered at him. Finally she shrugged. "Then I'll settle for dinner."

When he landed from the morning mission, an easy counter to pack two, Lucky volunteered to leave on the base shuttle for Danang to pick up Manny DeVera's F-105, which had been left there for repairs. When he returned the following day, Linda Lopes had returned to Bangkok.

This time she left no notes.

CHAPTER FOURTEEN

Captain Billy Bowes

It was the second time Billy had led a flight into combat, the first time he'd led in pack six. They were headed out over the flatlands, the tough and dangerous area where Manny DeVera had been hit and lost his cool. The northeast railroad.

Talon flight crossed eastward over the midpoint of Thud Ridge at 10,000 feet altitude. Billy was leading, Joe Walker on his wing, Liebermann and Horn making up the second element. His thoughts lingered on Liebermann, how he accepted Billy's leadership even though he wanted to lead a flight of fighters into combat more than anything.

Billy hadn't wanted to lead, but all it had taken was a word from Lucky Anderson that he needed him. Billy admired the man so much that he would do about anything he asked, and since this time it involved keeping C-Flight together, the argument had been unassailable.

Anyway, Major Lucky had said he'd try to get them *all* upgraded to lead status; Captain Liebermann, and Lieutenants Horn and Walker as well. When that happened, when

Major Lucky no longer needed his help, Billy would go back to his secret war. Stinging the enemy where it hurt them most, and fuck the restrictions.

He looked over at the second element, then waggled his wings for Liebermann to close it up. Bob was a fair pilot when he loosened up, but he tried to get flying moxie through a scholarly learning process and by religiously following the rules. Billy had taught his student pilots that once they felt *comfortable* flying a bird, the rest would come. It was obvious Liebermann hadn't learned to do that. But Billy liked Bob and all the other pilots in C-Flight and intended to do everything in his power to keep them safe.

They flew in a series of four-ships as they'd done when he'd first arrived at Takhli, fragged to locate and destroy rolling stock targets on the dangerous northeast railway.

Big Eye airborne radar had called MiGs at "Bullseye zero oner zero for twenty miles," using the new code system designed to make it easier for them to figure out where the MiGs were. "Bullseye" was Hanoi, and just as the planners thought, the jocks *always* knew where they were in relation to Hanoi. And since Big Eye had called ten degrees at twenty miles from Hanoi, that meant there were MiGs in their vicinity. They'd been briefed that Big Eye had added some kind of system that decoded enemy transponders, so their warnings were regarded as especially accurate.

Out over the flatlands now and not far from the railroad, so it was time to change switch settings from shooting MiGs to dropping bombs.

"*Talons, let's set 'em up for air-to-ground,*" Billy called.

"*Two.*" "*Talon three, wilco.*" "*Talon four,*" came the responses.

Billy selected centerline station, where he carried his seven-fifties, and dialed in forty-five-degree dive-bomb settings. He double-checked that he was up properly, then scanned the sky ahead and to either side.

Cumulus clouds towered in all directions, and he led Talon flight around an especially dark and ominous one that lay before them.

"*THIS IS BIG EYE. DOGMEAT AT BULLSEYE ZERO ONER FIVER AT THIRTY-FIVE MILES. I REPEAT, THIS IS BIG EYE. DOGMEAT AT BULLSEYE ZERO ONER FIVER AT THIRTY-FIVE MILES.*"

Billy mentally calculated their position. The MiGs were

close. He gave the sky another visual sweep and listened as the Wild Weasel flight, forward and right of Talon, dueled with a SAM site.

No way he'd trade jobs with the Weasels, sparring with the big missiles, especially in shitty weather like this. He wondered how his cousin Mal had put up with ninety-five missions of the dangerous duty. Then he remembered what he was doing, dive-bombing targets while SAMs and a hundred guns tried to kill him, and he guessed everything was relative.

Dark puffs ahead at their altitude. The guns along the railroad were active. He saw more bursts, concentrations of fours and sixes. Fifty-sevens and eighty-fives, he decided, as more and more of the big guns opened up, trying to zero in on a jinking covey of Thunderchiefs.

A flight of F-4 Phantoms high above turned right, heading toward Haiphong, and he supposed they'd spotted something there.

0648 Local—Bac Giang Province, DRV

Air Regiment Commandant Quon

Quon called for his six MiG-21's to split into two sections of three, and they immediately responded. He was left with a Vietnamese captain and lieutenant in loose trail, each staggered a hundred meters above the MiG before him. The Russian, Aleksandr Ivanovic, led an East German and a Polish pilot in a similar formation toward the flight of Mee radar-hunters east of them.

Quon's element was given a new VHF radio frequency, and after his pilots had called the switch, and positive identification was verified by the controller, he radioed, *"Red Quon requests directions to target."*

The response was immediate. *"Red Quon, turn to zero five five . . . four targets at eight kilometers."*

Since the Mee fighters were on the opposite side of the large dark cloud in that direction, Quon advised the controller to provide constant target information. Then, already in a hard turn, with his throttle full forward, he called for his section to prepare for K-13 heat-guided rocket attacks.

He planned to surprise the Mee pilots by using the wispy edges of the cloud for cover.

A draft of air bounced his jet mightily, but he tensed his stocky body and ignored it, continuing to skirt the edge of the cloud, eyes drawn forward in anticipation.

"Is it you, *Lokee?*" he asked quietly as he double-checked that he was set up to fire K-13 rocket number one.

0651 Local—Northeast of Hanoi, Route Pack Six, North Vietnam

Captain Billy Bowes

Big Eye had warned of three different groups of MiGs, and then one of the Weasels sighted a MiG-21 and called for a hard turn.

The railroad was only a dozen miles ahead, beyond the big cloud they were skirting. A flight of Thuds was in their pop-up there, attacking a rail siding on which they'd found a few boxcars, and someone in their group said the flak was heavy.

Billy kicked the rudder in first one, then the other direction, checking their six o'clock position. Something was nagging deep inside that all hell was about to break loose, and he'd grown to trust his intuitions.

As they approached the far side of the big cloud, he began to breathe easier. Only a few more seconds and they'd be clear. He hated clouds, not for what they were but for what they might be hiding. He'd been eyeing it warily, imagining MiGs and gremlins out of the various shapes of swirling moist air.

He glanced out past Liebermann to Horn, flying off to his right, then to his left at Walker. Everyone was jinking nicely and appeared alert.

"*Talon two has a bogey at three o'clock,*" called Joe Walker.

Billy whipped his head right, searched the edge of the cloud there.

"*Atoll, Talons, Atoll! Break right!*" radioed Walker, and Billy was already throwing his control stick to the right when he saw two, then three delta-shaped aircraft emerge from the gloom of the cloud.

A missile darted between Liebermann and Horn, leaving its white wisp of smoke. Close.

Talon flight was coming around now, turning into the MiGs, sluggish with the weight of the bombs but no longer sitting ducks. Billy had all three delta-winged MiGs in sight. Very close. Not silver, but a flat green color, the leader with a dark red sash painted around its fuselage. One by one the MiGs flashed past their quarry and for a few seconds were behind them and lost to Billy's vision, but somehow he *knew* they would reattack.

"*MiG-21's!*" he yelled as the flight continued their hard turn. "*Dump your bombs and tanks and get 'em ready to fight, Talons.*" He eased the turn slightly, punched the jettison switch, and felt the weight drop away, then resumed his hard turn.

"*Two.*" "*Four,*" came the response to his call.

What the hell was wrong with Liebermann? he wondered.

"*Talon three will retain my bombs,*" called Liebermann crisply, for they'd been briefed by the brass to keep their bombs to drop on the target and to avoid engaging MiGs.

There was no time to argue. Billy kept his Thud turning as hard as its stubby wings could manage while he frantically changed the weapons selector to the guns-air position.

0653 Local—Bac Giang Province, DRV

Air Regiment Commandant Quon

Blue-tails!

Once past the Mee, Quon immediately led his nimble MiGs into a hard right turn to reengage. He watched the Thunder plane leader and two others jettison bombs and fuel tanks. No longer such easy prey there. But the aircraft on the leader's right wing failed to jettison and was wallowing in its turn and becoming separated from the others.

Quon's MiG-21's easily outturned the Thunder planes. The lead Mee had come only half-circle when Quon was rolling wings level and slapping at the rocket-head enabling switch. He cut off and tracked the one with the bombs and fuel tanks still hanging, and positioned ever closer, glancing periodically at the ready light. It continued to blink, refusing to come on steady.

The Thunder-plane pilot before him tried to turn tighter but could not, yet was safe because the fornicating rockethead refused to lock on. Quon was reaching forward for the selector switch to change to another rocket when the pilot before him reversed direction and engaged afterburner . . . providing a superb target for the K-13 heat-seeking rocket.

Steady light. Quon immediately fired, fervently hoping there'd be sufficient separation for the fuze to arm, for he was close.

During his reversal the stupid Mee pilot straightened for a split second, and it was enough. As Quon feared, the rocket's warhead did not explode, but it homed so true that it tore away the upper-engine exhaust and sheared off the vertical stablizer.

The Thunder plane slewed out of his vision, going down.

"Red Quon, break off," radioed the controller. *"Phantoms at seven kilometers, closing."*

0655 Local—Northeast of Hanoi, Route Pack Six, North Vietnam

Captain Billy Bowes

"Weeep, weeep, weeep," sounded Bob Liebermann's emergency beeper.

Billy had watched the shoot-down, and felt sick.

He'd told Bob about the MiG, told him to stay out of burner, to put his nose down and disengage. The Thud could outrun anything on earth down there. But he hadn't, just as he hadn't jettisoned his bombs, and now the sound of his emergency beeper told Billy he'd punched out of his airplane.

"Weeep, weeep, weeep."

Billy had no time to shut off emergency guard channel and wished Bob would turn his chute beeper off to help his concentration. He was closing on the rearmost MiG, still in a right-hand turn and hoping for a shot. There'd been no time to change his switches to get radar ranging from his gunsight, so he'd have to estimate it.

As he'd anticipated, the MiG driver saw him and reversed, so Billy held down his trigger as the MiG veered in front of him, spewing out 200 rounds in a wild, high-angle snapshot. He missed, and the MiG kept turning hard left, so Billy also reversed and engaged afterburner to take on the leader, the green MiG with the red stripe that had bagged Liebermann.

"Thud in the fight with the MiG-21, this is Trigger lead. Get out of the way so we can get a missile shot," sounded over the strike frequency.

The F-4's had arrived. *About time,* he thought.

"I'm gonna shoot this guy first, Trigger," called Billy.

"His wingman's on your ass, and you're about to get an Atoll up your tailpipe," said Trigger almost conversationally.

Billy kicked rudder and swiveled his neck to see a MiG-21 leveling its wings, in position and ready to fire. *Oh, Jesus can they turn,* he thought, and his next reaction was done without thinking.

He came out of burner and slapped the speed-brakes switch.

It was quick. He slowed from 590 knots to 550 almost immediately, and the MiG on his tail slid past as if he'd stopped dead in the air.

"Good going, F-105," yelled Trigger lead. *"We're engaging, Triggers."*

Billy immediately retracted his speed-brakes, but he was out of the fight. He tapped afterburner to regain airspeed and called for a position on his two remaining flight members.

"Talon four is five miles west, lead."

"Talon two's joining off your right wing," called Joe Walker, and Billy saw him when he glanced around.

He looked back at the MiGs, diving and twisting in the distance.

"Trigger two is Fox one," called an F-4, and a Sparrow missile zipped cleanly through the loose MiG formation.

"Fox one" meant they'd fired a midrange radar missile. "Fox two" identified their shorter range, heat-sinking Falcons or Sidewinders.

Billy led Walker into a left-hand turn toward Henry Horn, whose bird looked lonely by itself.

"Fox two," called another Phantom, without identifying himself, and Billy watched another missile miss. An AIM-4 Falcon, the shittiest missile in the inventory. The F-4Ds were close, but they weren't equipped with a cannon. They could outclimb and outdive the MiGs and damn near turn

with them, but they didn't have a gun to shoot them with. It was a crime to send a fighter to war without a gun, he thought.

"*You take a hit, Henry?*" he asked Horn, worrying about his flight. He did not like the thought of anything being amiss this far from safety. Enough had gone wrong.

"*I don't think so, Talon lead. The number two MiG was all over me like ugly for a couple seconds, but I dumped my nose like you were telling Bob and got the hell away.*"

"*Weeep, weeeep—*" Bob Liebermann's beeper was finally shut off, and that was a good sign, because it meant he was healthy enough to switch it off.

Billy transmitted over guard channel, hoping Bob had his survival radio out. "*Talon three, Talon lead. Can you hear me, buddy?*"

A hiss of static, then something about being okay.

Billy sucked in a sad breath. "*Beat it out of there if you can, Talon three. There's no rescue up here.*"

"*Roger, lead. I'll think of something. There's a lot of farms around here, and a village close by, so I'd better hurry. Give 'em hell, Talons.*"

Billy kept his voice even. "*See you later, Talon three.*"

"*Talon three's out.*" Liebermann's survival radio went off the air.

The remainder of Talon was very quiet as they began to rejoin, heading west.

From the F-4 Phantoms Billy heard, "*Trigger two is Fox one . . . splash.*"

The "splash" call meant Trigger two had downed one of the MiGs with a radar-guided Sparrow missile.

All in all, Billy figured as he and Joe Walker joined up with Henry and began to look one another over for damage, it had been a hell of an initiation. *Welcome to leading a flight in pack six*, he said to himself. He said a silent farewell to Bob Liebermann as they continued back toward Thud Ridge. If Bob had only been smart enough to know *which* of the silly-assed rules to ignore, he'd likely have made it through the fight. But then, maybe not. The northeast railroad was a hell of a place to have to fight, he thought as he looked back at a trio of SAMs arcing through the air, and a flight of Thuds maneuvering to dodge them.

All three Talons seemed okay, and since there didn't seem to be much enemy activity where they were, he assumed it was over the for day. Too bad, with the Thuds cleaned up for action as they were.

Two of the MiG-21's escaped, he thought, and that pissed him off again.

He called for a fuel check and then calculated they could all make it to the tanker with no problems. Of the three, he had the most fuel.

Enough for a slight diversion?

They were approaching Thud Ridge at 9,000 feet.

The MiGs had short legs, which meant they couldn't carry enough fuel to fight for long without landing. He wondered if they would land at Phuc Yen, at the southernmost end of Thud Ridge.

Just maybe . . .

"Talons, let's change to squadron common frequency," he said. He didn't want to broadcast his idea over the strike frequency.

0712 Local—Phuc Yen PAAFB, DRV

Air Regiment Commandant Quon

One Thunder plane killed, one MiG-21 lost to the fornicating Mee Phantom. He hoped his pilot had survived, for he was a good one, and too few of his Vietnamese airmen were sufficiently adept at flying the tricky small-tail MiG-21's. The other MiGs, led by Captain Ivanovic, had been discovered during their attack and escaped to China.

Quon's MiGs were low on fuel after the wild maneuvering to escape the Phantoms, and had to land quickly. It would've been handier to land at Kep, but that had become an authorized target for the Thunder planes, so he led his wingman back to the safety of Phuc Yen, still off-limits to the Mee pilots.

When he got on the ground, he would call to see if the Mee pilot he'd shot down had been captured, for he *knew* this one was from the despicable Pig Squadron.

He made a long, straight-in approach, remembering he had his show to perform. Whenever they flew, the ground crews watched as they returned, to see who would perform a victory roll, meaning he'd scored a kill. Thus far Quon had performed seven of them, four in the MiG-17 and three in his red-bannered MiG-21. This would be number eight.

As they approached the big base, he noted that he was down to a scant 500 liters of petrol. He decided on a quick flyby, then to immediately come about to land.

Near the end of the runway he pulled the nose slightly up and prepared to maneuver. The tower radioed something, but he ignored it in his concentration. He entered the roll maneuver nicely, nose held slightly high, and recovered smoothly, then gained a bit of altitude and turned downwind.

The tower operator was screaming words about a Thunder. . . .

He never saw his attacker, only felt his MiG-21 begin to lurch wildly and come apart.

He yelled a question over the radio as the small-tail slewed sideward, pinning him to the seat. When he pushed hard on the rudder, the aircraft corrected only slightly.

A glance into his mirror showed fire burning aft of the cockpit. His heart thumped as he fought the controls.

A Thunder plane loomed before him, pulling up into its recovery arc. He could even see the white letters *RM* on the tail.

They were not supposed to attack here!

The shrill scream of the engine abruptly stopped, and the silence was like an omen of death. He fearfully looked out and saw that his right wing had been shredded.

The MiG pitched up, out of control, and slewed sideward before beginning to tumble earthward. Quon was screaming uncontrollably, clawing for the ejection handle, but his hand was held away by the terrible force of the spin. He was begging for mercy when somehow he found and pulled the handle.

1030 Local—Intelligence Debriefing Room, Command Post, Takhli, RTAFB, Thailand

On the flight back to base, Billy and Henry and Joe had agreed that he'd been in hot pursuit of the MiG, which was the only reason he could legally be where he'd been to shoot it down.

Joe said he'd seen a chute, which meant the MiG driver

had escaped death, and Billy felt somehow cheated. But even if the bastard was now safe and drinking with his buddies, it felt good to get his MiG kill.

Halfway through the intell debriefing, things started to turn to shit. Colonel Lyons came in and listened for only a moment before he jumped him, arguing first that Bowes had not been authorized to engage MiGs. When he heard the rest of the story, Lyons blamed him for the loss of Bob Liebermann, and that pissed Billy off.

"I don't feel proud of losing a member of my flight, Colonel," Billy said, "but I sure as hell didn't contribute to his getting shot down. If he'd dumped his bombs and tanks or disengaged like I told him to, he'd have made it.

That made Lyons even more irate. "You were *explicitly* told neither to engage MiGs *nor* to drop your bombs."

"We were told not to jettison *unless it was necessary*. For Christ's sake, Colonel, the MiGs had already fired a missile and we were fighting to save our lives!"

"Then why didn't you immediately engage burner and get your men out of there instead of trying to outturn MiG-21's."

Billy opened his mouth to respond when he realized that, regardless of being an asshole, the colonel had a point.

Lyons pressed his advantage. "You were derelict in your duty as flight leader."

Billy avoided the colonel's eyes. He thought of Liebermann and wondered.

Lyons spat the next words out hatefully. "Why didn't you just point your gun at his head and pull the trigger before takeoff, Captain? You would have gotten the same results, and we wouldn't have lost an airplane."

"He's alive, sir," said Billy, flushing with anger and self-recrimination.

"You don't know that, do you?" Lyons said.

"I talked to him on the ground."

"But you don't know if he's *still* alive, do you?"

Billy's response was slow coming. "No, sir."

Lyons nodded his head at the debriefing report in front of Billy, on which he'd been describing his MiG kill. "I also suspect your reason for shooting at a MiG in the restricted area."

"I was in hot pursuit, sir." But now Billy's words came out sounding uncertain.

Lyons glared. "Perhaps an inquiry will find differently." Billy felt miserable.

"As of this moment, Captain Bowes, you are *off* flight status," Lyons said triumphantly.

354th TFS Duty Desk

Major Lucky Anderson

Lucky was talking to Bad Injin Encinos, the squadron commander, when Henry Horn went into the squadron building and told what had happened to Billy Bowes.

Encinos's expression clouded. He mumbled something about work, then went into his office and closed the door.

Lucky looked at Horn evenly. "Tell it to me one more time, Henry," he said. They walked into the privacy of the C-Flight office, and he listened.

When he'd heard it all, Lucky raised a single finger. "Only one question, Henry. You say Billy was in hot pursuit?"

Horn looked away and swallowed. "Sort of, sir. The MiGs weren't always in sight, but . . . we figured where they'd be going."

Lucky waited until Horn looked back at him, then spoke quietly. "If anyone asks, just remember one thing, you guys *were* in hot pursuit."

"Yes, sir," said Henry, relieved.

Lucky nodded a final look of encouragement and walked out of the squadron building toward the command post. Angry clouds boiled to the west of the field. They'd likely get another frog-drowner in a few minutes, he thought, so he hurried his step.

Billy Bowes and Joe Walker emerged from the command post door and approached, looking despondent. They saluted and Billy said, "I've got something to tell you, boss."

"Later," he said. "I've got something to do right now. See you both back at the squadron soon as I'm done."

"It's important," tried Billy.

"So's what I have to do. You guys go to the squadron and get a beer, and wait for me there."

He hurried on.

Inside the command post he asked for Colonel Lyons and was told he was in his office. He went there, knowing what he had to do and that it would be distasteful.

Lyons was alone in his office, speaking on the phone in a smooth voice, as if he were sweet-talking a female. He glanced out and saw Anderson and motioned for him to wait.

Lucky went inside and closed the door, careful to press the privacy lock to keep others out.

Lyons's mouth sagged. He told whomever he was talking to that he'd call back and slammed down the receiver.

"What the hell are you doing, Major?" he said in a loud and outraged voice.

"Well, Colonel sir, I figured that since you fucked with one of my men, we'd better straighten it out, and I didn't think you'd want anyone hearing you change your mind."

Lyons's face grew crimson with outrage. He sputtered.

Lucky leaned against the door, taking it in.

"Get out of here!"

Lucky wagged his head. "No, sir."

"That is a direct order, Major. Get out before you make matters worse for yourself."

"I'll answer that with something I wish Captain Bowes had thought of. Get fucked . . . Colonel, sir."

Lyons's mouth dropped. "Are you demented?"

Lucky pondered. "Possibly. I hadn't thought of it like that. But I'm not leaving until we've had our talk."

Lyons stared at Lucky's face with distaste. "I *will* press charges, Major. Be assured that you will answer for your actions."

"Do you remember a certain chief master sergeant named Wallace who retired from here two weeks ago?"

Lyons stared.

"He told me he hated your fucking guts, Colonel, sir."

Lyons forced a thin smile. "I do not remember being overly impressed with the chief, either."

"He also wrote out a statement and signed it, and I was a witness. I suppose you remember calling him in and ordering him to take you off the flying schedule any time you were supposed to go *anywhere* but to pack one."

Lyons stared hatefully.

"I've checked and it's true. You haven't flown a mission

outside of pack one. I figure Colonel Parker, maybe even General Moss, might be interested in that single-paged document signed by the chief. I don't know what you call it. Dereliction of duty? Giving an illegal order? Taking the easy missions so the dumb-shit lieutenants and captains are the only ones who get shot at?"

Lyons looked away. His hands clenched and unclenched before him. "It's just that I don't feel with . . . ah . . . all of my other duties, I am properly prepared to fly . . ."

"To fly where they might be shooting?" asked Lucky.

Lyons glared at him but did not speak.

"And if being called a despicable, fucking coward doesn't matter to you, Colonel, sir, I've got a couple more items tucked away you might be even more surprised at. I think it might be interesting, what with your laying charges against Captain Bowes and myself, and my accusing you of all kinds of shit. It might even get downright exciting."

Lyons was chewing his lower lip.

"It's your call . . . sir."

"What do you want?" Lyons finally said in a low voice.

"Number one, stop any action you're thinking about taking concerning Captain Bowes. Two, it was hot pursuit, but we'll forget all about his MiG kill since it might upset assholes at headquarters who think like you. And three, I don't want any of your bullshit about taking him off lead orders or off the schedule, or anything else. Don't ever fuck with my men again, Colonel. Not with any one of them. Because next time, I won't give you the chance to crawfish out of it."

Lyons stared.

"You got all that, Colonel, sir? If you don't, we can sure as hell take this thing a whole lot further."

A few minutes later Lucky was walking back toward the squadron. When a few drops of rain sprinkled down, the forerunner of a real drenching, Lucky picked up his pace.

Lyons was such a lightweight that he'd not doubted the outcome, even though it had all been a bluff. Chief Wallace had indeed bitched about Lyons's order, but there was no deposition, and he had nothing else on him. But he knew that people like Lyons believed they were exempt from decency, and did a lot of things they wouldn't want aired, and Lucky had known he'd fold.

He didn't feel good about what he'd done. It was a bloody shame the Air Force had those few officers like Lyons around, who could give the rest such a bad name.

He would return to the squadron, he decided, and give the guys a minor chewing out about not following rules, and then tell Bowes he'd not get credit for a MiG kill. He wouldn't be too tough on them. Losing a member of the flight was bad enough. And deep inside he was damn glad Bowes had shot down the guy who'd done it. He'd have done the same.

Monday, June 12th, 1100 Local—Hoa Lo Prison, Hanoi, DRV

Air Regiment Commandant Quon

A week following the ignominious shoot-down in front of his entire air regiment, Quon hurried to the Hanoi prison. They'd finally captured the pilot of the Thunder plane he'd shot down. More important, the man's name, a long and especially difficult one, was on the list of Mee pilots who had strafed and killed his son.

Knowing the pilot was from the Pig Squadron and then shooting him down had been especially pleasing, but that pleasure had been spoiled by the subsequent embarrassment. Quon had landed in his parachute in the city of Phuc Yen, only a kilometer from his base. Neither the people there nor his own men had wanted to believe that the great Quon had been downed so easily. There'd been no interviews or mention in the party newspaper, but the word had been quickly and widely spread through word of mouth.

Even worse than that humiliation was his anger at himself, for he'd been shot down by a pilot of the Pig Squadron. The hunter humiliated by his prey. Thus he especially savored his trip to the prison. He felt increasingly pleased as he entered the prison's admission hall and went directly to the commandant's office.

The senior lieutenant was awaiting him and greeted him with the bow accorded senior officials. "Comrade Quon, I am once again honored to . . ."

"Where is the prisoner?" he snapped.

"We have had two interrogation sessions, and after much work I have the information you wished." The commandant was fawning, but seemed hesitant.

Was he worried that he might lose another prisoner to Quon's anger? In a dark rage Quon had determined not to shoot the Mee. Too easy, he'd decided.

"Where is he?" Quon iterated doggedly. He had a meeting in the afternoon and did not wish to be late.

"He is in one of the holding cells where we place new arrivals. He suffers from the interrogations. As you ordered, we went to work very soon after he arrived."

"What did you learn?"

"He admitted he was assigned to *Lokee*'s flight, and that he flew the day your son was killed. He was the second one to strafe your son's aircraft, just as the other pilot told us."

Quon again relished the fact that he'd been the one to shoot him down. "He admitted firing his gun?"

"Yes. He was not sure he hit the taxiing airplane, but he fired his cannon at it."

"Take me to him."

The senior lieutenant licked his lips cautiously. "The holding cell is a filthy place, comrade Quon, for we have the prisoner secured in leg-stocks, and he has relieved himself there. You might be offended by the smell."

Quon's eyes flashed with emotion.

The senior lieutenant quickly acquiesced and hurried to lead the way out and down the hallway. They passed a guard station and entered a block of cells.

Quon felt weary and sore. He'd ached miserably since the shoot-down. Mainly his back, but also his neck and even his legs pained him so greatly at night that it was difficult to sleep. The aching continued during the daytime, but he suffered without complaint. It was the lack of sleep that bothered him most.

"Some of the cells here are empty," the lieutenant said. "This is where we bring the pilots after they are shot down."

"Which one?" Quon snapped, wishing for no more conversation.

The lieutenant pointed. He motioned at two guards and told them to open it.

A dim bulb glowed overhead. A figure huddled in a corner, fettered in leg-stocks and manacles. The stench of blood, feces, and urine was strong.

Quon approached.

The man had a heavy stubble and was filthy, clad only in shorts and bloody undershirt.

The interrogator with the carp's face came in, looking quizzically at Quon, carrying the length of pipe he'd had with him on Quon's previous visit.

Quon motioned silently, then pulled the pipe from his grasp.

"Leave me," he whispered.

The senior lieutenant began to argue, but Quon turned a cold eye upon him, and he left.

Quon looked down on the Mee, the man he'd vanquished in the sky.

"Are you a friend of *Lokee?*" he asked.

The pilot grunted. Was it in recognition?

He poked him harshly in the face with the pipe, eliciting a yelp of pain. "You are the second one, *Leebuhmunn.*"

A flicker of attention at the mention of his name.

"There are only two more." He remembered his son, and that this was one of the animals who'd killed him. Then he thought of his fear as he'd pulled his ejection handle. He thought of the awful face of *Lokee.*

Quon began to beat the pilot methodically in the head with the pipe, continued until there was no trace of life remaining, continued even then until his rage had subsided.

As he stalked from the room, puffing from his exertion, he noticed that his hands and the sleeves of his tunic were bright with the Mee pilot's blood. He decided he must bathe and change before attending his staff meeting. The fact that he might be late was irritating.

1500 Local—Bach Mai Hospital, Hanoi

Colonel Xuan Nha

Lieutenant Quang Hanh read to him from the pages of *Nham Dan,* the party newspaper distributed just that morning. The article was about Colonel Nguyen Wu, patriot and hero, who'd been called to go south by their brethren in the National Liberation Front. They had specifically requested

Colonel Wu's advice about what to do regarding the terror being rained upon them by the American imperialists and their lackey Saigon puppet troops.

General Van Tien Dung was quoted as saying that it was a most important mission the colonel had embarked upon. The selfless way that Nguyen Wu had volunteered to help their brethren, he said, was an example for others to emulate.

The article gave highlights of Wu's childhood, how he was first victimized by the French oppressors, and then by the Americans. It told of his rapid rise through the ranks, noticed by his superiors because he never asked more of his men than he was willing to do himself. He led, said the article, by example and sacrifice.

He was the architect, said the writer, of the modern defenses of the Democratic Republic, and it was through his astute guidance that the Republic's rockets, artillery, and interceptors were constantly victorious. He had not been previously acclaimed, said the *Nham Dan* reporter, only because he preferred to work in the background, in harmonious relationships with all others.

Nham Dan asked its readers to decide whether Colonel Nguyen Wu, selfless and brave, should be awarded a hero's welcome upon his return from his dangerous journey.

Xuan Nha was smiling as Lieutenant Quang Hanh put down the newspaper.

"What does it mean?" asked Quang Hanh, which was a question readers of *Nham Dan* asked only when they were with trusted friends.

"It means," said Xuan Nha, "that General Dung has changed his mind about Colonel Wu. Perhaps my wife has visited with him. I know she holds the editors of the newspaper in her hand."

Quang Hanh looked at the newspaper with a dubious eye. He'd worked with Nguyen Wu for two years and knew that absolutely none of the newspaper's words were true. They'd learned that Nguyen Wu had not gone south at all, but had left the convoy in the mountains west of Vinh and had hidden in that city with relatives.

Xuan smiled again, this time at the naïveté of his lieutenant, who often liked to quote the official party source.

"Tell me," he asked, "is there any mention of Quon's heroism in the issue?"

Quang Hanh shook his head.

"The tides of truth ebb and flow," said Xuan Nha, "and we must learn to work with them. Perhaps even," he said vaguely, "to influence them."

The seeds of a plan began to form in his mind.

Saturday, June 17th, 1900 Local—Bachelor Officers' Quarters, Nellis AFB, Nevada

Major Benny Lewis

By the seventeenth day of June, Benny began to wonder why he'd not gotten a response to his queries concerning the status of Bear Stewart. More than two and a half months had passed since they'd been shot down and the Bear killed, almost sixty days since he'd written the first letter, so he could not understand the reticence on the part of his old squadron commander. Mack MacLendon was a straight shooter with his people, yet neither of his letters had been answered.

Benny was also feeling feisty, for the previous morning he'd pinned on major's leaves. He disliked officers who threw their weight around after a promotion, but he felt that *just perhaps* it might make a difference.

He decided that on Monday morning he'd write another letter, this one addressed to Colonel Parker, the Takhli wing commander. Perhaps *he* might be able to help.

The telephone rang.

It's her, said the inner voice.

Benny grinned in anticipation as he picked it up.

"Is this the residence of *Major* Benjamin Lewis?" she asked.

"As a matter of fact it is," he replied.

"How does it feel?" asked Julie Stewart with a smile in her voice.

"The oak leaves are awfully heavy, but I think I *may* be able to manage."

"I'm very proud of you," she said.

"I'm still in shock. I keep thinking someone's going to find out and give the promotion to the right person."

"Don't be humble, flaunt it."

They laughed.

"I had my checkup at the hospital this afternoon, after I landed from my flight." She'd returned from an overnighter to Honolulu.

"And . . . ?" he asked.

"I'm healthy as a horse and the baby's got a strong heart-beat."

That's great! exclaimed the inner voice.

"Wish I could see you," he said, then wondered if he should have.

"*No* one should see me like this. I'm as fat as a cow. I waddle up and down the aisles of the airplane."

"How was the trip?" he asked.

"One thing about being pregnant, the guys don't joke as much. They used to ask if it was true they'd get lei'd when we landed in Hawaii. Now they call me ma'am and try to avoid looking at me."

"That's your imagination," he said.

"I'm going to be *obese* by the time I deliver."

"By the way, this is my private phone. I've got a room at the BOQ now." He'd left the number with her operations desk. "Ready to copy my new address?"

She paused as she wrote it down, then nagged him. "You should still be in the hospital, Benny Lewis."

"I've got a deal with them. I'll spend all the nights I'm feeling bad over there in their torture bed, and the rest of 'em here."

"And just how many times have you gone to the hospital to spend the night?"

"I only moved in here yesterday, and so far I haven't felt bad."

"You're impossible."

"I'm getting better. They even let me out of the back brace for a couple of hours every now and then."

"*Hmmph.* It's too early for that. I talked to your secretary last week, and she said you're entirely too active."

"So you visited the doctors today," he said.

"You're trying to change the subject."

"They give you a firm delivery date for the baby?"

"Late September, same as before. That doesn't change, silly. By the way, when I was at Travis, I talked with the nurse who took care of you."

"Lady Dracula?"

"Her name is Pam and she's very nice. When you were

here, she was concerned about you and you just took it wrong. She said she's been seeing some guy who works for you."

"Moods Diller."

"She really likes him and thinks you're mean for not letting him visit more often."

"If I let him, Moods would be up there every week, and not because of Lady Dracula."

"Pam," she corrected.

"He's working on a technical project, and he goes there to see engineers at Stanford, not a blood-sucking, skinny nurse."

She ignored him. "Pam has asked to be transferred to Nellis Air Force Base so she can be closer to him."

"Damn," he said, fearing the worst.

"She succeeded, and I'm happy for her. She'll report there in two weeks, and she promised to keep a close eye on you and your progress, just like she did before."

His heart sank. "Thanks."

"You need a watcher, Benjamin Lewis."

"I thought I was doing okay."

Her voice changed subtly. "You have any prospects for a steady girlfriend?"

Watch it, Benny! the inner voice warned.

"No." Did he say it too firmly? he wondered.

"Well until you get one, I plan to watch out after you."

"You think I should get a girlfriend?"

Don't ask her that, dummy.

"Darned right I do." She was quiet for a moment. "You're a nice guy, Benny, and you'd be good for some girl."

See what you started, said the voice.

He felt awkward, found it difficult to tell her he hadn't been that interested in women lately, that whenever he met someone, he compared them with Julie and they came up short.

Go ahead and tell her, counseled the voice.

"I'd have to check her out, of course," said Julie.

"I miss you," he said suddenly.

That's better.

She was quiet. Finally, "Maybe I can come down and visit after the baby's born."

"Three months? Why so long?"

"Benny, you just made major early. Think of your career.

It wouldn't look . . ." She caught her breath. "Anyway, I won't be able to travel with the baby for a while after it's born. It'll probably be more like four months before we'll be able to travel."

Too long, complained the voice.

"Too long," Benny said.

"By then," she added, "you'll probably have someone, and I'd just get in the way."

"I won't have someone," he said quietly.

Not bad.

She said nothing.

"You want me to come up there, Julie? I could spend a couple days. Maybe we could talk. Go out to dinner or something."

"I don't want you traveling *anywhere* with your back."

The conversation grew difficult. Too many forbidden words had been spoken.

That night as he slept, he dreamed again about the distant popping sounds as the Bear shot it out with the gomers.

It was not a nightmare, not at all tragic as it had been at the time, only a memory he would never forget. As he roused into the twilight of consciousness, the sounds faded.

That was for you, said the inner voice, *but don't forget about Julie and the kid.*

CHAPTER FIFTEEN

Thursday, June 29th, 0655 Local—South of Haiphong, North Vietnam

Captain Billy Bowes

The Takhli strike force was flying northward over the South China Sea, approaching North Vietnam from the water side. They'd finished refueling and were forming into the protective gaggle. Since Thanh Hoa was located near the sea, they wouldn't spend much time over land, but that target was well defended, and they'd have to take care.

Lucky had decided it was time to upgrade the two lieutenants to flight-lead status, and today Horn was leading and Walker was number three on the strike into pack four. C-Flight flew as Tuna flight, positioned at the rear of the Takhli gaggle, which was following on the heels of a similar force from Korat Air Base. Lucky flew on Henry's wing to make sure he got things right. Billy was flying as number four, on Lieutenant Joe Walker's wing, and would be last to drop his bombs.

Which was just right for what Billy had in mind.

The targets were a collection of petroleum tanks near Thanh Hoa, a port city ninety miles south of Haiphong. Surely, Billy reasoned, the tanks would be destroyed before his turn came. If they'd not been hit by then, he would bomb them. If they had . . .

The target area was several miles downstream from Thanh Hoa, at the mouth of the Ma River. There foreign ships off-loaded fuel and supplies onto a small wharf area. At one side and several hundred yards from the wharves, fuel was piped into a dozen large storage tanks. Those were today's target. But in an area at the opposite end of the wharves, well camouflaged by netting, Billy Bowes felt that a trove of war matériel was likely being amassed, probably to be taken up the Ma River at night.

The camouflaged supply area, not the tanks, was Billy's intended target. They'd been specifically briefed to avoid that area, so close to the wharves, and any ships either docked or waiting to offload there. To Billy Bowes that meant his target was a good choice.

Ahead of them SAMs were fired at the Korat formation, which was now outbound. A great, billowing cloud rose from the target area.

Billy switched to poststrike frequency and listened to the Korat flight leaders giving the success code word. *"Bold Webster,"* they said, one after the other, meaning they'd destroyed their assigned targets.

He switched back to the Takhli strike frequency just in time to hear the mission commander tell everyone to double-check their armament switches.

As they approached the coastline, he could see four ships waiting to off-load and another tied up to the wharf. *Bastards.* Off-loading war matériel for their commie buddies. British and French ships, and a lot more from so-called friendly nations, were supplying the assholes who were trying their damnedest to kill Americans, including Billy's family and friends. Too bad he couldn't take out a ship. *Just one,* to show them they were fucking with danger when they supplied America's enemies. But that would be obvious and surely reap repercussions. He would stick with the supply area. If anyone asked, he'd blame it on a bad bomb, just as he'd done before. This time he was flying his own bird, and there was no strike camera.

As they drew closer, he could see that two of the largest petroleum tanks were burning and billowing huge columns of black smoke.

Colonel B. J. Parker was mission commander. He led his

flight down the chute first. Billy watched. Not bad for an old guy on the shitty end of forty. The bombs exploded into a third tank, but it was empty so there was no secondary explosion or fire.

The second, then the third flights went into their dives and set fire to two more full tanks. The remainder were obviously empty.

Then it was Tuna flight's turn.

1155 Local—354th TFS, Takhli RTAFB, Thailand

Major Lucky Anderson

Bowes looked in the doorway. "You wanted to see me?"

Lucky motioned him inside. He slowly unwrapped a fresh cigar and mouthed it, keeping his eyes on him and watching for clues.

"Shut the damn door."

Bowes did so, then stood awkwardly, waiting.

"You bombed the wrong target."

Bowes tried to smile but it didn't work, so he swallowed. "I missed the tank farm, sir. Bad bombs."

Lucky slowly shook his head from side to side. "If some guys I know had thrown bombs that far, I might have agreed, because they're ham-fisted bozos. You just plain and simple set up and bombed the wrong target."

"I offset the wrong direction and maybe used a bad approach, but I just got some bad bombs, sir."

Lucky wanted very badly to believe him, but he knew better. He wondered if Bowes even understood why he was angry.

He didn't want to turn him over to the headquarters pukes and lawyers so they could disgrace him. The real criminals were the politicians who made the restrictions and kept them from winning and kept killing American pilots and gomers alike. Breaking their stupid rules would be a shitty reason to burn the best young pilot in the wing.

He wasn't pissed off by what Bowes had done, but because he was *lying* to him, and to Lucky deception was kin to betrayal. He chewed harshly on the cigar, mashing it to pulp.

Lucky shook his head and lowered his voice. "You poor,

dumb bastard. You've got big balls and hands like velvet, and nothing in your fucking head but sawdust."

Bowes drew himself up to stand at attention. This was a serious ass-chewing.

"You think you hid what you did pretty good, don't you? You think everyone else is a dumb shit. So far I've had three different people tell me about your bombs going off within a couple hundred yards of the ship tied up to the wharf."

"I . . . uh . . ."

"You had a bad bomb, right?"

Billy stared at him.

"Bowes, lie to me once more, and I'll turn you over to the headquarters pukes. I'll take a lot of shit from you guys, but I won't stand for lying, not in the air or on the ground."

Bowes stared straight ahead, his expression increasingly troubled.

Lucky slowly reared forward, then roared into Billy's face, *"You like being a fucking liar?"*

Bowes paused. He slowly shook his head.

Lucky sat down and lowered his voice. "What was your aim point?"

Bowes's answer was crisply given. "Surface wind was from zero-one-five at six knots, so I aimed thirty feet north of the target."

"What target?"

"The camouflaged area north of the wharf."

Lucky chewed the cigar.

"I thought it might be a munitions storage area."

"You thought?"

"Yes, sir. It made sense. Petroleum goes to the tanks, munitions and supplies to the camouflaged area."

"How about a POW camp?"

"Sir?"

"What if it's a POW camp? Maybe where they're holding Tatro and Liebermann and the other guys."

Billy paused. "I don't think so. Those are marked on the maps in intell."

"All of them? I doubt that."

Bowes was quiet.

"How about a hospital, or a school, or maybe an old folks' home?"

"Camouflaged and next to a wharf?"

"Did you get any secondary explosions?"

"None that I saw."

"I watched your bombs hit and there weren't any. So it isn't likely there were munitions there, is it?"

Pause. "Perhaps not."

"You hate the gomers, don't you, Bowes?"

"I've got personal reasons for my feelings."

"Fuck your personal feelings. You're supposed to be a professional fighter pilot."

"Yes, sir."

"You think the North Vietnamese are the first assholes our country's ever fought? Turk Tatro's a southerner, right? You ever hear of a place called Andersonville? That's where the Confederates systematically starved their prisoners to death, and one of those was an ancestor of mine. Think I ought to hate Turk?"

"No, sir, but . . ."

"You got Cherokee blood, right? They were a brilliant people, but they were ruthless when they captured their enemies. I had an ancestor that was killed on a Kansas homestead by a band of Indians. Not Cherokee, but their cousins. Hell, maybe I ought to hate you."

Bowes's lips were held tightly together.

"Most of our enemies have been animals, Bowes. Mean and despicable bastards. The gomers are assholes, but so were the Nazis and the Japanese and the North Koreans."

Bowes tried to interject something about his family, but Lucky wouldn't allow it.

"War's a violent business, Bowes, but it's our business and we're supposed to be able to handle it. We're the tools of the politicians, no matter if they're smart or dumb shits. They represent the people, we don't. If they say fight, we fight. If they say turn tail and run, we say yes, sir, and do it. To do otherwise is either mutiny or treason. You don't understand that, you should take up a new line of work."

Billy Bowes stared straight forward.

Lucky stopped talking and chewed on his cigar, feeling it was unlikely he'd gotten through. He sighed mightily, finished with sermonizing.

"Bowes, you've made the guys in C-Flight look shitty, like we're out of control," he said quietly. "I don't think we deserve that reputation, but I guess it's true."

"If you want, I'll ask to be reassigned, sir."

Lucky chewed his cigar on that, then decided to ignore

it. "You let me down. I asked for your help, and you pulled this *shit*."

A flicker of emotion crossed Billy's face. "That was not what I intended."

"You just wanted to get even with the gomers, right?"

"I just want to beat the bastards, and *they're* not letting us do that."

"You ignored the lawful orders of your superior officers, then you lied to me. You've destroyed your credibility and made a mockery of my judgment, Bowes."

Billy frowned and became introspective, and Lucky knew he'd finally gotten through. But did he really believe what Bowes had done was wrong? He knew some about Bowes's family history. If he'd been in his shoes and had lost that many family members . . . ?

Lucky walked to the window and peered out toward the flight line. Dark clouds were boiling overhead. Few light clouds came their way. When they got to Takhli, they by-God dumped rain. The crew chiefs were busily lowering aircraft canopies and putting tarps over tool kits and start carts in preparation for another wetting.

He turned and regarded Bowes, who looked unhappy.

"I'll make you a deal."

"Sir?"

"A deal. You can take it or leave it."

Silence.

"You get another wild-assed idea like this one, tell me about it. Tell me what's coming off, and what to expect, and convince me it'll help win the war. If you want to hit a munitions-storage area, first prove to me that's what it is, and then we'll *talk* about what to do about it. Unless I say different, you follow the rules, period. But don't *ever* surprise your flight in the air or lie to me again."

Billy slowly nodded his agreement.

"You don't want to do that, then ask to be put into another flight and go your own way, and stay the fuck away from me and away from C-Flight."

Bowes had assumed a grim look.

"If you stay, there'll be no more lies, and no more shit like this. Understand?"

"Yes, sir."

"Now get the hell out of here," said Lucky. He ignored

the salute and turned back to the window. He heard Bowes close the door. It began to rain.

Great sheets of precipitation swept across the tarmac.

He sighed and mouthed the cigar a few more times. Then he went to his desk, sat down, and fumbled through the base phone list to find the medical clinic's number. He could no longer trust Bowes, not until he'd proved he meant what he'd agreed to. But Lucky sorely needed *someone* he could trust to back him up in the air.

He called to find out when Captain DeVera would be released for flying duty and was connected with Doc Roddenbush, who was in charge of the clinic. Roddenbush said Manny was complaining about pain when he moved his fingers. The doc could find nothing wrong, but the human hand was a complex mechanism, and he wanted to give it a few more days.

Before Lucky Anderson left his office, he scribbled notes onto the steno pad he kept in the lower drawer.

29 JUN 67

LT H.: FINISHED HENRYS EVALUATION REPORT— 9/4

CPT B.: UNAUTH TARGET—LEAD IN LOWWER ROUTE PACKS UNTILL HE PROOVES TRUST—

CPT M.: RESOLVE MED. PROBLEM—BUILD CONFIDENCE.

Sunday, July 2nd, 1600 Local—Command Post

Colonel Thomas F. Lyons

The classified message dated 011520Z JUL 67 was from CINCPACAF/CC, a four-star general named Roman at Hickam Air Force Base, and was addressed to the commanders of all flying units participating in OPlan ROLLING THUNDER. Bomber Joe Roman, who'd worked for Curtis LeMay and become a hero in World War II, was a casual friend of Lyons's father.

His father considered Roman to be a boorish, loud, and ofttimes pig-headed fool. The kind of person he considered useful only to the military, he would create disaster in any corporation. But of course his father also thought that about his youngest son. The fact that Tom had risen so quickly through the ranks did not surprise his father, for it had been due to his influence rather than his wayward son's achievements.

It bothered Tom Lyons not at all that his promotions were due to political influence. *Privileges were due the privileged.* It was as simple as that.

Several times in his career he'd telephoned his father when things began to go sour. Each time, although he never knew precisely how, his problem had vanished. Demerits were erased that might have prevented him from graduating from undergraduate pilot training. An accident board had changed its collective mind about pursuing an embarrassing line of investigation. More recently, several marginal evaluation reports had disappeared and he'd miraculously been selected for colonel.

He was grateful for his father's help. But his next step, to general officer, would be a tough one, and he worried about the influence of General Moss, the three-star at Seventh Air Force headquarters who disliked him. Moss had inherited both money *and* a military heritage. His family had produced generals since the Civil War. He was doubly powerful.

Lyons's contact in the colonel's assignments branch at the Military Personnel Center in San Antonio had advised that he *might* have a problem with his next assignment. Meaning that a flag had been placed on his records jacket by someone with clout. He could think of many who disliked him, but only one who was in a proper position to do that. Lieutenant General Moss.

Which made Lyons realize that he must either do something to gain the attention of even higher-ranking generals, or allow Moss to keep him from further advancement.

When Tom Lyons reread the message from the four-star general at PACAF headquarters to the wing commanders, he knew precisely what he could do to gain high-level attention.

1. (U) ON 30 JUN 67 THE GOVERNMENT OF
NORTH KOREA ISSUED AN OFFICIAL
COMPLAINT IN THE UNITED NATIONS

THAT ON THE PREVIOUS DAY SEVERAL
AMERICAN AIRCRAFT ATTACKED AND
BOMBED ONE OF THEIR UNARMED SHIPS
NEAR THANH HOA, NORTH VIETNAM. THIS
ATTACK WAS WITHOUT PROVOCATION,
RESULTED IN DAMAGE TO THE SHIP, AND
LEFT THREE NORTH KOREAN CITIZENS
SEVERELY WOUNDED. TIME OF THE INCIDENT
WAS REPORTED BETWEEN 0700 AND
0715 LOCAL TIME, 29 JUN 67.
2. (C) THE 8, 388, AND 355 TFW'S
PARTICIPATED IN OFFENSIVE ACTIVITIES
NEAR THE LOCATION OF THE INCIDENT
DURING THAT PERIOD. THOSE
COMMANDERS WILL TAKE IMMEDIATE
ACTION TO IDENTIFY PILOT(S) RESPONSIBLE
FOR THIS ILLEGAL, IRRESPONSIBLE, AND
MOST UNPROFESSIONAL ACT. I EXPECT
YOUR INVESTIGATIONS TO BE CONDUCTED
VIGOROUSLY, AND TO PROVIDE TIMELY
RESULTS.
3. (C) THIS IS THE SEVENTH INCIDENT
IN THE PAST FOUR MONTHS IN WHICH U.S.
AIRCRAFT HAVE BEEN REPORTED IN
FLAGRANT VIOLATION OF RULES OF
ENGAGEMENT. SUCH REPORTS ARE NOT
ONLY EMBARRASSING TO THE OFFICERS AND
MEN OF THIS COMMAND, THEY ARE ALSO
DETRIMENTAL TO THE SUCCESSFUL
CONDUCT OF THE CONFLICT.
4. (U) IT IS THE DUTY OF SENIOR OFFICERS
OF ALL COMBAT UNITS OF THE PACIFIC AIR
FORCES TO ENSURE THAT ASSIGNED
PILOTS STRICTLY OBSERVE ALL RULES
OF ENGAGEMENT IMPOSED BY HIGHER
AUTHORITY. ANY, REPEAT, ANY VIOLATIONS,
WHETHER KNOWN OR SUSPECTED, WILL
BE IMMEDIATELY AND WITH DUE
DISPATCH FORWARDED FOR MY PERSONAL
ATTENTION. SIGNED: JOSEPH T. ROMAN,
COMMANDER IN CHIEF, PACIFIC AIR
FORCES.
CONFIDENTIAL IMMEDIATE

The wing commander had passed both the message and the investigative task to his Special Projects officer, and Tom Lyons had immediately interviewed all flight leaders on the mission in question. None had seen anything out of the ordinary, or at least anything they wished to report. Two flight leaders had seen bombs that had been errant and missed the target, but that was common and they swore none had hit the ship. Regardless of how Lyons threatened or cajoled or what he promised for reward, no one changed their stories.

He'd concluded that this particular infraction had either been accomplished by pilots of another unit or was being covered up by the flight leaders.

That was not important.

Although he did not yet know precisely how he would proceed with it, he knew he'd discovered his vehicle to draw favorable attention to himself, and a potential route to general officer's rank.

He started by preparing a message for B. J. Parker's signature, addressed to CINCPACAF/CC, saying that although their investigation had proved unfruitful, the 355th TFW shared the general's concern about the gravity of the subject violations and had assigned Colonel Thomas F. Lyons the important task of running Operation TAKHLI PATRIOT, to ferret out any illegal activities on the part of assigned combat pilots. Operation TAKHLI PATRIOT would be given top priority within the wing, and periodic reports would be provided directly to CINCPACAF/CC showing progress in properly indoctrinating unit pilots, and reporting any future violations.

Colonel Parker had liked the message and immediately signed it out, saying, "That should satisfy the bomber-loving"—smile,—"*did I say that?* . . . general."

All of which made Tom Lyons so happy that he'd telephoned the sexy morsel named Jackie Bell at her Peace Corps camp near Nakhon Sawan.

Since the spick captain had pulled out of the game, which was the first sign of good judgment he'd seen from DeVera, Lyons had been closing for the kill.

He wanted to fuck the sexy little blond more than about anything, had wanted into her pants since he'd first met her, but she'd proved to be elusive and he'd had interference. First the cold-bitch GS-15 from Bangkok had asked him how tough it was being away from his wife and three kids

... *right in front of the girl* ... and with Colonel Parker looking on he couldn't lie. Then, after he'd later convinced her he was splitting up with his wife and she'd begun sympathizing about how traumatic it must be ... the goddam spick captain had interfered and waltzed her away from his table and out of the club. When DeVera had finally become smart enough to drop out of the picture, she'd asked so many questions about his wounded hand and how he was doing that Lyons had hardly had a chance to get personal.

But tonight the cold bitch was away in Bangkok and the spick captain was out of the picture, and he'd sent a driver to pick up the blond at her camp so they could share a special dinner in his trailer. He'd even called a friend of his father's at the Bangkok embassy and had them send up a variety of good French wines and brandies.

He had been close a couple of times with her. Once he'd even gotten a hand inside her blouse and felt a superbly firm breast before she'd twisted away.

She always left with his promise to provide administrative supplies or pumps or spades or something else from the long list of things she said her camp needed, even though he felt her requests were just a game she played to be with him more often. Still, to help grease things tonight, he'd sent a truckload of lumber to the camp with instructions to the driver to make sure the project leader *and* his female administrator knew who had authorized it.

He stopped, staggered by a sublime thought. He wondered, the way she acted when it got right down to things, if Jackie Bell wasn't a virgin? He'd bedded some tough ones, including wives of close acquaintances and subordinates, just by telling them what it was like to live with *old* money or how he'd help with their husband's promotion, or whatever else seemed appropriate for the occasion. It didn't make sense that this little bitch would ignore all of that and put someone like him off unless there was something golden about her ass.

He decided that she was indeed a virgin, and the thought excited him. She'd have the honor of becoming the fourth *real* notch on the old musket, along with precisely forty-one smaller ones, who included two of his parents' maids, his wife, her older sister, three of his secretaries, an Air Force nurse, and an assortment of high-class hookers. But who counted?

Friday, July 7th, 1030 Local—Ponderosa BOQ

Major Lucky Anderson

Lucky went into the BOQ day room and spoke for a while with a couple of new lieutenants, then asked one where he could find Captain DeVera.

"Probably in his room," said one. He gave directions. "He spends a lot of time there."

"Thanks." Lucky went to the refrigerator and liberated a beer, adding a quarter to the can on the counter. Then he walked through the hall and knocked at Manny's door.

DeVera looked like shit when he peered out. "Oh, hi, boss," he mumbled.

Lucky sipped beer and stared.

"You need something?"

Billy Bowes walked by, on his way to his room, and nodded sheepishly at Lucky, as he'd done since the ass-chewing. Lucky ignored him.

"Let's take a walk, Manny," he said.

"Do I need to put on a uniform?" He was wearing a T-shirt, jeans, and thongs.

"You're fine as you are. See you outside." Lucky went through the day room, then outside where he sat at one of the picnic tables and sipped cold beer as he waited.

A couple of minutes later Manny came out and sat across from him. He smelled of mouthwash, and his eyes were hidden behind sunglasses.

"You been drinking already, Manny?"

DeVera shrugged. "Not much to do, being off flying status."

"A lot of paperwork's piling up at the squadron."

Manny mumbled, "I'll get right to it."

"I need you back in the cockpit, Manny. I can't lead 'em all."

DeVera looked uncomfortable. "How about Billy? He's on flight-lead orders."

"So are the others now, but it's not the same. I need you because of your experience in the Thud."

DeVera paused for a long moment. "Doc Roddenbush won't let me back on status."

"I just talked to him. He says you complain about your

hand hurting, but you refuse to go to the hospital at Clark so they can look at it."

DeVera shrugged.

"It's been six weeks now, Manny."

"You think I'm lying about the pain?"

Lucky regarded him evenly. "I think it's time to either shit or get off the pot."

"Goddammit, I . . ." DeVera looked away, in obvious turmoil.

"You know, the other day I was talking to Henry Horn, and he told me something because he was feeling guilty and had to unload his mind. You're assistant C-Flight commander, so I feel I should share it with you."

Manny looked back sharply. "Is Henry okay?"

"He didn't think so. Said he's scared shitless every time we go north. Doesn't matter if we're going to the lower packs or up to pack six, he said he starts thinking about how a golden beebee's going to shoot him down."

Manny released a ragged breath.

"He said he thinks he's a coward. The only reason he didn't talk about it earlier was because the rest of us never act like *we're* afraid."

DeVera's eyes were downcast, as if he were inspecting the wood on the tabletop. "You shitting me?" he finally asked.

"I'd never lie to a member of my flight. I'm telling you because you're my assistant, and I thought you ought to know. You think I'm lying, then I should shut up right now."

DeVera didn't look up from the table, but he appeared interested. "Henry's a steady guy," he ventured.

"I think so too. Billy flies a better stick, and Joe is smoother, but Henry is damned reliable, and maybe that's best of all."

"Yeah."

"Anyway, Henry's got fifty-nine missions now, and he's worrying about not making it home to his wife and new daughter."

"What did you tell him?"

"Not a lot I could tell him about his chances of making it through a tour. All I could do was give him some advice about how to deal with his shakes and jangles."

"Yeah?" Manny pursed his lips in thought.

"I told him I do what a guy who'd flown combat in Korea told me a long time ago."

Manny leaned just a bit closer.

"When we come off the tanker and start toward North Vietnam, I give myself this little pep talk, like it's a football game we've gotta win and I want to get myself charged up."

Manny looked up to stare at him through the sunglasses.

"Then I think about all my options, how if a MiG shows up I'll handle the switches and fight him, and if we get a SAM launch how I'll handle that. I think about which way I'm going to come off the target, and then how I'm going to bring the guys home."

"Maybe it's hard for Henry to stop thinking about ... negative things."

"What I don't do is take my mind off what *I'm* going to do. I concentrate on getting charged up, and what I'll do. I keep my mind on the offensive and think how I'm going to kick the shit out of the target. Let the enemy worry about losing, because I'm not going to." He waited for DeVera to participate.

Manny was thinking about it and took his time. "Maybe it's different with Henry about the way he's got to handle his problem. You think of that?"

"Maybe. But my way works, Manny, and it's worked for fighter jocks for a long time. Colonel Mack over at the 357th squadron told me he was told about that trick all the way back in the Second World War. So why try to change something that works?"

Manny blew a long, tortured breath. "What if the enemy *does* shoot you down?"

"When I'm coming down in my chute, I'll think of how I'm going to get away so I can be rescued. And if I fail and they capture me, I'll think of how I'm going to resist them."

Manny was nodding very slowly.

"Whenever I fly, I figure the poor bastards have a problem on their hands, Manny, because by God they do."

"So what did Henry say to all that?"

"You know Henry. He listened hard and said he'd take the advice."

"He's a good man," Manny said again.

"Yeah, so keep it quiet, okay? He thinks people might think he's a coward."

Manny raised an eyebrow. "You ever had those thoughts? Worrying about getting killed or shot down?"

"No, guess I haven't. But that's probably because I use the advice I gave Henry and never let myself come off the offensive."

Again Manny slowly nodded.

"Anyway, I wanted you to know. I figured since you'll want a few easy counters down in packs one and two while you're coming back up to speed, you might want Henry to fly a few down there with you so he can try what I told him and build his confidence."

Lucky stood, done with what he'd come to do.

"Thanks, boss," said Manny DeVera, but he said it very low, and Lucky acted as if he hadn't heard.

Captain Manny DeVera

Major Lucky drove away in a squadron pickup, back toward the main base, and Manny went inside. The two lieutenants were still there, talking about a python one of the guys in the 333rd squadron had bought for five bucks, and how the guys in their Ponderosa had told him that either the snake or they had to go.

Then one of the lieutenants asked if he could pick up anything for the rest of them, because he was going to take the van to the exchange to buy cigarettes.

Manny told the lieutenant to hold up, that he'd need a ride to the base clinic as soon as he put on his flying suit.

He went to his room and changed, thinking about what Major Lucky had told him.

Henry Horn was a good shit and shouldn't feel bad about having human worries, Manny thought. If Henry just knew what Manny had been going through, he'd likely feel better. But of course he wouldn't know, because the Supersonic Wetback wouldn't let on. At least not for the present, he wouldn't.

He was going to the clinic to ask Doc Roddenbush to put him back on status. If the gomers killed him, so fucking what? That would be better than living in hell.

Thursday, July 13th, 0945 Local—Li Binh's Villa, Hanoi, DRV

Colonel Nguyen Wu

He was elated. More, he was ecstatic! Nguyen Wu had returned to Hanoi two days before to a hero's welcome rally at Ba Dinh square and had just been appointed to a position he'd previously only dreamed of. The perfect position for him.

He was to be Assistant Commissioner of People's Safety within the Ministry of Internal Affairs, his duties to oversee the reeducation of criminals, dissidents, traitors, and incorrigible recalcitrants. Whenever the party told the Ministry of Justice to classify a person as any of those, Nguyen Wu would supervise his reeducation.

Nguyen had just spoken to the Commissioner, whom he'd previously heard mentioned only in careful whispers, and had been charged with his new duties. The Commissioner had been impressed by the assignment of such a young military colonel as his assistant, and even more impressed that the suggestion to assign him had come from the Lao Dong party.

The Commissioner controlled the secret police and other important state functions and reported directly to First Minister Pham Van Dong. The people called him the "Commissioner of Death" in whispers, but that was more often shortened to just "the Commissioner." He was undoubtedly the most feared man in the Democratic Republic.

Li Binh had told him the Commissioner had once been a friend of Xuan Nha's. But his uncle's name had not come up during the interview, only that of his aunt Li Binh, the newest member of the People's Central Committee. The Commissioner knew where the power lay.

He'd said that Wu's new position would require diligence and honesty.

What was Nguyen Wu if not diligent and honest?

After a very few minutes of conversation, mostly discussing the health of his venerable aunt Li Binh, Nguyen Wu knew they would get along well.

With his interview complete, Nguyen Wu hurried to his aunt's villa to thank her properly for what she'd done for him. He would show her the joy and gratitude he felt. He admonished himself to be clever and make her gasp with wonder as she sometimes did when she was carried away with her pleasure.

Li Binh thought she understood his strangeness, believed he could copulate with her only in very dim light because he was shy. She must never realize that it was her power that aroused him, that when he caressed her lean body, he dreamed of a man's, or that he needed the darkness because each time he plunged into her thin body, he imagined it was being done to himself.

Nguyen Wu preferred the raw masculinity of brawny men and didn't dare let her discover how often he found true comfort with old Sergeant Ng or some other rugged soldier. He shuddered to think what Li Binh might do if she was to find out.

His mind reeled with excitement as he entered the front door of the villa, but the womanservant said Li Binh hadn't yet arrived. She was still at the early meeting of the Central Committee, giving her report of how things had gone in Paris.

He took tea from the womanservant, whom he despised. She was subservient enough, but often she hinted that she would willingly spread her legs for him. Which was why he disliked the presumptuous whore.

He wondered if Xuan Nha had bedded her when he'd been master of the home. It seemed something his arrogant uncle might do.

So what do you do now, uncle?

He laughed. It was unlikely that Xuan Nha, once called the Tiger of Dien Bien Phu, would ever bed *anyone* again. Who would have a maimed man who was so unsightly? Surely not Li Binh. She was sickened more by the very sight of him each time she visited.

His mind wandered back to his new appointment.

It was precisely what he'd wanted from the beginning. A position not easily observed or critiqued by others, yet one that could be powerful. No man would trifle with him, for there were ways to steer the investigations performed by the Commissioner's people. And once he got his hands on a person he disliked to reeducate him . . .

He thought of Quon, who he knew had engineered his banishment to the South, and his mind filled with hatred.

Perhaps, he wondered . . . but then cast the thought aside. It would be too much to hope for.

Thanks to his wonderful aunt it was he, not Quon, who was the hero mentioned in the party newspaper. The newspaper's adulations must stop now that Wu held the new, secretive position, but Quon would have difficulty regaining the party favor he'd once held.

Quon was distraught over his son's death. Li Binh had told him that Quon's fascination with revenge was taking more and more of his time and energies, and that the generals were increasingly upset with him.

Although Nguyen Wu vowed never to act rashly again, as he had with his plan to discredit Quon's MiGs, or the other one to kill Quon's son, those plans had indeed worked. He had become the hero and Quon the outsider.

Li Binh knew nothing of those plans, for he'd been afraid to tell her.

He sipped his tea thoughtfully, then quickly rose to his feet as the ever-energetic Li Binh burst happily through the door of the villa. He sank to his knees before her, expressions of love and gratitude spreading across his face.

1120 Local—Bach Mai Hospital, Hanoi

Colonel Xuan Nha

It was a good morning for Xuan Nha. The pain had diminished even more. All of the bandages that had swathed his torso had been removed, and regardless of the feeling of squirming worms from the scar tissue, he knew he was healing. In a show of vanity he now even sported a linen eye patch over his missing right eye.

Quang Hanh kept him abreast of the spectacular news about Colonel Nguyen Wu's return. Two days earlier Wu had appeared at the People's Army headquarters to turn in his study of air defenses in the South to General Dung's office. Then he'd gone to Ba Dinh square and a "spontaneous" people's rally, to be acclaimed as the latest Hero of the Republic. Yesterday's *Nham Dan* had again been filled with reports of his heroism, and told how The People had thronged about Wu at Ba Dinh square and held their fists high to show how they shared his enthusiasm for the War of Unification.

Xuan Nha telephoned Lieutenant Colonel Tran Van Ngo, who was running things for him at the headquarters until he healed, and told him to join them at the hospital room. As they waited for Tran to arrive, Quang Hanh continued to read the article haltingly, as if he could not believe the newspaper had actually printed such lies about the man he knew.

Poor Quang Hanh, thought Xuan, *still does not wish to understand.*

When Tran arrived, Xuan ordered the door closed behind him, and the three of them huddled and spoke in hushed voices.

Tran said Nguyen Wu's study had been forwarded to him from General Dung's office. It was comprehensive and spelled out specific needs for air defenses in the South. It called for Soviet-built 23 mm, dual-barreled anti-aircraft guns, as well as for additional rapid-firing 37mm guns, and even outlined a field-training program for soldiers in the South. Tran told him that the men of his rocket-and-artillery forces, both at the headquarters and in the field, were nervous that Colonel Wu would retake his old position and reap vengeance upon them.

Xuan only grunted in response, but he was pleased about the animosities and fears. They fit well with the plan he'd decided upon.

"*Did* he visit the headquarters?" asked Xuan Nha.

Tran shook his head. "When I heard he was back, I prepared to relinquish the office, but he has not come near the place."

"It might be prudent," said Xuan Nha in his frog's rasp, "to learn what my nephew has been doing since his return."

Tran looked about hesitantly, and even then considered his words. "I receive reports, unofficially of course, from the men. They tell me where he goes."

So Tran was having him followed. *Very good.*

"I know you once told us never to become involved in politics and connivery, but . . ."

"That time has passed," croaked Xuan. "Nguyen Wu presents a threat to the Republic and . . . to us." He paused then and glanced back and forth with his single eye. "Both of you are at risk, as I am, and we must act quickly."

Quang Hanh looked frightened. He'd faced death in the past, but never anything like this. Whenever it served his cause, Nguyen Wu turned against even his closest confidants. The men beneath him were used for his own aggrandizement. Those who posed a threat to his career were disposed of through disgrace or reassignment.

Xuan Nha was at least as dangerous as his nephew, but he was a soldier, and the focus of his terrible temper had always been directed upon cowardice, gross ineptitude, or the failure to follow orders. They could live with Xuan's flaws, for he was a brother warrior.

"So what have you discovered about Wu's activities?" Xuan asked Tran.

"Only where he goes, comrade Colonel. This morning, for instance, he visited the Ministry of Internal Affairs for more than an hour. He spoke with the Commissioner."

The Commissioner of Death? What would Nguyen Wu be doing there ... unless ...

Xuan silently considered.

Wu might want no more of his previous position. Had Li Binh obtained a new one for him? That made sense, considering their relationship.

"When he left the Commissioner's office," Tran added, "Colonel Wu went directly to your home."

"This morning?"

"Yes, comrade Colonel. You're wife joined him, and they were still inside when I received your summons. The servants were sent out of the main house, so they are alone."

Xuan Nha had become ambivalent about the fact that Nguyen Wu might be caressing Li Binh's skinny body. But there were things she did not know, or she wouldn't be so receptive to her nephew. Like many women, Li Binh was disgusted that so many Vietnamese men preferred intimate male companionship. It was odd, since she knew so many secrets, that she'd been blind to the truth about her own nephew.

Of course it could not be Xuan who would tell her.

On the occasions Li Binh had visited him since her return from Paris, they'd spoken only once about her nephew. Xuan Nha had seen the warmth in her eyes and had been careful to speak highly of Wu's selfless contributions to the national defense. She'd seemed worried about him at the first meeting, but had not mentioned her nephew since.

Had she discovered that Wu had been hiding in Vinh and contacted him? She'd spoken hatefully about Quon during subsequent meetings, which gave strength to the idea. Only Wu could have guessed it was Quon behind the trick to send him South.

And now she'd altered things so the ruse was turned in her nephew's favor.

Xuan Nha wondered. Would Nguyen Wu return to his old position, or had he gained a position within the secret-police apparatus? He felt a shudder of foreboding at either eventuality. He was especially vulnerable, tied to this hospital room as he was. He must act, set his plan into motion without delay.

"So Colonel Wu has not visited his old office or contacted the men there?"

"So far," said Tran Van Ngo, "he has shown not the slightest interest in us."

The radio-telephone buzzed, and Lieutenant Quang Hanh went over to speak with the command center about the results of the morning Mee attack.

Xuan motioned Tran to his bedside. "I wish to walk," he said.

Tran Van Ngo helped support him as he got out of bed and hobbled painfully across the room to a chair. Xuan sat slowly as Lieutenant Quang Hanh rejoined them.

"The morning attacks went poorly for us. A rail siding was destroyed, and a mobile rocket battery was badly damaged by radar-hunters."

Xuan grunted. "Let us continue our previous discussion before we speak of business."

Both men stood quietly, waiting for his guidance.

"Quang Hanh," began Xuan Nha slowly, "has discovered an interesting fact about the communications breakdown on the day Quon's son was killed by the Mee?"

Quang Hanh became concerned. "The communications officers were reluctant to speak of it, Colonel. I told them their secret would go no further."

"Their fears are understandable," croaked Xuan Nha. "If the radios had not ... *malfunctioned* ... that morning, the aircraft would not have been caught on the ground."

Quang Hanh looked uneasy.

"And Colonel Wu ordered it?" asked Xuan. He had not

pressed Quang Hanh when he'd first been told, but somehow he knew it was true.

Quang Hanh fidgeted uneasily. "Yes," he finally said in a low voice. Quang Hanh continued the whisper, even though the three of them were alone. "It was made to appear that a power surge caused the radios to malfunction. The order came from Colonel Wu's communications officer, but there was no record made."

"That is also understandable," said Xuan Nha. "Quon would have had Nguyen Wu killed if he'd known it was deliberate."

"Perhaps it is best forgotten, Colonel Nha," Quang Hanh said in a hopeful voice.

"I believe you are right, Lieutenant. It will be officially forgotten."

Xuan Nha looked back and forth between the two men. With only the one eye, he had to move his head to do it.

"But," he continued, "rumors are always being circulated within the People's Army, and there are two that I feel would work in our advantage."

"Rumors?" asked Quang Hanh with surprise. Rumormongering was a punishable crime in the People's Army, and Xuan Nha had always sternly enforced the rule among his men.

"Both rumors involve my nephew. I want you to start them very carefully, so no trace can be made back to yourselves . . . or to me."

Lieutenant Colonel Tran Van Ngo looked thoughtful, still digesting the news that Nguyen Wu had engineered the radio failure.

"Do you have contacts at Phuc Yen Air Base, Tran?"

"Many, comrade Colonel."

"Trustworthy men?"

"I have worked closely with them in life-and-death situations."

Xuan Nha told him what he wanted circulated there.

"An easy task," said Tran Van Ngo.

"But I told them I would not let the secret go further," pleaded Quang Hanh.

Xuan Nha stared harshly at his lieutenant, who quickly lowered his eyes. "The second rumor will be quite different and much easier to start. It involves Colonel Wu's personal preferences, and I wish it to become common knowledge among the people of Hanoi. This one is for you to do, Lieutenant Hanh."

Lieutenant Quang Hanh heard the second rumor and was assigned the task to have it spread very covertly among the civilian populace. When Xuan had finished with his orders, they returned their attentions to the morning's air raids, but it was apparent from the distant looks of his two men that they were thinking of what they must do.

Fleetingly, Xuan Nha thought of how political he was turning. A few months earlier he would never had considered such Machiavellian twists. But his world had changed, and he'd vowed never again to be a victim, either of bullets *or* of politics.

It would reach Quon, the hint that Colonel Wu had ordered the radio failures, and even if Quon disbelieved it, he would surely wonder. That one was meant to show Quon his true adversary was Nguyen Wu and not some Mee fighter pilot who'd seen and strafed an interceptor on the ground. Xuan Nha owed him that.

As for the other rumor, Li Binh's tentacles heard every nuance floating through the populace. She would surely react to the news that not only did many people know of her affair with her nephew because of his boasting, but that he was secretly laughing at her, because Nguyen Wu was a very active homosexual.

Nguyen Wu would be kept busy trying to quell the revelations. So busy that he would not have time to plot against his uncle Xuan Nha.

There were many ways to serve one's country, thought Xuan Nha. If things turned out as he'd planned, his forces could continue to destroy enemy aircraft, perhaps even deny the Americans success on destroying that first critical bridge. They must not allow that campaign to begin, for it would severely damage the war effort.

If they could persevere a while longer, Xuan Nha was confident that the American politicians would halt the bombing of the Democratic Republic. During a visit Li Binh had told him of her contacts with Mee diplomats, how they were eager for some sort of deal, willing to trade even tiny concessions for stopping the bombing.

She'd met with one very secretive delegation from an unnamed high-level American government source who wished to stop all bombing. If they did so, they asked, would her country respond in a positive way? She'd told them the Democratic Republic would act only *after* such actions were taken, but that she would personally work to see what she could do.

To Xuan Nha it had been a staggering revelation.

It meant the American government had become so cowardly and corrupt that victory might indeed be achievable for the Democratic Republic. Not by winning military battles, of course. Even though the American politicians tied the hands of their soldiers, their military might was so awesome that no one could defeat them in the field, and their air forces had proved they could destroy any target they wished, regardless of the defenses. But through an amazing mixture of connivery and treason, American politicians were working to give victory away.

His nephew would fit in well with that group, thought Xuan Nha. It was easy to imagine Colonel Nguyen Wu as an American politician, twisting this way and that in his convictions as he tried to further himself.

CHAPTER SIXTEEN

Monday, July 17th, 0400 Local—Command Post, Takhli RTAFB, Thailand

After a two-and-a-half-month delay, CROSSFIRE ZULU was turned back on. Another attempt would be made upon the Paul Doumer bridge, this time with *hard* bombs.

In early May, when Pearly Gates at Seventh Air Force had put together his team of henchmen to run the combat test phase of OPlan CROSSFIRE ZULU, he'd asked Lucky Anderson to be his contact at the 355th Tac Fighter Wing. When Lucky had tried to beg out, saying he had his flight to run and a war to fight, Colonel B. J. Parker stepped in. B.J. had received a phone call from Lieutenant General Moss, saying how happy he was that Major Paul Anderson was helping his guy at Seventh Air Force. Colonel Parker had enthusiastically agreed that it was a good thing. And so, by God, would Lucky.

Major Lucky Anderson

Benny Lewis, a longtime friend, was his contact at Nellis Air Force Base. Lucky had received a package of tactics information from Benny and had agreed to forward results of the

combat test to Nellis for analysis by the tacticians and
number crunchers.

After examining the awful results from the AGM-12 Bullpup fiasco, the test-and-evaluation people at Nellis had explored various exotic methods to destroy bridges and survive
in a high-threat environment. Those included classified tests
on a new family called smart bombs, but they couldn't be
completed in time. There was little innovativeness about
their final suggestions for the next try at the big bridge. The
Nellis weapons people felt they should resort to vanilla-
flavored heavy bombs and some doctored World War II tactics.

When Benny suggested they try 1,000-pounders, he ran
into heavy opposition. While Pearly Gates was running
CROSSFIRE ZULU, General Moss had taken a personal interest in the tactics-and-weapons selections. As Benny told
Lucky Anderson on the phone, "Moss is still a fighter jock
at heart, and trying to get him to stay out of a tactics discussion's like asking a wino to ignore an open bottle of
muscatel—he knows he *should* stay out of it, but he can't
help himself."

General Moss was happy they'd stopped considering anything new. He said it was time for the fancy engineers to get
out of the way so the fighter jocks could do their job. They'd
learned how to knock 'em down in the *big* war. They'd used
the largest bombs they could lug to the target, "bridge-
busters" they'd called them, and they'd taken the bastards
down.

He thought they should try 3,000-pounders.

But Lucky knew that Moss and the pilots in the *big* war
hadn't faced SAMs and tremendous concentrations of radar-
directed guns, and that they'd been able to go after enemy
fighters where they lived. He'd considered it all and then
sided with Benny Lewis's suggestion that they try not the biggest, but the most aerodynamic bombs that might do the job.

For the second test Benny suggested they send out
twelve strike birds, protected by flak suppressors, Wild
Weasels, and F-4's, and carry Mk-83 1,000-pounders.

General Moss *still* recommended the bigger 3,000-pound
bombs.

Benny Lewis had called Pearly Gates on the scrambler
phone to argue. His experts at Nellis had concluded the
1000-pounders would have less drag, so the pilots could fly

faster and maneuver better, and they'd be more accurate because they could be carried on the centerline multiple-ejector rack. The 3,000-pounders couldn't be carried on the MER, but instead had to be attached to wing-station adapters, and bombs dropped from the wings were sometimes less accurate. He asked Pearly to pass that on to General Moss.

When Pearly Gates had arrived at Takhli the previous day, he'd told Lucky that General Moss had relented only because he knew both Lucky and Benny and trusted their judgment. But he'd said to tell them both he was betting a six-pack they'd change their minds.

Which gave Lucky pause. Moss seldom bet, but when he did, he almost never lost.

At 0405, with sleepy-eyed Pearly Gates looking on from a corner of the room, Lucky kicked off the mission briefing and outlined the weapons, flight profile, and delivery tactics.

Next Colonel Mack, the mission commander, briefed the target and what he expected from the pilots. Then Lieutenant DeWalt, wearing shiny new first-lieutenant bars, briefed they would face five SAM sites, with their thirty missile launchers, within twenty miles of the target area, and that the number of guns guarding the bridge had not decreased since their last try.

But that time they'd used Bullpup missiles, and the attack profile had exposed them to the gunfire. Lucky felt better about the use of hard bombs. This time they could release even higher than normal because they'd be using the sleek, accurate Mk-83's, and that meant they'd remain in optimum range of the big guns for a shorter time.

As Colonel Mack gave the group a few final pointers, Lucky observed Manny DeVera, who would be leading Viking flight on the effort while Lucky stayed on the ground with Pearly Gates and gathered test results. Manny seemed solid and was even cracking jokes. Still, Lucky wished it were him leading his men into battle, and Manny collecting results.

0715 Local—Route Pack Six, North Vietnam

Captain Manny DeVera

The positive, give-'em-hell philosophy Lucky had told him about had worked fine during Manny's four missions down in the lower packs, but he'd *never* had a problem there, and this was his first return trip up north. It had always been the specter of pack six, seeing the collections of flak and SAMs coming up and knowing the MiGs were out there waiting, that had created the problem. Or so he'd guessed before takeoff. But he'd kept himself busy with mission details and worrying about things like fuze settings and delivery parameters, so it hadn't seemed bad.

Since they'd dropped off the tanker and started toward the target, he'd given himself the pep talk as Lucky had explained, then kept his mind thinking of how he'd handle various emergency situations if they arose. Periodically he scanned the sky about them, even though his Viking flight was in the center of the sixteen-ship formation.

He guessed Lucky's advice was helping, for so far all he'd felt was bitterness toward the fucking gomers because they'd scared the shit out of him, and by God no one should be able to scare the fucking Supersonic Wetback and get away clean.

"*Close it up, Viking three,*" he growled to Bowes, who was leading the second element and had let himself get farther out than what Manny estimated was 1,500 feet.

Bowes pulled in a bit closer and Manny was mollified.

"*THIS IS BIG EYE. POPEYE AT BULLSEYE THREE THREE ZERO FOR TWELVE. I REPEAT, THIS IS BIG EYE. POPEYE AT BULLSEYE THREE THREE ZERO FOR TWELVE.*"

MiGs northwest of the target.

The queasy knot threatened.

If they were jumped by MiGs they would . . . Shit, think! . . . *If they were jumped, they'd take defensive action and let the Phantoms handle it.*

Right?

Right.

He checked his weapons settings. Four Mk-83's on the centerline MER. Set to ripple position. Master arm switch armed. Sight set for forty-five-degree dive bomb.

Ready and loaded for bear.

They approached Thud Ridge, crossed it at the high peak in its center, where Lucky had said they should.

"*Cowboys . . . now,*" called Colonel Mack, who was Cowboy lead.

One after the other, they made crisp forty-five-degree right turns, also as briefed.

Within seconds they were all headed directly down the ridge toward a point a couple of miles east of the bridge. They would dive to their right and release high, at 8,000 feet, then swing back around to recover over the ridge.

SAMs arced upward in the distance, and the Weasels lofted their Shrike radar-homing missiles toward a downtown Hanoi missile site.

Sic 'em.

Manny ran through his mental drill. If they had SAMs launched at them, they would hang firm and let the ECM pods do their work. Trust the damn things, whether they worked or . . . Quit it! *Trust 'em.*

"*This is Cowboy lead,*" called Colonel Mack from up ahead. "*Target visibility is good.*" There were towering buildups of clouds all about them, but obviously none were over the target. The mission was on.

Getting close now.

Manny's nerves began to crawl, creating a tingling feeling all over his body.

Cowboy flight was first in, turning up on their right wings and nosing over into their dive-bomb deliveries to drop CBUs on the guns.

The RHAW rattled warning sounds, and three different strobes were accompanied by the AAA light, meaning three Firecan radars were painting him.

Manny shivered uncontrollably.

Major Max Foley led his flight down the chute. Viking was next.

Gotta be quick about it. Lucky had wanted them in and out in a hurry.

Wind from the east at fifteen knots. That meant offset downriver . . . eastward . . . at . . .

Oh shit! He looked down into hell, for so many bursts were exploding around the Thuds down below that . . .

"*Viking, let's go to work,*" urged Billy Bowes in a quiet voice.

He was beginning to breathe hard, felt the sweat running into his eyes and stinging.

Gotta do it.

He cocked the airplane up on its right wing, then pulled over and into his dive bomb. *Fuck you, bridge.* The sweat was hurting his eyes. He blinked hard and looked for the target.

Jesus. Flak everywhere down there, but there was no bridge. Something was bad wrong.

He had to search for his sight picture. He'd delayed too long and was over downtown fucking Hanoi! He came around harder to his right, leveling out to a very shallow dive and flew back toward the river . . . along a gauntlet of guns.

The gomers began to search for Viking flight in earnest, zeroing on them, for they were the most obvious target, and the sky filled with even *more* flak.

Manny DeVera raged at himself for delaying the dive. Then, *I'm coming, bridge.*

Dark bursts buffeted his Thud, then shook him again.

Still too far out. He flew on, passing through 10,000 feet in his slight dive. He glanced down and thought he saw 650 indicated. Which meant almost 800 knots true airspeed.

Two bursts shook him simultaneously. More flak in his path. Too much.

He turned over on his back and pulled the stick, then eyed the bridge and turned back wings level, diving. *You fucker!* he yelled at the target.

He was at forty degrees. Close enough to forty-five degrees that he could compensate for the error. He watched the altimeter unwinding through 8,000 feet.

His mind clicked and he remembered his offset and aimed short of the target. That's better. Through sixty-five hundred feet. Pipper on the offset point. He pickled, remembered he should have corrected less because of the lower dive angle, and then, as he was pulling back on the control stick, the aircraft shuddered.

"Viking lead's hit," he immediately announced in a shaky voice.

His Thud was still flying and responding to control inputs, so he pulled back harder, until he was enduring six gravities of stress. The foggy phenomenon created by moisture, high angles of attack, and high speed in the Thud grew at the canopy bow until he could not see the world outside.

Still flying and . . . the gauges were good and the master caution light was still off, so the bird wasn't badly wounded. *Which way to turn?* He started left, but changed and whipped the stick back to the right and selected afterburner.

The burner took forever to light. He finally felt the kick in the seat and hurried north toward the rejoin point, wondering how badly he'd been hit.

Viking flight and all the others made it back to the ridge, where Colonel Mack pulled them together into the big ECM pod formation and herded them westward.

"This is Cowboy lead," radioed Colonel Mack as they approached the Red River. *"Anyone hit the bridge?"*

Max Foley said he thought he'd hit a northern span, but hadn't knocked it down.

It was Manny's turn. *For Christs's sake*, he bitched to himself, *I didn't even look.* He was pretty sure he'd missed, because he'd not corrected enough, but as lead he should know if anyone in his flight had hit the target.

He queried his Vikings. Henry Horn, who was Viking four and last on the target, said Billy Bowes's bombs had narrowly missed the southern span, but the bridge was still standing.

Manny critiqued his performance a dozen times on the trip back. He'd clanked up only once, by delaying his roll-in, but in the face of all the defenses, that once could have been a killer. Viking was fortunate not to have lost anyone, and it wasn't his fault they hadn't.

Then his embarrassment grew, for when they looked the birds over, Manny had not been hit at all. Two others had suffered flak damage, but he'd just been shaken by a near miss.

Life remained miserable for the Supersonic Wetback. But he remembered what Lucky had told him, and he began to think of how he'd do it next time.

Asshole bridge!

0940 Local—Command Post, Takhli RTAFB, Thailand

Major Lucky Anderson

The pilot reports were gloomy. Two Mk-83 bombs, each capable of laying waste to a city block, had either hit or exploded just beside the Paul Doumer bridge, yet it was still standing. Possibly damaged, but no one knew how badly.

It was downright and utterly disappointing, except for

one fact. The gomers had shot like hell, yet the strike force
had taken no losses.

Manny DeVera remained quiet about his role, but a couple of the guys from the 333rd squadron who'd been behind
Viking bitched. He'd delayed so long with his roll-in, they'd
had to fly back toward the target to get a proper setup for
their bombs.

But the Vikings hadn't done badly. Henry Horn told
Lucky that all their bombs had been close, that Manny's had
been a bit short, Joe's had straddled the bridge, and one of
Bowes's bombs had either hit or been so close it should've
done the trick. His own bombs had been a little long.

"How'd the rest of the mission go?" Lucky asked Henry,
fishing for a report on how well Manny had led the thing
without actually asking for it.

Looking tired and drawn, feeling the postmission low as
they did when the adrenaline was pumped dry, Henry just
shrugged and said that except for the delayed roll-in it was
pretty much of a standard, "one tenth of an air medal" mission.

Since they received an air medal for every ten missions
they flew, Henry meant it had been routine and uneventful.
And that made Lucky feel better about things. He liked it
when missions went off as planned and there were so few
surprises that everything appeared routine.

As soon as they'd collected the pilot debriefings, Lucky
followed Pearly Gates out to the waiting T-39 Sabreliner.

An hour later they were at Udorn Air Base, walking toward
one of the trailers at the ready area near the end of the runway. It was a "photo-processing intelligence facility," shortened to PPIF and called "pee piff" by the recce pilots. Each
PPIF housed automated film-processing equipment and
specialists. The RF-4C that was just then landing carried exposed poststrike assessment film of the Doumer bridge in its
camera bays.

Two reconnaissance birds had been sent out, but one had
been shot down by intense AAA fire near the bridge.

"Those guys have balls of steel," said Lucky, looking at
the RF-4C slowing as it rolled down the runway. "They've
gotta fly straight and level over the target to get their photos."

Pearly Gates, huffing to keep up, agreed.

"Just maybe," said Lucky on a more cheerful note, "the bridge was damaged worse than the guys' thought."

"God, I hope you're right," said Gates, and Lucky was reminded that the bridges campaign was Gates's project.

"Wish we could have given you better results," he said.

Pearly nodded. "We've got a window of opportunity to be turned loose on a campaign to really sting the North Vietnamese. We wait much longer and they'll get cold feet."

"Who's they?"

"The big leaguers. The Secretary of Defense and the President."

Lucky whistled. He couldn't think that high.

"Mainly the President. He and the Secretary of State have to prod the SecDef a lot, because he says we can't beat the North Vietnamese with air power, and it's like he keeps throwing roadblocks at us so it'll come true. What do the pilots think of the Secretary of Defense?"

"They believe he should go back to building Edsels. At Korat they've got a full-size teakwood Edsel grill hanging in the O' Club bar."

Pearly chuckled. "I told General Moss about that, and he laughed for ten minutes. He'd like to see it, but they take it down when he visits. He distrusts all politicians, but he's got a big-time dislike for the SecDef, and although he'd never say it out loud, he doesn't think much of the President."

Lucky frowned. He thought Johnson was trying his damndest, that he was just hamstrung with lousy advice from the *Wunderkinder* cabinet left over from the Camelot years. It was difficult to think badly of the President, who was also his commander in chief.

They arrived at the PPIF and watched the RF-4C turn off the runway and release its drag chute, then swing around and brake to a stop beside the PPIF. A crew chief threw chocks in place under the tires, and while both engines were still running, film technicians unbuttoned camera bays to retrieve the film canisters.

Lucky was impressed. "They're real pros," he said.

But Pearly Gates was just frowning and waiting, hoping for better news than the Takhli pilots had given him.

•   •   •

Early the next morning, as they finalized the inch-thick report with its photos and diagrams and pages of initial analysis, Lucky looked wearily at Pearly Gates.

They were in a small back room of the Udorn command post, working in short sleeves and beginning to smell ripe from their night-long efforts.

"You think we need another recce run?"

Pearly Gates shook his head. "No use to endanger more recce crews, having 'em run the gauntlet again. One RF-4C's enough to lose."

Lucky sat back in his chair. "You going to see General Moss when you get back?"

"He'll be my second stop. First will be a place called the Recce Tech, where they'll blow up portions of the film we've got here."

"Tell the general I owe him a six-pack. He was right about the bombs being too small. But tell him we've got our tactic. Most of the guys released high and stayed out of the worst of the gunfire, and we still got some near hits."

"I'll tell him," Pearly said gloomily.

"What's next, Pearly? We going to try again right away?"

Gates rubbed his eyes, then ran his hand through his close-shorn, kinky hair. "I don't think so. It'll take a while to get approval, now that we've got two failures in a row. The guys at PACAF and Air Force have to do their Monday-morning quarterbacking and tell us 'see there, I told you so,' and all that."

Lucky stood up. "Then I can get back to doing other things."

"You just keep working this thing, Lucky. Stay in contact with Benny Lewis at Nellis and with me in Saigon, because next time we go for it, we've got to get it right. This makes two strikes, and if we get another chance and blow *that* one, they'll stop us for sure."

Lucky walked over and poured himself one last cup of coffee from the pot on the warmer, then refilled Pearly's cup. All the while he was thinking how happy he was that he didn't live in a world of politics and bullshit like General Moss and Pearly Gates.

Pearly sipped hot coffee and sighed. "Thanks."

"You think this campaign will be a good one, once we get started?"

"Hell, Lucky, I don't know, but at least we'll be doing

something to sting 'em. This is one crazy war, trying to get the politicians to let us fight. It took three years before they let us go after their *little* air bases. General Moss is still fighting an uphill battle to turn you guys loose on their main MiG bases."

"Unbelievable."

"When I talk to my buddy at OSD, that's the SecDef's office, he tells me how the Secretary's convinced we should stop bombing North Vietnam, saying we're just strengthening their resolve like the Germans did with the British during World War II. It doesn't matter that we have a potful of intelligence reports saying different, that every time we hit something new, they squeal, Ho Chi Minh gets sicker, and Giap pulls in more troops."

That outburst made Lucky even more determined—he didn't *ever* want to go to work at a headquarters.

"Which means," summarized Pearly, "that if we can't begin a good campaign that shows the President the SecDef is full of crap, he'll probably listen to him and stop the bombing. And that means it'll be one hell of a long and tough fight for our ground troops."

Lucky sipped coffee.

"So I want you to stay on top of it, Lucky. We lose this one, we lose big-time."

"You just get us another chance. We'll knock the damned bridge down." He stared evenly at Pearly Gates. "That's a promise."

Thursday, July 20th, 0730 Local—TFWC/TAF, Nellis AFB, Nevada

Major Benny Lewis

Benny and Moods were already at work, had been there for an hour working on reports and preparing correspondence. The civilian analyst would come in at eight, take his hourly breaks, and at four-thirty he'd be out the door. He made half again as much money as Benny and was not nearly as good with his figures as Moods Diller on a bad day. Benny used him for trivial tasks and was fortunate the civilian didn't refuse to do them. It was almost impossible to fire civilian em-

ployees. That was the way it had been with feather
merchants since the Second World War.

Benny finished reading the message summarizing the results of the latest CROSSFIRE ZULU test, and muttered
about excrement.

"They miss again?" asked Moods.

Benny nodded, feeling grumpy.

Moods hesitated before machine-gunning. "Another few
weeks, I'll have my smart bombs ready."

Benny told him to just shut the fuck up about his fucking
smart bombs, then stalked down the hall to get a cup of coffee and perhaps put himself in better humor.

At the coffee nook the secretary brandished the pot, saying she had to make a new one. The last taker had left the
pot empty and the burner on, so she'd have to scour it.

"Men!" she exclaimed, and he ducked away.

He went up to the first floor and wished the colonel well
on his morning-long meeting with two visiting senators. After he'd left, Benny poured coffee from the colonel's private
pot and returned to the basement.

Moods tried to soothe him. "I read th' message. They're
really not *bad* results."

"Bullshit." Benny snatched the message back and read it
again. *Damage to structure . . . photos show loss of concrete
and rebar hanging down . . . est. 36 hrs to repair structure,
24 hrs to rpr tracks & roadway sfc.*

At the end of the message was an added paragraph that
made little sense until he thought a bit harder.

4. (U) FOR L.A. AND B.L. FM R.M. RESULTS
INDICATE U 0 6 BUD. THNX. 3000'S?

He laughed, and the shitty mood partially evaporated.

"General Moss passed a message to Lucky and me," he
told Moods.

Moods looked harder before smiling his understanding.

"He bet us a six-pack we were wrong," said Benny. "This
makes it seven times he's been right when he's bet a six-
pack. We've won twice."

"When'll th' guys get their next chance at th' bridge?"

"I dunno," said Benny. "Colonel Gates says it has to be
within the next month or the whole program might be shut
off. Some high-level politics are involved."

They both worked on their various paperwork drills for the next fifteen minutes, then grunted greetings to the civilian number cruncher who came in with his paperbag lunch in one hand and a steaming cup of coffee in the other.

Benny put the civilian to work filling out reports before going back upstairs for another cup of coffee, since the downstairs pot was empty again.

The colonel's secretary was in, a thirtyish brunette with a nice smile and breasts that swung like cantaloupes in her loose sweater. She asked if he was doing anything that night . . . there was this great show at Caesar's Palace she'd love to see.

He said he already had something going, which he didn't, and left.

You sure? asked the inner voice. *Those are damned nice cantaloupes.*

She'd attended the parade where he'd risen from his wheelchair to be awarded a total of sixteen medals, including three Silver Stars, four Distinguished Flying Crosses, and a Bronze Star. Afterward she'd breathlessly told him how wonderful and brave he'd looked, and asked him out for the first time.

She was separated from her husband, she'd said, and the voice inside him had said she sounded horny. He'd not taken her up on that offer or the others she'd made since.

Each time he begged out, the voice inside him had been increasingly disgusted.

As he cautiously descended the stairs to the basement, he thought again about last night's telephone conversation. Julie had said there was still no change in the Bear's status, and she was going through a heavy, melancholy mood. She'd been dreaming again that the Bear was hurt and trying to get out of North Vietnam.

It just wasn't right, what they were putting her through.

Neither Colonel Mack nor B. J. Parker had responded to his letters. It wasn't like them just to ignore him like that.

It came to him then, as he was walked back into his office and took his seat, what he had to do.

Moods was talking on his telephone, and the number cruncher was still working at the task he'd given him. Benny picked up the message from Pearly Gates and reread it.

Moods put down his phone and whooped. "They're

shippin' five laser-guidance kits . . . be here in two weeks for testing. . . . Hot damn!"

Moods was ecstatic over any development with his projects, depressed about almost everything else. Benny ignored him and thought more about the idea spawning in his mind.

He walked down the hall to the secretary's office.

"I need a set of travel orders," he told her.

She peered morosely at him. "You the one who *forgot* to make coffee when you drained the pot *again*?"

"Nope. I've been stealing my coffee from upstairs."

"*Hmmph*. I've had to clean the thing twice now and it's only eight-fifteen. You guys are as forgetful as my husband. Bad enough having one, now I got ten of you guys screwing things up. Men are good for only one thing."

He grinned.

She glared. "And not what you're thinking, Major."

"Then what *are* we good for?"

"Parallel parking. Women have a mental block about parallel parking. If it wasn't for that, we could do without you because everything else we do better."

"I need a request for TDY travel orders."

She sighed and picked up her pencil and a blank Temporary Duty Order request form. "Where to?"

"Seventh Air Force in Saigon, then to Takhli, Thailand."

Her eyebrows furrowed. She still played sheriff for Julie, telling him when she thought he was overdoing it. "Purpose of trip?"

"Classified. And keep the itinerary open so I can go back and forth between the bases as required."

"The colonel's got to sign the request. Since you're traveling out of country, it'll come out of his travel fund."

"I know."

She smiled meanly. "And you've got to submit a waiver signed by the hospital commander with the request for orders. You're still on limited duty, y'know."

Shit, said the voice.

"A waiver? You're kidding," he lamented.

"Nope," she said with a hint of triumph. "Still want me to type up the request?"

Benny nodded glumly. He knew there was not a chance in hell his flight surgeon would recommend that he was ready to travel. "The hospital commander, you say?"

She nodded, looking smug.

He wondered how the Bear would have handled it. Mal Stewart had been a brazen master at this sort of skulduggery.

C'mon Benny, think, the voice inside him said.

He'd heard something about the colonel who commanded the Nellis Hospital.

That's it.

He got the unsigned Medical Waiver/Authorization to Travel form from the secretary, who gave him an exasperated look, and told her, "Be back in a while."

You'll need an accomplice, said the voice.

He went upstairs and waited for the colonel's secretary to get off the phone.

Good thinking.

Benny was bold. First he asked her to meet him after work for a drink at the O' Club.

"Oh, yeah," she said breathlessly.

This one's a piece of cake, said the voice.

"Something else," he said in a more confidential tone. "I need you to find out some information for me."

First she verified what he'd been told about the hospital commander. After five more minutes of telephone work, she handed Benny a detailed account of the colonel's schedule.

Efficient.

"One *more* thing," he asked her.

She stared at him with eager eyes.

Not bad looking, the voice said. *Maybe a little skinny in the shank, but the tits are great.*

"If you can get just a little time off now, I need some help with something in my BOQ room."

She almost crumpled. "Oh, yeah." She immediately called another secretary and asked her to take her calls until she got back from an "important" meeting.

Then she accompanied him to his room and giggled constantly as she helped him remove the back brace.

"I can't get the thing off by myself," he apologized.

As he began very cautiously to slip back into his shirt, she stopped giggling and purred that he had a *wonderful* build.

She ran a fingernail across his chest.

He continued with the shirt, then paused as the inner voice complained.

Who'd it harm, Benny? You've got time, and anyway, the voice said, *you owe her.*

She was very gentle, riding lightly on top of him with the cantaloupe breasts swinging to and fro, staring at his face to make sure she eased up when she saw the slightest pain there.

"Oh, *yeah!*" she squealed finally, as she ground down and tossed her head back in ecstasy. She slowed her writhing motions when he stiffened and groaned, shuddered as she felt his hot fluid, then ground down again and rode him relentlessly until he was fully spent.

He was surprised to find how much he'd needed it. As she carefully wiped away his plentiful juices with a hand towel, he felt bad, as if he'd taken advantage of her.

You don't think she enjoyed it? You gotta learn more about women, Benny. She'll keep that smile for a week.

An hour later, and precisely on schedule, he hurried into the hospital commander's office.

"Good thing you caught him," said the secretary when she saw the form in his hand.

"Why's that?" he asked innocently.

"He's leaving on a ten-day trip. He came in for his briefcase before he leaves for the airport."

"Is my staff car waiting?" called the hospital commander from the other room.

"Yes, sir," she called back. "The driver phoned from the lobby."

The full colonel hurried out of his inner office and glanced at Benny. "Help you, Major?"

Benny held the waiver form out to him. "I'm going on a trip for the general, but I've got to get this signed first."

The colonel blinked. "The general?"

"Yes, sir."

"What's wrong with you?"

"I had some pains in my back, sir. They're okay now."

The colonel bit his lip in thought. "I really should check with your flight surgeon."

"It's Major Young, sir." Young had the day off.

"Backaches?"

"Yes, sir, but they're gone. I could delay the trip, but you know the general."

The colonel signed in an unrecognizable flourish, told the secretary he'd see her in ten days, and left.

"You're fortunate you caught him," the secretary repeated.

Benny grinned. "Sure am."

The voice inside chuckled.

On his way out of the hospital, Benny ran into Lady Dracula, who had indeed been transferred to Nellis. She, being a captain, saluted. Then she glared hard, for she'd discovered he was working more than the two hours a day he was now allowed. Moods Diller admitted she'd asked and that he'd screwed up and told her.

"Where's your back brace?" she demanded, eyes narrowing. It was obvious he wasn't wearing the bulky contraption.

"I'm going to my room to put it on," he answered. "Feels good to take it off for a few minutes every now and then."

She looked doubly incensed. "If I see you without it again, I'll speak with Major Young and have you moved back into the hospital. He should never have allowed you out anyway."

"See you later . . ." He could never think of her name, always thought of her just as Lady Dracula.

She went inside, still looking angry. Moods said she was a real sweetheart.

He walked toward the Fighter Weapons Center building, slowly because the back was beginning to act up without the brace. After his club date with the secretary he'd have to ask her to help put it on again.

Yeah, said the voice. *Cantaloupes.*

This time he smiled.

The trip was on. He'd go to Saigon and give Pearly Gates assistance running the combat test, then drop by Takhli to give Lucky Anderson a hand before they flew it. He was good at air-to-ground tactics, and surely he'd have something to offer.

And since he'd already be there, he would have Bear Stewart's official status changed from MIA to KIA.

For Julie, so she could get on with her life.

The voice inside was pleased.

When he showed the secretary the waiver and asked her to go ahead and process the request for orders, she looked puzzled. "He signed it?"

"That's the hospital commander's signature. If anyone doubts it, they can verify it with his office."

She shook her head in amazement. "When do you want to depart?" she asked, the troubled look slowly leaving her face. She'd done her best.

He thought about the hospital commander's schedule, about some more healing time for his back, and about the fact that Pearly thought it would be at least two weeks until they got the next go-ahead for CROSSFIRE ZULU.

"How about ten days from now, on the thirtieth."

Bach Mai Hospital, Hanoi, DRV

Colonel Xuan Nha

The wounds were continuing to heal. Xuan now put on a uniform each morning at 0530 before beginning his work, just as he'd done for so many years before being caught in the bombing attack. He was growing accustomed to using one hand for everything he did. The worst part about dressing, he'd found, was holding his trousers together while he buttoned them. The rest was getting easier.

Although he never left the hospital, the doctors were concerned that he was overly exerting himself, and that he might open the fragile sheath of scar tissue.

"I am getting as soft as a woman," Xuan complained to them. "I must have exercise."

"Not yet," they told him. "Later, perhaps."

But Xuan Nha exercised his remaining right arm by tensing it often, and each night he walked down the hospital corridor and back to his room, venturing farther each time. He didn't want to remain longer than was necessary in the hospital. Not only did he dislike the place, he was too vulnerable there.

Thursday, July 20th, 1500 Local

Xuan Nha sat at his desk in a corner of the room, for somehow the act of sitting made him feel more productive than when he worked from the bed.

"Reports from the afternoon attacks?" he croaked to

Lieutenant Quang Hanh, and his communications officer lifted a field telephone to call the command center.

Lieutenant Colonel Tran Van Ngo quietly entered the hospital room and handed Xuan Nha a folder. Quang Hanh looked up from his radio console, then quickly averted his eyes, as if he might shield himself from what was transpiring if he didn't look.

"Well?" asked Xuan in his frog's voice, putting the folder aside. Tran had gone to Li Binh's villa, ostensibly to retrieve the folder from Xuan's papers.

Tran remained expressionless. "I spoke to your wife's womanservant."

"And?"

Tran smiled. "Nguyen Wu moved from your home yesterday evening."

So what they'd heard was true. Xuan Nha began to feel better about things.

"Did she say *why* he moved?"

"Almost," said Tran. "She said that Madame Li Binh was very angry, but then she would say no more. She became frightened."

"If Li Binh knew she was telling household secrets, she would have her head."

"The womanservant wrinkled her nose when she spoke of Colonel Wu."

Xuan arched an eyebrow.

"I believe she heard that he likes men as much as she does." Tran gave a slow smile. "I was forced to show her my skill with my elephant's trunk. She was appreciative, but still she would not tell me more."

Xuan laughed. It emerged as a guttural, rasping sound.

He remembered his wife's womanservant. She was obeisant and easily frightened, but she was also utterly insatiable. Whenever Li Binh had been away and he'd gotten the urge, he'd fucked her thoroughly. At a snap of his fingers she'd step out of her trousers and bend over a chair or whatever else was handy, and once it started, she never wanted it to stop.

He'd fucked her, but so had his driver, the menservants, and likely any male, like Tran, who happened by. It made sense that she wouldn't appreciate Nguyen Wu's competition for men's penises, which she craved so for herself.

He relished the thought of his nephew being evicted

from the villa, pleased that one of the rumors had *almost* worked as he'd planned it. Almost, for apparently Nguyen Wu still held his position at Internal Affairs. He'd hoped that Li Binh would ruin him completely, but apparently their blood ties hadn't allowed it.

Xuan motioned to his communications officer.

Quang Hanh looked troubled as he rose from his radios and joined them. He had not liked the duties Xuan had given him . . . not at all. But he was dedicated to Xuan Nha and knew that he survived or drowned with his leader.

"This afternoon's missions were all near Vinh, comrade Colonel," he said. "No targets or damage in the Hong Valley."

Another day had passed without another try at the bridges. Was it over? Did they dare move some of the guns away? Or at least stop sending most of the newly arriving guns from China to the bridges?

Twice the Mee had initiated large-scale raids against the Long Bien bridge, and twice they'd failed. The last attempt had been only three days before. Like the first time, they'd damaged but had not destroyed the structure. Twenty-four hours later it had been reopened to critical road traffic, and the following day to rail traffic from China and Haiphong.

But were the Mee done with it?

Only, he decided, if the Mee politicians stopped them. The tenacious Mee pilots would keep trying until they were stopped by their leaders.

So he must continue to bolster the number of guns at the bridges, even if other targets were more vulnerable. In the meantime he'd ask his wife about her continuing diplomatic campaign to have the bombing stopped altogether. It would be easier to speak with her now, with her nephew removed from the picture. Perhaps one day he and Li Binh could work closely together again. He remembered those times fondly.

He shifted his thoughts to the present. Since the first rumor had worked, he wondered about the second.

"Have you heard from Phuc Yen?" Xuan asked Tran Van Ngo.

Tran shrugged. "Only that many whispers have spread among the men there. They do not specifically name Nguyen Wu, but it's said that someone very high in the rocket forces ordered the radio malfunctions."

"Has Quon been told of the rumor?"

"I do not know, comrade Colonel. I visit the radar controllers at Phuc Yen twice each week, but I do not dare ask *too* many questions. I only know that the whispers are loud."

After a moment of hesitation Xuan shrugged. It did not matter greatly. If Quon didn't wish to listen that was his concern.

He turned his gaze on his two men. "Can either of the rumors be traced?"

First Tran, then Quang shook their heads.

Xuan slapped his single hand down upon the desktop and smiled. "Good. The matter is forgotten."

Lieutenant Quang Hanh looked relieved, and Lieutenant Colonel Tran Van Ngo became businesslike as he produced maps showing proposed deployment locations of the defenses.

Tran had come to the same conclusion as Xuan, for he'd recommended that even more guns be placed about the bridges.

1610 Local—Phuc Yen PAAFB

Air Regiment Commandant Quon

Quon had heard the whispers—that Nguyen Wu had ordered communications between the radars and the interceptor bases to be blocked—but he didn't believe them. Rumors, he knew, were frivolously turned into truths in the eyes of military men who were shielded from what was happening about them.

Since the Lao Dong party allowed only its versions of truth to the men of the VPAAF, their antennae were always out for tidbits of knowledge. The more outrageous the hints and whispers, the more interesting and widespread they became. This one involved treachery and the demise of a hero; therefore, it was a popular story on the air base.

That rumormongering was a crime, and that passing information harmful to the war effort was punishable by death, couldn't deter the men from their whispers. So Quon shrugged off what he'd heard and even grew angry when he heard it was still being circulated.

Nguyen Wu did not have the testicles to engineer his son's death. Such trickery could have come from only one source, the enemy, and he now knew that enemy's name.

Lokee.

Nguyen Wu had returned from the South to a hero's welcome and taken a civilian government job. Since he was out of the picture and could no longer interfere with his MiGs, Quon was satisfied. Xuan Nha and his surrogate, Lieutenant Colonel Tran Van Ngo, were doing a creditable job of controlling the defenses, and each week Quon grew more pleased with the professionalism of the pilot-controllers at the Phuc Yen P-1 radar.

He found it easy to push Nguyen Wu from his mind.

Anyway, the man called *Lokee* was filling his thoughts more each day, and he was increasingly driven to find and kill him.

1700 Local—Ministry of Internal Affairs

Assistant Commissioner Nguyen Wu

Although he no longer wore a uniform or was listed in the roles of the People's Army, Nguyen Wu demanded that his new associates in Internal Affairs call him by the title of Colonel. It was salve for his wounded spirit, but not nearly enough.

They were laughing at him. All of them! Every man and woman he passed in the halls of the building he worked in, every peasant and soldier on the street.

Ridiculing *him*.

It had started so abruptly that he was still shaken.

The previous evening his aunt, his once beloved mentor, had ousted him from her villa as she might a scavenging dog. He'd not suspected, had harbored no idea it was coming, had arrived home to the astonishing spectacle of his belongings being tossed out onto the pebbled driveway by her manservant. Out in the open, vulnerable to the drizzling rain, his clothes becoming soggy and ruined. He'd thought the man had gone mad.

When he cursed at the cowering manservant, he'd been told that Madame Binh was inside and wished to see him.

Puzzled, knowing some great mistake had been made, he'd gone in and the truth had been coolly spat at him.

She knew. She said it was common knowledge, known to every peasant on the streets, that he acted the woman's part with every common soldier who would have him . . . *and* . . . that he was his aunt's lover.

Her arguments had been undeniable. She'd proved the whispers to be true. And then the rumor had been compounded by other truths, and she'd decided what must be done.

There'd been no heat of anger in her. She was like that when she was most dangerous.

One, it was widely known that he panted after every coarse soldier on the street.

Two, he'd bragged about the things he did to his aunt when he could not find a man to pleasure him.

Three, he spoke disparagingly about his aunt's husband to both his lovers and subordinates, even bragged about how he'd destroyed and replaced him.

She paused.

And *four*, Feodor Dimetriev had quietly spoken to her that very morning, and she had discovered that Wu had used her name to coerce the Russian officer into a despicable act.

She had recited her facts carefully. Then, while Wu's head was still spinning with it all, she'd forced him to write a list naming every man he had copulated with . . . *ever*. He'd sat there benumbed and had done it, had written all the names he could remember, because she would have had him killed if he had not.

She'd told him that.

Then she had taken the paper and waved it before him, saying he was looking at a list of dead men. Not because of what they'd done, and certainly not to protect Nguyen Wu. They were dead men because she would allow no tales or black marks against her own name.

He'd tried to explain.

She'd refused to listen and told him if he persevered, she would add *his* name to the list before she gave it to the Commissioner.

It was her calmness that had terrified him and set him to blubbering. He'd cried out about how much he adored and needed her.

She'd given a curt shake of her head. It was over.

What about his position in Internal Affairs? he'd cried.

She said he could remain in his job, but he *would* be watched, and if he ever mentioned he'd shared a bed with his aunt . . . if he ever used his aunt's name to coerce anyone or further himself . . . if he ever again had sex with a man . . . if he ever again spoke poorly of her, or about anything else about her, including her husband . . . she would order that he be sent south to fight, and she would further order them to tie satchel charges to his body and march him at gunpoint toward the American lines. She'd said to take heed, for she'd had that done to better men than he would ever be.

She'd nodded brusquely toward the door and he'd left quickly, and when the door had closed behind him, he'd stood in the rain staring dumbly at the sodden mound of clothing.

A weapons carrier had stopped in the driveway near the mound, and a low-ranking soldier called out from the canvas-covered cab. He'd been told to come here to take away trash in the driveway. Was this mound what they'd referred to?

There was a mistake, Nguyen Wu had told him. He'd paused then, wanting to sob. Just pick up the clothing and load it aboard the truck, he'd finally told the man as he'd walked sadly around to the other side and climbed in.

When the driver had finished placing the clothing in the rear and crawled back into the driver's seat, Wu almost made the fatal error of directing him to the quarters of a male friend. But he'd stopped himself and redirected him to a barracks for senior government officials.

Now, as he finished his work at his desk in the lonely office at the rear of the Ministry of Internal Affairs, he again bemoaned the fact that he was ruined.

He'd formed a team that morning to investigate . . . "certain lies" that had been told about him. He wanted to know where the rumors had originated and how far they'd spread.

He'd planned to squelch them before they became widely known.

The men quickly reported back that the most widely held rumors were that he was homosexual and bragged about fornicating with his aunt. Their informants said the word was

everywhere, and when they'd searched for sources, they'd
been led in circles.

After a long moment of despair, Wu told them to locate
everyone doing the whispering and to threaten them with
death if they continued to mouth the lies.

It was too widespread, they said. He'd caught one
smirking and screamed at him.

If they'd been his subordinates, he would have had them
destroyed, but these were secret policemen who worked for
the Commissioner. He dully told them to leave, and when
they were gone, he brooded.

Nguyen Wu knew who was trying to destroy him. The
same man who'd connived his removal from his previous job
and had him sent south on the dangerous fool's errand.

Quon.

He wondered what he might be able to do about it.

CHAPTER SEVENTEEN

Thursday, August 3rd, 1300 Local—Takhli RTAFB, Thailand

Major Benny Lewis

The C-47 groaned and squealed to a halt before the base-operations building, and the engines settled to idle.

Benny stared out at the base. The flight line, at least, looked the same. Row after row of F-105D Thunderchiefs were parked along the apron, extending for as far as he could see.

He craned his neck. Atop base ops was a sign reading "WELCOME TO TAKHLI—HOME OF THE GREAT 355TH TFW—PACAF'S PRIDE—COLONEL B. J. PARKER, COMMANDER."

Benny chuckled. B.J. was not a modest man.

As the loadmaster came back down the tilted aisle, the left engine clattered to a stop. "Takhli," he announced to the four passengers seated on aluminum and nylon-web seats along the sides of the fuselage. The base shuttle flight had stopped first at Korat and would now continue on to Udorn and Ubon, as it made its circuit of the Thai fighter bases.

Benny disconnected his seat belt and reached for his B-4 bag, with CAPT B. L. LEWIS still stenciled onto its side.

"Let me help you with the bag, sir," said an airman who was also deplaning, and Benny gratefully agreed, for his back was burning with new pain. It had begun a few hours after coasting out on the leg from Seattle, Washington to Anchorage, Alaska, and had progressively gotten worse. He'd doubled his dosage of muscle-relaxant pills, hoping to stop the clenched feeling, and of painkillers to keep his sanity.

Two days earlier, when he'd gone into the headquarters at Tan Son Nhut to pay his courtesy visit to General Moss, he'd slipped on the stairs and wrenched *something* back there. As he'd waited to get in to see the general, he'd sweated like a pig from the pain.

Moss had taken a single look, raised hell with him for traveling in that condition, and within minutes had a flight surgeon hurrying into his office. The doctor grumbled about the Nellis Hospital commander signing the travel waiver and placed Benny on his back for a full day. Then he'd given him even *stronger* muscle relaxants and more painkillers before he'd returned to the headquarters to talk with Pearly Gates and General Moss.

After ordering him to take it easy on the remainder of the trip, Moss said they'd make space on a med-evac bird to the States when he returned from Takhli. Benny had spent another night on the Tan Son Nhut hospital torture bed, and by this morning he'd felt good as he left for Bangkok. The shaking, shuddering C-47 base shuttle had taken care of that.

He made his way forward and gingerly climbed down onto the tarmac, then stood there looking at the big war birds. A flight of four fully loaded, camouflaged Thuds taxied by, and he felt his heart stir. He was back to where the action was.

He was accustomed to heat. It had been 107 degrees when he'd left Las Vegas. Yet the mugginess of Takhli's 90-degree heat made it seem worse. Sweat gathered in puddles on his skin, soaking his shirt in a ring about the back brace.

"Captain Lewis," someone hailed, and he turned to see Staff Sergeant Jerry Tiehl, his old crew chief, hurrying up with a beaming smile on his face. "Good to see you."

Benny grinned, and the pain and heat were partially forgotten.

"Damn." Tiehl saluted him. "Forgot, sir."

Benny returned the salute. "You still crew-chiefing Weasel birds?"

"I'm on my way Stateside. Shipping out tomorrow."

"Where to?"

"George Air Force Base in Southern California. I'm from LA, and this'll be the first time I've been stationed west of the Rockies." He looked closer. "You're a major."

"Miracles happen, Jerry."

They went inside base operations together, chatting about the old days, which had been just four and a half months earlier.

"Too bad about Captain Stewart," said Tiehl sadly.

"He went out the way he figured a man ought to."

"I think about him a lot, about how he used to joke with the crew chiefs and all. I heard he was put in for some big medal."

"An Air Force Cross."

When they finally broke up the reunion, Sergeant Tiehl motioned to a base ops tech sergeant. "This is Major Benny Lewis. He flew ninety-four and a half missions here a few months ago before he left one of my airplanes in North Vietnam."

The tech grinned. "Nice to meet you, sir. Anything I can help with?"

Jerry Tiehl interjected, "I want you to call over to the billeting office and threaten those guys with death if they don't assign him the best guest trailer on base. Then I want them to bring the key here, so the major can go directly to his quarters."

The base ops sergeant went to the nearest telephone and began dialing.

Jerry Tiehl turned back to Benny. "You got the NCOs looking out for you now."

"Thanks."

"You oughta get some rest right away, Major Lewis. You don't look so good."

Friday, August 4th, 1615 Local—354th TFS, Takhli RTAFB, Thailand

Moss's Fighter Mafia

On Friday afternoon the three of them, Lucky, Max Foley, and Benny Lewis, got together in the C-Flight commander's office, where Anderson had stacks of classified manuals, bomb tables, and scribbled notes laid out on his desk.

"By God, the gomers would just blow the thing up if they knew the three of us were together, plotting the demise of their bridge," said Max Foley.

"Good to see you two characters," said Benny. He moved cautiously, and the back brace was obvious beneath his shade-1505 short-sleeved uniform. Periodically he would become very still and wince, then unconsciously lick his lips.

"Benny, you're a fucking human wreck," said Max.

"You're not so pretty yourself," Benny told the skinny weapons officer, "and *you* don't have a reason."

"I'm the pretty one," Lucky growled to settle matters. "Now let's get to work."

They'd been together at Nellis, where they'd been called Moss's Fighter Mafia, and were accustomed to working with one another. At Nellis they'd tested, improved, and documented tactics to be used by U.S. fighter forces. Now they were to perfect tactics to destroy bridges, starting with the big one on the north side of Hanoi.

"A piece of cake," Max said. "We just keep laying on sorties until we knock it down."

Benny told them what Pearly Gates and General Moss had said about the importance of what they'd be doing. "You've probably only got one more chance at it," said Benny, "and you've got to make it convincing."

"How about picking another bridge?" said Max. "This one's a tough bastard."

"No," said Lucky. "It has to be the Doumer bridge. Everyone from the Pentagon up and down's looking at us, and this is the bridge they want."

Max shook his head sadly at the stupidity of headquarters pukes. "Well, when do we get our next chance?"

"Pearly Gates is working that end," said Benny. "He says it may be a week, maybe a couple of weeks. If he can't work it by then, General Moss thinks the whole idea will be scrubbed."

Benny winced and groaned.

"Bad one?" asked Max, frowning.

Sweat had popped out on Benny's forehead. "Spasm," he finally said, but he looked as if he were relaxing some.

"You oughta get the fuck back to the States," growled Max Foley. "We can handle this end of things."

"It's better now," said Benny. "I plan to hang around here for a few days until the planning's done, then go to Saigon so I can help Pearly Gates interpret the results."

Lucky shook his head at Benny's obstinacy. "Let's get on with things."

Max shrugged. "Way I see it, there's no surprises. We load M-118's and do the same thing we did last time."

"One thing we'll never do," counseled Lucky, "is send pilots to Hanoi using the same tactics twice in a row."

"I agree," said Benny.

"Okay," said Max, "so I lost my head for a minute. What changes are we going to make?"

1950 Local—Officers' Club Stag Bar

Captain Billy Bowes

Billy was drinking alone, enjoying his sphere of privacy in the loud bar, when a major in a headquarters-puke uniform made his way through the crowd to stand beside him. The major tried to shout over the babble of a nearby trio of pilots who were happy because they'd bombed the hell out of a railroad siding, sad because they'd lost their flight leader.

Billy leaned forward to hear better, then realized whom he was talking to. He'd heard about him being on base, but this was the first time he'd met him.

"Major Lewis?"

"Yeah."

They shook hands. His cousin Mal Stewart had written a lot about Benny Lewis.

"Good to see you," he said, then he remembered and nodded. "And congratulations on making major."

Benny Lewis didn't act overly impressed with his new rank, and Billy liked that.

The group of fighter jocks grew louder, and Lewis looked at them apprehensively. Billy knew he'd gotten a compression fracture of his spine when he'd ejected from the Thud.

"Let's go over to a table where we can talk," Billy yelled, and received an appreciative look. He got a fresh drink for both of them from Jimmy the bartender, then cleared the way to an empty table, glaring and pushing to make certain no one bumped into the injured man.

When they were seated, Lewis nodded. "I heard a lot about you from the Bear."

"Same with you."

Lewis began telling him how it had been to fly the Wild Weasel tour with Bear Stewart. Billy listened carefully, now and then puffing with pride as he heard how Mal had been as smart and brave as he'd thought.

"We hear he was put in for an Air Force Cross," said Billy.

"It's been approved. They wrote his wife it would be presented either when he was rescued or his status changed, meaning when they declare him dead."

"I haven't met her yet."

"She's one hell of a fine girl," said Benny Lewis, and Billy noticed something warm in his expression.

"You talk with her much?" he asked.

Benny nodded, and Billy detected something else. Hesitancy?

Billy Bowes didn't drink much, because he disliked the foggy feeling of intoxication. He came to the bar often, but normally he'd nurse a couple of drinks and sneak in several straight tonic waters in between. But he liked Benny Lewis, whom Mal Stewart had accurately described as looking like a cross between a pleasant-natured bulldog and a fireplug. He was so good at his calling, his cousin had said, if he was told to bomb the warts off a frog, he'd ask which ones . . . and mean it. So Billy listened raptly to his tales about their exploits and ordered another round.

Again Benny mentioned Julie Stewart, and again he got the faraway look.

Mal would have been pleased, thought Billy. His cousin was like that, wanting the best for his favorite people. Billy knew, because he'd been one of them.

"She's having it rough," said Lewis. "The Bear's still listed as MIA, and she keeps thinking *just maybe* . . . but it's not true, Billy."

Billy agreed. "They should change his status to KIA. Hell, the gomers killed him, then the guys bombed and strafed the fucking place until they said it would have been impossible for an ant to have lived through it."

"I heard them on the chopper radio when they were taking me out."

Billy remembered what Tiny Bechler had told him.

"They wanted to make damned sure none of the gomers came out of it alive."

"His burial ground," said Lewis.

"He would've liked it," said Billy simply. He went over and retrieved the new round from Jimmy at the bar and returned in time to see Lewis gritting his teeth with another bout of pain. He set the drinks down and sat, waiting for him to recover.

"Spasms," said Benny Lewis finally.

"You shouldn't be here. I heard Major Lucky saying that."

"It got worse during the flight over."

"So why _are_ you here?"

"I'm on a project that's pretty important to us." Lewis looked evenly at him. "And since I'd already _be_ here ... I figured I could try to convince them to change the Bear's status to KIA."

"Anything I can do to help?"

"I wanted to make sure it was okay with you before I proceeded further."

Billy Bowes thought about that for a few seconds. "I guess you know from talking to Mal that we're a pretty close family. We all write our grandma back in McAlester. She's like the center of the family ... lets the rest of us know how everyone's doing."

"The Bear told me. Said she was one proud Cherokee."

"Mal wrote good letters, usually five or six pages long. Some about the war, but mostly about his friends."

Lewis was listening closely.

"He wrote a lot about a guy named Glenn Phillips, and a lot about you. Said you two were as close as any brothers could be."

"We got like that. I guess it was because we shared the same dangers and kept one another alive. I can't explain it exactly." Lewis stared down at his drink, then shifted his eyes upward. "He died saving my ass, Billy. He could have gotten away clean, but instead he stopped the gomers from getting me."

Another silence.

Bowes finally spoke. "I'll let you in on something. Grandma Bowes talks about you with the same pride she reserves for us. She brags about your being from a rich family, but how they work hard for their money. About your uncle who owns three auto dealerships, and your father who owns the biggest insurance brokerage in Northern California."

"They're not all *that* wealthy."

"Well, to Grandma Bowes they are, and I'd hate to argue with her. She says you've probably got some blood from the People, meaning the Cherokee, because you're so brave."

Lewis looked self-conscious.

"I came over here thinking you're likely one of the best pilots in the Air Force, and guess what?"

Lewis cocked his head.

"Anyone says different, they've got a fight on their hands."

At that Lewis smiled.

"Now if you've thought it out, and you say it's best for Julie Stewart," Billy looked at Lewis, "or for anyone *else*, that Mal be declared KIA, you've got the family's approval."

"I would guess," said Major Benny Lewis, "that's a yes answer."

Sunday, August 6th, 1500 Local—Command Post

Major Benny Lewis

He went to see Colonel Lyons on Sunday, after they'd completed all the mission planning they could accomplish before the date was announced, and Benny prepared to return to Saigon.

He'd already seen Colonel Mack, whom he'd written the first letters to, had visited him in his trailer the same night he'd talked to Billy Bowes. After a long session of bullshitting over a bottle of good Scotch whiskey, he'd asked Mack if he'd received the letters.

Colonel Mack said he'd forwarded both letters to B. J. Parker, the wing commander, with his recommendation to follow Benny's advice and declare Bear Stewart dead.

On Saturday he'd visited B. J. Parker in his office and was warmly greeted. Parker said he'd given the letters to his special-projects officer, a full bull named Tom Lyons, who'd proved to be adept with paperwork and getting around bureaucracies. Lyons, said B.J., had some good contacts at PACAF headquarters and was the right man to handle it.

Colonel Lyons ran the command post and would be returning to Takhli on Sunday morning.

At 1400 on Sunday, Benny entered the command post and endured the most miserable confrontation of his life.

He was directed to Lyons's office, at the rear of the command post. When he entered, the colonel looked up and stared.

"Hello, sir. I'm Major . . ."

"Don't you salute?"

Benny did so, then again tried to introduce himself. "Major Lewis, sir, and I've . . ."

"I'm really quite busy." Lyons looked irritated.

"I'll only take a few minutes of your time. I have to catch a T-39 going to Saigon."

"Well, get on with it." Lyons sat back, hands coupled over the embryo of a potbelly.

"It's regarding three letters I sent from the States."

"*Which* letters? I get a lot of correspondence through here."

Benny noted the clean desk and empty in- and out-baskets. "I forwarded two letters to Colonel Mack and another . . ."

"I assume you mean *Lieutenant* Colonel MacLendon. There is a difference between the two ranks, you know."

Jesus! "Yes, sir."

"Go on," said Lyons. He impatiently glanced at his watch.

"The letters refer to the official status of Captain Malcom Stewart, who's presently being carried as MIA."

Lyons nodded.

"His wife is terribly troubled. She believes he might be wounded and trying to get out somehow. Of course he is not. So . . ."

"Do you know her?"

"Yes, sir."

"And just what is your relationship?"

"Pardon me?"

"Your relationship with Captain Stewart's wife?"

Benny knit his brow. "I don't understand."

"Are you close friends?"

"You might say that. Captain Stewart was my backseater, and she's . . ."

". . . she's very close?"

Benny bristled. "She is a very nice lady."

"And the two of you are . . . close."

"I am trying to do her a favor, sir."

"Did she ask you to? Did she ask that her husband's status be changed?"

"Not in precisely those words, but she did say . . ."

Colonel Lyons raised his hand to stop him and shook his head slowly from side to side. His voice emerged in a hiss. "This is one of the most despicable things I've ever heard of."

"Pardon me?" asked Benny, wondering if he'd heard correctly.

"I'm talking about a man, a field-grade officer, trying to take advantage of an Air Force wife by having her husband declared dead."

"Take advantage?"

"Have you been making love to her, Lewis? Is that it? Or is it that she refuses to do so until her husband is declared dead?"

Benny's mouth drooped in astonishment.

"*Yes*, I was given the letters for action, and they made me sick. I know some of the rabble in the States are protesting our involvement in the war and insulting our fighting men, even dragging our flag in the mud. But I've never seen *anything* quite so low as trying to take advantage of a fellow officer's wife by having him declared dead."

Benny sputtered, so outraged he was unable to form words.

"I'll tell you what I'm going to do about your letters, Major. I'm going to write one of my own to your commanding general. You're at Nellis, right? I plan to tell the general precisely what kind of animal he has working for him."

Benny opened his mouth to explain. "You're wrong . . . ," he managed.

"You want to take advantage of a woman, go out and find a whore, but stay away from the men's wives. *You are dismissed*, Major."

"You low son of a bitch." Benny was shaking with fury. He clenched his teeth tightly and stared for a moment, then turned and strode out of the man's office.

"Come back here, Major!" he heard, but he ignored him.

"Bastard!" he raged.

Max Foley was emerging from the intelligence office. "Something wrong?" he asked.

Benny didn't stop. He continued out the door and into the open air, where he stopped to take a couple of deep breaths, still trembling with emotion.

Max had followed him. "You okay?"

Benny didn't answer.

"What happened in there?"

Benny glanced back at the building. "I just came close to killing a man, Max, and he was wearing an Air Force uniform."

Max shrugged. "If you're talking about Lyons, no one would care much."

Benny was trying hard to cool down.

"Was it Lyons?"

"Yeah."

"He's a regular asshole, except when he's around B.J. He's got Colonel Parker buffaloed, but no one else. Anything I can help with?"

Benny gave a single, angry shake of his head and began walking toward base ops.

"Give me a call from Seventh Air Force," Max yelled after him.

He had to catch an airplane. Perhaps on the way to Saigon he would be able to think clearly again, but just then all Benny could think of was taking the bastard colonel by the throat.

The voice inside him was dismally quiet.

Thursday, August 10th, 2030 Local—Trailer 5A

GS-15 *Linda Lopes*

Linda had returned to Takhli tired of the charade and foolery surrounding her relationship with Paul Anderson. She was weary of worrying about how he felt about it, and of trying to honor his silly code of whatever it was that drove him to keep her out of his life. He was being imbecilic about it, and she'd had enough of doing nothing about it.

It had started the week before, when she'd decided, once and for all, *to hell with Paul Anderson. I'm going to get on with my life before the wrinkles are so established there won't be another chance,* and had accepted a date with the ambitious, distinguished-looking, and *very* available Chief of Operations of the Bangkok embassy.

They'd had a great dinner on a floating restaurant, brandy at the Siam Intercontinental, then eyed each other and smiled with knowing eyes before rushing to his sumptuous apartment, where he put on a Nat King Cole record and she'd purred and told herself she was going to give him something he would not soon forget. They'd almost fallen into each other's arms, and if he'd gotten to the point with things, it might have ended differently. But every now and then he'd interrupt their necking and pad over to the wine bottle so he could ply her with more booze. Then, when things were beginning to get heavy, when he was pawing and snorting like a bull and fumbling with her bra release like he was working on the Gordian knot, she'd realized she was more interested in the subtle, nutty flavor of the wine than in what he had in mind. She'd pushed him away and said *bullshit.* She'd left the poor klutz groaning and pleading about his needs and taken a cab back to her apartment in the American village.

By the time she got there, she'd realized it had all gone on long enough. It had been nine weeks since she'd proved to herself, and to Paul if he hadn't been so hardheaded that he wouldn't admit it, that he could not extinguish the fires they'd lit eight years earlier.

She rapped "shave and a haircut" on his trailer door, then watched the window and saw the light come on.

He peered out, blinded by the light of the porch lamp. "Linda?" He hid behind the door, obviously unclothed.

"Yeah."

"I was taking a nap. I'd ... uh ... ask you in, but ..."

"Nope," she said. She'd fortified herself with a martini before she'd trekked over from Trailer 9A. "I don't *want* in."

He looked confused, at least she thought he did.

"You've got an advantage over me, Paul," she said fearlessly. *No more beating around the bush or pulling punches.* "Since the accident I can't tell what you're thinking."

He blinked.

"But I know for sure that you're wrong, and I'm sick and tired of you trying to screw with *my* mind."

"I don't know what you're talking about."

"I was going to wait until tomorrow, but then I realized

you might find out I'm here and try to slither away like a low snake, like you did last time. Remember?"

"I had to go to Danang to pick up an airplane," he said cautiously.

"Yeah, I heard about how you volunteered for the job and took one of your guys'—Henry something?—place."

"Lower your voice," he pleaded. "The guys have to fly in the morning. Hell, *I* have to fly in the morning."

"Yeah, I know. But you're off tomorrow afternoon."

He stared and blinked, and it felt good to be one up on him.

"We're going to sit down over lunch at twelve sharp, Paul Anderson, and we're going to talk about a lot of things."

"Well . . . ?"

"Let me change that. We're going to sit down, and *I'm* going to talk about a lot of things. One of those things is going to be your god-awful face."

He did a slow take on that. His mouth threatened to droop open.

"I've done some homework, and I've found that if you want to, you can get a lot of facial reconstruction done."

"Jesus, who've you been talking to, Linda?" He sounded like a child whose mother had gone through his room and found dirty books.

"Three calls to the burn center at Brooks Air Station, for starters. They say you can begin as soon as you get back to the States. Two weeks per visit, and thirty days recovering each time you go."

"I don't want that."

"The hell you don't!"

"Shhh." He looked about nervously.

"I can get used to your face. I'm beginning to already. But you can't, so we're going to take a trip to the center every few months until you think you're presentable."

"Dammit . . ."

"And we'll also talk about where we want to be stationed back in the States, things like that."

He stared.

"Twelve noon, at the club. If you aren't there on time, I'll find you. I'll go to your squadron and cry a lot, and if you're not there, I'll go to Colonel Parker and tell him you've done me wrong." She furrowed her brow, then brightened. "I'll tell him you've given me some exotic venereal disease."

He looked panic-stricken—she was beginning to read him after all.

"Ciao," she said, waggling a raised hand, and walked back toward Trailer 9A, humming happily and thinking that Paul Anderson had tried to fool with the wrong lady.

CHAPTER EIGHTEEN

Friday, August 11th, 0455 Local—Briefing Theater, Command Post, Takhli RTAFB, Thailand

Major Lucky Anderson

Since the execution order hadn't yet come through for CROSSFIRE ZULU, and the planning had been completed, Lucky placed himself back onto the flying schedule. That morning they would return to the northeast railroad to locate and destroy rolling stock, which Seventh Air Force claimed was being hurried down from China in increasingly heavy numbers. Each aircraft carried four CBU-24's on the centerline station. Their Gatling cannons were loaded with high-explosive-incendiary rounds.

As mission commander Lucky would lead Yankee flight to the northernmost section of the railroad. He assigned other sections of the rail line to the three other flights of Thuds.

He gave a more thorough briefing than normal, for several of the pilots were new, including a cherubic lieutenant named Smith who'd been assigned to C-Flight. In pilot training Smitty had been Billy Bowes's student. Lucky placed them in the same room at the Ponderosa and told Billy to indoctrinate and teach him the essentials of combat.

"Release high," Lucky reminded them all before the briefing broke up, "for wide dispersion of the bomblets. Release lower if you want to concentrate them." He'd felt irritable all morning, but tried to keep it from his voice.

He looked around at the group. "Questions?"

"Yes, sir," responded Lieutenant Smith. "What if there's no trains and we can't find any rail cars at the sidings?"

Lucky had already covered the answer to that one and started to snap a response to "listen up, dammit." He cooled his irritation and passed the question on.

"Captain Bowes?"

He was beginning to trust Billy again. Since the ass-chewing there'd been no more breaches of trust, and he liked the way he'd taken Smitty under his wing.

Bowes turned to Smith. "If the target area is socked in by weather or we can't find a suitable target, then we'll lug the CBUs back to pack five and drop on the alternate target."

Their alternate target was a section of mountain road that contained several suspected truck parks. Exactly the sort of wasted effort they hated most.

Then someone in another flight asked about the marginal weather they anticipated, and Lucky, exasperated because he'd covered that one too, told them not to be stupid and to steer well clear of the biggest clouds.

"And finally," said Lucky, "everyone remember that it's a long way to the northeast railroad. If you have to dodge SAMs or look around for too long, gas can become critical, so watch your gauges and call Bingo fuel when you get down to six thousand pounds."

Bingo fuel was the amount required to make it back to a recovery airfield.

Without further comment Lucky collected his briefing material and stalked out of the room toward their flight-briefing room, unable to shake his shitty mood.

0709 Local—Northeast Railroad, Route Pack Six, North Vietnam

Captain Billy Bowes

They were flying in a spread formation with a half-mile separation between elements, and he and Smitty were far out to Major Lucky's right when Billy saw smoke in the distance.

"*Yankee three's got a train in sight, eight or nine miles up ahead,*" he announced.

Major Lucky paused before answering, probably to look at his map, for they weren't far from the Chinese buffer zone. He'd been grumpy all morning, both during and after the briefing, and had snapped at the flight members over the radio during the refueling, so everyone was trying to toe the mark.

Billy continued to scan up ahead, then turned and looked about the sky. Thus far it had been spooky quiet. They'd dodged several thunder-bumper clouds building in vertical developments, but there'd been no SAM firings, and they'd seen little flak on the railroad.

"*Yankee flight, the train's in the buffer zone,*" called Major Lucky gruffly, "*and we're getting too close. Prepare for an in-place turn.*"

The flight responded. "*Two.*" "*Yankee three.*" "*Yankee four.*"

"*Ready . . . turn . . . now!*"

All four aircraft had wheeled into a three-G left turn to reverse course when a SAM signal began to chatter on Billy's RHAW.

"*Yankee flight, roll out level,*" called Major Lucky. He didn't want the firing to come from their vulnerable six o'clock.

Billy quickly pulled out of his turn and flew wings level to get a relative bearing on the SAM site. The strobe grew, the LAUNCH light came on, and a squealing sound was loud in his earphones.

"*Yankee three's got a SAM launch at my seven o'clock,*" Billy immediately called. The LAUNCH light was steady, the strobe unwavering, so it was meant for his aircraft.

"*Turn to put him at your ten o'clock, three. Four, pull out well clear of Yankee three.*"

"*Yankee four, roger,*" called Smitty, pulling away as he'd been told and leaving Billy to face the SAMs. There was no reason to jeopardize both aircraft.

Billy selected burner, dropped the Thud's nose slightly to pick up maneuvering energy, and turned to place the strobe at his ten o'clock, all the while looking for the missiles.

He tried to spot the missiles against the green hillocks to

the north. You had to see them to dodge them, but *where the hell were they?*

"*Yankee three doesn't have . . .*"

"*Prepare to break, three,*" called Major Lucky.

There they were, close!

"*Got 'em in sight,*" Billy muttered over the radio, heart pumping. He waited a second longer, until they appeared *impossibly* close, then pulled . . . hard . . . tensing and gritting his teeth to endure the strain of seven g's. A missile flashed by, close to his canopy.

They launched them in threes, so he continued to pull hard on the stick.

He reversed and rolled the Thud on its back. Another missile tried to correct but skidded by harmlessly before detonating in a tremendous orange explosion.

"*That's the last one, Yankee three,*" radioed Major Lucky.

He'd become separated, and the remainder of Yankee flight was now a couple of miles southwest of Billy. He was turning toward them when his radio came alive.

"*Yankee four's showing a SAM launch, three o'clock,*" called Smitty.

Dammit! thought Billy, for it was Smith's first time in pack six, and Smitty wasn't experienced enough to make a proper SAM maneuver on his own.

"*Get ready to take it down, Yankee four,*" said Major Lucky.

"*Yankee two has an activity light,*" called Henry Horn.

"*Ignore it unless you get a solid launch light, two,*" said Lucky. "*These'll be headed for you, Yankee four.*"

One, two, and then three SAMs launched in furious flurries of dust and smoke at Billy's one o'clock, less than two miles distant. He was so close that the strobe on his RHAW was huge even though the SAM radar wasn't painting him.

Was the site in the restricted area?

The missile boosters were pushing the missiles toward Smith.

Fuck the restricted area. Billy had already rolled over and now dropped the Thud's nose into a steep dive attack to get his sight picture.

Fifty-five hundred feet. Fifty degrees dive angle. Not much time.

He pointed the Thud's nose at the center of the SAM site, pickled, and immediately pulled hard.

Flak began to puff about his Thud as he continued to sink.

Dropping very fast toward the ground.

Sinking farther yet. He read 2,500 feet altitude.

The RHAW strobe and SAM light abruptly went off. He'd killed the site.

White popcorn flak puffed around him. Then it stopped, and he figured it was because he was too low for them to track.

When he finally recovered, the altimeter showed less than 500 feet, but he was in afterburner and going very fast. He climbed, then rolled over on his back to examine the damage. The CBUs had hardly had time to open and had made four small circles from which smoke drifted aimlessly.

"Yankee three, what's your position?" called Major Lucky.

"Coming off the SAM site, sir." He continued to climb.

Pause. *"Did you release your weapons, Yankee three?"*

"Roger that."

"Hit anything?"

"Either that or I scared the hell out of him, Yankee lead. His radar went off the air, and he stopped guiding the missiles. I'm pretty sure I got the control van."

Another pause, then Lucky announced in a terse voice, *"Okay, Yankees, give me a fuel reading."*

"Two's got sixty-one hundred pounds."

As they sounded off with their fuel status, Billy realized that Lucky Anderson was unhappy.

1130 Local—354th TFS, Takhli RTAFB, Thailand

Major Lucky Anderson

Lucky's mind churned with anger as they walked into the C-Flight office.

Billy Bowes had bombed a SAM site inside the Chinese buffer zone. He'd done precisely what Lucky had told him not to.

Dammit!

Lucky closed the door and turned to face Bowes, who wore a stiff, defensive expression.

"The last time we talked, I told you never to go after another fucking unauthorized target."

"It was a SAM site, Major, and he was firing on my flight."

"*My* flight, dammit!"

"It was Smith's first time up there and he'd never even seen a SAM. He doesn't know his ass from his elbow yet. Without an element leader there to show him how to dodge it, there was a good possibility he couldn't handle it."

"How the hell do *you* know that?"

"Because I know Smith, sir. I was his instructor pilot at Moody, and I probably know more about his flying ability than anyone in the Air Force."

"Did you know you were in the buffer zone when you dropped?"

"I thought I probably was."

"But you dropped anyway. Dammit to hell, when are you going to learn discipline?"

"I was told that once a SAM site fires at you, it's fair game."

Lucky sighed and shook his head. "Who told you that?"

Billy looked thoughtful. "I don't remember for sure. One of the Weasel pilots, I believe."

"Maybe that's guidance for the Wild Weasels, Bowes, but it isn't for the rest of us. Read the goddam rules for a change. For all you knew, you could have been in Red China, for Christ's sake."

"Major, I wasn't thinking of anything but saving my wingman's ass. If it'd been in China, I'd have bombed it."

They stood nose to nose, feet planted and glaring at one another.

Sudden anger swept over Lucky, and he pointed a shaking finger at Billy. "You're grounded, Bowes. Tell your fucking lies to the lawyers. I've had enough of your private war."

Billy looked startled, then shaken. Lucky boiled even more, wanting to hurt the fucking prima donna standing before him with the insolent look.

"And stay the hell away from the other guys in C-Flight until I take proper action."

Billy Bowes kept his voice very even. "I did not lie, and

bombing that site had nothing to do with what we talked about before. Major, you're being . . ."

"Get the fuck out of here!"

"Major, you're wrong."

"You're dismissed."

Billy stared for a heartbeat longer before giving a wiseass, highball salute and left the room without waiting for Lucky to return it.

By God, I'll have his ass, Lucky fumed.

But the door closed behind Bowes, and just as quickly as the anger had swept over him, it was gone. Lucky slowly sat at his desk, and as he calmed down, he wondered, *What the hell have I done?*

He ran a shaking hand through his hair and sighed, feeling ashamed.

What an asshole I've become, he thought.

He wondered about the cause of it.

What if he had been where Billy had been, and the site had fired its missiles? No thinking to it. He'd have attacked the bastard, just as Billy had. Bowes had reacted quickly and appropriately and had very possibly saved a man's life, *and he'd just chewed his ass for it.*

Why?

Had he been so preoccupied, so consumed by the thought of facing Linda Lopes over lunch that he'd taken it out on Billy?

Can't be, he reasoned, *but . . .*

If it was true, he should be doubly ashamed. It was a cardinal precept for a leader to keep his private life separate from his work. He'd always believed in that rule and abided by it. *Except this time.* Before the morning mission he'd stewed about Linda's visit, and it *had* affected his thinking.

So what should he do about Billy Bowes? The guy was a fucking hero and he'd treated him like shit. He mulled it all over in his mind for a moment or two, and the impact of what Billy had done continued to sink in. He retrieved the steno pad from the drawer and laboriously printed:

11 AUG 67: CAPT. B.—SUBMIT FOR DFC— "DODGED MISSILES, DESTROYED SAM SITE AT GRATE RISK TO HIS OWN LIFE TO PROTECT WINGMAN—ETC."

He thought about it for a moment longer, then scratched through "DFC" and penned "SILVER STAR?" above it.

After the dreaded lunch with Linda, he'd find Billy. Maybe explain that he was having a personal problem and . . . *No* . . . Just apologize and tell Billy he'd done good work.

He returned the steno pad to the lower drawer, then rose and sighed and began to think of how he could best prepare himself for Linda.

Max Foley opened the door and peered inside.

"What the hell do you want?" Lucky snapped. Foley should have knocked.

"Jesus, I'm sorry. You having your period, Miss Anderson?" The way Max was grinning could mean only one thing.

"We get the go-ahead?" Lucky asked.

"You betcha. The frag order just came in. The Doumer bridge with M-118 three-thousand-pound bombs. Takeoff at thirteen-fifteen. Time over target at fifteen hundred."

Lucky's mind raced. "Jesus, Max, that gives us only an hour and a half before takeoff. There's no way we can make it."

"B.J.'s asking Seventh Air Force to push everything back an hour so the guys can change the weapons loads."

"Still doesn't leave much time. Let's get over to the command post."

"You don't hurry, you'll be eating my dust."

On his way out Lucky told the duty officer to call the club, have them page a Miss Linda Lopes, and tell her he couldn't make it for lunch but that he'd see her for dinner, and . . . this time there wouldn't be any snakes involved.

The duty wog didn't understand about "snakes," so he repeated the message, then went out to join Max Foley.

As they hurried toward the command post, Lucky pondered only once about the lunch discussion. *Saved again,* he thought. Then his mind turned to the tactics they'd use on the afternoon mission against the Paul Doumer bridge.

Captain Billy Bowes

Billy watched the two majors hurry from the squadron building and idly wandered outside himself, wondering what the rush was all about. Since leaving the C-Flight office, he'd felt like shit in a gunny sack. During the past weeks he'd worked hard to regain Major Lucky's trust, and now he'd blown it again. Hell yes, he'd known he was in the Chinese buffer zone when he attacked the site, but if what he'd done was wrong, then somehow it was hard to make sense of *anything* they were doing here.

Lucky Anderson had said he'd been wrong, so he supposed he was. Major Lucky wasn't one to fuck with your mind. Billy regretted the silly highball salute he'd given, because it had not at all reflected the way he felt, *but dammit* . . .

Standing outside the squadron building, he saw the flight line was going into a sort of frenzy. Bomb cradles were being rushed toward the aircraft, and the crew chiefs were acting as if they were going to download *everything* on the airplanes, even those already loaded in standard combat configurations.

Some kind of special mission?

He wanted to go to the command post to see what was happening, but he remembered what Lucky had told him . . . that he was grounded and to stay away from C-Flight . . . so he supposed that meant he was to stay away from the entire flying operation.

He began walking aimlessly toward the main part of the base.

1240 Local—Command Post

Major Lucky Anderson

To kick things off, B. J. Parker took the floor and gave a spiel about how important the mission was and how they'd been working to change the weapons and tactics to make it work.

"This time," he said, "let's knock the damned bridge down, because I'm sure as hell tired of going back there."

Then B.J. sat down and left things to Max Foley and Lucky.

Max gave a soliloquy on M-118's, how the things had been manufactured during the Second World War, but how they were still good bombs with *fair* aerodynamics for their size.

Which was not especially true. Flying with the big

blivots was a bit like flying with your speed-brakes out, they created so much drag. But they wanted to get the guys' confidence up, and there was no reason to be negative about things the pilots already knew.

Then Max gave his tactics pitch. When he told the hand-picked pilots they were going to get to fly in individual flights rather than a gaggle, they felt good about it.

Even when he told them the *reason* for not flying the big formation—that radar returns from the big bombs were so bright, the ECM pods wouldn't do them a lot of good, so he wanted them free to maneuver—they *still* felt good about it. They enjoyed flying like fighter pilots, rather than in bomber formations.

"You'll be using more fuel than normal because of the drag," Max said, "so don't be surprised if you come off the target with less than usual. But you should have about seven grand left, so you can use afterburner to get out of the area and away from the guns."

Lucky took his turn and talked about the flight profile, pointing at the large wall map

"We're going to fly down Thud Ridge to the target," he told them, "but this time we're going down its western side to a different pop-up point, here, just past the Phuc Yen MiG base. Pop up northwest of the bridge and roll in directly down the river. We're trying for saturation. We'll have so many Thuds coming at them, so closely spaced, they won't be able to shoot at *all* of us. Wind should be ten knots or so from the east, so offset about fifty feet downriver. Get a good sight picture the first time, because you're only going to get one chance at it. No reattacks, because there's too many guns in the area. If your bombs don't come off, jettison them into the river.

"After you've released, keep flying straight ahead. Make a dogleg or two if you want, but I want everyone in, bang . . . bang . . . bang, and then everyone out of there. We'll rejoin southeast of Hanoi near this island in the river and form into our gaggle for the egress out to the water and our tankers."

Lucky and Max took turns answering questions about the weapons, flight profile, and tactics.

"Don't expect the two bombs to hit together," said Max. "They're on the wings, which means they're separated by more than twenty feet to *start* with. And they won't come off the airplane precisely together, so you'll slew a little and throw the second bomb a few more feet."

"All you need to do is hit with one bomb," interjected Lucky. "One three-thousand-pounder will knock down a span."

Colonel Parker would lead the chopper flight and be twenty-five seconds in front of Max. The chopper flight's CBUs should still be going off among the guns at the sides of the river when Max Foley was delivering his bombs. After Max led the first aircraft onto the target, there would be three more flights of Thuds. The last of those would be Lucky's Barracuda flight.

Henry Horn was Lucky's number two. Three was Manny DeVera, and four was Joe Walker. He'd wanted to include Billy Bowes, with his uncanny bombing ability, but when he'd called the squadron, they'd been unable to locate him.

What Lucky Anderson did not tell anyone, either in the mission briefing or the briefing for Barracuda flight, was the reason he wanted to be last. If it went that far and things had not gone well, he planned to do whatever was required to knock down the damned bridge.

1340 Local—Flight Line

Staff Sergeant Larry Hughes

Just two hours earlier they'd received the orders to select eighteen birds, download their standard configurations, and upload with centerline fuel tanks and 3,000-pounders on the wings. Which meant they would change all the weapons, all the pylons, and all the fuel tanks with only a single hour's slip in the schedule. That was an impossible task, so of course they did it.

Larry's bird, 820, with CAPT W. BOWES painted in bold letters on the left canopy rail and SSGT L. HUGHES on the right, was one of two spares. It would be launched only if a primary aircraft went bad or crashed on takeoff.

They'd been told it was an important target, so like the other crew chiefs, Larry worked his butt off to get the airplane ready in the impossible period of time. He got all the wing tanks and pylons and the 750-pound bombs and the MER downloaded, but then he had to wait.

Since 820 was a spare, they brought the centerline tanks and M-118 bombs only after the sixteen primaries had been loaded. When the grumpy captain pilot arrived to preflight it and taxi to the arming area, where the spares would be pre-positioned, they were still uploading wing adapters for the bombs. The pilot wanted to raise hell with *someone*, but there was little to do but stand off to one side and glare while Larry and the load team worked their asses off.

When the pylons were in place and the bombs were loaded, there was a glitch when one of the bomb-load crews found a problem with a fuze.

The primary aircraft began starting engines. The pilot started to come over and bitch again, which would have just slowed them down more, when Major Lucky arrived, carrying his map case and helmet and lugging his parachute.

"My airplane had a bad gyro, chief. How's your bird?"

"Fine, if you guys'll give me a chance to finish loading it."

Major Lucky ran off the other pilot and returned, looking at his watch and asking Larry how much longer it would take.

Larry did not pause in his labors. "Every time you ask another question, it holds us up that much more."

Major Lucky backed off, grinning apologetically but looking fidgety. Ten more minutes passed before Larry waved to him and gave a thumbs-up.

Major Lucky Anderson hurried over, but when he looked up at the name on the canopy, he frowned as if he'd forgotten something. "Call Captain Bowes," he said, "and ask him to meet me at debriefing when I get back. I've got something important to tell him."

"Will do, sir," said Larry Hughes.

The other airplanes had begun to taxi by then, so Lucky crawled on up the ladder without checking things, accepting Hughes's word that everything on 820 was working.

The engine start and flight control check went smoothly and everything looked good. As the bird taxied out of the stand, Larry saluted as sharply as possible.

Major Lucky returned the salute, nodded crisply, and pushed the throttle forward, taxiing away in such a blast of exhaust that a nearby start cart almost tumbled.

"Asshole!" yelled a crew chief who was a friend of Larry's.

Larry Hughes stiffly walked over and put his hand on his friend's shoulder. "You call that particular pilot an asshole again, you and me are going to come to an understanding."

He turned then and watched 820 disappear down the taxiway.

He'd done his part. The major had a good bird.

CHAPTER NINETEEN

Friday, August 11th, 1545 Local—Route Pack Five, North Vietnam

Captain Manny DeVera

They were approaching the Red River when his airplane began acting up. By that time Manny had himself so hyped and ready to knock down the damned bridge that he *knew* he was going to do it. But the air-turbine motor, which was located just beneath the pilot in the Thud and created a terrible racket even when it was running smoothly, started making an even more god-awful howl. The sound became intermittent, whining loud, then dropping off, whining, then dropping again. The utility hydraulics pressure gauge rose and fell with the sounds from the ATM.

If the ATM went out, he'd lose his backup hydraulics, stabilization system, and primary instrument readout. It was a semiserious problem even in peacetime. It would be foolhardy to go into a combat situation with it.

He hesitated before he called the problem. They seldom lost an ATM. There'd been problems with them at first, when the early Thuds were coming off the assembly line, but those were the old B-models and with the newer D-models, problems with the ATMs were rare. Manny worried that someone might think he was faking it. He listened carefully and watched the utility-pressure gauge for a full minute before deciding it was a no-go.

"*Barracuda lead, three's got a fluctuating ATM,*" he finally called. "*I think it's about to go out on me.*"

They talked it over for only a couple of radio transmissions before Major Lucky sent him home. He sent Henry Horn, who was flying as Barracuda two, to escort him, and advised them to dump their bombs at the Termite Hill and land at Udorn.

Henry pulled in closer and the two aircraft made a sweeping turn, to head back and out of danger.

1547 Local—Route Pack Six

Major Lucky Anderson

Lucky watched as Barracudas two and three turned westward and away from the remaining two ships of the flight.

"*Close it up, Barracuda four,*" he called.

"*Four,*" came Joe Walker's acknowledgment, and he slid into place on his right wing.

They were not far behind the flight in front of them, but Lucky nudged the throttle forward and closed the gap even more. If they were jumped by MiGs, six Thuds were better than a two-ship, and by flying closer, they'd be better hidden in the ECM jamming.

They'd crossed the Red and were halfway across to Thud Ridge when a SAM signal rattled its warning on the RHAW. They looked out sharply, but there was no launch. Then they approached Thud Ridge and turned right to fly down its western side.

"*THIS IS MOTEL. BLACK BART AT BULLSEYE, TWO SIX ZERO FOR THREE ZERO. I REPEAT. THIS IS MOTEL. BLACK BART AT BULLSEYE, TWO SIX ZERO FOR THIRTY.*"

MiGs thirty miles west of Hanoi, a long way from their flight. Still, they looked out sharply.

The Weasels were in the target area being harried by three different SAM sites. Twice they called SAM launches, then again. In the confusion of things they also called that target visibility was good.

The SAMs were very active, noted Lucky.

A few seconds later Colonel Parker radioed that he was in the pop-up for his bomb delivery, and Max called that he was hot on his heels.

Lucky felt adrenaline charging his system.

Two Firecan AAA radars and a Fansong SAM radar tracked them from the east, but he figured they were no problem. The threat was *before* them, and he made damned sure he was jinking unpredictably to foil the guns.

"*Barracuda four has three bogeys at three o'clock level,*" called Walker.

Lucky swiveled and searched, then saw the MiGs. They were several miles distant and traveling north.

"*Barracuda lead has them in sight. Three MiG-17's five miles west of Phuc Yen, Pistols.*"

The Phantoms didn't answer, so he assumed they were on another radio channel.

Since the MiGs didn't pose an immediate threat, he pushed them into a secondary tier of consciousness. Maybe later, after he'd dropped his bombs, they'd become more interesting.

Max Foley came off the target, and one of his flight said they were shooting like hell. Then B. J. Parker called that one of his flight had been hit by flak but was still flying.

The second flight was delivering bombs now, and the flight immediately before Barracuda was nosing up into their pop-up.

When Phuc Yen Air Base was at their immediate right, Lucky plugged in afterburner and began a series of wide S-turns as he climbed, to gain a few seconds of separation.

A covey of three surface-to-air missiles sped through the second dive-bombing flight, flashed, and created their tremendous orange airbursts. The flak was heavy, so thick, it looked impossible to fly through. Smoke from the tremendous number of guns along the river and throughout the sprawling city had created a low layer of haze. Above it was the white blanket of 37mm, and above that the big guns' bursts tracked individual targets. The visual obstacles and the distance made it impossible to tell if a span of the bridge had been knocked down by the first two flights.

Someone called from the third flight and said the target was standing.

Lucky snaked on upward to 12,000 feet.

"Barracuda four, start your roll-in," he ordered. *"And don't wait around for me."*

Joe Walker immediately called, *"Four's in,"* and smoothly nosed over into his dive attack.

Lucky banked, watching and circling ever southward.

Walker released high, as Lucky had directed so they could stay out of *some* of the flak, and his bombs dropped toward the target. They bracketed it, one short and the other long. The concussive waves rippled outward as if huge stones had been dropped into the river.

Lucky's RHAW rattled and squealed, indicating a SAM launch. He looked harder at the CRT, then back into the distance. *Two* different SAM sites had fired missiles at him.

As he approached his desired roll-in point, he turned up onto his left wing, then rolled inverted and pulled the nose down toward the target. He was in a steep dive, more than fifty degrees nose down, aimed directly at the bridge.

He dived upside down for a few more seconds, watching as one covey of SAMs approached, going fast but too high, and missing because the operator hadn't anticipated his maneuver. He saw the second group of three missiles. This time the SAM operator had compensated, and they were turning toward an intercept point with his Thud. He watched and waited, and when they were very close, he jinked hard into them, groaning as he pulled the g's, then reversed back toward the target.

His heading was 060 degrees, and he was flying directly down the length of the bridge. He offset, aiming at the water thirty feet right of the third northern span, settled there.

He looked at his unwinding altimeter: 6,000 feet . . . 5,700 feet . . . 5,500 feet. Pressing the target, tracking it nicely.

Five thousand feet. *Good sight picture.*

He pickled, felt the bombs release, and pulled. Continued pulling until he felt several g's pushing him into the seat. The foggy bubble effect clouded his canopy, but he figured there was little to see out there anyway.

The blasts from the huge bombs swatted and almost upended the bird.

He tried to initiate a right turn, but the aircraft was sinking and hardly flying. Through 2,500 feet and still sinking.

He selected afterburner.

Fifteen hundred feet and sinking!

The burner lit, kicked him, but the altimeter now read 1,000 feet, and he was *still* descending. Slower now, but there was little room left.

His Thud began to recover.

He began his right turn, and looked. It took a moment to see it, for he was very low.

The span was missing.

He whooped and immediately radioed, *"Barracuda lead declares Giraffe!"* which was the mission-success code.

There was no time for discussion. He immediately heard the sounds of an emergency beeper. He guessed that the guy in B. J. Parker's flight had punched out of his bird. Lucky cursed about the loss, as he climbed through 4,000 feet.

The RHAW was suddenly squealing. SAM launch. Eight o'clock. *Damn.* He hated them from the rear where you couldn't see them. He was also flying too slow, and had too little maneuvering energy.

He began a left turn, so he could at least see the damn things to *try* to dodge them, wondering how close . . .

The impact was tremendous, throwing him sideways against the bulkhead. Then another shook him. The aircraft shuddered, shaking like a car rolling on a flat tire. The engine surged, quieted, surged again, and he knew it was about to quit on him.

Thud Ridge was there, not far away at his ten o'clock. He banked. The controls were stiff but responsive.

He tried the radio, but it was dead.

The shuddering continued. He looked out and saw that the metal covering the left wing had been warped upward and was, panel by panel, being blown away. Except for the mangled metal skin and a jumble of wires and landing gear, there was hardly any wing left.

He glanced at his rearview mirror, saw flame licking behind his cockpit and was not surprised. From habit he also checked and noted that his MASTER CAUTION, TAILPIPE OVERHEAT, and FIRE lights were on, and it interested him because he'd never experienced all three like that. The orderly way the other telelites were coming on, one after another as the various systems became inoperative, fascinated him.

He looked back at the ridge. Not far at all now.

The surging continued. The jet might be able to fly far-

ther, but the green, sparsely populated forests of Thud
Ridge were only a couple of miles distant. It made sense to
eject there rather than into the sea of people in the valley on
the other side. He picked an especially rugged, high area of
the ridge and decided that was where he wanted to punch
out. If the airplane continued to respond, he would pull up
before he ejected so the bird would proceed over the ridge
and crash on the opposite side. The farther from his parachute, the better.

He rotated his left ejection-seat handle. The canopy
lifted, then was swept away in the slipstream. He waited for
a flash fire, for those sometimes occurred when you jettisoned the canopy. There was none, but he could feel heat
from the fuselage behind him where the main fuel tank was
burning fiercely.

As he waited to pull the trigger and initiate the ejection
sequence, he had glimpses of old thoughts, but they were
orderly and useful ones. Time had slowed to a crawl, and as
he approached the position over which he'd determined to
eject, he mentally went over his procedures ... what he
would do in the chute and immediately after he hit the
ground.

Half a mile from the eject point. Closer ... closer ...

He pulled the Thud's nose up into a ten-degree climb,
tucked his feet back against the seat, released the control
stick, and grasped the other ejection handle with his right
hand. He counted *one, two,* and pulled the lever.

1735 Local—Command Post, Takhli RTAFB, Thailand

Captain Manny DeVera

The first pilots were showing up at the debriefing tables,
looking drawn and weary.

Manny waited. After shutting down the ATM and pick-
ling off his bombs at the Termite Hill, he'd had to ham-fist
the bird to keep it in the air. But he'd insisted they return
all the way to Takhli rather than land at Udorn or another of
the forward bases.

The crew chief had confirmed the problem with the
ATM, and that made him feel better somehow. He'd wondered if he had deluded himself about it and chickened out.

After drinking a cool beer at the squadron, he and Henry had wandered to the command post to wait for the guys to arrive for debriefing and see how the mission had gone. Lieutenant Colonel Encinos was already there in the debriefing room, speaking in reverent tones to Colonel Lyons. The two were seen together a lot. The guys in the squadron said the Bad Injin was feeling better now that he'd found someone to brownnose. They said he'd tried it with B. J. Parker but that Parker had shunned him, so he'd taken up with Lyons, who acted as if the deferential treatment were his due. Manny saw that Billy Bowes was also waiting in the room, wearing a grim look, so he waved him over to join them.

"What are you doing here, Billy?"

Bowes paused a bit before answering. "Major Lucky flew my bird. Before he took off, he told my crew chief he wanted to see me at debriefing."

Colonel B. J. Parker came in the door. He'd just landed and his face was still creased with the red marks left by his oxygen mask. He glanced about, cast a nod toward Lyons and Encinos, then came over and joined the group from C-Flight.

Parker rocked back onto his heels, as he liked to do, and pursed his lips, silently eyeing DeVera. Then he said, "Good to see you made it back okay, DeVera."

Manny shrugged. "Sorry I bugged out on you, Colonel."

"You can't fly combat with a broken bird. Are they gonna have to replace the ATM?"

"Yes, sir."

The colonel wearily exercised his shoulders and looked at Manny again. "Lucky's not coming back. No one saw him go down, but we heard the beeper. We weren't sure *who* we'd lost until we counted noses. It was a real donnybrook up there."

Manny muttered, "Jesus. The boss?"

Parker motioned toward the message center. "We're waiting for confirmation from the recce people, but Lucky called the success code just before we lost contact. If anyone knocked the bridge down, it was him. It was standing when the rest of us left it."

Manny choked up. "Jesus," he whispered again.

"Where'd he go down, sir?" asked Henry Horn.

"We don't know for sure. Don't even know what got him."

The three members of C-Flight looked mournful.

Lyons and Encinos came over. Encinos looked deferential and Lyons wore his haughty expression.

"I just heard about Major Anderson," said Lyons. Manny swore that a smile lurked beneath his surface, and his disdain for the man intensified.

Encinos's expression grew sad, as if he'd tasted bitter alum. "It's a great loss to the squadron. I don't know how I'll replace Lucky. Perhaps . . ."

Parker looked at him with a grim expression. "Hell of a way for Captain DeVera to make flight commander, isn't it?"

Encinos was puzzled for only a split second, then began to nod vigorously. "Just what I was going to say, Colonel."

Lyons regarded Manny with distaste, obvious in his disagreement.

Encinos was still bobbing. "I've got great faith in Captain DeVera. I was just . . ."

Parker shifted to Billy. "Lucky said he had something to tell me about you after we landed, Captain Bowes. You know what that was about?"

Billy Bowes, already distraught, looked like an added weight was dropped onto his shoulders. "Yes, sir."

"Lucky said it was one of the most heroic things he'd seen since he'd gotten to Takhli."

Bowes's expression turned incredulous. "Sir?"

"Said it happened on the morning mission. Didn't have time to tell me what it was."

Henry Horn was watching closely. He interrupted before Billy could speak. "This morning Captain Bowes attacked a SAM site that threatened our flight, sir. During this afternoon's flight briefing, Major Lucky asked if I'd help write up the medal."

Bowes's mouth gaped.

Joe Walker came into the debriefing room, thin-lipped and angry. Doc Roddenbush pushed a cup of mission whiskey into his hand. Walker bolted it down, then walked over.

"Shit," was all he said.

Major Max Foley came into the room from the command center, and also came over to join them. He looked dog-tired.

"I just got off the phone with Benny Lewis at Seventh Air Force," Max said to Parker.

Manny noted that Colonel Lyons's expression also tightened at mention of Benny's name, and he wondered who the man *did* like.

"What did Benny have for us?" asked Parker.

"Film's not processed yet, but the recce pilots report one span's down on the north side of the bridge."

"Shit hot!" yelled a pilot who'd overheard. Several others picked up the chorus, and the mood in the room was transformed into a happier one.

Manny DeVera's head spun with it all.

Parker and his horse-holders left them then, and Manny, Billy, Joe, and Henry were left to commiserate the loss of their leader.

"Get your debriefing over," Manny finally told Joe Walker, "then we'll go to dinner. Lots of things to talk about, and I'm going to need support from everyone in the flight."

"I'll see you guys over at the club," said Billy Bowes, who'd recovered some of his composure. "I'm going out to talk with my crew chief. That was our bird Major Lucky went down in, and Sergeant Hughes is going to take it hard."

He left.

While Walker was going over the mission with Lieutenant DeWalt and they waited for him, Manny thought of many things. Among them was the fact that a lot of people seemed to have crossed Colonel Lyons the wrong way. He'd noticed reactions to the mention of Major Lucky, Benny Lewis, Billy Bowes, and, of course, his own appointment as C-Flight commander. At dinner he would advise the guys to steer clear of Lyons. Things were screwed up enough without looking for trouble from that source.

When Walker had finished and they were preparing to leave, Manny asked Lieutenant DeWalt where Major Lucky had ejected. DeWalt said they didn't even know *when* he'd gone down, for no one was sure when they'd first heard his emergency beeper.

"He could have gone down about anywhere in pack six," said DeWalt.

On that sour note Captain Manny DeVera joined the others as they filed from the debriefing room.

1800 Local—Phuc Yen PAAFB, DRV

Air Regiment Commandant Quon

Quon had flown two missions that day and begrudgingly admitted to himself that he was getting too old for that sort of thing. Since bailing out of his MiG in late June, he'd grown aches as never before. When he flew now, he used one of the unbearably hot Russian antigravity suits, but even so, the gravity forces were becoming too much for his body to endure.

It was difficult enough, evading the Phantoms and trying to get at the more vulnerable Thunder planes. But now that the auxiliary bases were no longer safe havens, they had to return to Phuc Yen, and since the time Quon had been shot down in his approach pattern, the MiG pilots remained wary until they were safely on the ground.

Periodically observers at Phuc Yen warned of Mee Phantoms and Thunder planes lurking over the nearby Viet Bac mountains, waiting for fuel-starved MiGs to return to their roosts. At such times Quon's MiGs were diverted to bases in southern China, and on two occasions MiGs had been lost because they'd run out of fuel trying to get there.

He decided to fly less often, perhaps only once or twice a week.

Quon entered his office and glared at the mounds of papers in the wooden communications baskets. He had little time for them, for General Tho would arrive in two hours accompanied by a Russian Air Force colonel. He and Quon would entertain the Russian and try to convince him that they should receive additional MiG-21 interceptors, preferably the modern and stable PF big-tails. Tomorrow the Russian would inspect the flying operation, and Quon had encouraged his pilots and mechanics to be most correct.

It was dark outside and Quon was forced to work by lamplight, as an example for the others. Electricity was no longer readily available. Since the last Mee attacks upon the Hanoi electrical distribution yard, only generator power had been available at Phuc Yen. But diesel fuel to power the generators was also scarce, since it was prioritized for the supply convoys. So Quon had directed that electricity be provided only for essential operations.

Since his last trip to Hanoi, the subject had become a bitter one for Quon. Power was off in most of the capital city, and at night the people lived like ancient cave dwellers, their only light from tallow lamps, candles, or small, illegal bonfires in alleys. All petroleums, including lantern fuel, were used for the "critical war effort." But of course there were rows of large generators constantly powering the People's Army headquarters, Ba Dinh Hall, and the important government offices, even when there was no one inside.

He would wager that Colonel Nguyen Wu had lights and even air-conditioning at his office at the Ministry of Internal Affairs. Wu was a conniver, the kind of elusive sneak who could be dropped into a *bo*-bucket of shit and emerge with a flowery smell.

As he lifted the first piece of correspondence from the nearest stack of papers, he frowned, then dropped it back on the stack, and thought.

Today the Americans had destroyed a span of the Long Bien bridge. On two previous attempts they'd not succeeded, and Xuan Nha had predicted they would not begin an all-out campaign against the *other* bridges until they'd succeeded at Long Bien. Long Bien, he'd said, was their test, the one most heavily defended and perhaps most important, for across it came supplies from both China and Haiphong harbor.

If what Colonel Xuan Nha said was true, and the Mee had successfully completed their test, they could expect a series of bombing attacks upon other bridges. He decided to meet with Xuan Nha and Colonel Trung. So far the most successful defenses had proved to be Trung's artillery. How could he get his interceptors to . . .

His adjutant came into his office, interrupting his thoughts. "A radio message was just received from Hanoi for your attention, comrade Commandant."

"Yes?"

"Two Mee aircraft were shot down by artillery at Long Bien." His adjutant referred to a note. "Both have been located. One had the white letters *RU* on the tail, the other *RM*."

Quon held his breath. *RM* was the Pig Squadron initials.

"One of the pilots has been captured, and they expect to have the other by first light in the morning." The adjutant stopped reading from his notes. "Our liaison officer at the command center said you wanted this kind of information."

Quon felt his pulse quicken. Other blue-tail aircraft had been shot down in the past month, but none of those pilots had been on his list. Had his luck changed?

"Contact my driver and have him pick me up immediately," Quon said, standing. "I will go to Hoa Lo Prison."

"But the general will be here in less than two hours, comrade Commandant."

"You are a good adjutant," Quon said with a grin. "Make an appropriate excuse. I will be back before the pig-fornicating Russian colonel finishes his second bottle of wine."

CHAPTER TWENTY

1st Day, 1900 Local—Southern End of Thud Ridge, North Vietnam

Major Lucky Anderson

He'd done precisely what his survival instructors had told him not to do. He'd hit the ground, hastily gathered his few essential items into a panel hacked out of his parachute, and threw the remainder aside. Then he'd determined directions with the survival compass he carried in his vest, tossed his sack over his shoulder, and began to put as much distance as possible between himself and the point where he'd hit the ground. First through the thick growth, pushing his way through brush and vines and stinging bamboo, crawling over fallen tree trunks, moving ever northward. When he'd come to a rude dirt path that wandered in that direction, he'd gotten on it and ran like the wind, not caring that he might be leaving tracks.

His immediate concern was to get the hell out of there. The possibility of being cornered by soldiers closing in on the area was greater, he reasoned, than being successfully tracked down. During the summer monsoon it rained daily, and it was likely that his tracks would soon be washed away.

And there were few men around who could catch Lucky Anderson when it came to long-haul running.

He had reasoned it out before he'd made his second swing in the parachute and was now simply carrying out his plan.

Half an hour after he'd gotten on the road, he burst into a small clearing with a thatch shack at one side, but he gritted his teeth and ran on past that one and then a second dwelling. No one had been outside, but if there had been, he'd have done the same.

He ran until it became too dark to see obstacles on the path clearly, and he feared he might do something dumb like sprain an ankle. Then, chest heaving from the long, difficult effort, he slowed to a walk. At 1900 he stepped off the path into a thicket and sat back against a ledge, rubbing his legs and working his shoulder muscles, and drained the second of his three plastic baby bottles of water.

Remember to refill them the first chance you get, he told himself.

He was traveling northward on the eastern slope of the series of mountains they called Thud Ridge.

How far had he come?

He'd found the road and begun running on it at 1640. He furrowed his brow and computed his normal rate and the times he'd had to slow down for obstacles. Then he added the short distance he'd walked after darkness. He was at least three, and no more than five, miles from where he'd landed.

He tried it again and decided he'd come four miles. Fortunate miles, he told himself, for there'd only been the two houses and no travelers on the path. Several times on the mountainside he'd been able to look out on the flatlands and had seen villages, cities, and farms there. Those he had to avoid at all costs.

The sliver-moon peeked out from the cloud it had been hiding behind, and he eased himself upright. The night must become his time to travel. When he'd been running on the road, he'd thought it fortunate that he was a runner and that he enjoyed hiking and camping. Henceforth that might do him little good. He wouldn't be able to run at night, and his outdoor knowledge was of far different places. In the darkness many things would be different, easy things would become difficult. He had a lot to learn if he was to evade capture for long.

It began to rain, lightly at first, but quickly building in tempo.

He found shelter beneath a tree trunk that grew at an angle. After an hour the rains stopped as quickly as they'd begun, and he continued northward. He was thoroughly soaked and miserable, and his progress was slow as he slipped and slid along the narrow path.

1930 Local — Hoa Lo Prison, Hanoi, DRV

Air Regiment Commandant Quon

The prisoner was strung up in the interrogation room when Quon arrived. When he strode into the room, the senior lieutenant bowed appropriately and spoke in an obsequious voice, trying to remain between Quon and the prisoner, who'd been stripped and was receiving his initial beating.

Quon pushed the prison commandant aside and stared. The prisoner was not *Lokee*. Quon sighed with disappointment.

"His name?"

"*Cah-tah*. He is not on your list, comrade Quon."

"His unit?" Quon's interest began to lag.

"He has not yet told us."

Quon felt discouraged. His intuition had let him down.

He stared at the prisoner for another moment, then looked at the interrogator. "I must have the information very quickly, for I have an important obligation."

He sat and watched, interested in the brute-force technique of the interrogator who asked his questions and manipulated the prisoner into interesting, almost impossible positions using ropes. He asked his questions and used a bright cigarette tip on the man's head and body. He asked his questions, and by the time he'd removed three of the pilot's fingernails, he'd been told everything Quon wanted.

Quon became elated when the interrogator interpreted.

The other aircraft that had been shot down might indeed be *Lokee*'s. The last flight to bomb the bridge had been called *Ba-koo-dah*, and *Lokee* had been one of those. When the prisoner had been shot down and the Thunder planes had circled him and were talking on their radios, they had said a *Ba-koo-dah* had been shot down.

As Quon listened to the interrogator, he smiled. So close now. He walked over to get a closer view of the prisoner, and the senior lieutenant prison commandant grew panicky.

"Please, comrade. If certain party officials find out that prisoners are being killed for no reason . . ."

"For no reason?" Quon turned on the man. "Is the murder of my son no reason?"

The senior lieutenant raised his hand to his mouth, as if guilty of blasphemy. "Of course not, comrade Quon." He tried to explain. "But as each prisoner arrives, a report of his name and condition is forwarded to the"—he dropped his voice to a whisper—"Commissioner of People's Safety." He spoke of the official who controlled the secret police, the man called the Commissioner of Death.

"The Ministry of Internal Affairs shares control of Mee prisoners with the People's Army," said the senior lieutenant. "We are accountable to both."

Quon sighed. The lieutenant was truly fearful, and he supposed there was justification. "If anyone questions, tell them to speak with me, comrade Lieutenant." ·

That didn't seem to mollify the prison commander, so Quon looked at the prisoner and smiled. "Tell them this one arrived in good health and cooperated well."

The Mee pilot's eyes were half-shut, and he was gasping from his awful pain.

"Reward him," said Quon. "Feed him and tell him that because of what he said, I will catch *Lokee* and kill him like the monster he is."

"We cannot tell prisoners such things, comrade Quon."

Quon's enthusiasm was undampened. "Do as you wish. But I *order* you to treat him well, for he has made me very happy."

The return drive was even slower than the trip to Hanoi had been. With the Long Bien bridge impassable they had to find a way to cross the Hong Song, and the night traffic was queued in impossibly long lines at the ferry slips near Hanoi. The driver detoured northwest to Son Tay, more than fifty kilometers out of their way, and used Quon's influence to place them in front of the line. After crossing the Hong, they backtracked eastward to Phuc Yen.

By the time they'd returned to the base, the Russian colonel had long before retired to his room. General Tho was livid with anger that Quon hadn't been there to greet and entertain them. Quon accepted his admonishments, saying he would atone by presenting them with a superb tour the next day. When Tho calmed enough to ask where he'd been, Quon told him.

General Tho knew about Quon's mission of vengeance and thoroughly disapproved.

"Forget this silliness, and about this man you call *Lokee.* Your son was killed in battle and died heroically. A warrior cannot ask for more. *You* should not ask for more."

"I may be very close," said Quon. "Either *Lokee* or his wingman was shot down and is hiding in the southern Viet Bac. He may be no more than a few thousand meters from where we stand."

"Forget it, I tell you," said Tho.

"I radioed intelligence in Hanoi and told them to find if it is truly *Lokee,* and to tell the search team to capture the pilot alive."

Tho shook his head wearily.

Quon stared at his superior officer evenly. "This thing I must do."

Tho looked evenly at his old comrade. "I hope *this thing* does not destroy you."

1950 Local—Guest Trailer 9A, Takhli RTAFB, Thailand

GS-15 *Linda Lopes*

She was not a maudlin person, for she'd learned at an early age that it was better to reason her way through bad news than spend her time wringing her hands. She was very good in emergencies, her bosses had always told her, and this one qualified. The guy she'd loved for eight tough years was in deep trouble.

Colonel B. J. Parker had been considerate enough to come and tell her about it. They were not at all sure where he'd gone down, he said, because everyone else had been rejoining south of the target. They thought he *might* have gone down somewhere near the northern side of the city of Hanoi, near a bridge he'd tried to bomb. No, Parker had corrected himself. The bridge he *had* bombed, and had destroyed a span of. It had still been standing when the rest of them had left the area, but they'd received a jubilant call from Tan Son Nhut Air Base saying the reconnaissance film showed a span of the bridge was definitely down.

Lucky's had been the only bombs to hit.

"If he was fortunate," Parker had told her, "he's been captured by North Vietnamese soldiers." He'd explained that was better than being captured by civilians.

So Linda had returned to her trailer to hope and pray that Lucky had been captured by soldiers and not by civilians enraged because they'd been attacked by American bombs.

Sometimes the North Vietnamese released names of the pilots they had captured. She said another prayer that his would be on the next list. Then Linda Lopes, who'd heard she was called the Ice Maiden by some, and a cold bitch by others, began to hold herself and rock, and to sob uncontrollably.

2015 Local—Plans & Programs, HQ Seventh Air Force

Major Benny Lewis

General Moss had told them to call him at his quarters as soon as the results of the strike were in and interpreted. Ten minutes earlier Pearly had made that call, and now Moss was on his way. They waited in his office.

The two RF-4C recce birds that had crossed over the northern side of Hanoi at 1636 local hours, immediately after the strike, had returned directly to Tan Son Nhut. At 1812 local time they'd landed, and their film had been offloaded and processed in the Recce Tech, the best-equipped and most efficient photo-intelligence facility in the world.

Photo interpreters had analyzed the poststrike film negatives, frame by frame, as they emerged from the autodeveloping system. Within fifteen minutes the initial estimates had been made. Then the best and most revealing frames were selected, some forty-seven of them for this particular job, and a thorough bomb damage assessment had been made. That process included enlarging selected frames and poring over each for signs of target and collateral damage, damage to defenses, and other information of intelligence value.

It was said that a good photo interpreter could tell the size and weight of a human from a single frame, from two frames he could tell his age and unit, and from three frames his IQ and mother's maiden name. The PIs at Tan Son Nhut were very good and, using their magnifying glasses and interpretive skills, had formed a comprehensive picture of what had taken place in the hour and nine minutes between the pre- and poststrike recce sorties. This they wrote onto summary sheets that accompanied the seventeen photos they selected.

Lieutenant Colonel Pearly Gates carried a manila folder.

A total of forty-eight aircraft sorties involving nine different types and models of aircraft had participated in the attack. Twelve MiGs had threatened and been driven away, and seventeen more had been deployed into the Chinese buffer zone during the attack. Nine SAM and sixty-four artillery batteries had engaged the aircraft. Some 145,000 gallons of petroleum, 127,000 pounds of bombs and munitions, 21 surface-to-air missiles, and 9,900 artillery rounds had been expended. One hundred and one Americans had been airborne to support or participate in the strike, and 1,348 North Vietnamese had actively defended the bridge. One North Vietnamese MiG-17 pilot, seventy-three artillerymen, and four civilians had been killed or wounded, and two American pilots were missing in action. The results of that grand effort were summarized in the twenty-three pages of photos and summary sheets contained in the folder.

Pearly pushed his glasses back on his nose, a nervous habit Benny had noticed in the man. "Forgot to tell you. My admin sergeant said you got a call from Nellis while we were in the control center."

"Anything important?" Benny's mind was elsewhere.

"She said your boss is *some* pissed off. I guess the hospital commander's raising hell about your pulling the wool over his eyes when he signed your waiver to travel."

"Oh, shit," said Benny. For the past days he'd been preoccupied with the air strike, and he'd completely forgotten.

"Your boss says for you to get your ass back there pronto if not sooner, because the hospital commander's about to press charges."

"You got any connections, Pearly, so I can get an early flight?"

"I'll get you out on the med-evac bird like the general wanted."

"You'd better make it ASAP."

"We've got med-evacs going both to Travis and San Antonio."

"Make it Travis." He wondered if he should take time to drop in on Julie and see how she was faring.

"I'll call your colonel in a couple hours when it's morning there. Tell him General Moss is putting you in for a gong to your Bronze Star for your effort here, that he's also writing a personal commendation to go into your records."

"Think Moss'll do it?"

"Sure. Moss thinks a lot of his mafia."

"You're part of the group. He appreciates having someone on his staff here who'll tell it to him the way it was."

"Yeah, but he's got a special feeling for you guys from Nellis."

The general hurried into the office, wearing a polo shirt, white shorts, tennis shoes, and a bronze tan. He waved them into his inner office, then sprawled behind his massive desk.

"I'm supposed to play a set of tennis with the fucking honorable congressman from Massachusetts. I dislike that slimy politician more every time I meet him, and I'm looking forward to whipping his ass."

Pearly started to pull the summary from the folder, but Moss raised his hands.

"Did they knock it down?"

"Yes, sir. One span's down and two more are damaged."

Moss grinned at Benny. "Told you guys the three-thousand-pounders would do the trick."

He noticed Lewis's grave look.

"Losses?"

"Two of them, sir," said Pearly Gates.

"That's unfortunate. Who knocked it down?"

Benny spoke up. "From all we can gather, it was one of Lucky Anderson's bombs."

Moss chuckled. "So Lucky came through again."

"He's down, General."

Moss immediately sobered and stared. At Nellis, Lucky

had been his handpicked mafia leader. He had genuine affection for him.

"Lucky sent the rest of them ahead so he'd be last on the target," said Benny. "A couple minutes later he called the success code, then no one heard anything from him again."

"Did they hear an emergency beeper?" asked Moss.

"Yes, sir," said Pearly. "Colonel Parker was circling a pilot who went down about twenty miles south of the target when he heard it. He couldn't take the force back for him, and we don't know where he went down. The Wild Weasels said two sets of SAMs were fired from Hanoi, but they didn't have him in sight."

"That's a hell of a loss for the Air Force. A *hell* of a loss." Moss looked at the ceiling and stared there. "That's an expensive bridge."

"Yes, sir, it is," said Lewis.

Moss blinked and lowered his gaze. "I had a gut feeling we'd knock it down. As soon as we got the initial success code, I called Admiral Ryder and told him we'd done it."

Ryder was USCINCPAC, the admiral in charge of Pacific-theater operations.

"He said to get on with the program and knock down the rest of the damned bridges, that he'd take care of the authorization." He pinned his look on Pearly Gates. "Go ahead and release the proper ATO."

The air tasking order would be transmitted to the units to spell our their targets.

"Yes, sir," said Pearly Gates.

"What's on the menu for tomorrow?"

"Both Thud bases will hit the bridge at the Canales des Rapides in the morning. The Navy'll strike two bridges near Haiphong tomorrow night."

Moss drew a deep breath, then slowly released it. He regarded Lewis. "Thanks for coming over, Benny. You've been a great help. Guess you'll be going back now."

"Tomorrow, sir."

"Take better care of that back."

"Will do, General."

"They treating you right at Nellis?"

"Yes, sir. I've got a good job."

"I told the general there he was getting a good man last time I spoke to him."

"Thank you, sir."

"Anything I can help you with?"

Benny immediately thought of Mal Stewart's official status.

"Well?"

His face burned again with the shame Colonel Lyons had put him through at Takhli. "No, sir," he finally said.

"You guys never delivered on your six-packs. Trying to welsh on a bet?"

"I'll have one sent to your quarters tomorrow before I leave."

Moss nodded firmly. "I'll collect the other from Lucky when he gets back."

2200 Local—Command Post, Takhli RTAFB, Thailand

The new air tasking order had arrived thirty minutes earlier, and the frag order outlining Takhli's role had been broken out for the next morning's mission. They were to return to Hanoi with 3,000-pound bombs, this time to attack the five-span bridge over the Canales des Rapides, just four miles north of the Doumer bridge.

The rail line that ran out of Hanoi went over the Doumer bridge, then split, east toward Haiphong and north over the Canales des Rapides toward China. Cutting the bridge would stop the rail traffic from China before it reached the big rail yard at Gia Lam. There was to be no letup now that they'd knocked down the first bridge. The campaign to destroy the enemy's key bridges and shut down their rail and road traffic had been turned on.

Captain Manny DeVera

Max Foley said the headquarters planners thought if they could knock down the big, tough Doumer bridge, the rest would be easier. But as he studied the target, he said he was not at all sure they were right.

"The Doumer bridge is big," agreed Manny, "and look how much trouble we had hitting the damn thing. The Canales bridge is a lot smaller, and it'll be that much harder to hit."

Max grinned. "Think we ought to try Bullpups again?"

"Fuck you, Major."

"Just asking," said Max.

Max knew and liked Lucky Anderson as well as anyone, had worked for him at Nellis, and had known him even before that. It was the first time he'd shown anything but a grimace since the afternoon mission had landed.

"I talked to Benny Lewis on the phone," said Max. "He's returning to the States in the morning."

"Land of the big BX," said Manny. He looked at Max. "Lyons makes a sour look every time Lewis's name is mentioned. Something happen between those two?"

"Something, but I don't know what. Benny came out of his office all pissed off last week, but he wouldn't tell me what it was about."

Manny fished. "What do *you* think of Lyons?"

"Same as everyone else, I guess. No one except the Bad Injin and B. J. Parker likes the egotistical bastard. Lucky Anderson had his number and Lyons pussyfooted around him. But with Lucky out of the picture, you watch your ass. I *know* he doesn't like you."

"B.J. likes him?" Manny asked. B. J. Parker and Max Foley were friends.

"Lyons talks about all the influence his family has in Washington and how he knows a lot of politicians, and B.J.'s impressed. He would not at all mind making brigadier general."

"Yeah. B.J.'s ambitious."

"Why're you asking about Lyons? Jealous because he's chasing your girl?"

Lyons had been seen with Jackie Bell a lot since Manny dropped out of the game.

"She's a big girl," said DeVera. "Anyway, it's over between us."

Manny knew he couldn't complain. His emotions had been on a roller-coaster ride during the past couple of months. It would have been unreasonable to expect her to act like a nun, waiting for him to come to his senses. Maybe, he thought, when he got his act together regarding C-Flight, he'd give her a call and see if she was still interested.

But first Manny DeVera still had things to prove to himself. As determined as he was, and though he was able to put things into better perspective since Lucky's talk, he did not at all look forward to going back to pack six.

Which he would do first thing in the morning when he would lead C-Flight into combat and try to knock down the bridge over the Canales des Rapides.

BOOK III

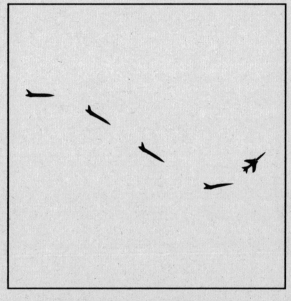

SAM Evasion Maneuver

Saigon, Republic of Vietnam

Peacemaker now had an apartment downtown. Not anything sumptuous like the newsman's, of course, but not shabby either. A quiet black-market air conditioner kept it cool, and it was nicely furnished. The newsman had suggested it. The rent payments were handled for him, as were payments for the twice-weekly maid service, the stocking of the bar, and the superb pot stash.

When he'd hesitated because of the potential for security problems—the west-side location was adjacent to an off-limits area filled with known Viet Cong sympathizers—the newsman said to forget his worries, he was well protected. And when Peacemaker had mouthed the logical question, the newsman had laughed and said don't even ask.

There was also a steady but discreet flow of women, some of whom he recognized as dancers from the Blue Pheasant, to handle his infrequent sexual stirrings and share a mind-blowing pipeful of Asian hemp.

He waited impatiently for the newsman's friend with another list of targets, this one so long he'd been forced to mimeograph two pages of data. It gave the coordinates of all bridges that had been approved for attack during the CROSSFIRE ZULU campaign.

The back door opened and the newsman's friend appeared, silently and unannounced. He was one of the Asian businessmen he'd first met more than two months earlier in the Blue Pheasant bar. Tonight he wore rumpled slacks and a flowered shirt. Peacemaker had learned that although he drove one of the city's thousands of taxicabs, he was really much more.

Peacemaker pulled the two sheets from his shirt pocket and handed them over. The cab driver smiled and bobbed his head as if eternally grateful.

The cab driver asked if he wished for companionship. Doreece was waiting in his taxi.

Sure, he said. It had been a long, tough day at the office, staying out of the officers' way as they'd gathered the results of the first successful strike on the Doumer bridge.

Then the cab driver had a strange request. He asked the names of the pilots who'd been shot down on the afternoon air attack. Peacemaker didn't like the sound of that one. It made what he was doing ... too personal?

He said he didn't know.

It was important, the cab driver said insistently. It was the request of the newsman. Background for a story.

Increasingly Peacemaker had come to realize it was not only the newsman who wanted his information, but the Viet Cong as well. The fact had bothered him at first, but then he'd rationalized it by remembering that this was an unjust war, one his country should not be engaged in. Back in the States, people who held similar beliefs to his were calling the pilots who bombed the North Vietnamese war criminals and baby killers.

But still, he'd never given them a pilot's name before.

He knew only one of the two names, and that only because his stupid colonel and the visiting major from the States had lamented about how he'd been a friend to them both.

He hesitated too long, making it apparent he knew something. Again the cab driver insisted, this time not looking friendly at all. Peacemaker's heart raced as he tried to think of the possible consequences of giving an answer.

The cab driver's eyes narrowed and his look grew mean.

Peacemaker finally huffed a sigh and said maybe one of them was a major named Lucky Anderson. He remembered hearing something like that, he said.

The cab driver resumed his bobbing, happy demeanor as he went to the back door.

The girl named Doreece would be right in, he said as he left.

CHAPTER
TWENTY-ONE

Saturday, August 12th, 0650 Local—Route Pack Six, North Vietnam

Captain Manny DeVera

The morning sun seemed brighter than usual, a relentless orange orb directly before them, its glare making him uncomfortable and creating pain in his forehead.

They were Wasp flight and were in the middle of the twelve-ship gaggle, each of them loaded with a 3,000-pounder on each wing and a centerline fuel tank. Thus far the flight had been uneventful; no SAM launches and only a single, distant MiG sighting.

Two minutes until time over target.

The Wild Weasels announced there were numerous clouds in the target area, but that the area immediately surrounding the bridge was clear. It became a discretionary call, up to the mission commander whether to proceed or turn back.

Major Max Foley chose to continue. *"Keep a good eye out for SAMs and MiGs,"* he called, *"and don't press the target."*

Pressing a target meant releasing lower than the minimum altitude, which Max had briefed as 7,500 feet. That would keep them above most of the 37mm barrage fire, the intense and deadly blanket of popcorn flak the gomers put up over high-value targets.

The strike force approached Thud Ridge at its midpoint, then turned to fly down its eastern side, directly toward the bridge. The mountains in the southern half of the ridge were cloaked by low clouds. Only the taller ones peeked up through the cover.

One minute and thirty seconds to go.

Thus far Manny had felt apprehension, but only enough to make his blood pump faster. He'd been using Lucky's technique, keeping his mind filled with *what ifs*, going over the target's peculiarities and how they would destroy it. It was the headache from the sunlight that plagued him.

The Canales des Rapides bridge was a sturdy five-span structure a quarter of the size of the one they'd attacked the previous day. Guns had been massed in all directions around the thing. It was so close to the Doumer bridge that they'd be in the coverage of the same six SAM sites.

One minute from the target.

He'd decided to go for the very center of the bridge. Which, if his geometric eye and bombing were good enough, would take down the middle span.

Max Foley, flying in front of the gaggle by a few seconds, called he was at the checkpoint, which meant he was preparing to roll in on the guns with his cluster bomblets. On that cue the flights within the gaggle began to climb and separate slightly from one another. They would dive-bomb the bridge with minimum separation between aircraft and again try to saturate the enemy gunners. One or two aircraft might not be difficult targets for the AAA, but six or eight should prove challenging.

Suddenly Manny's RHAW lit up with strobes and lights like a pinball machine gone berserk.

"Wasp three has SAM activity," announced Billy Bowes.

Manny felt his skin begin to crawl. The headache grew more persistent.

Thirty seconds.

"Wasp three, call if you get a good missile-launch indication," Manny advised. His voice was steady enough, even if he did feel the familiar knot of fear growing in his stomach.

"Roger, Wasp lead," Billy answered.

Max Foley announced his flight was rolling in at the same

time the Weasel flight lead said he was firing a Shrike radar-homing missile.

Large clouds were visible up ahead.

Manny's heart began to race faster. *Fucking clouds,* he thought.

As they approached closer, the first strike flight announced they could see the target and immediately winged over and disappeared from view.

Wasp flight was next.

Manny began to look for the target. A wide hole appeared in the clouds. Hanoi in the distance . . . he ran his eyes back past the Doumer bridge and . . . the target appeared tiny down below.

Too close.

"Wasp flight is in the dive," he announced immediately, and at the same time rolled inverted and tucked in, then rolled back upright. The bird's nose was pointed toward the bridge.

Flak began to blossom about him. The lump grew and raised from his gut to his throat. The headache was blinding in its intensity.

Almost sixty degrees dive angle. Too damned steep.

Manny jinked out to his left, downriver, and after a few seconds came back around hard.

He'd lost the target! *Where was the fucking bridge?*

"Say your position, Wasp lead," came Henry's voice.

"I got him east of the target, two," radioed Billy Bowes. *"Wasp three and four are also jinking out wide."*

A dark burst rattled his Thud mightily, and Manny caught his breath in a short whimper. His head threatened to explode!

He looked harder. His attention was drawn by bombs erupting at his ten o'clock, and he saw the bridge. Manny turned sharply toward it, and at the same time noted he was diving through 7,000 feet, already below their minimum release altitude.

Cursing, he steadied and pickled his bombs off, knowing they'd be shitty but not daring to press lower. He began his pullout and a right turn toward the rejoin point.

When the gaggle had re-formed and they were heading back westward, Max Foley queried the flights and received negative responses.

No one's bombs had hit the target, but Manny DeVera's headache was beginning to disappear.

1040 Local—Briefing Theater, Command Post, Takhli RTAFB

Captain Billy Bowes

Following the intell debriefing, Major Max Foley called everyone into the briefing theater. When asked why, he shrugged as if he weren't sure.

"While we're waiting," said Foley, "I want to apologize to everyone here. The weather was shitty and I pressed it."

"Hell," said Pudge Holden, the Wild Weasel flight leader for the mission. "I should've called it better. We had a couple of SAM sites cornered right then, and I wasn't too sharp with my weather report. Sorry about that, Max."

"Not much good can be said about what we accomplished up there today, except most of the bombs were so bad, I doubt the gomers knew which target we were after."

Laughter. The pilots liked Max Foley.

"And we didn't lose anyone," added Manny DeVera.

"Yeah," said Max, "that's *really* the good part, especially with all the clouds."

"How long we going to have to wait?" grumbled a major from the 357th squadron. "I've got better things to do than just sit here."

Max Foley shrugged. "I was told to assemble you guys in here. I got better things to do myself."

Billy sipped on his Coke and waited, as did the other fighter jocks in the room. By the time twenty minutes had passed, the pilots had grown restless and began cracking jokes about everything from bomber pilots to Ho Chi Minh's cathouse at Yen Bai . . . and the Mickey Mouse leadership that had them waiting around like grade-school kids.

Colonel Tom Lyons slipped quietly into the room and called Major Foley over to confer. A couple of times Billy saw Foley give grim shakes of his head. Finally Lyons leaned back against the wall at the rear of the room while Foley retook the podium.

It was not Max's way to mince words.

"*Supposedly* someone's bombs went flying half the way to Hanoi and hit in a residential area."

The room grew quieter. Then someone said, "Gee, I sure hope we didn't *hurt* anyone. They might think there's a war going on or something."

"A big fire was *supposedly* started in some houses there, and some pinko correspondent was on the phone to somebody tout suite, because they started receiving phone calls back here before we landed."

Each time Max emphasized the word "supposedly," Lyons glared.

Several groans and *fuck-ems* sounded from the pilots.

Colonel Lyons spoke from the back of the room. "Don't take it lightly, gentlemen. General Roman has asked that anyone who bombs a restricted target be reported immediately."

Someone muttered, "Fuck him too," and Lyons's head whipped around to identify the culprit. He scribbled something on a pad.

Major Foley held up his hands to quiet the increasing noise level. "So how many of you guys think it could have been your bombs that went long?"

Half a dozen hands went up, including Manny DeVera's and Henry Horn's.

Billy's bombs had missed the target, but they'd been close. He didn't raise his hand.

When he saw that Lyons was taking notes, he nudged DeVera. "I saw yours hit," he said. "They went off in the water. You didn't hit any fucking houses, Manny."

Manny brightened. "You sure?"

"You got yourself into a shitty position, but you made a good correction. You didn't do bad, considering you were offset like that."

Manny pulled down his hand, but Lyons had completed his note taking.

1530 Local—C-Flight Office, 354th TFS

Lieutenant Colonel John Encinos

The 354th squadron's operations officer was a friend of Lucky Anderson's, and since they liked to assign an officer of equal or higher rank as summary courts officer, he'd volunteered for the job. As such he would inventory Anderson's personal belongings and place them in cartons to be shipped to Lucky's next of kin, his parents living in Ohio. The ops officer had finished with the trailer and was ready to start on Lucky's office.

Encinos worked his master key in the lock. "Soon as I heard he'd been shot down, I locked his office so no one would take anything." He said it as if proud of his achievement.

"I won't be long," said the ops officer. "Lucky traveled light."

Encinos led the way inside, looking about the room and frowning unhappily at the stack of paper in the in-basket. He suspected that many of his memos went unread. His attention was drawn to the bottom drawer of the desk, which was still ajar as if Lucky had put something inside and left in a hurry. Visible in the drawer was a lone steno pad, which Encinos picked up.

Probably the book Lucky said he kept on his pilots, because on the outside he'd printed in bold marker:

KEEP OUT!

PRIVATE PROPERTY

MAJ PAUL ANDERSON

Encinos was intrigued. He turned and saw that the operations officer was busy filling in the heading of an inventory form, so he hurriedly leafed through the pad. On each page a different date was printed at the top, and below were notes about the men in Anderson's flight.

Things like:

23 APR 67

CPT T.: WANTS R&R TO HICKAM IN JUL TO VISIT FAMLY/CANT FORGET TO ARANGE IT!

CPT D.: AGRESIVE & LERNING.

LT W.: SMOOTH AS GLAS THIS MSN. SUPER JOINUP. GOOD A/R.

LT B.: SUPERB HANDS & GOOD EYES; READDY FOR MORE.

CPT T.: COL B.J. SAYS OK HE WILL PUT TURK ON OFFICIAL ORDERS AS CLASSIFIED COURIER (OR SOMTHING). TOLD T. & HE IS HAPPY & ANXOUS TO SEE HIS WIFE & DAUTERS.

Encinos read a few more entries and was about to put it down when he saw:

29 JUN 67

LT H.: FINISHED HENRYS EVALUATION REPORT— 9/4

CPT B.: UNAUTH TARGET. LEAD IN LOWWER ROUTE PACKS UNTILL HE PROOVES TRUST—

. . . Jesus!

He slapped the pad closed, his mind churning with possibilities. Tom Lyons had said he was working hard to find who was making the wing look bad by bombing unauthorized targets. Here it was!

Should he take it directly to Colonel Parker?

No. Parker would just chew his ass for looking in a private notebook. Especially one that was properly marked, as Lucky Anderson's was.

They were periodically briefed that the only documents not officially reviewable were those privately purchased notebooks that had been marked as Lucky Anderson's was. Those documents were not to be scrutinized by superior officers or anyone else.

He should immediately put the steno pad back where he'd found it.

"Find something, sir?" asked the ops officer.

Encinos hid the pad at his side and snapped, "Go ahead and finish with your duties."

The major looked at him for a quiet moment, then shrugged and began to go through the desk, inventorying as he went.

Encinos needed advice. He walked from the room, his

features drawn into a frown. He told the lieutenant manning the duty desk that if he was needed, he'd be at Colonel Lyons's office.

1810 Local—Plans & Programs, HQ Seventh AF, Tan Son Nhut Air Base, Saigon, RVN

Lieutenant Colonel Pearly Gates

Just after noon Master Sergeant Turner, NCOIC of the Documentation section, had said he wanted to speak with Pearly at the end of the day, which was rather strange because Pearly kept his door open at all times to the people in his branch. But he'd honored the request, feeling the sergeant likely had his reasons. Probably, he figured, he wanted more manpower to help with the ever-growing work load.

The sergeant ran a tight ship. Pearly liked the way he operated, making damned sure Pearly was advised of everything that went on in the important matters, and not trying to baffle him with bullshit on the unimportant ones.

When he closed the door behind himself, Turner did not hesitate. "Remember when you told us to watch for anything that looked funny, because there might be a security leak?"

Pearly grew tight-lipped. *Christ, not in his own group!*

"Well, something's funny, and I don't mean ha-ha, Colonel."

"Go on."

"When you told me to look closer, I started keeping a log of when the guys worked late and when they signed off the safes and the vault and all, and keeping track of the numbers on the mimeograph machine. I came up with seven times that things were run off on one of the copiers after hours and haven't been logged. Those machines are supposed to be used only for classified material."

Pearly pulled off his glasses and furiously polished them, listening intently.

"Sometimes it's one and two pages. Sometimes more. So next I decided to find out who could have been doing it. I came up with two possibilities, Colonel, because those were the guys working late those nights."

Pearly nodded, impressed with his efficiency.

"Sergeant Slye and Airman O'Neil."

Pearly frowned. Both O'Neil and Slye were good men. Slye liked to go downtown a bit too much for Turner's liking, and he'd kept the peace symbol on his desk after Turner had suggested he remove it, but he did his job well. And aside from Sergeant Turner himself, Airman First Class O'Neil was the steadiest man in Documentation.

"I didn't want to get too excited about it until I knew more. I mean, I didn't want to bring it to you if someone was just doing something harmless. Hell, sometimes we all cheat a little bit and use the machines for personal use. Like sometimes I write one letter and copy it so I can send it out to several friends and relatives. So I felt that first I should find out what was being copied."

Pearly pulled on the glasses and blinked as the room came into focus. He wished he didn't have to listen.

"There's a second-image capability on both of the copiers in the vault, where duplicate copies are made and stored in a secure bin underneath. Normally we keep that function turned off because it's a pain to work with and just creates that much more classified waste. You've got to get into the bin to turn it on and off and to take out the extra copies, and if the bin gets full, it'll make the machine jam."

"I forgot we even had that capability."

"I don't think either Slye or O'Neil even know about it. Anyway, the last few nights before I left, I've been switching them both on and then checking in the morning what was in the bins against what was written down on the copier logs."

Pearly nodded, hoping . . .

"Mind if I smoke, sir?"

"Go ahead." Pearly's voice came out strained.

Turner lit up a cigarette and pondered. "When I checked this morning, I got a surprise."

"What did you find?"

"Our summary of next week's air tasking order. There was no mention on the copier log, but there it was."

"Jesus! The entire summary?"

"Just the first two pages. Dates, times, and target coordinates, Colonel."

Pearly closed his eyes and his head sank into his hands.

"Last night two guys worked late. Sergeant Slye and Airman O'Neil again. Unless someone else came in while they were working, one of them ran it off on the machine."

Pearly raised his head. "And you're sure that neither had good reason to copy it?"

"Positive. Neither has anything to do with targeting documents. O'Neil files changes and amendments to the OPlans, and Slye keeps track of the Top Secret documents."

"Jesus," Pearly said again, for both positions gave the men access to highly classified documents.

"You want me to go to the OSI with it, sir?"

Pearly thought, then shook his head. "Not yet. I'll take it from here, Sergeant."

Master Sergeant Turner looked relieved. "Anything else I can do to help?"

Pearly gave him a wan smile. "Tell me none of this happened. That'll help."

"I don't like it either, sir. I hope to hell it's something harmless."

"You've done a good job, finding out what you have."

"Both of those men work for me, and I feel like I've let you down by letting it happen, Colonel. I should've been more alert."

Pearly pressed his glasses back firmly into place, thinking.

"It won't happen again, I can assure you of that. I plan on being the last one out of the office from now on, and I won't let another ATO summary out of my sight."

"Where do you keep them?"

"Safe number two in the vault, sir. Second drawer."

Pearly nodded, still thinking. Finally he said, "Well, we're going to play a little game before I turn this thing over to the spooks, Sarge."

Turner raised an eyebrow.

"I want you to type up a fake amendment to the tasking order, changing the targets, and put it into the file. Right in front where it can't be missed."

Turner nodded.

"Use these target coordinates." Pearly studied a wall map and determined the coordinates for first Phuc Yen and then Kien An air bases in North Vietnam, which he wrote down for Turner. Next he briefed the sergeant on further security precautions they'd take. When Turner left to type up the fake air tasking order amendment, the look on Pearly's face remained drawn.

He'd keep the real ATO summaries in his own safe, to which only he had the combination. If the fake target coordinates were being provided to the enemy, there should be a hasty buildup of defenses around Phuc Yen and Kien An.

If . . .

He thought of the two men Turner had mentioned and found it hard to believe that either would do anything detrimental to their country like turn secrets over to an enemy.

Sergeant Slye was a gangling farm boy from Arkansas who'd wanted to cross-train into a flight-crew job, but couldn't qualify because he couldn't swim. Since his rejection he'd become dejected and somewhat of an eight ball, but Pearly couldn't imagine his being conniving enough to steal secrets. He was just too naive and open.

Airman First Class O'Neil was a hard worker, a Bostonian who'd told Pearly he wanted to return to school and finish his degree as soon he got out of the Air Force. Twice he'd saved his section from security write-ups by finding classified documents that others had left out.

It had to be someone else. Perhaps it was just a mistake. *God*, but he hoped it was a mistake.

But if the North Vietnamese started bringing in guns and SAMs and positioning them around their MiG bases at Phuc Yen and Kien An . . .

1945 Local—Officers' Club Dining Room

Captain Billy Bowes

DeVera had asked him to join him for dinner. He seemed unhappy, not only about missing the target that morning, but about things in general. It was the first time Manny had confided his troubles, and Billy didn't feel good about being dumped on with all those woes. But he listened because Manny was a friend and because they were together in C-Flight. Lucky Anderson had built that into them, that they had to be able to rely upon and lean on one another. They missed his unique leadership style, glaring and gruff when they screwed up the essentials, giving encouragement when they needed it, understanding their faults on the ground but pressing for perfection in the air. "Like Major Lucky said . . . ," was uttered often within the group.

"Remember when Major Lucky said he didn't like surprises?" Manny said. "Well, I've sure as hell learned what he meant."

"He liked things to go smoothly," agreed Billy.

"Standard mission was what he called the good ones," said Manny. "Meaning everything's covered in the flight briefing, and we perform according to the plan."

Billy nodded.

"Well, we didn't do that today," said DeVera with a discouraged look.

"Don't beat on yourself," said Billy. "There's no way to dive-bomb a target when the weather's shitty and you can hardly see the thing. Like Major Foley said, it was a bad call even to try it. We shouldn't have pressed the weather."

Manny was looking at him evenly, sort of hanging on to his words as if he needed them, which made Billy feel even more uneasy.

Not far from them, seated at the colonels' reserved table, were Colonel Lyons and the blond Peace Corps administrator. Billy tried to remember her name . . . Jackie something? Lyons was acting especially possessive, which was likely for Manny's benefit. DeVera refused to look in their direction, like they weren't there.

"You're assistant flight commander now, Billy," Manny was saying, "and I'm going to need all the help you can provide."

"We'll all help. You know that."

"But you in particular, Billy."

Which made him feel uncomfortable again.

"How're you with paperwork?" asked DeVera.

"I hate the shit. We were swamped with it in Air Training Command, and I hoped it would be better once I got here. Henry Horn is the only one of the bunch who can write well."

"Henry's got a lot more missions than the rest of us. He's at seventy-six now. Another few weeks and he'll be gone. You're the one I'm gonna have to lean on for help."

There was no way out of it. He paused before he said, "I'll help you get it done. But I gotta tell you, my spelling's not much better than Major Lucky's."

DeVera forced a grin. Lucky was an atrocious wordsmith, and his spelling was worse.

Billy stared down at his half-eaten hamburger. "Before you place too much trust, Manny, there's something else you should know."

DeVera waited.

"A couple months ago I bombed a target I shouldn't have."

"The warehouses?"

Billy lifted his vision and pinned him. "You knew?"

"All of us knew. Henry, Joe Walker, Turk, all of us."

Some secret, thought Billy. "I also hit what I thought was a weapons area near the docks at Thanh Hoa harbor."

"I only knew about the warehouse. You're too good to miss that badly on a clear day."

Billy felt defensive. "I can have a bad day with the best of 'em."

"I haven't seen many. Major Lucky said you were the steadiest he'd ever seen under fire. None of us gave a shit about your private war, so long as no one else got the blame. Anyway, Henry told us you'd stopped it."

Billy furrowed his brow, but he knew he had to say the words. "That last day, before Major Lucky was shot down . . . ?"

"Yeah?"

"He was all pissed off because I bombed a SAM site that may have been in the buffer zone. He said I was grounded, and I think he was about to turn me in."

"He told the rest of us he was putting you in for a medal for it. He even asked Henry to help write it up, because he was along on the mission. He said he'd asked that you meet us when we landed, so Henry could get with you for the write-up."

Billy Bowes thought about that. "I thought Henry was just covering for me in front of the colonel."

"Henry thinks you're a shit-hot hero, and so does Smitty. Hell, *especially* Smitty. It was his ass you saved."

Billy rubbed at his jaw. "Well, that does change things."

"I told Henry to go ahead and submit the write-up. I think we can justify a Silver Star."

"Forget the medal," Billy said. "Just knowing everything's okay is good enough."

Manny DeVera paused, and when he spoke, his voice

was very quiet. "You're cool as hell under fire, Billy. I'm not. In fact, there's something *you* should know about *me*."

Billy Bowes sat back and observed Manny for a long moment, and somehow he knew that Manny DeVera was about to tell him he was a coward. He didn't believe it. Like the others in C-Flight, he knew Manny had a confidence problem, but he was no coward.

Joe Walker had told him he thought it was worse for Manny than it would be with someone else, because he'd always been so macho confident and pushed himself so hard. Joe thought he was probably just having the same fears as most rational men but refused to accept it. Billy wasn't prepared to deal with anything as heavy as Manny was about to lay on him. There were too many crosses of his own to bear.

He shook his head and said in a low voice, "Manny, I don't want to hear what you're trying to tell me."

DeVera released a pent-up breath, looking relieved. "You're right. Some things are best left unsaid."

"It's not that . . ."

Smitty approached the table with a grin on his cherub's face.

"The other guys and I are in the stag bar," he said. "You two want to join us?"

"Sure," said Billy, happy to escape the conversation.

Manny shook his head. "You guys go on. I'm going over to the squadron and do some catching up. The Bad Injin's turning out memos faster than I can file them."

Colonel Lyons led Jackie Bell toward the door. She was laughing in a low voice, but she paused to cast a bold glance at their table. Manny pretended not to notice.

1800 Local—San Francisco, California

Julie Stewart

When she turned off the water, she heard the telephone ringing in the next room. As she hurried out of the shower, she made the mistake of glancing at her pregnant body in the mirror. She shuddered, then quickly cloaked herself in the terry-cloth robe that hung beside the bathroom door.

God, but she was obese.

The telephone rang again, and she hurried, leaving a wet path.

It was her mother, calling from her home in New Jersey. It was nine P.M. there, and she said she'd wanted to call before Julie went to bed.

"The child's going to be a giant," her mother said. She'd examined the photograph Julie had sent with her last letter along with an airline ticket.

"Just a second, Mom. I just crawled out of the shower and I've gotta dry off."

She laid down the telephone and went, still dripping, into the bathroom and grabbed a towel, refusing to look in the mirror again. When she'd blotted off most of the water, she returned to the living room and picked up.

"Sorry."

"I was saying the child is going to be a giant."

"Don't say 'child,' say 'he.' I want a boy, and I want him to be big and look just like his father. He was so handsome . . . I wish you could have met him, Mom."

"His photos show he has big ears. I hope the child doesn't have big ears like that."

"Mom!"

"And you say he has bad vision."

"One eye was nearsighted just enough to keep him out of pilot training. He didn't wear glasses unless he was driving or flying."

She didn't tell her that Mal Stewart had been too vain to wear them.

"Have you received any more word about him?"

"They've still got him listed as missing in action."

"Well, don't give up hope."

Oh, God! Here it was again. "I told you, Mom. His friends who were there say he was killed."

After the short pause she always gave, her mother said, "Sometimes they know things they can't tell the men. I'm sure if the Air Force was all *that* sure, they'd declare him dead. One thing I learned in my years as a military wife was that the Air Force takes care of their own. It would be cruel to let you go on hoping for no good reason."

Julie's heart leapt again, as it often did when they talked. Was what her mother said true? But the men who'd been there said it wasn't, that he was dead.

"I don't want you to give up hope, Julie. Not so long as they say he might be alive."

"Mom, I know the Air Force says he's MIA, but his friends say he was killed, and they wouldn't lie to me." She paused, then cried out, "I just don't know, Mom!"

Her mother changed the subject. She thanked Julie for the airline tickets she'd sent, and said she looked forward to coming out to stay with her during the delivery and to help take care of the infant.

They talked for ten more minutes, but although she spoke words, Julie understood very little. She was too busy trying to keep the horrors about Mal Bear from her mind.

After she hung up, Julie pulled off the robe and shower cap and finished drying herself. Then she powdered her pudgy body, careful to get under her breasts where a rash threatened to form. She examined herself and watched in fascination as the baby moved. She pulled on maternity pajamas, her fluffy pink mules, and an old, comfortable housecoat that tied at the throat and gaped at the belly because of her roundness.

And all the while she tried hard not to think about what her mother had said.

But the horrors won, as they always did.

Could he be alive?

They'd seen him surrounded by enemy soldiers, being mutilated, so they'd angrily bombed and strafed and killed everything down there.

Had Mal somehow survived?

Could he have escaped and be trying to get back to her? If he had, he was surely horribly maimed and in constant pain.

She sobbed once, but caught herself.

What was truth, when you just didn't know? It was ... anything at all, whatever your imagination told you. She wished Benny would call so she could talk to him and hear his sure voice, but he was away in Saigon or somewhere, helping conduct the war.

Wonderful, square, always pleasant Benny.

He'd promised to be there when the baby came. That was good, for she'd need his strength. As much as she loved her mother, she wanted Benny to be there even more.

One month to go, and it could not pass quickly enough. But what then? She wondered what kind of mother she would be, and that set her to worrying. Then she wondered what it would be like raising a boy without a father.

If Mal was alive . . .

But Colonel Mack and Major Sam Hall had written her and said he was not, and Benny had also said he could not possibly have lived through it.

What was truth? *You don't know.* She cried, as she did every time after talking with her mother.

The downstairs doorbell rang, and she wondered who it could be, since she wasn't expecting company. After a long moment of trying to pull herself together, she went to the door and pressed the intercom button.

"Yes?" Her voice quavered.

"It's Benny Lewis," said a pleasant male voice. "How do I work this thing so I can come up to visit?"

She was still sniffing. "Benny?"

"Yeah. How do I get in?"

His voice thrilled her. "Benny!"

She caught her breath, her heart bouncing around inside her like a Ping-Pong ball.

"Just push the latch when you hear the buzzer," she cried out, then depressed the door-opener button as she looked wildly about the apartment.

While he was coming upstairs, she busied around the room, picking up magazines and other signs of her sloppiness, wondering how her prayers had been answered so quickly. Staid, wonderful Benny, who was always there on the phone when she'd needed him.

Mal Bear had called him square, but he'd done so with great fondness.

She heard knocking at the door. She threw it open and grabbed him in a hug, then just as quickly released him. "Oh, damn! Did I hurt you?"

He was grinning. "Hurt me again."

"Silly." She showed him in.

After a few steps he stopped and frowned. "Hey. What's wrong with your eyes?"

"Nothing is wrong with my eyes. Now you go over to that couch and *sit*. How long have you been on your feet?"

"Not long. I got a med-evac flight from Saigon to Travis, and they had me strapped to a mobile torture bed, just like at the hospital. I got to be miserable the entire trip."

He sat gingerly in the stuffed couch she'd indicated, frowning at her face and tear-swollen eyes.

She went on the offensive. "I spoke with Pam at the Nellis Hospital, and she told me how you connived your way into getting the hospital commander to sign the medical waiver so you could travel."

"You mean Lady Dracula?" He sighed dramatically. "I guess I'll have to face her when I get there tomorrow."

"Don't worry about Pam. She's doing everything in her power to hold off the wolves until you get back. But she says the hospital commander is really mad. She had to fib and tell him you were doing much better than she thinks you really are."

"Lady Dracula?" he asked incredulously.

"Pam. Oh, you're *impossible*, Benny Lewis."

"Your eyes are red."

"Because I've been crying. Satisfied?"

His brows furrowed angrily. "Has someone been here?"

"No, and don't worry about me."

"C'mon, tell me. I'll kill the guy before I leave."

"It wasn't a guy. It was my mother, and she's in New Jersey."

"I'll fly out there and beat her up."

"Silly."

"Is she bigger than me?" He drew back in mock fright. Benny was solid and tough looking. Mal had told her he lifted 200-pound weights for exercise.

She giggled. "She's even shorter than me."

"Then I'll tear off her arms and legs."

Julie laughed heartily and he grinned back. He seemed a little different from when she'd seen him last. He'd been awfully straitlaced, almost *too* much the perfect gentleman. Always lovable, of course, but now he seemed to joke more at himself.

"It's so *good* to see you," she said.

"Let's get back to the tears."

She shook her head. "You don't want to know."

He cocked his head.

"Mom says that no matter what you guys say, the Air Force wouldn't call Mal Bear MIA if they knew he was dead."

He shook his head. "The Air Force isn't a *they*, Julie, it's just a bunch of guys like me. The Bear's not coming back.

I talked to his cousin Billy, he's a pilot at Takhli now, and he agrees the Bear should be declared KIA." He started to add more, but stopped short.

"Mom says they have information you guys don't."

"There is no *they*." He looked at her narrowly. "Do you think I'd be saying it if I didn't *know* he was dead? He was like a brother. I loved the ornery bastard."

Her jaw quivered and she sniffed. *Dammit, don't cry in front of him.* She firmed herself up and whispered, "Let's change the subject."

"Good idea."

"I was just . . ." She looked at herself. "Oh, God."

"Something wrong?"

"I just got out of the shower and I've been crying and I look . . . terrible."

"You couldn't look bad to me, Julie."

She ran toward the bedroom, waving an arm toward the kitchen. "Booze is in the cupboard on the right. Fix yourself a drink while I change."

Twenty minutes later she emerged, freshly combed, made-up, and wearing a new maternity dress with yards of material to hide in.

He eyed her. "You look nice."

"Maybe better, but not nice. Sorry I can't reduce a bit around the middle for you, Benny."

"Guess you will in about a month." He peered at her stomach and grinned as he waved a tumbler of whiskey. "You look like you're carrying a beach ball in there."

"My mother says he's going to be a giant with big ears."

"He?"

"I want a boy, and if I keep saying 'he,' maybe it will be."

"The Bear wanted a girl."

"He was wrong," she said cheerily.

She poured herself a gin and tonic. "My doctor says I can have one ounce of alcohol a day," she said. "I got my first prenatal checkups at Travis, because I was spending so much time going over to see you there, but now I see a civilian doctor here in the city. A little Jewish guy who's funny and very capable."

"He'd better be."

"He served his internship in the Air Force, stationed in Germany. He was at Bitburg when I was a kid at Spangdahlem, just seven miles away." Julie had been a service brat, her father a senior Air Force NCO. "Small world, huh?"

"Yeah."

"I really like him." She remembered then that she hadn't eaten. "Hungry?"

"A little."

As she fixed sandwiches, they talked about Benny's trip to the war zone. He told her about a friend named Lucky Anderson, who had a badly burned face and was the most capable leader he'd met in the Air Force. Benny was troubled by what had happened, and she could tell he thought a lot of Anderson. She didn't know how to make it better, so she just listened.

After they'd eaten and she'd served him a snifter of Courvoisier, his eyelids began to droop.

"Days and nights are mixed up," he muttered. "My body-clock's screwed up."

"I'll get a couple of blankets so you can sleep on the couch," she said. "Be right back."

"No!" He said it so forcefully it surprised her.

She stopped and gave him a puzzled look.

"I'll get a hotel. I left my bag down in the lobby. Just call me a cab."

"You're a cab. Now stretch out on the couch."

"Dammit, Julie . . ."

"Dammit *yourself*, Benny Lewis, you are not going out to get a hotel room at nine o'clock at night. Period."

He gave her a stubborn look.

"No man I love is going to go out at this time of night and get a hotel room when I've got a perfectly good . . ."

He looked so startled that she paused. Then, softly, "You didn't know I loved you?"

"I . . . uh . . ."

"You are very, very dear to me, Benny Lewis."

He collected himself. "Like a brother?"

"Like someone I can turn to for help, and who's always there." Then she lightened up and laughed. "You're a good-looking, teddy bear of a guy. I'll bet the women in Vegas are lined up, waiting their chance at you."

He grinned. "Yeah. The cops complain because they're congesting traffic."

A few months before, he would never have joked like

that. She liked the little, noticeable changes. It reminded her just a bit of . . . Mal?

"I'm going to phone downstairs to a couple I know and get the husband to bring your bag up," she said. "The exercise will do him good, and I *don't* want you lugging it up here."

He narrowed his eyes again and started to respond.

"No arguments."

She made the call, saying her brother was in town visiting, and he had a bad back.

When she hung up, he gave her a wry grin. "Brother? My name's on the bag."

"Half brother?"

He looked at her with a raised eyebrow. "You love me like a half brother?"

"Maybe I do." She stared at him evenly, surprising herself but unable to stop. Finally she spoke in a husky tone. "No, not a half brother."

Their eyes were still locked. He muttered something about getting the hotel room.

"Say it one more time and I'll scream."

He was the one to look away.

She inhaled a breath. "I'm going to have the baby at St. Joseph's Hospital here in San Francisco. I'll give you directions while you're here. You promised to be there, remember?"

He nodded, obviously relieved that she'd changed the subject.

The downstairs neighbor knocked at the door.

Half an hour later, while Julie was getting him a second cognac, Benny fell asleep on the couch. She quietly poured the brandy back into the bottle and turned off the lamp. Then she waited a bit before straightening him. He did not wake up. She removed his shoes and pulled a blanket over him.

Satisfied, she stood back and stared at him for a long time before going to her room.

CHAPTER TWENTY-TWO

Day 4, 0130 Local—Thud Ridge, North Vietnam

Major Lucky Anderson

The moon was perfect, enough to illuminate his way yet not so bright that he could be easily seen. He was holed up at the edge of a mountain village, waiting for them to sleep so he could pass through. Although the path had degenerated and his progress had become laboriously slow, it still presented the best route northward. To his left there was sheer rock, too steep to climb, and to his right were open fields, too near the populated flatlands.

It was not a large village. There were only nine or ten thatch mountain huts there, but he'd counted at least thirty people and knew there were more inside. Perhaps fifty of them? Certainly more than he wished to confront, so he lay at the edge of the clearing and watched as they went about their business in the flickering lights of their cooking fires.

No vehicles would come to the village, for there were no passable roads here. An ancient tractor was parked at the edge of the rock-strewn field below the village, a skeletal reminder of another time, but it was obviously inoperable.

His interest stirred as they brought out three yapping dogs on ropes, two midsized yellow ones and a small black pup, to the closest fire. He grimaced when they broke their forelegs with clubs and untied the ropes. Women emptied a fire pit and placed large round stones and banana leaves while children screamed with delight and watched the squealing dogs try to crawl away. Then a man deftly gutted one of the yellow ones while it was alive, and the noise was worse yet.

It was then, during their preparations for roast dog, that he felt there was sufficient noise and confusion. Bent over, he scurried to the next group of bushes, intending to go from that one to the next and on around the uphill edge of the village.

One of the men must have heard him, for he walked closer and peered into the thicket. Lucky flattened and remained still until the man left to berate two children who were beating one of the dogs senseless with sticks.

Lucky had misjudged the situation. He was too close, not twenty yards from the nearest fire, and found himself trapped in the small thicket with open areas behind and before him.

So, he reasoned, he would wait until the village slept.

When the gutted dog stopped struggling, the children danced about and pointed to another, and the man started on that one.

He wondered what the hell was giving them their insomnia. According to his watch's luminous dial it was now 0145. He'd passed other villages during his nightly treks, but they'd been dark and, except for a few noisy dogs, quiet. He'd assumed everyone had been asleep.

These were not the backwards tribesmen they'd been briefed about. They lived too close to civilization. Using the downhill path, which ran down the middle of the large field, it could be no more than a mile to the farms and heavily inhabited area beyond. They dressed in conical wicker hats and dark clothing, and only a few wore footwear.

He tried again to determine what was keeping them awake, but could not.

Two young women walked past his thicket, holding hands and whispering secrets. They stopped to talk in the area between him and the forest he'd emerged from.

Great. No way to move in *either* direction now. He groused about it for another moment, then settled in for a longer stay.

He thought about the day.

At 1400 he'd used a survival radio to contact a high-flying formation of Thuds. Not a long transmission, just enough to let them know he was alive and evading. After three days on the run it had felt good to talk with fellow fighter jocks. They'd asked for his position, and he had refused to give it, so they'd become suspicious. Maybe they thought he was a gomer with a captured radio, he guessed. He'd told them he would talk to them in a couple more days, and they'd proceeded on.

A couple more days?

Confident, aren't you? he joked with himself.

Damn betcha, he answered.

Each day he plotted his course for the night's travel. Tonight he'd planned to make it three miles farther, but since he was now caught in the middle of the village, he'd have to delay things. He disliked such surprises now just as he had when he was flying.

His map showed that a place to cross over to the western side of the ridge was only three miles ahead, beyond the 5,200-feet-high peak directly uphill from the village. He hoped the mountain pass was uninhabited, but there was no way to know. Small villages, such as this one, weren't shown on his map.

On the opposite side of Thud Ridge he would follow a mountain stream that flowed down into the small Dai River, which was possibly swollen by monsoon rains. After crossing the Dai, he planned to hurry into a group of hillocks called the Dong Luc on his map.

From the western edge of the Dong Luc, he would observe and create a plan for crossing the Red River Valley. There'd be villages and a thousand farms to pass, as well as dozens of small streams and canals and two wide rivers to cross. Thirty very tough miles from the Dong Luc to the western mountains. Some had come close, but no downed pilot had ever made it all the way across the valley. An American in a flight suit would stand out among the Vietnamese like a Doberman in a pack of terriers.

As he lay there listening to the loud squeals of the third and final dog, he began to list his inventory of critical items, and to wonder if there was not more he could leave behind to lighten his load.

There were the two detailed maps folded into his g-suit

pocket. He'd covered them with protective plastic film and put them there the week after he'd arrived at Takhli; then he'd forgotten them. Now they were his most treasured possessions.

He had finished the second pemmican bar that afternoon, so there was no worrying about which food to keep. There was none. He'd found berries and nuts near his daytime hiding places, so perhaps food would be no problem. During his three survival-training courses he'd learned that man can go without eating for long periods, but that he *must* have water.

In the ever-present heat, and with the added exertions of travel, he consumed a lot of water, but with the predictable morning rains, clean water was plentiful.

So did he need all three eight-ounce baby bottles?

Probably, he thought. Rice paddies in Asia were fertilized with human and animal waste, and the streams would carry runoff from those. So . . . when he was traveling in the valley, he would be forced to use the cleanest *looking* of what he found. He didn't want a massive case of dysentery slowing him down, and that would likely happen if he did not have the bottles to carry him from place to place. He decided to keep them all.

He had three survival radios, two in his survival vest and another he'd taken from the survival kit. One of those could be sacrificed, smashed until inoperable and left behind.

He also had three lengths of nylon parachute cord that might come in handy at some time during his trek. They were light enough to keep.

Then there were other items, some useful, others redundant or unnecessary. For instance, he carried a Marine-issue bayonet knife as well as a standard survival knife. He'd keep the razor-sharp bayonet. He mulled through the items he carried, one by one, and the decisions were easy until he got to the firearms. There he had a problem.

Like all Thud pilots, he'd been issued a Smith & Wesson .38 Special revolver and twenty-four rounds of ball ammunition. Like a smaller number of pilots, he carried a second weapon.

A few pilots carried a broken-down M-16. A *very* few carried an illegal .22 pistol with a silencer.

When he'd received his orders to go to Takhli, he'd taken the advice of a friend and ordered a Phoenix Special. A week later he'd landed at Luke Air Force Base during a weekend cross-country flight, drove into Phoenix to a small gun shop, and after a demo had paid his $200 and picked up a nondescript package.

The ex-Marine who owned the gun shop had served on a recon team during the Korean conflict and knew there were unique needs for fighting men in unique situations. He sold such wares only to military men who might have such a need, on their way to combat.

The Phoenix Special used the frame and most of the action of a Colt Woodsman semiautomatic .22 LR pistol, but half of the six-inch barrel had been replaced by a small canister filled with a mixture of raw cotton and steel wool. The automatic blowback feature had been eliminated, so each time you wanted to fire it, you had to work the slide to chamber a round and cock the hammer.

When Lucky had fired the demo weapon, it had been so silent, he could hear the low *tick* of the firing pin, yet the single round had punched a two-inch exit hole in the dead rabbit hung up as his target. The ex-Marine had shown him how to repack the cotton-steel wool after each firing. He'd said if he did that, each barrel could be used four times before the noise became unacceptably audible.

The Phoenix Special had been dismantled, dipped in gel, and packed with an extra barrel and twenty rounds of low-velocity, lead-jacketed, cross-scored steel bullets, which splintered into four fragments when they hit a target.

Lucky decided to keep the Phoenix Special. Although he was a fair shot with the .38, and its effective range was much greater than that of the .22 LRs, there was no way he could survive a shoot-out with an enemy armed with rifles. The only real use he might have for a pistol would likely be at close range, and he could think of no reason to desire noise. He would bury the heavy .38 and its ammo with the other unnecessary gear.

The three dogs had been skinned and nested between large leaves in the fire pit, and a fire was being built on top.

But why now? It was 0215 and they were preparing for a feast? What the hell was it, he wondered, a birthday party?

At 0245 the villagers, rather than retiring to bed, began to gather in front of the largest fire and take turns with windy orations.

He sighed and wondered. Then he saw the shrouded shape of a body beside the fire. A wake? Women gathered, looking forlorn, and a man began pointing and gesturing. The orator became louder and sounded as if he might be saying nice things about the body. As more villagers gathered around, and more speakers spoke in loud voices, Lucky carefully surveyed the area about him. No one was between him and the forest to his rear.

He'd delayed long enough.

He carefully backed across the clearing until he was again in the forest, and after a few deep breaths of relief, began to make his way down the mountainside to circumvent the place. It would take time from his planned schedule.

As he listened to the diminishing sounds of the speeches, Lucky thought about Linda. She'd think all this "local culture" was interesting, maybe compare it to the Irish tradition.

He'd been thinking a lot about her during his trek.

Tuesday, August 15th, 0830 Local—Commandant's Office, Phuc Yen PAAFB, DRV

Air Regiment Commandant Quon

People's Army intelligence had confirmed for him, through their Saigon sources, that *Lokee* had indeed been shot down over the Democratic Republic, but after four days there'd been no trace of the hated pilot except his parachute and the pile of discarded items where he'd landed. The search team believed their quarry, like most Mee pilots they chased down and captured, was hiding not far from where he'd come down. The sergeant in charge of the search team told Quon that the Mee pilot's capture was imminent. So although he was increasingly impatient, Quon was not yet discouraged. The sergeant said no Mee had ever been rescued from the Viet Bac, the mountains stretching north from Hanoi, and that capture was not only probable but a sure thing. Some, he said, just took longer than others.

People's Army intelligence had an ultra-high frequency radio monitoring station on the roof of one of the headquarters buildings to monitor Mee pilots' radio transmissions and provide warning of attack. They advised Quon's adjutant that they had picked up two air-to-ground conversations with "Barracuda lead," which the prisoner had said was *Lokee*'s radio call sign. The ground transmissions had been weak and garbled, so the pilot was likely behind a hill, but they'd come from an azimuth of 355 degrees. The direction-finding ability of the receiver station was accurate only within ten degrees, but that was good enough to establish that *Lokee* was indeed in the Viet Bac, confirming what the search-team sergeant had told him.

The grizzled and capable sergeant was said to be the most capable hunter of men in the Democratic Republic, the veteran of dozens of successful manhunts for American fliers and People's Army deserters. He'd even determined what *Lokee* had with him.

They knew the standard survival items included in the emergency pack. With that, what they'd found discarded, and what had been learned from interrogations of Pig Squadron pilots, they knew that *Lokee* carried his issue .38-caliber revolver with twenty-four bullets, a hunting knife, a bayonet knife sewn to the right leg and a sealed pouch sewn to the left leg of his antigravity suit, three radios, three plastic bottles of water, a signal mirror, two flares, a bottle of water-purification tablets, a first-aid kit, a small compass, a plastic-covered map, two hard food bars, a cigarette lighter, several cigars, which he put in his mouth but oddly did not smoke, a small flashlight, a square of material he'd cut from a parachute panel, and three lengths of nylon parachute cord.

Of his mental condition they knew that *Lokee* had once endured great pain and had been toughened by it. He had a woman who lived in Bangkok, but he was not married to her. A Mee prisoner said that while he appeared to take little interest in women, he thought *Lokee* cared for that one more than he'd admit but was ashamed because of his burns. He was a natural, capable, and very aggressive fighter pilot. But while *Lokee* loved flying, he was an unorthodox military officer who cared little about rank or protocol.

Lokee kept himself in excellent physical condition. At Takhli he'd run and exercised daily and had built incredible endurance. The search-team sergeant worried about that and reports of the Mee pilot's aggressive nature, for Quon insisted that he be captured alive.

Sitting in his commandant's office, Quon went over the information again and again in his mind as he stared out at the maintenance hangars and aircraft shelters without seeing them. Three MiG-17 interceptors taxied off the runway and back toward their shelters, returning from safe haven in China, but he hardly took notice.

He had just gotten off the field telephone with General Tho, who had demanded to know where he'd been the previous afternoon, and when Quon had told him he'd visited the team looking for *Lokee*, his superior officer had grown very quiet.

Quon had admitted that he was obsessed by the search for *Lokee*, had even suggested that he be temporarily relieved of his duties until the Mee assassin was found.

General Tho had quietly answered that he would stand for no more. If he relieved Quon, it would not be a temporary thing. His senior officers were expected to lead their pilots to protect the People's Republic, to subjugate their private lives for the duration of the war.

A moment of silence had followed, and then General Tho had asked if he'd understood.

He did.

Would Quon return to his duties and forget about the search for the Mee pilot?

He said he could not forget, so long as *Lokee* was free.

Tho had ordered him to assign a subordinate to the task of monitoring the search team and to return to his duties.

Quon knew Tho well, knew that he was out of patience, so he'd reluctantly agreed. He would assign his adjutant to the search and give appropriate time to his duties. He apologized and told Tho that he could rely on him to attend fastidiously to his command in the future.

Tho had seemed mollified, and their conversation had returned to the business of war, for the Mee were intensifying their campaign against the bridges, and even though they were suffering losses, they were all too successful.

Supplies were bottlenecked at rail sidings near the Chinese border and on the docks of Haiphong. The attacks on the bridges must be stopped. His mind had been distracted during the conversation. He tried to remember what he'd told Tho they should do about the attacks.

He blamed his forgetfulness on the burned American pilot, the man he'd grown to despise more than any other. The man he was growing to know so well.

He told his adjutant to contact the search-team sergeant and get another progress report.

"Does the commandant wish to fly one of the aircraft tomorrow morning?"

They'd received an intelligence report that the Mee would target both Phuc Yen and Kien An airfields sometime during the next week. All day artillery-and-rocket batteries had been pouring into prepared sites around the two bases. For their safety, half of the MiGs would be flown out to China, others to remote auxiliary airfields near the northern border.

It had been a week since he'd gone up, and Quon seldom went that long between flights. He knew he *should* join his pilots during the evacuation, but . . .

"No," he finally said. "There is too much for me to do here."

He did not dare fly, for he might miss out on the capture of *Lokee*. Even if it meant staying at Phuc Yen and weathering the American bombing attack, he would stay.

1000 Local—Hoa Lo Prison, Hanoi, North Vietnam

Major Glenn Phillips

For the first time in two weeks, Glenn was able to communicate with other prisoners, and most of the news and the rumors and even the innuendos were bad.

He got most of his information while visiting the *bo*-dump, the filthy shit depository in the courtyard, while he was suffering a painful bout of dysentery. First there was a note hidden in a *bo*-dump hiding place, to be read by the P going there. Then a P working at breaking up bricks in the courtyard began hammering out a flurry of letters when he saw him, using their tap-code. And finally there were muttering sessions as other P passed him in the yard. It all came in bits and pieces, but information was treasured more highly than gold in the prison.

After getting the jigsaw pieces, it was always challenging to try to put it together so it made sense, and to *try* to separate fact from fancy.

In the bad news: The V were going through the P from the 354th squadron again, beating the hell out of them and bending them until they told everything they knew about Lucky Anderson. Then beating them for information about the strafing attack at Kep, the same information that had been beaten out of them back in April.

It was believed that at least two P from the 354th had been killed during their initial interrogations after being shot down, and it was rumored that the number was higher. At least one of those had been shot, the rumor said, and at least one, perhaps more, beaten to death.

Another rumor, yet unconfirmed, was that Lucky had been shot down and was evading, and that the V were hot on his heels.

The good news was that he obviously hadn't been caught, because they continued to try to get information about what he carried with him when he flew.

When he was caught, the V had something special in store for him. *Lokee* was a hot topic with the V, and they spat out the name as if it were a dirty one.

Glenn reflected on the time at Nellis when he, Benny Lewis, and Max Foley had worked for Lucky on weapons projects, all under the watchful eye of then Major General Moss.

They'd all been superb pilots, but Lucky had been the most professional of the group. He remembered how Anderson had never wanted to be the one in charge of the projects, but how Moss, the other pilots, and Lucky's leadership ability had conspired to put him there.

He remembered a night when Lucky had hurried into their shared BOQ room, packed his gear, and told him he was going camping for the weekend. A tall, distraught brunette had appeared a few minutes later, asking for him, and Glenn had caught on right away that she felt something special for Lucky. When Lucky had returned from the desert and asked about her, it was just as apparent that he was as upset about things as she'd been.

A strange, highly capable, withdrawn fellow was Lucky Anderson. Glenn felt a bit helpless that all he could do was offer prayer. But during his time as a prisoner, Glenn Phillips, once the most eligible, hard-driving, high-flying fighter pilot in the Air Force, had learned that prayer was more

powerful than he'd ever believed. So he said a series of special prayers for his good friend.

A warrior's prayers.

He prayed the next news they heard about Lucky
Anderson was that he'd been rescued.

And if what he'd heard was correct about the V being after him so intensely, and if Lucky wasn't rescued, he prayed
they'd hear that he'd shot it out with the V and been killed.

1300 Local—TFWC/TAF, Nellis AFB, Nevada

Major Benny Lewis

"Tell, uh . . ."—he tried to recall Lady Dracula's name—
"Nan?"

Moods Diller frowned, then brightened. "You mean
Pam?"

"Yeah. Tell her thanks for calming down the colonel over
there."

The hospital commander was finally satisfied that he
would toe the mark and take better care of his back. Benny's
penance was to check into the hospital each morning for
physical therapy, including a periodic session on the rack,
which was what he called the metal bed that sent random
electrical shocks into the muscles of his back.

"Why don't you thank her yourself?" said Moods.

"You tell her, okay?" He'd tried to talk to her, but she
hadn't slowed down with her complaints long enough to
hear him. Sometimes he felt she'd interceded with the colonel only to make sure she remained his preeminent ha-
ranguer.

"Sure," said Moods. He was unhappy, almost morose,
even though the LGB tests were going well.

Several laser kits had been shipped to him by the Texas
team during the past weeks, as had a zot machine small
enough to be mounted in a pod under the right wing of an
F-4 Phantom, and manipulated by controls in the rear cockpit. The first drop-tests had gone reasonably well. Only two
hits out of eight, but the misses had been explainable and
the hits had been squarely on target, so Moods was convinced they were in the home stretch.

He was working with the weapons officer at Danang Air

Base in South Vietnam and had him as excited about what they were doing as Pearly Gates had once been. When the bugs were out of the kits and the zot machine, and they'd selected a host bomb, Moods planned to take them to Danang and try them in combat, he hoped against one of the bridges they were having so much trouble with, like the small one at the Canales des Rapides or the obstinate one at Thanh Hoa.

But there were still problems, one of which was the fact that they couldn't design modules that would work properly on all the bombs as they'd planned. The various bombs' shapes, circumferences, and centers of gravity were just too different. So Moods and his cohorts at the various test-and-evaluation offices had to settle on a single host bomb.

Moods Diller favored existing Mk-84 2,000-pounders. They were relatively new and aerodynamic, were still being manufactured at munitions plants, and didn't require special adapters like the 3,000-pounders. He'd convinced the officers at the development centers until there was only a single holdout, but that one was a powerful adversary. The guys at the Weapons Lab at Eglin Air Force Base in Florida favored entirely new bombs, completely reengineered to have the guidance modules installed at the factory.

For the dozenth time Moods explained the problem to Benny, who had elected to stay out of the squabble.

"I need it resolved," he pleaded. "They've *gotta* let me use Mk-84's."

"You work it out," said Benny, eager to get back to his work.

"Dammit, Benny, if they have to redesign a bomb . . . gonna delay things . . . I'm on the verge of making this thing work. If we prove the concept . . . not right to hafta sit on our asses while they build new bombs."

"The whole project falls under the charter of the Weapons Lab, not us."

"Yeah, but I'm here, not there." He was not bragging, just stating a fact. "Benny, they're just flexin' muscles . . . showin' me who's boss."

"Maybe if the Weapons Lab gave you a tailor-made bomb it *would* be better, you think of it like that?"

"I don't have the time. . . . Th' guys're losing too many people, dropping gravity bombs."

Benny stared.

"If Lucky'd had my laser-guided bomb . . . wouldn't've had to press low 'n' *maybe* he wouldn't've been shot down."

That argument struck a chord. Benny thought about it, then shook his head. "I'll tell it to you like it is, Moods. You've cried wolf so damned many times, saying you were *almost* there, not many people believe you anymore."

Moods Diller sighed. "Yeah, I know."

"Every week you say, 'I'll have it next week.' Then it's another week, then another. Some people are beginning to believe you've got a great idea for the *next* war."

Moods looked miserable, and his voice came out so slowly, it seemed normal. "I'll have the guidance problem ironed out in a couple weeks. If they have to build a new bomb, the estimates are it'll be nine months to a year *min-imum* before they'll have it ready and tested."

Benny was not sympathetic. "Perhaps by then all the bugs will really be out of your LGB kits, and just *maybe* they'll work."

Quit being such an old maid and listen, said the voice inside him. It had been a while since he'd heard it.

Moods looked thoroughly beaten.

Asshole, said the voice. *This guy's giving it all he's got and he needs your help.*

Benny narrowed his eyes and thought about it.

Moods shook his head sadly.

"Okay, Moods," sighed Benny. "Give me your rationale again."

Diller told him.

Benny cocked a finger and pointed it directly at him. "How long would it take to change your design so the modules fit to Mk-84's?"

"I've already got the design on paper . . . the Texas contractors say they can build a prototype in two weeks."

"How long until you get the bugs out of the laser-guidance kits?" Benny shook his head sternly. "I want a concrete answer, Moods. Something I can take to the bank. No more wags." A wag was what they called a "wild-assed guess." Benny looked evenly at him. "I don't want to back you and make *both* of us look dumb."

Moods almost laughed out loud. "You'll help?"

"How long, dammit?"

Moods jotted timelines on his pad.

Benny moved over beside him. "Let's make sure we add

a few days to get money shifted from the discretionary fund, transit times for shipping the bombs, plenty of time to work out design bugs, and then a quick-reaction contract to produce a few kits."

Half an hour later they'd come up with a rough milestone chart. In three months Moods could travel to Danang for his LGB test . . . *if* they used existing Mk-84 bombs.

Benny stared at the figures, then nodded. This time he believed them.

Whatcha going to do now, Ace? asked the voice, rather proud of him.

Benny picked up the telephone and dialed an autovon number.

"Who you callin'?" asked Moods Diller.

"Friend of Lucky Anderson's who runs a division at the Armament Lab."

Moods looked dejected again. "That's at Wright Patterson. It's the people at *Eglin* who're giving me the problems."

"Yeah? Well guess who the two-star at Eglin works for?"

"The three-star at Wright Pat?"

"You got it."

CHAPTER
TWENTY-THREE

Thursday, August 17th, 0900 Local—HQ Seventh Air Force, Tan Son Nhut Air Base, Saigon, RVN

Lieutenant Colonel Pearly Gates

The previous night the Navy had taken a try at *their* bridges, and Pearly was trying to interpret the results. CINCPAC had told Seventh Fleet to work closely with Seventh Air Force on CROSSFIRE ZULU, but since it had been an Air Force idea, the airdales remained selective about what they told them. The Navy had always been reluctant to release results to the Air Force, whom their admirals called the "junior service," and that hadn't changed. Which was fine, thought Pearly, except he needed to know what to brief his boss.

Navy A-6 Intruders had been fragged to destroy two bridges west of Haiphong. The message Seventh Fleet had released said one was damaged and the other "heavily" damaged.

So what the hell did that mean?

He'd talked to one of the Navy liaison officers assigned to the headquarters, an elusive full commander, and found out nothing except: "Our guys are reliable. They say it's heavy damage, they mean it."

"So is the bridge down or is it just damaged?" he'd asked.

"Like they said, it's *heavily* damaged."

He sighed. "So they knocked down a span?"

"Well, *I'd* say if a span was knocked down, it's heavily damaged. Of course they'd've said it was destroyed if the damage was *really* heavy."

Pearly had tried a different tack, asking the commander for recce photos of the "heavily damaged" bridge. He was told they were unavailable. The commander said he was sure they'd be forwarded in the morning, after tonight's missions, which made Pearly suspicious.

Pearly went to work with what he had. He marked the Doumer bridge in red. The one the Navy said was heavily damaged he marked in yellow, meaning the damage was of a more temporary nature. The other Navy bridge and the one over the Canales des Rapides he marked in green, meaning they were undamaged.

The weather had been bad the past few days and they'd been able to get few of their missions completed, but he still wished he had better results to show the generals. He wandered down to the TACC, the Tactical Air Control Center, and confirmed the afternoon mission from Takhli was to be against the Canales bridge, and that Korat would bomb the bridge at Thanh Moi. The F-4's were joining the campaign, and both Danang and Ubon would go after the big bridge at Thanh Hoa.

The weather was forecast to be marginal.

He told the FDO that he'd return later for results, because the elephants were dancing.

It had started when his contact at CINCPAC, the lieutenant commander at Camp H. M. Smith, said they were getting flak from the Pentagon about CROSSFIRE ZULU. An Assistant Undersecretary of Defense was waffling about their approval of the OPlan and wanted justification for continuing the campaign, based upon *direct* results they were getting from bombing the bridges: how much reduction in the tonnages of supplies getting through to enemy troops in South Vietnam—things like that.

It's too damned early for results, Pearly had said, but he was preaching to the choir, for the Navy officer agreed with him. Still, he had to answer the questions. The lieutenant commander asked for a detailed report of damage to the bridges as well as combat losses attributed to the campaign, as those were required to supplement his report.

But then the elephants had begun to dance, and the three- and four-stars had gotten into the picture. And when the elephants danced, staff officers scurried to try not to get caught underfoot. When the lieutenant commander briefed the mixed results to his boss at CINCPAC, Admiral Ryder had called General Moss to tell him that if they couldn't start showing success, he feared the SecDef would convince the President to stop the effort. The SecDef was letting it be known more vigorously than ever that he favored cessation of all bombing of the northern regions of North Vietnam. He said the bombing was doing no good whatsoever there.

Which was why Moss wanted the meeting with Pearly, and why Pearly needed the results of the afternoon bombing sorties.

If they could destroy the bridge over the Canales des Rapides, they would halt rail traffic from eastern China. Eliminating the bridge at Thanh Moi would cut the Haiphong-Hanoi rail line. The bridge at Thanh Hoa was a major conduit from Hanoi southward.

He puffed out a sigh, hoping the weather would cooperate, and the afternoon's Air Force strikes and the Navy's night raids would bring results.

To make matters worse for Pearly, the recce photos showed that defenses had been dramatically increased at Phuc Yen and Kien An, the bases he'd identified as targets on the fake air tasking order. The traitor, the man releasing targeting information to the enemy, the one who was killing his fellow Americans, was in Pearly Gates's organization.

Now that he knew the security leak came from his branch, he had to tell the proper authorities, and he knew he must start with General Moss.

What a crying, awful mess.

1000 Local—Ponderosa BOQ, Takhli RTAFB, Thailand

Captain Manny DeVera

Manny had worked with Billy Bowes the past few evenings to catch up with the paperwork left by Major Lucky. Things like memos from the wing deputy for operations, and the squadron commander, with suspenses which were long overdue. He'd finished with them the previous night. Since he wasn't on the morning schedule, he'd slept in until seven, then attended personal matters. He'd finished a letter to his stepparents and wrapped a birthday present for Sister Lucia, both things he'd delayed because of the paperwork drill.

He'd never known a close family. Manny had been nine when he'd been placed with his adoptive parents in San Antonio, and although they'd provided him with all the essentials, there hadn't been the warmth Manny knew he'd have had with his real mother and father. But of course he'd never known his real parents, and the staff at the children's home had told him nothing except their name was DeVera and they'd never be coming back.

At the children's home his favorite had been Sister Lucia, even though she was the strictest and seldom coddled him or told him how special he was, as the others tried to do. He was not alone in trying to please Sister Lucia. The other kids liked to say that when she said something, she by God meant it.

After he'd been with his new family for a couple of years, he'd returned to visit the rock-tough old nun and found she'd not changed an inch.

"It's a hard world, Manuel," she'd often say, never using the familiar "Manny" as his new parents and the other sisters did. When she was pleased with him, she'd add, "But you will succeed as long as you always remember to work very hard, respect God's will, and never spend a day without thanking Him for giving you breath and the chance to do your best."

Sister Lucia was as devout an American as she was a Christian, but her patriotism held a special flavor. While she knew that pride was sinful, she said there was no harm being very pleased that God had made Manny a Westerner, a Texan, and a Mexican-American.

According to Sister Lucia, the east coast of the United States had been settled and shaped by Anglos, but most of the rest of it was the result of hardworking Spanish pioneers. And of course it was much better to live where things had been set up properly in the first place, as they'd done.

Easterners huddled in huge cities on their coast, trying to turn things into Little Europe. Show one a high mountain or an arid plain, and he'd likely make a long face and want to go home. Show the same to a Westerner, she said, and he would come to terms with it and live there in harmony.

Of course, she'd say, there were *some* Easterners who had *acted* like Westerners. Like George Washington, Thomas Jefferson, Abraham Lincoln, and the hero of her own time, Franklin Roosevelt.

And never forget, she would say, that it was Mexican-Americans who had taught the other Westerners their special kind of fortitude.

According to Sister Lucia, Texas would never have been freed from the strangle-grasp of conniving Santa Anna by Sam Houston and his small band of Anglo and German settlers—they'd still be living in the state of Tejas in northern Mexico—had it not been for the brave support and the shed blood of the Mexican community. *Read the Hispanic names of men who died at the Alamo,* she would say, *and remember who fed the soldiers and gave them information about their enemy.*

And what would America be, Sister Lucia would ask with a frown, *without Texas?*

According to Sister Lucia, Mexican-Americans still supported America well. There were higher percentages of Hispanic volunteers serving in World War II and Korea than from any other ethnic group, and they'd won a higher percentage of medals for bravery.

Manny DeVera had finished his second year of college, working night and day to do it, and when he'd been accepted for flight-cadet and pilot training by the United States Air Force, it had been Sister Lucia he'd told first. She had not only let him get away with his moment of boasting, she'd placed her hands over her mouth and shaken her head in wonder, and then hurried him to the other sisters so he could tell them.

His adoptive father had felt it his duty to counsel Manny and ask him to reconsider, since he would be wasting a hard-earned education. Anyone can fly airplanes, he'd said.

When he'd volunteered for combat and was about to be sent to fly and fight in Southeast Asia, he'd returned to San Antonio.

Sister Lucia had grown misty-eyed when he told her.

"If I'd had a son . . . ," she'd started, but then she'd drawn herself stiffly upright and did not finish. Instead she'd changed the subject and fussed at him for not regularly attending mass. She said she would pray for him each morning and night until he returned.

His adoptive mother had accepted his going as a tragedy, and his stepfather was angry that he'd again ignored his advice.

Sister Lucia wrote weekly, telling him how wonderful it must be to live in the exotic East. He never mentioned the war, so she did not either, but he read her letters and treasured her words, and promptly answered them. Besides Sister Lucia, a couple of girlfriends who had endured to become *real* friends, and the members of C-Flight, there was no one to give a good damn whether Manny DeVera survived or was shot down in flames.

He finished his labeling of the package containing the present for Sister Lucia's seventy-fifth birthday. The birthday would be in four days, and it wouldn't get there in time, and for that he was truly sorry. He looked at his neat handiwork. He was good at wrapping packages.

That afternoon he would see if he was as good at dropping bombs. An hour earlier he'd gotten a phone call from Billy Bowes telling him they were on again, which meant they would be returning to the damned bridge at the Canales des Rapides.

1045 Local—Command Post

Captain Billy Bowes

Manny entered the command post and Billy waved him over.

"Sorry I'm late," Manny said. "Had to take care of a couple personal things."

Billy showed him first the flight plan, then the lineup card he'd completed. Manny was shown as flight lead, and Henry would fly his wing. Billy was number three and Smitty number four in the flight.

Manny looked over each card in detail. Finally he said, "Looks good to me."

"If you need to catch up on more private stuff, paperwork or anything, I'll fly as lead and plug Joe Walker into my spot. We'll probably run into bad weather and have to find an alternate target in pack five anyway."

Billy felt awkward saying it, thinking about what Manny had tried to tell him in the dining room a few days before. This would be another tough mission, and he wanted Manny to know he could make up his own mind on those things.

But Manny shook his head. "I'll lead."

"So far the weather looks a *little* better than it's been the last few days. Not good, but not bad enough to scrub the mission before takeoff."

They'd been weathered out of route pack six for most of the five days since their last try at the Canales bridge. Twice they'd been airborne, but the Weasels had reported cloud buildups over the target, and they'd judiciously turned back.

Manny shrugged. "We'll just have to do our best. Who's mission commander?"

"Colonel Mack. Bad Injin Encinos was going to take it, but he got sick or something."

Manny nodded without comment. Thus far their squadron commander had not proved to be another John Wayne.

"I'm waiting on a call they're trying to put through in the command center. Soon as I'm done, why don't we go have a quick lunch?"

"Sure," said Manny; then he gave him an inquisitive look. "They're putting the call through *for* you?"

"On the scrambler phone. I'm trying to reach my cousin at Danang on a classified line. Our command post got a call from Korat. One of their flight leads got a radio transmission from the ground up in pack six yesterday. Said the guy identified himself as Barracuda lead."

"That was Major Lucky's call sign."

"Yeah." Billy grinned. "Means he's still up there on the loose."

"Jesus, that's good news! Where is he?"

"He wouldn't give his location. Probably didn't want to broadcast it to the gomers. So I was going to call David, that's my cousin at Danang."

"What can he do?" asked Manny.

"He's in Special Forces. Got some kind of job that has to do with communications and spook work, or at least that's what I *think* it is. I just thought that maybe the Army's got some way of triangulating Lucky's radio calls so they can tell us where he is."

"Sounds interesting," said Manny. "I'll wait for you."

1512 Local—Route Pack Six, North Vietnam

Captain Manny DeVera

Twice they'd been forced to break up the gaggle as coveys of surface-to-air missiles zipped out of the clouds, heading directly at various aircraft. The cloud cover was low, banked at 10,000 feet. They flew up at 20,000 feet, but the missiles had a head of steam built up before they came darting out at them, and they had little time to react.

The crew leading the Wild Weasel flight was one of the least aggressive in the wing and weren't enamored with challenging the SAMs in poor weather. When they got to Thud Ridge, they just orbited there to fire Shrike homing missiles at Fansong SAM radars to the south. They radioed that the weather *looked* to be good in the target area.

Today the Weasels would provide little protection from the SAMs.

As they approached, they could see that there was indeed a hole in the weather. It was a long, skinny one extending from Thai Nguyen to the northern edge of Hanoi, so the bridge was at the far end of the clearing. Puffs of flak forming over the target appeared almost as a part of the clouds, making it hard to tell the bad stuff from the awful stuff. The fighter pilots liked the clouds just a little better than artillery bursts, but wished neither was there.

Colonel Mack MacLendon was in his dive delivery, trying to neutralize the target defenses with his cluster-bomblet units, yet also trying to stay out of the clouds. Manny's Rifle flight was immediately behind Mack and would be first to drop on the Canales bridge. He flew over the right edge of the oblong hole, along its western side, for although it was hidden by clouds, he knew there were no guns on the steep and craggy Thud Ridge.

"*Rifle's in the dive*," was all Manny said as he rolled over, inverted.

He leveled his wings in his dive-bomb attack, and the HSI, the gyrostabilized horizontal-situation indicator, read precisely forty-five degrees.

Good dive angle, he whispered into his oxygen mask.

The nose of the aircraft was squarely on the target.

The Wild Weasels began shouting about SAMs, but he ignored them.

Wind from the east they'd briefed before takeoff, and since he saw no visual reference down below, like smoke blowing one direction or the other, he had to believe them. He offset downstream, trying to estimate thirty feet, placed his pipper, and then waited for the target to crawl up there.

Altitude was ... 7,900 ... 7,700 ... 7,500.

Good sight picture. He pickled the bombs off.

Flak bracketed his bird as he pulled off to his left. Too close. He went into the clouds momentarily, and that was precisely when the flak burst hit his bird.

Whoomph! The Thud shuddered, and he knew he'd been hit.

A flash of fear numbed him. The Thud flew clear of the cloud and he was climbing out, turning slightly left as Colonel Mack had briefed, trying to think clearly.

They were to exit to the southeast and cross the coast north of Thanh Hoa.

He spotted a flight up ahead. Likely Mack's group.

He remembered his briefing to his flight and called, *"Rifle lead's in the clear, south of the target."*

Rifle two said he was not far behind him, then three and four radioed that they were in burner trying to catch up.

They were back together and joining with Mack's flak-suppression flight when Manny realized he'd lost his shakes and jangles. His Thud had been hit while he'd been blind and in a cloud, yet he'd had only the quick moment of panic. Was the unreasonable fear gone? ... the terrible time over?

Before they coasted out, Mack called a SAM break and a missile flashed smoothly between his number two and number three. Rifle wasn't threatened, so they hung together in their own formation, keeping a close watch on the clouds below.

Colonel Mack called "feet wet," meaning they'd passed over the coastline. It was impossible to tell visually, because the earth below was shrouded in clouds. A couple of minutes later Manny directed Rifle flight to their squadron radio frequency and asked if anyone had seen his bombs hit.

"Rifle two saw them, lead," said Henry. *"You got a near miss right beside the center of the bridge. Shook the hell out of it, but it didn't go down. I think the winds went calm on us, and we overcompensated. Mine hit in the same place as yours, just east of the bridge."*

Damn.

"*How about yours, Rifle three?*" asked Manny.

"*You see my bombs, four?*" asked Bowes. "*I went into the clouds too.*"

Smitty's voice was shaky. It was only his third trip to pack six, so that was understandable. "*You took out the northern approach to the bridge, three. You hit short of the bridge itself, but you put a big crater right at the approach.*"

Bowes didn't answer.

"*You see your own bombs impact, four?*" asked Manny.

"*No, sir, but I'm pretty sure they hit short. I was trying to avoid going into the clouds, and I dropped too soon.*"

"*Anyone get hit?*" asked Manny.

"*I think I took one in the wing,*" said Henry.

"*Yeah, so did I. Let's check each other over and make sure there's nothing we don't know about, then we'll go to Red Crown frequency and give our reports and get a steer to our tanker.*" Manny paused for a second. "*Wish we could give 'em a success code, Rifles.*"

As they began to look one another over, Billy made a radio call in his quiet and confident voice. "*Rifle lead?*"

"*Yeah?*"

"*Maybe we didn't win the war today, but all things considered, I'd call that a good, standard mission,*" said Bowes.

"*I'll second that,*" called Henry Horn. "*No surprises.*"

Manny thought about it, and suddenly he felt pretty damn good about things. "*Yeah. Maybe you're right.*"

1620 Local—Plans & Programs, HQ Seventh Air Force, Saigon

Lieutenant Colonel Pearly Gates

Red Crown airborne command post had received the pilot reports of the afternoon bombing results and relayed them to the Saigon control center. The results were mixed.

Korat reported that the Thanh Moi bridge was down on one side, and they didn't think the side still standing had enough surface to permit vehicular traffic. Takhli reported the northern approach to the Canales des Rapides bridge was badly damaged, but that the spans were all still standing. Danang reported the heaviest flak they'd ever encoun-

tered, the loss of an F-4 to a SAM, and ... probably no
damage to the Thanh Hoa bridge because it had been covered by clouds.

Pearly went from the command center directly to General Moss's office, then waited outside for twenty minutes
while Moss spoke to the senior B-52 liaison officer.

"Watch out for him," whispered the general's secretary.
"He's in one of his moods."

The big bombers had bombed in pack one twice during
the past week. It was the farthest north they'd ever ventured
and was understandably a very big deal to the B-52 people.

The bomber pilot left Moss's office frowning.

Pearly cautiously looked in.

"Come on in," Moss growled, "and close the door behind
you."

Pearly did so.

Moss rubbed vigorously at his jaw while Pearly took his
seat. "You got results yet?"

Pearly started to show him his map with the red and yellow marks, but Moss raised his hand and stopped him.

"Just tell me."

"Two bridges down and four damaged, sir."

Moss brooded, eyes narrowed and, Pearly knew, ready to
strike out at *someone*. Then, very slowly, the general began
to relax.

"Jesus," Moss finally said. "I'm starting to get wound up
over bullshit."

"The B-52's?"

"PACAF's all excited because they dropped all that tonnage on the infiltration routes. No one gives a shit if they hit
anything, just how many pounds of bombs they drop."

"I'd rather have *them* working on the truck parks than
fighters," said Pearly defensively, for he'd been the one to
request the missions. Since requests for B-52 utilization had
to be approved by PACAF, and often Strategic Air Command and the Pentagon got into the picture, it hadn't been
easy.

Moss ignored him, angrily shaking his head. "Send 'em
up to the DMZ to knock out some truck parks and NVA
temporary headquarters, and next thing you know, they're
acting like they're winning the war single-handed."

"It's the first time they've bombed in North Vietnam," explained Pearly.

"Hell, they were flying at thirty thousand feet, and as far as I know, the NVA never fired a shot at 'em."

"Probably not, sir."

"Anyway, General Roman wanted the lead crews *immediately* put in for DFCs, so we said yes, sir, and did it. Made them sound too much like heroes, I guess, because we just got a message from the air staff asking us to reevaluate using them up there. They heard about the medals and said we're putting high-priority aircraft in jeopardy."

"You want me to scrub their mission for tomorrow?"

"You think they're doing any good?"

"NVA prisoners say they're scared to death of them, General. One minute they're fat and happy around their camp fire, the next minute the world's erupting. The B-52's drop a lot of bombs, and right now we want to show as much damage as possible to the infiltration routes."

Moss pondered, then nodded. "One more time. Then have 'em back off. Many more missions up there, and we'll run out of medals."

"Yes, sir."

Moss eyed him and changed the subject. "Admiral Ryder called about an hour ago."

Pearly waited. It must have been something important. An hour before, it had been almost eleven P.M. in Hawaii, and few full admirals worked that late.

"He's nervous about the bridges campaign. I remembered some inputs from General Westy's intelligence people that the tonnage of war matériel coming south is dropping, so I told him that and about how we're starting to knock down bridges. I told him it'll get even better as the weather clears."

"Maybe that'll help."

Moss shook his head in disgust. "It's the rain slowing down the NVA supply line, Pearly. There hasn't been *time* for the action up north to slow things down here."

"I know, sir, but if we keep it up a little longer, the results will start to show."

Moss began to brood again. "You get on back to work. God knows someone around here has to. I'll spend my next hour answering the air staff's concerns, then I've got a meeting with a senator on another fact-finding tour, looking for truth from us lying, military monsters. And *then* I've got to have a midnight talk with General Roman about the possibility that our fucking cowboy fighter pilots might have bombed another unauthorized target."

Pearly stood to leave.

"Tell the guys out in the wings we'd better start knocking down more bridges, Pearly, or the politicians are going to call the whole thing off."

"Maybe that's what the guys'd like, sir. They're getting clobbered up there."

"Bullshit," said Moss. "For the first time in a while I think we just may be doing some good. And if I can feel it, I know the pilots out there feel it too."

Pearly braced himself. "I've got one more thing, General."

"Spit it out," Moss growled impatiently. "I've got work to do."

Pearly sucked a breath and told him about the compromised target list, then how he'd faked the tasking order and how the North Vietnamese had built up those defenses.

"It's one of my people, sir."

Moss sat stiffly, eyes locked forward sphinxlike. Pearly waited for the explosion.

Among the options Moss was undoubtedly considering was firing Pearly on the spot. Gates couldn't blame the general if he chose that route of action. American pilots had been killed or captured because of his reluctance to believe the leak could be coming from his branch. He had misplaced his trust. A leader was responsible for the actions of his men.

"You want me to call in the OSI, sir?"

Moss did not answer for a long while, just sat there staring. When he finally spoke, it was in a quiet voice, and the words were not at all what Pearly had expected.

"It's a strange war, Pearly. Back in the States we've got government officials releasing military secrets to the press, and the judicial system doesn't know how to handle it because there's no declared war. Schoolkids are rioting, and when the cops try to stop them, the press calls it police brutality. Politicians are scared of the press and refuse to help. We've got servicemen deserting to Canada and Sweden, and our so-called allies are sheltering them. A strange war, threatening to destroy the fabric of our democracy."

"Yes, sir, it is."

"If your man is found out by the OSI and legal charges

are preferred, a hundred top-notch lawyers in the States will rush to come to his defense. The worst that will happen to him will be some jail time and a less-than-honorable discharge, and I'm not even sure of that. He'll become a celebrity with the peace movement. In any event, our headquarters will be disgraced, and the brush will likely extend to our fighting men."

Pearly shifted uneasily on his feet.

"There are a lot of heroic men here who deserve better."

"Yes, sir."

"I wonder how many pilots have been killed because of the leak?" Moss asked quietly. "You're a numbers man. How many?"

Pearly spoke haltingly. "As many as thirty airplanes went down because of . . . of the immediate defensive buildups in the past six months."

Moss shook his head slowly. "Thirty pilots."

"More like forty. Some were two-place F-4's and A-6's."

Moss leaned back in his chair.

"You say you've narrowed it down to two of your men?"

"Two are most likely suspects, sir."

"What are their names?"

"Sergeant Slye and Airman First Class O'Neil, sir. I still don't know which one's giving out the information. I can't believe it's O'Neil, but then it's hard to think it's either of them. Sergeant Slye is . . ."

"Just the names. I don't want to hear anything more."

"Slye and O'Neil, sir."

General Moss wrote the two names on a pad. "You've contained the damage for the future?"

"I've placed both men on a special project, cataloging outdated amendments and changes to contingency plans. Neither of them's happy about it, but nothing they're working on now would be harmful if it was leaked. Perhaps embarrassing, but not harmful."

Moss made up his mind. "I won't tell you what to do about it, Colonel. It's your shop, and your people."

Pearly was surprised. "Sir?"

Moss was measuring him closely. "Handle it. Do what's right."

"Yes, sir," said Pearly Gates, wondering what the right thing was, and how he would do it.

Day 14, 0200 Local—Red River Valley, North Vietnam

Major Lucky Anderson

He was lean, down to one-fifty pounds he thought, for he'd labored hard and eaten little for the past eight days. The worst of the hunger had left him. Now there were just the times during the night while he was traveling when his stomach would knot up to tell him something was wrong. He was growing weaker, but all of that was about to end.

He trotted through the field, carrying the dead chicken in his new hat, treasuring it and salivating whenever he thought of it.

Not a big chicken, just one of the scrawny kind the poor gomer farmers kept in their yards. They were never fed, just allowed to forage in the dirt and compete with every other living thing for food. This one had looked in the wrong place. The hen had clucked and probably wondered what the hell the thing was lying there covered in the mud, but it had not wondered long after it pecked at the hand he'd painstakingly positioned there.

Not a sound had it croaked when he'd grasped the neck and squeezed. A silent kill except for the wild flapping. He'd held on desperately for more than a minute, squeezing hard and hoping no one heard. Finally it had stopped flopping about, and he'd pulled it down into the muck with him. He'd lain there then, immersed among the reeds at the side of the canal not more than a hundred yards from a farmhouse.

He'd clutched the dead chicken for two more hours, until half an hour after sunset. Then he'd sneaked up to the unfortunate farmer's shack and taken a ratty-looking conical hat from his porch. The gomer and his family had been inside talking, six feet from him on the opposite side of the thatch wall, and he'd taken his hat and bird and crept away feeling like a million dollars.

He was partway across the valley, between the two wide rivers, the Lo and the Red, traveling very slowly because of all the people living in the valley.

Crossing the Lo had been difficult and cost him two days. The first time he tried, he'd come a hair's breadth from being discovered by a river boatman. He'd scurried back from the water's edge, burrowed into his rice paddy, and thought the next night's plan through more carefully. He'd made it across by kicking behind a small, decrepit boat he'd liberated.

His maps, matches, and the Phoenix Special were waterproofed, the maps by their plastic sheathing, the matches and ammo in the sealable plastic bag with the pistol. Everything else was soaked, as he was, for he'd found it was easiest to hide in mud and water. He preferred thickets of reeds found along a river or canal's bank, but he'd sometimes settle for an abandoned rice paddy. His skin was wrinkled and puckered when he emerged each evening, and he picked off leeches and dug fleas and nits from his hair until he tired of it, but he felt he was safest in the water.

Every other day he tried to contact the Thuds overhead to tell them he was still evading. Twice he'd missed them, but he had talked to them four times since leaving Thud Ridge. Once he was sure it was Colonel Mack he'd spoken to. The other discussions had been with strangers.

They all cheered him on, telling him things like *"hang in there, buddy,"* but he knew they thought he had no chance of making it, because no one else had.

They don't know Lucky Anderson, he growled to himself, although the words were bravado. It was not his way to think about dismal alternatives until they were forced on him.

The survival radios were great, he'd thought at first, just as waterproof as they'd been briefed. He'd decided to write a letter to whoever the hell manufactured the things when he got out, to thank them for making a great product. Then, two days earlier, one of the damned things had quit on him when he was talking with Colonel Mack, and he cursed himself for leaving the third one behind on Thud Ridge. One radio left now, and he would need it for the pickup, so he planned to use it sparingly.

He found a small road going his direction, put on the gomer hat, and clutching the chicken, continued traveling west by southwest. With the moon down to a sliver there was little to illuminate his way, so he proceeded cautiously.

The headpiece inside the thatch hat was woven to fit a much smaller head, and he was having trouble balancing it in place. He stopped and carefully put the dead chicken down, then stretched the headpiece with his hands, keeping at it until he could wear it. It wasn't a great job, for he'd torn the woven mesh on one side, making the hat perch lop-sided on his head, but at least it stayed in place.

Other than the hat he wore only the flight suit and boots. He'd discarded the g-suit on the ridge. His socks had deteriorated into ragged strips after the sixth day, so he wore the boots over bare feet. His few remaining belongings he carried in the pockets of the filthy flight suit.

He hurried down a long portion of the road, for he could see no one there in the dim light. It felt good to stretch out his legs and walk like that.

A voice barked out from the side of the road. He noticed a shadow there.

He kept walking, not knowing what else to do.

The voice called after him, but he continued on.

If it was an NVA soldier, he might be shot, he thought, but he sure as hell didn't know how to answer, so he just kept going, clutching the chicken to his chest. Maybe the guy was just commenting on having just seen the world's biggest gomer.

He heard no one following, so he continued the pace and felt better about things.

Then he heard the revving of diesel engines.

Coming his way? He slowed, still cradling the precious chicken in his arms, and continued down the center of the hole-pocked road.

He saw dim lights moving south to north, perpendicular to his route. A main road? He also heard a babble of distant voices and the sounds of more and more vehicles.

He continued walking for several more minutes, then stopped and stood very still. An intersection was less than a hundred yards ahead, and there were a hell of a lot of people there.

He edged off the road and into a dark field, wondering. There were hundreds of lights blinking and moving as far as he could see in both directions on the main road, humans carrying flashlights and lanterns.

A long line of traffic came from the south, paused at the intersection, then continued northward. Vehicles were also stopping half a mile farther down the road.

Highway 2. He'd remembered it from the map and had been looking for it, but he hadn't anticipated it would be *this* busy. And the checkpoints? He wondered what the hell they were looking for. After a few minutes of pondering he gave up and just thought about how he might get across the thing without being detected ... and without losing his chicken.

The road he was traveling was a small one, running parallel to a larger one the map showed a mile or two to the south, which also intersected Highway 2. He didn't want to wander far from his present route, because it was the shortest way across the valley. But how the hell was he going to get across the road?

He cautiously made his way farther into the field, then sat and thought *fuck it*, he'd stay put for a bit while he thought over the thorny problem.

He started to pluck the chicken, which was a tough job without hot water to douse the thing in, and began to steel himself so he'd be able to eat raw bird. After he'd spent half an hour on the plucking job, he had an audacious idea.

There were a million fires flickering throughout the valley, maybe more, because many of the rice farmers kept a small fire going outside their thatch houses. What the hell would be suspicious about one more? Why not build a small fire, cook the bird, and dine in style?

He wandered about the field as silently as possible until he'd found several abandoned and drained rice paddies. He picked the one with the highest banks, to help shield a small fire from view, and went about collecting wood. When he'd built his small tepee of sticks and had another stack beside it, he used one of his precious matches. As soon as the fire was surely started, he held the chicken to it and singed off the remaining feathers.

Distant voices drifted over the field.

Fuck 'em, he joked, they could find their own chicken. As the skin crackled in the heat, he was unable to stop salivating.

In the gloom of predawn, Lucky began to search for a place to hide for the day. He'd spent most of the night eating and celebrating his fortune, his way blocked by the horde of people on and near the road. He liked to wait for the half light of morning to pick his hiding places, because whenever he'd tried it in darkness, he'd selected poorly.

And as he looked around in the false dawn, it became apparent why he'd seen all the people on the road the previous evening. He was camped, had cooked and eaten the chicken, only a couple of hundred yards from an NVA SAM site. A loaded missile launcher was set up there, clearly visible, and he could see two more in the distance.

Jesus! They'd been setting up the things during the night, while he'd been eating his chicken and thinking how fucking smart he was. The lights immediately south of him hadn't been from the road, they'd been the gomers setting up and loading their launchers.

And then he saw that on either side of the highway, for as far as he could see in either direction, were series of artillery batteries, with the long snouts of big guns sticking up out of the six revetted positions of each battery.

There'd been no checkpoints, just gomers telling the trucks where to haul the guns.

He looked about slowly, counted maybe a hundred trucks parked helter-skelter everywhere. Including in the fucking field he was in. Over each truck was draped a camouflage net, and beside each was a slouching, bored, and well-armed guard.

When he'd recovered sufficiently from his shock to start thinking of a way to get the hell out of the area, a siren sounded in the distance. Then a Klaxon horn at the SAM site began making an awful racket.

They've seen me, was his first reaction, and he hunkered low to get out of their view before he started thinking more clearly.

It was time for the morning strike. That was what they were after, not a dumb-shit fighter jock they'd *already* shot down.

Lucky stuffed the legs, wings, and neck of the chicken—he'd saved those for today's feast—into the pockets of his flight suit. He double-checked that the Phoenix Special was ready for firing and slipped it into the left upper pocket, zipping it closed until only the butt was exposed.

He heard a distant *whump-whump-whump,* then much louder sounds as some of the nearer guns began firing.

The noise became deafening.

Lucky almost looked up to see what they were shooting at, but returned to his senses. He clapped on the gomer hat and held it in place as he ran toward the highway. He couldn't think of a better time to cross the highway.

He hurried faster.

A tremendous roar and a crack so loud it made him stumble and clutch his ears. *Jesus!* Then a second SAM passed overhead, and he regained his composure and was again running hard when the third one created its sonic boom.

He crossed the road, heard loud yelling coming from the nearest gun position as the men worked, then an ear-shattering *BA-BOOM, BA-BOOM, BA-BOOM* as their gun fired in concert with the others.

He almost fell into a gun pit filled with two soldiers manning one of the smaller guns, changed directions and intercepted a farm road and ran even harder down it, continued until the sounds of the guns stopped. He ran on until he saw people on the road in the distance. That was when he finally slowed to a walk.

He adjusted his hat so it would perch in place and stalked off the road, past a farmhouse toward a raised dike, hoping it held a reservoir or canal to serve as his bedroom.

Dumb shit, he started to grumble at himself as he climbed the dike and examined the reservoir there. Then he revised his estimate. He was full of gomer chicken, felt almost human, and he'd crossed the big, busy highway.

He found a suitable patch of reeds and peered back over the dike. He was far enough from the farmhouses. While he continued to watch for people, he fieldstripped the Phoenix Special and placed it and the matches into the plastic pouch.

Five minutes later he saw a second strike force in the distance. He pulled out his radio, selected 243.0, ensured the volume was very low, and transmitted.

"*F-105's, this is Barracuda lead, transmitting in the blind,*" he radioed.

After a couple of tries he contacted them and told them he was still evading. He ended his transmission by telling them, "*It won't be much longer now until I'm ready.*"

His contact asked something, but he was through, and he carefully shut off his final radio to conserve its battery.

1500 Local—MAC-SOG Liaison Office, Danang Air Base, South Vietnam

Sergeant First Class David Bowes

Bowes worked as an administrative NCO at the MAC-SOG liaison office at Danang, a three-man group formed to coordinate air support for Special Forces A- and B-Team operations. The previous week he'd received a call on the scrambled, secure phone from his cousin at Takhli, and this morning he'd received another, and both times he'd told Billy there was nothing his group could do about the problem.

"I don't think there's any way we can find out where he is," he'd told Billy, and he'd told the truth. He had tried to get the people at the Monkey Mountain communications site to help, but they'd told him they had other priorities.

"If we can find out where he is, you think there's any chance your people could go in and get him out?" Billy had asked.

"We don't operate up there," David had told him for the third or fourth time, "because of an executive order against offensive ground operations inside North Vietnam."

Billy had sounded discouraged.

David hated that, for he'd liked Billy ever since he'd been a cocky young kid. He and Mal Stewart, another cousin, who'd been only a year younger than David, had agreed that Billy had the intelligence and drive to get a college education.

Before he'd enlisted in the Army, David had talked to Billy's high-school teachers and asked them to keep encouraging him, and he'd told Mal to keep him advised on Billy's progress. Later, when Billy won his scholarship to Oke U, both he and Mal, who'd enlisted in the Air Force by then, had helped with letters of encouragement and whatever meager amounts of money they could spare. Then Billy had been enrolled in Air Force ROTC, and the U.S. government had taken over the financial load of Billy's education.

It had been a proud day when he and Mal—Mal not long out of OCS and wearing lieutenant's bars, and he the stripes of a Spec-4—had attended the graduation at the Norman campus. It had surprised no one when Billy announced his intent to attend pilot training.

Theirs was a close-knit family. When Billy's brother and then Mal had been killed in action, flurries of letters and telephone calls of anger, compassion, and support had been circulated. Certain things had been instilled in each of the clan members. Among them were dictums always to honor blood ties and never to lie to one another.

But now it had been necessary to lie to his younger cousin, for it was closely held that Special Ops aircraft based at Nha Trang periodically did insert long range recon patrols into North Vietnam. The missions of the groups, called India Teams by the Air Force and by their recon-team code names by the Special Forces coordinators were so closely held that David seldom knew what was going on. The fact that the teams even existed was classified, but he did know a few of the members.

Special Forces recon teams were normally inserted to operate in the sparsely populated southern regions of North Vietnam. Farther north there were supposedly only the indigenous teams, meaning NVA soldiers who were at least *thought* to have been turned, but neither the brass nor anyone else trusted them. And of course that was where they'd have to operate if they were to find Billy's flight commander.

There was one team leader he mentally zeroed in on. A shadowy fellow called Black, who he'd heard led a unique recon team named Hotdog, and who was presently on temporary duty at Danang.

Sergeant Black was not the man's real name and possibly not his rank. David Bowes did not even know if Sergeant Black was in the military or was perhaps some kind of civilian spook agent. He did know that he was considered capable, one of the best at whatever he did, and that his team had been dropped into and extracted from *somewhere* on previous occasions. The locations were so closely held that David hadn't known where they'd operated, but from the security level alone he felt it must have been an interesting locale.

Shooting in the blind, David called over to the Special Forces camp, dubbed the NCC, for Sergeant Black.

Half an hour later a man wearing civilian clothing came into his office and dropped into a chair. He looked at David Bowes with dark and expressionless eyes.

"You wanted to see me?"

Hell, thought David, *I don't even know if the bastard's an American.* He looked a bit Japanese, but he was too stocky and thick-chested. He had a Caucasian's nose, but his face was round and his eyes Asian. He looked a little Negroid, but his hair was straight as a shock of black wheat.

Sergeant Black

Sergeant Black was all-American. Not only did his eyes get misty when he heard "The Star Spangled Banner," he knew every word of his anthem. He could quote the Declaration of Independence and Lincoln's Gettysburg Address verbatim, and felt honored to be accorded the privilege of fighting for the finest country ever to appear on planet earth.

He had royalty in his bloodline, in murky but traceable lineage back to King Kamehameha I, the most resolute and capable leader to emerge from a long line of tough Polynesian warrior kings. He also had a smattering of Portuguese and Japanese blood, from ancestors brought in to work the huge Hawaiian plantations on Lanai and the big island, as well as a dash from an early-American missionary who had dallied too long with a convert.

He'd joined the military as a young man in trouble with the Honolulu law, told either to enlist or face charges for the beating of a *haole* tourist who'd tried to force himself on his sister. No choice at all there, so he'd dropped out of his first year at the University of Hawaii and said hello to a grinning Army recruiter.

He loved the United States Army as much as he loved America, for to him they were inseparable, so it turned out not a marriage of convenience but one of love. He liked to think he was the best in the world at what he did, which was to covertly find out what the enemy was up to without getting his team compromised. So far he had been promoted, awarded a Silver Star Medal, and put in for a Distinguished Service Cross, so someone up there agreed.

He lounged in the chair as he heard what SFC Bowes had to say, and felt his interest grow.

"This guy's got a badly burned face, you say?"

"From an aircraft fire of some kind," said David Bowes. "I met him once and he looks like shit, but he doesn't seem to let it bother him."

"And now he's trying to make his way across the Hong Valley?"

"They *think* he's somewhere there. He's been on the run for two weeks, and the North Vietnamese don't have a good fix on him, but we don't know exactly where he is either, because he's smart enough not to give his location over the radio."

"So what do you want from me?" asked the man called Sergeant Black.

David Bowes looked at him squarely. "I can't ask for a damn thing except your interest."

"You got it. I admire this Anderson guy's balls." He stood up to leave. "Keep me informed, Sarge."

"Will do." Then Bowes looked askance at him. "Tell me what the fuck your rank is, Black, so I'll know how to talk to you."

"You already know. Shit, man, you called me sergeant, didn't you?"

"Yeah, but are you a fucking E-4 or an E-7 or what? Hell, maybe I'm overstepping myself by even talking to you like this."

"I think you're doing just fine, Sarge." He nodded pleasantly. The United States Army captain called Sergeant Black quietly left, thinking it might be interesting to find out more about Major Lucky Anderson.

Black's bunch of renegades, the recon team code-named Hotdog, was being prepared for insertion on a very interesting mission up north, but it might be several weeks before they'd be given the green light. Timing was everything in the world of Special Operations, and they didn't dare rush things.

Too bad, he thought. By the time they were dropped in, Anderson would likely be captured.

He tried to push the matter from his mind, but the image of the faceless American pilot came back to him. While it was highly unlikely he would make it across the Red River Valley, it would sure feel good to help him get out if he did.

Before returning to the NCC and his men, Black looked up his contact at Monkey Mountain, the hill at one side of the big base from which bristled hundreds of camouflaged antennae. From Monkey Mountain the Army Security Agency, Air Force Communications Service, and National Security Agency people monitored radio transmissions from South and North Vietnam, Laos, Cambodia, and southern China.

Sergeant Black asked his ASA contact for a private favor, to advise him of any radio transmissions to or from a downed pilot, call sign "Barracuda lead," on the survival-radio frequencies. He wanted a position and anything else they could give him.

The Monkey Mountain spook said he'd try to work it in, but he doubted they could spare the receiver time to scan the five frequencies and try to get a positive position. Priorities already had them working overtime, he said.

"When can you spare the receiver time?" asked Sergeant Black.

All he received was a slow shake of the head and a raised eyebrow.

They bartered.

Black promised him ten watermelons from the bunch they were flying in from the Special Forces camp at Nakhon Phanom, Thailand. The watermelons from NKP were especially sweet and juicy and were treasured by Americans throughout Southeast Asia.

The spook said his men would *make* time for Black's request.

CHAPTER TWENTY-FOUR

Captain Billy Bowes

They were Red Dog flight, and again they were going after the damned bridge over the Canales des Rapides, which still hadn't been knocked down. Takhli had been sicced on the thing six times, Korat five times, Ubon once, and the Navy a couple of times, but no one had hit it.

In the meantime they'd gone back to destroy another span of the Doumer bridge, which must have been frustrating to the gomers who'd worked like dogged machines to repair it. They had also successfully bombed two other bridges. But the damned Canales bridge was small, elusive, and tough.

The saying went around that the world was hinged by the Canales bridge, and if they destroyed it, the world would come apart, and that was why the gomers had about 200 big guns protecting it.

They'd laughed, and then they'd gone out and lost another pilot and missed again.

Today they would succeed. Billy Bowes felt it, even though he was nursing an engine that refused to develop sufficient thrust. It was a bird that had just been assigned to Sergeant Hughes to replace 820, and Hughes hadn't yet had time to perform his magic. The crew chief had told him he didn't trust the damned airplane, that he just didn't have a good feel for it yet. He'd wanted Bowes to take a spare aircraft instead, but Billy had insisted. He liked flying his own airplane, with his and Hughes's names painted on the canopy rail.

After start-up Billy had seriously considered aborting when his engine-pressure ratio had been low. Also the engine decay—the rate of RPM drop-off when he chopped the throttle to idle—had been poor. But the outside temperature had been cooler than normal, and he'd talked himself into making the takeoff since it shouldn't take quite as much runway as usual.

He'd regretted the decision during takeoff roll, when the Thud accelerated slowly and he'd kept rolling and rolling down the runway. He'd lifted off when he could see only green and no more concrete before him, and then had trouble keeping the damned Thud airborne.

Too close, he'd nagged himself as he finally joined up with lead five miles north of Takhli. But since then, except for the fact that it didn't want to develop enough power, he'd not had trouble with the engine.

They crossed the muddy Red River, with Red Dog at the tail end of the gaggle, and listened to the Weasel flight as they started to work the SAMs in the valley ahead. The Wild Weasel pilot reported that two sites were active between the Red River and Thud Ridge.

The strike force commander was John Encinos, their squadron commander whom the guys called Bad Injin, a nickname that made Billy bristle and think of his Cherokee blood whenever he heard it. Encinos was very quiet. Probably, Billy thought, because he was scared shitless.

It was one of the few times they'd seen him fly this far north, and certainly the first time he'd led a mission in pack six. Normally he'd put himself on the pack-six schedule only when the weather was so shitty over Hanoi, he knew they weren't *really* going to be bombing there. This time he'd been on the schedule for an easy flight to pack two, but the target had been changed and he'd been trapped, because B. J. Parker had been in the command post watching.

One of the pilots had snickered about it, and said it was

going to be hard for the Bad Injin to fake it with the North Vietnamese shooting at him.

So far Encinos had remained very quiet, providing neither leadership nor interference with the flight leads' calls.

The two Fansong SAM radars began flickering their strobes on the RHAW scope, and Billy found himself getting edgy. Dodging SAMs took a lot of maneuvering energy, and with the reduced power he was getting, he wondered if it wasn't time to call Manny and tell him about his Thud's marginal engine. But if he told him, Manny would send him back with Smitty, and that would reduce their chances for a successful mission by that much. After thinking about it, he decided he could make it okay.

Someone up ahead in the flak-suppression flight, led by Colonel Encinos, called that they had a valid SAM launch.

Billy kept his eyes peeled forward for a moment, looking for the SAMs and for the flight up there. He found the Thuds in the distance, four winged specks on the horizon approaching the midpoint of Thud Ridge. Then the dots begin to scatter like startled quail.

No orderly calls and maneuvering, just three aircraft breaking away from one of them who just continued jinking wildly from side to side but not changing his flight pattern.

Break! Billy started to call, because he could see the first SAM coming up, darting toward the lone Thud at great speed.

Someone beat him to it. *"SAM, Falcon lead. Break!"*

But by the time the words were out, the first SAM explosion had momentarily engulfed the Thud. The airplane emerged and flew on, now straight ahead and not jinking at all. Then two more SAMs hit the bird, one after the other. John Encinos's aircraft was torched by the second SAM, and the third one burst it into a thousand pieces.

The SAM operator had scored three hits with three SAMs, all on the same target.

Overkill, thought Billy.

The largest chunks were visible, burning and tumbling earthward. There were no sounds of an emergency beeper, so one of the falling pieces was the Bad Injin in his seat.

The remaining three ships of the flak-suppression flight turned for home, for they'd jettisoned their CBUs and tanks when they'd dodged the SAMs.

Billy Bowes looked about the sky, scanning for MiGs. His gaze finally settled on his wingman, Smitty.

"Move it out a little farther, Red Dog four," he called tersely.

Captain Manny DeVera

Manny was horrified by the scene played out by Bad Injin and the SAMs, but did not dare let his mind ponder it.

Remember what Lucky told you, he thought. *Concentrate on what you'll do.*

Today the damned bridge was going down, period.

They flew past the Ridge, and then five miles farther before the flights, one by one, turned southward.

They would bomb the bridge from east to west, pause to rejoin over the ridge, then skedaddle back across the Red. Manny's Red Dogs would be the last strike flight on target, and last out of the valley.

The Bad Injin hadn't briefed it that way. He'd just kept asking the flight leaders how *they* intended to do things, and even Lieutenant DeWalt had been embarrassed by his indecision. Finally Max Foley and Manny had stood up and taken over, and had gotten a plan together. Max was leading the first strike flight, he the last, so they figured they could keep a good watch over the two flights in between and get it all to come out reasonably well.

Manny radioed that the flights hadn't gained enough separation and were still crowded too closely together. Max called for his flight to accelerate and for the others to drop farther behind.

Abeam Thai Nguyen the second flight called a SAM launch, and by the time they'd dodged the missiles, they'd scattered almost as badly as the flak-suppression flight had.

Two pilots had punched off their bombs so they'd have better maneuvering energy. Which was shitty, because when you jettisoned your stores, you were wasting a planeload of bombs. Those two were now just along for the ride, thought Manny. Dropping the bombs and tanks was not necessary if you dodged the SAMs properly, as Major Lucky had taught C-Flight, and Manny decided to talk to the other guys about that.

"Red Dog three's got a MiG-17 in sight at our ten o'clock low, going away."

Billy Bowes, with his magical eyes.

"*Roger three,*" replied Manny. "*Keep your eye on him in case he turns back.*"

"*Wilco.*"

He saw the target area up ahead. First the wide Red River, then the river Y and the smaller branch to the north, and finally the bridge that had been giving them such a hard time.

Max and his crew were there already, looking small in the sky as they hurtled earthward in their dive-bomb attacks.

"*Red Dog four has a SAM activity light,*" called Smitty in a shaky voice.

No need to respond. If it changed to a LAUNCH light, he might worry about it.

Spouts of smoke and debris in the target area. Then great geysers where other bombs hit the water. He looked closer.

No hits by Max Foley's flight. The bridge appeared insolent down there, mocking them, impervious to their attempts.

The two aircraft of the second flight with bombs remaining were in the dive, each tracked by flurries of dark flak bursts. They missed the bridge, and so did the third flight. By then there was a lot of smoke lingering around the target, and from eyeballing the direction it blew, he'd judged the wind to be fifteen knots, east to west.

"*Red Dog lead's in the dive,*" he announced, and rolled in.

A little shy of forty-five degrees. Which meant he'd adjust his sight picture just a bit, right?

Yeah.

He aimed thirty feet east of the bridge to compensate for the wind, added a couple more feet for the adjustment, and glanced back and forth from altimeter to his sight picture.

He did not jink, although they were shooting well and the flak was *too* damn close. He wanted very badly to knock down the bridge, and then he wanted never to return.

Steady, steady . . . now.

He released at 6,500 feet, smoothly stroked in the afterburner and jinked left as he waited, sinking lower until the afterburner kicked in and the aircraft began to accelerate and climb.

He raced toward the hills for a few seconds, then turned hard right and looked back.

Great spouts of water and debris from his bombs were still hanging in the air.

The bridge was down in its center!

Henry's bombs hit as he watched and went off just beside the bridge, so close that the fallen section from his own hit was blown sideward. The arch rocked and swayed, and then a second span fell.

C-Flight had knocked down two spans of the toughest bridge in North Vietnam.

He reversed his course and sped for the ridge, feeling jubilant.

1650 Local—Plans & Programs, HQ Seventh AF, Tan Son Nhut Air Base, Saigon

Lieutenant Colonel Pearly Gates

"General Moss wants to see you ASAP," the female staff sergeant called in to Pearly.

Pearly rose wearily and began to prepare himself mentally. For the past three weeks, following his revelation about the leak coming from his own office, his meetings with Moss had been strained. He trudged toward the general's office thinking of the good news he was bearing. The Takhli strike force had radioed a success code on the bridge at the Canales des Rapides. If the BDA photos confirmed it, that was very good.

If Moss fired him, at least he'd go out on a high note.

He entered the general's outer office and the secretary motioned.

"He's inside with Mr. Smith," she whispered, meaning he was with a CIA agent.

"Should I wait?" he asked.

"He wants you to go right in," she said.

He rapped once on the door, military style, and peered inside.

Moss waved vaguely at him. He was talking to a man wearing a short-sleeved bush jacket.

"You have any idea who it might be?" Moss was asking.

"Not yet. We'll find them, but they're elusive," said Mr. Smith.

Moss glanced at Pearly. "Mr. Smith thinks the information leak may still be open."

Pearly grew a heavy feeling in his chest. "Is classified information still getting out?"

Mr. Smith looked at him without expression.

Moss spoke to Smith. "You can talk in front of him. Go back over it again."

The agent's face remained impassive as he recounted his story. "For a while now we've had an API reporter under surveillance. Three months back he began sending in releases containing information he could only have gotten from the Cong, so we took a look. Couple of days ago we went through his apartment and found some interesting notes."

Pearly's heart began to pound. "You think he's the leak?" He prayed it was so.

"Probably part of it. He's been visited regularly by a known VC agent. A cabbie we used as a source from time to time until we learned we were being trick-fucked by the commies."

"Jesus," said Pearly, shaking his head.

"But the reporter doesn't have access to anything classified, so he's getting his information from someone inside the system. When we went into his apartment, we found notes written in two different hands. A few were written on notebook paper, with some drawings showing the perimeter defenses around the embassy compound. Then there were a bunch of old napkins with North Vietnamese coordinates."

Pearly tried to remain calm. "Could I get the coordinates?"

Mr. Smith glanced at the general.

Moss nodded.

The agent handed over a typewritten page, which Pearly examined. He went to the map on Moss's wall and moved his finger from one set of coordinates to the next.

Power plants, barracks, and rail sidings.

"Are those new targets?" asked Mr. Smith.

"Old ones," said Pearly. "We haven't hit most of them for months."

"You sure?" The agent looked discouraged.

Pearly nodded. He looked over at General Moss, wondering if he shouldn't tell the agent that someone in his office had copied target coordinates, that he'd run his own scam, and the North Vietnamese had moved their defenses accordingly.

Moss's face was neutral.

He'd told Pearly to handle the problem, and to *do what's right*.

Pearly withheld his secret.

The agent sighed. "Perhaps the ARVN major was the source of the leak after all. The time frame's right. Maybe he gave the coordinates to the reporter. Maybe. We're still wary. We can't find out how the major could have gotten access to targeting data. Can't figure out why he wouldn't have just gone directly to the VC. And it was the VC cabbie who gave the tip on him to the OSI."

Moss said, "Pick him up and question him."

"Killed himself, remember?"

"The reporter I mean."

"We've probably already overstepped ourselves by searching his place. The word's been passed straight from the State Department: *Don't fuck with the press.*"

"Not even on something as serious as this?"

"No matter what."

"How about the VC cab driver?"

"Went underground. We can't locate him."

Moss pursed his lips. "So where do you go from here?"

"Keep the reporter under surveillance. See where he goes, who he meets with. Next time the Vietnamese kick reporters out of the country, we'll make sure he's on the list."

The CIA agent turned to Pearly then, as if he'd remembered something. "You got a guy named Slye working for you? A staff sergeant?"

Pearly nodded, trying not to betray his excitement. Slye, the Arkansas farm boy turned barracks lawyer, was the one he'd come to suspect. He sorely wanted the CIA, or someone, to take over the problem and do the right thing for him.

"Slye was on our original long list of possibles. Then he was reported to be hanging around in Cholon at a couple of the off-limits bars, so we took a look."

Pearly waited expectantly.

"He's clean. Slye gets taken by the whores downtown, but the only crime he's committing is inflating the prices for the other guys. He made no contacts with anyone, including the API reporter. When we planted a bar-girl, he paid her double the going rate for a short time and wouldn't tell her anything when she pressed him. Said he was a cook and didn't know any secrets and paid her double for another hour. I think the poor bastard fell in love. Keeps going back to the same sleazy bar looking for her."

Pearly frowned. With Slye out of the picture, that left O'Neil, and he could not believe the serious-minded airman would do anything to betray his country. Gates had all but cleared him of suspicion and even now had doubts.

Moss thanked the CIA agent. He shook hands and left.

When they were alone, Moss took a paper from his desk drawer and looked at the two names Pearly had given him.

"Eliminates one of your suspects, doesn't it?"

"It would appear to, sir."

"Don't take much longer deciding, Pearly."

"No, sir."

Moss's voice changed tone. "Anything new?"

"Takhli reported a success code against the Canales bridge."

"Finally."

They talked about the CROSSFIRE ZULU campaign, and Moss was almost back to his old self, interjecting philosophies and war stories here and there.

"Any news about Lucky Anderson?" Moss finally asked.

"A couple of radio calls, but they still don't have his location. Intell thinks he's either on Thud Ridge or out in the Red River Valley, but they're not sure."

"He's still evading?"

"Yes, sir. As of yesterday anyway. They picked up a weak radio transmission."

"Damn near a month now since he went down."

"Almost."

"Anything you find out, make sure you pass to me."

"Yes, sir, I will." Pearly rose to his feet.

"Call B. J. Parker and congratulate his wing on knocking down the Canales bridge," said Moss as Pearly was leaving. "That was good work."

•   •   •

As Pearly returned to his floor, his mind was flooded with thoughts of doing "the right thing," to appease both General Moss and his own wounded soul.

Forty men had been shot down because of the security leak. If the normal rate was applied, that meant ten men were dead, fifteen captured and in prison, and fifteen rescued. And if the normal rate applied, more than half of those rescued had been injured during ejection.

Do the right thing.

"Sir?" asked a voice.

He raised his eyes and focused through the thick lenses.

Airman O'Neil was before him, his uniform and bearing correct as usual, his look more serious than normal.

"Sorry. Caught me deep in thought," Pearly muttered apologetically.

"I just wanted you to know, sir, that I've changed my mind about the commissioning program that Master Sergeant Turner talked to me about earlier. I plan to go to personnel and apply first thing in the morning, if I can get the time off."

Pearly swallowed and tried to smile, tried not to look the least bit suspicious. "If you can qualify, it'll mean the Air Force will send you to your last two years of school."

"I've thought about it a lot recently. I like the Air Force and believe I'd like to make it a career."

"I'm . . . ah . . . very pleased."

"I respect both you and Sergeant Turner for working with me like you have. It'll make me work harder in the program, to prove that neither of you have misplaced your trust."

"I appreciate that."

"By the way, sir. Sergeant Slye and I have just about finished the project Sergeant Turner gave us. Going over the outdated amendments, I mean."

"And what do you think of working with Staff Sergeant Slye?"

O'Neil hesitated. "The truth, sir?"

"The truth."

"Sometimes he's a little too sloppy with classified material, and he asks too many questions about things he should have no interest in. Other than that and coming in hung over every morning, I guess he's okay."

"What kind of questions does he ask?"

"Oh, about targets, things like that."

"But you didn't tell him anything, did you?"

"Of course not, sir. He has no need to know, but he seemed to have a lot of information about them already. He's sort of spooky."

"Thanks for the information."

"I've said too much, Colonel. I certainly don't mean to get Sergeant Slye in trouble."

"Don't worry about it. I'm not the kind to act rashly. But keep me advised if you see anything else out of the ordinary, okay?"

"Yes, sir. I will."

Pearly continued toward his office, his mind busy with what he'd just heard.

Was what O'Neil told him about Sergeant Slye true? Could the CIA have erred about Slye? Or was O'Neil aware they were closing in and trying to cast doubts about others?

Do the right thing.

What the hell was the right thing?

1945 Local—Officers' Club Stag Bar, Takhli RTAFB, Thailand

Captain Billy Bowes

"Scratch one gomer bridge," Manny DeVera said proudly.

"Not bad," said Billy with a wry look, "if we don't count all the times we went there."

"Two spans down," crowed Manny, ignoring him.

"I'd've hit the damn bridge too, if you guys hadn't hid the thing in the water," joked Billy. Which was right, because his bombs had hit in the void where the two spans had stood.

"God I wish Major Lucky and Turk Tatro were here," said Henry Horn.

"An' Bob Lieb . . . Liebermann," added Joe Walker.

Joe was more inebriated than Billy could ever remember seeing him, and it wasn't yet eight o'clock. Joe's bombs had destroyed the southern approach to the bridge.

"The thing is totally, fucking unusable," said Manny. "They're gonna play hell fixing that sucker like they do the Doumer bridge."

Joe Walker looked at Billy just a little cross-eyed. "Nex' time we go back to the Doumer, le's fix that bastard too."

"You do it by yourself, Joe," said Billy. "I'm tired of going there."

Joe looked hurt that Billy didn't want to join him.

"Hey, man," said Horn. "You want to go there again, let me know."

Joe turned to Henry, who'd been his friend since their first year at the Academy.

"You'll go with me, won' you, Henry?" asked Joe.

"Fuck no," said Horn with an amazed look, "but I'll wave when you take off."

They all laughed, especially when Joe Walker poured his beer over Henry Horn's head. Henry sputtered and blew, and said Manny DeVera was laughing too hard and poured his glass of whiskey on *his* head. Then Manny doused Billy with his sticky Scotch and Drambuie MiG-15, and not to be outdone, Billy poured his whiskey on Joe, who was laughing so hard that he hardly noticed.

"You started it, Joe. You buy the next round," said Manny.

"That's not fair," said Joe. "Hell, I'm the one who *missed* the fucking bridge."

"Then you sure as hell ought to buy," said Henry, "just for the privilege of drinking with your betters."

"Look here, honkie boy," said Joe Walker, "you keep it up and I'll *personally* teach you about war."

"What the fuck's a honkie?" asked Billy suspiciously.

"You don't know?" asked Joe.

"No. Something new?"

Joe Walker looked amazed that anyone could be so dumb. "Honkie's what the blacks are calling white boys back in the States," he said.

Billy was more than a bit drunk himself. He drew himself up and glared. "So what are they calling Indians?" he demanded.

A pilot turned to them from the bar, offering a sad look. "I heard about the Bad Injin," he said. "Too bad."

"I'm confused," said Henry. "Who said anything about the Bad Injin?"

Joe and Henry looked at one another, shaking their heads.

"Who gives a fuck about the Bad Injin?" growled Billy Bowes to the pilot who'd offered his condolence.

The pilot gave them a mean look, as if they'd committed sacrilege.

Joe and Henry began to laugh.

"Silly fucker should've got himself killed earlier, giving Indians a bad name like that," Billy muttered darkly.

That started the C-Flight lieutenants laughing harder. Everything seemed hilarious to the two. If someone had told them the Russians had nuked Washington, they'd have laughed.

Billy looked disgustedly at them, then turned to Manny. "I heard you sweet-talking and spouting bullshit on the phone. Was that your Peace Corps dolly?"

"Maybe," said Manny, looking innocent.

"Everybody's sure getting tired of seeing Lyons hustling her," said Billy. "About time you took her back."

Manny shrugged, but a smile was growing.

"You headed up to her camp?"

"No."

"You oughta. We're not on the morning schedule."

"She's coming here," said Manny.

Billy nodded, feeling better about it. Lyons was a true asshole. With him skulking around trying to catch someone bombing a restricted target, everyone was worried he might settle on them. He didn't *deserve* to be squiring a pretty girl around as he was doing.

2320 Local—Guest Trailer

Captain Manny DeVera

Although they'd been in the trailer for no more than an hour, she'd already demonstrated her ankle-grabbing trick twice. Now she was on top, rocking ever so slightly, and he was just beginning to grow to the occasion when she decided it was time to discuss things between them.

"Let's talk later," he said in a gravel voice.

She rocked and worked the muscles, and made him groan.

"Damn," he hissed. "That's wonderful."

She pushed and squirmed until she had him fully inside, into the hot center of her, and then shuddered and cried out for a while before she slowly began to milk him again.

When he'd finished, she became very still.

"I missed you," he finally said.

"I couldn't have told that," she said in a petulant tone, "the way you acted like I didn't exist."

"You didn't look so lonely."

"Don't ever snub me and think I'll be lonely. There's other fish out there."

He grew quiet about it, not wanting to hear more.

She wasn't through. In fact, she giggled.

"Was he that good?" He tried not to sound as if he were sulking.

"Who?" she asked innocently.

"Lyons."

She giggled again. "He thinks I'm a poor, frightened virgin."

"What're you talking about?"

"Colonel Lyons. He's been wining and dining me like I'm the queen of England. Keeps telling me about his family and their *old money,* and how he can't live with his wife anymore because she's so *common.*"

He snorted.

"He says he'd consider marrying me, if I'd just be reasonable and go to bed with him. Keeps telling me how it won't hurt much, and how someday I'll even enjoy it."

"Lyons says that?"

"Then I tell him I just can't, 'cause what would my mother think if she found out, and he groans and grabs his balls and runs off to the bathroom."

"You're shitting me."

"Three times he's done that now."

"And you haven't given him any?"

"All I want from him are some supplies every couple of weeks. We've already got the best-equipped Peace Corps camp in Thailand, maybe in all Asia, because of him."

Manny laughed uproariously.

"But don't get too obnoxious about how much I missed you. There's a couple guys at the camp who're ready to take your place in a minute, if you push me away again."

"Probably long-hair, draft-dodging hippies."

"They're fun, and they're more my age than *you* are."

"I'm not old," he said defensively. "Twenty-eight isn't old."

"That's the same line Colonel Lyons uses. He says"—she

lowered her voice—"*I'm not so old. I was promoted very quickly, you know.*"

"That's mean, Jackie, comparing me with him. He's at least ten years older than me."

"You tell me to fuck off again, I'll show you mean, hon."

"I needed some time to myself. I went through a bad period for a while."

"I waited."

Then he remembered her words. "But you didn't get lonely, you said."

She paused before speaking. "I meant *next* time I wouldn't let myself get lonely." Was there a hint of guilt in her tone?

Before he could question her further, she began rocking, and again he felt himself stirring. It had been a long time.

He rolled over with her, holding her gently, and let her reach down for her ankles . . . then started to give her a wild ride. Their accumulated juices made it a frictionless, slippery task. She grunted loudly each time he drove forward, her utterances mingling with the slapping sounds of their wet bellies. This time there was no one next door, so she made her sounds with abandon.

He drove her hard into the mattress, uncaring that the bed squeaked and the headboard thumped against the wall in a constant tempo. This time it took longer before he finally felt the delicious spasms and moaned with each surge of exquisite release. When he'd drained himself, he pushed fully into her and held tightly in place, and she began to make new sounds. A cooing that grew in volume as she began to shudder and stiffen her body.

She locked her legs in place, pressing her heels hard into his calves, and ground herself tightly to him as the sounds from her throat grew louder. She was at full volume then, pressing tightly to him and squealing. . . .

A pounding sound erupted on the door of the trailer.

Jackie sucked a sharp breath and stopped, lying very still and quiet beneath him.

The pounding again, this time more stridently.

"Fuck 'em," whispered Manny. He raised himself onto his elbows. "Ignore it."

The pounding sounded again.

She slithered from under him and fumbled for her

clothes, trying to catch her breath. She found and switched on the desk lamp.

"Tell 'em to go away," grumbled Manny.

Jackie pulled on panties and clutched her blouse closed before she cautiously went to the door.

Manny sat up and was reaching for his shorts as she opened the door and peered around it.

She said, "What do . . ."

"You lying bitch!"

And then she squealed as the door was thrown open and she was dragged outside.

Manny said fuck the shorts and rushed out into the darkness. He saw two people struggling a few feet away and then watched her reel away and scream.

Some asshole had hit her!

Manny leapt toward her assailant and began to punch him in the body, heard the groans and grunts as he connected. He drew back his fist then and sank it deep into a soft gut.

The man sucked in a series of breaths. "Eckkk! . . . Eckkk! . . . Eckkk!"

"Bastard," Manny growled. He grabbed the guy and dragged him to the ground and sat astraddle him. He punched him hard in the face.

The man caught his breath and sobbed. "Stop!"

Manny hit him in the mouth and felt teeth giving.

He squealed like a frightened, wounded pig.

"Rat fucker!" cried Manny, and hit him again.

Jackie ran around them and reopened the door of the trailer.

"I quid!" screamed Tom Lyons, caught in the momentary light. Blood was trickling from his mouth.

"You damned betcha you quid," said Manny, and hit him again.

Lyons squealed. "My *node*," he cried, trying to protect his blood-gushing nose.

Jackie had disappeared inside the trailer, but she switched on the porch light. Lyons's face was distorted and he was crying like a baby.

Manny got to his feet and dragged Lyons up by his shirt front.

"I quid," cried Lyons between sobs.

"You touch her one more time, asshole . . . you even *look*

like you're going to touch her . . . and I'll make you wish you
had it *this* good."

"I won'! I quid!"

Then Manny DeVera turned Lyons around and kicked
him in the ass with the side of his bare foot. Tom Lyons
stumbled, righted himself, and fled, running toward his
trailer only thirty yards distant.

Manny stood there, angry and huffing from exertion.

A major, the operations officer who now acted as commander of the 354th, hurried up and stood looking at him.
Manny stared back. Then he squared his shoulders and
grinned sheepishly.

"What the hell was all the noise about?" asked the ops officer.

"Stepped on a rat," said Manny.

The major looked over at the full colonels' trailers as Tom
Lyons slammed his door and locked it.

"A *big* rat," said Manny.

Silence.

Jackie pulled the curtain back and watched from the window.

"You want a towel or something?" asked the major.

Manny thought about his nudity. "Naw, thanks," he finally said. "Sometimes I go for midnight walks like this. Old
Mexican tradition. Lets the skin breathe." After thinking
about that for a moment, he casually turned to walk to the
Ponderosa, which was half a mile distant.

The trailer door cracked open. "Manny DeVera, get in
here," she said.

The ops officer grinned awkwardly, mumbled something
about hating fucking rats, then went back toward his trailer.

Jackie swung the door wider. "You're naked, hon. Come
on inside."

He peered at her face as he went in. She had a bruised
lip and was holding a washcloth to it.

"You okay?" he asked.

"I used to hit my brother harder than he hit me."

He chuckled and patted her on the shoulder. "You're
tough."

She grinned back at him. "Tough enough for the Supersonic Wetback?"

He nodded his head, impressed. "You damn right, you
are."

"How's Colonel Lyons?"

"I hit him harder than you hit your brothers," said Manny, looking at his skinned knuckles.

They both laughed nervously, coming down from their emotional highs.

"Well, I suppose I won't be getting any more supplies from *this* base," she said.

They laughed louder.

He was shaking with humor, but was able to stop long enough to say, "And I don't guess he's going to marry someone he suspects just might not be a virgin."

That time they howled with their laughter.

CHAPTER TWENTY-FIVE

Captain Manny DeVera

Manny was leaning back in one of the uncomfortable theater seats, drinking soda pop and thinking about Jackie and the crazy night, when a grizzled major wearing fatigues entered the room.

"Help you, sir?" asked a lieutenant.

"I'm looking for a Captain Manuel DeVera." He pronounced it *Duh-Veer-uh*.

"Right here," called Manny.

The major's pants were bloused and stuffed into the tops of shiny combat boots, and he wore a security-police badge on the left pocket of his fatigue shirt.

Manny shook his head, thinking Lyons had wasted no time in pressing charges. He'd wanted to go to B. J. Parker first thing that morning to tell him about the matter, but Parker was in Saigon visiting Seventh Air Force headquarters. And then he'd heard that Lyons had left that morning for Bangkok, so he'd figured he'd been smart enough to let it go.

He'd obviously thought too highly of the bastard.

"Talk to you?" asked the major in an *almost* friendly tone.

"Long as it doesn't take much time," said Manny. "I've got to fly this afternoon, which means I don't have much time before I've got to start flight planning."

"I just talked to your acting squadron commander. You're off the schedule."

"It's that serious?"

"Serious enough to talk about."

Manny stood. "My office is next door."

"Let's go to mine, Captain."

Manny sighed. "Well, I'd better tell the duty desk where I'll be."

"I've already done that."

They went out to the major's vehicle, a blue Air Force pickup with a light-bar on top.

"What did the bastard tell you?" asked Manny as they got in.

"Let's not talk about it until we get to my office and I read you your rights."

"Fuck my rights. The bastard hit a woman, so I decked him."

The major looked at him strangely, then shook his head. "Let it wait, okay?"

They drove in silence to the base commander's group of buildings. The cop shop was off to one side by itself, and Manny didn't fail to notice the small fenced stockade at its rear.

The major led the way inside and stopped at the desk, where he read him his rights under article thirty-one of the Uniformed Code of Military Justice in the presence of a burly tech sergeant. Then the three of them went into a small office with bare walls, furnished only with a table and chairs.

As the tech sergeant closed the door, Manny began to suspect that he might be in deeper shit than he'd thought.

"What's this about?" he asked, eyes narrowed.

"It sounded like you knew, back in the pickup," said the major.

"I'll hear it from you, then I'll tell you my side."

"You'll get your chance." He waved Manny into a chair and sat down opposite him. The tech sergeant leaned against the wall near the door, staring at Manny.

The major opened a folder, took out a paper, and read from it.

"The commander of the 355th Combat Support Group has ordered this inquiry into actions you are suspected of taking on two dates, those being . . ."

The base commander? Two dates? Manny was confused.

". . . April twenty-eighth and July twenty-ninth, 1967. On those dates it is alleged that you purposefully and illegally bombed targets that were specifically restricted by written and verbal lawful orders of your superior officers."

"What?" said Manny, not believing what he'd heard.

"You want me to read it again?"

"Yeah."

The major did, very slowly and clearly.

"That's bullshit," snorted Manny.

"We've got certain evidence to the contrary. Now it's your turn to prove it wrong."

"You mean I've got to prove myself innocent of a bunch of bullshit. Hell, I don't even know if I was flying on those dates."

"You were. We checked the schedule. This is just an informal inquiry, Captain DeVera, but I've got to tell you that if it goes further, you may be facing a court-martial."

"For dropping a couple of bad bombs?" he asked incredulously.

"For conspiracy against the government of the United States of America."

1150 Local—354th TFS Duty Desk

Captain Billy Bowes

The ops officer, who was acting squadron commander until a replacement arrived for Lieutenant Colonel Encinos, called Billy into his office and motioned for him to take a chair.

"Captain DeVera is in some kind of trouble," said the major. "I was just advised by the legal office that he's relieved of his position and all flying duties until it's straightened out."

Billy was stunned. After his initial shock he muttered, "Can't be anything bad. Hell, Manny wouldn't *do* anything bad." Then he frowned. "This have anything to do with Colonel Lyons and the Peace Corps dolly?"

"I don't know. All the legal officer said was that Manny's got to go through an informal inquiry, and that he might be facing something worse."

"Jesus."

"You're acting C-Flight commander until it's over."

Again Billy asked, "This have anything to do with Colonel Lyons?"

The major looked as if he knew something but didn't know whether to talk about it.

"Lyons hates Manny's ass," said Billy.

The major was a good shit, but the matter was beyond the normal domain of a fighter jock. After more hesitation he told Bowes what he'd heard and seen the previous night outside the guest trailer, which was not much except squeals and cries and Manny standing there buck-ass naked.

"It's gotta be Lyons behind this," said Billy.

"Lyons took the nine o'clock base flight to Bangkok this morning."

"Anyone see him?"

"He was all beat-up, but he wouldn't tell what happened."

Billy felt helpless. "Is there anything I can do to help Manny?"

"Not that I can think of. Hell, we'll all do what we can, Billy, but you're still going to have to take his place as C-Flight commander until it's straightened out."

When he emerged from the ops officer's office, Billy spotted Lieutenant Smith and waved him over. "You're going onto the flying schedule, Smitty."

Smith looked desolated. "I'm supposed to have the day off."

"And I just took it away."

"I was going to town with my *pu-ying*," Smitty complained. He had a Thai girlfriend, one of the Thai base commander's several daughters, and she liked to shop.

Billy didn't feel at all like arguing, so he gave him a glare. "Save your money. Now go get started on the flight plan. I'll be over there shortly."

"Who's flight lead?"

"I'll lead and you'll be on my wing. Henry and Joe will make up the second element."

Smitty nodded dejectedly, wanting to argue but not wanting to piss Billy off *too* badly.

Manny DeVera came in. He saw Billy and started over, wearing a grim expression.

"Go get started," Billy told Smitty. "I've gotta talk to Captain DeVera."

"I haven't had lunch yet," tried Smitty.

"Then get a fucking candy bar. Now go on, dammit."

Smitty started for the door, giving Manny a woeful look and trying to look sad enough that he might overrule Billy and give him back his day off.

"What's wrong with him?" asked Manny DeVera.

"Fuck Smitty. What the hell's happening with you?"

"You won't believe it," started Manny.

Wednesday, September 13th, 0320 Local—Phuc Yen PAAFB, DRV

Air Regiment Commandant Quon

Where is Lokee? his mind beseeched.

The UHF radio tracking station in Hanoi had picked up another transmission on the rescue frequency a few days earlier, but it had been so weak, they couldn't get a direction.

Why was the signal weaker? Had he moved farther away, or was his survival radio's battery being depleted?

It had now been thirty-four days and the rescue team had not found him, and Quon suffered from insomnia and stomach cramps from the thought that he might be getting away.

The rescue sergeant complained that they would have located him long before if it hadn't been for the morning downpours that eliminated traces of his passage. They had discovered an American-made survival knife, a demolished radio, and a .38 revolver where they'd been buried at the base of a knoll in the Viet Bac and then partially unearthed by the rain. Were they his? The sergeant thought so, but how could they be sure?

Why would he discard the revolver and radio? It was all very puzzling.

Quon had assigned the task of monitoring the progress of

the search team to his adjutant, as he'd promised General Tho. But as the search dragged on, instead of forgetting about the scarred Mee pilot, his mind had become obsessed with visions of the man's horrible face. The Mee pilot would first smirk, then begin to chuckle, and then laugh uproariously.

Not only had he killed his son, he *laughed* about it. As time passed, it became increasingly difficult to separate the fantasies from his real knowledge of the man. When the search team sergeant made excuses, Quon would shout that the Mee was laughing at him, and he must find the pilot or else . . .

But of course he knew the sergeant was the best, and he didn't dare have him replaced. He sighed and rose, preparing to travel to the Hoa Lo Prison and sit in as they interviewed yet another Mee prisoner from the Pig Squadron. He felt it was important to be there. Perhaps it was being face-to-face with a man who had met and knew the monster *Lokee*.

The adjutant knocked and entered.

"Is my automobile ready?" Quon asked tersely. Daytime surface travel for high-ranking officers was now strictly prohibited, but he often ignored the ban.

"I just spoke with the prison commandant on the telephone, comrade Quon. The lieutenant says they are being inspected by officials from the Ministry of Internal Affairs and he cannot receive you."

Quon cursed.

"He says the officials specifically forbade him to interview another prisoner for you until they investigate certain matters. The lieutenant said he is being asked difficult questions, comrade Quon, and begs that you go there no more."

Quon was livid that a civilian would interfere, but he knew it would be of little use to fight it. He jerked his head angrily toward the door, and the adjutant hurried out.

He paced the floor for several minutes, trying to calm his anger and thinking about the ineptitude of civilian officials in general. Finally he sat, still angry, and brusquely opened the latest new order from General Tho's VPAAF headquarters. The number of such orders had sharply increased since the Mee had begun to concentrate their efforts on bombing bridges and transshipment points.

ORDER NUMBER 412A

1/The newest American bombing campaign must be stopped. Each time a bridge or rail yard is damaged or destroyed by enemy air pirates supplies are delayed. Our brave soldiers fighting in the South must not be isolated. The problem is of the highest importance.

2/Air losses to enemy aircraft are again rising and must be reduced, and more Yankee Aircraft must be destroyed. Air Regiment Commandants will ensure the following Steps are immediately taken.

—The general staff has determined that sufficient numbers of VPAAF pilots have been trained in combat flying duties in all aircraft. From this date only Vietnamese patriots will be allowed to fly VPAAF interceptor aircraft on combat patrols. This order excludes all foreign pilots from flying combat.

—This order does not apply to helicopters or other aircraft which remain under the control of our allies. Soviet Air Force advisors may continue to fly VPAAF interceptor aircraft on test and training sorties.

3/All VPAAF pilots must be prepared to fight to the death to stop the bombing.

There was an urgency to the order that Quon hadn't noticed since the Mee bombing of the Thai Nguyen steel mill, once Ho Chi Minh's great pride and showplace. But like the frantic messages they'd received then, the order was contradictory and confusing, and the words were mostly grand posturing.

If things went awry, General Tho could later say he'd ordered his commanders to win. It would be Quon's reputation in jeopardy, not the general's.

General Tho knew they were already doing everything possible to stop the Mee. Quon's interceptors had shot down only two Mee aircraft in the past month, but they had engaged them often, and several times Thunder planes and Phantoms had been forced to drop their bomb loads before arriving at their targets.

Aleks Ivanovic, the Russian pilot-advisor who had been his son's friend, briefed the regiment pilots that it was more important to cause two planes to drop their bombs than to shoot one of them down. He briefed that once the Mee had dropped their bombs and turned toward them, they should quickly disengage and seek another target, for their job there was done.

Ivanovic is developing into a good tactician, thought Quon. For a long time after the raid at Kep, the Russian had seemed too withdrawn.

The order to stop foreign pilots from flying combat, especially in the MiG-21's, was troubling to Quon, for his Vietnamese pilots were still having trouble mastering the small-tails. Later he'd try to talk General Tho out of the restriction, but for the present he knew he must comply.

He would wager that the order had been relayed from the Lao Dong Central Committee, the aging group who believed that only Vietnamese warriors could be depended upon. They were distrustful of all Tay, including the Poles, Germans, and Hungarians who manned the second air battalion of MiG-21 small-tails.

Of course they were also distrustful of the Chinese, the North Koreans, Laotians, and Cambodians, regardless of how they tried to appear as helpful communist brethren.

Politics, Quon huffed.

He called in his adjutant and told him to summon the senior representatives of the foreign pilots, including the chief Russian pilot-adviser. Then the adjutant was to call in Quon's air battalion commanders so he could give *them* the directive.

He was not yet sure whether to tell his pilots to be more bold, or to withdraw more judiciously to conserve their forces. Fine words on a message could tell them to stop the Mee yet lose no aircraft to the enemy, but he had to be specific and tell them how they should go about doing the impossible.

He decided that a mixture of tactics, according to the pilots' abilities, would be best. They should engage the enemy if they felt sure of success, but flee north toward China if the enemy obtained any slight advantage. But Quon did not continue to think his reasoning through, for he was not as clearheaded as he had been in other times. Quon had not flown a combat mission since *Lokee* had been shot down. He knew he *should* be flying, if only as an example to his pilots, but . . .

While he waited, his thoughts wavered and again returned to the Mee pilot called *Lokee,* who was still evading capture.

Where are you? his mind shouted.

Day 35, 0320 Local—East Bank of Red River, North Vietnam

Major Lucky Anderson

It had now been nineteen days since he'd finished off the gomer chicken, nine since he'd eaten his first rat, and two since he'd eaten the last, a big one with a body almost a foot long. What the hell . . . he'd had his plague shot, and the rats hadn't tasted bad at all. Hungry again, he had pleasant memories of how they'd tasted like greasy rabbit.

The big rodents were plentiful, but elusive and difficult to catch and kill. He'd eaten four of them, all done in with the Phoenix Special. He'd missed only once, but each shot used some of the silencing material. The next time he'd taken more care and waited for a better shot. When he'd killed the last rat, he had used the fifth shot from the barrel, and just as the ex-Marine gunsmith had cautioned, it was too loud. So he'd discarded that barrel and inserted the other one and felt shitty about it until he'd taken his first bite of succulent rat. He'd finished it at a single sitting and decided it was a good trade for the gun barrel. But that had been two days before, and now he wasn't so sure, for he was hungry again. He'd alternately grumble that the sparse amounts only served to remind him of his hunger, then he'd realize the food kept his energy at a minimum acceptable state and again feel grateful.

He had to get across the Red River. He'd been at various sites overlooking the big, muddy river for more than a week, and none of them had appeared good for crossing. The place he now peered down upon was little better. Too many people lived along the riverbanks. There was also constant activity on the river during the nights, which was when he had to make his move.

The number of barges and boats was startling. He'd looked down at the Red River from the air coming and going from pack six, but had never realized how much of a lifeline it was. He'd wager that as many supplies were carried down the river as by rail, and that tonnage was spectacular.

Dropping the bridges alone wouldn't do. They needed to mount a campaign to cut it all off, the road, rail, *and* the water traffic. The key would be to hit them where it hurt most, right in Hanoi. The barges he looked out upon would shortly be tied up to a busy Hanoi dock.

If he got out, he'd make sure General Moss heard about what he'd seen and . . .

Dammit! It wasn't *if* but *when* he got out of North Vietnam.

He returned to thinking out his immediate task, his third attempt to cross the Red. Both of the other times had been thwarted by flukes. Once a loud dog had brought out its owner. The next time he'd already been in the water and ready to shove off on a couple of large boards he'd tied together with his nylon cord. Then a boat had diverted directly toward him and he'd quickly retreated, leaving his makeshift raft and the nylon cord behind.

He stared across the river at distant lights and knew it was as inhabited there as it was on this shore. He had picked a relatively narrow portion of the river, but though the map showed it was only a quarter mile wide here, it looked much farther across to the lights.

The three houses lined up on the riverbank before him were separated by gaps of five feet. On either side the thatch huts were continuous, built either with common walls or with walls almost touching, so he'd chosen these.

He crouched and scurried across the roadway, then flattened himself between two houses.

No noises from inside.

He crept to the corner and surveyed the dark river silently in the moonlight. Waves washed against the bank, creating a gurgling sound. From farther out came other sounds, a low, rushing noise from the river and the puttering of engines. He heard wood creaking and made out the outlines of two boats tied up to pilings twenty feet out in the water.

He considered, but dismissed, the boats. *They were too big. Too noticeable.*

He continued to look around until he found a small drying rack. He dismissed it because he didn't know if the damn thing would even float.

A sharp aroma assailed his nostrils.

He crept closer and pulled off several strips of drying fish and stuffed them into his pockets, then another which he immediately began chewing on. He hated dried fish. *It tasted wonderful.* After a few bites, he'd finished that first

strip and could barely restrain himself from biting into another. He crept forward then, looking about for something to
float across with, as he'd done at the Lo River.

If he'd only kept the inflatable g-suit.

But he had not, so he continued to look.

Nothing. No boards or flotsam of any size. Just the two
large boats. The river was too wide to swim, especially as
weakened as he was from lack of nourishment. He had to
have *something* to help keep him afloat during the crossing.

He wondered if he shouldn't go back and consider another crossing point.

*No time for that. Screw around much longer, and the odds
are going to catch up. It's got to be tonight.*

He looked harder. On a porch there was a washtub, like
the one his mother had used to carry wet clothing in. He
pondered, then rejected it. Too bulky and difficult to keep
afloat.

He looked back at the water. Something was bobbing
near the shore. A closer inspection showed it was a bloated
dead fish.

He released a breath and waded into the mucky water,
chest-high to the boats. He grasped the gunwales and
started to crawl into the first one, knowing he couldn't steal
it. They'd miss the boat and surely call out a search.

He crawled the rest of the way in and looked about. The
moon had passed behind a cloud, but he could make out the
shapes of heavy oars at either side and some wooden boxes
at the stern. He went to the boxes and tugged, but they
were secured to the boat. Inside one there was a heavy
rope, but he could think of no use for it.

No engine, but he could smell fuel, so they must have
somehow detached it and taken it inside.

He considered the oars, went back and lifted one. *Heavy
bastard.* He carefully placed it into the water and found it
floated just fine. He followed it over the side.

Before he'd progressed ten yards, he'd found that an oar
was not a good swimming partner. By the time he had gone
twenty yards, he'd lost his gomer hat and was considering
going back to shore. After twenty more yards he was starting
to get the hang of it. He held on with his left arm and did
a flutter kick, and was even able to rest periodically. He
made his way in pretty good fashion into the center channel
of the river.

That's the way, he rooted, but even with the periodic pauses he was tiring.

Then he heard the puttering sound of an engine and looked to see the dark shape of a barge bearing down on him, not thirty yards distant. He kicked like crazy, but the damned barge was coming too fast. When it was very close, he grabbed the oar with his right hand and ducked down until only his eyes and the top of his head were showing, hoping, since he was off-centered, the bow swell might sweep him to one side.

He felt a sharp pain as the barge struck his shoulder and pushed him along before it. He shoved away hard with his free hand, but the thing struck him again, and he exhaled sharply and felt nauseated and panicky. Just as he was about to be sucked under the prow, he was swept to the far side and the barge was moving by. The side loomed closer and he shoved again, but as he did, he lost his grip on the oar. It thumped loudly against the barge and was immediately swept away.

A human shape leaned over the side to investigate, so Lucky ducked and let himself sink below the surface. He remained underwater, waiting ... waiting until his lungs begged for air ... then kicked and stroked upward. He broke water and sucked a deep breath.

The barge was gone, but so was his oar, and he was being swept farther downstream. It took a moment to regain his wits and orient himself, and even to convince himself that he must go on. He was dog-tired, his arms and legs feeling like sodden weights—and he was only halfway across.

He began to swim.

It was twenty more minutes before he could touch bottom on the western shore of the river, and although he was weary to the bone, there were just too many lights there. Painfully he slogged farther downstream before finding a darker place, between lights, where he waded slowly out of the muck and onto the riverbank.

He was impossibly tired, his shoulder and side throbbed from the barge's impacts, and for the first time Lucky Anderson gave serious consideration to giving up the struggle.

He staggered into the dark, open area, chest heaving.

The thought of going on, of walking any distance, was repugnant. His mind tried to work a solution, wondering what the hell he could do, for he'd emerged in the middle of a town, and he didn't have the energy to go farther.

A flat-bottomed boat was turned upside down nearby, so he slogged over to it and sat heavily, then just let his muscles shudder and react in spasms. He heard voices upstream, but couldn't muster the energy to look in that direction. They were not close, so screw them.

Someone laughed.

He wondered which town he was in. There'd been several downstream, but he had planned to emerge between them. He'd wanted to come out well north of Phuong Xa, a relatively large city on the map, but he glumly supposed he was on the outskirts of the place.

Get moving!

He could not. His body wanted to stay there and wait and rest.

Get moving!

He tried to rise, but slipped heavily back down.

Voices, coming toward him.

He groped around for the hat, then remembered it was gone.

Dammit!

He fished in the pocket, pulled out the waterproof pouch with the pistol inside, and struggled to open it. He ripped the protective plastic and cursed his shaking fingers. The pistol and the matches would no longer be kept dry.

The voices grew closer, and dim shapes came from around a dark building.

He almost dropped the barrel, but grasped it and tried to screw it into place. The task was beyond the facility of his shaking fingers.

One of the shapes spoke sharply, and in the dim light he could see they both carried rifles. Soldiers. Again he tried to screw in the barrel, and again failed.

One of the shapes shifted the muzzle of his weapon in his direction. They were only twenty yards distant.

He'd come so far only to . . .

He felt the grooves, then reversed the barrel, which he'd been trying to screw in backward.

Dumb shit!

One soldier spoke loudly and the other muttered, fumbling with something, yet Lucky had the feeling they were not really excited. They continued to advance closer until they were only several feet from the boat. He did not trust himself to rise.

The pistol was together except for the clip, which he also had trouble handling. It clicked into place finally, and he slowly ratcheted a round into place.

The second soldier switched on a flashlight as Lucky raised his arm before himself, aiming at the one with the poised rifle.

The light settled on his chest and he wavered, then steadied his aim. As the beam blinded him, he squeezed the trigger.

Pop.

A single grunt from the one with the raised rifle. He slowly released his weapon and crumpled.

Lucky doggedly ratcheted another bullet into the pistol, wondering why the other one was waiting. He raised his shooting arm as the soldier finally dropped the flashlight and awkwardly handled his weapon. When he aimed, the soldier was fumbling with his rifle.

Pop.

The man yelped loudly, staggered, and went to one knee.

Lucky ratcheted again and slowly rose, then walked closer on his leaden legs. He felt no excitement, no rush of adrenaline to fuel him as it had in other crises. There was only the numbing weariness.

He passed the prone soldier and approached the kneeling one. The man was breathing harshly, making a hissing, wet sound. Lucky stood over him, trying to decide what to do next. He couldn't afford to leave them. Even if the wounded one died, the situation told too much.

He looked about, but there was nothing except dark buildings about him and water behind him. He listened, heard only a diesel engine out on the river and the wheezing sounds from the soldier. He pushed the pistol into its pocket and zipped it closed, then grasped the kneeling soldier under his arms. The man groaned but helped raise himself to his feet. Lucky supported him and they walked toward the river, the soldier making the wheezing, gurgling sounds. At the river's edge Lucky slogged on into the muck, still supporting him. The soldier tried to say something but only gagged and coughed. At waist-high Lucky released him, then shoved him hard out into the water, watching as he thrashed. He went back and got the other one and dragged him by the shoulders into the river. They were small men, but the effort of the two trips was almost too much.

It began to rain.

He grasped the dead soldier's collar and dragged him through the water until he found the one he'd deposited there, now half-floating, half-submerged, hands out and facedown. Lucky pushed them both out into the river until he was up to his chest before he released them. They floated slowly away, borne downstream by the current.

He considered going after them, to puncture their lungs so their bodies would sink, but decided he was so utterly out of strength, he'd likely drown himself. He waded toward the bank, stumbling often. Ashore, he searched the area and picked up both rifles, both men's caps, and the flashlight, then sat heavily onto the boat again. He rested there for ten wonderful minutes, until his numbed brain began to function.

A water buffalo moaned loudly from downstream. An interesting sound. Sort of a cross between a cow's bellow and a donkey's squeal.

He tried on both soldiers' caps, but they were ridiculously small, and he ended up tossing them into the river. He handled the rifles, for it was too dark to really see them, and found them large and heavy. He fleetingly wished they'd been carrying AK-47's, then realized if they'd been carrying AK's, things would likely have turned out differently. One at a time he chucked them into the water. He examined the flashlight, decided it was also deadweight, and tossed it too.

He heard a chatter of voices. A sharp laugh.

His watch read 0535, two hours since he'd entered the river on the other side.

Not long until dawn. Time to move out.

He pulled out a piece of dried fish and gnawed on it as he walked along the dark, muddy street in the downpour, heading directly away from the riverbank.

Twice he held up at street corners when he thought he heard voices, and each time he realized he was just being spooky. No one else was silly enough to be out in the downpour.

After five weeks he'd finally crossed the Red River. The thought was a nice one, but he didn't feel the joy he'd anticipated. It was not the fact that he'd just killed two men that sobered him. He'd been fortunate and they had not. He'd felt no different shooting them than when he'd pressed the pickle button in his cockpit to drop bombs. Dying was precisely what he wanted his enemies to do.

But Lucky Anderson had been swept far south of his planned route, and now had to cross six more miles of densely populated farmland and rolling hills before he could reach the western mountains.

Tuesday, September 19th, 2130 Local—St. Joseph's Hospital, San Francisco, California

Major Benny Lewis

The taxicab dropped him at the emergency entrance to the aging, dark-brick hospital. Benny hurried inside, asked his question, and was directed down the hall and up to the third floor.

The elevator ride took forever. At the second floor a janitor got in and gave him a strange look, as if he'd come from another planet. His crumpled uniform?

He'd returned to his BOQ room from dinner at the club to find a note on his door, a message from the BOQ office, reading: *MRS. STEWART CALLED AT FIVE-THIRTY SAYING THE HANGAR DOOR'S ABOUT TO OPEN.*

Jesus, what a sense of humor.

The voice inside him had squealed for him to hurry, which had been unnecessary because the note had roused him to a state of near panic.

He'd thrown clothing into a gym bag and driven like a maniac to base ops, where he'd remembered to call his boss and tell him he'd be gone for a few days on personal business. Then he'd rushed to the operations desk and found the duty NCO.

No military flights going anywhere in the direction of San Francisco, the base-ops sergeant had told him.

Oh shit, the panicky voice inside had said.

He'd called a buddy named White in the Wild Weasel training squadron. They had a T-39 Sabreliner, a small jet transport they used to test new electronic equipment.

White said he couldn't just take off in the bird like that without authorization from his squadron commander.

"Get it!" Benny had yelled.

"You okay?" White had asked quietly, trying to calm him.

"I'm having a baby, for Christ's sakes!"

After a pause White had told him to get the flight planning done and file the clearance, and that he'd get authorization and be right down. "But be ready to explain the upcoming miracle of nature," he'd joked.

They'd landed at San Francisco International. A cab was waiting because Benny had called for it when they'd come within radio distance of the airport tower.

You'd imagine, Benny thought in the slow elevator, a guy'd get used to women having babies. His ex-wife had delivered two, and both times he'd come unglued. This time was no different.

The third floor . . . finally. Pink elephants in tutus danced on the wall. Maternity-ward art, he remembered, was odd.

At the nurses' station he asked for Mrs. Stewart. The floor nurse glowered protectively and asked if he was family. Her brother, he lied. She mentioned and said she was in 312.

"She's doing fine," she said to calm him.

He hurried down the hall, almost barged past the room, then stopped and eased the door open. There were two beds, both occupied. A short, stocky middle-aged lady blinked at him, standing guard beside the nearest one. A bottle dripped liquid into the veins of the patient there.

Julie had trouble focusing. When she saw the uniform, a happy smile spread across her face, and Benny Lewis felt a giddy feeling course through him.

"Nothing to it," she croaked, the drugs affecting her voice.

Her beach ball was gone. The sheet over her belly was almost flat.

"Dammit," he whispered. He was late. "How'd it go?" he asked stupidly.

"Easy as skinning a grape," she said.

Skinning a grape?

"Mom *said* it'd be easy. We Wright women are built for having babies," she said proudly. Wright was her maiden name.

He awkwardly stepped closer, and she reached out for his hand and squeezed it. "I told Mom you'd be here."

He glanced at her mother, who observed him with a too-neutral look.

"Hi."

"Hello," said Mom.

"Mom, this is Benny Lewis."

"He's your husband's friend?" her mother asked quietly.

Benny stared at her, noting the present tense, as if the Bear were alive. He nodded finally. "We flew together."

"I've heard of you."

"I've heard a lot about you too, ma'am. I knew your husband at Spangdahlem. We pilots there were a bit in awe of him."

Chief Wright had been the maintenance line-chief at the base in Germany.

She remained cool, so he tried again. "It's good to finally meet you, ma'am."

She nodded, too curtly, and he saw her glance at Julie's grasp on his hand.

"The baby?" he asked Julie. "Is it okay?"

Julie frowned. "Mal Bear was right, dammit."

He grinned. "A girl?"

She nodded wistfully. "I've already held her, and all the right parts aren't there for a boy."

"She's a lovely child," said the mother, looking squarely at Benny. "His father will love her."

Julie regrasped Benny's hand, holding tighter. She shuddered suddenly.

"Are you okay?" he asked.

"Tell her Benny," she cried out. "Tell her so she'll *stop* it!"

Her mother took a slight step back.

"Tell her!"

"It's not a good time," he tried.

Tell her, said the voice.

He turned to the mother. "Captain Stewart was killed, Mrs. Wright. He was killed by the North Vietnamese ... while saving my life."

The mother turned on a stony expression.

"See, Mom," said Julie. "See!" She shouted the last word, and the woman in the next bed rose up to see what was wrong.

Her mother looked contrite. "I didn't mean to upset you, honey."

"But you do, Mom. You do every time you talk about it." Julie was crying and gripping hard on Benny's hand.

A nurse entered, the one he'd met at the desk. After observing the scene, Julie crying and clutching his hand, she nodded curtly to both visitors.

"You'll have to leave."

Julie looked at him. "Don't go," she pleaded.

"I won't," he said, and ignored the nurse's angry look.

Several minutes later she slept. He waited until her grasp eased, then stepped past the tight-jawed nurse and left the room.

Her mother was in the waiting room, staring wistfully out at the cribs beyond the viewing window.

"I'm sorry," he said, not knowing what else to say.

She continued to stare.

"Which one is she?" he asked.

She pointed. The baby was ruddy and wrinkled, with wisps of dark hair.

"She's tiny," he whispered.

The infant opened her mouth and made an O with it. He laughed. "She yawned," he said, as if it were a wonderful thing to yawn.

"Her ears are small," said Julie's mother, looking on with a critical expression.

"The Bear wanted a daughter," he said.

"That's what Julie said. She wanted a boy who looked like he does." Present tense again, as if she were determined to use it. "It's all very confusing, Major Lewis. She gets angry when I tell her to have faith that her husband will return. That's what a good Air Force wife must do until she's told differently."

He wanted to stop her, and the only way he knew was to present the brutal truth.

"Mrs. Wright, the last time they saw the Bear, he was being hacked to pieces. The pilot of the rescue plane said it looked like they were using swords or machetes, and . . . he's very dead, Mrs. Wright."

She was shaken by the description but kept her stern look. "The Air Force hasn't reported him killed."

He tried to explain. "We made a mistake at Takhli early this year. No one saw a chute from an airplane that was shot down, so the flight reported the pilot went in with his airplane. Three days later a newspaper ran photos of him being paraded through Hanoi. That was when the wing staff decided to stop jumping to conclusions and call them all MIA for a while."

"See," she said. "You can't be positive."

"This time it's different." He knew he wasn't getting through but was unwilling to give up. "There's no doubt about Captain Stewart."

"I won't be convinced until they change his official status," she said stubbornly.

"I respect that, Mrs. Wright. But please stop confusing Julie. She'll have her own doubts, even after he's declared dead. You're just making it worse."

She looked away.

The old bat, said the inner voice, but he ignored it. She was just trying to provide her daughter with proper, "good military wife" guidance.

He stared at the baby for a long while before turning to leave.

"Will you be back?" asked Mrs. Wright.

"Yes, ma'am. Visiting time in the morning, I'll be here. You see, I promised."

"You promised Julie?"

"I promised Julie *and* the Bear. His last words to me on his survival radio before he was killed were to look after his wife and child. I plan to do that as best I can."

She did not respond.

"Good evening, ma'am."

CHAPTER TWENTY-SIX

Day 44, 1845 Local—NVA Barracks/Field Training Area, North Vietnam

Major Lucky Anderson

He'd been held up in the scrub-brush foothills for seven days, trying to get past the sprawling barracks complex and the adjacent field-training areas, all of which were teeming with enemy soldiers. They were young and exuberant recruits, obviously being prepared for combat in South Vietnam. Daily they fanned out like ants and swept about in mock battles, and that was what had been holding him up.

He'd holed up right before their noses, in a cranny dug into the only standing corner of a bombed-out building half a mile from the barracks. From there he watched and planned and waited. He'd called two different groups of Thuds passing overhead, but stopped the practice when his radio had grown noticeably weaker. He had to conserve the remaining battery power until he'd pushed well into the mountains and was in a proper location for rescue.

That week he'd fired the last two quiet rounds through the silenced barrel, killing another monster rat and a small, nosy dog for food. He had eaten both raw, and even in his ravenous condition had gagged on the meat. The next shots would make more noise, each louder than the previous one. He had eleven bullets left, but was hesitant to use them this close to the soldiers.

Unlike the militia soldiers he'd killed in Phuong Xa, these carried AK-47's and seemed nervous. That, in Lucky Anderson's eyes, made them doubly dangerous, so he chose his route of travel carefully.

He couldn't go south, for that was a heavily populated area and would take him too far from the flight routes of the Thuds on their way to pack six. He couldn't venture far to the north, for that way was blocked by heavily traveled farm-to-market roads. For three nights running he'd cautiously ventured out to pick a route through the area. Finally he'd picked the most audacious one. Straight as an arrow, directly across their training fields.

Tonight was the right time. There'd be a quarter moon. Enough illumination to see well enough to travel, but not so light they'd easily be able to see him from any distance. He'd spent the day mentally girding himself for the trek, staring for long periods at the map. He'd calculated that he must pass through four miles of training area before reaching the mountains. He'd computed his time of passage several times, and finally allowed himself thirty to forty-five minutes of steady running to reach the mountains.

At dusk he crossed the main road and plunged ahead, weaving past two new encampments. At first he walked briskly, head held low and eyes alert, avoiding the encampments at the perimeter of the training area. Then he began to trot, head constantly swiveling, circumventing occasional camp fires and grass huts.

Voices hailed him from a thicket a hundred yards away, and he saw two, then three figures emerge and gesture at him in the gloom. Another shout, then another. But at the distance, and in the growing darkness, he doubted they could tell anything about him. He continued the jogging pace, bent over and leaning into a sort of shuffle, as he'd seen some of them doing. Another thicket shielded him from their view, and after a long minute, when there had been no shooting or sign of pursuit, he slowed his pace. He was already tiring.

Twice he almost ran into company-sized bivouacs, but he was able to keep moving along, using the small, shuffling steps of the soldiers he'd observed. He periodically noted the time by lifting the luminous dial of his Glycine Airman watch to his face. When half an hour had passed, there were no more soldiers and the hillocks were getting steeper. He slowed to a brisk walk, huffing, turning north toward the star Polaris, trying to intercept the road the map showed would take him through the mountains. He had trouble finding it. When he'd walked for half an hour, he grew concerned. *Can't afford to miss it,* he whispered to himself. The rugged mountains would be impenetrable if he could not find the roadway to lead him through their passes. He'd crossed a small path fifteen minutes before. Had that been it? He almost turned back, but decided against it and continued northward.

He'd been searching for an hour and a half when he gave up and turned westward to climb over the high foothills, through large, rocky fields and occasional pockets of low trees, then through vines and undergrowth. Another hour passed, but he knew he hadn't come far because of the increasingly thick jungle. When he began to scale a steep precipice, he knew it was not just another of the foothills, for the shadow of the thing rose high into the night sky.

He'd broken through to the western mountains, but had no way through them. After climbing for a while longer, he stopped at an outcropping of rocks and rested, wheezing and blowing, aching in places he hadn't known he had muscles. He looked hard out at the dark world below, but could see little. He decided to wait where he was, and look for the mountain path in the light of morning. As he searched for a hiding place, he came upon a drooping limb from a young teak tree. He cut the thing away with his bayonet knife, then carved off the small branches and bumps until it was smooth.

A walking staff.

He carefully carved forty-four nocks in the wood and separated those days into the proper weeks and months by creating lines between them. It was Saturday, September 23rd, his forty-fourth day of evasion. With the staff he would no longer have to wake up each evening and try to figure that out, and say little riddles to himself as he walked all night so he wouldn't lose count. For some reason it was important to Lucky Anderson to keep track of such things.

Saturday, September 23rd, 1920 Local—Officers' Club Dining Room, Takhli RTAFB, Thailand

Captain Manny DeVera

Billy Bowes waved his hands over the tabletop. He held one hand before the other, then inverted the first one.

All of C-Flight was seated at a single large table, as was Jackie Bell. She'd visited often since Manny had been restricted to the base. She sat beside him, watching Billy's hands as they flew over North Vietnam.

"Then," Billy said, "the MiG splits for the deck, going about Mach twelve and Joe's back there shooting like hell and trying to figure out where the bullets are going."

Joe Walker grimaced. "I tell it a little differently."

"Am I wrong?" asked Billy Bowes. "You think you hit it?"

"I wasn't even close, but you oughta give me credit for scaring the hell out of the MiG pilot."

"All you get is to buy us a drink when we go to the bar," said Henry Horn.

Everyone but Joe laughed.

"Maybe I was trying to run him into the ground. Anyone can *shoot* a MiG, but how many can get him to commit suicide?"

Manny stopped laughing and asked what had happened. "Have your switches set up for strafe and forget to reset them?"

"Yeah. Cost me a MiG kill, too," said Joe with a petulant look.

"Say, Jackie?" asked Henry. "What do your long-hair Peace Corps people think about us military swine?"

Jackie, fast becoming a regular part of the group, paused before answering. "They're split," she finally said. "Some think you're okay. Some think it's a dumb war, and we shouldn't be in it. Others think all military people are heartless baby killers."

"Aww," said Joe, happy to pass the attention to someone else. "They're thinking of Smitty when they say things like that."

Smitty, who was cherubic and innocent looking, grinned at Jackie. "I'm just your regular run-of-the-mill, combat-trained killer," he said. "But Joe's not. He just scares 'em."

Joe glared.

"Joe's a member of the SPCG," said Henry. "The Society for the Prevention of Cruelty to Gomers."

"Aww, c'mon, guys. Let me off the hook for missing the MiG, okay?"

"Teach you to call *me* names," said Henry indignantly.

Since he'd learned Henry was sensitive about his receding hairline, Joe had been using a cockney accent to call him " 'enry 'orn, the 'airless 'onkie."

As he sat listening, Manny realized he was happy. Even if he couldn't fly with them, he enjoyed their company.

Billy Bowes looked over at him. "When's all the crap going to end so you can get back to work?"

Manny shrugged. "Got me."

"Hell, it's been two weeks now, Manny. You'd think they'd tell you *something*."

"Yeah, you'd think so."

"What the hell have they got that makes 'em think you did anything?"

"Today they showed me a copy of a page from Major Lucky's notebook."

An incredulous look came over Billy's face. "You shitting me?" he asked.

"Nope. It's his printing. The Bad Injin gave it to Lyons before he got killed, and Lyons gave it to the cops."

"What's it say?" Billy didn't look convinced.

"That I bombed an unauthorized target."

"And your name's on it?"

"It just says Captain D, but Lucky just used initials in his book, and I'm the only *D* in the flight."

"Is the book marked 'private,' like they say to do?" Billy asked. "If it is, they're not supposed to use it."

Manny shook his head. "This was just a single sheet. Supposedly Lucky gave it to Bad Injin in case he got shot down. Told him he wanted him to press charges if anything happened. That's what Lyons says, anyway."

Billy snorted. "That's a goddam lie. Whenever Major Lucky got pissed off at you, he'd tell you right to your face. I oughta know. It's a setup, Manny."

"Okay, let's say it is. Now you tell me how I prove it. It's a single sheet, so I can't tell if it's marked 'private' or anything. Major Lucky's writing was so lousy he usually printed everything, and it looks like his printing. The spelling's shitty, and you remember he couldn't spell worth a damn.

And it says that I bombed an unauthorized target. *And* Bad Injin Encinos isn't around to explain how he got it."

Billy glared out at the room, then looked back at him. "What's the date on the sheet?"

"July twenty-ninth. That day I led a flight attacking a barracks west of Hanoi. The gomers said we bombed a hospital."

"They *always* say we bombed a hospital, a school full of kids, or an old folks' home," growled Henry.

Billy's eyes narrowed. "Could it have been *June* twenty-ninth? That was the day Lucky got pissed off at me for dropping on the wrong target at Thanh Hoa."

Manny thought. "No, it says *J-U-L* for July."

"You sure it wasn't changed from *J-U-N*? I don't trust Lyons."

Manny reflected, then gave a shake of his head. "I guess the date *could* have been altered. I only saw a copy, not the original. But changing the date and the initials would be illegal as hell, and I don't think even Lyons would stoop so low as to pull that kind of shit."

Billy Bowes smirked, as if Manny were being naive. Joe Walker was frowning and beginning to look troubled by what he heard.

"That the only date they're pissed off about?" asked Billy.

"They're investigating some others. Remember that time in late April when I threw my bombs toward Gia Lam airport?"

"You missed the airport, for Christ's sake."

"Doesn't matter. Some Aussie reporter claimed bombs went off in a residential area. I think I can beat that one. A lot of people were watching and saw me get hit as I released."

"I remember," said Henry, "and by God I'll tell 'em that."

Manny continued. "It's the note that's the problem. Who the hell's going to say Lucky Anderson lied?"

"And with Bad Injin dead," Joe Walker said darkly, "it's Lyons's word against yours."

Jackie Bell spoke up. "I told Manny we should go to Colonel Parker about what happened between Tom Lyons and him that night. I think it might help if he knew."

Manny looked evenly at her. "Just stay out of it, and don't mention that night again."

It was the dozenth time he'd told her that, and he'd

made up his mind on the matter. Why let her foul her reputation by saying he'd spent the night in her trailer, especially when it would likely do him as much harm as Lyons?

"What's the worst they can do to you?" asked Henry.

"At first they said a general court-martial and possible jail time, but now the legal officer says it'll more likely be a summary court-martial and a fine if I'm found guilty."

A summary court-martial involved only a single senior officer sitting in judgement.

"That'd be enough to ruin your career," said Joe quietly. "Even if you were found innocent, people would just remember you were court-martialed and forget the rest."

Manny nodded. "Yeah, but before it can *go* to court-martial, they've got to find cause during this inquiry, then make formal charges against me and hold a preliminary hearing, and *then* comes a court-martial."

"It's like a bad dream," said Jackie bitterly.

"It's stupid," Joe said. "They ought to drop the whole thing."

"The legal officer thought that's what would happen once the initial noise settled down. Then he said someone at PACAF called and scared the shit out of the base commander, so he bucked it up to the wing commander, and now everyone's excited about it again."

"That's where it should have been in the first place," Henry said. He nodded with conviction. "Colonel B.J. will have 'em drop it."

Joe Walker was still in his worrying mood. "Don't be too sure," he said. "B.J.'s awfully ambitious, and if PACAF's determined, he just might bend over for them."

But Manny felt better now that it was up to the wing commander. He'd known B.J. since Parker had been a squadron commander in Germany and brought his pilots down to Libya to practice on the El Uotia gunnery range. Manny had briefed him and his pilots dozens of times on weapons and range procedures, and B.J. had thought highly of him.

"I'll still bet Lyons is involved up to his pretty blue eyeballs," said Billy Bowes. "Like calling people at PACAF headquarters when things started dying down and it didn't look like anyone here wanted to hang you high enough."

"I wouldn't put it past the asshole," said Smitty; then he looked at Jackie and blushed. "Sorry," he muttered.

"I couldn't agree more," said Jackie. "Colonel Tom Lyons is a pedigreed asshole." She didn't speak in a subdued voice, and several guys at adjacent tables turned to grin their agreement.

Thursday, September 28th, 0745 Local—Route Pack Five, North Vietnam

Captain Billy Bowes

Five days after the dinner discussion, Billy talked to Major Lucky for the first time since he'd been shot down. The radio call on guard frequency was weak and hardly audible, and he would likely not have heard it at all if he hadn't been thinking about the pilot with the scarred face.

"... *cuda lead calling in the blind on guard. Barracuda lead ... guard in the ...*"

After a few seconds of digesting what he'd heard, Billy switched to the emergency channel.

"*This is Bison lead. Go ahead, Barracuda lead.*"

"*Roger, Bison ... cuda lead. I'll be ready ... out of ... in ... days.*"

Billy tried to put the transmission together in his mind, but could not.

"*Your transmission is broken, Barracuda lead. Please repeat,*" called Billy.

"*... cuda ... out.*"

Although he tried to contact him twice more, Billy heard no more from the ground.

"*This is Bison lead. Anyone able to hear all of that transmission?*"

"*Lead,*" called Henry Horn. "*I think he said he was ready to be picked up.*"

Billy had not made that connection, but he wondered if Horn had heard more than he had.

"*I think he said he'd be ready for rescue in a few days,*" called Major Max Foley, who was strike force commander.

That was more in line with his own thinking. "*Anyone hear how long before he'd be ready?*"

No one answered.

"*Maybe we should go back and try to raise him again,*" called Henry.

"*Negative, three,*" he radioed, wanting to do just that but knowing it wasn't the smartest thing to do. As he thought it over, a Fansong SAM radar rattled its strobe onto the CRT of his RHAW system.

"*Bison lead's got a strong tracking SAM signal at ten o'clock.*"

They were entering pack six, on their way to bomb the bridge at Bac Giang, a heavily defended target east of Hanoi.

"*Bison two's got an ACTIVITY light,*" called Smitty, which meant the SAM operator had turned on his missile-guidance beam.

A few seconds later the LAUNCH light illuminated, and they watched for missiles from their left. As usual, Billy saw them first.

"*Bison lead's got three SAMs in sight at nine o'clock,*" he announced. "*Everyone check they've got their music on?*"

He ensured that his own ECM pod was turned on, and the green light illuminated, then looked back at the missiles. They were coming on fast, darting directly toward them. He pushed the nose of his Thud slightly downward and fire-walled his throttle.

"*They're for us, Bison two. Prepare to maneuver.*"

"*Two.*" Smitty's voice was steady. He was very good, very reliable.

The missiles were close . . . just a bit closer and . . .

He pulled up hard, and after enduring eight seconds of heavy g-forces, eased up and slid off to the right.

"*Bison lead, the missiles are clear,*" called Henry.

Billy reversed back toward the rest of the big formation. The others had pulled away to allow him and his wingman to maneuver. Within a few more seconds Smitty was back in formation, and the others were closing to proper intervals between aircraft.

The formation proceeded across the south end of Thud Ridge and then ten miles farther before swinging right, toward Bac Giang and the bridge there.

2350 Local—Western Mountains, Route Pack Five

Sergeant Black

"*Twenty-one minutes to go,*" said the Air Force loadmaster, and Black nodded his thanks.

He sipped at the paper cup of awful, lukewarm coffee. Then, when he remembered it would be more than two weeks before he'd get another, he savored it.

He glanced back at his men sitting in the rearmost seats of the C-130 Hercules, which was painted flat black and flown by the Air Force Special Operations crew from Nha Trang. The team was barely distinguishable in the dim glow of red light used to preserve their night vision. *All* lights would be shut off when the big rear door was opened and they prepared to exit, to avoid being seen from the ground.

He gave his team a thumbs-up signal and echoed the loadmaster's call. *"Twenty-one minutes until we jump,"* he said in impeccable Vietnamese.

"No threats," broadcast Cecil the Crow over the aircraft intercom. The Crow, a highly trained electronic-warfare officer, sat at a console immediately behind the aircraft's cockpit, hidden by a set of blackout curtains and monitoring his scopes and headset for signs of enemy radar or communications activity. They said Cecil was the best of the Crows. His sensitive receivers were pretuned to known radar and radio frequencies, and with them he vowed he could "tell what the gomers down there were eating for fucking dinner."

If a threat of any kind appeared ahead, or if there was absolutely *any* indication the enemy knew they were coming, they would abort and sneak home via one of several preplanned routes. The Special Operations air war was quite different from others, for they avoided all confrontation with the enemy. To do their jobs appropriately was to successfully *evade* a fight. To be discovered would mean sudden, fiery death. The North Vietnamese Army could easily shoot them down with any of a thousand of their sophisticated antiaircraft weapons, or even with their million-odd unsophisticated ones.

"Friday, I've got the Yen Bai Firecan on the air at our two o'clock. He doesn't see us." "Friday" was the aircraft commander's unlikely first name. "Firecan" was the code name of a fire-control radar for antiaircraft artillery.

"Anything new, Cecil?" asked Friday. They knew where the threats were supposed to be and were most likely to move to, and those were planned for in advance and circumvented. They'd planned for the Yen Bai Firecan. He was asking if anything was out there that they'd *not* planned for.

"Nope. Quiet as a mouse," said the Crow to the pilot.

They didn't call out positions, like "pilot" or "navigator," because they knew one another's voices. Special Ops aircrews were the loosest and seemingly most ill-disciplined group in the military, but they were damned good at their jobs and were proud of it. Like the Air America CIA contractors, Special Forces, and the SEALS, they reported to MAC-SOG, and not through regular service channels.

"Friday, come right ten degrees to zero-oner-fiver," called the navigator, and the pilot made an abrupt turn that made Sergeant Black want to puke. He didn't like airplanes or flying in the things, especially the kind of hot-rod flying some of the Special Ops pilots liked to do.

Sergeant Black wore a blackout uniform, issue jungle fatigues dyed very dark, with subdued E-6 rank on the collar. The Geneva Convention called for proper uniforms or you could be executed as a spy, so for some stupid rationale his bosses required it, like if he was captured in uniform he would be invited for crumpets at Chez Ho Chi Minh. So he wore the fatigues and carried a Geneva Convention card that lied about his rank and name and even his serial number. As soon as they were established on the ground, he would remove the rank and destroy the card, as he always did, and become a shadow. He was good at it. And when required, he would put on an NVA sergeant's uniform, the various pieces of which were distributed among his men's packs. Fuck the brass and their ladies'-tea-group concepts of warfare. Until they were exfiltrated, he and his men must remain either invisible or indistinguishable from the sea of fish they operated in.

His six-man team did not wear bogus uniforms. They'd deserted from the 321-B Division of the Vietnamese People's Army, and were willing to give their lives to rid the world of the Hanoi communists. A year before, they'd kidnapped an American sergeant, carefully convinced the shaken soldier that they wished to turn themselves over to the Americans, and came marching into a Special Forces A-Team camp near the DMZ with wide grins and their hands behind their heads. Fortunately the astonished Special Forces team had not immediately killed them.

Other NVA troops had given themselves up, but as far as he knew, none had done so in such spectacular form. But the Special Forces brass hadn't trusted them and suspected they were plants from the NVA. Sergeant Black had been fifth in the line of interrogators to speak to them. Two months later, in a trial run, they'd been inserted by chopper to observe activity on the Ho Chi Minh Trail. They went in unarmed with five Americans who had orders to kill them at the first sign of betrayal. Instead they'd saved the lives of the Americans. After their return they'd been joined up with Sergeant Black, his name and rank changed because the brass were still wary of the renegades and wanted them to have a minimum of hard information.

Special Forces A-Teams normally consisted of twelve men, long-range recon teams of five men. Hotdog was a special seven-man insertion team. Not twelve, because twelve guys too often couldn't easily link up in a dark jungle after being dropped in. Not five, because Sergeant Black liked to have the extra eyes and firepower. But most of all he'd kept the six renegade NVA together because they were accustomed to working with one another and had built intense loyalties.

Black reasoned that Hotdog would fight for the Americans, but it might be too much to ask that they do it wholeheartedly. He'd made a good decision, for Hotdog fought like demons, would fight to the last breath of life, to save one another and keep their team intact. Black had grown to admire and like the tough little renegades.

This was Hotdog's fifth insertion, their third into North Vietnam. They'd done well, and he was damned proud of them. After another trip or two he'd follow up on his guarantee of a free ticket to the States, where he pledged to be their sponsor for citizenship. He'd advised them to avoid the mainland, because *haoles* ran things there and sometimes had trouble getting along with the different races. They needed good people like them in the islands. When he described his home in paradise, their eyes would drift and they'd grow slow grins.

Their lieutenant motioned Sergeant Black closer, because it was difficult to hear over the awful noise of the C-130's four engines.

"Fifteen minutes to drop," came the navigator's announcement, and Black echoed it to the men in Vietnamese before leaning toward the lieutenant.

"When are we going after Majah Lokee Anduh-sun?" asked the lieutenant.

It was a valid question, for it hadn't been covered as a

part of their briefings. Officially they were to reconnoiter supply routes, a barracks-and-training area, and a new prison camp being built west of Hanoi, as well as defenses throughout that area, but Sergeant Black had told the men that they were also going to try to find the pilot with the badly scarred face.

The Special Forces brass didn't trust his ex-NVA and told him not to mention the pilot's name or description. Black thought that was ridiculous, because they'd be the ones searching for him. So he'd told them, but said to keep quiet about it because the brass would be pissed off if they knew he'd ignored their counsel.

He confided, "We will look on our way in, and if we do not find him, we will make another search on our way to Point Zulu."

They'd be inserted at Point Victor by parachute and in seventeen days be exfiltrated by chopper at Point Zulu. The exfiltration checkpoints were memorized by Black and never put on paper, in case one of the indigenous members was captured.

"Hokay, Sarge," said the NVA lieutenant.

"Quit that," he growled. He'd taught them a little English and some island pidgin, but he didn't like them speaking it when they were on a mission.

"Hokay, Sarge," the lieutenant retorted impishly, and Sergeant Black glared.

He showed the lieutenant the map he'd been studying, an old, well-detailed 1950 French road map. Newer roads and developments had been roughly inked in.

He pointed to a location south of Yen Bai. "He crossed the Hong Song about here. That was two weeks ago, but he's been moving slowly. Last radio contact was here, ten kilometers from our drop point. I think he's following that mountain trail."

"When was his last radio call?"

"Oh-seven-forty-five this morning. His transmission was weak, and they were only able to get an approximate position."

Accurate only within seven kilometers, his Monkey Mountain liaison had estimated.

The lieutenant studied the map closely. He moved his finger westward a few klicks.

"Somewhere there," Black agreed. "He is likely hiding in

the daytime and traveling at night, so he will not be easy to locate."

The lieutenant nodded confidently. "We will find him."

"We will not have long to look. Perhaps only two days."

"*Ten minutes*," came the navigator's announcement, and the C-130 began another descent, this time to fly even lower, to skim over the treetops.

"Jesus," said Sergeant Black, and started to become more frightened as the aircraft pitched and bucked in the turbulence caused by the mountain effect. This was the worst part for him. When they flew so damned low above the pitch-black jungle, he always thought of shitty things, like smacking into the sides of hills. He'd be happier when they gained altitude to jump out of the damned, dangerous contraption.

"*No threats*," announced Cecil the Crow in a pleasant voice.

Sunday, October 1st, 1045 Local—Hoa Lo Prison, Hanoi

Major Glenn Phillips

Some days were worse than others at the Hanoi Hilton. The worst for Glenn were the ones when he got into his depressed moods and began thinking they would never be released or freed. That the war would just continue to be dragged out by the politicians, and the people back in the States would get so tired of it, they'd stop giving a damn about the guys they might leave behind. Especially guys dumb enough to let themselves be shot down. Then his mind would rebel against that thought, because they were Americans, by God, and Americans don't leave their men behind. Someone in charge, maybe President Johnson, would decide that if a war is worth fighting, it's worth winning, and the next thing they'd see would be a bunch of U.S. Marines outside kicking the V's asses out of the way so they could free the prisoners.

He'd thought about it all the day before and finally had gotten himself in trouble, for the more he'd thought, the angrier he'd become.

He wasn't acting as an American ought to.

Yesterday evening he'd refused to bow when two guards came into his cell.

The rule was that whenever a V entered your cell or you passed one in the yard, you were to bow to the waist. But he'd just stood there and said, "Can I help you?" as if he were in his bachelor pad back in the States answering his door. It hadn't been a planned thing but a capricious one, to show the V that regardless of where he was, he was an American, and, by God, Americans don't bow. Not to kings or queens or fucking V, Americans don't bow.

It had been a silly gesture, and he'd known it, but somehow it had been important to him. They'd taken him to the interrogation room and beat the hell out of him, then did their rope tricks. Once he'd noticed through a painracked fog that a skinny shin, *his* skinny shin, was pressing against the back of his head.

The entire episode was unimportant to anyone except Glenn Phillips. All they wanted to do was teach him a lesson and get him to bow, not try to get nuclear secrets or anything. But for a while it had been important to Glenn.

He'd finally said, hell yes, he'd bow next time. Then after a few whacks with a rubber hose they'd stopped.

In a way he'd won, though, because when the V were through with him and tossed him back into the cell, he hadn't been able to bow at all. All he'd been able to do was lie there making retching sounds as they locked him in the leg-stocks on the concrete bunk. Then he'd curled up in pain, and they'd beaten him with the rubber hose to get him to straighten enough to put the heavy iron cuffs on his wrists.

He hurt all over, but it was the pain from the leg that had been badly broken during his ejection that was most nauseating. He'd lain in the half-curl position all night and was there when the turnkey had come to unlock the iron cuffs and give him his morning meal.

He'd tried to eat the stuff, but his face hurt when he did, because his lips and nose were swollen from the rubber-hose beating. The turnkey was the same mean little bastard who had started it all, and he'd just laughed when he saw Glenn was having trouble with the food, and again when he saw him picking out a few maggots.

A few of the turnkeys were almost human in the ways they treated the prisoners, but this one was a rat-faced asshole, and the P had to be cautious around him.

A while after Ratface had left, he heard a distant tapping

and put his ear against the wall to hear better. Later one of the P came by sweeping the hall, making a slap-slap sound, and as he did so, he tapped out words in their code.

It was another hour before he'd put the news together.

The V had moved a group of P to another camp, probably to nearby Cu Loc, which the P called the Zoo.

Which was okay, for the Zoo was no better or worse than here at the Hanoi Hilton, except there were a couple of bad-ass American-hating Cubans who'd arrived at the Zoo to help teach the V how to beat up on the P.

The senior camp officer said to listen to the words of their SROs, because that was the way it was, period.

Obviously some of the P were giving an SRO, the senior ranking officer in a cell block, a bad time. As the only major, Glenn was SRO of the area called the Sahara by the P, but he'd had no problems with the five other P there with him, and there wasn't much leadership involved, anyway.

The last news was more exciting.

Lucky Anderson was still on the run. At least the V hadn't caught him as of three days before, when they'd questioned another group of 354th fighter squadron guys.

Superb news!

After he'd digested it all and he lay there thinking of his friend trying to escape, he felt the rebellious mood returning.

Cool it, he tried to tell himself, but the news made him feel damn good.

"Keep going, Lucky," Glenn shouted through battered and swollen lips, "and don't stop until you get out! Then come back in a Thud and kill these bastards!"

He laughed out loud, and it felt good.

The badass turnkey heard him and came in with two other guards. They iron-cuffed his hands again and beat him with their fists and the hose until he howled and cringed like a dog. Then Ratface beat him until he stopped screaming.

Day 52, 1230 Local—Western Mountains

Major Lucky Anderson

He'd continued ever westward since breaking through the military-training area and into the western mountains. The first night he'd stayed on the mountainside, and when light came, he found himself looking down on a pleasant pass and a group of ancient, deserted pagodas. He'd continued to travel up high for a while, paralleling the road below. Then the mountain had grown steep and difficult, and he'd been forced down onto the small, rugged roadway that wove its way through canyons and mountain passes.

Every couple of miles there was a collection of huts on the well-traveled path, and each tiny village had to be avoided carefully, for in them he'd seen men with rifles. Thus far he'd been successful at remaining unseen. On occasion he'd almost run into late travelers on the wide path, but each time he'd been able to slip into a hiding place before they caught sight of him.

Three days earlier, unable to suppress the urge, he'd called a formation of Thuds he'd seen in the distance and was alarmed at the weak condition of the radio's batteries. He thought the voice who had answered as Bison lead was Billy Bowes, but he'd cut the conversation short to conserve batteries. He'd still had twenty miles to go before he would be in position for a good, clean pickup by the rescue people.

Had he drawn the power too low? he worried, but he dared not test the radio's batteries, for even that action drained them ever so slightly. From experience he knew that when they rested, batteries rejuvenated themselves a bit. He was letting them do just that.

He was growing shaky from hunger. This time he was so weak, he knew he couldn't last much longer without food. Since acquiring the walking stick, it had become dear to him, and not only because it was his calendar. Increasingly he used it to support himself as he walked. He was that weak. But whenever he'd seen game, mostly jungle rats that looked like large weasels, and tiny, spotted deer, he'd either been too near a village or suspected one was around the next bend. The pistol would make noise now, and he didn't dare press his luck. His only food had been occasional sour fruit, small wild tubers, and crickets he found near the path.

Just that morning it had been food that had caused his latest and almost fatal concern. He cursed himself when he thought of it.

The sky had been growing light with false dawn, so he'd been looking for a hiding place for the day. As he'd stared across the creek that ran beside the path, a deer had cautiously stepped out of a nearby thicket and warily looked about. Lucky had immediately frozen in his tracks and stared as a shaky-kneed fawn ventured out behind the doe.

He'd salivated at memories of the taste of venison.

Should I? he was thinking, and was slowly drawing the pistol from the breast pocket of the flight suit when the doe and fawn bolted. He'd stared after them, feeling sad and starved and cheated. Then he'd heard a much closer sound and turned back toward the pathway.

The family had come upon him suddenly, and both he and they stared.

They were typical travelers of the beaten path. A man, his woman with a baby slung on her back in a crude wicker carrier, and two young children walking before them.

They'd stared at him.

Dammit! he'd raged, and angrily pulled the pistol free.

The man had raised his arms defensively, and the woman chattered her alarm, terrified. The children had just stared at his face, mouths agape.

Kill them and hide the bodies, his reason told him. *They're the enemy.*

Lucky Anderson had raised his pistol at the man, stared for a moment longer, then had sullenly lowered it and trudged on by. He'd looked back at them only once, as they fled around a turn in the mountain path, and felt like crying.

All morning he'd continued to travel, stopping only to circumvent other groups of travelers and two small collections of huts. His troubled mind cried out for a plan, but it was difficult to think clearly, and all he could come up with was to keep going ahead.

He knew he should hole up for at least a few hours in the early evening, to get much-needed rest, but he grudgingly decided that he must travel through the day and night. Then he would surely be far enough from the valley for rescue, he reasoned, and it would not matter if the family had turned him in.

He walked just off the path so the boots wouldn't leave their marks, trying to remain silent and alert, increasingly supporting himself with the walking staff as he grew wearier.

He saw movement on the bank of the small stream and froze.

A jungle rat with its litter, eating the remnants of a dead fish.

He *must* have food. Was he too close to a village? He

thought not, and again began to pull his pistol from the pocket, very slowly, so he wouldn't alert mama rat.

But then, although he heard nothing, he sensed that something or someone was approaching on the path, and he melted into a nearby group of bushes, cursing his luck.

He sucked in and held a breath as six NVA soldiers appeared on the path with wary eyes and ready weapons. They moved smoothly and quietly, looking professional. Fifty yards from his hiding place their leader made a hand signal, and they spread out onto the hillsides, searching the area thoroughly and coming ever closer.

Mama rat and her brood bolted for cover, and one soldier pointed. The leader motioned him back to his task.

Lucky lay perfectly flat in his tiny area, breathing cautiously, peering out at the group with a single slitted eye, knowing he was about to be caught.

They came on toward him. As he was preparing to hide the pistol and radio so they wouldn't be captured with him, they stopped cold in their tracks.

The leader made a sharp motion with his hand, and Lucky saw another man, sturdily built and serious looking, dressed in black garb and carrying a stubby machine pistol, descend the northern hillside to join him. The two conversed in low tones, then the man in black filtered back into the jungle not ten feet from where Lucky lay. The others immediately came down from the hillsides and joined together, listening to words from their leader. When they proceeded past him, Lucky shuddered involuntarily. They were the most capable soldiers he'd yet encountered and had obviously been searching for *someone*.

If they hadn't been told to break it off, he'd have been taken. He was so shaken that he decided it was time to get the hell out of the valley, regardless of the extra day it would take before he could be picked up.

1410 Local—Phuc Yen PAAFB, DRV

Air Regiment Commandant Quon

Quon was sitting in on the briefing that Kapitan Aleks Ivaňovic was giving to the Vietnamese pilots, listening as the young Russian told them how to engage Mee Phantoms.

His adjutant came into the room and motioned for him. In the hall he said the search-team sergeant had called on the radio telephone.

Quon paused. It was an important briefing.

"Has he found *Lokee?*" he asked.

"There was a sighting this morning."

Quon hurried to his office and picked up the receiver.

Word had been relayed to the search-team sergeant from the Hanoi Command Center. A family had come face-to-face with an apparition who could only have been *Lokee*.

Quon caught his breath, excitement racing. "Where?"

"In the Tay Bac, near a small village called Lang Xom." The sergeant paused. "It will take us two days to travel there."

The Tay Bac was a rugged mountain area west of the Hong Valley, many kilometers from the sergeant's ongoing search near the Viet Bac.

"You are *sure* it is he?"

"The family who saw him was frightened because the man had no face. It is *Lokee,* comrade Quon. Somehow he crossed the Hong Valley and made it into the Tay Bac. If I hurry there with my team, we will be able to capture him before he is rescued."

Just as in aerial combat, once the quarry was spotted, Quon became calm. His stomach grew easy and his nervousness abated. "Where are you now?" he asked.

"I am at the Song Lo, comrade Quon, with a forty-man team. We have found where he crossed the river using an old, broken rowboat to float across."

Quon looked at his wall map and a village there. "How far are you from An Lao?"

"Just three kilometers."

"Go there. I will send two helicopters to transport you and your men to the Tay Bac." He thought a moment. "Will your forty men be enough?"

"Enough to contain him in the valley where he was seen. Then I will bring in more men from the Xom Dong training barracks to close the trap."

Excitement welled through him. "Find him!"

"I promise you that, comrade Quon."

"You've promised many times already. This time don't promise, just do it."

1545 Local—Western Mountains, North Vietnam

Sergeant Black

They'd looked for the downed pilot for two and a half days, scouring the mountain on which Black had thought he was hiding and the nearby path for sign of his passage. But then Black had noticed a ragtag group of local militia traveling west on the road toward them, and he'd contacted the team and told them to approach and question the militiamen.

When the lieutenant appeared, the mountain villagers were impressed, for they seldom saw officers. Their leader thought he and his men were the search team sent by Hanoi.

What team? the lieutenant asked.

A man and his family had seen a monster on the mountain road who had threatened to kill them with an evil-looking pistol. The militia had contacted Hanoi on the radio they kept at their village.

And?

Hanoi said they knew of the monster. He was a dangerous Mee named *Lokee*. They said to pursue him diligently until a search team arrived, but not to kill him.

The garrulous militia leader had tried to impress the lieutenant with his position as headman of his village. He told him about his love and great esteem for Ho Chi Minh.

Weren't the lieutenant and his men from Hanoi?

Near Hanoi, the lieutenant had confided, *but not from Hanoi itself.* The lieutenant used a cover story; they were from the Tu Ky Training Center looking for recruits who'd deserted.

The militia leader had been let down. Hanoi had promised they would deploy a team to the valley very quickly and seal it off so the Mee killer couldn't escape. They'd mentioned a commendation for his diligence, and even a reward if they caught *Lokee* alive.

The lieutenant's chest heaved as he briefed Black, for he'd hurried back with his news.

Black stared down at the mountain trail with a wistful expression. Half an hour earlier they'd heard the distant sounds of at least one and probably two helicopters. Likely they'd brought the searchers sent by Hanoi.

Not only was it now necessary to curtail their search for

the downed pilot, they just *might* have been compromised. And since compromise was the worst possible fate for a recon team, Black ordered the team to withdraw eastward.

Half an hour later the lieutenant stopped and again called him down the mountainside.

One of the men had found boot prints and the mark of a walking staff, which were surely traces of Anderson's passage. They were fresh, not more than a few hours old. He suggested that they backtrack and make a thorough sweep during the night, for it would take another day for the search team to become organized.

"No," said Black, and he brusquely motioned them on down the trail. He had a gut feeling that things were beginning to fall apart. "Perhaps we can look on our return trip if they have not found him," said Black, but he knew that was unlikely.

Two hours later they were walking down the trail in the semidarkness when they came face-to-face with the advance guard of the NVA search team. Black quietly slipped into the dark jungle, leaving the indigenous team to their wiles.

The lieutenant went onto the offensive and set about questioning the grizzled veteran sergeant in charge of the team.

They were indeed looking for a Mee killer named *Lokee* who had been sighted not far away. The sergeant said his team would shortly be joined by several hundred men from the provincial barracks, who would tighten a noose around the area.

He was good, that sergeant. The lieutenant's rank hadn't discouraged him from asking what he and his men were doing there, and even wondering if they couldn't join his search. The lieutenant gave the cover story he'd given the militiamen: that they were from the Tu Ky Training Center pursuing deserters. He would check with Tu Ky to see if they could be spared, he said. In the meantime they must continue their own search.

Later he told Black he didn't think the sergeant had been totally convinced.

After hearing him out, Black judiciously decided they had to get the hell out of the area—quickly. This time the lieutenant did not disagree.

Black almost aborted the entire mission right then and thought of circling back to the exfiltration point. But after they'd separated themselves ten klicks eastward from the search team and were settling in for the remainder of the night on a peaceful hillside, he decided to change to an alternate cover story and proceed.

They'd made their first radio call the morning after parachuting in, that they'd been inserted and were together. Their next transmission was to be in four more days, before withdrawing toward Point Zulu, and he wanted at least part of the mission to be a success.

Too bad about Major Anderson, he thought. Unless he could contact someone on his survival radio and get himself rescued in one hell of a hurry, the poor bastard had little chance of getting out of North Vietnam.

CHAPTER
TWENTY-SEVEN

Day 55, 0520 Local—Karst Area, Western Mountains, North Vietnam

Major Lucky Anderson

The NVA team that almost caught him had concerned Lucky so much that he'd immediately started up the rugged ridge north of the narrow valley. That was fortunate, for the next morning when he'd looked down from the crest, he'd seen a much larger search party making their way through the valley.

He hadn't delayed after that single look, but had continued making his way through dense jungle until he'd descended into the next valley. There he found another east-west mountain path, this one more narrow and less well traveled than the previous one. He'd wearily circumvented a village that night, and during the day he'd curled under a fallen tree and slept like the dead.

The following evening the new path took him out of the thick forests to twist through the ugly, barren red limestone karsts he'd often noted from the air. He remembered thinking what great hiding places their caves would make. Now, as he passed among their great shadows, a feeling of foreboding filled him. The countryside was barren of vegetation, and there seemed to be absolutely no food, not even the occasional tubers or sour, tough-skinned fruit.

Twice during his sojourn through the mountains, when Lucky had felt particularly secure with his hiding places, he'd removed his ragged flight suit, washed it in a rocky stream, and bathed. Both times he'd examined and gauged his gauntness from how prominently his ribs protruded. Now he knew it was worse. He was emaciated, and estimated he'd lost fifty pounds during the trek.

He must call in the rescue forces, for he was fast approaching the limits of his reserve.

The previous night he'd walked for only three hours before stopping to rest in a small roadside cave. Although exhausted, he'd had his days and nights reversed for so long that he'd found it difficult to nod off in the darkness, so he'd lain quietly and rested and thought of what he must do the following morning to make the rescue an easy one for the choppers.

Lucky arose well before dawn, restless with anticipation, and went through his ritual of checking to see that the pistol was ready for firing, then of carving a notch in the staff.

Fifty-six days on the run.

He drained the old water from his two remaining baby bottles and replenished them from a small stream. One leaked worse than the other, so he always drank that one first.

He looked about one last time, ready to move out.

"It is time," he solemnly declared, "to go home." The sound of the words thrilled him. He'd dreamed of saying them since his feet had first touched ground on Thud Ridge.

He climbed up onto the path and carefully walked on the side of it, as he'd trained himself to do, so the distinctive tread of the boots would not be obvious. It was difficult here, where there was only dust and rock, not to leave a trail. As he walked in the gloom of the false dawn, he stared at the sides of the rugged mountain. Most karsts were flat-topped, like American mesas. He was searching for one, and an easy way to get up. After half an hour he came to a break in the steep limestone karst formations. Off to his right was a gentle slope leading upward. He hurried, scrambling and climbing, unmindful for the first time in eight weeks of leaving signs of his passage.

At 0700 he was on top, in a superb location for a pickup. He could see forever, and there was a large, flat area. The rescuers would easily be able to tell if there were gomer soldiers in the area to be neutralized, and the chopper could land beside him.

He sat cross-legged and fished out his radio and . . . the single precious flare that he'd saved for the occasion. He waited for the fighters to come.

With the filled water bottles he could stay for two days. Hopefully the Thuds would be flying a combat mission into pack six today and fly their normal route, but he could wait another day if he must. The gomers were searching in the next valley, not this one.

Ten minutes later he saw the strike force, far to the west and flying very high, already in their large formation. With trembling hands he picked up the radio, then with great difficulty calmed and scolded himself to have patience. He wanted them closer so he wouldn't waste transmitting time with the weak radio.

Gotta remember, he briefed himself. *It's the transmitting that takes the power.* Once he switched it on, he could receive all he wanted but must talk very little.

Maybe he'd take Linda to dinner tonight. Big steak. Two steaks? No, he'd have to take it easy on the old stomach for a while. Maybe a single steak, and a potato and corn. He loved corn on the cob. He pulled out the radio's antenna and watched the dots in the sky.

He and Linda would have a good long talk and settle things between them. It was time for a settling. He'd been a dumb-shit fool. If she wanted to put up with an ugly wretch, he could at least listen to what she had to say. The Thud strike force was almost overhead. He switched to transmit/receive and depressed the button.

"F-105's, this is Barracuda lead transmitting in the blind."

There were no side tones when he transmitted, and the battery needle showed no movement from the red zone.

He tried again. Nothing. No side tones or static.

He frantically checked the battery. *The radio was dead.*

The strike force passed just north of him, continuing toward the Red River Valley, unaware that one of their own was far below, foolishly reaching upward and pleading for them to take notice.

Wednesday, October 4th, 1300 Local—Ponderosa BOQ, Takhli RTAFB, Thailand

Captain Manny DeVera

Manny was getting discouraged again.

It had been almost a month since the inquiry had begun, and still it wasn't resolved. He didn't know if the matter was going to the next step, an official preliminary hearing of formal charges, or if the whole thing would be dropped. He was on an emotional roller coaster. One day the legal officer would be cheerful and say it was all bunk, and the next day he'd say the brass were determined to hang someone, and even if the evidence was shaky, they had DeVera to experiment with. Manny was now buddies with the major from the legal office. If the matter went any further, they'd decided to send him to the Philippines, where they had a proper judge advocate general office and court facilities, and enough lawyers to proceed with things. As soon as the Takhli legal officer knew he wasn't going to be in that picture, he confidentially told Manny he thought it was all a bunch of crap. But the matter wasn't cleared up, and Manny was confined to base and unable to resume his duties.

He was lying on his bunk, thinking those things, when someone out in the day room loudly called the place to attention. Manny sat up, wondering, and was peering at the open doorway when Colonel B. J. Parker strolled up the hall and stood there looking at him.

B.J. smiled. "Caught you napping on the job."

On the job? Was he here to tell him to return to work, that the charges had been dropped? Manny's heart pumped faster as he quickly got to his feet and regarded his wing commander with a grin. "I'm working out grand strategies to win the war, Colonel."

"May I come inside?" asked B.J. too politely. No joking around, as he often did with DeVera.

"Yes, sir," said Manny, glancing around at the room in case something was amiss. It appeared shipshape. Two bunks, a desk, and a chair. He'd put up some pictures of airplanes and had a photo of Jackie Bell on the desk. They hadn't assigned a roommate since Liebermann had been shot down, so it was all his.

B.J. took the only chair and looked up at him, so Manny

quickly sat on the bed B.J. probably didn't like being looked down to, and Manny sure as hell didn't want to piss him off.

"Is there anything to all this bullshit, Manny?"

He answered without hesitation. "No, sir. I've never tried to drop bombs anywhere but on an assigned target."

B.J. nodded, staring sadly, and suddenly Manny knew he was not bringing good news.

"Lucky's note is pretty convincing stuff," said B.J.

"Yes, sir. I don't understand it at all."

"He had a reputation for telling it like it was."

"Colonel, I was his assistant flight commander, and he never *once* mentioned anything to me about dropping on civilians or unauthorized targets."

B.J. raised an eyebrow at him. "Never?"

"No, sir. I went through a period when I had the shakes and jangles flying up in pack six, but he worked with me until I got my problem under control."

B.J. nodded slowly, then lowered his eyes, as if he were about to do something he had no heart for.

"He never mentioned any other problems," added Manny. He knew his words sounded lame and wondered how he might be more convincing.

"I wish to hell Lucky was here so he could tell us what the note was all about." B.J. sighed. "But he's not, and I've had to make a hard decision."

"It's your call, Colonel," said Manny in his quietest voice.

The disposition of matters such as this were left to the commanding officer. No one else was in the loop. The legal officer had made that clear. He'd told Manny that B. J. Parker could stop it all with a simple refusal to let it go further because of the shaky evidence. But he'd also said that pressure was being brought to bear from PACAF headquarters.

"I wish it was that simple," muttered Parker, and Manny wondered if he wasn't here to try to explain himself. "A four-star's got me by the neck on this, and he won't let go."

"I didn't do a damn thing illegal, Colonel," Manny tried.

B.J. sighed. "I've got a full colonel who swears he was given a note that says you did. I've got the note, in Lucky's hand, that says you bombed an unauthorized target. And higher headquarters tells me that *someone's* bombs hit an unauthorized civilian target that day."

Manny steeled himself.

"I'm preferring charges. You'll be going to Clark Air Base in the Philippines for the preliminary hearing. They're the ones with court-martial authority, and they're bringing in a senior officer from Hickam to run it."

"Jesus," said Manny. He hadn't known it would hit him this hard. He'd had all that time to prepare himself, but now he realized he'd never thought it would really happen.

"I've dropped the charges for that first date, when you were hit by flak. It's just the one date now, the one shown on Lucky's note."

He felt numb. As B. J. Parker rose to his feet, he followed.

"These things work themselves out, Manny. Tell 'em the truth and it will be resolved."

Regardless of his friendly demeanor, Manny DeVera realized he was facing no friend in B. J. Parker. He slowly came to attention, head stiff, and eyes locked straight ahead.

"I've written a letter about my personal knowledge of your capabilities and your courage in combat." Parker held it out to him. "It also says you've been put in for a Silver Star medal for destroying the bridge at the Canales des Rapids."

But he knew Parker didn't believe him and was throwing him to the wolves, and Manny felt no different toward him than he did toward Lyons. *To hell with them both*, he thought bitterly.

After an awkward moment Parker quietly asked, "Do you want the letter?"

"No, sir!" He barked the words out crisply, as he had as a flight cadet.

He kept his eyes locked forward and his face frozen as the wing commander nodded sadly and left the room.

1410 Local—Commandant's Office, Phuc Yen PAAFB, DRV

Air Regiment Commandant Quon

The sergeant had radioed again. He wanted to split his force and send more than half back to the Hong Valley.

Three nights earlier, when they'd first arrived in the Tay Bac, they'd met another, much smaller, group of People's

Army soldiers led by a lieutenant. He'd thought it strange that such a small group was led by an officer and had called for Hanoi Command Center to confirm their story. Then he'd continued the search for *Lokee*.

They'd found *Lokee*'s trail, had several good imprints from the distinctive tread of his Mee boots. But he had fooled them for a full two days because he'd crossed over into the next valley. They'd now also crossed the mountain and found new signs of his passage, and felt they were drawing close.

But back to the lieutenant and the six men he led. Hanoi had contacted Tu Ky Training Base and found that no such team had been sent to the Tay Bac.

"So?" asked Quon, impatient to return the conversation to the quest for *Lokee*.

"The lieutenant was an impostor. A very good impostor, for there is a lieutenant at Tu Ky with the same name, but he was there at the training base. I must find and capture that group of soldiers, comrade Quon. They are either spies or saboteurs."

"They are there to rescue *Lokee*," hissed Quon. "Continue to search for *Lokee* and you will find them."

"But, comrade Quon, the lieutenant and his men left in the direction of the Hong Valley. If we continue here, we will miss them, and they might cause great damage."

Quon was resolute. "They are trying to rescue *Lokee*. I order you to continue to look for him. If you see the rescuers, shoot them on sight, but you must find *Lokee*."

1545 Local—Five Miles West of the City of Son Tay, North Vietnam

Sergeant Black

As Hotdog approached the big, populated valley, Black had donned his NVA sergeant's uniform, and their charade had changed. Now when they were occasionally questioned, they were survivors from the 310-A Division, a unit that had been decimated during a battle with American Marines. They'd been sent home to join a new battalion that would augment the 310-A. They carried a properly sealed order to that effect, with the valid signature of the 310-A Division's adjutant. In another week they were to join a new battalion forming at the Dao Lang barracks and return south with it.

It was a good cover, but it wasn't fireproof. Most of the mauled NVA division's officers had been killed in combat and their adjutant captured. At least some of that could be discovered with a radio call to the right people at the People's Army headquarters in Hanoi. So regardless of appropriate uniforms and their possession of many of the current passwords used by various units in the area, they tried to avoid official contact.

They'd walked for thirty kilometers, then hitched a ride on a poorly tuned Soviet weapons carrier that continually backfired and belched black smoke and finally gave out. Then they'd fortuitously come across a small Army barracks with several dozen bicycles parked in racks, protected by a single sleepy guard, and had made a quiet midnight requisition. They'd biked the rest of the way to Son Tay, chattering and eyeing and waving at the prettiest girls, and acting as 310-A survivors would on a short leave back home.

They made good time, stopping only when area sirens announced the approach of American air parties. Then they'd dismount and shout angrily, and like other soldiers try to shoot down the Mee with their rifles. More than a dozen times during the bike ride, both coming and going, they'd seen large Russian helicopters clop-clopping their way to and from Hanoi, and the lieutenant told Sergeant Black that none of them had seen that many before.

Which made Black wonder if they weren't coming from some nearby helicopter base.

Near the Hong River at Son Tay that morning, they'd observed the new prison camp. Sergeant Black had gotten a glimpse of American prisoners wearing dirty white uniforms with maroon stripes, moving rocks and debris under the watchful eyes of a group of arrogant, slovenly guards. His throat had constricted and grown a lump at the sight.

They'd carefully taken it all in, and the lieutenant had approached the camp guards to ask directions so he could get a closer look at things. The prisoners, he'd reported back, looked undernourished and in poor health.

By noon they'd been on their way, not daring to tempt luck more than they had, and with each kilometer Sergeant Black regretted more that they'd not found Major Anderson. Soon he'd face the same fate as the group in the camp. In fact, from what they'd learned in the mountains, he wondered if the North Vietnamese didn't have worse in store for Anderson.

But Black also knew they couldn't return to the area of the search. There were too many soldiers there, and with each encounter Hotdog's chances for compromise were increased. He picked a return course to the Zulu exfiltration point which took them well south of the search area. So much for helping the major he was himself beginning to think of as *Lokee*. Since there was nothing they could do about the pilot, he tried to push him from his mind so he could concentrate on other things.

As they pedaled westward, they watched the skies. The Russian helicopters were coming from the foothills of the western mountain range, from an area only a few kilometers south of their route. Intrigued, Black decided to make that small detour.

1915 Local—Commandant's Office, Phuc Yen PAAFB, DRV

Air Regiment Commandant Quon

Quon was summoned from his evening meal to speak on the radiophone with the search-team sergeant.

"The false lieutenant and his team of spies were seen in Son Tay today, comrade Quon. I have been ordered to terminate this search and go after them."

"Who gave such an order?" stormed Quon.

"My major at Hanoi. He has received great pressure to find the spy team, and I must withdraw with my men. There are others here now who can continue to search for *Lokee*."

"How close are you now?"

"We have closed our net to within seven kilometers, and I know *Lokee* is inside. Three hundred men will stay here to find him while we go after the spy team, comrade Quon."

"You will *also* stay."

"But comrade Quon . . ."

Quon broke the connection and rang the colonel who commanded the sergeant's superior officer. After a short argument the colonel agreed that the sergeant would continue the search for *Lokee*.

All People's Army units within fifty kilometers of Son Tay would be alerted to look for the band of spies, and when found, they would be shot on sight. If they hadn't been caught by the time *Lokee* was discovered, the sergeant would then join the search for the spies.

Thursday, October 5th, 0600 Local—Seventeen Miles Southwest of Son Tay

Sergeant Black

By nightfall they'd holed up and prepared the radio for the next morning's radio call; then the lieutenant had taken two men to reconnoiter and verify the existence of the helicopter base. Their 0200 report confirmed only that there was some sort of fenced military base there. Sergeant Black decided it was worth a look-see of his own in the light of day, so he'd asked the lieutenant and the two men to return with him. They'd crawled to the camp's perimeter and dug in in the darkness, waiting for dawn so they could observe what was there.

As the sun sprayed tendrils of red across the eastern sky, Black sucked in a breath of wonder. Huge camouflage nets covered an operational base with full maintenance facilities. He counted a dozen of the big Russian helicopters parked insolently beneath the nets.

As he watched and waited, a helicopter's engine began to whine, and its eight tremendous blades began rotating. The blades chattered, then roared, then slowed to a steady clop-clop. A couple of minutes later the huge bird's engine surged, and it lifted off. Forward at first, until it had cleared the high camouflage nets, then gaining altitude and turning to fly over them and roar away, eastward toward Hanoi.

He heard a low whistle and glanced back to see the lieutenant motioning his head to the south. He looked there.

Shee-it!

A tracked, armored vehicle was coming directly toward them, likely making a routine check of the perimeter. If they remained where they were, the damned thing would run over them.

Time to fake it.

Sergeant Black rose nonchalantly and strolled to catch up

with the three other men, who were also up and chattering as they casually walked from the area.

The vehicle headed directly toward them, slowed, and stopped a few meters distant.

The lieutenant spoke for them, telling their cover story to the sergeant in command of the vehicle and motioning toward Sergeant Black to add a war tale about how he'd been wounded in the South after heroically shooting down an American helicopter with a machine gun. He told windy stories about the other two men, and the NVA sergeant grew impatient.

Dammit, get rid of 'em, Black thought, but he knew the lieutenant was doing the proper thing.

The sergeant finally waved them on.

"This is a restricted area, and you must leave immediately, comrade Lieutenant," he said forcefully. "I will check with my office and tell them to not bother you, so long as you depart immediately. What is your unit?"

The lieutenant again told him their unit was the 310-A and said they would be very quick about leaving.

Buddy, you ain't lying there, thought Black.

The personnel carrier revved its engine and was off, continuing around the perimeter.

That group looked at one another with grim expressions. If the sergeant called their unit and cover story in to Hanoi, they'd been compromised. They hurried back to the others, where Black strung the radio's wire antenna over a tree limb and prepared for transmission.

At precisely 0700 Black called over the pretuned low-frequency radio. He started with their code name and today's password. *"Hotdog, Pigeon,"* he radioed.

The listener answered with two beeps, which meant he'd received him loud and clear.

First Black related what they'd found at Son Tay. That one was simple, for he followed a memorized checklist. *"Yes. . . . Medium, three. . . . One. . . . Yes. . . . Yes. . . . Eight. . . . Seventeen. . . . Five,"* he radioed, and the first task was done.

It was indeed a prisoner-of-war camp, it was defended by three 57mm AAA batteries, they'd noticed one SAM site in the area, the camp was active and held prisoners, they had seen eight guards and seventeen prisoners, five of them well enough to positively identify.

He waited and a few seconds later heard a single beep, which meant to repeat . . . which he did. Then he received a beep-beep.

"More coming," he transmitted.

Beep-beep.

"Twelve Sunday Hags plus full support at Tango-Foxtrot-Seven-Two-Five-One," he said, which told them there were twelve Soviet helicopters plus a full support base at the coordinates, which he'd defined down to a gnat's ass.

Beep.

The sounds of a machine gun, and then another, rattled in the distance. They heard the sounds of more than one APC now. He glanced around at the men of Hotdog team, giving them a "keep your cool" look. Then he repeated his message on the radio.

Beep-beep, they acknowledged.

Louder machine-fun fire. Closer?

"More coming," he transmitted.

Beep-beep.

"Big Hawk, negative. Probable." Telling them that Hotdog had searched for the downed pilot and had not made contact. And . . . that he'd likely been captured.

Beep-beep.

More engine revving sounds from the searching APCs.

"More coming," he said again, for finally he had to tell them that Hotdog had been compromised.

Beep-beep.

"Charlie, Charlie. Expedite. Hotdog out."

Beep-beep-beep-beep, said Monkey Mountain. Which meant *Get the fuck outa there.*

As he started to reel in the wire antenna, he heard a revving engine and the clatter of tracks growing close. The lieutenant gripped his shoulder, and he swung around to peer through the brush toward the road.

The APC was approaching fast up the nearby roadway. The same NVA sergeant was in the turret, looking around grimly and pointing the mounted machine gun wherever he looked.

The rest of the team hit the dirt. Black crouched lower but continued to watch. The silly shit couldn't see him. He was fucking invisible in the bush.

The sergeant began firing wildly into heavy foliage at one side of the road. *Rrraaaap.* He fired into the brush at the other side. *Rrrraaaaap.* Then he stirred the gun about its swivel mount. *Rrrraaaa-rraaaap.*

He swung the muzzle in his direction, and Sergeant Black dropped for the ground.

Rrraaa-aap.

He'd been too slow.

"Shit!" he exclaimed, and curled up, clutching at his side. *God it hurt.*

He almost screamed as the agony swept over him, but he clenched his teeth, and then the lieutenant was there, trying to help.

The Soviet armored personnel carrier with its loud engine and noisy tracks continued down the road. The sergeant continued to fire wildly at the sides of the road, oblivious to the fact that he'd hit his mark. *Rrrrraaaa-aaap. Rrrraaa-aaaaap.*

Hurting very badly, Sergeant Black looked down and wondered if he was dying.

CHAPTER TWENTY-EIGHT

Day 57, 1430 Local—Western Mountains, North Vietnam

Major Lucky Anderson

He'd traveled northwest for two days since burying the useless radio, but he'd done so slowly. *Find a source of food,* his mind had begged him with every step. In those two days he'd eaten two frogs, a lizard, and a few insects he'd found sharing his hiding places in the barren karst land.

No more insects, though, except crickets. A fat shiny-green beetle had tasted bitter, and when he'd forced it down, he'd immediately felt terrible pains in his gut and began to wretch. After he'd puked it up and the pain finally subsided, he'd become leery of all insects, except crickets, of course. Crickets were tasty and went down well. The problem with them was that you'd have to eat them by the handful to fill yourself, and they weren't always easy to catch.

He'd been drinking rainwater, which collected in natural limestone basins after each downpour, but while water was most important, he knew he must now have food . . . and not just an occasional cricket. Increasingly his strength was failing him, and he was beginning to have trouble thinking through the simplest of problems.

Hope and willpower had helped sustain him during the journey, but since the failure of the survival radio, much of that had left him. Now each new day presented him with perplexing mental puzzles and impossible physical demands.

The gomers were after him, drawing ever closer, methodically searching each karst and barren hillock. He was sufficiently lucid to know they must be avoided, but it was increasingly difficult to do so. By day he hid in small caves carved into the stone by wind and rain. He moved only at night, and then mostly when it was raining. So far he'd eluded them, but they were drawing in from all directions, and unless he could break out of their net, it was only a matter of time before they captured him.

He had just the two goals, to get food and to break through the gomer net, and he was working on a plan to do both.

He lay on a rocky formation, looking down on a group of thirty soldiers as they chattered among themselves, preparing to move out. They'd camped there the previous evening, and the wonderful smells from their cooking pots had drawn him. They'd advanced farther into the net than the others, so for most of the day they had delayed, waiting patiently, periodically splitting into small teams to search the area. They were thorough, but there were too few of them, and he'd become adept at hiding in small, improbable places.

During their last search they'd left only two soldiers behind to guard the camp. If they did that again, he intended to kill the guards, then fill his pockets with food and run straight down the rocky path at their rear until he was clear of the net.

He hadn't run for a long time now, but he felt that with a few bites of food in him he could do it. Outrun them all. Once clear, he'd hide and again become covert about things. Another audacious plan, but he'd convinced himself it could work, just as the one had that had taken him through their training area.

The worst that could happen would be to be killed, and he cared increasingly less about that. The best that could happen would be to break free of the net with a full stomach and continue the seventy-mile trip to the TACAN station at the Laotian border. Then he'd be taken out by the CIA's hired help, maybe by one of his friends who had left the Air Force to fly with Air America. He knew they resupplied the

tribesmen who refueled the TACAN station's generator and
guarded the site.

Maybe he would . . .

. . . but first . . .

. . . first he had to . . . take out the guards and get food to
provide fuel for his body and mind. Each day when he slept
in his fitful naps, he'd awake not knowing whether he was
conscious or hallucinating. He even drifted into reveries
when he was walking.

Something was wrong with the plan.

He thought it through again.

The guards might be hard to kill. They were carrying
AK-47's, and he had only the small-caliber pistol.

Anything else wrong?

It's a stupid plan, part of his mind tried to tell him. *Just
get through the net and worry about food when you're clear.*

Then he remembered the mouth-watering smells of food
from their cook fire and convinced himself that *most* of his
plan was sound, and that would have to be enough.

Change the plan. The guards have AK-47's. He stared
sullenly at the group as they prepared to move out.

*Pick the right time and just quietly steal in and out of
their camp. Take food from the two pots beside the fire pit
while the guards aren't looking.*

They'd never suspect he would do that. He felt *very* intelligent.

He thought about food for a while longer, and memories
of eating became overpowering and impossible to push
away.

The men formed into two groups, as they had earlier, and
as before they left only two guards behind. He hoped they'd
be as lazy as the previous pair had looked to be.

The soldiers fanned out and began to scour the area.

A chopper flew past, and Lucky looked up warily. The
big green helicopter with the red star on its side continued
on its way east toward the Red River Valley.

They'd not seen him. He'd covered himself with the om-
nipresent red dust and knew he appeared as a part of the
rocks upon which he lay.

He waited, lying on the small rocky outcropping beside
his hiding niche, watching as the two guards horsed around
for a while, then settled into their routines. One wandered
to the east side to stare after the departed soldiers. Lucky

watched as the other one began to work with pots and big bags of rice, preparing the evening meal for the men.

"Jesus," Lucky muttered, and he thought of food. "Jesus."

A voice from behind startled him. He turned to see an NVA soldier looking at him, AK-47 trained directly at his back. They stared at one another, and the Vietnamese became slack-jawed with fright, then yelled out a string of words.

Lucky Anderson's freedom had come to a rude end.

When six of them had gathered, they all stared just as the first one had.

"*Lokee!*" one hissed.

They spread-eagled him where they'd caught him, face to the sky, and the one who'd found him went through his flight-suit pockets and took everything. There wasn't much. The pistol, knife, signal mirror, and the flare. The matches, compass, and dog-eared plasticized maps. Two badly cracked and empty baby bottles and a short remnant of cord. Finally the soldier removed his boots and the flying watch from his wrist. Those were his only remaining possessions, and they took them. Then they covered him with their weapons and barked shrill orders to one another as they herded him down off the rock.

There was more yelling and laughing as they marched him into the camp, prodding him with gun barrels.

He stumbled and fell. They prodded. He tried to get up and fell again.

They laughed and jabbed with the gun barrels, and one of the soldiers kicked him in the side. Another soldier, this one wearing two small stars on his shoulder, screamed at the one who'd kicked him and pointed, mentioning the word *Lokee* again.

The same soldier who'd kicked him hesitated before touching him, but helped him to his feet and supported him as they walked into the camp.

Even through his mental fog, Lucky realized he was a prize. He motioned toward the pots, where the cook was preparing the meal. The ranking man, the one wearing the two small stars, looked inquisitively at Lucky, then brightened and motioned toward his mouth. Lucky nodded and crumpled again as waves of weakness swept over him.

Two-stars said something and the others laughed. Then he barked orders and signaled for them to continue.

They bound him securely, taking no chance that he might escape. First they tied his hands behind him, then his elbows together, which hurt like hell, so he screamed until they loosened the ropes a little. Next they tied his feet and then his knees. To make sure, they set up a guard to stand over him, AK-47 at the ready. By that time the others had been called in from their search and were gathered about, gawking. One came very close and touched him on the shoulder, then sprang back, laughing while the others heckled him.

Two-stars called two men out and explained something carefully. Several times he looked over at him and mentioned the word *Lokee*. They both nodded energetically before taking off at a trot back up the path to the west. Messengers?

The cook knelt before him, holding a bowl heaped with rice that was generously laced with dark pieces of meat. He fed him with a large spoon, and Lucky ate voraciously until the bowl was finished. It was sticky and stank of fish, and tasted as good as any tenderloin. The cook held a cup of water so he could drink, then cocked his head inquisitively and asked something.

Lucky nodded.

The cook fetched more food, and although he knew he shouldn't, he ate that entire bowl too. By the time he'd finished, his stomach ached with sharp, toothache-like pangs.

An hour passed, and the crowd watched closely as he writhed uneasily with his aching stomach and bloated bowels, and they laughed each time he could no longer contain yet another powerful release of gas.

The sounds of a revving diesel engine came closer, and finally an aging half-tracked vehicle labored up the path and into the camp. A tough and leathery-looking soldier dismounted and nodded curtly at the soldiers. He wore three small stars on his shoulders, and Lucky guessed he was some sort of senior enlisted man.

He stopped, bent down directly before Lucky, and stared carefully at his face. He made a distasteful expression and very slowly nodded. Three-stars stood and chattered to the driver of the half-track. He went to the vehicle, strutting proudly, and a few minutes later spoke vigorously into the microphone of a whining radio.

After a long radio conversation, three-stars returned and hunkered down again.

"You *Lokee?*"

Lucky realized the man was speaking English. He stared.

"You name?"

He spoke with difficulty. "Major Paul Anderson."

The man nodded and smiled. "Lokee."

Friday, October 6th, 1620 Local—People's Army HQ, Hanoi, DRV

Air Regiment Commandant Quon

He'd been called to a meeting of the general staff at the headquarters, and it was apparent to Quon that he was in trouble with both General Dung and General Tho. Every time either had spoken to him, they'd done so coolly, with no trace of their old camaraderie.

Two more bridges had been destroyed, both near the Chinese border. Trung's guns had downed one of the invaders, and Xuan Nha's rockets another. The fighters from Phuc Yen had not engaged the Mee, yet one of his lieutenants had been killed in his small-tail MiG-21 while trying to get away from a Phantom that had caught him fleeing toward China. The Phantom had fired a missile, and the young pilot had panicked and wrenched his bird into a hard turn. The MiG's nose had slewed sideward, and the airplane had entered a deadly, flat spin.

Quon had tried to explain that he'd been ordered to place his Vietnamese pilots at the controls of the spin-prone MiGs before they were ready. The generals hadn't listened. The commandant from Kien An had looked away, likely happy that it wasn't him under scrutiny.

Quon had said he'd personally look into the training they were getting from the Russian advisors, and the generals asked why he hadn't been more diligent in that task in the past.

He didn't tell them that he'd become so consumed by the search for his son's killer that his performance had suffered.

He simply promised the generals that he would do better in the future and left the meeting breathing hatred for *Lokee*. If it weren't for the disfigured Mee pilot, he wouldn't have had to endure the humiliation.

Following the meeting he'd come to the Command Center with General Tho to review the performance of their forces during the afternoon raids. Tho listened to a major tell them about the day's raids. Another bridge down, this one at Hung Yen, south of Hanoi. Two more had been damaged in the far north. Reports of yet another attack were arriving from Bac Giang. The general listened somberly as he was told about the failure of MiG interceptors from Kien An Air Base, whose pilots were having the same difficult problems as Quon's pilots at Phuc Yen.

As General Tho berated the colonel from Kien An, Quon noticed his adjutant beckoning. He sidled over to him, unseen by Tho as he continued to speak harshly to the other air regiment commandant.

"What do you want?" Quon hissed impatiently.

"The sergeant just radioed that he has captured *Lokee*."

A heavy weight was instantly lifted from Quon. "Alive?"

"He is unharmed, comrade Quon. Thin from the lack of food, but otherwise well."

Quon's nostrils flared as he thought of it. He felt giddy.

"Have them hold him where they've caught him," he whispered. "I must accompany the general to another meeting, which will last until late."

The adjutant nodded.

"Arrange for a helicopter to pick me up at the senior officers' quarters very early in the morning. I'd like to be in the hills and gone before the early Mee attacks."

"Do you plan to bring the Mee pilot back with you?"

Quon laughed very low so General Tho wouldn't overhear. "Only partway back."

The adjutant looked puzzled.

Quon intended to proceed to Kep and then throw *Lokee* out of the helicopter from a thousand meters height, to land precisely where his son had been killed.

He rejoined Tho and the colonel from Kien An, knowing that nothing the general told him could make him unhappy.

1645 Local—354th TFS Duty Desk, Takhli RTAFB, Thailand

Captain Manny DeVera

Manny was leaning over the counter talking with Joe Walker, who was duty officer, and with a couple of other squadron mates when the legal officer entered. This was alien territory for nonfliers, and he looked ill at ease as he peered around.

Manny waved him in. "Any of you guys get in trouble and need a shark," he said cheerily, "this guy's your bet."

The major winced at the word "shark." "May I see you privately, Captain DeVera?"

Lieutenant Walker and a couple of the others gave the lawyer cold looks as he followed Manny into the C-Flight office.

Billy Bowes looked up from the desk. "You want me to leave?" he asked Manny.

Manny looked back at the legal officer.

The major nodded. "For a few minutes, please."

"Take your time," said Billy. He gathered his papers and departed, closing the door.

The legal officer stared at the nameplate on the desk.

CAPTAIN M.G. DEVERA
"The Supersonic Wetback"
- WORLD'S GREATEST FIGHTER PILOT -

"I thought you were relieved of duty," said the major.

Manny shrugged. "I took the desk plaque to my room a couple times, but the guys keep taking it and putting it back. They say I'm still their flight commander, no matter what they're told."

Manny sat behind the familiar desk and leaned back. The major sat opposite him.

"You'll be leaving tomorrow for the Philippines. There's a military flight departing from Bangkok at noon, so you'll have to take the nine o'clock base shuttle down there."

"Good. I'm tired of sitting on my ass and just waiting."

"As soon as you get to the Philippines, they'll admit

you to the hospital and perform a series of psychological tests."

"To see if I've flipped out and become a baby killer?"

"Something like that."

"What's the charge?"

"Disobeying a legal order. They tried to make a couple others fly, like mutiny and dereliction of duty, but they felt those would just muddy the issue, so they dropped them."

"How many counts?" asked Manny. He was getting the lingo down.

"They're going with the one incident on July twenty-fourth. One charge and one count. That's good." But the major was wearing his grave look, not the happier one he'd had when Manny had last spoken with him.

"Something changed?" Manny asked.

"The headquarters legal people at Clark are talking general court-martial again, and that's serious. They're flying in a hard-ass full colonel from Hickam to run both the preliminary hearing and the court-martial. I've been talking to a couple of friends at Hickam, and they say General Roman called him in and said he wants to make an example of you."

Manny DeVera looked out the window, at the rows of parked aircraft there. *God, they're beautiful,* he thought. He wondered if he would ever again crawl into a fighter cockpit.

"You'll need a good lawyer," said the JAG. "You know any?"

"Just you."

"I'm talking about civilian lawyers. Someone with solid defense experience. You can have any lawyer you want, you know, and you'd better pick a good one."

"I've been in the Air Force too long to trust a civilian with anything as important as this."

The legal officer grimaced at his naïveté. "I've got a friend in the judge advocate general's office at Clark. He's young, but he's good."

"Will he take me?" asked Manny. "He may want to think twice if they're bringing in the hanging judge from Hickam."

"It'll be a fair hearing. I know the colonel they're talking about. He's tough as a nail and doesn't back off, but no matter what any general tells him, he'll be fair. The fact that he was put under pressure may even work in your favor. And yes, the captain will represent you. I've talked to him about it, and he's interested."

"What do you think? What's going to happen?"

"I think that unless you can get someone to prove the page from Major Anderson's book was faked or altered in some way, the matter will go to trial. That alone will damage your career. I know it's not supposed to if you're found innocent, but it sure as hell won't help it any."

"You think they might find me guilty?"

"Who knows? How much faith do you have in the military system, Manny?"

"The military raised me from a pup. I haven't known anything else since I was twenty years old. I trust the system. I don't trust that bastard Lyons, and I don't like what I've heard of General Roman, but people like them aren't the Air Force."

"Maybe not," said the major, "but you'll find they have a lot of influence."

Manny thought about that for a moment and felt a chill in the room.

"Call your lawyer buddy at Clark," he said.

1945 Local—General Officers' Quarters, Tan Son Nhut Air Base, Saigon, RVN

Lieutenant Colonel Pearly Gates

The tennis courts outside General Moss's quarters were lit, and Moss was volleying with his chief of staff, the colonel who ran his administrative staff. He chased a high ball to the back of the court and smashed it directly toward the colonel, who awkwardly drew in his racket and managed a weak return.

Moss lobbed the ball over the backpedaling colonel's head.

"Thirry—ruvv," announced the Vietnamese referee, and a ball boy chased after it.

"Caughtcha sleeping," Moss called amiably. He was ungracious in victory, nasty and unforgiving when he lost. He knew it and did not try to change himself.

Maybe, Pearly thought, that was part of what made him a good fighting general.

Pearly Gates edged onto the court and waited under the lights.

"You here to see how it's done, Pearly?" called Moss.

"Business, General."

"Can't wait until morning?"

"I'd rather it not, sir."

"Be right with you."

Moss smashed a serve at his chief of staff's knees. In less than two more minutes he'd won his game. The colonel went to the bench, shaking his head and sipping water. Moss retrieved his towel and came over to Pearly, obviously irritated that his game had been interrupted.

"Trying to impress me by working late?" he growled.

Pearly glanced at the nearby security-police bodyguards and lowered his voice. "I was called over to MAC-V, General. MAC-SOG's onto something pretty hot."

The Military Assistance Command–Studies and Observation Group worked directly for General Westmoreland, out of the operational control of the military-service commanders. MAC-SOG controlled a number of Air Force aircraft, mostly C-130's and C-123's, which gave Moss, the senior Air Force officer in Vietnam, great heartburn.

"Fucking prima donnas," he snorted.

Pearly kept his voice low. "They have certain, ah . . . assets . . . in place west of Hanoi who've located a bunch of Russian helicopters."

Moss blotted sweat from his brow as if not listening.

"It's right on the line between packs five and six, General. According to our guidelines we're authorized to strike 'em, as long as it doesn't interfere with our priority missions."

"How many choppers?"

"Ten or twelve big ones, General. As well as an entire support base."

Moss nodded.

"We've never known much about their helicopters, except what our spooks hear on their radio frequencies. We believe they have quite a number of the things, but we've always thought they kept them under wraps at their restricted bases, like at Gia Lam or Phuc Yen."

"And MAC-SOG found some and they want us to take 'em out?" Moss's voice was not forgiving. MAC-SOG had *stolen* his airplanes.

"Their assets up there are in trouble. They radioed that they'd been compromised and are on the run. MAC-SOG doesn't have more details. Their assets didn't call in this morning."

"Were they supposed to?"

"The spooks at Monkey Mountain monitor for them at oh-seven-hundred, when the North Vietnamese are preoccupied with our airstrikes. When they're in trouble like this, the team's supposed to call in every morning they can do so without being compromised."

"Maybe they've been captured and the helicopters moved."

"May be, sir. But MAC-SOG is asking if we'll go in and give the North Vietnamese Army something to worry about besides chasing their team."

"Are the helicopters in shelters?"

"We looked over a couple of recce pictures, and the photo interpreter thinks they're just parked under camouflage nets."

General Moss grew his narrow-eyed, fighter-jock expression, and Pearly knew he was finally getting interested.

"Defenses?" snapped Moss.

"Very few big guns and only one SAM site in the area, fifteen miles to the east. They've probably got a lot of small arms there, but not much else. It's like they don't want to draw attention to the chopper base." Pearly paused. "There's one other consideration."

"What's that?"

"According to our spooks who intercept their radio chatter, a lot of the conversations are in Russian. We think a number of the chopper pilots are Soviets."

The general paused, then nodded. "Makes it all that much sweeter."

"Yes, sir, it does."

"But we'd have to get the job done before the SecDef finds out and goes squealing to the President to get us to chicken out."

Now Pearly knew the general was *very* interested.

Pearly quickly pressed on. "We either hit the base right away or forget it, General. I can't see the North Vietnamese keeping the choppers there for long."

Moss draped the towel over his shoulder. "We have any high-priority targets up north tomorrow?"

"Nothing big in the morning. Two new bridges in the afternoon."

Moss smiled smugly. "And MAC-SOG's asking for help." A statement of satisfaction.

"Yes, sir."

The general's eyes glittered. "If we do it, they'll owe me for it."

Pearly played his ace. "They said one reason for dropping their assets in where they did was to try to locate one of our downed pilots, sir."

Moss looked at him sharply.

"Major Paul Anderson."

Anderson's loss continued to bother Moss. He'd asked to be briefed every time a pilot talked to Lucky Anderson on the ground, wanted to know every word Lucky had spoken, as if it might be a key to getting him out. After each of Pearly's briefings he'd spoken wistfully about the days when Anderson had worked for him at Nellis, and how valuable he was to the Air Force.

"They went in after him?" asked the general.

"Yes, sir, but they were unsuccessful. They believe it's likely the North Vietnamese captured him. They couldn't elaborate further."

Moss looked grimly at the ground. "Well, he gave it one hell of a try." Then he regarded Pearly with a purposeful stare. R. J. Moss paid his debts. "Get on the scrambler phone and alert the command posts at Takhli and Korat before you send out the order. Have a couple flights from both Thud bases load fuel tanks and ammo only."

"Both bases, sir?" asked Pearly.

"Yeah. Suggest they go in at low level and strafe. This is one they'll enjoy."

"Yes, sir, they will," said Pearly.

Moss pursed his lips for a thoughtful moment, then turned back toward the tennis court.

"Your serve!" Moss yelled to his chief of staff as Pearly hurried away.

2155 Local—Intelligence Area, Command Post, Takhli RTAFB

Captain Billy Bowes

The supplemental air tasking order had been deciphered and fragmented thirty minutes before, and Major Max Foley had called Billy to the command post. "How about you and your C-Flight animals taking the second flight?" he asked.

"I dunno," said Billy. "The guys have been working pretty hard, and I told 'em they were getting tomorrow off."

"It's going to be an interesting mission, Billy." Max explained they'd be attacking a dozen helicopters, how they had to be covert about it or the choppers might scatter like quail and move to an alternate location.

"We just sneak in and strafe 'em while they're on the ground?" asked Billy.

"Yeah. No bombs or anything. We go in at low altitude and shoot the hell out of them." Max grinned.

Billy liked what he'd heard. "We'll take it."

It was a good mission, and Billy wanted C-Flight to get a piece of it, even if he had to use someone from the outside to fill in for Lieutenant Horn. Henry was into his final five missions, so Billy had to give him the option of backing out. After a pilot reached the magic number ninety-five, he was offered easy counters down in the lower packs until he finished.

"You need me to help with mission planning?" he asked.

"I'll handle it. Just have your guys show up early. Say at oh-three-forty-five?"

"Will do, Major." Billy left to join the rest of the flight at the club, where they'd gathered to say farewell to Manny DeVera and wish him luck in the Philippines.

2215 Local—Officers' Club Stag Bar

Billy got himself a tonic water and ice before joining C-Flight at the end of the bar.

"I leave on the nine A.M. for Don Muang," Manny was saying. "Then I'll take a flight to Clark and sit on my ass until Monday."

"Don't give us that," said Henry Horn. "Saturday night in

the PI where they've got round-eye nurses and schoolteachers, and the Supersonic Wetback'll sit on his ass?"

Manny smiled, but it was a weak one.

The silence was long and awkward. Manny drained his glass. "Thanks for the drinks. I promised Jackie I'd give her a call, since she couldn't make it tonight. It won't be easy to get through from the Philippines, so it might be a while before I get to talk to her again."

Joe Walker spoke up in a gruff voice. "I've got the morning off tomorrow, Manny, so I'll drop by base ops and see you off."

Billy started to tell Joe about the morning mission, but Manny was shaking his head.

"Be better if you guys don't show up," said DeVera. His eyes were watery.

He shook hands all around, looking each one of them in the eye, as if mentally storing something away. Then Manny looked around at the group, nodded, and left.

"Fuck!" exploded Joe Walker, watching his back.

Henry shook his head. "I love that crazy bastard."

"I heard tales about the Supersonic Wetback at every fighter base I ever visited," said baby-faced Smitty. "I wasn't even sure he really existed until I got here."

They stared as Manny left through the side door.

Billy finally broke the silence. "I volunteered us for the morning go," he said.

Smitty whipped his head around. "You didn't! Dammit, Captain, I've got to go to town tomorrow morning. I've had to put it off three times already."

"Then tomorrow will make four times. We've got a three-forty-five show at the command post."

"Hell, Smitty," said Horn, grinning maliciously, "Billy's saving you from poverty. That girlfriend of yours is going to break you."

Smitty glared at him, then changed to a pleading look aimed at Billy Bowes.

Bowes ignored him. "Henry, you've got your choice on whether or not to go on this one." He lowered his voice. "It's right on the border between packs five and six."

Horn grinned. "Maybe I oughta stay here and look up Smitty's girl."

"You stay away from her," glowered Smitty. His demeanor was so cherubic that it was difficult for Smitty to look mean. He managed to appear sullen, as if he was about to pout, but not at all threatening.

"I'll tell her you ran out of money," Henry kidded. "Then I'll take her shopping and see if she's properly grateful."

"Smitty, I'll see you at the oh-three-forty-five briefing," said Billy before he turned his attention back to Horn. "You coming, Henry? If not, I'll get someone else."

"What kind of mission?" asked Henry Horn.

"All I can say here is it's going to be different and very interesting."

Henry leered at Smitty, twisting the tips of his bushy mustache like a Simon Legree. "Maybe Smitty's girlfriend would be interesting too."

"She's a nice girl," said Smitty, "not one of the whores from downtown you guys are used to."

"She's such a nice girl," asked Joe Walker, "how come she carries a change machine and wears a mattress on her back?"

"You shouldn't talk bad about her. She's the Thai base commander's daughter."

"Yeah, but by which wife?" asked Joe Walker. "Makes a big difference in status."

Smitty hesitated. "Her mother's number-two wife. Don't mention that when she's around, because it makes her feel bad. She thinks her mom should be number one."

"Hell, Smitty," said Horn, "the way you keep buying things for her, by the time you leave, she's going to own Ta Khli."

"Open up her own cathouse," said Joe Walker, and this time Smitty came close to a malevolent glare.

"You coming with us?" Billy asked Henry again.

"I'll tag along. Can't let you guys go screwing things up."

Smitty looked relieved.

Henry waved to Jimmy the bartender. "One more before we turn in."

Everyone but Billy ordered.

While they waited, they endured a long moment of silence. "Lara's Theme" was playing on the jukebox, and a soft voice was crooning, "Somewhere my love . . ."

Joe Walker gruffly voiced their thoughts. "Think we'll ever see Manny again?"

Henry Horn turned toward him and snorted. "Goddam right we will. They can't hang him with that kind of shit."

Then they grew silent, staring into the distance as the sad song played on.

CHAPTER TWENTY-NINE

**Saturday, October 7th, 0623 Local—Senior Officers'
Quarters, Hanoi, DRV**

Air Regiment Commandant Quon

The helicopter arrived eight minutes late, but though Quon
was a fanatic for timeliness, the fact failed to darken his
mood.

His adjutant apologized for the tardy aircraft.

"Russians are piloting it," said Quon. "They are slow and
ponderous people."

"I shall be at Phuc Yen when you return, comrade
Quon."

"And I," said Quon, "will fly this afternoon and show our
pilots how the small-tail MiG should be flown."

The major smiled, for Quon had not been himself for several weeks.

"Contact the *Nham Dan* reporters and tell them to be
there when I land, for I plan to kill a Thunder plane. Tell
them I *will* kill a Thunder plane, and to look for my victory
roll."

"Yes, comrade Quon," said the adjutant, looking pleased
that Quon had returned to his former level of exuberance.

Why did I become so withdrawn? thought Quon. He

would call General Tho when his immediate task was done, to speak of old times and apologize.

Quon boarded the waiting helicopter, resplendent in his dress-white uniform with its gold-and-blue epaulets and golden wings over his right breast pocket. He'd worn the dress uniform because he'd wanted to look as good as he felt.

Day 58, 0636 Local—Western Mountains, North Vietnam

Major Lucky Anderson

Just before daybreak a large, many-bladed helicopter landed in a flat area at the northern edge of the camp, but Lucky feigned apathy. He'd cursed himself throughout the night. The things he'd done, approaching the camp, devising a plan as silly as his had been, seemed ridiculous. But of course he was now thinking from the advantage of having a full belly and an increasingly functional mind. He'd been fed well again that morning and already felt new vestiges of physical strength returning to him. They'd also untied him to let him urinate, and his shoulders and arms had screamed from pain as they were released. Immediately after he'd done his chore, they'd slipped the flight suit back over his shoulders and retied him.

As his mind had begun to function, he'd kept it busy, and by early morning he'd entered into a new role to keep his captors off guard. All morning he'd ranted to himself, muttering about inconsequential things like spin-recovery procedures for the T-6 trainers he'd learned to fly in, and the batting order of the Cincinnati Reds. When they'd helped him up to urinate, he'd sagged in their grasp to make it obvious he was in no condition to run. It hadn't worked, for they'd cinched his bonds as tightly as before, but he'd clenched his arms and wrists as they tugged, and later, when he'd relaxed them, the ropes were not nearly as taut. It was a tiny victory, but perhaps an important one, for as he grew more lucid, Anderson mentally and physically prepared himself to escape.

As he chanted the inconsequential things, he mapped the area and locations of soldiers. He flexed his shoulders and legs often, trying to keep the circulation going, and the gomers didn't seem to notice or care. Not that they were stupid. An armed guard continually stood nearby, watching his every move, hardly taking his eyes away even when, in the gloom of dawn, the Russian chopper landed and the rotor blades slowed to an idle.

A compact gomer in a white uniform, with gold epaulets on his shoulders and upswept wings on the right breast of his tunic, emerged from the helicopter and looked about. The leathery-skinned sergeant hurried forward and greeted him by bowing sharply from the waist.

A high-ranking pilot?

They talked for a while, and three-stars motioned toward Lucky as they walked to a cloth upon which his belongings were displayed. The officer handled the silenced .22 and glanced contemptuously at the prisoner before dropping it back onto the cloth.

As they approached him, the three-star sergeant pointed about the area, obviously explaining how they'd snared him.

Was this the way they handled all captured pilots? Somehow he felt it was not.

Lucky noted the look on the pilot's face, the taut mouth and eyes that narrowed as they looked into his, and saw something fervent and hateful in the expression.

The officer barked a few words and three-stars interpreted.

"He say . . . do you rimmembah . . . kill Thanh?"

Lucky rolled his eyes and tried to recite the top of the Reds batting order.

The officer jabbered, and again the sergeant spoke.

"He say you rimmembah!"

Fuck 'em, thought Lucky, and he continued to mumble. Once they saw through his lunacy game, he intended to give only name, rank, and serial number; until then he'd continue the craziness.

The sergeant bobbed his head at Lucky and motioned toward the helicopter. "He say . . . we go with him. We stop one time . . . until Mee air pirates go away . . . then we go to Kep."

Lucky understood most of it. They would fly somewhere to wait out the morning bombing mission, then proceed to Kep. Kep Air Base? Was that where they took new prisoners?

He grinned at three-stars and babbled excitedly.

The officer stared, hatred glittering from the eyes, face twitching with animation. He spoke again to the sergeant.

"He say . . . when we get to Kep . . . he teach you to fly!" The sergeant nodded happily.

And suddenly Lucky knew what would happen to him once they arrived over Kep. He stopped his crazy act and evenly returned the officer's stare. There was communication. A smile slowly crept onto the man's features, and it was one of triumph.

Two soldiers untied his feet, then supported and half carried him to the chopper.

As they loaded him aboard, Lucky feigned that he was very weak, which wasn't at all hard to do. While they pushed him into a corner to lie on his stomach against a bulkhead behind the chopper pilots, a soldier knelt nearby, his AK-47 trained squarely at his midriff. The gomer pilot, followed by the grizzled sergeant, boarded and took canvas seats facing forward.

The high-ranking officer strapped in, casually rested a booted foot on Lucky's neck, and barked something to the guards. He unholstered his pistol and rested it on his leg as the soldiers scurried off the helicopter.

The officer spoke sharply to the pilot, and through half-closed eyes Lucky turned to see that Caucasians manned both forward seats. *Asshole Russians,* he thought. As if reading his mind, the high-ranking gomer stepped down hard on his neck. It hurt like hell, but Lucky remained quiet as his face was pressed into the corrugated metal floor.

As they prepared for takeoff, Lucky tried to form an escape plan. Nothing he could think of seemed appropriate. He writhed and tried to turn so his tied hands would be out of view, but the gomer pilot bellowed and stomped even harder, which made Lucky want to yell out. He did not.

As the Soviet helicopter lifted off, Lucky was still without a plan of escape. They had something special in store for him, and if it was what he thought, he'd damned well better hurry with *some* kind of idea.

0657 Local—Route Pack Five

Captain Billy Bowes

They flew with a mile's spacing between the two four-ship flights, directly toward the bright, orange morning sun peeking over the horizon. They'd set up the spacing as they passed over BRL TACAN, and as they crossed pack five, they'd slowly descended from 8,000 to 6,000 feet altitude.

Major Foley led the first flight, call sign Bass. Billy was Trout lead. Only the Wild Weasel flight accompanied them, flying forward and to their right, not so far ahead that they might betray their intention to turn toward the real target.

F-4 Phantoms had been fragged to fly MiG-CAP, but no one had yet seen or heard them, and none of the Thud pilots cared. The Thuds were lighter and more agile than usual, for they carried no bombs, and their internal Gatling guns made them at least as dangerous to the MiGs as the Phantoms.

The cannons were loaded with phosphorus-tipped incendiary rounds, to wreak maximum havoc on the helicopters. The same rounds would be just as effective against MiGs, and anyway, the MiG-drivers had appeared especially hamfisted the last few days. Billy thought of the song about the barroom mouse and whispered, "Bring on your goddam cat."

The plan was to drop even lower when they reached the foothills west of Yen Bai, then to turn to the southeast, toward the coordinates of the chopper base. Although they'd carefully studied the maps, the next tough chore would be to find the thing. The gomers were good with camouflage.

Thus far they'd spoken little on radio. They were able to maintain radio silence better than usual because of the small force size, and because they'd briefed the mission thoroughly and every pilot knew precisely what he was to do.

Five miles before them the guns of Yen Bai began to shoot: 37mm flak formed in its white layer, then darker 57mm rounds began bursting in groups of six. They would not fly through the Yen Bai flak. A mile in front of them Bass flight began their right turn and descent.

Billy motioned to Smitty, his wingman, to prepare to maneuver, as he paused for a ten-second count before beginning his own turn. The remainder of Trout flight followed.

He descended to 5,000 feet, just above the small arms' reach, and began a smooth jinking motion with the bird, flying southeast above the foothills.

He checked the clock on the panel before him. Oh-six-fifty-eight. Two minutes until their scheduled time over target. Timing was important, for the flights from Korat Air

Base would be hot on their heels, their TOT just minutes after their own. There was to be no interval between attacks that might allow any surviving helicopters to get away.

SAM and AAA radar activity made his RHAW system rattle and buzz, but the strobes were small and the sounds faint. The Wild Weasels had swung several miles out into the Red River Valley, and were flying parallel to them to shield them from the SAM action around Hanoi. The Weasels were playing decoy, presenting fat and vulnerable-looking targets, trying to get the gomers to concentrate on them.

The Weasels called a SAM launch, then fired a Shrike homing missile before setting up to perform their SAM evasion maneuvers. They twisted through the sky east of the shooters, building up airspeed and energy for the tactic.

After another glance to ensure the SAMs weren't coming their way, Billy carefully scanned the remainder of the sky. Nothing there. He looked back to the east.

The Wild Weasels had smoothly evaded the SAMs and were turning toward Hanoi, soaring to get into position to bomb the site, now keeping the missile-site operators' attention focused upon survival rather than the shooters.

Thus far it was going smoothly, but as Major Lucky had taught them, he concentrated on the challenges they *might* face.

If you're prepared for every contingency, there'll be no surprises.

Since there was no ground fire from the foothills, Billy led Trout flight into a shallow descent to fly a few hundred feet lower. He wanted to be able to see the camouflage nets, which were not easily discerned from above. They were much easier to see from one side or the other.

"Bass, see the building off at our ten-thirty," announced Max Foley. *"The target should be just a couple miles south of it."*

There was no response, but eight sets of eyes were now looking there.

"Lead, this is Bass two. I see something that looks out of place at our eleven o'clock. There's a patch of foliage that's a different color."

Pause . . . then, *"I've got it in sight, two."* Max sounded excited. *"Double-check your switches for guns-ground, Bass."*

Again no response was anticipated, but the adrenaline flowed harder as the pilots of both flights checked their switch and sight settings.

Billy remained silent. Max Foley was doing his normal good job.

Bass flight began to fly in a left-hand arc, and Billy stared at the rectangular patch of foliage that was just slightly lighter in hue than the green trees and grass about it.

Then his mind was made up, because a road led into one side of the rectangle, disappeared, and reappeared on the opposite side.

It was camouflage netting.

And when his mind accepted what it was, he began to discern other phenomena, like the regular, man-made shape of the netting, and he even saw how it was elevated in places. The covered area was large, several hundred feet long and a couple of hundred wide.

Bass flight had dropped into extended trail, flying one behind the other, so Billy waggled his wings and Trout did the same.

Max led Bass into a thirty-degree dive, directly toward the nets. He was drawing close before energetic streams of 12.7mm and 14.5mm began to hose about the sky.

"They're protecting something down there," yelled someone in Bass flight.

A trail of smoke issued from Max's gunport as he fired his Gatling cannon. Something torched and burned brightly beneath the camouflage, then a flash and fingers of bright fire reached upward as it exploded. The phosphorus was doing its job. Two large and a dozen smaller fires were blazing merrily beneath the camouflage net.

Billy pushed over into his dive attack, offset so he would fly down the length of the rectangular area.

Bass two, then three, and then four fired long bursts into the camouflage and pulled off.

It was Trout's turn.

The nets on the end toward them began to fall, then the entire thing collapsed, and Billy could see several dark, fiercely burning shapes. At 2,000 feet slant range he depressed the red trigger switch, aiming for the nearest shape.

A bit low. *Perfect.*

He walked the rounds upward, pausing for a split second at three of the shapes and a small hangar, and finally, very close to the ground, he pulled sharply up and into a left-hand turn. Ground fire zipped past his canopy like angry bees.

"*Shit hot!*" someone yelled, unable to restrain himself. Henry Horn?

He'd obviously hit the helicopters.

Billy looked farther left and saw Max's flight stretched out as if they were on the downwind leg at a stateside gunnery range. They would turn back inbound and strafe again to make sure none of the choppers escaped before the Korat flights arrived.

Beyond the second Thud, Billy saw something in the distance, coming slowly, hard to see because it was almost the same color as its background. He peered harder. It was indeed moving.

The shape was turning and descending toward the treetops.

"*Trout lead has an airborne chopper in sight at my eleven o'clock,*" he announced.

He watched the helicopter moving lower yet, fleeing.

"*Trout three and four, follow Bass in the strafe pattern. Trout two, follow me,*" called Billy.

"*Two,*" responded Smitty.

He slowed as he broke out of the pattern and flew toward the chopper. As he closed, it began to fly in a frantic and erratic pattern. It would be difficult to hit the slow-moving, evasive target, but he was determined to try.

There was no telling what the chopper was carrying. *Maybe*, he thought, *it might be someone important.*

0702 Local—Over North Vietnam

Major Lucky Anderson

Lucky had no earthly idea what was happening. The chopper had chugged along for ten minutes, had made a turn, and the tempo of the blades had changed, quieting as if they were on an approach for landing. But then the pilots had begun to yell excitedly and the engine had roared to life and the chopper had turned and dived and they were going like a bat from hell, swinging first in one direction, then in another.

Lucky rolled helplessly about the floor, thrown against one bulkhead, then sliding the opposite way until he was slammed against that side. On the second slide he tried working to free the ropes, but he was being thrown about so violently, the task was beyond him, and he judiciously concentrated on protecting himself.

Simultaneously, holes appeared in the aft bulkhead, the engine quit, and the three-star sergeant's torso burst and splattered gore throughout the cabin.

The engine was silent, and the chopper was clop-clopping downward.

Autorotating for an emergency landing?

Lucky pushed himself under the dead sergeant's legs onto a coil of rope, kicking and wedging himself into place. Then he curled into a tight ball, anticipating . . .

The impact was hard but bearable, as if they'd hit into treetops. The chopper tilted onto its tail, and after a short pause Lucky could feel that they were plummeting.

Again he braced himself. The second impact was more severe, but was tempered by the crumpling of the tail section. The fuselage slowly fell forward and came to a jolting rest.

Silence . . . the smell of kerosene growing stronger.

Gotta get out.

Lucky kicked mightily and pushed his way from under the dead sergeant, then slithered across the floor.

The high-ranking officer looked dazed. His pistol had been wrenched from his grip, and he held his hands, fingers extended, before himself, eyes wide and staring at them with a numbed expression. Blood ran down, soaking one sleeve.

Lucky didn't pause to look further. He stood, fell, then stood again and studied the door latch.

The high-ranking pilot said something in a low mutter.

Lucky turned his back to the door and worked with his hands until the latch was pulled up and around. He shoved hard. The sliding door budged. He turned and pushed, then reared back and butted it with his shoulder. It moved again, was now several inches open.

It was enough.

He slithered through and tumbled out onto the ground. They were in dense jungle.

He looked slowly about and finally found a piece of broken Plexiglas that looked sufficiently sharp for his needs. He turned and knelt, and picked it up with his bound hands.

"*Lokee!*" came an outraged shout from inside.

He hurried on shaky legs into the underbrush and away from the helicopter, not knowing which direction he was traveling and at least for the moment, not caring.

0715 Local—Ta Khoa Province, DRV

Air Regiment Commandant Quon

The enormity of what had happened grew. A Thunder plane had shot them down, and now . . . *Lokee* was escaping!

Quon released his seat belt, but he felt agonizing pain in his left arm when he tried to move forward. He examined and saw that a sharp, thin fragment of aluminum had been torn from the aft bulkhead and skewered his upper arm. The tip of it protruded from his bicep.

"*Lokee!*" he shouted again. He wanted to follow the escaping prisoner, but he was pinned, for the jagged piece of metal was connected to the bulkhead. He stared at the wound, then braced and slowly forced himself forward until he was freed. Blood flowed down his arm, soaking his tunic sleeve, but he ignored it.

"*Lokee!*" he bellowed even louder. The smell of fuel was sharp in his nostrils.

The Russian copilot was moving about in the forward cabin, frantically trying to tend to the pilot, who'd been half-decapitated by a tree limb.

"He is dead," grumbled Quon in Russian. "Leave him. We must find the prisoner."

The copilot released the pilot's seat belt and shoulder harness and tried to pull him out of the seat.

"Leave him," repeated Quon as he pushed his way into the doorway opened by *Lokee*. He squeezed through the small space and dropped to the jungle floor, looking about warily.

"*Lokee*," he whispered.

The American was nowhere in sight. Which way had he gone?

The copilot had dragged his fellow Russian to the door

and was outside, attempting to pull him through when a fire started at the crushed aft section of the helicopter.

"Get out of there, you fool!" shouted Quon. "It is burning!"

As fire spread toward the fuselage, the copilot backed away until he stood beside Quon. "He was a hero," the Russian said with a catch to his voice. "He brought us down alive."

"He is dead," Quon said simply.

"Will it explode?"

"The tank was ruptured, so it will only burn. Let us go now."

The co-pilot blinked and looked at Quon. "We should wait here to be rescued."

"No!" shrieked Quon. "We must find help, and then we must recapture the monster."

1830 Local—Officers' Club Dining Room, Takhli RTAFB, Thailand

Captain Billy Bowes

The others had finished eating and left. Billy was by himself in the dining room, waiting for No Hab to bring his hamburgers and idly contemplating whether to go downtown and get his ashes hauled by one of the bored Thai whores, or to tackle unfinished paperwork.

The paperwork's argument waned when he remembered it had been more than a month since he'd last visited the ladies of Ta Khli.

That argument solved, he looked about the dining room.

B. J. Parker was at the colonel's table across the room, speaking with Colonel Lyons.

They aren't so different after all, he thought. Then he wondered if, when you made full bull, they didn't cut off your balls.

It was a crying, fucking shame, what they were doing to Manny. Morale had been affected in all three squadrons, and the pilots thought of Colonel Parker in a new light. Before Manny's troubles, Parker had been regarded as one of them. A fighter jock who'd made it to colonel and wanted to go higher, and what the hell was so wrong with that? But now, no matter what he said about "all that pressure," B. J. Parker was the one bringing charges against DeVera.

Perhaps it would have cost Parker his career to go against the four-star's wishes, but that was part of being a leader. You supported your men first, *then* you worried about yourself. It could have been any one of them instead of Manny. Everyone had a bad bomb every now and then. No one was immune from flinching a little at bomb release when a flak burst went off beside the cockpit. Some threw a bomb more often than others, but no one got great bombs every time they dropped.

The guys who knew him said there weren't many better than Manny DeVera when it came to collecting the dime bets after a training mission on a bombing range. And everyone who knew him knew he was no conspirator. A few remembered he'd gone through a bad period, but he'd not been alone. And he'd come out of his nervous state to regain his place as one of the best gunners in the wing, which made him just that much more special. Manny'd been the one, for Christ's sake, to drop the goddam Canales des Rapides bridge.

"Join you for a minute, Captain?"

Billy emerged from his thoughts, looked up, and saw Parker standing before him with a serious look on his face.

He quickly stood. B. J. Parker cocked his head inquisitively.

"Oh—yes, sir," said Billy, remembering what Parker had asked, and at the same time wondering what the wing commander wanted.

Parker sat across from him and regarded the room for a moment as Billy cautiously retook his own seat.

"Heard you did okay up there today," said Parker.

"We got the helicopters on the ground. Major Foley counted ten of them."

"How about the one you went after?"

"I think I hit him, but I took my eyes away for a couple of seconds, and when I looked back, he was gone. Lieutenant Smith thinks he went down, but he could've landed."

Parker nodded. "I read the debriefing reports." He grew a pained expression. "Heard anything from the Supersonic Wetback?"

Billy bristled that Parker should use the term Manny reserved for friends.

"No, sir," he finally said.

After another pause Billy followed his impulse. "He's in-nocent, Colonel." Parker raised an eyebrow, surprised he'd spoken up. "Manny DeVera didn't do anything wrong. Hell, he was always harping at the rest of us to keep *our* bombs on the target."

"Yes, well ... I was shown a piece of paper, solid evi-dence, that said he dropped on a restricted target."

"That's bullshit, sir. If it says that, the paper lies."

Parker frowned.

"Ask anyone in C-Flight. Manny DeVera might be a little wild at partying, but he's a straight arrow when it comes to flying and duty and being an Air Force officer."

"I thought so too. I've known him for a long time, you know. Since he was a lieutenant. But the evidence and"— Parker shook his head—"I'm getting a lot of pressure. . . ."

Billy suppressed more anger. *A fucking excuse from a wing commander?*

Parker looked out at the room.

Might as well go all the way, thought Billy. "Did you know about the hassle between Captain DeVera and Colonel Lyons, sir?"

Parker looked as if he didn't want to talk more about it. "What hassle?"

Billy told him what he knew about Manny taking Lyons's girl from the club, and how Manny had reclaimed her after he'd beaten his problem.

Parker listened half-attentively, not interrupting but not seeming to be impressed.

Billy sucked a breath and told what he'd heard about the fight at the trailer.

"Captain DeVera hit the colonel?" asked B. J. Parker in-credulously.

"Lyons either slapped or hit the girl, Colonel."

"She said Colonel Lyons slapped her?"

"Well she didn't come out and *tell* us that, but Lyons did *something* to her before Manny slugged him. She wanted to go to you with the story, but Manny told her not to."

Parker narrowed his eyes. "Did Captain DeVera tell you all this?" he asked, and Billy realized he was intimating that Manny had made excuses.

"No, sir. Manny didn't want to say anything that might hurt Miss Bell's reputation. I picked it up here and there."

He related what the acting squadron commander had told him.

"But the major didn't actually see anyone hit anyone else?"

"No, sir, but . . ."

"You're sure all this isn't just rumor?"

"Yes, sir."

Parker looked as if he were struggling with a decision, and Billy became hopeful.

Then Parker shook his head. "You didn't give me anything to say that Manny DeVera didn't purposefully attack the wrong target. And nothing to verify that Colonel Lyons did anything wrong or was trying to *get* Captain DeVera."

"Don't you think it's awfully convenient that neither Major Lucky nor Colonel Encinos are here to question what Lyons is telling you, sir?"

Parker's mouth tightened.

"Manny DeVera was set up by Lyons, Colonel."

Parker's face was fixed in a hard expression. "You mean *Colonel* Lyons, I assume. That's a damned strong charge, Captain, considering you don't know what went on between them, and you don't have proof that DeVera didn't drop on an unauthorized target."

Parker rose to his feet stiffly, followed closely by Billy.

B.J.'s voice was crisp. "Some day, Captain, you'll learn you have to go with the evidence before you, and that you can't follow rumors and gut feelings."

Billy remained quiet. He'd already overstepped himself.

"Good evening," said B. J. Parker, and he strode from the dining room as if leaving something distasteful.

"Fuck," muttered Billy darkly.

But even if he'd gotten into trouble with Parker, he somehow felt good about what he'd done. Even if he hadn't listened, he'd told him what he and most of the other pilots thought.

And just *maybe* he'd planted a seed of doubt.

Billy wondered if he shouldn't have told Parker about his own transgressions, how he'd gone after the unauthorized targets and how he *still* felt no remorse about bombing them.

No Hab had arrived with his overcooked hamburgers before he made up his mind that it wouldn't help to throw himself on the fire that was beginning to engulf Manny DeVera.

He resolved to go downtown, find a good-looking LBFM, a little brown fucking machine, and try to screw his troubles away.

CHAPTER THIRTY

Western Mountains, North Vietnam

Major Lucky Anderson

He was lost, knew only that he was in forested mountains, that the strike planes flew on a path north of him, and that he was heading west toward Laos. He had no idea how far he'd have to travel. Each morning he watched for the Thuds and Phantoms on their way to the Red River Valley, so he could walk in the direction from which they came. He'd done that for the past two days, going toward Channel 97, call sign BRL, the TACAN navigation station which served as a checkpoint for the strike force. And . . . the CIA-sponsored tribesmen there.

He had nothing to shoot or capture animals with. He'd tried lying in wait to club jungle rats with his new walking staff, but they were far too wily to fall for it. He occasionally found and ate berries and sour fruit, and he'd once found eggs in a nest and had gulped down their viscous liquid. While that wasn't sufficient to maintain his strength, together with the boost the gomer meals had provided, it would have to be enough.

The critical question remained. *How far must I go?*

The thing he hated most was his lack of footwear, for

with each step his feet became more raw. There were thorns and bristles, and worst of all, stinging bamboo, but even when he avoided those, the jungle provided a thousand other plants and stones to hurt his feet.

He'd tried wrapping his feet with the tough leaves of plants and tying them in place with vines, but he couldn't keep them on. Then he'd ripped the sleeves from his flight suit and worked with the piece of sharp Plexiglas to fashion bindings for his feet. That helped, but he knew they wouldn't last much longer, for they were already shredded.

He continued to travel ever westward, and even though his pace was slow, his feet continued to blister, swell, and suffer.

Day 60, 0715 Local

He waited, scanning the western sky for aircraft. Finally he saw them, still far out. A series of specks at first, then drawing closer and growing wings.

He drew a mental line down to the horizon and memorized prominent landmarks there, so when he awoke in the evening he'd know which direction to walk. With that done, he grasped the piece of Plexiglas and for the hundredth time rubbed the glossiest side onto the fabric of his flight suit. He held it up, noted the position of the morning sun, and moved it until he saw the reflection on a nearby tree. Very slowly, he steered the beam up toward the formation of aircraft.

Lucky had practiced different ways of signaling rescue aircraft in all three of the Air Force survival courses he'd attended. Mostly he'd used mirrors designed for the task, but the instructors had also encouraged the pilots to learn how to make do with other materials, such as pieces of shiny metal and Plexiglas. The glare had seemed bright enough when he'd tried it the previous day on other formations of aircraft, even though there'd been no response. He'd decided to use it whenever he saw an American aircraft, because just maybe . . .

He continued to sweep the reflected light methodically across the formation of fighters, hoping someone up there was looking and would see the recurring flashes.

When they'd passed by, Lucky replaced the glass into the

pocket of his flight suit, then began looking for a good hiding place for the day. He settled on a small thicket on the hillside.

Monday, October 9th, 0722 Local—Route Pack Five, North Vietnam

Captain Billy Bowes

The flashing first caught his attention when it came from a position on the ground far ahead of the gaggle and continued as they approached. When Billy called their attention to it, several others agreed that someone was down there trying to contact them. There was a cadence to the flashes, indicating they were man-made.

As they passed, Billy wrote down the coordinates shown in the counter of his Doppler nav system. While the Dopplers were often inaccurate, he'd updated as they'd passed over BRL TACAN station on the border, and there hadn't been time for it to wander *too far* off course.

They were not likely to have the luxury of the TACAN station for much longer. Intell reported BRL was about to come under attack, that the previous evening a sizable group of Pathet Lao troops had approached the mesa on which it was located. C-47 gunships had been called in to support the station by spraying the area with their miniguns, and several fighter strikes had bombed near the base of the mesa, but the attackers were well hidden in thick forests. Intell felt it was only a matter of time before the Pathet Lao took the site.

If it was a downed pilot flashing them from the ground, he hoped to hell he wasn't headed toward the TACAN station.

A thought glimmered. *Could it be Lucky down there?*

Fuel permitting, Billy decided that on their way out Red Dog flight would try to find the coordinates and see if the flashes reappeared.

"*We've got some weather up ahead*," called B. J. Parker, who was strike force lead. "*We'll swing north around it.*"

Parker had been cool toward him this morning, but he'd expected that and didn't regret what he'd said to him. *Someone* had to speak up for Manny, for Christ's sake.

Billy could see towering clouds in the distance and wondered if there would be more in the target area. They were bound for the Bac Giang bridge, east of Hanoi. Henry Horn's bombs had knocked a span down two weeks before, but it had since been repaired. Henry had volunteered to fly this mission, although it was his ninety-seventh, saying he didn't want to leave unfinished business behind.

The 355th wing had now heavily damaged or destroyed six different bridges and had gone back to batter the Doumer bridge three times. They'd come to regard the Doumer as the easiest of the lot, because it was so large. Now it was the small ones they disliked.

The gomers were resourceful at patching up badly damaged bridges. Still, when they went to bomb the rail sidings and truck parks north of Hanoi, they found them filled to overflowing with bottlenecked supplies, so they were obviously having effect.

They were slowly paralyzing the bastards by attacking their bridges, thought Billy.

He glanced at the coordinates he'd written on his kneepad, thinking for another moment about Lucky and how he'd knocked down the Doumer that first time. Then he slowly scanned the skies about them, looking for MiGs. It was time to go to work.

The Red River slowly crawled beneath his aircraft, and they passed into pack six.

0731 Local—North of Bac Giang, Route Pack Six

The flak was heavy, 57mm and 85mm tracking all about the individual aircraft as they dived. Billy eyed it carefully and decided to delay his dive for a couple more seconds so he could hook back toward the target and attack from the south.

Red Dog was last on target, and thus far the bridge was still standing. They were diving from 16,000 feet. High, but not so high they couldn't see the target.

His RHAW system began to chatter, and a powerful SAM strobe pointed toward Haiphong. Then, for the second time on the mission, the LAUNCH light illuminated.

"Red Dog two shows a SAM launch," called Smitty.

Billy responded by winging over and entering his dive attack. He feinted first to his right, then after a couple of seconds he adjusted hard left, which should throw off the SAMs. He forgot about them and concentrated on the dive-bomb problem.

Passing nine thousand feet.

There is a period during the final seconds of a dive bomb when, if he is going to hit the target, the pilot must hold the aircraft steady and true, neither jinking nor taking any other defensive action. Billy entered that zone. He'd throttled back and was now holding the bird steady on its forty-five-degree dive bomb.

Eight thousand feet.

A bright flash! The explosion was violent and wrenched the bird sideward, slewing it through the sky.

SAM?

He was still falling earthward.

Billy fought the controls, then pushed in left rudder and felt a response. He shoved the throttle outboard to the A/B notch, eased the stick back, and the bird began to recover.

Still flying.

With afterburner lit, he swung left and was jolted again, this time by flak bursts.

He checked his telelites and gauges. His primary hydraulic system was out. The needle quivered as the fluid drained, then settled at zero. Now there were only the limited hydraulics supplied by the utility system.

The altimeter read 6,000 feet, and he was climbing, headed north.

He still had his bombs aboard. Should he reattack, considering the severe hydraulic-system problem? He left the flak and made up his mind. With a pang of apprehension, he sucked in a breath and held it as he turned in an arc toward the target.

He'd finished the turn and was headed back toward the bridge, flying level at 7,500 feet, when he came out of afterburner.

The bridge was still standing. Its previously destroyed middle span, rebuilt with scaffolds and wooden structures, was unharmed.

Billy pushed the nose over and aimed for the rebuilt section. Flak was everywhere, before and about him, for now they had only the single Thud to shoot at. He ignored his pounding heart as he concentrated on the target. He'd set up-well. He acquired a good sight picture, adjusted for the slight wind, and pickled off the bombs at 6,000 feet. He shallowed his dive angle, but did not pull out. Flak still surrounded him, but most of the rounds were passing behind him. *I'm going too fucking fast for you bastards,* Billy gloated.

He engaged afterburner for even more speed and shallowed his dive even more, heading directly toward the heart of the city of Bac Giang.

At 2,000 feet he felt the concussions from his bombs.

He leveled at fifty feet, flying at Mach one and accelerating. His peripheral vision was blurred because of the vortices created by the speed. He stared only forward, holding the bird down very low, skimming over rooftops.

As Major Lucky had taught them, the laws of physics hadn't been revoked. There was no way the enemy could hit a target this low and going this fast.

He slowed to Mach one when he approached Thud Ridge.

Billy caught up with the rest of Red Dog beyond the Red River, where Henry Horn had them waiting. Henry looked him over and called that he'd taken several hits in his left wing, and that there were so many holes in his vertical stabilizer, it looked like a sieve.

Since Billy was flying a wounded bird, and because he was short on fuel due to his extensive use of afterburner, they were unable to drop down and search where they'd seen the flashes from the ground. Still, they looked there as they flew by.

Horn reported he saw another flash of reflected light he was sure was man-made. *Sure as hell,* he radioed, *someone's down there trying to get our attention.*

0940 Local—Command Post, Takhli RTAFB, Thailand

During the debriefing Lieutenant DeWalt was interested in what Billy had to say about dropping the span of the bridge, but when he mentioned the flashes, he grew wary.

"Could it have been glints off of water?" he asked.

"Not likely," said Billy.

Colonel Tom Lyons was standing at the nearby doorway, taking it in.

Henry Horn spoke up from the next debriefing table. "They were man-made flashes. I've seen 'em too many times before. Someone was down there trying to get our attention."

"I see," said DeWalt, unconvinced. "If you *really* think it was a signal-mirror flash, I'll include it in the remarks section."

"I'm sure enough," said Billy. "I'll give you the coordinates." He peered at his map and began correlating what he'd written on his kneepad with the contour lines.

Doc Roddenbush, the head flight surgeon, was beside Lyons, doling out paper cups of mission whiskey to pilots who'd finished their debriefings. He tried to speak to Colonel Lyons, but Lyons brushed him off and came over to Billy's table.

"Did you establish radio contact with anyone on the ground, Captain?" Lyons asked.

Billy held his finger on the most likely spot before he looked up.

"No, sir," he answered.

"Without radio contact your coordinates are useless."

"The last time I spoke with Major Anderson on the ground, his radio was very weak, Colonel. There's a possibility his batteries gave out and he's trying to signal us this way."

Lyons gave him a derisive smile. "Don't you think that's a rather remote assumption?"

"I think it's worth checking out."

"I think not."

Billy stared at him incredulously.

"If it was a man-made signal, and I think that is doubtful . . ."

Henry Horn broke it. "It *was* man-made, Colonel."

Lyons turned to him with a frown. "I do not appreciate being interrupted, *Lieutenant*."

Henry started to retort, but slowly closed his mouth.

"As I was saying, if it was man-made, it's likely an enemy trap. It would be criminal to send rescue forces up there on a wild-goose chase and needlessly expose them to danger."

Billy stared at the colonel for a moment, then shook his head from side to side. "That's bullshit."

Lyons's face grew dark. "Would you care to repeat that remark, Captain?"

"We can't just ignore what we saw. If Major Lucky or any other American pilot's up there trying to get our attention, we've got to follow up and try to get him out."

"It was *not* a man-made signal," said Tom Lyons.

Billy exploded. "How the fuck would you know? Lieutenant Horn has been up there ninety-seven times now, and he says it was man-made. You weren't there, and you've never *been* there!"

Lyons was startled by the outburst.

Billy stared hard, waiting for the retribution he knew would come.

Lyons spoke in a crisp voice. "Your remarks are both inaccurate and disrespectful, Captain Bowes. I'll speak with your commander about your insolence, and I will examine your debriefing report for inaccuracies before it is sent out."

Lyons glared for emphasis, then left the room.

Billy figured his chances of ever making major had just been reduced to zero.

"That asshole," someone murmured.

Doc Roddenbush came over to Billy and held out a cupful of Old Overholt, today's rotgut mission whiskey. "I think maybe you need this," the Doc said.

Billy declined.

"He can't change our reports, can he?" asked Henry in an incredulous voice, staring at the doorway from which Lyons had departed.

Lieutenant DeWalt licked his lips apprehensively, obviously frightened of Lyons.

Billy knew it would do no good, but he read the coordinates from his kneepad.

DeWalt wrote them down on a separate paper, not on the report.

"That's all I've got," said Billy, feeling shitty about everything in general. Henry Horn and Joe Walker met him at the door, and they walked out together.

"Unbelievable," Henry muttered.

"I think we should go to Colonel Parker," said Joe.

Billy shook his head bitterly. He remembered the previous evening. "He's in too tight with Lyons. He wouldn't believe us."

Just then the wing commander emerged from the main
door of the command post and started toward his office.

"Sir," called out Henry Horn.

"Goddammit," hissed Billy. "You've got ninety-seven missions now. Don't fuck it up."

B. J. Parker turned and noticed them, then returned their
salutes.

"Could we speak with you, Colonel?" asked Henry.

B.J. glanced at his watch. "Make it quick. I've got a staff
meeting in twenty minutes."

1523 Local—HQ Seventh Air Force, Tan Son Nhut AB, Saigon

Lieutenant Colonel Pearly Gates

The WAF staff sergeant poked her head in the door of his
office. "I know you didn't want to be disturbed, Colonel, but
Airman O'Neil wants to see you."

Pearly looked up from his work, the following week's target selections for the OPlan CROSSFIRE ZULU bombing
campaign. The three pages were spread out before him.

"Can't it wait?" he asked.

"He says it's important."

"Have him take it up with his NCOIC." Sergeant Turner
handled the day-to-day operation of his section, including
personal problems and complaints about assigned duties.

He'd heard that O'Neil was unhappy about his latest task,
to catalog and cross-reference several series of unclassified
procedural manuals.

"He says he can talk only to you."

Pearly collected the pages of the classified document,
thinking hard as he delayed his answer. He opened a side
desk drawer and manipulated other papers before nodding.

"Tell him to come in."

He closed the cover of the SECRET—SENSITIVE INFORMA-
TION document.

O'Neil entered and saluted sharply. "Airman First Class
O'Neil reporting, sir."

"Take a seat," Pearly said.

O'Neil looked troubled as he sat across from him.

"Can I help you?"

"I've got some information, sir, and I don't know what to do with it."

Pearly observed O'Neil's tired eyes. He was jittery, as if he'd jump and run if you said "boo." This was the same man who'd been so cool a few weeks earlier.

"It's about Sergeant Turner, sir."

Pearly waited while O'Neil chewed on his lip, framing his words. During the past week he'd told Pearly of his suspicions about three different co-workers. Now it was his boss. He was obviously running scared.

"I worked late last night," O'Neil said, "and before I left, I saw Sergeant Turner take something out of number-three safe and copy it. Then he put the copy in a folder and carried it out of the building with him, Colonel."

"That right?" Pearly turned on an appropriate concerned look.

"I dunno where he took it, because I went on back to my barracks. Tired, you know. But I couldn't sleep, thinking about it. I know he's our NCOIC and all, but ... it's not right doing what he did, is it Colonel?"

"Not if it was classified material. You think that's what it was?"

"We've got nothing in safe number three *but* classified, sir."

Pearly was frowning. "Sounds like this one might be something serious."

"Think I should go to the OSI, sir?"

"You're supposed to report security violations to your supervisor, but in this instance you're certainly justified in coming straight to me. I'll make sure the proper people are notified. I hope you're wrong about this, O'Neil."

"I do too, sir. I really respected Sergeant Turner. But I couldn't have looked myself in the mirror if I'd just let it pass."

"A man has to do his duty."

Do the right thing, the general had told Pearly.

"Thank you for your time, sir," said O'Neil, rising.

"Go back and act as if nothing's happened. I'll make sure this gets to the right people."

"One more thing, Colonel," said O'Neil. "Sergeant Turner has me doing some awfully boring duties right now. Maybe ... maybe he's doing something wrong, and he's got me doing these other things so I can't get nosy."

"I'll look into that too."

"There's no problem with me, is there, sir? About classified or anything?" O'Neil was looking at him closely to gauge his reaction.

"From everything I've heard, you're highly regarded by everyone in your section. Even Sergeant Turner says you're very diligent. I'll look into the duties you're working on."

"Thank you, sir." O'Neil saluted and started to leave.

Pearly started to rise himself, but stopped as if remembering something.

"Help you with something, sir?"

"Take this revision back to the vault and turn it in. Tell them I'll need two copies before close of business tonight, and to call me when they're ready. I've already got General Moss's signature, so it's ready to go. This one's got a quick trigger."

Pearly noticed no change of expression as O'Neil took the SECRET—SENSITIVE INFORMATION document from the desktop.

"Happy to help, sir."

"I've got several other things brewing, so I appreciate it," said Pearly, already delving into the in-basket for his next piece of work.

At 1715 a staff sergeant called from the vault to tell him the two copies of the revision were ready and waiting.

"I'll be right there," he said.

On his way back to his office, the two copies in hand, he stopped by the Documentation section. At 1600 O'Neil had gone to his barracks, complaining about a migraine headache. Pearly took Master Sergeant Turner aside and told him to have someone check at O'Neil's barracks to inquire about his headache. "Then," he said, "come see me in my office."

Five minutes later Turner reported that O'Neil had stopped at his barracks only long enough to change clothes before he'd headed downtown.

They had a good idea where he was headed. Three days earlier Master Sergeant Turner and a couple of his NCO buddies had followed O'Neil to an apartment in an off-limits district of Cholon. The sergeants had nosed around and found that O'Neil went there a couple of times a week. Turner had given Pearly the address, cautioning that it was definitely not the kind of area you'd want to wander into unsuspectingly at night.

Pearly handed the two SECRET copies to Master Sergeant Turner. "Take those back to the vault and have 'em destroyed."

"Another scam you're running? Like when you listed the fake targets?"

As Pearly removed his eyeglasses and began to polish them, a leaden weight filled his chest.

Day 62, 0240 Local—Mountainous Region, North Vietnam

Major Lucky Anderson

For three days he'd tried to signal every formation of aircraft that passed over, but none had seemed to take notice. With each discouragement Lucky became less sure about making it to the TACAN station. His feet were so sore that each step was agonizing, and the enemy was about to close in again. Twice he'd seen troops during the past two days. Both sightings had been distant, but they had been NVA troops, nevertheless, and he remembered only too well the last time they'd come for him.

The previous day he'd hidden on a mountainside with a view to the east and watched a convoy of Soviet-built trucks snaking their way along a road a couple of miles distant. He knew the gomers disliked moving on the roads in the daylight hours, so he'd guessed they were likely after something they thought was important—him. A bit later he'd seen troops on the adjacent mountain crest, scouring the area there.

He'd tried to step up his pace by beginning the nightly trek earlier than normal and had almost stumbled into a group of people working crops in a rough field. He didn't *think* they'd seen him, but there was no way to be sure. He'd drawn back and made a wide detour of the place, using up more valuable time.

Now it was very dark, and he was having trouble making his way through a stretch of steep, heavily forested hillside. He was dog-weary, his feet hurt like hell, he couldn't see where he was going, he was half-starved, and on top of all that the fucking gomers were out there dogging him.

He found a fallen tree and sat on it to rest, trying to quell the bout of self-pity.

A dim light blinked twice off to his left, from up the hill-side, then a low, barely audible whistle sounded.

What the hell?

He looked about carefully, then back toward the source. He waited, wondering what might be his smartest reaction.

Had someone seen him? Maybe. Otherwise why the light?

He should do *something*.

Hide? Not if they already knew where he was, for Christ's sake.

Run? His feet were sore as boils. The rags tied to his feet were threadbare, and he could feel every twig he stepped on. Running was definitely out.

He sensed something drawing closer and slipped over to the opposite side of the fallen tree and crouched there.

"Majuh Anduhsun?" The words were spoken in a low voice.

Shit! His heart thumped as he pressed to the side of the tree, molding himself to it. There was very little light, so it might not be easy to find him.

Someone came up the crude trail he'd been following and stopped on the opposite side of the tree.

"Majuh Anduhsun?"

He held his breath.

Other sounds from up the hillside, these moving directly toward him.

Fuck it. He let himself breathe.

The light came on and pinned him for a moment. Then the man flashed it three times down the hillside.

"Come, Majuh Anduhsun." The first voice.

Lucky slowly rose from his hiding place, wondering if he shouldn't try using the sharp piece of Plexiglas. Maybe cut the bastards with it and . . . *what then, dumb shit?*

He sighed. Twice captured.

The second man laughed, very low. "You smell rike shit. How you gonna ged away like that?"

"Well fuck you too, buddy," said Lucky. What the hell kind of soldiers were these, who'd track you down, then in-sult you?

"Ret's go, Majuh Anduhsun."

"You need he'p, bruddah?" asked the other one.

"No," said Lucky. "I don't need your fucking help." He raised his hands and started over the fallen tree.

"Low you han's, bruddah. Whut you wan' . . . Sarge Brack mad ad us?"

The other one agreed. "Low you han's, Majuh Anduhsun. You wid frien's."

Their pidgin English was so poor, he could hardly understand them, but he thought they were telling him to lower his hands. He was not sure, so he played it safe and kept them shoulder height as they made their way down the hillside.

After fifty yards they stopped in a small clearing and waited.

Several soldiers arrived, then one separated from the other, moving painfully toward him.

"Good to see you, sir," the gomer said in a low voice with no trace of an accent.

Anderson remained quiet.

"I'm Sergeant Black, sir. United States Army."

The words staggered him. Following a silly flash of hope, Lucky realized the man was lying. He kept his mouth shut and wondered why they were acting so strangely.

"We're gonna have to move out, Major. There's about a hundred NVA camped a couple miles southeast of us who would like to have a piece of your ass."

Lucky blurted, "You're an American?"

"Yes, sir."

"How the hell did you find me?" Lucky asked suspiciously. He did not trust him. From what he could see, he looked like a gomer.

"When I made my radio call-in yesterday morning, they said you might be in this area. We arrived about noon and found the NVA showing up too. I figured we'd better locate you in a hurry so we could get out of here."

Lucky looked at the others, who were carefully watching the perimeter of the small field. "Who the hell are those guys?" he asked. "Don't try to tell me *they're* Americans."

"Don't even ask. You hungry?"

"Yeah."

Black handed him something. "Rice ball. I'll get some water for you too."

"I just had a drink from a stream, so I'm not thirsty."

Lucky crammed the tasteless rice into his mouth without wasting a grain.

"We gotta be moving out."

"The bastards took my boots when they caught me, and my feet're pretty beat-up."

Black rubbed his jaw, trying to figure a solution to the problem. Finally he conferred with his men. They dumped a few articles of clothing from their packs and carefully bound Lucky's sore feet.

Lucky's heart pounded with mounting excitement as he realized it was no dream. It was really happening!

"You gonna be okay like that, Major?"

"How far have we got to go?"

"About thirty klicks. First ten we've gotta do right away, then we'll be able to slow down and take our time. We've got a place to hole up and wait for a chopper to take us out."

The mention of a friendly helicopter sounded wonderful. "I'll make it so long as I don't have to run."

One of the men came over and spoke in Vietnamese.

"There's one request the guys have, sir, and it doesn't involve running. Something so we won't *all* get caught."

"What's that?" Lucky looked at the Vietnamese, who were obviously impatient.

"They want you to stop and wash off, because they could smell you from fifty feet away." It was just light enough to see that Black was smiling. "Can't say I disagree, sir."

Lucky Anderson laughed for the first time in a long while, and although it wasn't much of an outburst, it felt very good.

When they moved out, Lucky realized he wasn't holding them up with his painful hobbling. They kept one man on point, another at the rear, and one on each side to monitor the flanks. The two largest and strongest of the Vietnamese supported Black as he walked and were very gentle about it. The task of the final man was to erase sign of their passage, and he did his job efficiently. Good mutual support, thought Lucky. They'd make good fighter jocks.

When they stopped for a breather, between bites from his third rice ball Lucky asked Black how he'd been wounded and was told about the helicopter base and an NVA sergeant spraying the countryside with machine-gun fire. An unlucky round had taken Black in the side.

"No big deal," Black said. "But it hurt like hell."

"Sarge," said Lucky with a shake of his head. "Thank God you're doing it, but I wouldn't trade jobs with you for anything they promised me."

Black shrugged. "It's what I do. Hell of a lot better than flying airplanes. Damn things scare the shit out of me."

Saturday, October 14th, 1645 Local—Commandant's Office, Phuc Yen PAAFB

Air Regiment Commandant Quon

With each pulse Quon's arm hurt like a dull toothache.

They'd found signs of *Lokee*'s passage from the helicopter crash site and followed them, and for five days the search force had followed. A group of farmers had seen a very large man on the second day. But when the soldiers had begun to close in, he'd vanished.

During all that time Quon had remained morose and angry, sleeping little and hardly emerging from his office. When he'd first arrived back at Phuc Yen, he'd allowed the *bach si* to tend him, to sterilize and stitch up the wound and place his arm in a sling. When the doctor had tried to see him thereafter, he'd shunned him.

The awful, laughing face of *Lokee* seldom left his thoughts.

Why hadn't the Russian helicopter been on time? They might have all been killed at the helicopter base by the Mee attack, but it would have been satisfying to see *Lokee* killed by his own pilots.

Why hadn't he killed him when he'd had him?

Why? He sighed mightily, then slowly gained his feet. He could do this no more. It was time to go to work, to fly and to lead his men again. He would avenge his son by killing Mee pilots as efficiently and mercilessly as possible.

His son? He'd hardly thought of Thanh for days. It had changed to become something between himself and the Mee pilot with the terrible face. Quon knew that somehow the pilot had been rescued. He felt it. For the moment at least, *Lokee* had won.

The faceless pilot would fly his Thunder plane again, and it was there that Quon would find him.

We are not done, Lokee.

He called to his adjutant, but there was no response. A slender civilian with a sunken face appeared in the doorway. The man smiled. It was a moment before he recognized him.

"What are you doing here?" he asked in a dull voice.

"You are looking bad these days," said Nguyen Wu in a friendly tone.

Quon glared as Wu came into his office and looked about.

"Not impressive for such an important man. You deserve much better, comrade Quon."

"I am busy. We can talk at a later time."

"Oh, we shall talk, Quon. We shall talk, and you will tell me many things."

Wu leaned against the desk and motioned for the two men who'd appeared at the door to wait. They wore plain, nondescript uniforms with no badges of office.

"If you are difficult, these men and their associates will also talk with you, Quon. I must warn you that they are crude and not nearly as pleasant as I am."

Quon understood then. He sighed, resigning himself to whatever was to happen. Had he somehow expected it? "You have cleared this with General Tho?" he tried.

"With a higher authority than Tho, old friend. I have the signature of General Dung, among others. Your welfare has been entrusted to me. We will work together, you and I, to turn you into a much better and more patriotic man."

"What are the charges against me?"

"Charges? There are no charges. There will be no trial for such a great hero as yourself. You are a special case, and I have promised the party to take special care of you."

Quon breathed no easier.

"We are here to *help* you, comrade Quon," said Wu in a pleasant and soothing voice.

He motioned to the two men.

CHAPTER
THIRTY-ONE

Sunday, October 15th, 0730 Local—HQ Seventh Air Force, Tan Son Nhut Air Base, South Vietnam

Lieutenant Colonel Pearly Gates

"Come on in," called Moss, motioning to him.

Pearly walked in with his Bomb Damage Assessment folder, feeling particularly good about what he had to say.

"What've you got *this* time?" Moss growled, but he was joking.

Pearly pushed his glasses into position, then sat across from Moss and pulled the map from the BDA folder. He placed it before the general. It was filled with bright red X's. "There are seventeen bridges down and unusable right now, sir."

"And . . . ?"

"And the flow of supplies coming south have been slowed down, just as we forecast. That's been confirmed by MAC-SOG using three different sources."

"You believe 'em?"

"Yes, sir. Two of the sources are Special Forces recon teams they've inserted to observe the trail firsthand."

Moss called out to his secretary and asked for fresh coffee. A few minutes later she brought in a pot and two cups. Moss motioned, and she shut the door behind herself.

"Go on," said Moss, pouring a cup.

"Traffic is down by a third, General, and it's falling every week."

"But it's still getting through."

"Yes, sir. There's no way to stop it all without going after the Hanoi and Haiphong transshipment points."

"I got a call last night. The SecDef's saying the bridge campaign's a waste of time. He wants to terminate our entire effort up north and concentrate on traffic coming across the borders."

Pearly was shocked speechless. He used the silence to push his spectacles back on his nose and try to quell the queasy feeling growing in his gut.

Moss sipped his coffee. "I'm supposed to evaluate the suggestion, and comment."

Pearly shook his head. "Sir, we've tied up a hell of a lot of enemy troops up north with this campaign, just like we meant to."

"How many?"

"Upward of five hundred thousand, sir."

"Is that a firm figure?"

Pearly looked at him silently, then miserably shook his head. "I don't know how I could get firm figures. Intell doesn't have them."

"The SecDef is going to suggest to the President that we restrict all bombing above the twentieth parallel. He was gracious enough to ask our opinion on *that* too."

"Jesus," Pearly whispered.

"He says we can stop the supplies if we concentrate on closing off the borders. Wants to plant sensors along the border so we can tell where they're coming through."

"The borders are just jungle, sir."

"He says we can stop the trucks."

"There aren't many trucks coming in. By the time they get anywhere near the border, they've loaded everything onto wheelbarrows, water buffalo and horses, and *mainly* onto bicycles. We're sending multimillion-dollar jets after bicycles."

"I know how the supplies get here, Pearly. I'm just telling you about the kind of mail I have to answer."

"If we stop bombing up north, we might as well pack up

and go. There's no way to win if we don't put pressure on them up there."

Moss sipped coffee, peering over the rim at Pearly and listening quietly.

"Sir, we've got to increase the pressure, not decrease it. We've never *really* got to sting them yet."

Moss cocked his head inquisitively. "The same message says every time we knock down a bridge, they just move their supplies another way. Like in boats and ferries and over submerged bridges. That true?"

"Yes, sir, just like I briefed you they'd do. But it takes a lot of people and effort for them to do that, and the tonnage goes down."

Moss sighed. "I know all that. I was just trying to play devil's advocate so I might get a new argument. General Westy and the Joint Chiefs are fighting the SecDef on stopping the bombing, but they need fresh ammunition."

Pearly felt his ears burn with anger.

"I don't think the SecDef's going to win this particular argument, Pearly. Too many people realize that if we stop bombing up north, we're tossing in the towel."

"It scares me he even thinks like that, General. Think about how our POWs would feel if they thought we'd deserted them. If we don't keep bombing, we'll lose all leverage to get them out."

"How many bridges did you say are knocked down?"

"Seventeen. It would've been twenty, but they've got three patched up."

"Determined bastards."

"Amen to that. By the way, the Navy's done good work on this campaign, sir."

"Yeah. Much as I hate to, I periodically pass my congratulations to the admiral."

Pearly rose to leave. "That's all I have, sir."

Moss held up a hand to stop him. "I've got a note in my desk with a name on it."

"Sir?"

Moss lowered his voice. "Airman First Class O'Neil?"

"He hasn't come to work for two days now, General," Pearly said in a monotone.

Moss smiled humorlessly. "Maybe he's on his way to Canada or Sweden, to give speeches about baby-killing American pilots and pass out secrets to the press."

"I don't think he's gone far, General," he said. O'Neil was holed up in his apartment. Sergeant Turner's NCO friends in the security police were unofficially keeping an eye on the place.

"They'll give him sanctuary, you know. Good buddies, the Canucks and Swedes."

Pearly's heart fell just thinking about the damage O'Neil could do. Not only that, he would become a hero to the antiwar organizations with his revelations. Perhaps even to the growing number of loud politicians in Congress. He could not allow that to happen. His day, begun on the high note, was turning sour as he thought about what he must do.

Moss's intercom buzzed, and he brusquely tapped the button that turned it on. He'd asked for no calls during his conversation with Pearly. "Yeah?" he growled.

"Wing commander from Udorn's on the line with a message for you, General."

"What the hell does he want that's so important?"

"He says they're just now picking up a pilot named Anderson."

A grin flickered, then began to grow on Lieutenant General Richard Moss's face. "Put him on!" he said jubilantly.

Pearly Gates settled back into his seat, listening in and feeling that maybe it wasn't such a terrible day after all.

0945 Local—Medical Dispensary, Udorn RTAFB, Thailand

Major Lucky Anderson

An unmarked chopper had picked them up at Point Zulu the previous afternoon to fly them to a small camp in eastern Laos. The dirt runway and the camp were maintained by a Special Forces A-Team whose medic fussed over Sergeant Black's wound and Lucky's feet. But it was the cook who'd been most popular, for he'd fed them hot meals *without* rice.

From there Lucky was to return to the care of the Air Force at Udorn, while Black and his crew waited for an Air America C-123 to airlift them to the Special Forces headquarters camp at Nakhon Phanom, a small base 130 miles due east of Udorn.

"We've got fresh watermelon at NKP," Sergeant Black

had said. "You can't imagine how good that watermelon tastes, Major. You ever get there, try it."

The entire Hotdog team had gathered when the big Jolly Green helicopter landed, and watched the paramedic hurry out to help Anderson board. Lucky had started forward with him, then went back to shake hands again and pour out more effusive praise for Sergeant Black and his men. The NVA renegades had grinned awkwardly. Black said to forget it.

"In fact," he'd said with an eye trained directly on Lucky's, "*please* forget it."

Several times he'd told Lucky to develop amnesia about Hotdog and their participation in his rescue. Black felt if certain American politicians even *suspected* they operated inside North Vietnam, their activities would be curtailed. He'd intimated that Lucky was not the first fighter jock to be pulled out by a Special Forces team, but if word got out, he'd surely be the last.

He'd prompted Lucky to say his Thud had made it to the western mountains before he'd bailed out, and he'd stayed with friendly mountain tribesmen before being picked up by the Jolly Green. Sergeant Black had described the Ma tribe so his narrative would ring true.

Lucky said he'd stick to the story, no matter who asked.

To make his story credible, at 0550 the Jolly Green helicopter had landed at the Laotian camp, then ferried him directly to Udorn Air Base, where they landed at the helo pad beside the base medical clinic.

The doctors at Udorn made a fuss over him, worrying about his lack of nutrition and his mental state, even though he kept telling them it was his feet that were bothering him.

"They'll heal," said a flight surgeon who wore thick glasses and a worried expression.

Lucky was x-rayed in every conceivable position, donated copious amounts of blood and numerous urine and fecal samples, and was told he'd likely contracted every bug known and unknown to man. They fed him, gave him a massive shot of penicillin, and told him he'd be med-evacuated to Clark Air Base in the Philippines.

He told the doc he had to make a telephone call.

"I don't know," said the worried flight surgeon.

Lucky gave him a conspiratorial look. "It's a matter of national security," he whispered. "There's a VIP at the Bangkok embassy, who *must* hear what I've got to say."

The flight surgeon relented, but he accompanied him as a hospital tech wheeled him down the hall and into the admin office.

Lucky had the command post patch him through to the USAID office in the Bangkok embassy. While he waited for them to connect him with Linda, he turned his meanest glare toward the corpsman and the flight surgeon, who looked on with mounting interest.

"Dammit, it's sensitive information," he said ominously, and they reluctantly left.

She answered.

"Hi, lady."

A long pause.

"Paul?" Her voice was breathless.

"You got any vacation time built up?" he asked her.

"Oh my God! Paul!"

"They're flying me to the Philippines for medical observation, and I figured . . ."

She was crying. "Are you okay?"

". . . and I figured if I didn't invite you over there, you'd call me a snake again."

When he finished a few minutes later, he felt much better about himself and a lot of things. He yelled out, and the hospital tech came in and wheeled him out of the office and back down the hall toward the examination room. Then a staff sergeant came out and nabbed them.

"You've got a call from the wing commander at Takhli," the sergeant said.

He was wheeled back to the same telephone, and this time they knew to leave.

Colonel Parker was happy as hell that he'd made it out of North Vietnam, and happier yet when Lucky told him he intended to return to Takhli after the doctors at Clark saw him.

He made a request.

Damn right he could take a couple of weeks' R and R to Hawaii before he reported back, said B. J. Parker.

How're my men doing? asked Lucky about C-Flight.

Parker told him about what was going on with Manny DeVera.

Lucky said he didn't believe it.

There was the incriminating page from Lucky's steno pad dated July 29, B.J. said, that they were using as evidence.

Lucky hesitated, confused, then thought he knew what Parker *might* be referring to. "What about the rest of the pad?"

"I wasn't told about that," replied B.J. "I was told you gave the one page to Lieutenant Colonel Encinos in case you were shot down."

"That's bullshit. I never gave the Bad Injin anything," said Lucky. "Ask him."

"Colonel Encinos was hit by a SAM. He's KIA."

"Well, the page you're talking about was from a steno pad in my bottom desk drawer, marked 'private.' I bought the pad myself and kept notes for my use only."

Parker became quiet, which allowed Lucky to reflect further on what he'd written in the steno pad.

"Not only that, Colonel," he said, "the entry on that particular page was about another guy, not about Manny DeVera." He paused, remembering more, then exploded. "Hell, it wasn't the same date or the same initial. What the hell's going on there?"

"It said 'Captain D.' I read it myself," said Parker.

"Then someone changed it. I wrote it and I remember it clearly. Anyway, I used an *M* when I wrote about Manny, not a *D*."

"You sure of all that, Lucky?"

"I'd stake my wings and my commission on it, as well as on Manny DeVera."

"Thanks," said Parker with a heavy sigh. "You've just cleared something up." He paused for a moment longer. "You'd do that, wouldn't you?"

"Do what?"

"Stake your career on protecting your men."

"That's part of taking the oath and accepting the commission, isn't it?"

B.J. was quiet again. Finally, "Yeah, it is."

"Where's Manny?" Lucky asked, his anger smoldering.

"He's at Clark in the middle of a preliminary investigation. They're trying to set him up for a court-martial."

Anger welled in Lucky's chest. "Who is *they*, sir?"

B. J. Parker did not answer. He said only, "You're being sent to Clark?"

"Yes, sir. They've got to wash some bugs out of my system and let my feet heal."

"I'll call the JAG office there and have 'em hold things up until you've given them a written statement."

Lucky's anger was reflected in his voice. "Colonel, we don't need this kind of shit while we're doing our best to fly and fight."

Parker agreed. "Call me when you get to Clark. I've got something else to talk to you about, but it'll wait. And . . . welcome back, Lucky."

As soon as Lucky had hung up the phone, the admin sergeant stuck his head into the doorway. A look of awe was registered on his face.

"You've got a call from General Moss on line three, Major. He said to ask you where his damned six-pack was before I put you on the line."

"Six-pack?"

Then Lucky Anderson smiled as he remembered the bet the general had made with him and Benny over the 1,000-pounders.

"While I'm talking to the general," Lucky said to the sergeant, "send someone over to the base exchange to get me a pack of cigars."

"What brand, sir?"

"Doesn't matter. Just get the biggest and best ones they've got."

1115 Local—HQ 355th Tactical Fighter Wing, Takhli RTAFB

Colonel B. J. Parker

He was answering an admonishment from PACAF headquarters, this one about a poor rating given the base during a recent tidiness inspection, when he heard a rap on his door.

Tom Lyons looked in, grinning. "You wanted to see me, B.J.?"

Parker looked at him, watched as he slouched into the room and leisurely took a seat.

Lyons spoke first. "I wanted to talk with you too. About the sloppy way the guys are debriefing after their missions. I feel . . ."

"Don't call me B.J.," interjected Parker. "I don't like it."

Lyons chuckled. "I understand. It's just that I've heard it so much from so many others, that I . . ."

"And I don't remember asking you to sit down, Colonel." Tom Lyons blinked at him.

"Stand up, goddammit!"

Lyons slowly gained his feet, frowning.

"About an hour ago I got off the phone with the vice commander at PACAF . . . ," started Parker.

"I know the general. He . . ."

"Dammit, Lyons!" raged Parker, pointing his finger. "Don't interrupt me."

Lyons drew himself into a loose semblance of attention.

B. J. Parker calmed himself before continuing. "I apologized for bringing up false charges against one of my men and asked him to pass my regrets to General Roman. Captain DeVera was not the person referred to on the page you gave me. The page was from a private notepad, and it had been altered."

Lyons looked surprised. "Altered? What could make you think that?"

"Major Paul Anderson was rescued this morning . . ."

Lyons looked shocked. "I didn't hear about a rescue attempt."

Parker glared at the interruption. ". . . and he told me about the steno pad."

But Tom Lyons was too slick for that. He tried to look surprised. "Lieutenant Colonel Encinos handed that page to me just like I gave it to you. You say it was changed?"

"For Christ's sake, Lyons. Don't try to lay the blame on a dead man who at least had the balls to fly up north."

Lyons looked hurt.

Parker shook his head sadly. "I put an innocent man through hell."

"Perhaps not all *that* innocent, Colonel. There are the other dates in question regarding Captain DeVera."

"It's over!" roared Parker.

"Perhaps not," said Lyons slyly. "General Roman is very interested in the case. His aide told me . . ."

"His vice commander called back ten minutes ago. General Roman feels this incident has embarrassed him, and that *certain people* let him down. You're one of them, Lyons."

For the first time Lyons was speechless.

"You seemed surprised that Major Anderson was rescued," said Parker.

"It was just that he was up there for so long," Lyons said quickly. "I'm very happy for him, of course."

"A few days ago some of the pilots came to me and told me you tried to suppress information about his possible location."

"Jesus no. I wouldn't try to do that."

"That's not what intell says. A lieutenant there claims you threatened to change the debriefing reports if they mentioned the signal flashes the aircrews saw."

"I only said I wanted to review the report for accuracy, not *change* it."

"Like a young captain told me a few days ago, *that's bullshit*. Anyway, I phoned the coordinates in to Saigon, and I hope to hell they were instrumental in helping find him."

Lyons was slowly shaking his head, as if being done a terrible injustice.

"Until I can get rid of you, Lyons, and hopefully that will not take long, I'm giving you new duties. I wish I could assign you to shoveling shit for some local farmer, but since that might be frowned upon, I'm making you special assistant to the base commander in charge of monitoring base cleanliness. By the way, Lyons, that was the suggestion of a three-star general who says he can *guarantee* you'll never get a better job."

"Jesus, you want me to apologize, I will, but I didn't do *anything* wrong." Lyons was beginning to grovel, and it was an embarrassing thing to watch.

"You did," said B.J. "You did some very wrong things, and I was foolish enough not to listen when others told me about them."

Lyons's look turned shrewd. "Forget this, and I promise you'll never regret it. I believe I told you that my family has certain . . . *political* connections . . . which can help . . ."

"Did you hit the girl, Lyons?" Parker interrupted.

Lyons's mouth drooped. His silence answered the question.

"Get the hell out of my office, and take your slimy *political* connections with you."

Lyons's voice became shrill. "You can't do this! If you take me down, your career will go with me."

"Fuck my career. Now get the hell out of here."

1245 Local—Ministry of Internal Affairs, Hanoi, DRV

Assistant Commissioner Nguyen Wu

The prisoner sat in the chair in the middle of the barren room, arms tied securely behind his back, eyes downcast and full of pain and sorrow. They'd done their jobs well. There were few visible marks from the all-night beating. Only the puddle of piss beneath the prisoner revealed anything truly amiss.

The interrogator looked to Nguyen Wu with a question on his face.

"Did he admit to plotting against the Republic?" asked Wu.

The interrogator shrugged. "He confessed to everything on your list, comrade Colonel. It is all written down and properly signed."

Nguyen Wu turned to the prisoner and shook his head. "Oh Quon, you lied to me," he chided. "You said you would die before confessing your son was a coward."

The prisoner did not react.

"What shall I do with you, old friend?"

"Kill me," came a low response. The words were said pleadingly.

"Do not be absurd. We only wish to determine the bad traits you have that must be changed during your reeducation."

"Please."

Nguyen Wu's voice changed to a low hiss. "You shall have no such satisfaction."

He turned to go.

"What next?" asked the interrogator.

"Beat him until he waters his pants again," said Nguyen Wu, with a satisfied expression on his face.

1930 Local—Field Grade Quarters, Tan Son Nhut Air Base, Saigon

Lieutenant Colonel Pearly Gates

Pearly handled the pistol to become familiar with it. He did not like firearms and was nervous in their presence, but he wanted to do what he had to do properly. After great agonizing he could think of no other way to handle the problem. So many lives had been jeopardized by the man. If he lived, there might be others.

Pearly wondered how he would handle his conscience after he'd done it. The Judeo-Christian upbringing General Moss had once referred to was strong in him. If he was successful in what he was about to do, he would always know he'd killed a man.

No, not *if* he was successful. He *had* to be successful. The right thing must be done.

He pushed his glasses back onto the bridge of his nose and methodically worked the action of the Colt M1911A1 .45 automatic. Sergeant Turner had told him it was a weapon commonly found in Saigon, for thousands had been provided to the ARVN. Sergeant Turner had asked no questions when he'd given it to him, but Pearly knew he was aware of what he would do with it.

He let down the hammer, then inserted the clip with its seven rounds of ball ammunition. The bullets too were quite standard.

Although Pearly would have liked to pass the awful task to another, he knew it must be done by himself. He was responsible for the tragedies, the airplanes and pilots. The buck stopped at his desk. Turner had understood and hadn't tried to dissuade him.

He wore civvies, a light shirt and trousers, and a waterproof windbreaker to repel the predicted evening shower. He pushed the pistol into his waistband, checked to see that it was hidden under the jacket, and for the hundredth time he sighed.

Knocking at the door.

Master Sergeant Turner asked if he could come in.

"He's run," said Turner.

Pearly's heart pounded. "Where to?"

"They don't know. He came out of the apartment at the same time a taxi was pulling up. He jumped in, and the driver took off like a scalded ape. They found the cab abandoned a few blocks away . . . empty."

Pearly stared at him, feeling sick in the pit of his stomach, as if he were about to throw up.

"I got my buddies looking, but it's going to be damned hard to find him, Colonel. Saigon's a big city and there's a million places to hide."

Pearly felt miserable. He'd waited too long and O'Neil had escaped. His worst fears were coming true.

CHAPTER
THIRTY-TWO

**Tuesday, October 17th, 1000 Local—354th TFS Pilots'
Lounge, Takhli RTAFB, Thailand**

Captain Billy Bowes

Bowes watched the last members of C-Flight enter the
room and take their seats. Two of them still carried their in-
processing papers. New guys, who'd have much to learn in
their first few missions.

He went to the fridge and fished around for a cold beer,
found one and pried off the top.

"C-Flight's all here," said Joe Walker.

Billy walked to the table set up in front of the group and
balanced a buttock on it as he took a swig of beer. It tasted
cold and refreshing.

"Once every week," he started, "we'll have these
meetings. Not that I enjoy them or anything. I've got a hell
of a lot of more important things to do with my time than
hold meetings, but things change at a rapid rate here, so
we'll meet and talk about what you can and what you can't
do, and how to survive when you fly up in pack six."

He looked out at them and felt a pang of protectiveness.
They were a cross section of pilots you might find anywhere
in the U.S. Air Force, but to him they were special. They

were in his C-Flight, and he hoped he could keep them alive long enough to get a good start on their one hundred missions.

"What's this I hear about all the restrictions?" growled a new captain.

"There's so many, you'll want to puke," said Joe Walker.

"We really have to follow them all?" asked the captain.

"Last time I looked," said Billy Bowes pointedly, "the civilians still ran things in America. Yeah, we follow them all."

The captain looked troubled by the answer.

"What's this I'm hearing about Major Lucky?" asked Lieutenant Smith.

"I heard the same rumor," said Billy. He looked out at the group. "Can't confirm or deny it, but there's word going around that our former C-Flight commander will be coming back as squadron commander."

"Where's he been?" asked a new, very young captain.

"He was shot down," said Joe Walker. "Hairiest mission I've been on yet."

"You were there?"

"I was flying his wing," Joe said proudly.

Billy interrupted. "It's a long story, so you guys can talk about that tonight at the bar. Right now let's talk about flying combat. Let's start with introductions. I'm Captain Billy Bowes, and I came out of Air Training Command. I've got forty-two combat missions now, but I've still got a hell of a lot . . ."

"Captain Bowes," Smitty interrupted, "was my IP at Moody, and he was the best flight instructor there. Now he's the best damned combat pilot at Takhli. You guys listen to him."

1600 Local—TFWC/TAF, Nellis AFB, Nevada

Major Benny Lewis

Strangely, Moods became more subdued as his project's success grew closer.

The preliminary testing had been completed, and his smart-bomb project, although one of the most classified in the Air Force, was capturing the attention he'd always felt it deserved. But with the attention came increased involvement of every headquarters puke inside and outside of their chain of command.

The Air Force test-and-development centers at Eglin, Wright Patterson, and Edwards were scrambling for bigger pieces of the action, as were the Navy's centers at Patuxent and China Lake. Several times control of the project had almost been stolen away. Only the determination of TAC headquarters supporters and the 1A priority they'd given the project kept Moods Diller in the loop.

Finally a compromise was reached. The Armament Lab at Eglin would take over the project immediately after combat testing, which Moods would supervise.

Twelve LGB kits were being hand-built by the sole-source prime contractor, and Mk-84 bombs had been earmarked and were being diverted to Danang for the combat test.

Moods Diller was convinced he was about to change the face of aerial combat. "One target, one bomb" was the way he put it. He'd get his chance to prove it when he accompanied his kits and bombs to South Vietnam within the month ... precisely on the timeline he and Benny had roughed out together.

They talked about it Tuesday afternoon, as they began to wrap up the day's business.

"I wanta become part of the fighter mafia," he told Benny.

"Hell, Moods, you've been a part of it all along. There's no initiation rites."

Moods raised an eyebrow. "Yeah, there is. It's called trust. I don't think I had that ... before we made out that schedule and I showed everyone I could stick to it."

"Maybe so, Moods. You've proved it works ... *so far*." He grinned at him.

Two more captains now worked for Benny, but they'd taken desks with the civilian number cruncher in another room, leaving Benny and Moods with more elbow space.

One of the captains leaned into the doorway, saying, "The daily summary just arrived." Secret daily and weekly summaries were released by Seventh Air Force in Saigon, to keep Air Force units in other areas of the world abreast of what was happening in the war.

"Anything new?" Benny asked.

The captain referred to the summary in his hand. "Lost

an F-100 yesterday in South Vietnam, but they got the guy out okay. Couple birds down up north. An F-4 crew was rescued, but they're still looking for a Thud jock. Supply traffic going to South Vietnam is down. Let's see. Oh, yeah. Some major was rescued up north after he spent a long time living with a mountain tribe. They mention a little about what it was like."

Benny nodded, deciding he'd read it later.

"What's the major's name?" asked Moods Diller.

The captain flipped to the second page of the message. "Anderson, Paul C. Ander—"

Moods whooped.

"Let me see that!" Benny said.

Sure enough, Major Paul C. Anderson had been recovered after spending two months in the jungle. The message described how he'd been taken in by a small, nomadic tribe in the western mountains of North Vietnam, and how his life with them had been primitive but relatively uneventful. The tribe would be rewarded with presents of pigs and goats.

"I thought you said Lucky went down near Thud Ridge," said Moods.

"That's what they thought, but truthfully I don't give a damn *where* he went down as long as they got him out."

Moods Diller whooped again, and Benny joined his laughter, delighted about his buddy's rescue. They created such a racket that the others came in to see what was going on.

"This calls for a drink," Benny told the captains. "Shut down the office and let's go to the club. I'll buy."

"I'll drink," grinned Moods.

As they filed out of the office, the phone rang insistently, but Benny led them away. "To hell with business. One of our guys got out!"

2030 Local—Bachelor Officers' Quarters

Four hours later the phone was also ringing as he opened the door of his BOQ room.

"Benny?" wailed a sad voice.

"How're you doing, Julie?" He felt more than a bit inebriated and tried to clear away some of the fog.

"I've been trying to call you since four-fifteen." A long pause, then she cried, "I need you here."

Benny's mind raced. He thought he could get away, but he was scheduled to present an important briefing the next morning.

"Tomorrow afternoon all right?"

"I guess."

"What's happening?"

"I got a visit from a colonel and a chaplain from Travis field this afternoon. Mal Bear's been declared KIA."

He was silent.

She drew a ragged breath. In the background he heard the baby begin to cry.

Benny said, very softly, "He died last April, Julie, not today."

"I know. It's just . . . I need your shoulder to cry on, Benny."

"I'll be there."

"Next week I'm supposed to go to Travis, where the commander will present Mal's medals to me. Can you be there for that too?"

"Sure."

"I'm sorry I'm being such a baby about things."

"That's bull. I don't want you to change an inch." Had he said that?

"Thank God for you, Benny."

And somehow he knew it was time to press her for something he'd wanted since coming to Vegas. "I think you should move down here so we can be closer."

"We'll talk about it when you get here, okay?" She answered so quickly that he knew she'd been thinking about it.

"I plan to be as convincing as possible," he said boldly.

"Maybe you won't have to be. I gave my notice to the airline yesterday. I'm quitting my job."

"I'm glad."

"I don't want to be away from the baby while she's so young. They offered me office work, but I haven't given them an answer." She was calmer now.

"Have you talked with your mother about the Bear's status yet?" he asked.

"When I couldn't get you at your office, I called her. I told her I was going to ask you to come here so I could cry on your shoulder. She didn't think that was a good idea."

"She'll come around. I'm lovable, remember."

She sniffed, then suddenly giggled. "Are the women still congesting traffic trying to get you to go out?"

He went along. "Now the casinos are complaining because all their showgirls are in the line."

She didn't think that was funny. "They'd damn well better *not* be!"

He didn't feel guilty. There was no one. There had been the single liaison with the secretary, but he'd not repeated it. He'd stopped kidding himself about what he wanted.

There was no more hesitation in her voice when she suddenly blurted, "You might as well get used to me, Benny Lewis, because I plan to elbow my way to the *front* of the line."

He grinned happily. They shared the same dream.

When she finally broke the connection, he realized that the inner voice had not spoken to him for some time now, and he knew it wouldn't return. He was a little different because of it, somehow a little better. They would remain his secret, the inner discussions. If he mentioned them to others, they would think him odd. But it had nothing to do with his mental stability, and there was no reason to speak of it.

I'll take good care of her, were Benny's final words to the voice.

Wednesday, October 18th, 1045 Local—Hoa Lo Prison, Hanoi, North Vietnam

Major Glenn Phillips

Things had been downbeat for Glenn the two weeks following his defiance and the resulting bad beatings. The ratfaced turnkey had baited him unmercifully, and he'd drawn Fishface's wrath the last time he'd been taken in for a periodic indoctrination meeting.

Fishface had wanted him to write a letter home on an official form, telling his parents how well he was being treated and how they should send money to help his guards continue his great standard of living.

He'd quibbled and gotten himself a minor beating, which surprised him because Fishface was the meanest V in the prison.

Then Fishface had brought him back in and said he could redeem himself by volunteering to go to a Hanoi suburb and help repair bomb damage to a school the criminal American terrorists had bombed. He'd said he'd rather not, and wondered why Fishface was being so nice.

They hadn't beaten him badly that time either, but he did spend the next six days in leg-stocks and iron cuffs so he'd see the error of his ways. When the irons were finally removed, he could not stand, and he worried that the circulation had been cut off for so long that he might have gotten gangrene. But his luck held, and the blood finally coursed enough that he could hobble around the cell.

For the last couple of days no one had bothered him with dumb demands, and he thought things might be starting to go better. He wanted to stay out of trouble with the V for a while so his body could heal some more, which was difficult enough with the lousy, starvation rations they gave them.

The rat-faced turnkey came into his cell and peered at him with a mean look, and he bowed as he'd said he would. The turnkey cursed and cuffed him hard because he'd stumbled on his bad leg. Ratface seemed to be gloating about something, and the two guards with him were subservient.

Then they pushed a new prisoner carrying his bedroll and mosquito net into the room, and after Ratface had shoved him around a bit, they abruptly left.

Glenn was overjoyed. He'd had a few roommates before, but they'd all been badly wounded, as if he were a medic or something and could repair them. This guy was skinny, but he looked fit enough. He figured the prison was getting overcrowded, and the V could no longer afford the luxury of keeping them isolated.

The two shook hands and talked like crazy, because aside from their freedom, human contact was the thing the prisoners craved most.

He was a Marine fighter jock, shot down near the DMZ in an A-4 Skyhawk, and he'd been in jail for one year, three months, and twelve days.

Glenn told him he'd been there for ten months.

They passed news between themselves like schoolkids sharing goodies from lunch boxes. You hear about *this*, one would say, and the other would listen intently, then he would add something he'd pieced together, and the first guy would listen.

In the marine's last room the guy next door had been from the 354th squadron, and they'd shared news via the tap system. When he told him his name, Glenn remembered him from Takhli.

"The guys from the 354th have had it pretty rough the last few months," said Glenn Phillips.

The marine agreed. "My neighbor went through some bad times. Like when the V beat the hell out of him in front of a high-ranking gomer wearing wings."

"A V pilot?"

"That's what he thought. They kept asking him questions about this guy. . . ."

"Lucky Anderson?"

"Yeah. They'd ask all kinds of dumb questions about Anderson. The gomer pilot would sit there and listen and get them to ask more questions and keep on beating until he answered."

The V had been asking their questions about Lucky for a long time now, thought Glenn. He wondered about his friend's safety, and where he might be.

"Then, ten days ago the questions stopped."

"They stopped?" Glenn was surprised.

"You didn't hear? It's been going around the jail."

Benny grinned. "The V have had me preoccupied with other things."

The marine looked at his still-swollen face. "I can tell."

"So they stopped asking about Lucky?"

"From what they told my neighbor later, he thinks this Lucky Anderson got away."

Glenn dared not move for fear he'd wake up and the dream would change. He'd been praying every day for so long. . . . "He escaped?" Glenn hardly breathed the words.

"That's what everyone thinks, and from the way the V acted, it makes sense."

"He escaped." Glenn's grin widened. Jesus, it felt good even to *think* that Lucky had gotten away from them.

The marine nodded. "A couple of weeks ago it was *Lokee* this, *Lokee* that, but now the V don't even want his name mentioned, and they're acting like they never asked any questions at all. The prison commandant's been replaced, and one of the good turnkey's said that's the reason, for asking all the questions and something else he wouldn't talk about."

Glenn's mind spun with it all.

"You know Fishface?" asked the marine.

A darker look came over Glenn's face. Fishface was their chief tormentor. He was the meanest interrogator of the bunch, his atrocities equaled only by the Cubans.

"Fishface is in deep trouble. The rumor is he killed some new guys by tromping on 'em too hard for information, and the gomer brass are pissed off about losing their bargaining chips, meaning us prisoners. Yesterday they took Fishface off. Marched him out between two guys who looked mean as hell, and he hasn't come back."

A warm and happy feeling came over Glenn Phillips.

That afternoon they met the new prison commandant, but he seemed no better than the one they'd had. The rat-faced turnkey had been promoted to replace Fishface as chief interrogator. To make a proper impression, he started things off by calling in Glenn and another P he disliked and beating the hell out of them because of their poor attitudes.

After they'd returned him to his cell, Glenn couldn't sleep because of the intense pain from Ratface's beating on top of the previous ones he'd gotten. As he lay there, curled into a ball and hurting, he kept his mind occupied by imagining all the wonderful ways that Lucky might be enjoying his freedom.

Later he hallucinated and dreamed that Lucky and Benny and all of his other friends had finally been told to go ahead and do whatever was necessary to win the war.

Finally he became aware that his new roommate was gently shaking his shoulder and wearing a concerned look.

"It won't be long now," Glenn whispered happily to the marine. "They'll be coming for us soon."

1215 Local—Base Operations, Clark Air Base, Philippines

Major Lucky Anderson

The charter TWA flight was to land in twenty minutes, the base-ops sergeant told them. Right on time, he said.

They walked outside, in front of the base-operations

building, and looked about at the busy Clark Air Base flight line.

Lucky was wearing a shade 1505 uniform, with shiny new oak leaves and command-pilot wings. The uniform was tailored and sharp looking, ironed in precise, military creases, and his hair was freshly cut and neatly combed. Even his issue sunglasses had been polished and cleaned of every speck of lint. He felt like a teenager on a first date, anticipating Linda's arrival but a little scared he'd screw it up.

He toyed nervously with his crutches as Manny DeVera pointed out a flight of F-4 Phantoms lining up at the end of the runway in preparation for takeoff.

Both of his feet were swathed in bandages, and he'd been told he *must* stay off them for at least another week. He'd first tried to bribe the flight surgeons at the hospital, then had threatened bodily harm, and finally had pleaded to be allowed to meet her plane. Nothing had worked, so DeVera had sneaked in the new uniform and helped him steal the crutches so he could get out of the place.

He glanced over at Manny. "Do I look okay?" Still thirty pounds underweight, he was worried he might look like a bony scarecrow.

Manny looked him over. "Okay compared with what?"

"Asshole," said Lucky.

Manny laughed. "You never looked so good in your life to me, boss. You really think all this court-martial horseshit is going to stop?"

"If we're not scheduled on the same plane out of here, I'm not going. I leave when you're cleared, Manny. Not before."

"I thought you were going to take your lady to Honolulu?"

"If she's willing to go, I will, and I'll arrange it for you too. A few days on the beach wouldn't do any harm. But I'm not going anywhere until you're cleared."

"Jesus that sounds good."

"Even the prosecutor says it's just a matter of doing the paperwork to get it turned off. The judge is going to visit me at the hospital in the morning and take my statement, and that should do it."

"You want me to kiss your feet now or later?"

"Make it later. Better not get the bandages soggy."

Manny laughed again. Then his expression turned serious. "I talked to Billy Bowes on the phone last night, and he
says there's a heavy rumor you're taking over the squadron
when you go back. That true?"

The flight of fighters took off from the long runway, on
their way to one of the combat bases across the South China
Sea. They continued to look on until the Phantoms were
safely in the air.

"Yeah," Lucky finally answered. He still felt uneasy
about taking on the responsibility, but he'd accepted because B.J.'s offer was in line with the rest of the changes
he was making with his life. His records would go before
the promotion board in a couple of weeks, and the
squadron-commander title would look good. And if things
went right with Linda . . .

"You'll be good for the squadron," said DeVera.

"You guys give me enough help and we'll make it work.
The way I see it, it's going to be a hell of a challenge for everyone at Takhli while we finish the job up north."

"You'll have our support." Manny meant it.

"I think that's the airplane," said Lucky, looking out at a
big bird on final approach.

"Stay cool, boss," advised Manny DeVera, the old pro at
handling women. "Don't let her think you're nervous or excited or anything."

Lucky Anderson hardly heard him, for he was already
hobbling toward the door, a grin of anticipation on his battered face.

POSTSCRIPT

Saigon, South Vietnam

Peacemaker

O'Neil felt good for the first time in days.

First there'd been the abrupt warning over the telephone that he'd been compromised and that he must leave the base immediately.

When he'd rushed to the apartment, he'd found a note from the API correspondent, telling him to wait in the apartment, for he would be contacted and taken out of harm's way. There was also a copy of the last target list he'd given them. Across the typed target coordinates the word LIES was written in red pen. Interjected in the midst of the text beneath the coordinates, which O'Neil had not read in his zeal to get the pages to his benefactors, was a statement underlined by the same red pen, reading: The penalty for treason is death.

He'd remained in the apartment, scared and wandering about in a daze, going out only to shop for essentials, until he'd received a note warning that he was under surveillance. He'd almost panicked and run. But then, true to their word that they'd protect him, they'd helped him escape from the apartment.

The taxi driver had deposited him in a tiny, filthy room in a Chinese whorehouse not far from the Nghe Canal, where he'd grown even more despondent and miserable, spending long hours thinking awful thoughts and fearing the worst. The American military establishment would find and arrest him. They couldn't allow him to escape, for he knew too many of their secrets. And the VC couldn't afford to have him captured, because he'd met some of them and knew about the Blue Pheasant and several of their other operations.

During his first night of isolation at the whorehouse, listening to loud Chinese voices and squeaking beds, smelling the unpleasant odors of urine, opium, and sperm from the surrounding cubicles, O'Neil had sobbed desperately and felt very sorry about himself and what he'd done.

The next day he'd first thought about turning himself in. He perfected the idea, built upon it until he realized it was the only sensible solution. Tell the OSI how he'd been kidnapped by the Viet Cong. Maybe describe a few of them for authenticity. The more he'd thought about it, the more he decided that was the best course to take. He'd be protected by the laws of his nation, be innocent until proven guilty. What could they have but suspicions? No one had seen him copying secrets or giving them to anyone. It would be his word against theirs. If they charged him, he'd fight it. Get a good civilian lawyer. The API correspondent would help him find the best; he owed him that. Then O'Neil had another clever thought. If they persevered in their folly, he'd threaten to expose the government's secrets.

He asked for stationery from the silent old woman who brought his food, then wrote a note to the API newsman about some of his thoughts and gave it to her. He addressed the envelope to the correspondent, marking it PRIVATE, and signed the letter with the single word PEACEMAKER. The old woman seemed to know what to do with it, for she grinned and nodded when she took it.

On the third day at the whorehouse, O'Neil received an answer from the correspondent that changed his thinking.

Arrangements had been made. He'd be taken to a freighter tied up to a pier only a dozen blocks from the whorehouse. The ship would proceed down the Kinh Te channel to the open sea, where he'd become a free man. After a couple of port stops to drop off and take on freight, they'd arrive in Montreal, where the correspondent's friends would

*meet him and help him apply for landed immigrant status. A
job awaited him at the API office in Toronto, Ontario.*

*O'Neil laughed aloud in his joy and immediately forgot
about turning himself in. His mind became filled with what
he would do when he reached Canada. Even earlier! On the
voyage he'd write scathing articles about the American involvement in Southeast Asia. His byline would be Peacemaker, the code name he'd given himself when he'd met the
API newsman.*

Perhaps he'd even write a book about his experience.

They came in the middle of the night to take him to the ship.

*O'Neil followed them out the back way to the waiting taxi.
He wanted to see the API newsman a last time before leaving, to thank him and tell him how much he'd like to work
with him some time in the future because he had some dyna-
mite ideas about exposés, but he wasn't in the cab. There
were just the three businessmen he'd met that time in the
Blue Pheasant, wearing the same stupid, friendly expressions.*

*The taxi driver drove up Duong Avenue, away from Cho-
lon toward the docks of Saigon, so he figured they'd changed
ships. Then they swung south across the Mong bridge, and
he began to wonder and ask questions.*

*The driver said they were going to the Ben Tau wharf, on
the other side of the canal.*

*Ten minutes later, when they'd passed by the Ben Tau
turnoffs and were picking up speed as they entered the dark
countryside, the Peacemaker knew, and began to sob and
croon, "Nooooo."*

TRUTH & FICTION

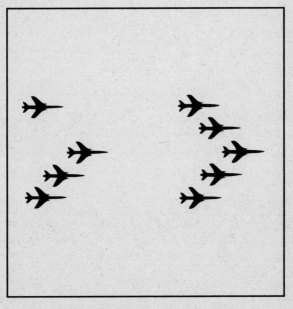

Missing Man Formation

TRUTH AND FICTION

Descriptions of locales are generally accurate for the period. The 355th Tactical Fighter Wing was located at Takhli, Thailand, during the period of *Lucky's Bridge*. Southeast Asians, having never seen a bulldog, identified the 354th TFS emblem as a pig and called the 354th the Pig Squadron. Depictions of Asian tribes were taken from discussions with an adventurer who knew and spent his life among them, as well as from personal experiences.

The bridges campaign had difficulty getting off the ground, but was finally turned on in August and lasted through November of 1967. The OPlan nickname CROSS-FIRE ZULU is not historically accurate. AGM-12 Bullpups were not used on the first attack on the Doumer bridge, but they were misused against other high-threat-area targets, and results were generally as described. The air attacks mentioned occurred at those target locations on or about the dates mentioned. A pilot from the 354th TFS was first to knock down a span of the Doumer bridge, on the date and using the ordnance described.

Electro-optic and laser-guided smart bombs were developed during the period . . . and their operational readiness was accelerated for the bridges campaign. LGBs were introduced for combat testing shortly after the campaign ended.

A friend related to me how the teams he dropped into North Vietnam were mostly all-indiginous, much as the NVA renegades described as Hotdog, and were very short-lived. A Special Forces team leader told how his group reported the helicopter base and witnessed the attack. On the day depicted in the book, ten Soviet helicopters were destroyed by Thuds from Takhli using internal M-61 Gatling cannons.

Like most military men, airmen of that time were mostly apolitical, yet selected politicians were especially disliked for constantly placing roadblocks in the path of victory. A teakwood Edsel grill was prominently displayed at the Korat Officers' Club bar, not in admiration of the Secretary of Defense.

Members of the 355th TFW were charged with attacking unauthorized targets and subsequently court-martialed, and the entire wing's morale suffered. The real-life stories were different and much more dramatic than those described in *Lucky's Bridge*. An account may be found in Jack Broughton's nonfiction book, *Going Downtown* (Orion Books, 1988).

There were no American females assigned at Takhli during the period. Only the occasional USO showgirl, Peace Corps worker, government official, or newswoman honored the base with her feminine graces. A friend recently told me that the first assigned female, a secretary, arrived on November 5, 1967 . . . but who keeps track of such things?

The fighter-pilot songs in *Lucky's Bridge* are as they were sung. I'm sure some have been updated by pilots who flew in Desert Storm, for singing is a time-honored Air Force tradition. "Beside a Laotian Waterfall" will sound just as sweet when sung as "Beside a Saudi Sand Dune," and the change is just fine, for World War I fighter jocks sang it as "Beside a Belgian Watertank."

Some related items of interest regarding later conflicts:

. . . Laser-guided bombs were used effectively during the Libyan campaign. LGBs and electro-optical smart bombs were both employed with spectacular results during Desert Storm.

. . . After being deactivated at Takhli when the 388th TFW moved there from Korat, the 355th TFW was reactivated at Davis Monthan Air Force Base in Arizona and equipped with A-10 Warthogs. During Desert Storm, 355th OA-10's were used as forward air controllers and helped decimate enemy tanks and bunkered positions with bombs and 30mm Gatling guns.

While I especially enjoyed writing this fictional account of fighter pilots at work, I do not pretend to have captured the true courage of the real players, many of whom I was honored to serve with. I am still awed by the memories of men who flew their missions against such odds, flying to the pop-up point and climbing, then turning and diving into not the *possibility*, but the *probability* of sudden, fiery death.

A country that produces such men will prevail.

ABOUT THE AUTHOR

TOM "BEAR" WILSON was a career United States Air Force Officer with three thousand hours of flying time, mostly in fighters. During his five hundred hours of combat flying, he earned four Silver Star medals for gallantry and three Distinguished Flying Crosses for heroism. He also served in various roles as instructor, flight examiner, tactician, staff officer, and unit commander. After leaving the military, Wilson enjoyed diverse careers, including: private investigator, gunsmith, newspaper publisher, and manager of advanced programs for a high-tech company in Silicon Valley. Mr. Wilson recently completed his third novel, TANGO UNIFORM, a sequel to LUCKY'S BRIDGE.

"Tom Wilson is a brilliant storyteller. He was there, and he puts you there, too."—Larry Bond, author of *Cauldron*

TOM WILSON
TANGO UNIFORM

North Vietnam, 1967–1968. As the enemy masses for its greatest assault of the war—the Tet Offensive—the American high command receives a daring new plan that could result in a quick and decisive victory. It's called Line Backer Jackpot, a large-scale bombing campaign with no restricted targets, no holds barred. This is the ultimate aerial battle, the one the F-105 pilots of the 333rd Tactical Fighter Squadron have long been waiting for. Washington, however, has yet to approve the plan, and for now the pilots must fly into the heat of the withering enemy fire knowing they can't hit back full force. But neither the politicians back home nor the war lords in Hanoi can contain the fighter jocks' courage or their conviction—the willingness to die by fire so a cause may live. Beyond the awesome firepower, beyond the daily struggle to succeed and survive, *Tango Uniform* is the story of the honor and the glory that can turn a few proud men into warrior-heroes.

Turn the page for a preview of **Tango Uniform**, *on sale in March 1994 wherever Bantam Books are sold.*

"Marlin lead's off the target to the right," he announced as his bird began to recover from the dive attack. He could see the flak clearer now that he was no longer tracking the target—so thick and heavy it rated an Oh-My-God. *Don't think about it. Stay calm. What's your next move?*

Bursts flashed harmlessly past, misses but close enough to make him feel vulnerable. He pulled harder to get away—realized he was being predictable in the constant turn and began to jink eastward. He glanced out to his right, toward Hanoi, and saw bright red bowling balls flashing through the sky—all seemingly directed at his airplane, like he was some kind of magnet.

As he approached the southern extremity of Thud Ridge, Manny reversed left, wanting to hug up beside its first high mountain.

"Valid SAM launch, Scotch Force. This is Red Dog lead. Valid launch!"

He eased off his turn and looked out sharply. Until they rejoined in the cooperative jamming offered by the pod formation, they were vulnerable to SAMs.

"Homing on us, Red . . ." The transmission immediately shut off.

Manny soared a bit as he approached a hill, then quickly swung his head back around to stare out at the valley, still wondering if the SAM could be targeted for him.

Nothing in sight.

"Break, Red Dog four! Br . . ."

Someone was breathing heavy over the radio, holding down the transmit button.

"Red Dog four's hit!"

One of the Wild Weasel crews.

"Get out, four! Get out!"

The Weasel Thud must be burning. Manny did a tiny dogleg right and left, so his flight could catch up. He consciously stopped an urge to breath harder. *Stay on the. . . .*

Weeep, weeep, weeep. An emergency beeper was sounding its plaintive cry, then a second when the other Weasel crewmember's chute opened.

Damn! Manny thought bleakly. Two men down.

As he turned back to face the mountain, Manny's airplane was staggered by a mighty jolt, then another, then a third! Each was accompanied by a tremendous explosion, deafening even in the sealed cockpit. The Thud reeled drunkenly—the controls instantly sluggish.

Oh shit! *Calm yourself, dammit. Keep thinking of what you should do next.*

Gain altitude! was Manny's initial thought, and he instinctively hauled the stick back and checked that the throttle was full forward.

Smoke gathered low in the cockpit, and he could see light down there. The bird was hit, and he knew it was a mortal one. He forced himself to remain calm as he wondered how far west he could get if he stuck with the bird. He couldn't yet turn for home, for the ridge blocked his way, so he continued climbing as he flew northward.

Someone radioed that he had a visual on a SAM, then another voice said it was a burning aircraft. He listened to Animal Hamlin's New Jersey accent explaining, saying something about *Marlin lead* and . . . *bright fire.*

Manny's fire was burning so intensely, they'd mistaken him for a missile! He tried to respond, but heard no side-tones to tell him the radio transmitter was operative.

Someone yelled for him to *get out*, as they'd done with the F-4 a few seconds earlier.

All of those things happened almost instantaneously, but time had entered another dimension and dawdled unnaturally. Manny glanced toward his feet to watch the thick smoke curling there, then observed his gauges as the oil pressure gauge went to zero.

No way to fly without oil pressure. *Stay calm. What's your next move?*

As he watched the telelite panel his Utility, P-1 and P-2 lights came on.

Can't fly far without hydraulics, either. Things were going to hell. *What's your next move?*

Weeep, weeep, weeep. A new beeper squealed.

". . . lead, *Honda three's* out of the airplane. I got one good chute in sight!"

Another emergency beeper sounded. The Honda three front seater.

The carnage wasn't yet complete.

". . . *Honda four's* hit!"

". . . *losing control of the* . . ."

". . . *get out, get out.*"

". . . *dammit.*"

Two more beepers wailed, and the accumulation of sounds

from the locator beacons drifted in and out of unison. Manny shut off emergency guard frequency to eliminate the racket.

In a period of seconds, two F-4s had been downed. With the Wild Weasel crew already out, six men were floating earthward. A bad day for the good guys. None of those would be picked up, for the rescue force couldn't come in this far.

Steady your breathing. Keep thinking of what to do next. Manny's heart remained calm. He was determined to make it out as far as possible.

As soon as he could see over the ridgeline, he cranked the stick to the left. The bird responded . . . falteringly so, but he was turning. He settled on a westerly course of 285 degrees, which he reasoned was the fastest track between his position and the nearest mountain wilderness across the wide valley.

Climbing still . . . more smoke boiling up from below. *Come on, baby,* he breathed. *We've got a long way to go.* He didn't wish to join the others below in their chutes, sure to be killed or captured. *Remain calm.*

He was past the ridge and over the flats, headed westerly at six-ninety knots, the Thud gamely struggling upward.

Can't *get* high enough, he decided, and continued to climb. He scanned his altimeter . . . it was dead. He glanced at his airspeed gauge and found it inoperative. No inputs from the pitot system, and he couldn't trust the rest of the instruments.

"*. . . left ten degrees.*" called Yank Donovan.

"*. . . you read, Marlin lead?*" Like the others, the first part of Animal Hamlin's transmission was also lost.

Manny turned the bird southward a bit, as Donovan had directed, then again tried his radio—without luck. He couldn't transmit. Although the first words of transmissions were clipped, he could receive. His breathing remained calm, his thoughts lucid . . . as if he was an observer of the *Titanic* before it went belly up. He began a high-pitched laugh, then cut it off.

"*. . . through sixteen thousand feet,*" he heard Animal explain in the cool voice. Yank Donovan asked something and Animal replied he was coming up on Marlin lead's right side . . . that the airplane was burning and shredded. He said he could see right through the Thud's belly to the engine, like it was a cut-away model. There was a big chunk torn out of the right wing, and three feet of the aft fuselage was missing.

"Keep flying baby," Manny urged his Thud. *Stay calm. Think of what you do next.*

"*. . . keep your distance in case it blows,*" radioed Colonel Donovan.

Manny's eyes smarted and wept from the smoke. He leaned close to the canopy plexiglass and saw an aircraft shape looming on his right. Animal Hamlin. The presence made him feel better. He leaned forward to check the situation indicator for his heading, but found that both electrical systems had shut down since his last look. He extended the ram air turbine for emergency power, but there was no change. He leaned well forward until he was close enough to see the needle on the whiskey compass, and corrected to 285 degrees, magnetic.

Another voice. *". . . out, Marlin lead. You're burning!"*

He studiously ignored the advice. The farther he could make it to the west, the better his chance for rescue.

Animal's voice. *". . . through twenty thousand feet, Marlin lead. You're burning on the right side of your bird. Dark smoke. I think oil from your ATM's feeding the fire. Make sure you've got the ATM shut down so it'll stop pumping oil."*

Manny felt for the air turbine motor switch.

". . . little better. Not burning quite so bright back there now." He owed Animal a drink for that advice.

Manny's feet were getting hotter. He looked to see if there were flames, but the smoke was too thick.

Animal's distinctive voice. *". . . doin' good, Marlin lead. Awfully good. Turn ten degrees left again, though. You're in a slight bank and keep drifting north."*

Manny fed in a few degrees correction . . . what he thought to be ten degrees. Found himself starting to breath too rapidly and calmed it.

". . . out, Marlin lead!" someone yelled hoarsely.

Animal's cool voice returned. *". . . on the right side of your bird. Gotta start thinking about gettin' out, Manny. Coming up fast on the Red River, if that's what you been waiting for. Level off a bit now. You're in a slight climb again, and . . ."*

Hamlin didn't finish his sentence. Manny's radio had gone completely dead.

He couldn't see at all now, partly because of the smoke, mostly because his eyes were watering profusely. He blinked and leaned forward but couldn't see the whiskey compass.

Gotta get rid of the canopy, he decided, and had trouble finding the manual lever. He pulled. The metal bow was thrust up into the airstream and the canopy disappeared. Manny had anticipated a flash fire, and was clutching desperately onto the left ejection handle in case he had to immediately abandon ship . . . but there was no flash fire and the smoke diminished. He blinked repeatedly to flush water from his eyes, wondering how tear ducts could carry so much liquid, then glanced over and saw that Animal's Thud was locked into position at his side. Hamlin gave him a nod and thumbs up. It felt exhilarating to be able to see. He grinned and laughed into his mask as he returned the wave, then blinked some more and stared down over the side.

The Red River was directly before them, not more than a couple of miles distant. All he had to do was . . .

"Ungghhh!" he grunted, for the Thud pitched nose up into a steep climb. He stabbed with his left foot at the rudder and the red-hot pedal fell against his leg, searing the skin and causing him to yell out in pain.

The damned rudder pedal had melted free! He tried to kick it away, and felt his rubber boot sole grow sticky on contact.

He was fighting the stick as the bird soared, but little seemed to be working. He hung from his straps, now inverted, and the Thud did some kind of odd, twisting trick and he was fluttering earthward in a spin.

There was absolutely no control!

Time to get out, he sagely decided. He had sufficient altitude for a clean ejection. He took a couple of seconds positioning himself, as he'd practiced a thousand times in the simulator, then released the controls and grasped the ejection handle.

The Thud slowly righted itself and began a recovery arc, so he regrasped the control stick and felt sluggish response. Past the Red now. If he could only make it . . .

"Unghhhh!" he groaned and blacked out as the bird's nose pitched into a nine-g pull-up which he'd thought impossible. This time he was tossed to one side as the aircraft reversed and began to flutter, only half-flying, sinking earthward again.

"I got your number, baby," Manny coaxed, still panting from the g's.

He released the control stick.

No effect. The Thud continued to fall.

Dammit!

He grasped the control stick again. There was absolutely no response. *Remain calm.*

Manny fleetingly wondered if he was still beyond the river as he groped for the ejection handle, said a very quick prayer, pulled his heels back, sucked a shaky breath of oxygen, then pulled both ejection levers.

The explosive blast kicked him hard in the butt.

Major Lucky Anderson

The gooney bird shimmied and whined throughout the takeoff from Don Muang airport, as if it was the right of a lady of her age to act as she wished. C-47s had been designed and first built in the thirties and had been a mainstay of every conflict since. Other cargo birds, like C-119s, had been designed to replace her, but she was still flying while they'd mostly been relegated to boneyards or sold off to other countries. Goons were not pressurized—on this one Lucky could see daylight through gaps where the passenger door didn't fit properly—so they had to fly down low enough that the passengers or crew wouldn't need oxygen. As reliable and endurable as a railroad pocket watch, gooney birds shuddered for no apparent reason and you could see their wings articulating up and down, phenomena that scared the hell out of young jet pilot passengers, but she'd complain and groan and keep flying, and get you there every time. In Thailand goons were used to shuttle passengers and low priority cargo between the various bases.

Lucky was headed back. Returning to Takhli to finish his combat tour, and do it as a squadron commander. Not only that, when he'd been in Hawaii, he'd received a call from Flo, General Moss's spinster secretary, saying he was on the LC list. She'd said he owed her dinner, and Lucky had said *yes ma'am.* One of Flo's favorites had been promoted, and she expected her due. Then she'd connected him with General Moss, who'd added his terse congratulations and said the promotion list wouldn't be released for a few days, "so act surprised when they tell you."

"Major?" A young brunette with shoulder-length hair, large blue eyes, rounded face and pixie features sat beside him. She'd watched him curiously since watching Linda embrace him at the airport. Her name was Penny Dwight, she'd told him after they'd been seated near the back of the C-47, and she was going to Takhli to be the wing commander's secretary. She didn't seem horrified as some women did when they saw his burns, simply took a long, critical look, then acted as if it was normal for a guy to have no face to speak of.

She'd chattered a lot since they'd strapped into the aluminum bar and nylon mesh seats that ran down each side of the old aircraft's interior. When she'd learned that Linda was his fiancée, she'd told him she'd once been engaged too, but she mentioned it no more and seemed to be suffering no traumas over whatever had happened. When she'd gotten the chance to come overseas, she said she'd jumped at it. Lucky's first impression was that she was thrilled with the exotic assignment, and seemed more than a bit naive and flighty. He wondered what she would become at Takhi. The place changed everyone who went there.

"You've been to Takhli," she said. "What's it like?" Her voice was breathless, As if Takhli was some kind of exotic place like Bali or Tahiti.

"It's in the central Thailand savanna. Hot and dusty. Rains a lot in the summer months like everywhere over here, but between rains there's a lot of heat. Should be cooling off some now, and we'll have a few months of drier weather."

"I've always thought of Siam as being all jungle."

"Mostly farmland in the central portions. There's dense forest to the west, in the Kwai River area over toward Burma, and in the far east, near the Mekong River, and south, down in the panhandle all the way to Malaysia, but not in the central and northern parts of the country. Just grassy savanna and farmland."

"Good. I'm deathly afraid of snakes."

He started to tell her that there were plenty of big snakes around Takhli, that the words Ta Khli meant place of the king cobra, but he stopped himself. She'd be the first American female assigned. If he scared her off, the guys would never forgive him.

She turned in her web seat, craning her neck to look out the window. Kind of pretty, Lucky thought, if she'd change her hair (the long hair didn't go well with her rounded face) and stop slouching. Of course he was accustomed to the meticulous way Linda carried and groomed herself, and the comparison was unfair. Anyway, the guys at Takhli would finally have an American female presence. He wondered if it wasn't the doing of their new wing commander.

"We'll be landing in twenty-five minutes," announced the burly loadmaster as he made his way back through the passengers.

1444L - Route Pack 5, North Vietnam

Captain Manny DeVera

He was freefalling, tumbling earthward from twenty thousand feet plus, wondering if the chute would open at twelve thousand as advertised. The silence seemed loud since he'd left the roar of the engine. He could hear only a slight rushing sound outside the helmet.

Through the long freefall he kept the oxygen mask in place—at altitude, life-sustaining oxygen was force-fed from a small green cylinder at his side. A mechanical, chirping sound came from behind as a tiny motor activated and extracted the pin binding the parachute together. A couple of seconds later he felt a tug as the chute deployed, then a harsher jerk and he swung in a tremendous arc.

"Whooo-eee," Manny yelled. "Ride 'em cowboy." During the next wide swing to his left he pulled on his right risers. The swinging motion slowed.

Now below 12,000 feet, he'd no longer require oxygen, so he tugged at the right side of his mask and pulled the bayonet connector free. The fresh air was delicious.

He moved his limbs. Sore from flailing, but he'd not been going fast in the spin and except for a throbbing, obviously dislocated left shoulder, he was intact. The shoulder hurt with a mounting intensity which was difficult to ignore—but he was alive, and that was something. *What's your next move?*

Look around! He was indeed beyond the Red River, but only barely, descending toward a village in a crook of the wide stream. *Gotta slip the chute,* he decided.

First things first. The seat kit was hanging beneath him, and the raft was inflated and deployed on a long lanyard beneath that, like a bright yellow banner saying, "Hey guys, here's the Supersonic Wetback."

He had friends who'd successfully ejected from a Thud only to be crumpled by the frigging seat pack when they hit the ground. Manny felt with his good, right arm at one side of his butt, found the catch on the seat pack and disconnected it. He reached around and—with more difficulty—found the second. The pack and raft dropped away.

Ignore the pain.

Another glance at the village far below. If he continued, he'd land smack in it's middle.

He crawled up the risers a bit and tugged on a small, red banner. Nylon cords slipped free and panels at the rear of the chute became disconnected, reconfiguring it so the air would flow through and give him forward progress. Now the chute was steerable ... you could go left or right if you pulled down on those risers, and faster forward if you selected both front ones ... not fast enough, though ... not nearly enough. He estimated he'd still land in one of the farmers' fields, short of the first densely-foliated mountain ridge.

He decided to add more slippage to the chute so he could go faster. He crawled up the nylon straps again, hooked his useless left arm in the vee, and this time pulled very hard on the forward risers to increase the air flow out the rear. The chute began to take him faster toward the mountains. Maybe. . . .

He needed even *more* distance—as much separation as possible. He was pulling hard, but it was difficult with the painful arm. Manny kicked up a leg, took a couple of stabs at it, then succeeded in catching his left foot over the left riser vee. He pulled down with the left leg and his good right arm. The chute billowed and flapped, but he was *really* moving westward now, well past the first forested ridge and headed toward a second. He looked back and saw the yellow raft fall to earth, taking a mighty bounce in a field beside the village.

He'd slipped a half-mile, enough to help baffle pursuers, but he wanted more.

Lower now, but not so low he couldn't continue to slip the parachute. He tugged down harder with the good arm and leg, until the chute flapped wildly and began to collapse, then he eased off just enough to refill it with air.

He sailed over a second ridgeline, which he'd estimated was almost two miles from the village. There were no roads or habitation he could see below him, but he didn't dare let up, relentlessly applying the pressure on the risers and traveling ever westward.

He was much lower when he skimmed over a third, lower ridge. A big swatch of what appeared to be elephant grass was dead ahead. He decided to steer for it.

1458L - HQ 7th Air Force
Tan Son Nhut Airbase, South Vietnam

Lt General Richard J. Moss

Lieutenant Colonel Pearly Gates was standing before him, wearing a frown, when Flo buzzed. "Colonel Leska on line two, General."

Moss picked up. "Shoot, Buster."

"Sorry to bother you, sir, but I was just informed of something you should know about. Captain Manny DeVera just went down in North Vietnam. He's on the list."

"Pearly just came in to tell me. We don't have a location on him yet. How about you?"

"Not yet, sir."

"I just advised the control center that I want a maximum effort in there to get him out. They've got the rescue people alerted and on their way in."

"Thank you, sir."

Moss hung up, grim-faced.

"Perhaps we shouldn't allow the people we've got aboard the program to fly combat," Pearly offered.

Moss shook his head. "We need all the feedback we can get, so we can keep Gentleman Jim properly advised." He gave Pearly an unhappy look. "I've got a couple senators waiting for me to give 'em a rah-rah briefing on the air war. Don't hesitate to interrupt if you hear anything."

1504L - Takhli RTAFB, Thailand

Major Lucky Anderson

Halfway through the straight-in approach, with the gooney bird groaning and wheezing dramatically, the pilot announced that everyone should stay in place after they'd taxied in.

There was a ceremony of some sort being set up.

The goon touched down, then soared again before finally settling. As they slowed the rear of the bird skittered as the tailwheel touched. The pilot turned off halfway down the runway. As he taxied past the endless rows of F-105 Thunderchiefs, Lucky found himself staring.

He loved the heavy fighters. Every airplane had its unique personality. In his mind the Thud was an iron lady who fiercely protected her pilots. She was rock steady, and you could make tiny corrections that were impossible in other fighters. Tough, she'd suffer terrible damage without complaint. He'd seen birds come home with missing vertical stabilizers and others with large portions of wings or aft sections shot away. Even when mortally hit, she'd try to get her pilots to safety before going down. She couldn't turn on a dime, but she was extremely fast at low altitudes, and if you wanted to get away from anything in the sky, all you had to do was stroke afterburner and angle the nose down. If she'd been human, she'd be a perfect mate for the warriors who flew her. She was big mama, and tried her damnedest to take care of her men.

The C-47 taxied up in front of base operations, and the left engine was shut down so the passengers could safely deplane.

As the prop was clattering to a stop, the rear passenger's door opened and a tall, easy-going captain in a flight suit peered inside. He looked past Lucky and discovered his target. A grin grew on his face as he brushed unruly hair into place with his hand.

"Miss Dwight?"

The new secretary unbuckled, looking unsure, and made her way toward the door on still-shaky legs. Lucky was curious as to how she'd fare among the mob of horny fighter jocks, crew chiefs and other womanless men at Takhli.

"I'm Captain Dusty Fields, Ma'am. We have a little reception for you," the captain said, taking her hand to help her down.

There were throngs of men waiting in front of base operations. As Penny Dwight emerged from the goon and stepped onto the tarmac, she looked startled as they began to cheer. Happy fighter pilots tossed flowers in her path as she walked onto a long red carpet. Crew chiefs and muscular load crews bowed in exaggerated poses. Burly line chiefs gawked.

Lucky pulled his sage-green hang-up bag from beneath the web seat.

The loadmaster was standing near the door, frowning as he observed the antics of the men outside. "Act like they've never seen a woman before," he said.

"She's the first round eye to be stationed here," Lucky explained, watching the procession which now included two happy non-coms holding umbrellas over her head to shield her from the sun. Lavish garlands of flowers were placed around her neck by grinning fighter jocks.

Lucky deplaned, glanced about to orient himself, then started across the ramp toward the 354th TFS, the squadron he'd been assigned to before he'd been shot down. A blue pickup pulled up beside him, and Colonel George Armaugh, the wing deputy for operations nodded to him.

"Welcome back, Colonel."

Lucky shifted his bag to his left hand and saluted with his right. "Colonel?" He acted surprised at the rank, as General Moss had told him to do.

"You're on the LC list. Congratulations."

"Thank you, sir."

"Jump in and I'll drive you."

Lucky nodded toward the 354th squadron building, which was not far. "I'm just going over there."

"Things have changed. You're getting the 333rd squadron."

"Oh?"

"And the new wing commander wants to talk to you. You know Buster Leska?"

"Don't really know him, but we've met." Lucky placed his bag in the back of the pickup and crawled into the passenger's seat.

Armaugh drove slowly down the flight line. "We just got word that four birds went down on the alpha strike this afternoon. Two of 'em were ours."

Lucky grimaced in response.

"A Wild Weasel crew was shot down in pack six, with no chance of rescue, and a D-model made it out to the edge of pack five. Dunno if we can get him out either. It'll be close, according to how far he made it, I'd say."

"No position yet?"

"Somewhere near Yen Bai. That's all we know so far."

"That makes it doubtful. Who was it?"

"The Supersonic Wetback."

Lucky's jaw tightened. Manny DeVera had worked for him. He was a good friend.

He stared bleakly out the window, then looked about. "I thought we were going to the wing commander's office."

"He's on his way to the command post, trying to find out more about the shoot-downs. He knew DeVera in Europe and thinks highly of him. One of the first things he did when he took over was name him to replace Max Foley as wing weapons officer."

"I'll be darned."

"Manny's doing a good job," Armaugh said. He drove out of the aircraft parking zone, crossed the street, then pulled to a stop before the command post door. "I've gotta go out and monitor things while the birds recover. I'll talk to you later so you can tell me how it went with Colonel Leska, and I'll give you my pitch about what I expect from *my* squadron commanders."

Lucky pulled his bag out of the back, then deposited it at the guarded command post entrance before he went inside to look for the wingco. He found the chalk-white-haired colonel sitting alone in his position at the rear of the command center, staring at the status boards.

Leska noticed him and waved him over. "Captain DeVera's down," he said evenly.

"I just heard." Lucky sat beside him, wondering about his level of concern. A lot of good fighter jocks were being shot down.

"They've got the rescue effort holding in there until the

fighters make radio contact and get a positive position. Two Sandies and two choppers."

Lucky fished a fat cigar from his pocket and popped it into his mouth, a habit he'd acquired long before. He didn't smoke the things, just mouthed and chewed on them when he wanted to think hard on a subject.

Leska nodded at one of the operations sergeants in the front of the room. "He's got Sandy Control at Udorn on the line. No word about Manny's status so far." He turned his gaze on Lucky. "I guess you got to know the rescue folks pretty well yourself."

"Enough to have great respect for 'em. Manny went down near Yen Bai?"

"Just south-west from there. Yank Donovan's running the rescue effort. He relayed word that they hadn't seen unfriendlies in the immediate area."

Donovan hadn't yet arrived at Takhli when he'd been shot down, but Lucky knew him. He was a superb pilot, but a difficult man to like. "Yank's good," he finally said.

Leska gave him a questioning look.

"Got an ego a mile wide," Lucky regretted the criticism as soon as the words were out, so he quickly added, "but he's good in the air."

They sat through five minutes of inactivity and no new word about the rescue.

"You're getting the 333rd squadron," Leska said idly.

"That's what Colonel Armaugh just told me. They're a good bunch of guys."

"I've been flying with them—watching over 'em while you were off in Hawaii and they were without a commander. That'll make 'em double happy to see you arrive."

"Thanks."

They sat quietly, waiting for word about the rescue attempt. And Lucky continued to wonder at the level of concern the wing commander was showing over one of his pilots.

1519L - Route Pack 5, North Vietnam

Captain Manny DeVera

He couldn't believe his eyes! It hadn't been a field of nice, yielding elephant grass like he'd thought. Instead it was a big batch of the tallest bamboo Manny had ever seen, fifty or sixty feet high and up to eight inches in diameter. He held his legs tightly together as he dropped through their tops, and felt fortunate he wasn't skewered like a chunk of goat on a kebab spit.

The chute caught up on one of the things, and just as he started to relax, it slipped and let him fall to the ground, hard, where his right foot crumped and his butt slammed down so mightily onto his heel that he wanted to yell.

He paused for a hurtful, breathless second and *did* yell. "Jesus!" he bellowed. Then Manny remembered Sister Lucia's admonishments, as well as the deep shit he was presently in. He quickly crossed himself and muttered how sorry he was about speaking the name in vain. He sure as hell didn't need to piss off the big guy.

As he switched off the emergency beeper and unlatched from the parachute, he tried to peer about, but could see only the thick bamboo stalks. Pain coursed through him from the disconnected shoulder, fiery stinging from the injured tail— hurting so badly that he almost puked.

Nothing he could do about the ass-bone. *Gotta* do something about the shoulder. Manny knelt and dropped his arm onto the ground, whimpering as it contacted, then tried to grasp the base of one of the smaller bamboo stalks. The hand was numb and wouldn't function.

He found a vee of two shoots and wedged the hand firmly, then stepped down hard on it with his left boot, blew out a breath, and very slowly stood, pulling hard.

Oh God! He continued pulling. The shoulder pain eased some as the arm stretched, then the thing popped back into place and he squealed in agony. After taking another apprehensive breath and tugging one last time, he staggered, then stood stock still, puffing. The arm still throbbed, but nothing like before. Feeling began to return. He found he could flex his fingers and move his hand.

Manny heard the drone of jets overhead, and immediately fumbled in a survival vest pocket for a handheld radio. *You didn't make it far enough,* his mind said soberly. *No way they'll come in this far to pick you up.*

Then he remembered the other thing. He knew about the plan called Jackpot.

The 357th Squadron, led by Lt. Col. Mack MacLendon, flies out of Takhli Air Base in central Thailand. Orders have come from Washington to destroy a prized North Vietnam steel mill. For American pilots, the toll is sure to be high. But those who survive will remember their valiant brothers when they fly into battle again—tomorrow.

TERMITE HILL

TOM WILSON

They were hard-core fighter jocks, supertough, super-cool, supersonic cowboys who took the fight to the enemy. They lived hard, fought hard, and died even harder, flying guts-for-grandeur into the red-hot fire zones over North Vietnam.

This is the story of an elite corps of pilots, their courage and camaraderie, their lives and loves.

❑ 29310-9 $5.99/$6.99 in Canada

Now there are two great ways to catch up with your favorite thrillers